THE ALBANY CYCLE

Book I

ALSO BY WILLIAM KENNEDY

Roscoe

The Ink Truck

Quinn's Book
The Flaming Corsage
Legs
(Collected in The Albany Cycle, Book II)

NON FICTION

O Albany!: Improbable City of Political Wizards,
Fearless Ethnics, Spectacular Aristocrats, Splendid Nobodies,
and Underrated Scoundrels

Riding the Yellow Trolley Car

WITH BRENDAN KENNEDY

Charlie Malarkey and the Belly Button Machine

Charlie Malarkey and the Singing Moose

THE ALBANY CYCLE
Book I

Billy Phelan's Greatest Game
Ironweed
Very Old Bones

William Kennedy

Scribner

First published in Great Britain by Scribner, 2002
An imprint of Simon & Schuster UK Ltd
A Viacom Company

Grateful acknowledgement is made to Warner Bros. Music for permission to reprint an excerpt from 'Bye Bye Blackbird', in *Ironweed*, lyrics by Mort Dixon and music by Ray Henderson. Copyright 1926 by Warner Bros. Inc.; copyright © renewed. All rights reserved. Used by permission.

Grateful acknowledgement is made for permission to reprint excerpts from the following copyrighted works in *Very Old Bones*: Poem by Catallus translated by Edith Hamilton from *The Roman Way* by Edith Hamilton. Reprinted by permission of the publisher, W.W. Norton & Company, Inc. Copyright 1932 by W.W. Norton & Company Inc., copyright renewed 1960 by Edith Hamilton. 'The Dwarf' from *The Palm at the End of the Mind* by Wallace Stevens. By permission of Alfred A. Knopf, Inc.

1 3 5 7 9 10 8 6 4 2

Simon & Schuster UK Ltd
Africa House
64–78 Kingsway
London WC2B 6AH

Simon & Schuster Australia
Sydney

A CIP catalogue record for this book is available from the British Library

ISBN 0–7432–2102–8

Typeset by Palimpsest Book Production Limited,
Polmont, Stirlingshire
Printed and bound in Great Britain
by The Bath Press, Bath

Contents

Author's Preface

The Albany Cycle of novels is an evolutionary development. I did not set out to create it, but began by thinking of a large-scale novel that would satisfy my obsession with the history of the city, one of the oldest in the nation. Back in the early 1960s, before I had published any books, I wanted to go back to earliest times and write of life among the Dutch colonists in the 17th century wilderness as they settled among the Iroquois and carved out a settlement. I'd move on to the Revolution, when General Burgoyne became the guest of Albany after losing the battle of Saratoga and the war. I'd tell the story of the waves of Irish coming in to build the Erie Canal and the railroads, be with Albany's 44th regiment when it left Albany to take on the Confederates. Herman Melville was schooled in Albany so I would bring him into the mix, along with Henry James's family fortune, and Teddy Roosevelt racing newspaper reporters up the Capitol steps. I'd track the Albany political machine that began in the 1920s and watch it become invincible, unspeakable and hilarious. I'd follow Jack (Legs) Diamond, the celebrity gangster, as he dazzled the town during Prohibition, I'd explore my family's grief in the Depression, my adolescent memories of World War Two, and my own time in the military during the Korean War era. Maybe I'd end with my journey to Washington for Jack Kennedy's funeral.

This was ridiculously ambitious, and absurdly haphazard, and I soon knew it; but the impulse to pursue it did not fade. I wrote the novel *Legs*, and out of that world came *Billy Phelan's Greatest*

Game, which begat *Ironweed*, each new book a consequence of characters migrating from one story to the next. There are seven novels so far, and I'm collecting toward an eighth.

In this volume, Book One, the three novels in which the Phelan family is dominant are collected for the first time, and appear as they were sequentially written, which is also the sequence of the periods in which their stories unfold: *Billy Phelan* taking place in late October 1938; *Ironweed* a few days later; *Very Old Bones* in 1958. But time is fluid in all, and *Billy Phelan* and *Ironweed* go back to the turn of the 20th century, *Bones* to the early 1930s and late 1880s.

There is also the early novel I called *The Angels and the Sparrows* precursor to *Very Old Bones* in which I created the Phelan family. It was a grim and episodic work that no one would publish, and for that I'm grateful. It belongs on the shelf. But when I was writing *Billy Phelan*, I reached back to that novel and lifted out Francis Phelan, an incipient bum, unmarried, unpleasant, and vagrant, but somehow valuable; and I made him Billy Phelan's father, gave him a family and a reason to be vagrant and drunk, and brought him back to Albany. He became coherent and forceful in *Billy Phelan*, a man at the bottom of the world who, even so, was ambiguously vital to me. He was demanding his own book, and so I obliged with *Ironweed*.

When *Ironweed* was published, and *Billy Phelan* and *Legs* republished, all at the same time in 1983, someone – not me – fixed on the notion of the 'Albany Trilogy', which I suppose is what it was; but I was already well into a fourth work, and there would be a fifth: that new version of *The Angels and the Sparrows*, which came to fruition as *Very Old Bones*, published in 1992, a vastly different work from the early novel, and a much fuller rendering of the Phelan siblings, parents, and ancestors.

By this time the Trilogy had a new name, the 'Albany Cycle' – my term – for I saw that what I was creating was an open-ended set of non-sequential tales, each focusing on a single individual who would carry the stories of others, each book written to stand by itself, independent of others in the Cycle; and yet all the books interwoven. My characters, I saw, begat one another, and all were counting time in the shared continuum of common ground, common history. I also began to see that I was slowly working out an evolved version of my original conception of writing one book, a prolonged conversation with time and place that would be as large as my imagination allowed, perhaps larger if I got lucky.

And the begetting continues.

William Kennedy, Albany
April 2002

BILLY PHELAN'S GREATEST GAME

For Brendan Christopher Kennedy, a nifty kid

The great archetypal activities of human society are all permeated with play from the start.

— JOHAN HUIZINGA

The 'eternal child' in man is an indescribable experience, an incongruity, a disadvantage, and a divine prerogative; an imponderable that determines the ultimate worth or worthlessness of a personality.

— CARL JUNG

1

Martin Daugherty, age fifty and now the scorekeeper, observed it all as Billy Phelan, working on a perfect game, walked with the arrogance of a young, untried eagle toward the ball return, scooped up his black, two-finger ball, tossed it like a juggler from right to left hand, then held it in his left palm, weightlessly. Billy rubbed his right palm and fingers on the hollow cone of chalk in the brass dish atop the ball rack, wiped off the excess with a pull-stroke of the towel. He faced the pins, eyed his spot down where the wood of the alley changed color, at a point seven boards in from the right edge. And then, looking to Martin like pure energy in shoes, he shuffled: left foot, right foot, left-right-left and slide, right hand pushing out, then back, like a pendulum, as he moved, wrist turning slightly at the back of the arc. His arm, pure control in shirtsleeves to Martin, swung forward, and the ball glided almost silently down the polished alley, rolled through the seventh board's darkness, curving minimally as it moved, curving more sharply as it neared the pins, and struck solidly between the headpin and the three pin, scattering all in a jamboree of spins and jigs.

'Attaway, Billy,' said his backer, Morrie Berman, clapping twice. 'Lotta mix, lotta mix.'

'Ball is working all right,' Billy said.

Billy stood long-legged and thin, waiting for Bugs, the cross-eyed pinboy, to send back the ball. When it snapped up from underneath the curved wooden ball return, Billy lifted it off, faced the fresh setup on alley nine, shuffled, thrust, and threw yet another strike: eight in a row now.

Martin Daugherty noted the strike on the scoresheet, which showed no numbers, only the eight strike marks: bad luck to fill in the score while a man is still striking. Martin was already thinking of writing his next column about this game, provided Billy carried it off. He would point out how some men moved through the daily sludge of their lives and then, with a stroke, cut away the sludge and transformed themselves. Yet what they became was not the result of a sudden act, but the culmination of all they had ever done: a triumph for self-development, the end of something general, the beginning of something specific.

To Martin, Billy Phelan, on an early Thursday morning in late October, 1938, already seemed more specific than most men. Billy seemed fully defined at thirty-one (the age when Martin had been advised by his father that he was a failure).

Billy was not a half-bad bowler: 185 average in the K. of C. league, where Martin bowled with him Thursday nights. But he was not a serious match for Scotty Streck, who led the City League, the fastest league in town, with a 206 average. Scotty lived with his bowling ball as if it were a third testicle, and when he found Billy and Martin playing eight ball at a pool table in the Downtown Health and Amusement Club, the city's only twenty-four-hour gamester's palace, no women, no mixed leagues, please, beer on tap till 4:00 A.M., maybe 5:00, but no whiskey on premises, why then Scotty's question was: Wanna bowl some jackpots, Billy? Sure, with a twenty-pin spot, Billy said. Give you fifty-five for three games, offered the Scotcheroo. Not enough, but all right, said Billy, five bucks? Five bucks fine, said Scotty.

And so it was on, with the loser to pay for the bowling, twenty cents a game. Scotty's first game was 212. Billy turned in a sad 143, with five splits, too heavy on the headpin, putting him sixty-nine pins down, his spot eliminated.

Billy found the pocket in the second game and rolled 226. But Scotty had also discovered where the pocket lurked, and threw 236 to increase his lead to seventy-nine pins. Now in the eighth frame of the final game, the match was evening out, Scotty steady with spares and doubles, but his lead fading fast in front of Billy's homestretch run toward perfection.

Word of a possible 300 game with a bet on it drew the bar stragglers, the fag-end bowlers, the night manager, the all-night pinboys, even the sweeper, to alleys nine and ten in the cavernous old room, spectators at the wonder. No one spoke to Billy about the unbroken string of strikes, also bad luck. But it was legitimate to talk of the bet: two hundred dollars, between Morrie Berman and Charlie Boy McCall, the significance being in the sanctified presence of Charlie Boy, a soft, likeable kid gone to early bloat, but nevertheless the most powerful young man in town, son of the man who controlled all the gambling, all of it, in the city of Albany, and nephew of the two politicians who ran the city itself, all of it, and Albany County, all of that too: Irish-American potentates of the night and the day.

Martin knew all the McCall brothers, had gone to school with them, saw them grow up in the world and take power over it. They all, including young Charlie Boy, the only heir, still lived on Colonie Street in Arbor Hill, where Martin and his father used to live, where Billy Phelan used to live. There was nothing that Charlie Boy could not get, any time, any place in this town; and when he came into the old Downtown alleys with Scotty, and when Scotty quickly found Billy to play with, Charlie just as quickly found Morrie Berman, a swarthy ex-pimp and gambler who would bet on the behavior of bumblebees. A week ago Martin had seen Morrie open a welsher's forehead with a shotglass at Brockley's bar on Broadway over a three-hundred-dollar dart game: heavy bettor, Morrie, but he paid when he lost and he demanded the same from others. Martin knew Morrie's reputation better than he knew the man: a fellow who used to drink around town with Legs Diamond and had hoodlums for pals. But Morrie wasn't quite a hoodlum himself, as far as Martin could tell. He was the son of a politically radical Jew, grandson of a superb old Sheridan Avenue tailor. In Morrie the worthy Berman family strain had gone slightly askew.

The bet between Charlie Boy and Morrie had begun at one

hundred dollars and stayed there for two games, with Martin holding the money. But when Morrie saw that Billy had unquestionably found the pocket at the windup of the second game, he offered to raise the ante another hundred; folly, perhaps, for his boy Billy was seventy-nine pins down. Well yes, but that was really only twenty-four down with the fifty-five-pin spot, and you go with the hot instrument. Charlie Boy quickly agreed to the raise, what's another hundred, and Billy then stood up and rolled his eight strikes, striking somberness into Charlie Boy's mood, and vengeance into Scotty's educated right hand.

Martin knew Scotty Streck and admired his talent without liking him. Scotty worked in the West Albany railroad shops, a short, muscular, brush-cut, bandy-legged native of the West End German neighborhood of Cabbagetown. He was twenty-six and had been bowling since he was old enough to lift a duckpin ball. At age sixteen he was a precociously unreal star with a 195 average. He bowled now almost every night of his life, bowled in matches all over the country and clearly coveted a national reputation. But to Martin he lacked champion style: a hothead, generous neither with himself nor with others. He'd been nicknamed Scotty for his closeness with money, never known to bet more than five dollars on himself. Yet he thrived on competition and traveled with a backer, who, as often as not, was his childhood pal, Charlie McCall. No matter what he did or didn't do, Scotty was still the best bowler in town, and bowling freaks, who abounded in Albany, gathered round to watch when he came out to play.

The freaks now sat on folding chairs and benches behind the only game in process in the old alleys, alleys which had been housed in two other buildings and moved twice before being installed here on State Street, just up from Broadway in an old dancing academy. They were venerable, quirky boards, whose history now spoke to Martin. He looked the crowd over: men sitting among unswept papers, dust, and cigar butts, bathing in the raw incandescence of naked bulbs, surrounded by spittoons; a nocturnal bunch in shirtsleeves and baggy clothes, their hands full of meaningful drink, fixated on an ancient game with origins in Christian ritual, a game brought to this city centuries ago by nameless old Dutchmen and now a captive of the indoor sports of the city. The game abided in such windowless, smoky lofts as this one, which smelled of beer, cigar smoke and alley wax, an unhealthy ambience which nevertheless nourished exquisite nighttime skills.

These men, part of Broadway's action-easy, gravy-vested sporting mob, carefully studied such artists of the game as Scotty, with his high-level consistency, and Billy, who might achieve perfection tonight through a burst of accuracy, and converted them into objects of community affection. The mob would make these artists sports-page heroes, enter them into the hall of small fame that existed only in the mob mind, which venerated all winners.

After Billy rolled his eighth strike, Scotty stood, danced his bob and weave toward the foul line, and threw the ball with a corkscrewed arm, sent it spinning and hooking toward the one-three pocket. It was a perfect hit, but a dead one somehow, and he left the eight and ten pins perversely standing: the strike split, all but impossible to make.

'Dirty son of a biiiiiitch!' Scotty screamed at the pair of uncooperative pins, silencing all hubbub behind him, sending waves of uh-oh through the spectators, who knew very well how it went when a man began to fall apart at the elbow.

'You think maybe I'm getting to him?' Billy whispered to Martin.

'He can't even stand to lose a fiver, can he?'

Scotty tried for the split, ticking the eight, leaving the ten.

'Let's *get* it now, Scotty,' Charlie Boy McCall said. 'In there, buddy.'

Scotty nodded at Charlie Boy, retrieved his ball and faced the new setup, bobbed, weaved, corkscrewed, and crossed over to the one-two pocket, Jersey hit, leaving the five pin. He made the spare easily, but sparing is not how you pick up pinnage against the hottest of the hot.

Billy might have been hot every night if he'd been as single-minded as Scotty about the game. But Martin knew Billy to be a generalist, a man in need of the sweetness of miscellany. Billy's best game was pool, but he'd never be anything like a national champion at that either, didn't think that way, didn't have the need that comes with obsessive specialization. Billy roamed through the grandness of all games, yeoman here, journeyman there, low-level maestro unlikely to transcend, either as gambler, card dealer, dice or pool shooter. He'd been a decent shortstop in the city-wide Twilight League as a young man. He was a champion drinker who could go for three days on the sauce and not yield to sleep, a double-twenty specialist at the dart board, a chancy, small-time bookie, and so on and so on and so on, and why, Martin Daugherty, are you so obsessed with Billy Phelan? Why make a heroic picaro out of a simple chump?

Well, says Martin, haven't I know him since he was a sausage? Haven't I seen him grow stridently into young manhood while I slip and slide softly into moribund middle age? Why, I knew him when he had a father, knew his father too, knew him when that father abdicated, and I ached for the boy then and have ever since, for I know how it is to live in the inescapable presence of the absence of the father.

Martin had watched Billy move into street-corner life after his father left, saw him hanging around Ronan's clubroom, saw him organize the Sunday morning crap game in Bohen's barn after nine o'clock mass, saw him become a pinboy at the K. of C. to earn some change. That was where the boy learned how to bowl, sneaking free games after Duffy, the custodian, went off to the movies.

Martin was there the afternoon the pinboys went wild and rolled balls up and down the middle of the alleys at one another, reveling in a boyish exuberance that went bad when Billy tried to scoop up one of those missiles like a hot grounder and smashed his third finger between that onrushing ball and another one lying loose on the runway. Smash and blood, and Martin moved in and took him (he was fourteen, the same age as Martin's own son is this early morning) over to the Homeopathic Hospital on North Pearl Street and saw to it that the intern called a surgeon, who came and sewed up the smash, but never splinted it, just wrapped it with its stitches and taped it to Billy's pinky and said: That's the best anybody can do with this mess; nothing left there to splint. And Billy healed, crediting it to the influence of the healthy pinky. The nail and some bone grew back crookedly, and Martin can now see the twist and puff of Billy's memorable deformity. But what does a sassy fellow like Billy need with a perfectly formed third finger? The twist lends character to the hand that holds the deck, that palms the two-finger ball, that holds the stick at the crap table, that builds the cockeyed bridge for the educated cue.

If Martin had his way, he would infuse a little of Billy's scarred sassiness into his own son's manner, a boy too tame, too subservient to the priests. Martin might even profit by injecting some sass into his own acquiescent life.

Consider that: a sassy Martin Daugherty.

Well, that may not be all that likely, really. Difficult to acquire such things.

Billy's native arrogance might well have been a gift of miffed genes, then come to splendid definition through the tests to which a street like Broadway puts a young man on the make: tests designed to refine a breed, enforce a code, exclude all simps and gumps, and deliver into the city's life a man worthy of functioning in this age of nocturnal supremacy. Men like Billy Phelan, forged in the brass of Broadway, send, in the time of their splendor, telegraphic statements of mission: I, you bums, am a winner. And that message, however devoid of Christ-like other-cheekery, dooms the faint-hearted Scottys of the night, who must sludge along, never knowing how it feels to spill over with the small change of sassiness, how it feels to leave the spillover there on the floor, more where that came from, pal. Leave it for the sweeper.

Billy went for his ball, kissed it once, massaged it, chalked and toweled his right hand, spat in the spittoon to lighten his burden, bent slightly at the waist, shuffled and slid, and bazoo-bazoo, boys, threw another strike: not *just* another strike, but a titanic blast this time which sent all pins flying pitward, the cleanest of clean hits, perfection unto tidiness, bespeaking power battening on power, control escalating.

Billy looked at no one.

Nine in a row, but still nobody said anything except hey, and yeah-yeah, with a bit more applause offered up. Billy waited for the ball to come back, rubbing his feet on the floor dirt just beyond the runway, dusting his soles with slide insurance, then picked up the ball and sidled back to the runway of alley nine for his last frame. And then he rolled it, folks, and boom-boom went the pins, zot-zot, you sons of bitches, ten in a row now, and a cheer went up, but still no comment, ten straight and his score (even though Martin hadn't filled in any numbers yet) is 280, with two more balls yet to come, twenty more pins to go. Is Billy Phelan ready for perfection? Can you handle it, kid? What will you do with it if you get it?

Billy had already won the match; no way for Scotty to catch him, given that spot. But now it looked as if Billy would beat Scotty without the spot, and, tied to a perfect game, the win would surely make the sports pages later in the week.

Scotty stood up and walked to the end of the ball return to wait. He chalked his hands, rubbed them together, played with the towel, as Billy bent over to pick up his ball.

'You ever throw three hundred anyplace before?' Scotty asked.

'I ain't thrown it *here* yet,' Billy said.

So he did it, Martin thought. Scotty's chin trembled as he watched Billy. Scotty, the nervous sportsman. Did saying what he had just said mean that the man lacked all character? Did only relentless winning define his being? Was the fear of losing sufficient cause for him to try to foul another man's luck? Why of course it was, Martin. Of course it was.

Billy threw, but it was a Jersey hit, his first crossover in the game. The ball's mixing power overcame imprecision, however, and the pins spun and rolled, toppling the stubborn ten pin, and giving Billy his eleventh strike. Scotty pulled at the towel and sat down.

'You prick,' Morrie Berman said to him. 'What'd you say that to him for?'

'Say what?'

'No class,' said Morrie. 'Class'll tell in the shit house, and you got no class.'

Billy picked up his ball and faced the pins for the last act. He called out to Bugs, the pinboy: 'Four pin is off the spot,' and he pointed to it. Martin saw he was right, and Bugs moved the pin back into proper position. Billy kissed the ball, shuffled and threw, and the ball went elegantly forward, perfect line, perfect break, perfect one-three pocket hit. Nine pins flew away. The four pin never moved.

'Two-ninety-nine,' Martin said out loud, and the mob gave its full yell and applause and then stood up to rubber-neck at the scoresheet, which Martin was filling in at last, thirty pins a frame, twenty-nine in the last one. He put down the crayon to shake hands with Billy, who stood over the table, ogling his own nifty numbers.

'Some performance, Billy,' said Charlie Boy McCall, standing to stretch his babyfat. 'I should learn not to bet against you. You remember the last time?'

'Pool match at the K. of C.'

'I bet twenty bucks on some other guy.'

'Live and learn, Charlie, live and learn.'

'You were always good at everything,' Charlie said. 'How do you explain that?'

'I say my prayers and vote the right ticket.'

'That ain't enough in this town,' Charlie said.

'I come from Colonie Street.'

'That says it,' said Charlie, who still lived on Colonie Street.

'Scotty still has to finish two frames,' Martin announced to all; for Scotty was already at alley ten, facing down the burden of second best. The crowd politely sat and watched him throw a strike. He moved to alley nine and with a Jersey hit left the baby split. He cursed inaudibly, then made the split. With his one remaining ball he threw a perfect strike for a game of 219, a total of 667. Billy's total was 668.

'Billy Phelan wins the match by one pin, without using any of the spot,' Martin was delighted to announce, and he read aloud the game scores and totals of both men. Then he handed the bet money to Morrie Berman.

'I don't even feel bad,' Charlie Boy said. 'That was a hell of a thing to watch. When you got to lose, it's nice to lose to somebody who knows what he's doing.'

'Yeah, you were hot all right,' Scotty said, handing Billy a five-dollar bill. 'Really hot.'

'Hot, my ass,' Morrie Berman said to Scotty. 'You hexed him, you bastard. He might've gone all the way if you didn't say anything, but you hexed him, talking about it.'

The crowd was already moving away, back to the bar, the sweeper confronting those cigar butts at last. New people were arriving, waiters and bartenders who would roll in the Nighthawk League, which started at 3:00 A.M. It was now two-thirty in the morning.

'Listen, you mocky bastard,' Scotty said, 'I don't have to take any noise from you.' Scotty's fists were doubled, his face flushed, his chin in vigorous tremolo. Martin's later vision of Scotty's coloration and form at this moment was that of a large, crimson firecracker.

'Hold on here, hold on,' Charlie McCall said. 'Cool down, Scotty. No damage done. Cool down, no trouble now.' Charlie was about eight feet away from the two men when he spoke, too far to do anything when Morrie started his lunge. But Martin saw it coming and jumped between the two, throwing his full weight into Morrie, his junior by thirty pounds, and knocking him backward into a folding chair, on which he sat without deliberation. Others sealed off Scotty from further attack and Billy held Morrie fast in the chair with two hands.

'Easy does it, man,' Billy said, 'I don't give a damn what he did.'

'The cheap fink,' Morrie said. 'He wouldn't give a sick whore a hairpin.'

Martin laughed at the line. Others laughed. Morrie smiled. Here was a line for the Broadway annals. Epitaph for the Scotcheroo: It was reliably reported during his lifetime that he would not give a sick whore a hairpin. Perhaps this enhanced ignominy was also entering Scotty's head after the laughter, or perhaps it was the result of his genetic gift, or simply the losing, and the unbearable self-laceration that went with it. Whatever it was, Scotty doubled up, gasping, burping. He threw his arms around his own chest, wobbled, took a short step, and fell forward, gashing his left cheek on a spittoon. He rolled onto his side, arms still aclutch, eyes squeezing out the agony in his chest.

The mob gawked and Morrie stood up to look. Martin bent over the fallen man, then lifted him up from the floor and stretched him out on the bench from which he had risen to hex Billy. Martin blotted the gash with Scotty's own shirt-tail, and then opened his left eyelid. Martin looked up at the awestruck mob and asked: 'Anybody here a doctor?' And he answered himself: 'No, of course not,' and looked then at the night manager and said, 'Call an ambulance, Al,' even though he knew Scoty was already beyond help. Scotty: Game over.

How odd to Martin, seeing a champion die in the embrace of shame, egotism, and fear of failure. Martin trembled at a potential vision of himself also prostrate before such forces, done in by a shame too great to endure, and so now is the time to double up and die. Martin saw his own father curdled by shame, his mother crippled by it twice: her own and her husband's. And Martin himself had been bewildered and thrust into silence and timidity by it (but was that the true cause?). Jesus, man, pay attention here. Somebody lies dead in front of you and you're busy exploring the origins of your own timidity. Martin, as was said of your famous father, your sense of priority is bowlegged.

Martin straightened Scotty's arm along his side, stared at the closed right eye, the half-open left eye, and sat down in the scorekeeper's chair to search pointlessly for vital signs in this dead hero of very recent yore. Finally, he closed the left eye with his thumb.

'He's really gone,' he told everybody, and they all seemed to wheeze inwardly. Then they really did disperse until only Charlie Boy McCall, face gone white, sat down at Scotty's feet and stared fully at the end of something. And he said, in his native way, 'Holy Mother of God, that was a quick decision.'

'Somebody we should call, Charlie?' Martin asked the shocked young man.

'His wife,' said Charlie. 'He's got two kids.'

'Very tough. Very. Anybody else? What about his father?'

'Dead,' said Charlie. 'His mother's in Florida. His wife's the one.'

'I'll be glad to call her,' Martin said. 'But then again maybe you ought to do that, Charlie. You're so much closer.'

'I'll take care of it, Martin.'

And Martin nodded and moved away from dead Scotty, who was true to the end to the insulting intent of his public name: tightwad of heart, parsimonious dwarf of soul.

'I never bowled a guy to death before,' Billy said.

'No jokes now,' Martin said.

'I told you he was a busher,' Billy said.

'All right but not now.'

'Screw the son of a bitch,' Morrie said to them both, said it softly, and then went over to Charlie and said, 'I know he was your friend, Charlie, and I'm sorry. But I haven't liked him for years. We never got along.'

'Please don't say any more,' Charlie said with bowed head.

'I just want you personally to know I'm sorry. Because I know how close you two guys were. I'da liked him if I could, but Jesus Christ, I don't want you sore at me, Charlie. You get what I mean?'

'I get it. I'm not sore at you.'

'I'm glad you say that because sometimes when you fight a guy his friends turn into your enemies, even though they got nothin' against you themselves. You see what I mean?'

'I see, and I've got nothing against you, Morris. You're just a punk, you've always been a punk, and the fact is I never liked you and like you a hell of a lot less than that right now. Good night, Morris.'

And Charlie Boy turned away from Morrie Berman to study the corpse of his friend.

Martin Daugherty, infused with new wisdom by the entire set of events, communicated across the miles of the city to his senile father in the nursing home bed. You see, Papa, Martin said into the microphone of the filial network, it's very clear to me now. The secret of Scotty's death lies in the simple truth uncovered by Morrie Berman: that Scotty would not give a sick whore a hairpin. And Papa, I tell you that we must all give hairpins to sick whores. It is essential. Do you hear me? Can you understand? We must give hairpins to sick whores whenever they require them. What better thing can a man do?

2

Martin Daugherty, wearing bathrobe and slippers, sat at his kitchen table, bleeding from sardonic wounds. In the name of the Father, in the name of the Son, who will savor the Father when the Son is gone? He salted his oatmeal and spiced it with raisins, those wrinkled and puny symbols of his own dark and shriveling years. He chewed a single raisin, thinking of Scotty dead, his own son gone to the seminary. But the boy was alive and free to change his mind in time, and the bitter-sweetness of this thought flowed on his tongue: treasure lurking among the wrinkles.

'You're mad entirely,' Mary Daugherty said when she saw him smiling and chewing, grim and crazy. She broke into laughter, the lilt of Connacht, a callous response to madness in her morning kitchen.

'You can bet your sweet Irish ass I'm mad,' Martin said. 'I dreamed of Peter, carried through the streets by pederast priests.'

That stopped her laughter, all right.

'You're at the priests again, are you? Why don't you let it alone? He may not even take to it.'

'They'll see he does. Fill him full of that windy God shit, called to the front, cherub off Main Street. Give the helping hand to others, learn to talk to the birds and make a bridge to the next world. Why did God make you if it wasn't to save all those wretched bastards who aren't airy and elite enough to be penniless saviors?'

'You're worried he'll be penniless, is that it?'

'I'm worried he'll be saved entirely by priests.'

The boy, Peter, had been sitting in a web of ropes, suspended beyond the edge of the flat roof of home. Billy Phelan, in another suspended web, sat beside Peter, both of them looking at Martin as they lounged in the ropes, which were all that lay between them and the earth. Martin marveled at the construction of the webs, which defied gravity. And then Peter leaped off the web, face forward, and plummeted two stories. His body hit, then his head, two separate impacts, and he lay still. Two priests in sackcloth scooped him into a wheelbarrow with their shovels and one of them pushed him off into the crowded street. Billy Phelan never moved from his web. Martin, suddenly on the street, followed the wheelbarrow through the rubble but lost it. In a vacant lot he confronted a band of children Peter's age. They jogged in an ominous circle which Martin could not escape. A small girl threw a stone which struck Martin on the head. A small boy loped toward Martin with an upraised knife, and the circle closed in. Martin rushed to meet the knife-wielding attacker and flew at the boy's chest with both feet.

He awoke and squinted toward the foot of the bed, where the figure of an adolescent, wearing a sweater of elaborate patterns, leaned back in a chair, feet propped on the bedcovers. But the figure was perhaps beyond adolescence. Its head was an animal's, with pointed snout. A fox? A fawn? A lamb? Martin sat up, resting on his elbow for a closer look. The figure remained in focus, but the head was still blurred. Martin rubbed his eyes. The figure leaned back on the legs of the chair, feet crossed at the ankles, leisurely observing Martin. And then it vanished, not as a dream fading into wakefulness, but with a filmmaker's magic: suddenly, wholly gone.

Martin, half-erect, leaning on his elbow, heard Mary say the oatmeal was on the table. He thought of the illustrated Bible he had leafed through when he'd come home after Scotty's death, compulsively searching through the Old Testament for an equivalent of the man's sudden departure. He had found nothing that satisfied him, but he'd put out the light thinking of the engraving of Abraham and the bound Isaac, with the ram breaking through the bushes, and he had equated Isaac with his son, Peter, sacrificed to someone else's faith: first communion, confirmation, thrust into the hands of nuns and priests, then smothered by the fears of a mother who still believed making love standing up damned you forever.

Had Martin's fuzzy, half-animal bedside visitor been the ram that saved Isaac from the knife? In a ski sweater? What did it have to do with Peter? Martin opened the Bible to the engraving. The sweatered animal at bedside bore no resemblance to the ram of salvation. Martin re-read what he had written years ago above the engraving after his first reading of the Abraham story: We are all in conspiracy against the next man. He could not now explain what precisely he had meant by that phrase.

It had been years since the inexplicable touched Martin's life. Now, eating his oatmeal, he examined this new vision, trying to connect it to the dream of Peter falling out of the web, to Peter's face as he left home two days before, a fourteen-year-old boy about to become a high school sophomore, seduced by God's holy messengers to enter a twig-bending preseminary school. Peter: the centerpiece of his life, the only child he would have. He raged silently at the priests who had stolen him away, priests who would teach the boy to pile up a fortune from the coal collection, to scold the poor for their indolence. The assistant pastor of Sacred Heart Church had only recently sermonized on the folly of striving for golden brown toast and the fatuity of the lyrics of 'Tea for Two.' There was a suburban priest who kept a pet duck on a leash. One in Troy chased a nubile child around the parish house. Priests in their cups. Priests in their beggars' robes. Priests in their eunuch suits. There were saints among them, men of pure love, and one such had inspired Peter, given him the life of Saint Francis to read, encouraging selflessness, fanaticism, poverty, bird calls.

Months ago, when he was shaping his decision, the boy sat at this same kitchen table poking at his own raisins, extolling the goodness of priests. Do you know any good men who aren't priests? Martin asked him.

You, said the boy.

How did I make it without the priesthood?

I don't know, but maybe sometimes you aren't good. Are you always good?

By no means.

Then did you ever know any men good enough to talk to the birds?

Plenty. Neil O'Connor talked to his ducks all day long. After four pints Marty Sheehan'd have long talks with Lackey Quinlan's goose.

But did the birds talk back?

You couldn't shut them up once they got going, said Martin.

Balance: that was what he wanted to induce in Peter. Be reverent also in the presence of the absence of God.

'I just don't want them to drown him in their holy water,' Martin said to Mary Daugherty. 'And I don't want him to be afraid to tell them to shove their incense up their chalices if he feels like coming home. There'll be none of that failed priest business in this house the way it was with Chickie Phelan.' (And Martin then sensed, unreasonably, that Chick would call him on the telephone, soon; perhaps this morning.) 'His mother and sisters wanted Chick to bring a little bit of heaven into the back parlor, and when he couldn't do it, they never forgave him. And another thing. I always wanted Peter to grow up here, grow up and beget. I don't want to see the end of the Daughtertys after the trouble of centuries took us this far.'

'You want another Daugherty? Another son? Is that what you're saying to me?'

'It's that I hate to see the end of a line. Any line. Think of all the Daughertys back beyond Patrick. Pirates stole *him* you know, made him a slave. That's how *he* got into the saint business.'

'Ah,' said Mary, 'you're a talky man.'

'I am.'

'Are you through now?'

'I am.'

'Why don't you be talky like that with the boy?'

'I was.'

'You told him all that?'

'I did.'

'Well, then?' said the wife and mother of the family. 'Well?'

'Just about right,' said Martin.

The talk had calmed him, and real and present things took his attention: his wife and her behind, jiggling while she stirred the eggs. Those splendid puffs of Irish history, those sweet curves of the Western world, sloping imagistically toward him: roundaceous beneath the black and yellow kimono he'd given her for the New York vacation. The memory of coupling in their stateroom on the night boat, the memory of their most recent coupling – was it three, four days ago? – suggested to Martin that screwing your wife is like striking out the pitcher. Martin's attitude, however, was that there was little point in screwing anyone else. Was this a moralistic judgment because of his trauma with Melissa Spencer, or merely an apology for apathetic constancy? Melissa in his mind again. She would be in town now with the pseudoscandalous show. She would not call him. He would not call her. Yet he felt they would very probably meet.

The phone rang and Miss Irish Ass of 1919 callipygiated across the room and answered it. 'Oh yes, yes, Chick, he's here, yes. Imagine that, and he was just talking about you.'

'Well, Chickie,' said Martin, 'are you ready for the big move today? Is your pencil sharpened?'

'Something big, Martin, really big.'

'Big enough,' said Martin; for Chick had been the first to reveal to him the plan concocted by Patsy McCall, leader of the Albany Democratic Party, to take control of the American Labor Party's local wing on this, the final day of voter registration. Loyal Democrats, of which Chick was one, would register A.L.P., infiltrate the ranks, and push out the vile Bolsheviks and godless socialists who stank up the city with their radical ways.

Patsy McCall and his Democrats would save the city from the red stink.

'No, Martin, it's not that,' Chick said. 'It's Charlie Boy. The police are next door, and Maloney too. Him and half the damn McCall family's been coming and going over here all night long. He's gone, Martin. Charlie's gone. I think they grabbed him.'

'Grabbed him?'

'Kidnapped. They've been using the phone here since four-thirty this morning. A regular parade. They'll be back, I know it, but you're the one should know about this. I owe you that.'

'Are you sure of this, Chickie?'

'They're on the way back now. I see Maloney coming down their stoop. Martin, they took Charlie out of his car about four o'clock this morning. His mother got up in the night and saw the car door wide open and nobody inside. A bunch of cigarettes on the running board. And he's gone. I heard them say that. Now, you don't know nothing from here, don't you know, and say a prayer for the boy, Martin, say a prayer. Oh Jesus, the things that go on.'

And Chick hung up.

Martin looked at the kitchen wall, dirty tan, needing paint. Shabby wall. Shabby story. Charlie Boy taken. The loss, the theft of children. Charlie was hardly a child, yet his father, Bindy McCall, would still think of him as one.

'What was that?' Mary asked.

'Just some talk about a story.'

'Who or what was grabbed? I heard you say grabbed.'

'You're fond of that word, are you?'

'It's got a bit of a ring to it.'

'You don't have to wait for a ring to get grabbed.'

'I knew that good and early, thanks be to God.'

And then, Martin grabbed the queenly rump he had lived with for sixteen years, massaged it through the kimono, and walked quickly out of the kitchen to his study. He sat in the reading rocker alongside a stack of Albany newspapers taller than a small boy, and reached for the phone. Already he could see the front pages, the splash, boom, bang, the sad, sad whoopee of the headlines. The extras. The photos. These are the McCall brothers. Here a recap of their extraordinary control of Albany for seventeen years. Here their simple homes. And now this. Here Charlie Boy's car. Here the spot where. Here the running board where the cigarettes fell. Here some famous kidnappings. Wheeeeee.

Martin dialed.

'Yeah,' said Patsy McCall's unmistakable sandpaper voice box after the phone rang once.

'Martin Daugherty, Patsy.'

'Yeah.'

'I hear there's been some trouble.'

Silence.

'Is that right or wrong?'

'No trouble here.'

'I hear there's a lot of activity over at your place and that maybe something bad happened.'

Silence.

'Is that right or wrong, Patsy?'

'No trouble here.'

'Are you going to be there a while? All right if I come down?'

'Come down if you like, Martin. Bulldogs wouldn't keep the likes of you off the stoop.'

'That's right, Patsy. I'll be there in fifteen minutes. Ten.'

'There's nothing going on here.'

'Right, Patsy, see you in a little while.'

'Don't bring nobody.'

In his bedroom, moving at full speed, Martin took off his blue flannel bathrobe, spotted with egg drippings and coffee dribbles, pulled on his pants over the underwear he'd slept in and decided not to tell his wife the news. She was a remote cousin to Charlie's mother and would want to lend whatever strength she had to the troubled family, a surge of good will that would now be intrusive.

The McCalls' loss intensified Martin's own. But where his was merely doleful, theirs was potentially tragic. Trouble. People he knew, sometimes his kin, deeply in trouble, was what had often generated his inexplicable visions. Ten years without this kind of divination, now suddenly back: the certainty Chick would call; the bizarre bedside visitor heralding the unknown; the death of Scotty followed by the kidnapping of Charlie. Coincidental trouble.

The inexplicable had first appeared a quarter century ago in late October, 1913, when, fresh from a six-month journalistic foray in England and Ireland, Martin found himself in Albany, walking purposefully but against logic north on North Pearl Street, when he should have been walking west on State Street toward the Capitol, where he had an appointment to interview the new governor, a namesake, Martin H. Glynn, an Albany editor, politician, and orator interested in Ireland's troubles. But a counterimpulse was on him and he continued on Pearl Street to the Pruyn Library, where he saw his cousin, a fireman with steamer eight, sitting on the family wagon, the reins of the old horse sitting loosely on his knees. He was wearing his knitted blue watch cap, a familiar garment to Martin. As their eyes met, the cousin smiled, lifted a pistol from his lap, pointed it at the horse, then turned it to his right temple and pulled the trigger. He died without further ado, leaving the family no explanation for his act, and was smiling still when Martin caught the reins of the startled horse and reached his cousin's side.

Nothing like that happened to Martin again until 1925, the year he published his collection of short stories. But he recognized the same irrational impulse when he was drawn, without reason, to visit the lawyer handling his father's libel suit against an Albany newspaper, which had resurrected the old man's scandal with Melissa. Martin found the lawyer at home, in robust health, and they talked of Martin's father, who at that point was living in New York City. Two hours after their talk the lawyer died of a heart attack walking up Maiden Lane, and the task of finding a new lawyer for his father fell to Martin.

That same year Martin tuned in the radio at mid-morning, an

uncharacteristic move, and heard of the sinking of the excursion steamer *Sweethearts* in the Hudson River below Kingston. He later learned that a girl he once loved had gone down with the boat. He began after this to perceive also things not related to trouble. He foresaw by a week that a *Times-Union* photographer would win six thousand dollars in the Albany baseball pool. He was off by only one day in his prediction of when his father would win the libel suit. He knew a love affair would develop between his wife's niece from Galway and an Albany bartender, two months before the niece arrived in Albany. He predicted that on the day of that love's first bloom it would be raining, a thunderstorm, and so it was.

Martin's insights took the shape of crude imagery, like photographs intuited from the radio. He came to consider himself a mystical naturalist, insisting to himself and to others that he did not seriously believe in ghosts, miracles, resurrection, heaven, or hell. He seasoned any account of his beliefs and his bizarre intuition with a remark he credited to his mother: There's no Santa Claus and there's no devil. Your father's both. He dwelled on his visions and found them comforting, even when they were false and led him nowhere and revealed nothing. He felt they put him in touch with life in a way he had never experienced it before, possessor of a power which not even his famous and notorious father, in whose humiliating shadow he had lived all his years, understood. His father was possessed rather by concrete visions of the Irish in the New World, struggling to throw off the filth of poverty, oppression, and degradation, and rising to a higher plane of life, where they would be the equals of all those arrived Americans who manipulated the nation's power, wealth, and culture. Martin was bored with the yearnings of the immigrant hordes and sought something more abstract: to love oneself and one's opposite. He preferred personal insight to social justice, though he wrote of both frequently in his column, which was a confusion of radicalism, spiritual exploration, and foolery. He was a comedian who sympathized with Heywood Broun, Tom Mooney, and all Wobblies, who drank champagne with John McCormack, beer with Mencken, went to the track with Damon Runyon, wrote public love letters to Marlene Dietrich whenever her films played Albany, and who viewed America's detachment from the Spanish Civil War as an exercise in evil by omission.

He also wrote endlessly on a novel, a work he hoped would convey his version of the meaning of his father's scandalous life. He had written twelve hundred pages, aspiring to perhaps two hundred or less, and could not finish it. At age fifty he viewed himself, after publication of two books of non-fiction, one on the war, the other a personal account of the Irish troubles, plus the short story collection and innumerable articles for national magazines, as a conundrum, a man unable to define his commitment or understand the secret of his own navel, a literary gnome. He seriously valued almost nothing he wrote, except for the unfinished novel.

He was viewed by the readers of the *Times-Union*, which carried his column five days a week, as a mundane poet, a penny-whistle philosopher, a provocative half-radical man nobody had to take seriously, for he wasn't quite serious about himself. He championed dowsing and ouija boards and sought to rehabilitate Henry James, Sr., the noted Albanian and Swedenborgian. He claimed that men of truest vision were, like James, always considered freaks, and he formed the International Brotherhood of Crackpots by way of giving them a bargaining agent, and attracted two thousand members.

His column was frequently reprinted nationally, but he chose not to syndicate it, fearing he would lose his strength, which was his Albany constituency, if his subject matter went national. He never wrote of his own gift of foresight.

The true scope of that gift was known to no one, and only his family and a few friends knew it existed at all. The source of it was wondered at suspiciously by his Irish-born wife, who had been taught in the rocky wastes of Connemara that druids roamed the land, even to this day.

The gift left Martin in 1928 after his fortieth birthday debauch with Melissa, the actress, his father's erstwhile mistress, the woman who was the cause of the paternal scandal. Martin returned home from the debauch, stinking of simony, and severely ill with what the family doctor simplistically diagnosed as alcoholic soak. Within a week Martin accurately sensed that his mystical talent was gone. He recuperated from the ensuing depression after a week, but rid himself of the simoniacal stink only when he acceded to his wife's suggestion, and, after a decade of considering himself not only not a Catholic but not even a Christian, he sought out the priest in the Lithuanian church who spoke and understood English only primitively, uttered a confession of absurd sins (I burned my wife's toenail parings three times) and then made his Easter Duty at Sacred Heart Church, driving out the odor of simony with ritual sacrilege.

He shoved his arms into the fresh shirt Mary Daugherty had ironed. A fresh shirt every day, Mary insisted, or you'll blow us all out the window with the B.O. Martin pushed into his black shoes, gone gray with months of scuffs and the denial of polish, threw a tie once around his neck in a loose knot, and thrust himself into his much abused suit coat. A sughan, Mary said. You've made a sughan of it. Ah well, all things come alike to all, the clean and the unclean, the pressed and the unimpressed.

In the bathroom he brushed away the taste of oatmeal, splashed his face with cold water, flattened his cowlick with the hairbrush, and then salt-stepped down the stairs, saying as he sped through the kitchen: 'I've got a hell of a story, I think, Mary. I'll call you.'

'What about your coffee? What about your eggs?'

But he was already gone, this aging firefly who never seemed to his wife to have grown up quite like other men, gone on another story.

Martin Daugherty had once lived in Arbor Hill, where the McCalls and the Phelans lived, but fire destroyed the house of his childhood and adolescence, and the smoke poisoned Katrina Daugherty, his mother, who escaped the flames only to die on the sidewalk of Colonie Street in her husband's arms, quoting Verlaine to him: '. . . you loved me so!' 'Quite likely – I forget.'

The fire began in the Christian Brothers School next door, old

Brother William turned to a kneeling cinder by the hellish flames. The fire leaped across the alley and consumed the Daugherty house, claiming not only its second victim in Martin's mother, but also his father's accumulation of a lifetime of books, papers, and clippings that attested to his fame and infamy, and two unfinished plays. Edward Daugherty left Arbor Hill forever after the fire and moved into the North End of the city, politely evicting the tenants in his own father's former home on Main Street.

This was the house Edward Daugherty's parents had built on the edge of the Erie Canal the year before Martin was born, and had lived in until they died. After Edward's first stroke, Martin moved into the house also, with his wife and son, to nurse his father back to independence. But the man was never to be well again, and Martin remained in the house even until now, curator of what he had come to call the Daugherty Museum.

Martin parked his car on Colonie Street in front of the vacant lot where his former home had stood before it burned. He stepped out onto the sidewalk where he'd once pitched pennies and election cards, and the charred roots of his early life moved beneath his feet. Chick Phelan peered out of the upstairs bay window of the house next to the empty lot. Martin did not wave. He looked fleetingly at the outline of the foundation of the old place, slowly being buried by the sod of time.

Patsy McCall's house was kitty-corner to the empty lot and Martin crossed the street and climbed the stoop. He, the Phelans, the McCalls (Bindy lived two doors above Patsy), and all the other youths of the street had spent uncountable nights on this stoop, talking, it now seemed, of three subjects: baseball, the inaccessibility of the myriad burgeoning breasts that were poking themselves into the eyeballs and fluid dreams of every boy on the street, and politics: Would you work for Billy Barnes? Never. Packy McCabe? Sure. Who's the man this election? Did you hear how the Wally-Os stole a ballot box in the Fifth Ward and Corky Ronan chased 'em and got it back and bit off one of their ears?

Martin looked at his watch: eight thirty-five. He rang the

doorbell and Dick Maloney, district attorney of Albany County, a short, squat man with an argumentive mouth, answered.

'You're up early, Dick, me boy.'

'Am I?'

'Are you in possession of any news?'

'There's no news I know of.'

And Maloney pointed toward the dining room, where Martin found Patsy and Matt McCall, the political leaders of the city and county for seventeen years. Cronies of both brothers sat with them at the huge round table, its white tablecloth soiled with coffee stains and littered with cups, ashes, and butts. On the wall the painted fruit was ripening in the bowl and the folks were still up at Golgotha. Alongside hung framed, autographed photos of Jim Jeffries, Charlie Murphy of Tammany, Al Smith as presidential candidate, and James Oliver Plunkett, who had inscribed the photo with one of his more memorable lines: 'Government of the people, by the people who were elected to govern them.'

'Morning, gentlemen,' Martin said with somber restraint.

'We're not offering coffee,' said Patsy, looking his usual, overstuffed self. With his tight haircut, rounded jowls, and steel-rimmed specs, this Irish-American chieftain looked very like a Prussian puffball out of uniform.

'Then thanks for nothing,' said Martin.

The cronies, Poop Powell, an ex-hurley player and ex-cop who drove for the McCalls, and Freddie Gallagher, a childhood pal of Matt's who found that this friendship alone was the secret of survival in the world, rose from the table and went into the parlor without a word or a nod. Martin sat in a vacated chair and said to Patsy, 'There's something tough going on, I understand.'

'No, nothing,' said Patsy.

The McCalls' faces were abulge with uncompromising gravity. For all their power they seemed suddenly powerless confronting personal loss. But many men had passed into oblivion for misjudging the McCalls' way with power. Patsy demonstrated it first in 1919 when he campaigned in his sailor suit for the post of city assessor and won, oh wondrous victory. It was the wedge which broke the hold the dirty black Republican sons of bitches had had on the city since '99. Into the chink Patsy made in the old machine, the Democrats, two years later, drove a new machine, the Nonesuch, with the McCalls at the wheel: Patsy, the savior, the *sine qua non*, becoming the party leader and patron; Matt, the lawyer, becoming the political strategist and spokesman; and Benjamin, called Bindy, the sport, taking over as Mayor of Nighttime City.

The three brothers, in an alliance with a handful of Protestant Yankee aristocrats who ran the formal business of the city, developed a stupendous omnipotence over both county and city, which vibrated power strings even to the White House. Democratic aspirants made indispensable quadrennial pilgrimages to genuflect in the McCall cathedral and plead for support. The machine brushed the lives of every Albany citizen from diapers to dotage. George Quinn often talked of the day he leaped off the train at Van Woert Street, coming back in uniform from France, and was asked for five dollars by John Kelleher on behalf of Patsy's campaign for the assessorship. George gave not five but fifteen and had that to brag about for the rest of his life.

'I have to say it,' Martin said, looking at Patsy, his closest friend among the brothers. 'There's a rumor around that Charlie was kidnapped last night.'

The gravity of the faces did not change, nor did the noncommittal expressions.

'Nothing to that,' said Matt, a tall, solid man, still looking like the fullback he once was, never a puffball; handsome and with a movie actor's crop of black hair. When he gained power, Matt put his college football coach on the Supreme Court bench.

'Is Charlie here?' Martin asked him.

'He went to New York,' Matt said.

'When was that?'

'None of your goddamn business,' said Patsy.

'Patsy, listen. I'm telling you the rumor is out. If it's fake and you don't squelch it, you'll have reporters crawling in the windows.'

'Not these windows I won't. And why should I deny something

that hasn't happened? What the hell do you think I am, a goddamn fool?'

The rising anger. Familiar. The man was a paragon of wrath when cornered. Unreason itself. He put Jigger Begley in tears for coming drunk to a rally, and a week later Jigger, Patsy's lifelong friend, quit his job in the soap factory, moved to Cleveland, and for all anybody knew was there yet. Power in the voice.

Martin's personal view was this: that I do not fear the McCalls; that this is my town as much as theirs and I won't leave it for any of them. Martin had committed himself to Albany in part because of the McCalls, because of the promise of a city run by his childhood friends. But he'd also come back to his native city in 1921, after two years with the A.E.F. and a year and a half in Ireland and England after that, because he sensed he would be nothing without his roots, and when, in 1922, he was certain of this truth he went back to Ireland and brought Maire Kiley out of her Gaelic wilderness in Carraroe, married her in Galway, and came to Albany forever, or at least sixteen years now seemed like forever. So to hell with Patsy and his mouth and the whole bunch of them and their power. Martin Daugherty's complacency is superior to whatever abstract whip they hold over him. But then again, old fellow, there's no need to make enemies needlessly, or to let the tone of a man's voice turn your head.

'One question then,' Martin said with his mildest voice, 'and then I'm done with questions.'

The brothers waited solemnly.

'Is Bindy in town?'

'He's in Baltimore,' said Matt. 'At the races with his wife.'

Martin nodded, waited, then said, 'Patsy, Matt. You say there's nothing going on and I have to accept that, even though Maloney looks like he's about to have twins on the stair carpet. But very obviously something is happening, and you don't want it out. All right, so be it. I give you my word, and I pledge Em Jones's word, that the *Times-Union* will not print a line about this thing, whatever it is. Not the rumor, not the denial of the rumor, not any speculation. We will not mention Charlie, or Bindy, or either of you in any context other than conventional history, until you give the go-ahead. I don't break confidences without good reason and you both know that about me all my life. And I'll tell you one more thing. Emory will do anything in his power to put the newspaper behind you in any situation such as the hypothetical one we've not been discussing here. I repeat. Not discussing. Under no circumstances have we been discussing anything here this morning. But if the paper can do anything at all, then it will. I pledge that as true as I stand here talking about nothing whatsoever.'

The faces remained grave. Then Patsy's mouth wrinkled sideways into the makings of a small grin.

'You're all right, Martin,' he said. 'For a North Ender.'

Martin stood and shook Matt's hand, then Patsy's.

'If anything should come up we'll let you know,' Matt said. 'And thanks.'

'It's what's right,' Martin said, standing up, thinking: I've still got the gift of tongues. For it was as true as love that by talking a bit of gibberish he had verified, beyond doubt, that Charlie Boy McCall had, indeed, been grabbed.

'You know I saw Charlie last night down at the Downtown alleys. We were there when Scotty Streck dropped dead. I suppose you know about that one.'

'We knew he was there,' Patsy said. 'We didn't know who else.'

'We're working on that,' Matt said.

'I can tell you who was there to the man,' Martin said, and he ticked off names of all present except the sweeper and one bar customer, whom he identified by looks. Matt made notes on it all.

'What was Berman doing there?' Patsy asked.

'I don't know. He just turned up at the bar.'

'Was he there before Charlie got there?'

'I can't be sure of that.'

'Do you think he knew Charlie would be at the alleys?'

'I couldn't say.'

'Do you know Berman?'

'I've been in his company, but we're not close.'

'Who is close to him?'

Martin shook his head, thinking of faces but connecting no one intimately to the man. Then he said, 'Billy Phelan seems to know him. Berman backed him in last night's match and did the same once before, when Billy played pool. He seems to like Billy.'

'Do you trust Phelan?' Matt asked.

'No man in his right mind would trust him with his woman, but otherwise he's as good as gold, solid as they come.'

'We want to keep tabs on that Berman fellow,' Patsy said.

'You think he's connected to this situation?' and both Patsy and Matt shrugged without incriminating Berman, but clearly admitting there certainly was a situation.

'We're keeping tabs on a lot of people,' Patsy said. 'Can you ask young Phelan to hang around a while with Berman, the next few days, say, and let us know where he goes and what he says?'

'Ahhhhh,' said Martin, 'that's tricky but I guess I can ask.'

'Don't you think he'll do it?'

'I wouldn't know, but it is touchy. Being an informer's not Billy's style.'

'Informer?' said Patsy, bristling.

'It's how he might look at it.'

'That's not how I look at it.'

'I'll ask him,' Martin said. 'I can certainly ask him.'

'We'll take good care of him if he helps us,' Matt said. 'He can count on that.'

'I don't think he's after that either.'

'Everybody's after that,' Patsy said.

'Billy's headstrong,' Martin said, standing up.

'So am I,' said Patsy. 'Keep in touch.'

'Bulldogs,' said Martin.

3

Martin drove downtown and parked on Broadway near the Plaza, as usual, and headed, he thought, for the *Times-Union*. But instead of turning up Beaver Street, he walked south on Broadway, all the way to Madison Avenue. He turned up Madison, realizing then that he was bound for Spanish George's bar. He had no urge to drink and certainly no reason to confront either George or any of his customers, especially at this hour. George, notorious in the city's South End, ran a bar and flophouse in Shanks's old three-story livery stable. He had come to America from Spain to build the Barge Canal and stayed on to establish an empire in the dregs, where winos paid to collapse on his cots after they had all but croaked on his wine.

The sour air assaulted Martin as he stepped inside the bar, but he understood the impulse that was on him and did not retreat. His will seemed unfettered, yet somehow suspended. He knew he was obeying something other than will and that it might, or might not, reveal its purpose. In the years when this came as a regular impulse, he often found himself sitting in churches, standing in front of grocery stores, or riding trolleys, waiting for revelation. But the trolley often reached the end of the line and took him back to his starting point without producing an encounter, and he would resume the previous path of his day, feeling duped by useless caprice. Yet the encounters which did prove meaningful, or even prophetic of disaster or good fortune, were of such weight that he could not help but follow the impulse once he recognized it for what it was. He came to believe that the useless journeys did not arise from the same source as those with genuine meaning, but were rather his misreadings of his own mood, his own imagination, a duping of self with counterfeit expectations. Five such fruitless trips in four days after his debauch made him aware his gift had fled. Now, as he gagged on the wine-pukish rancidity of George's, on the dead-rat stink and the vile-body decay that entered your system with every breath, he was certain that the impulse was the same as it had always been, whether true or false; and what he was doing was giving his mystical renewal a chance to prove itself. He ordered a bottle of beer and when George was looking elsewhere he wiped its neck clean with his handkerchief and drank from the bottle.

'I don't see you too much,' George said to him.

George was, as usual, wearing his filthy sombrero and his six-gun in the embroidered leather holster, and looked very like a Mexican *bandido*. The gun, presumably, was not loaded, or so the police had ordered. But any wino aggressive on muscatel could not be so sure of that, and so George, by force of costume alone, maintained order on his premises.

'That's true, George,' Martin said. 'I keep pretty busy uptown. Not much on this edge of things lately.'

'I see you writing in the paper.'

'Still at it. Right you are.'

'You never write me a story any more.'

'I've done you, George, again and again. You've ceased to be newsy. If you decide to renovate the premises and put in a bridal suite, then maybe I'll work up a story.'

'No money in that stuff.'

'You're probably right. Honeymooners are bum spenders. But business is good, I suppose?'

'Always lousy. You like a sandwich? Fry an egg for you?'

'I just had breakfast, thanks. The beer is fine.'

'Okay,' George said, and he pushed Martin's dollar back to him.

Martin sensed a presence then and looked toward the door to

see a tall, shambling man in a suit coat of brown twill, collar up, lighting a cigarette as he moved toward the bar. Despite what the years had done to the man, Martin instantly recognized Francis Phelan, Billy's father, and he knew his own presence here had a purpose. Forced confluence of Martin and the Phelans: Billy and Chick, now Francis, and yet more than that. The McCalls were part of it. And Martin's father, too, in his bed of senility; and Melissa, in town in the old man's play. A labyrinth.

'Francis,' said Martin, and Francis turned and squinted through half-waking eyes, pitiable visage. Martin vividly remembered the original: Franny Phelan: Albany's best-known ballplayer in his time. And he remembered too the dreadful day in 1901 when the scabs and the militia were trying to drive a single trolley through a mob on Broadway in front of Union Station, and Franny, in front of the Railroad YMCA, hurling a smooth round stone like a fast ball, and laying open the skull of the scab conductor. The militia fired wildly into the crowd as other stones flew, and in retaliation for the dead scab, two men who had nothing to do with the violence, a businessman and a shopper, were shot dead. And Franny became a fugitive, his exile proving to be the compost for his talent. He fled west, using an alias, and got a job in Dayton playing pro ball. When he came home again to live, he returned to life on the road every summer for years, the last three as a big leaguer with Washington. Franny Phelan, a razzmatazz third baseman, maestro of the hidden ball trick.

Such a long time ago. And now Franny is back, the bloom of drink in every pore, the flesh ready to bleed through the sheerest of skin. He puffed his cigarette, dropped the lit match to the floor, inhaled, and then looked searchingly at Martin, who followed the progress of the match, watched its flame slowly burn out on the grease of George's floor.

'Ah, how are you, Martin?' Francis said.

'I'm well enough, Fran, and how are you keeping yourself?'

'Keeping?' He smiled. 'Orange soda, with ice,' he told George.

'What color orange has your money got?' George said.

'Take it here,' said Martin, pushing the dollar back to George.

And George then poured Francis a glass of soda over ice, a jelly glass with a ridged rim.

'It's been years,' Martin said. 'Years and years.'

'I guess so,' said Francis. He sipped the soda, once, twice. 'Goddamn throat's burning up.' He raised the glass. 'Cheers.'

'To you,' Martin said, raising the bottle, 'back in Albany.'

'I only came to vote,' said Francis, smiling.

'To vote?'

'To register. They still pay for that here, don't they?'

'Ah, yes, of course. I understand. Yes, I believe they do.'

'I did it before. Registered fourteen times one year. Twenty-eight bucks.'

'The price is up to five now. It must've been a long while ago you did that.'

'I don't remember. I don't remember much of anything any more.'

'How long has it been? Twenty years, it must be.'

'Twenty-two. I do remember that. Nineteen-sixteen.'

'Twenty-two years. You see the family?'

'No, I don't go through that business.'

'I talked to Chick this morning.'

'Fuck him.'

'Well, I always get along pretty well with him. And he always thought well of you.'

'Fuck 'em all.'

'You don't see your kids either?'

'No, I don't see nobody.' He sipped the soda. 'You see the boy?'

'Quite often. He's a first-rate citizen, and good looking, with some of your features. I was with him last night. He bowled two-ninety-nine in a match game.'

'Yeah.'

'You want to see him? I could set that up.'

'No, hell no. None of that old shit. That's old shit. I'm out of it, Martin. Don't do nothin' like that to me.'

'If you say so.'

'Yeah, I do. No percentage in that.'

'You here for a while?'

'No, passing through, that's all. Get the money and get gone.'

'Very strange development, running into you here. Anything I can do for you, Franny?' Franny, the public name. What a hell of a ball player, gone to hell.

'I could use a pack of smokes.'

'What's your brand?'

Francis snorted. 'Old Golds. Why not?'

Martin pushed a quarter at George and George fished for the cigarettes and bounced them on the bar in front of Francis.

'That's two I owe you, Martin. What're you doin' for yourself?'

'I write for the morning paper, a daily column.'

'A writer like your father.'

'No, not like that. Not anything like that. Just a column.'

'You were always a smart kid. You always wrote something. Your father still alive?'

'Oh yes,' and ancient times rolled back, the years before and after the turn of the century when the Phelans and Daughertys were next-door neighbors and Martin's mother was alive in her eccentric isolation. Francis was the handyman who fixed whatever went wrong in the Daugherty home, Edward Daugherty cosmically beyond manual labor, Martin a boyish student of Francis's carpentry skills as he put on the new roof or enlarged the barn to house two carriages instead of one. He was installing a new railing on the back stoop the summer morning Martin's mother came down that same stoop naked, bound for the carriage barn with her shopping bag. Francis wrapped her in a piece of awning and walked her back into the house, the first indication to anyone except Edward Daugherty that something was distracting her.

Edward Daugherty used Francis as the prototype for the fugitive hero in his play about the trolley strike, *The Car Barns*, in which heroic Francis, the scab-killer, was immortalized. Legends and destinies worked out over the back fence. Or over a beer and an orange soda.

'He's in a nursing home now,' Martin said of his father. 'Pretty senile, but he has his moments when a good deal of it comes back. Those are the worst times.'

'That's how it goes,' Francis said.

'For some people.'

'Yeah. Some don't get that far.'

'I have the feeling I ought to do something for you, Fran,' Martin said. 'Something besides a pack of cigarettes and a glass of soda. Why do I feel that?'

'Damned if I know, Martin. Nothing I want out of you.'

'Well, I'm around. I'm in the book, up on Main Street in the North End now. And you can always leave a message at the *Times-Union*.'

'Okay, Martin, and thanks for that,' and Francis extended his right hand, which was missing two joints on the index finger. He will throw no more baseballs. Martin shook the hand and its stumpy digit.

'Don't blow any whistles on me, Martin. I don't need that kind of scene.'

'It's your life,' Martin said, but even as he said it he was adding silently: but not entirely yours. Life hardly goes by ones.

Martin bought an *Armstrong* at Jerry's newsroom, just up from the paper, and then an egg sandwich and coffee to go at Farrell's lunchroom, three doors down, and with breakfast and horses in hand he crossed Beaver Street, climbed the paintless, gray, footworn, and crooked staircase to the *Times-Union* city room, and settled in at his desk, a bruised oak antique at which the Albany contemporaries of Mark Twain might have worked. Across the room Joe Leahy, the only other citizen on duty and a squeaker of a kid, was opening mail at the city desk and tending the early phone. The only other life sign was the clacking of the Associated Press and International News Service teletypes, plus the Hearst wire, which carried the words of The Chief: editorials, advisories, exclusive stories on Marion Davies.

Martin never looked at the machine without remembering the

night Willie Powers, the night slot man, went to lunch and came back pickled, then failed to notice an advisory that The Chief was changing his front-page editorial on Roosevelt, changing it drastically from soft- to hard-line antipathy, for the following day. Willie failed to notice not only the advisory but also the editorial which followed it, and so the *Times-Union* the next morning carried The Chief's qualified praise of F.D.R., while the rest of the Hearst press across the nation carried The Chief's virulent attack on the president, his ancestors, his wife, his children, his dog.

There is no record of Hearst's ever having visited the *Times-Union* city room, but a week later, during a stopover at the Albany station on the Twentieth Century, The Chief received Emory Jones, who presented him with the day's final edition, an especially handsome, newsy product by local standards. The Chief looked at the paper, then without a word let it fall to the floor of his private compartment, and jumped up and down on it with both feet until Emory fled in terror.

Martin fished up salt, pepper, saccharin, and spoon to garnish his sandwich and coffee and, as he ate, studied the entries in the *Armstrong*. There in the third at Laurel loomed a hunch, if ever a hunch there was: Charley Horse, seven-to-one on the morning line. He circled it, uncradled the phone receiver and dialed the operator: Madge, lively crone.

'Any messages for me, kiddo?'

'Who'd call you, you old bastard? Wait while I look. Yes, Chick Phelan called. Not that long ago. He didn't leave a number.'

'You heard from Emory? He coming in?'

'Not a word from him.'

'Then give me a line.'

Martin dialed home and told Mary the news and swore her to secrecy. Then he called Chick's home. The phone rang but nobody answered. He dialed the home of Emory Jones, the Welsh rarebit, the boss of bosses, editor of editors, a heroic Hearstian for almost as many years as Hearst had owned newspapers, a man who lived and died for the big story, who coveted the Pulitzer Prize he would never win and hooted the boot-lickers and eggsuckers who waltzed off with it year after year. Martin would now bring him the word on the Charlie Boy story, fracture his morning serenity.

Martin remembered the last big Albany story, the night word arrived that a local man wanted for a triple murder in Canada would probably try to return to the U.S. Which border crossing he had in mind was uncertain, so Em Jones studied the map and decided the fellow would cross at Montreal. But on the off chance he would go elsewhere Emory also alerted border police at Niagara Falls, Baudette, Minnesota, and Blaine, Washington, to our man perhaps en route. When the four calls were made Emory sat down at the city desk, lit up a stogie, and propped up his feet to wait for the capture. We got him surrounded, he said.

'Em, that you?'

'Ynnnnnh.'

'I've got a bit of news.'

'Ynnnh.'

'Charlie McCall was kidnapped during the night.'

Emory yawned. 'You drunken son of a bitch.'

'I'm not drunk, nor have I been, nor will I be.'

'Then you mean it? You mean it?' Emory stood up. Even through the telephone, Martin observed that.

'I just left Patsy and Matt, and Maloney too, all at Patsy's house, and I pledged in your name we wouldn't run a story on it.'

'Now I know you're lying.' Emory sat down.

'Emory, you better get down here. This town is getting ready to turn itself inside out.'

The editor of editors fell silent.

'You really do mean it?'

'Whoever grabbed Charlie meant it, too.'

'But you didn't tell Patsy that about no story. You wouldn't say that.'

'I did.'

'You needle-brained meathead. What in the sweet Christ's name possessed you?'

'My Celtic wisdom.'

'Your Celtic ass is right between your eyes, that's your wisdom.

I'm coming down. And you better figure a way to undo that pledge, for your own sake. And this better be real. Is it real?'

'Em, are your teeth real?'

'Half and half.'

'Then Em, this story is even more real than your teeth.'

Martin found two more Chuck and Charlie horses in the *Armstrong*, checked his wallet, and lumped all but his last ten on the bunch, across the board, plus a parlay. Never a hunch like this one. He called the bets in to Billy Phelan, the opening move in his effort to bring Billy into the McCall camp, not that Billy would require much persuasion. Billy was a Colonie Streeter, was he not? Grew up three doors up from Patsy and next door to Bindy, knew Charlie Boy all his life. But Billy was an odd duck, a loner, you bet, erratic in a way Martin was not. Billy was self-possessed, even as a boy, but then again he had to be, did he not? Fatherless from age nine, when Francis Phelan left home, left wife, son, and daughter forever, or at least until this morning.

Martin's problem was similar, but turned inside out: too much father, too much influence, too much fame, too much scandal, but also too much absence as the great man pursued his greatness. And these, my friends, are forces that deprived a young man of self-possession and defined his life as a question mark, unlike Billy Phelan's forces, which defined *his* life as an exclamation point.

When his bets were made Martin swallowed the last of his coffee and went to the morgue and pulled all files on the McCalls. They should have had a file cabinet to themselves, given the coverage of their lives through the years, but thieves walked abroad. No clips remained of Patsy's victory in 1919, or even of the Democratic sweep of the city in 1921. Stories on the 1931 legislative probe into the city's assessment racket were gone. So were all reports on Patsy's doing six months for contempt in the baseball-pool scandal.

This was historical revisionism through burglary. Had freelancers looking for yet another magazine piece on the notorious McCalls done the filching? Or was it McCall loyalist reporters, who doubled on the city payroll as sidewalk inspectors? The lightfingering effectively kept past history out of the ready reach of reform-minded newsmen, or others snooping on behalf of uplift: Tom Dewey, the redoubtable D.A., for instance, who was making noises like a governor: Elect me, folks, and I'll send the McCall bunch swirling down the sinkhole of their own oily unguents.

Joe Leahy saw Martin shuffling through the McCall files and wondered aloud, 'What's up with them?'

'Ahh,' said Martin with theatrical weariness, 'a backgrounder on them and the A.L.P. Big power move that comes to a head tonight when the enrollment figures come in.'

'The McCalls taking on the reds? Can they really do it?'

'The power of prayer is with them. The bishop's behind Patsy all the way.'

'You writing something for the first edition?'

'Nothing for the first. When it happens, it happens.'

Martin turned back to the folders and Leahy walked off, a good Catholic boy who loved Franco and hated the reds. Untrustworthy with anything meaningful. Martin leafed through the Charlie Boy file, all innocuous stuff. Promoted to major in the National Guard. Engaged to sweet-faced Patricia Brennan. Initiated into the B.P.O.E. lodge number forty-nine. Named vice-president of the family brewery. Shown visiting Jimmy Braddock in his dressing room in Chicago before the fight with Joe Louis. Shown with his favorite riding horse, a thoroughbred named Macushla, birthday gift from Uncle Patsy of political fame, who keeps horses on a small Virginia farm.

Charlie was pudgy, the face of a smiling marshmallow on the torso of a left tackle. There he stood in his major's suit, all Sam Browne and no wrinkles. Where are you this minute, Charlie Boy? Tied to a bed? Gun at your brain? How much do they say your life is worth? Have they already killed you?

Martin remembered Charlie's confirmation, the boy kissing the bishop's ring; then at the party Bindy gave afterward at the Hampton Hotel, the bishop kissing Bindy's foot. That was the year the McCalls all but donated the old city almshouse to the Catholic diocese as a site for the new Christian Brothers Academy, the military high school where Charlie would become a cadet captain. Martin's wife, Maire, now called Mary, a third or maybe fourth cousin to Bindy's wife, sang 'Come Back to Erin' at the confirmation party, accompanied on the piano by Mrs Dillon, the organist at St Joseph's Church, whose son was simple-minded. And Mary, when the bishop congratulated her on her voice and patted her on the hand, felt fully at home in America for the first time since Martin had snatched her away from Ireland.

Martin's recollection of Charlie Boy on that afternoon was obscured by memories of Bindy and Patsy and Matt, whom he saw yet at a table in a far corner, objects of veneration, Albany's own Trinity.

The perils of being born, like himself, to a man of such fame and notoriety sent Martin into commiseration with Charlie. Bindy was an eminence, the power on the street. 'Celebrated sporting figure' and 'a member of the down-town fraternity' was as far as the papers ever went by way of identifying him. Cautious journalism. No one mentioned his direct power over the city's illegal gambling. No editor would let a writer write it. It was the received wisdom that no one minds the elephant in the parlor if nobody mentions it's there. Martin's own decision to tell Patsy there would be no story on the kidnapping: Was that conspiratorial genuflection? No end to the veneration of power, for the news is out: The McCalls hurl thunderbolts when affronted.

The memory of their confrontation with *The Albany Sentinel* was still fresh. *The Sentinel* had prospered as an opposition voice to the McCalls in the early days of the machine, but its success was due less to its political point of view than to the gossip it carried. In 1925 the paper dredged up 'The Love Nest Tragedy of 1908' involving Edward Daugherty and Melissa Spencer, purporting to have discovered two dozen torchy love letters from the famous playwright to the now beloved star of the silent screen. The letters were crude forgeries and Melissa ignored them. But Edward Daugherty halted their publication with an injunction and a libel suit. Patsy McCall saw to it that the judge in the case was attuned to the local realities, saw to it also that a hand-picked jury gave proper consideration to Patsy's former Colonie Street neighbor. *The Sentinel* publicly admitted the forgery and paid nominal libel damages. But it then found its advertisers withdrawing *en masse* and its tax assessment quintupled. Within a month the ragbag sons of bitches closed up shop and left town, and moral serenity returned to Albany as McCall Democracy won the day.

'Aren't you a little early this morning?'

Marlene Whiteson, a reporter whose stories were so sugary that you risked diabetic coma if you read them regularly, stood in front of Martin's desk, inside her unnecessary girdle, oozing even at this hour the desire but not quite the will, never quite the will, to shed those restrictive stays, leap onto the desk, and do a goat dance with him, or with anyone. But Marlene was an illusionist, her sexuality the disappearing rabbit: Now you see it, now you don't. Reach out to touch and find it gone, back inside her hat. The city room was full of hopefuls, ready to do Marlene, but as far as Martin knew, he himself came closest to trapping the rabbit on a night six years past when both of them worked late and he drove her home, circuitously. Need one explain why he stopped the car, stroked her cheek? She volunteered a small gift of smooch and said into his ear, Oh, Martin, you're the man I'd like to go to Pago Pago with. Whereupon he reached for her portions, only to be pushed away, while she continued nevertheless with bottomless smooch. Twist my tongue but stroke me never. Oh the anomaly. Coquettes of the world, disband; you have nothing to gain but saliva.

'What goodies do you have for us today?' Martin asked her.

'I have a message for you, as a matter of fact. Did you see this morning's paper?'

'I was just about to crack it.'

'I have a story in about Melissa Spencer. She sends you greetings and hopes she gets a chance to see you. She also asked about your father.'

'Ah. And is she well?'

'She looks absolutely gorgeous. For forty-nine. She is some sexy dame.'

'How long will she be here?'

'Just a week.'

Martin knew that. He had known for weeks she was starring in the touring production of his father's great work, *The Flaming Corsage*, the play Edward Daugherty had written in order to transform his melodramatic scandal with Melissa and her jealous lesbian lover, and the consequent destruction of his career and his wife, into anguished theatrical harmony. He used both Martin's mother, Katrina, and the young Melissa as models for the two principal women in the play, and, not unnaturally, Melissa, as a young actress, yearned to incarnate the role she had inspired in life.

Now, at forty-nine, no longer disguisable as the pristine Melissa of 1908, she was appearing in the play for the first time, but as the hero's reclusive, middle-aged wife. The casting, the result of assiduous pursuit of the part by Melissa herself, had the quality of aged perfume about it: yesterday's scarlet tragedy revived for an audience which no longer remembered this flaming, bygone sin, but for whom the reversal of roles by the famed Melissa was still quaintly scandalous. Melissa had acted in the play for six months on Broadway before taking it on the road, her comeback after a decade of invisiblity: one of the most animatedly lovely stars of the silent screen back once more in the American embrace, this time visible, all but palpable, in the flesh.

'She really is interested in seeing you,' Marlene said, opening the morning paper to her interview with Melissa and spreading it on Martin's desk. 'She's keeping a ticket in your name at the box office, and she wants you to go backstage after the curtain.' Marlene smiled and raised her sexual eyebrow. 'You devil,' she said, moving away from Martin's desk.

Martin barely managed a smile for the world champion of sexual fatuity. How surprised she would be at what Melissa could do with the same anatomical gifts as her own. He looked at Melissa's photo in the paper and saw Marlene was right. Melissa was still beautiful. When time descends, the ego forfends. But Martin could not read her story now. Too distracted to resurrect old shame, old pleasure. But Martin, you will go backstage one night this week, will you not? He conjured the vision of the naked, spread-eagled Melissa and his phone rang. Chick Phelan on the line.

'I saw you go in across the street, Martin. What'd they say?'

'Not much except to confirm what you said.'

'Now they've cut off all the phones on the block. I'm in Tony Looby's store down on Pearl Street.'

Chick, the snoop, grateful to Martin for introducing him to Evelyn Hurley, the love of his life, whom he is incapable of marrying. Chick will reciprocate the favor as long as love lasts.

'They probably don't want any busybodies monitoring their moves and spreading the word all over town. Anything else going on?'

'People coming in here know something's up but they don't know what.'

'Just keep what you know under your hat, Chickie, for Charlie's sake as well as your own. My guess is they're afraid for his life. And keep me posted.'

Martin called Walter Bradley, the Albany police chief.

'Walter, I hear the phones are out on Colonie Street.'

'What's that to me? Call the phone company.'

'We've been told, Walter, that something happened to Charlie McCall. I figured you'd know about it.'

'Charlie? I don't know anything about that at all. I'm sure Patsy'd tell me if something was going on. I talk to Patsy every morning.'

'I talked to him myself just a while ago, Walter. And you say there's nothing new? No kidnapping for instance?'

'No, no, no, no kidnapping, for chrissake, Martin. No kidnapping, nothing. Nothing at all. Everything's quiet and let's keep it that way.'

'You get any other calls about Charlie?'

'No, goddamn it, no. I said nothing's going on and that's all there is to it. Now I'm busy, Martin.'

'I'll talk to you later, Walter.'

In minutes Martin's phone rang again, Freddie Dunsbach of the United Press.

'Martin, we've had a tip Patsy McCall's nephew was kidnapped.'

'Is that so?'

'It's so and you know it.'

'Who said I know it?'

'I called Patsy. He denied it and then said to call you.'

'Me? Why me?'

'I thought you could tell me that. Right now we've got an eight-hour jump on you, Martin, or are you putting out an extra? You can't keep a story like this all to yourself.'

'There's no story, Freddie.'

'You really haven't heard about it?'

'I've heard a wild rumor, but we don't print rumors.'

'Since when?'

'Blow it out your ass, Fred.' And Martin hung up. The phone rang right back.

'Martin, I'm sorry. That was a joke.'

'I accept your groveling apology. What do you want?'

'Why did Patsy tell me to call you?'

'Damned if I know. Maybe to get rid of you.'

'I think we're going with the rumor, as an editor's advisory. Our source is a good one.'

'That's a bad idea.'

'We can't sit on it.'

'You can if it means Charlie's life.'

'This is too big. Hell, this is national.'

Martin snorted. Freddie Dunsbach, boy bureau chief. Arrogant yokel.

'It's all of that. But let me ask you. How long've you been in this town?'

'Almost a year.'

'Then you ought to know that if the McCalls are quiet on this thing, and the police are quiet, there's one hell of a reason. Patsy must've sent you to me because I told him I wouldn't print any rumors. I see the significance escapes you, but Patsy's concern is obviously for the safety of Charlie, if Charlie has in fact been kidnapped, which is really not provable if nobody admits it.'

'Does he expect us to bury our heads and ignore the story?'

'What Patsy expects is known only to the deity, but I know what I'd expect if I broke this story and Charlie was murdered because of it. Would you know what to expect in a case like that?'

Freddie was silent.

'Freddie, would you?'

'You're talking about reprisals for reporting the news.'

'You ever hear about the time Bindy McCall beat a man half to death for insulting his wife? What do you suppose he'd do to somebody who caused the death of his only son? The only child in the whole McCall family.'

'You can't run a news organization on that basis.'

'Maybe you can't. Maybe a five-minute beat – which is about all you'd get since we'd put it on the I.N.S. wire as soon as the word was out – is worth Charlie's life. Kidnappers are nasty bastards. You know what happened to Lindbergh's kid, don't you? And he was just a baby who couldn't recognize anybody.'

'Yeah, there's something in that.'

'There's more than you think. We could've had an extra out an hour ago with the rumor. But who the hell wins that kind of game?'

'I see, but –'

'Listen, Fred, I don't run the show here. You talk to Emory when he comes in. He'll be calling the shots for us and I think I know what he's going to do, which is nothing at all until there's a mighty good reason to print something.'

'It's going to be all over the world in a couple of hours.'

'Not unless you send it.'

'I'll talk to Emory.'

'You do that.'

Martin dialed Patsy, and the great gravelbox answered, again on the first ring.

'Are you sending people to me for a reason, Patsy?'

'You'll keep 'em quiet.'

'Hey, this thing is already spreading all over town. Some of these birds don't give a damn about anything but news. They'll blow it wide open unless they're convinced there's a hell of a good reason not to.'

Silence.

'Call Max at the office in five minutes.'

In five minutes precisely Martin called Max Rosen, law partner to Matt McCall.

'The story is this, Martin,' Max said. 'I answered a call here forty-five minutes ago. A man's voice told me to tell Patsy and Matt they'd picked up their nephew and wanted a quarter of a million ransom, a ridiculous figure. Half an hour ago we had a letter from them, with Charlie's signature, saying the same thing. They said if we told the police or put out any publicity that they'd kill Charlie. Patsy wants you to inform the rest of the press about this. He won't talk to anyone but you, and neither will I, nor anyone else in the family. We're not telling Chief Bradley much of anything, so don't bother him any more. I don't need to tell you what this means, do I, Martin, this confidence in you?'

'No need.'

'When there's something to be said it will be said to you, provided you can convince the rest of the press to preserve silence.'

'I'll do what I can, Max. But it's quite a big world out here. Full of nosy, irresponsible newspapermen.'

'The family knows that.'

'Do they also know I don't work miracles for a living?'

'I think they presume you do now.'

Emory Jones's hair was white, with vague, yellowish implications that he might once have been the fair-haired boy of somebody, a mother perhaps, somewhere. He said, whenever the whiteness of his hair arose for discussion, that peabrained reporters who didn't know the doughnut from the hole had given it to him prematurely. For years he had put up with them, he argued, because he had a basically sacrificial nature. He outlasted almost all of them, he argued further, because he had the forbearance of Jesus Christ in the face of the drooling, foaming, dementia praecox activity that passed for reporting on his one and only newspaper. The noted cry: 'That son of a bitch doesn't know the goddamn doughnut from the goddamn hole!' emanating from editor Jones's cubicle, meant a short professional life for somebody.

Martin Daugherty placed Emory in this context as he spotted the white hair, saw Emory rumbling across the crooked, paintless, freshly swept wooden floor of the city room. Here he came: pear-shaped, bottom-heavy, sits too much, unhealthy fear of exercise in the man, choler rising, executorially preempted by Martin's pledge, unspeakably happy at the unfortunate turn of events that had already boiled his creative fluids, which fluids, Martin could see, were percolating irrationally in his eyeballs.

Martin remembered a comparable frenzy in Emory's past: the period when Legs Diamond had been an Albany celebrity; the most outlandishly sensational running news event in the modern history of Albany. Emory, who whipped his slaves like a galleymaster to ferret out every inch of copy the story could bear, finally triumphed prophetically the night Diamond was acquitted of a kidnapping charge. He oversaw personally the hand-setting of the great fist-sized wooden type he saved for major natural catastrophes, armistices, and The Chief's sneezes: DIAMOND SLAIN BY ENEMIES; for the rumor had been abroad in Albany for twelve hours, and was indeed current the length of the Eastern seaboard and as far west as Chicago, that Diamond was, on that particular night, truly a terminal target. Emory had the headline made up a full six hours before Diamond was actually shot dead in his bed on Dove Street by a pair of gunmen. It was then used on the extra that sold twenty thousand copies.

Martin had already calculated that the extra that never was on Charlie Boy would have sold even more. When the news on Charlie did break, the coverage would dwarf the Diamond story. There had never been anything like this in Albany's modern history, and Martin knew Emory Jones also knew this, knew it deeply, far down into the viscous, ink-stinking marrow of his editorial bones.

'Did you undo that goddamn pledge?' were Emory's first words.

'No.'

'Then get at it.'

'It's not possible, Emory.'

Emory moved his cigar in and out of his mouth, an unnerved thumbsucker. He sat down in the wobbly chair alongside Martin's decrepit desk, blew smoke at Martin, and inquired: 'Why in the sacred name of Jesus is it not possible?'

'Because I don't think you're interested in being the editor who put the bullet in Charlie McCall's brain. Or are you?'

Martin's explanation of the sequence of events forced Emory to recapitulate the future as he had known it all morning. Martin let him stew and then told him: 'Emory, you're the man in charge of this silence, whether you like it or not. You're the man with the reputation, the journalistic clout. You're the only one in town who can convince the wire services and whoever's left among the boys up in the Capitol press room to keep their wires closed on this one for a little while. They'll do it if you set the ground rules, make yourself chairman of the big secret. Maybe set a time limit. Two days? Four? A week?'

'A week? Are you serious?'

'All right, two days. They'll do it as a gentleman's agreement if you explain the dread behind it. You'll be a genuine hero to the McCalls if you do, and that's worth money to this newspaper, if I'm not mistaken.'

'Keep your venal sarcasm under your dirty vest.'

'It's not sarcasm. It's cynical humanism.'

'Well, hell, I don't want to murder anybody. At least not Charlie.'

'I knew you'd get the picture.'

'But what will I tell them?'

'Emory, I have faith that you'll think of something. We both know you've got more bullshit than the cattle states.'

'Maybe Dunsbach's already put it out.'

'Maybe. Then your problem is solved, even if his isn't. But I doubt it. I was persuasive.'

'Then you do it.'

'I can't do it, Emory. I'm just a piss-ant columnist, not an omnipotent editor.'

'Willard Maney will go along. He's an Albanian.'

'And a McCall fancier.'

'And Foley at the *News*.'

'Another kinsman.'

'But those bastards up at the Capitol. I don't know them. You know them. You play cards with them when you're supposed to be out getting under the news.'

'Use my name up there if you like.'

'The wire services can pass the word up there.'

'Exactly. And the boys will very likely follow suit. Despite what you think, they're a decent bunch. And Emory, it's really not your responsibility anyway what out-of-town writers do. Then it's on them, and on their children. And what the hell, even an editor's advisory like Dunsbach's talking about wouldn't be all that bad if they made it clear to their clients that Charlie's life was at stake. Which is now a rotten fact.'

'That poor bastard. What he must be going through.'

'He may already be gone.'

Martin looked at the clippings on his desk, Charlie's face staring up from one as he attends a Knights of Columbus party. On almost any given evening when Charlie walked into the K. of C., somebody would make a fool of himself over this gentle young man who might carry a word of good will back to his father and uncles. Life preservation. Money in the bank for those who make their allegiance known. Shake the hand of the boy who shakes the hand of the men who shake the tree from which falls the fruit of our days. Poor sucker, tied to a bed someplace. Will I live through the night? Will they shoot me in the morning? Where is my powerful father? Where are my powerful uncles? Who will save the son when the father is gone? Pray to Jesus, but where is Jesus? Jesus, Charlie, sits at my desk in the person of an equivocating Welsh rarebit who doesn't understand sons because he never had any. But he understands money and news and power and decency and perhaps such things as these will help save the boy we remember.

We are now scheming in our own way, Charlie, to keep you in our life.

'I was putting together a backgrounder on Charlie,' Martin said, breaking the silence. 'Is there anything else you want me to do? There's also that A.L.P. business today.'

'The hell with that stuff now.'

'It's pretty big, you know. Quite a show of power.'

'They're a handful of reds, that's all.'

'They're not reds, Emory. Don't you fall for that malarkey. Probably only two or three are really Communists.'

'They're pinks, then. What's the difference?'

'We can discuss this fine point of color another time, but it's definitely worth a story, and good play, no matter what else happens along with it.'

'Whatever happens I don't want you on it. You stay on Charlie.'

'Doing what?'

'Find the kidnappers, what the hell else?'

'Find the kidnappers.'

'Check around Broadway. That's where they hang out.'

'Check around Broadway.'

'And don't get lost. Call me every hour. Every half-hour.'

'Every half-hour.'

And then Emory Jones, sucking on his stogie, rumbled off and slammed the door of his cubicle, then sat at his desk and picked up the phone to begin spreading the blanket of silence over a story whose magnitude punified even his own recurring glory dreams of news at its colossally tragic best.

4

'Please don't talk about me when I'm gone,' Mildred Bailey was singing over WHN, with the Paul Whiteman band behind her. And Billy Phelan, writing horses in his, or, more precisely, his sister's and brother-in-law's living room, wearing pants, socks, and undershirt, no shoes or belt, remembered the time she came to town with Whiteman. Played the Palace. She always sang like a bird to Billy's ear, a hell of a voice. Hell of a voice. Sounded gorgeous. And then she showed up fat. Dumpy tub of lard. Whiteman too, the tub. Billy remembered the night he played games with Whiteman at the crap table in Saratoga. He was dealing at Riley's Lake House, youngest dealer in town that season, 1931, and of course, of course he knew who Whiteman was when the big boy rolled the dice and lost the last of his wad.

'Let's have five hundred in chips, sonny, and an I.O.U,' Whiteman said.

'Who the hell are you? I don't know you,' Billy said. Sonny me, you son of a bitch. Hubie Maloy, the crazy, was at the table that night. From Albany. Always carried a gun. But Billy liked him. Hubie smiled when Whiteman called Billy sonny. Big-timer, throwing his weight around, that big gut, and figures everybody on earth knows his mustache.

'I'm Paul Whiteman.'

'Wyman?'

'Whiteman. Whiteman.'

'Ohhhhh yeah, Whiteman. You're the guy's got that hill-billy band playing over at Piping Rock. You don't mean nothing to me, bud. Go see the manager if you want chips.'

They fired Billy twenty minutes later. Orders from above. From those who didn't want to make enemies of Paul the Man. Lemon Lewis came over to the table and said, 'I hate to do it, Billy, but we gotta can you. I'll call over to Newman's and the Chicago Club, see what they got going.'

And two hours after that Billy was back to work, with cards this time, sleek and sharp, full of unpredictable combinations. Billy, maybe the best dealer around, pound for pound, you name the game, such a snappy kid, Billy.

He was in Saratoga that year because one night a month earlier he was hanging around Broadway in Albany when Bindy McCall came by, Bindy, in the tan fedora with the flowerpot crown, had connections and investments in Saratoga gambling, a natural by-product of his control of all the action in Albany, all of it: gambling houses, horse rooms, policy, clearing house, card games, one-armed bandits, punch boards. Playing games in Albany meant you first got the okay from Bindy or one of his lieutenants, then delivered your dues, which Bindy counted nightly in his office on Lodge Street. The tribute wasn't Bindy's alone. It sweetened the kitty for the whole McCall machine.

Billy touched Bindy's elbow that night.

'Hey, Billy.'

'Got a second, Bin? I need some work. Can you fix me up for Saratoga next month?'

'What can you do?'

'Anything.'

'Anything at all?'

'Craps, poker, blackjack, roulette. I can deal, handle the stick.'

'How good are you?'

'Haven't you heard?'

Bindy chuckled.

'I'll ask around someone who has. See Lemon Lewis.'

'All right, Bindy, fine. Obliged. Can I touch you for fifty?'

Bindy chuckled again. Billy's got brass. Bindy reached for the roll and plucked a fifty out of the middle.

'Use it in good health.'

'Never felt better,' said Billy. 'I pay my debts.'

'I know you do. I know that about you. Your father paid his debts, too. We played ball together when we were kids. He was one hell of a player. You ever hear from him?'

'We don't hear.'

'Yeah. That's an odd one. See Lewis. He'll fill you in.'

'Right, Bin.'

Billy saw Lewis an hour later at the bar in Becker's and got the word: You deal at Riley's.

'What about transportation?' Billy asked. 'How the hell do I get from Albany to Saratoga every night?'

'Jesus, ain't you got a car?'

'Car? I never even had roller skates.'

'All right. You know Sid Finkel?'

Billy knew Sid, a pimp and a booster and a pretty fair stickman. Put his kid through dentists' school with that combination.

'Look him up. I'll tell him to give you a lift.'

'I'll half the gas with him,' Billy said.

'That's you and him. And don't forget your source,' and Lemon hit himself on the chest with his thumb.

'Who the hell could forget you, Lemon?' Billy said.

It went fine for Billy for two weeks and then came the Whiteman scene and Billy went from Riley's to the Chicago Club, on earlier hours. The Club got a big play in the afternoon, even though the horses were running at the track. So Billy had to find new transportation because Sid Finkel stayed on nights. Was Billy lucky? He certainly was. Angie Velez saw him dealing at the Chicago Club and when he took a break, she asked him for a light.

'You weren't out of work long,' she said.

'Who told you I was out of work?'

'I was there when you gave it to Whiteman. Funniest damn thing I've heard in years. Imagine anybody saying that to Paul

Whiteman. You're the one with the hillbilly band. I laughed right out loud. He gave me an awfully dirty look.'

Billy smiled at this new dish. Then he asked her name and bought her a drink and found she was married but only dabbled in that. Hubby was a gambler, too. Brought her to Saratoga for a week, then left her there to play while he went home to run his chunk of Rochester, what a town. No town like Albany. Rochester is where you might go on the bum, only might, if they kicked you out of Albany. Billy couldn't imagine life outside Albany. He loved the town. And half-loved you too, Angie, now that you're here. 'Are you a spic?'

'I'm Irish, baby. Just like you. One of the Gagen girls. My old man's a Cuban.'

She was playing kneesies with him by then.

'You keep that up, you're liable to get raped.'

'Room two-forty-six in the Grand Union.' And she proved it with the key. That was the beginning of Billy's private taxi service between Albany and Saratoga for the rest of the month. Other things began that season in Saratoga: Billy's reputation as the youngest of the hot numbers at any table, never mind the game. Big winner. I could always get a buck, Billy said. What the hell, I know cards and dice.

Of course, at the end of the season Billy was broke. Playing both sides of the table.

Now Mildred Bailey was all through and Clem McCarthy was barking in with the race results on WHN, and can you believe what is happening to Billy? Friar Charles wins, the son of a bitch, five-to-two, the son of a bitch, *the son of a bitch!* Martin Daugherty, what in Christ's name are you doing to Billy Phelan?

Here's how it looked to this point: Martin bet ten across the board on Charley Horse, who wins it, four-to-one; puts a tenner across also on Friar Charles and now wins that one, too; and has a third tenner going across on Hello Chuckie in the sixth at Pimlico, and Hello Chuckie is two-to-one on the morning line. There is more. Martin also *parlayed* the three horses for yet another ten.

Now, Billy knows that Martin is a hell of a sport, always pays, and loses more than he wins, which has always been pleasant for Billy, who takes a good bit of his play. But my Jesus Christ almighty, if he wins the third, plus the three-horse parlay, Billy is in trouble. Billy doesn't hold every bet he takes. You hold some, lay off some. You hold what you think you can cover, maybe a little more, if you're brassy like Billy. Billy lays some off with his pal Frankie Buchanan, who has the big book in Albany. But mother pin a rose on Billy. For bravery. For Billy is holding *all* of Martin's play. Didn't lay off a dime. Why? Because suckers and losers bet three-horse parlays. I'll hold them all day long, was Billy's philosophy until a few minutes ago when Clem McCarthy came on with the Friar Charles news. And now Billy is sitting at his card table in the front room. (Billy came here to Thanksgiving dinner six years ago and never went back downtown to his furnished room.) His money sits on the floor, next to his bridge chair, in a Dyke cigar box, Dykes being the cigar the McCall machine pushed in all the grocery and candy stores in town.

Billy himself sits under the big, shitty print of Mo the Kid in the gold frame. Billy's figners are working with his number two Mongol pencil on the long yellow pad, and his eyes keep peeking out through the curtains on the front windows in case state cops step on his stoop, in which case Billy would be into the toilet p.g.d.q., those horse bets would be on their way down the city conduits toward the river, and even the most enterprising raider could not then bring them back and pin them on Billy's chest.

Stan whatsisname, the WHN disk jockey, was talking about Bob Crosby and Billy felt good hearing that because he knew Crosby, had heard him in Saratoga, danced to his music with Angie, talked music with him when he played The Edgewood over in Rensselaer. 'Between the Devil and the Deep Blue Sea' Crosby was playing now. The phone rang and Billy turned Crosby down. Frankie Buchanan with the results of the fifth at Arlington Park, Friar Charles official now. Billy then told Frankie about Martin Daugherty's very weird parlay.

'You're the weird one,' said Frankie, who was as weird as they come. One of the best-liked guys in Albany, Frankie, and yet he couldn't take the public. He'd come out at night for ham and eggs, and you'd have to sit with him in his car behind the Morris diner while he ate off a paper plate. Crazy bastards in this world.

'You want to give me the third horse or part of that parlay?'

'No,' said Billy, 'I can't believe the son of a bitch can pick three in a row, and parlay them, too. I never seen it done. I believe in luck but not miracles.'

'Okay, pal,' said Frankie, 'it's all yours.' And he left Billy wondering if he was really crazy. Billy could cut the mustard if the third horse ran out of the money, because the day's play was good. But if Martin Daugherty wins the parlay, Billy, it's up in the seven, eight hundreds, even if nobody else wins a nickel. And Billy Boy, you don't have that kind of cash. So why, oh why, is darlin' Billy doing it? Well, it's a gamble, after all. And Billy is certainly a gambler. Nobody will argue that. And Billy is already feeling the pressure rise in his throat, his gut, under his armpits, under his teeth and behind his jockey shorts. Christ, it tickles me somewhere, Billy thinks, and the money doesn't matter. Pressure. Sweet pressure. Here we go again, folks.

Crosby was just winding up 'Deep Blue Sea.' Billy remembered listening to it with Angie, saw her face. And then it was Morey Amsterdam on the radio. Popped into the studio as usual to ad lib with Stan. I gotta go up to the sixth floor, Amsterdam was saying. They're gonna lay a rug up there and I wanna see how they do it.

Telephone. Martin Daugherty.

'Yeah, Friar Charles wins it, Martin, so you got something good going. Shows seven dollars, four dollars, and three-forty. Tote it up, Martin, you're the money machine today.'

Stan was telling a caller, if you don't like my show, you crumb, don't listen, but if you want to make more of it than that I'll meet you at five o'clock out in the alley behind the studio and knock your brains out. And he gave the address. Wireheaded bastard, that Stan. Billy liked his style.

Then it was quiet with no phones and only Earl (Fatha) Hines – a kid, really, so why do they call him Fatha? – playing something wild, and somebody in the chorus, when he started to move it, really move it, yelling out, 'Play it Fatha . . . play it till nineteen ninety-nine.' And Billy smiles, taps his foot, feels the jazz, feels, too, that good old, good old pressure beginning to cut a pulpy wedge out of his fat-assed day.

Simpson, that bum, rang Billy's bell, looking for his sawbuck. Billy saw him coming up the walk, fished a tenner out of the cigar box, folded it once and put it in his right hip pocket. Ten down the sewer. But Billy had to pay. Tribute to Pop O'Rourke, Democratic leader of the Ninth Ward, who, six months ago, when Billy announced plans to write horses, approved the venture during Billy's formal call. The payoff? Give ten a week to Simpson, Pop said. He's down on his luck. He'll come by every week for it. Fair enough, Billy said. What else could he say? And he was still paying out the tenner.

'Hello, Bill, how you doin'?' Simpson said when Billy opened the door just enough to make it clear that it was not a welcoming gesture. The Simp's sport shirt was at least four days soiled and he needed a shave. Holes in the elbows of his sweater, boozer's look and the breath'd knock over two mules.

'Life's still tough,' Billy said to him.

'I thought maybe I'd come in and sit a while,' Simpson said as Billy was reaching for the ten in his pocket. And that line stopped Billy's hand.

'What?'

'Keep you company a while. I ain't doin' nothin', just hangin' around Brady's. Might as well chew the fat. You know.'

'No, I don't know nothing like that,' Billy said. 'You ain't coming in now or ever.' He opened the door all the way, stepped out, grabbed Simpson's dirty shirt, and lifted him backward down the stairs. 'Now get off this stoop and stay off. Next time you put a foot on it I'll knock your ass the other side of Pearl Street.'

'Don't get hot, Bill. I just wanna come in and talk.'

'I don't let bums in my home. Who the hell do you think you're conning? From now on I don't even want to see you on this side of the street.'

'Where's my ten?'

'You blew it, bum.'

And Billy slammed the door and called Pop O'Rourke.

'And he says he wants to keep me company for the day, chew the fat. Listen, Pop, I respect you, but that bum is looking to see my action. I have a good half hour, he'll want twenty instead of ten. Don't send him back, Pop, and I mean that. I don't like his slimy looks and I never did. I hit him once, I'll knock him off the stoop altogether. There's five steps and he'd clear the whole five if I hit him. I'll break both his arms, Pop. I don't want the bum ringing my bell.'

'Take it easy, Billy. He won't be back. He did wrong. He's a greedy person. I'll tell him.'

'Fine, Pop. Do you want me to send you the tenner?'

'No, not at the moment. I'll let you know if there's any other needy case around.'

'I'm a needy case, Pop.'

'But there are rules, Billy.'

'I play by them.'

'That's the good boy. Just don't get excited. I underwent a heart attack that way, and I can tell you that getting excited is one of the worst, one of the very worst things a man can do to himself. It takes you over when you don't expect it. Very sudden and we don't anticipate a thing. It's a terrible thing to do to yourself, getting too overly worked up, Billy. I wouldn't do it again for any man.'

'I'll catch you later, Pop. Thanks.'

'Billy, I'm very glad you called me.'

Billy hung up and scraped the horseshit out of his ear.

The first of Billy's family came home at three-forty. Daniel Quinn, age ten, resident little kid returning from fourth grade at Public School Twenty across the street, found his uncle on the couch with *True Detective* open on his chest, the lights out, shades drawn more than usual, the *Telegraph*, the *Armstrong*, the New York *News* and *Daily Mirror* on the floor beside the card table.

'That you, kid?'

'It's me, Unk. Aren't you working?'

'Get lost. I'm half asleep. Catch you later.'

And the boy went upstairs. But Billy's eyes were open again, his gaze again on the shitty print of Mo the Kid, more properly titled 'The Young Mozart,' hanging in an enormous gold frame above the couch. There sat the precocious composer, exceptionally upright, playing, no doubt, a tune of his own making, on a spinet in a drawing room baroquely furnished with gilded mirrors, heavy drapes, fringed oriental rug. The room was busy with footstools, ornamental screens, and music sheets strewn across the floor. The ladies in long, flowered gowns and chokers, clutching single sheets of music, and an older gentleman in a wig, breeches, and buckled shoes like the composer, all sat listening as the young Mo sent out his life-giving music. The three gave off non-human smiles, looking glazed and droopy, as if they'd all been at the laudanum.

The print would not have been on the wall, or in the house, if Billy had had his way. It was a gift to his sister, Peg, from their Aunt Mary, a reclusive old dame who lived in the old family home on Colonie Street, raised canaries, and had a secret hoard of twenty-dollar gold pieces she parceled out on birthdays. The picture always reminded Billy of his ill treatment by the people in that house after his father ran away and left him and his sister and their mother; ran away and stayed away eighteen years, and neither Billy, Peg, nor their mother ever heard from him again. In 1934 he came back, not to his own home but to that goddamn house of his sisters and brothers, his visit culminating in inadequately explained rejection and flight, and further silence. And so Billy hated the house for that reason, and also for the uncountable other reasons he had accumulated during his years as a never-quite-welcome nephew (nasty son of nasty Francis). The house was as worthless as the stupid picture in which Kid Mo offered up his stupid, invisible music to a roomful of dope fiends.

The picture would not leave his mind, even after he'd closed his eyes, and so Billy picked up the magazine and looked again at the about-to-be-raped model, fake-raped, with slip on the rise revealing thigh, garter, seamed stockings. In high heels, with her rouged lips, artful hair, artificial fear on her face, she cowered on the bed away from the hovering shadow of the artificial rapist. The change of vision from Mo to rape worked, and Billy slept the fearful sleep of an anxious loser.

Peg's keys, clinking at the keyhole, woke him.

Plump but fetching, graying but evergreen, Margaret Elizabeth Quinn was returning from her desk in the North End Tool Company, where she was private secretary to the owner.

'It's dark in here,' she said. 'What happened to the lights?'

'Nothing,' Billy said as she switched on the bridge lamp.

'Is Danny home?'

'Upstairs.'

'What's new? You have a decent day?'

'Great day.'

'That's nice.'

'No it's not.'

'Did Mama call?'

'No.'

'The receiver's off the hook.'

'I know it.'

'How could she call if the receiver's off the hook.'

'She couldn't.'

Peg cradled the receiver and took off her black-and-white checked shorty coat and black pillbox hat.

'You want pork chops?' she asked.

'No.'

'Liver? That's the choice.'

'Nothing, no.'

'You're not eating?'

'No, the hell with it.'

'Oh, that's a beautiful mood.'

'I'm beautiful out of business is what I am.'

Peg sat on the edge of the rocker, formidable lady in her

yellow, flowered print, full knees up, glasses on, lipstick fresh, fingernails long and crimson, solitaire from husband George small but respectably gleaming under the bridge light, hair marcelled in soft finger wave. Billy's beautiful sister.

'What's this you're saying?'

And he told her the Martin story: that, believe it or not, his three horses all came home. Some joke, eh kid? Sextuple your money, folks. Place your bets with Brazen Billy Boy, who lives the way we all love to live – way, way, way up there beyond our means.

Peg stood up, saying nothing. She pushed open the swinging door to be greeted by a near-frenzied collie, all but perishing from his inability to disgorge affection. From the refrigerator she took out the pork chops and put them into two large frying pans over a low flame on the gas stove. Then she went back to Billy, who was pouring a shot of Wilson's into a soiled coffee cup with a dry, brown ring at the bottom. The phone rang and Peg answered, then handed the instrument to Billy, who closed his eyes to drive out all phone calls.

'Yeah,' he said into the mouthpiece. And then, 'No, I'm closed down. No. NO, GODDAMN IT, NO! I mean I'm CLOSED. Out of business and you owe me fifty-four bucks and I need it tonight so goddamn get it up. I'll be down.' And he slammed the receiver onto the hook.

'Wasn't that Tod?'

'Yeah.'

'You don't have to eat *his* head off because you lost some money.'

'Lost some money? I'm dumped, broke. I can't work. Do you get that picture?'

'You've been broke before? You're broke most of the time.'

'Ah, shut up, this is bad news.'

'What possessed you to hold a three-horse parlay? I wouldn't even make that mistake.'

'I make a lot of mistakes you wouldn't make.'

'It doesn't make sense, with your bankroll.'

'I can't explain it.'

Billy gulped the Wilson's and the phone rang. Martin Daugherty. Peg handed him the phone.

'Yes, Martin, you're a lucky son of a bitch. Nobody in their right mind bets three-horse parlays. I know it, Martin. Yeah, sure I'll be downtown tonight. I'll have some of it for you. No, I haven't got it right this minute. Collections are slow, nobody paying this month. But you'll get paid, Martin. Billy Phelan pays his debts. Yeah, Martin, I held it all myself. Thanks, I'm glad you feel bad. I wish I could get mad at *you*, you son of a bitch. Knock your teeth out and make you spend your winnings on the dentist. What do I make it? What do *you* make it? Right. That's exactly right, Martin – seven eighty-eight eighty-five. Yeah, yeah. Yeah. See you tonight around Becker's, or maybe the poker game in Nick's cellar. Yeah, you son of a bitch, you sleep with the angels. What hotel they staying at?'

The kitchen gave off the rich odor of seared pork. Peg came out of it in her apron, carrying a long fork. At the foot of the stairs she called, 'Danny,' and from a far height in the attic came a 'Yeah?' and then she said 'Supper,' and the door slammed and the steps of Daniel Quinn could be heard, descending from his aerie.

'How much cash do you actually have?' Peg asked.

'About a hundred and seventy,' Billy said. 'Can you spare anything?'

Peg almost smiled. She sniffed and shook her head. 'I'll see.'

'George is doing all right, isn't he?' George wrote numbers.

'He's doing swell. He lost three dollars yesterday on the day.'

'Yeah. We all got a problem.'

'All of us,' Peg said. 'George wants to talk to you about a new book. Somebody named Muller.'

'I'm here if he wants me.'

'What about this money you owe? How will you raise it?'

'I can always raise a buck.'

'Can you raise six hundred?'

'What does *that* mean, can I? I've got to. What do you do when you lose? You pay.'

'The Spider never loses,' Danny Quinn said as he hit the last step down.

Billy drew the bath water, hot as he could stand for his hemorrhoid, back again. Got to get some exercise, Billy. Three baths a day in the hottest, the doc said, the sweat already forming on Billy's face, as he drew the hottest of hot baths. Has that guy Billy got any money? Has he! He's got piles! And he's in hot water, too, I'll say. Might be all washed up. He really took a bath, all right. But you never can tell about a fellow like Billy, because he runs hot and cold.

Billy eased into the water and spread his cheeks so the heat would rise up the back alley and draw some bloody attention to that oversized worm of a vein which was sticking its nose out, itching the goddamn ass off Billy. Are itchy assholes hereditary? But itchy no more right now. Now soothed. Now hot stuff. Now easy livin'. And Billy settles back against the tub and forgets about his asshole and its internal stresses and considers the evening ahead of him.

He will wear his navy blue gabardine and the new silk shirt he got at Steefel's through Harvey Hess. A fast half-dozen shirts for Billy and six, too, for Harv, who glommed them, wrapped them, and put them down as paid for in Billy's name, and all Billy had to do was go in and pick up his order. How sweet. Billy gave Harvey all his legitimate clothing action, or as much as Steefel's could handle, and why not? For wasn't Harvey Billy's grandest fish?

Harvey.

Why hadn't Billy thought of him before this? Harvey was of the opinion he could actually beat Billy at pool. Even after maybe two hundred games and yet to win even one. Still, Harv could say, I'll beat you yet, Billy, I'm learning and you got to admit that. Billy would admit anything to Harvey as long as he kept coughing up fivers and tenners. Such a mark. Billy remembered the night he and Tod had heavy dates with showgirls from the Kenmore and then Tod says, Billy, we can't keep those dates tonight. Why not? says Billy. Because, says Tod, it's payday at Steefel's.

Billy put Harvey on his list of problem solvers. He already

had $170. He would get $54 from Tod. Peg would be good for maybe $10, maybe only $5 if it was as tough with George as she said it was. And it had to be because Peg was no bull-shitter. So the arithmetic comes to maybe $234. And if Billy nailed Harvey for, let's be conservative, $25, that's $259, say $260 round figures; which means Billy still has to come up with say $530 round figures to pay off Martin. Quite a challenge, Billy, $530, and the first time in your life you ever went out at night and absolutely had to come up with five big ones. Always a first for everything. But Billy can raise a buck, right, Billy?

Billy saw the top half of his torso in the bathroom cabinet mirror. The vision always reduced him to a corpse, being washed and powdered in an undertaker's basement, like Johnny Conroy. He always turned the image quickly back to life, pulling chest hair to feel pain, pressing a finger against shoulder flesh to see it whiten, then return to rich redness, moving his mouth, showing his teeth, being alive in a way he wasn't sure his father still was. Is death hereditary?

Johnny Conroy: the corpse in Cronin's funeral parlor, 1932, raised with Billy on Colonie Street, wild kid. Used to run with Billy after the action, any action, run to the cliff at the tail end of Ten Broeck Street and leap, leap, faaaaaaaalllll, and lose the pursuit, faaaaaaaaalllll into the great sandpile in Hogan's brickyard, scramble off, free.

Johnny Conroy, free to die in the gutter over stolen booze, and they waked him at Cronin's.

Billy and Tod were taking Hubie Maloy home that night from Becker's, crazy Hubie who said, Let's stop and see Johnny, my old pal. But they're closed now, it's two in the morning, said Billy. I wanna go in, said Hubert, the wild filbert. And so Tod stopped the car and Hubert got out and went around the back of Cronin's and crawled in a window and in a few minutes had opened the side door for Tod and Billy, and in they went, half drunk or Billy wouldn't have done it. A burglary rap for sure. And there was Johnny in the open coffin with one basket of flowers, only one, ready for planting in the ay-em.

He don't look so bad, Tod said.

He don't look so bad for a corpse, Billy said.

And that's when Hubert undid Johnny's tie. And Billy watched it happen because he didn't understand Hubert's plan. Then Hubert pulled Johnny up from the casket and for the first time Billy really understood the word 'stiff.' Hubert took off Johnny's coat and shirt, and by then Billy and Tod were out the door and back in Toddy's car, parked safely up the street.

Hubert's nuts, said Tod.

Playful, Billy said and couldn't even now say why that word occurred to him. Maybe because he still, even now, liked Hubert, liked crazies.

Well, I don't play with him no more, said Toddy. He's got no respect.

And Billy said, You could say that. Because he had to admit it was true. Five minutes go by and Hubert puts out the light in Cronin's and comes out with all Johnny's burial clothes under his arm, suit, tie, even the shoes. He owed me, the bastard, Hubert says, and if I waited any longer I'd never even collect this much. And Hubert kept the shirt and tie for his own and sold the suit and shoes for twenty bucks the next afternoon at The Parody Club, to a grifter passing through with a carny. On Broadway they laughed for weeks over poor Johnny and, worse, poor old Cronin, who had an attack and damn near died when he walked in and saw the naked corpse, standing with his back against the coffin, all his bullet holes showing. For Hubert didn't tell folks he also took Johnny's underwear. Always said he wasn't wearing any.

Billy shaved and wet his straight black hair, brushed it back with the little part at the left, and was padding barefoot toward his bedroom, wrapped in a towel, when the phone rang. He waited and listened while Peg got it again. Ma. Billy stayed at the top of the stairs.

'We're fine, Mama, and how are things there? Good. Yes, everything is all right. Billy is getting dressed to go out, and George won't be home for an hour. The office is quite busy, yes, which is a nice change. You what, made an apple pie? Oh, I wish I had some. But it burned? Oh that's too bad. But it tastes good anyway. And now Minnie and Josie want to bake pies, too. Well, I hope I get a piece of somebody's pie. I bet yours'll be the best. Yes, Mama, Billy's working. He's going out tonight and pick up some money. Yes, it is nice . . .'

In his room Billy took out the navy blue gabardine and the silk shirt and the newest blue bow tie with the white polka dots. He fished in the drawer for the pair of solid blue socks with the three blue dots on the sides and took his black shoes with the pointed toes out of the closet. Billy never went out without being really dressed. But really. George was the same, and Peg and Ma, too. But George was too flashy. Dress conservative and you'll always be well dressed. George always imitated Jimmy Walker, ever since he worked for him up at the Capitol. He'd see Walker's picture in the paper in a sport coat with patch pockets and he'd be downtown buying one the next day. I never imitated anybody, was Billy's thought. I never even imitated my father. They couldn't even tell me how he looked dressed up, excpet what Ma said, he was so handsome. George is all right. George is a father. A good one. Billy hoped George would get the new book from Muller, but he didn't know who the hell Muller was.

Billy took his trig gray fedora out of the hatbox and thought: pies. And pictured Pete the Tramp stealing two steaming pies off a kitchen windowsill, then running off and eating them behind a fence.

Billy looked at himself in the full-length mirror on the back of the closet door. He looked good. Maybe handsome to some. Not like a man who owed seven eighty-eight to anybody. Whataya think, because Billy owes a few bucks he can't look good?

'Aren't you eating *anything*?' Peg said when he went downstairs.

'I'll grab something downtown.'

She didn't make him ask. She fished in the apron pocket and

handed him the bill, folded in a square. A twenty. He kissed her quick and patted her corset.

'That's all I can give you,' she said.

'I didn't expect so much. You're a classy dame.'

'Class runs in this family,' she said.

5

Billy got off the Albany-Troy bus at Broadway and Clinton Avenue and walked up Clinton, past Nick Levine's haberdashery, where the card game would be. He walked toward the theaters, three of them on Clinton Square, and stopped at The Grand. Laughton in his greatest role. As Ginger Ted. Ragged son of trouble. A human derelict on the ebb tide of South Sea life. Surpassing such portrayals as Captain Bligh, Henry VIII, Ruggles of Red Gap. An experience definitely not to be missed. *The Beachcomber.* Billy made a note to avoid this shit. Fats Laughton in a straw hat on the beach. He walked around the box office to check the coming attractions in the foyer. A Warner Baxter thing. Costume job with that lacy-pants kid, Freddie Bartholomew. Billy had already avoided that one at the Palace, coming back for a second run now. The Grand, then, a wipeout for two weeks. Billy headed for the restaurant.

There were four restaurants within a block of each other on Clinton Square but Billy, as always, went to the Grand Lunch next door to The Grand, for it had the loyalty of the nighttime crowd, Billy's crowd. Dan Shugrue, well liked, ran it, and Toddy Dunn worked the counter starting at six, an asset because he spoke the language of the crowd, which turned up even in daylight for the always-fresh coffee and the poppy-seed rolls, the joint's trademark, and because since Prohibition the place never closed and nobody had to remember its hours. Also there was Slopie Dodds, the one-legged Negro cook, when he worked, for he was not only a cook but a piano player who'd played for Bessie in her early years, and he did both jobs, whatever the market dictated. Nobody believed he'd played for Bessie until it came out in a magazine, but Billy believed it because you don't lie about that kind of thing unless you're a bum, and Slopie was a straight arrow, and a good cook.

The place was brightly lighted, globes washed as usual, when Billy walked in. Toddy, behind the counter, gave him half a grin, and Slopie gave him a smile through the kitchen door. Billy didn't expect the grin from Tod. Billy also saw his Uncle Chick sitting alone at one of the marble-topped booth tables, having coffee and doughnuts before going to work at the *Times-Union* composing room. It was the first time Billy had seen Chick in months, six, eight months, and even that was too soon.

'Hello, Chick,' he said, said it aloofly from the side of his mouth, that little hello that hits and runs.

'Howsa boy, Billy, howsa boy? Long time no see.'

'All right, Chick.'

Billy would have kept walking, but his uncle's gaze stayed on him, looking at those clothes, so spiffy, so foreign because of that; and so Billy spoke compulsively. 'How you been?' A man's got to be civil.

'Fine and dandy. Sit down.'

'I got some business here a minute,' and Billy's hand said, I'll be back, maybe. He walked to the counter, where Tod was already drawing a coffee, dark. Tod also shoved a spoon and an envelope at him.

'Forty there,' Tod said, jaunty in his counterman's white military cap of gauze and cardboard. 'All I can come up with.'

Billy didn't touch the envelope.

'That phone call,' Billy said.

'Forget it. Peg called me.'

'She tell you what happened?'

'All but the numbers.'

'Seven eighty-eight eighty-five. How do you like that, doctor?'

'You got a reason to be edgy.'

'I'm through till I pay it off and get another bankroll.'

'You got no reserve at all?'

'A wipeout.'

'Then what's next?'

'I thought I'd look up Harvey. You want to make the call?'

'For when?'

'When, hell. Now. I'm there if he wants me.'

Tod looked at his watch. 'Five to six. He's home by now. Shit. I got to work. I'll miss it.'

'I'll tell you about it. But I wanna make the game at Nick's.'

'How you gonna play with no money?'

'I got almost two bills.'

'And you got this forty,' and Tod shoved the envelope closer.

'Two-thirty then. I play with half that. I can't afford to lose more than that. I got to save something for Martin, unless I can swing him.'

'I'll call Harvey, good old Harv.'

'Hey, you hear I rolled two-ninety-nine last night? I beat Scotty Streck and the son of a bitch dropped dead from shock.'

'I saw the obituary in the afternoon paper. It didn't mention you. Two-ninety-nine? What stood up?'

'The four pin. Gimme a western.' Billy pocketed the envelope and carried the coffee to Chick's table, thinking: I could grunt and Toddy's get the message. Talk to Chick all week and he'll ask you is this Thursday. Chick wasn't dumb, he was ignorant. Anybody'd be ignorant living in that goddamn house. Like living in a ditch with a herd of goats. Years back, Chick got baseball passes regular from Jack Daley, the *Times-Union*'s sports editor. The Albany Senators were fighting Newark for first place and Red Rolfe was with Newark, and George McQuinn and others who later went up with the Yankees. Chick gave the passes for the whole Newark series to young Mahan, a tub-o'guts kid whose mother was a widow. Billy always figured Chick was after her ass. Chick gave Billy a pass two weeks later to see Albany play the cellar club. Who gave a damn about the cellar club? Billy can't even remember now which club it was. Shove your pass, Nasty Billy told his uncle.

'You're all dressed up,' Chick said, chuckling. 'Are you going to work?'

'Not to give you a short answer to a snotty question, but what the hell is it to you? What am I supposed to do, dress like a bum? Look like you?'

'All right, Billy, I was only kidding.'

'The hell you were.'

'Dress any way you want. Who cares?'

'I do what I want, all right.'

'Calm down, Billy, and answer me a question. You seen Charlie McCall lately?'

'I saw him last night. He bet against me in a bowling match.'

'You hear anything about him?'

'Since last night? Like how he slept?'

'No, no.'

'What the hell you asking then?'

'Can you keep a secret?'

'I'd be dead if I couldn't.'

'I hear Charlie's in bad trouble. I hear maybe he was kidnapped last night.'

Billy stared Chick down, not speaking, not moving except to follow Chick's eyes when they moved. Chick blinked. *Kidnapped*. With Warner Baxter.

'You heard what I said?'

'I heard.'

'Don't that mean anything to you?'

'Yeah, it means something. It means I don't know what the hell it means. You got this straight or you making it up?'

'I'm telling you, it's a secret. I shouldn't have said anything, but I know you know Charlie and thought maybe you heard something.'

'Like who kidnapped him?'

'Hey, come on, Billy. Not so loud. Listen, forget it, forget I said anything.' Chick bit his doughnut. 'You heard any news about your father?'

'Wait a minute. Why is it a secret about Charlie?'

'It's just not out yet.'

'Then how come you know?'

'That's a secret, too. Now forget it. What about your father?'

'Nothing. You know any secrets about him?'

'No, no secrets. Nothing since he came to see us.'

'And you kicked him out.'

'No, Billy, we wanted him, I wanted him to stay. Your Uncle Peter and I went all over town looking for him. You know it was your Aunt Sate had the fight with him. They always fought, even as kids. He was gone before we even knew he was out of the house.'

'Bullshit, Chick.'

'Nobody can talk to you, Billy. Nobody ever could.'

'Not about him they can't.'

'There's a lot you don't know.'

'I know how he was treated, and how I was treated because of him.'

'You don't know the half of it.'

Somebody said, 'Haw! My mother just hit the numbers!' And Billy turned to see a boy with a broken front tooth, about fifteen, brush cut, sockless, in torn sneakers, beltless pants, and a ragged cardigan over a tank-top undershirt with a hole in the front. His jackknife, large blade open, danced in his hand, two tables away.

'Saunders kid,' Chick said softly.

'Who?'

Chick whispered. 'Eddie Saunders. Lives up on Pearl Street near us. He's crazy. Whole family's crazy. His father's in the nut house at Poughkeepsie.'

'She had a dollar on it,' Eddie Saunders said. 'Four forty-seven. Gonna get five hundred bucks. Haw!' With his left foot he nudged a chair away from a nearby table, then slashed its leatherette seat twice in parallel cuts.

'Gonna get me some shoes,' he said. 'Gonna go to the pitchers.'

A lone woman in a corner made little ooohing sounds, involuntary wheezes, as she watched the boy. Billy thought the woman looked a little like Peg.

'Who'd she play the numbers with, Eddie?' Billy asked the kid.

The boy turned and studied Billy. Billy stood up. The boy watched him closely as he moved toward the counter and said to Tod, 'Where's my western? And gimme a coffee.' And then he turned to the kid.

'I asked who she played the numbers with, Eddie.'

'The grocery.'

'That's big news. Bet your mother feels good.'

'She does. She's gonna buy a dress.'

Eddie tapped the knife blade on the marble table top and let it bounce like a drum stick. Billy took the ironstone mug of coffee and the western off the glass counter and moved toward the boy. When he was alongside he said, 'You oughta close that knife.'

'Nah.'

'Yeah, you should.'

'You won't make me.' And Eddie made little jabs at the air about two feet to the right of Billy's stomach.

'If you don't close it,' Billy said, 'I'll throw this hot coffee in your eyes. You ever have boiling hot coffee hit you in the eyes? You can't see nothing after that.'

Eddie looked up at Billy, then at the mug of steaming coffee in his right hand, inches from his face. He looked down at his knife. He studied it. He studied it some more. Then he closed the blade. Billy set his western on the table and reached out his left hand.

'Now give me the knife.'

'It's mine.'

'You can have it later.'

'No.'

'You rather have coffee in the face and then I beat the shit out of you and get the knife anyway?'

Eddie handed the knife to Billy, who pocketed it and put the coffee on the table in front of Eddie. He put the western in front of him. 'Have a sandwich,' Billy said. He pushed the sugar bowl toward the kid and gave him a spoon a customer had left at the next table.

'Now behave yourself,' Billy said, and he went back to his table. 'Will you for chrissake gimme a western?' he said to Tod.

The dishwasher came in the front door with the Clinton Square beat cop, Joe Riley. Riley had his hand on his pistol. People were leaving quickly. Tod came around the counter and explained the situation to Riley, who took Eddie's knife from Billy and then took Eddie away.

'That was clever, what you did,' Chick said.

'Toddy taught me that one. I seen him use it on nasty drunks two or three times.'

'All the same it was clever, and dangerous, with that knife and all. You never know what crazy people will do. It was clever.'

'I'm a clever son of a bitch,' Billy said, and he reached for Chick's check and pocketed it. One up on you, Chick, you sarcastic prick. 'Doughnuts are on me, Chick.'

'Why thanks, Billy, thanks. Take care of yourself.'

Tod came around the counter with two coffees in one mitt and Billy's western in the other. He sat down.

'You play a nice game of coffee.'

'I had a good teacher. You call Harvey?'

'Yeah. He'll be down at Louie's.' Tod looked at his watch. 'Fifteen minutes from now. Damn, I wish I didn't have to work. I love to see old Harvey in action. He makes me feel smart.'

'Listen, you know what I heard? Charlie McCall was snatched.'

'No. No shit?'

'And I just saw him last night. He backed Scotty against me in this match.'

'That'll teach him.'

'They must've grabbed him after he left the alleys.'

'Wow, that's a ballbuster. Broadway'll be hot tonight.'

'Too bad I gotta play cards. Be fun just floatin' tonight.' Billy finished his coffee and then gave both his own and Chick's food checks to Tod, who knew how to make them disappear. 'Now I gotta go get fresh money.'

When Billy walked into Louie's pool room on Broadway across from Union Station, Daddy Big, wearing his change apron and eyeshade, was leaning on a cue watching Doc Fay, the band leader, run a rack. Tomorrow night, Billy would likely face the

Doc here in the finals of a six-week-old round robin. There were four players left and Billy and the Doc could beat the other two left-handed. But Billy and the Doc were also near equals in skill. They beat each other as often as they were beaten: Doc, a flashy shooter; Billy, great control through position and safe shots. Doc, as usual, was playing in his vest. Billy watched him mount the table with one leg, flatten out, stretch his left arm as far as it would take him, with the intention of dropping the fourteen ball into the far corner, a double combination shot he'd never try in a match unless he was drunk, or grandstanding. Ridiculous shot, really, but zlonk! He sank it. Sassy shooter, the Doc, no pushover.

Only one of the other ten tables was busy, Harvey Hess at that one, revving up his sucker suction. Billy could feel it pulling him, but he resisted, walked over to Daddy Big, whose straight name was Louis Dugan, known from his early hustling days because of his willingness to overextend the risk factor in any given hustle – once spotting a mark eighty-four points in a game of one hundred – as Daddy Big Ones, which time shortened to Daddy Big. He'd grown old and wide, grown also a cataract on one eye that he wouldn't let anybody cut away. The eye was all but blind, and so focusing on the thin edge of a master shot was no longer possible for him, which meant that Daddy Big no longer hustled. Now he racked for other hustlers and their fish, for the would-bes, the semi-pros, the amateurs who passed through the magically dismal dust of Louie's parlor.

Daddy Big had run Louie's since the week he came out of Comstock after doing two for a post-office holdup flubbed by Georgie Fox, a sad, syphilitic freak with mange on his soul. Because Fox had lifted Daddy Big's registered pistol to pull the job, then dropped it in a scuffle at the scene, Daddy ended up doing the two instead of Georgie, whom the police never connected to the job. But Bindy McCall, Daddy's cousin, made the connection, and sent out the word: Mark Fox lousy; which swiftly denied Georgie the Syph access to all the places the Broadway crowd patronized: the gin mills, the card games, the gambling joints, the pool rooms, the restaurants, the night clubs, even the two-bit whorehouses Georgie had never learned to live without. He lived two years like a mole, and then, the week before Daddy Big was due to return to Albany and perhaps find a way to extract some personal compensation for lost time from him, Georgie walked into Fobie McManus's grill on Sheridan Avenue, bought a double rye for himself and one for Eddie Bradt, the barman, and said to Eddie: 'I'm all done now,' and he then walked west to the Hawk Street viaduct, climbed its railing, and dropped seventy feet to the middle of the granite-block pavement below, there to be scraped up and away, out of the reach of Daddy Big forever. Bindy's reward to Daddy for time lost was the managership of this pool room, which Bindy had collected during Daddy's absence as payment on a gambling debt. And Daddy had a home ever after.

'Hey, Daddy,' Billy said, 'the Doc monopolizing the action?'

'He's got an idea he's Mosconi.'

'He thinks he can spot Mosconi.'

'I know some I can spot. And beat,' the Doc said, smiling at Billy. Good guy, the Doc. The ladies love his curls.

'Tomorrow you get your chance,' Billy said, 'if you got the money to back up the mouth.'

'I'll handle all you can put on the table. That's if you don't lose your first match.'

'I lose that, I'll get a job,' Billy said.

'You want a game here, Billy?' Daddy Big asked. 'I'm just keeping a cue warm.'

Daddy slurred when he spoke, half in the bag already. By midnight, he'd be knee-walking, with no reason to stay sober any more. Also, his teeth clicked when he talked, prison dentures. Sadistic bastards pulled all his teeth when they had him down. Yet he's still living, and Georgie Fox is gone. Georgie, turned into a cadaver in shoe leather, had hit Billy many a time for coffee money, and Billy'd peel off a deuce or a fin for the bum, even though he was a bum. Georgie was dead long before he hit the pavement, sucked dry by Bindy's order. Why didn't they just beat on him a little, Billy wondered. Lock him up or take away what he owned? But they took away the whole world he lived in. Billy always hated a freak, but he couldn't hate Georgie. I ain't et in two days, Billy. Billy can still remember that line. But Billy also says: You know what you do when you lose, don't you, Georgie? Do you hear me, freak? You pay.

'I already got a game,' Billy told Daddy, nodding his head in Harvey's direction.

The Doc heard that and looked up from the cue ball. He glanced at Harv, then smiled at Billy. 'So you do have dough, then,' he said.

'A hungry chicken picks up a little stray corn once in a while. How much we on for tomorrow night?'

'Fifty all right? And fifty more if my backer shows up?'

'Fifty definite, fifty maybe. You got it.'

Billy moved close to Daddy Big and spoke in a whisper. 'I heard something maybe you know already. About Charlie McCall.'

'Charlie?'

'That somebody put the snatch on him.'

'What the hell you say?' said Daddy, near to full volume. 'What, what?'

'It's what I hear, a rumor. More than that I don't know.'

'Who told you?'

'What am I, a storyteller? I heard it.'

'I didn't hear that. I know Bindy good as any man. You hear anything like that, Doc?'

The Doc gave a small shake of his head and listened.

'It's all I know,' Billy said.

'I don't believe it. Sounds like goatshit,' Daddy said. 'If that happens, I'd know about it. I'll call Bindy.'

'Let me know,' Billy said.

'Hey, Billy,' Harvey called across the empty table. 'You gonna play pool or you gonna talk?'

Billy looked at the Doc and said under his breath: 'Fish get hungry, too.' He clapped the Doc on the shoulder and watched Daddy Big waddling toward the pay phone. Then he went over to Harvey's table to reel in the catch.

* * *

Harvey Hess, a dude who wore good suits but fucked them up with noisy neckties and loud socks, had bitten the hook one night eight, ten months back when he saw Billy playing in Louie's and asked for a game. Billy recognized him immediately as a sucker. Billy recognized suckers the way he recognized cats. Harvey almost won that first game. The games were for a deuce after the first free one, and on subsequent days went up to five. Hearing rumors of Billy's talent did not put Harvey off. He merely asked for a spot. Ten points, then fifteen, and lately twenty, which made Harvey almost win.

Billy watched Harvey show off for him, finishing off two balls, both easy pickin's. Then Daddy Big came over to rack the balls, mark down the time, and give Billy the word that Bindy's line was busy. Harvey spoke up: 'Give me thirty-five points and I'll play you for twenty-five bucks.'

'Who the hell you think I am?' Billy said. 'You think I'm Daddy Big here, giving the game away?'

'Thirty-five,' said hard-hearted Harvey.

'Thirty,' Billy said. 'I never spotted anybody thirty-five.'

'Thirty-five.'

'Thirty-two I give you, for thirty-two bucks, buck a point.'

'You're on,' said Harv, and Billy felt the sweet pressure on the way. Harvey almost won, but it was Billy, finally, one hundred to ninety-two, winging it with a run of thirty-two in mid-game to come from behind twenty points. Daddy Big came back and told Billy: 'I knew that was goatshit about Charlie Boy. Bindy said he heard the rumor, too, and to kill it. He talked to Charlie in New York an hour ago.'

'What's this about Charlie?' Harvey asked. 'I sold him a gray sharkskin last week.'

'It's nothin',' said Daddy. 'Billy here's spreading the news he was kidnapped, but I just talked to Bindy and he says it's goatshit.'

'I took the third degree at the K. of C. with him,' Harvey said.

'I'll tell you why I bought it,' Billy said, shrugging. 'I heard a rumor last summer Bindy was going to be snatched, so the Charlie thing made sense to me.'

'Who snatched? I never heard nothing like that,' said Daddy.

'It was all over Broadway.'

'So was I, but I never heard it.'

'I heard it.'

'I never heard it either,' Harvey said.

'So you bums don't get around. What're we doing here, playing pool or strollin' down memory lane?'

'I'll play you one more, Billy, but I want forty points now. You're hot tonight. I never saw anybody run thirty-two before. You ran my whole spot. That's hot in my book.'

'I got to admit I'm feeling good,' Billy said. 'But if the spot goes to forty, so does the bet.'

'Thirty-five,' said Harv. 'I'm getting low.'

'All right,' Billy said, and he broke with a deliberately bad safe shot, giving Harvey an opening target. Harv ran four and left an open table. Billy ran ten, re-racked, ran four more, and missed on purpose, fourteen to four, and said: 'Harv, I'm on. What can I say? I'll even it up some and give you eight more points, forty-eight spot.'

'You give me eight more?'

'For another eight bucks.'

Harvey checked his roll, studied the table.

'No, no bet. I got a feelin' I ain't gonna lose this one, even though you got the lead, Billy. I'm feelin' good, too. I'm gettin' limber. Keep the bet where it is. You can't stay lucky forever.'

Lucky. The line blew up in Billy's head. He wanted the rest of Harvey's roll, but time was running. Nick's card game at nine-thirty with big money possible, and Billy wanted a cold beer before that. Yet you can't call Billy lucky, just lucky, and get away with it. Billy's impulse was to throw the game, double the bet, clean out Harvey's wallet entirely, take away his savings account, his life insurance, his mortgage money, his piggy bank. But you don't give them that edge even once: I beat Billy Phelan last week. No edge for bums.

Harvey faced the table. The seven ball hung on the lip, but was cushioned, and the cue ball sat on the other side of the bunch, where Billy, you clever dog, left it. No shots, Harv, except safe. Sad about that seven ball, Harv. But wait. Is Harv lining up to break the bunch? Can it be? He'll smash it? Not possible.

'What're you doing?'

'Playing the seven.'

Billy laughed. 'Are you serious?'

'Depth bomb it. The four will kiss the seven and the bunch'll scatter.'

'Harv, are you really calling that, the four to the seven?'

'I call the seven, that's enough.'

'But you can't hit it.' Billy laughed again. He looked again at the bunch, studying the angle the four would come off the end. No matter where you hit the bunch, the four would not kiss the seven the right way. Not possible. And Harvey hesitated.

'You don't want me to play this shot, do you, Billy? Because you see it's a sure thing and then I'll have the bunch broken, a table full of shots. That's right, isn't it?'

Billy closed his eyes and Harvey disappeared. Who could believe such bedbugs lived in a civilized town? Billy opened his eyes at the sound of Harvey breaking the bunch. The four kissed the seven, but kissed it head on. The seven did not go into the corner pocket. The rest scattered, leaving an abundant kindergarten challenge for Billy.

'You do nice work, Harv.'

'It almost worked,' said Harv, but the arrogance was draining from his face like a poached egg with a slow leak.

'Why didn't you play a safe shot?'

'When I've got a real shot?'

'A real shot? Willie Hoppe wouldn't try that one.'

'I saw you break a bunch and kiss one in.'

'You never saw me try a shot like that, Harv.'

'If you can do it, I can do it too, sooner or later.'

Billy felt it rising. The sucker. Lowlife of Billy's world. Never finish last, never be a sucker. Don't let them humiliate you. Chick's face grinned out of Harvey's skull. Going to work, Billy? Lowlife. Humiliate the bastard.

'Harv, you got to play safe even when you're ahead. Didn't you learn anything playing against me?'

'I learned plenty.'

'You didn't learn enough.'

And Billy leaned into the action and ran the table and broke a new rack and ran that and part of another. He missed a tough one and Harv sank eight and then Billy got at it and finished it off, a hundred to Harvey's twelve, which, with his forty-point spot was still only fifty-two. Billy put his cue in the rack, feeling he'd done his duty. Suckers demand humiliation and it is the duty of people like Billy to answer their demand. Suckers must be stomped for their love of ignorance, for expecting too much from life. Suckers do not realize that a man like Billy spent six hours a day at pool tables all over Albany for years learning how to shed his ignorance.

Doc Fay watched the finale, shaking his head at what he heard from Harvey's mouth. Harvey paid Billy the thirty-five dollars and put on his hat and suit coat. Billy actually felt something for Harvey then.

'You know, Harv,' he said, putting his hand on the sucker's shoulder, 'you'll never beat me.'

'You're good, Billy. I see how you play safe till the bunch breaks and then you get a streak going. I see how you do it.'

'Harv, if you play from now till you're ninety-nine (play it, Fatha), you still won't know how I do it.'

'I'll get you, Billy,' Harv said, backing toward the door. 'One of these nights I'll get you.' And then he was gone, only his monkey smirk still hanging there by the door above the image of his orange and purple tie. Doc Fay broke up with laughter.

'I thought for a minute there, Billy, you were wising up the sucker,' the Doc said.

'You can't wise up a sucker,' said Billy.

'Absolutely. It's what I said to myself when Harv says he knows how you do it. I said, Doc, *you* know and *Billy* knows.'

'What do we know?'

'That a sucker don't get even till he gets to heaven.'

'Right,' Billy said. 'I learned that in church.'

6

Red Tom Fitzsimmons, the four-to-two man at Becker's, a good fellow, stood behind his mustache and amidst his brawn in a fresh apron, arms folded, sleeves rolled, waiting for thirst to arise anew in his four customers. Martin Daugherty sat at the end of the bar underneath the frame of the first dollar Becker's ever made, and at the edge of the huge photo of Becker's thirtieth anniversary outing at Picard's Grove on a sunny day in August of 1932, which adorned the back bar. The photographer had captured two hundred and two men in varying degrees of sobriety, in shirtsleeves, sitting, kneeling, standing in a grassy field, clutching their beer, billowy clouds behind and above them. Emil Becker ordered a wall-sized blowup made from the negative and then spent weeks identifying all present by full name, and writing an index, which he framed and hung beside the blowup, which covered the wall like wallpaper.

Emil Becker died in 1936 and his son, Gus, put a check mark alongside his name, and a gold star on his chest in the photo. Customers then wanted the same done for other faithful departed, and so the stars went up, one by one. There were nineteen gone out of two hundred in six years. Martin Daugherty was in the photo. So was Red Tom. So was Billy Phelan, and Daddy Big, and Harvey Hess. So was Bindy McCall and his son, Charlie. So was Scotty Streck. The star was already shining on Scotty's chest and the check mark alongside his name.

Martin looked at Red Tom, and at his mustache: in the photo

and the real thing. It was a mustache of long standing, brooded over, stroked, waxed, combed, pampered.

'That mustache of yours, Fitzsimmons,' said Martin, 'is outlandish. Venturesome and ostentatious.'

'Is that so?'

'Unusually vulgar. Splendid too, of course, and elegant in a sardonic Irish way. But it surely must be unspeakable with tomato juice.'

'Give up and have a drink,' Red Tom said, pouring a new bourbon for Martin.

'It's pontifical, it's arrogant. It obviously reflects an intemperate attitude toward humankind. I'd say it was even intimidating when found on a bartender, a mustache like that.'

'Glad you like it.'

'Who said I liked it? Listen,' Martin said, now in complete possession of Red Tom's attention, 'what do you hear about Charlie McCall?'

Red Tom eyed the other customers, moved in close. 'The night squad was here asking your kind of question, Bo Linder and Jimmy Bergan.'

'You tell them anything a fellow like myself should know?'

'Only that the word's out that he's gone.'

'Gone how?'

'Disappeared, that's all.'

'What about Jimmy Hennessey?'

'Hennessey? What's he got to do with it?'

'Maybe something.'

'I haven't laid eyes on Hennessey in months.'

'Is he all right?'

'Last I heard, he was drying out. Fell down the church steps and landed in front of Father O'Connor, who says to him, Hennessey, you should stop drinking. Hennessey reaches his hand up to the priest and says, I'm waiting for help from the Holy Ghost. He's in the neighborhood somewhere, says O'Connor. Ask him to pick you up. And he steps over Hennessey's chest.'

'He must be dried out by now. The McCalls put his name on a go-between list.'

'A go-between list?'

'It'll be in the morning paper. Our guess is they're trying to find an intermediary to talk with the kidnappers about the ransom.'

Martin put the list on the bar and ran down the names: Joe Decker, a former soft-shoe artist who ran the Double Dot nightclub on Hudson Avenue; Andy Kilmartin, the Democratic leader of the Fifth Ward; Bill Shea, a Bindy McCall lieutenant who ran the Monte Carlo, the main gambling house in the city; Barney O'Hare, a champion bootlegger who served four terms as Patsy McCall's man in the State Assembly and no longer had need of work; Arnold Carroll, who ran the Blue Elephant saloon; Marcus Gorman, the town's best-known criminal lawyer, who defended Legs Diamond; Butch McHale, a retired welterweight and maybe the best fighter ever to come out of Albany, who ran the Satin Slipper, a speakeasy, after he quit the ring; Phil Lynch, who ran the candy store that was Bindy's headquarters for numbers collections and payoffs downtown; Honey Curry, a hoodlum from Sheridan Avenue, who did four years for a grocery store stickup; Hennessey, an ex-alderman who was one of Patsy's political bagmen until he developed the wet spot on his brain; Morrie Berman, the ex-pimp and gambler; and Billy Phelan.

'Kilmartin never comes in any more,' Red Tom said. 'O'Hare comes in for a nightcap after he gets laid. Gorman hasn't been in here since old man Becker told him and Legs Diamond he didn't want their business. Most of the others are in and out.'

'Lately?'

'All but Curry. No show for a long while.'

'Billy been in tonight yet?'

'He's about due.'

'I know. I whipped him today with a parlay. I think I hurt him.'

'He knows how to get well. You say this list is in the paper?'

Martin told him how the coded list arrived at the *Times-Union* as a classified ad and was spotted by a lady clerk as oddball enough to send up to Emory Jones for a funny feature story. The message was to CHISWICK, the names in scrambled numbers. Emory solved it instantly: A as 1, B as 2, the moron code. And when Martin next communicated, Emory had him check out everyone on the list. Max Rosen admitted the list was connected to the kidnapping but would say no more and didn't have to. Martin spent an hour in the phone booth discovering that none of those listed was available. Not home. In Miami. Away for the month. Except for Hennessey and Curry, whose phones didn't answer, and Billy and Morrie, whose recent movements Martin knew personally.

'Who's Curry hang around with these days?'

'He's cozy with Maloy, used to be. But he's always with a dame.'

'And Maloy?'

'I heard he was hanging out with a bunch down in Jersey. Curry too.'

Billy Phelan came in then. Martin saw him touch Red Tom for what looked like a twenty before he even looked the place over. Then he sat down beside Martin.

'Luckiest man in North America,' Billy said.

'A connoisseur of horseflesh.'

'With a horseshoe up your ass.'

'Talent makes its own luck, Billy. Like somebody bowling two-ninety-nine.'

'Yeah. I got a partial payment for you.' Billy signaled Red Tom for a refill for Martin and a beer for himself, and put an envelope in front of Martin. He kept his hand on it.

'I need a bankroll for Nick's game tonight. If I hold on to this and I win I pay you off entirely.'

'And if you lose, I lose this.'

'You don't lose. Billy pays his debts.'

'I mean this month.'

'All right, Martin, you need the cash, take it. I'm not arguing. I just work a little longer.'

'Keep the roll and maybe we'll both get our dues paid. But I have a question. What do you hear about Charlie McCall, apart from what we both know about last night?'

'Jesus, this is my big Charlie McCall day. Why the hell does everybody think I know what Charlie's up to?'

'Who's everybody?'

'Nobody.'

'Some significant people in town obviously think you might be able to help find him, one way or another.'

'Find him? He ain't lost.'

'Haven't you heard?'

'I heard he got snatched, but I just found out upstairs that's not straight. Daddy Big got it right from Bindy. Charlie's in New York. All I heard was a rumor.'

'Your rumor was right.'

'They took him, then? That's it?'

'Correct.'

'Daddy Big and his goatshit.'

'What goatshit?'

'Just goatshit. What about significant people?'

'Your name's in the paper that comes out tonight, one of twelve names, all in a code in a classified ad, which is obviously a message to the kidnappers about go-betweens. Nobody said anything to you about this?'

'Nobody till now.'

'You weren't on the original list. The ad came in about two this afternoon and I just found out your name was added about half an hour ago.' Martin told the ad story again, and Billy knew all the names. He signaled for a beer.

'I got a message for you,' Red Tom said when he brought Billy's beer. 'Your friend Angie was in today. She's at the Kenmore.'

'She say anything?'

'She said she needs her back scratched.'

'That's not what she wants scratched.'

'Well, you're the expert on that,' said Red Tom, and he went down the bar.

Billy told Martin, 'I don't belong on that list. That's either connected people or hoodlums. I pay off the ward leader, nickel and dime, and I vote the ticket, that's my connection. And I never handled a gun in my life.'

'You classify Berman as a hoodlum?'

'Maybe not, but he sure ain't no altar boy.'

'You know him pretty well?'

'Years, but we're not that close.'

'You know everybody on Broadway and everybody knows you. Maybe that's why you're on the list.'

'No, I figured it out. Daddy Big got me on it. If it come in half an hour ago, that's all it could be. Something I said about a plan to snatch Bindy last year. You know that rumor.'

'No. What was it?'

'Fuck, a rumor. I'm the only one heard it? What is this? It was all over the goddamn street. Tom, you heard that rumor about Bindy last year?'

'What rumor?'

'Around August. Saratoga season. Somebody was gonna snatch him. You heard it.'

'I never heard that. Who was gonna do it?'

'How the fuck do I know who was gonna do it?'

'It's your rumor.'

'I heard a goddamn rumor, that's all. I paid no attention, nothing ever happened. Now, because I heard a rumor last August, I'm on the McCalls' shit list?'

'This is no shit list,' Martin said.

When Red Tom went to serve another customer, Billy said, 'They think I'm in on it.'

'I don't think that's true,' Martin said, 'but it does make you a pretty famous fellow tonight in our little community. A pretty famous fellow.'

'Know where I first heard about Charlie? From my Uncle Chick, who don't even know how to butter bread right. How the hell did he hear about it? He asks me what I know about Charlie and all I know is last night at the alleys and then you and all your Charlie horses. You knew it then, didn't you?'

'Maybe.'

'Maybe, my fucking noodle.'

'Maybe, your fucking noodle then.'

'I'm standing with Charlie horses and you know the guy's glommed.'

'And that explains why I won?'

'Sure it explains why you won, you prick.'

'I didn't win anything yet,' and Martin pushed the envelope toward Billy.

'Right. Poker time. Money first, Charlie later.'

'Morrie Berman'll be in that game, right?'

'That's what he said last night.'

'Look, pay attention to what he says. Anything. It's liable to be very important.'

'What do you know that I don't?'

'That's an intriguing question we can take up some other time, but now let me tell you very seriously that everything is important. Everything Morrie says. We'll talk about it later when things aren't quite so public.'

'What are you, a cop?'

'No, I'm a friend of Charlie McCall's.'

'Yeah.'

'And so are you.'

'Yeah.'

And Billy drank up and stood up. He and Martin moved toward the door, which opened to the pull of Daddy Big as they reached it, Daddy in his change apron and eyeshade, questing sweet blotto at eventide. Billy grabbed his shirtfront.

'You turned me in, you son of a bitch.'

'What's got you, you gone nuts?'

'You told Bindy what I said about the snatch rumor.'

'I asked about it. Bindy asked me where I heard it.'

'And you finked on me, you fat weasel. And I don't know anything worth a goddamn pigeon fart.'

'Then you got nothing to worry about.'

'I worry about weasels. I never took you for a weasel.'

'I don't like you either. Stay out of upstairs.'

'I play tomorrow and you don't shut me out and don't try.'

'I shut out people who need to be shut.'

'Go easy, old man. There's three things you can't do in this world and all three of 'em are fight.'

Daddy Big broke Billy's hold on his shirt and simultaneously, with a looping left out of nowhere, knocked him against the front door, which opened streetward. Billy fell on his back on Becker's sidewalk, his fedora rolling into the gutter. Martin picked him up and then went for the hat.

'Not your day for judging talent,' Martin said.

Billy put on his hat, blotted his lip. 'He hits like he plays pool,' he said.

'So, that's new. Something you learned,' said Martin, brushing the dust off Billy's suit coat.

Martin walked with Billy up Broadway toward Clinton Avenue, thinking first he would go to Nick's cellar and watch the poker game but not play against his own money. Yet the notion of spectating at a poker game on such an evil day seemed almost evil in itself. His mind turned to thoughts of death: closing Scotty Streck's left eye, Charlie Boy maybe with a bullet in the head, dumped in the woods somewhere.

And passing the United Traction Company building at the corner of Columbia Street he saw Francis Phelan, again cocking his arm, just there, across the street, again ready to throw his smooth stone; and he remembered the bleeding and dying scab, his head laid open, face down on the floor of the trolley, one arm hanging over the top step. The scab had driven the trolley down Broadway from the North Albany barns, and when it reached Columbia Street a mob was waiting. Francis and two other young men heaved a kerosene-soaked sheet, twisted and knotted into a loose rope, over the overhead trolley wire and lit it with matches. The trolley could not pass the flaming obstacle and halted. The militiamen raised their rifles to the ready, fearful that the hostile crowd would assault the car, as it had the day before, and beat the driver unconscious. Militiamen on horseback pushed the mob back from the tracks, and one soldier hit Fiddler Quain with a rifle butt as Fiddler lit the sheet. But even as this was taking the full attention of the military, even before thoughts of reversing the trolley could be translated into action, other men threw a second twisted sheet over the trolley wire to the rear of the car and lit it, trapping the trolley and its strike-breaking passengers between two pillars of flame.

It was then that Francis uncocked his arm and that the smooth stone flew, and the scab fell and died. No way out. Death within the coordinates. And it was the shooting of the innocent onlookers which followed Francis's act that hastened the end of the strike. Violence enough. Martin saw two of the onlookers fall, just as he could still see the stone fly. The first was spun by the bullet and reeled backward and slid down the front of the railroad station wall. The second grabbed his stomach as the scab had grabbed his head, and he crumpled where he stood. Fiddler Quain lay on the granite blocks of Broadway after his clubbing, but the mob swirled around that horseman who hit him, an invasion of ants, and Fiddler was lifted up and swept away to safety and hiding. Like Franny, he was known but never prosecuted. The hands that carried the violence put honest men back to work. Broadway, then and now, full of men capable of violent deeds to achieve their ends.

'Listen, Billy,' Martin said as they walked, 'that business between you and Daddy Big, that's not really why the McCalls put you on the list. There's something else going on, and it's about Morrie Berman.'

Billy stopped walking and faced Martin.

'What Morrie says could be important, since he knows people who could have taken Charlie.'

'So do I. Everybody does on Broadway.'

'Then what you or the others know is also important.'

'What I know is my business. What Berman knows is his business. What the hell is this, Martin?'

'Patsy McCall is making it his business, too.'

'How do you know that?'

'I talked to him this morning.'

'Did he ask you to snoop around Morrie Berman?'

'No. He asked me to ask you to do that.'

'Me? He wants me to be some kind of stoolie? What the hell's the matter with you, Martin?'

'I'm not aware that anything's the matter.'

'I'm not one of the McCalls' political whores.'

'Nobody said you were. I told him you wouldn't like the idea, but I also know you've been friendly with Charlie McCall all your life. Right now, he could be strapped to a bed someplace with a gun at his head. He could even be dead.'

Billy made no response. Martin looked at him and saw puzzlement. Martin shaped the picture of Charlie Boy again in his mind but saw not Charlie but Edward Daugherty, tied to a bed by four towels, spread-eagled, his genitals uncovered. Why such a vision now? Martin had never seen his father in such a condition, nor was he in such a state even now at the nursing home. The old man was healthy, docile, no need to tie him to the bed. Naked prisoner. Naked father. It was Ham who saw Noah, his father, naked and drunk on wine, and Noah cursed Ham, while Shem and Japheth covered their father's nakedness and were blessed for it. Cursed for peering into the father's soul through the pores. Blessed for covering the secrets of the father's body with a blanket. Damn all who find me in my naked time.

Billy started to walk again toward Clinton Avenue. He spoke without looking at Martin, who kept pace with him. 'Georgie the Syph knocked down an old woman and took four bucks out of her pocketbook. I came around the corner at James Street and saw him and I even knew the old woman, Marty Slyer the electrician's mother. They lived on Pearl Street. Georgie saw me and ran up Maiden Lane and the old lady told the cops I saw him. But I wouldn't rat even on a bum like Georgie. What I did the next time I saw him was kick him in the balls before he could say anything and take twenty off him and mail it to Mrs Slyer. Georgie had to carry his balls around in a basket.'

'That's a noble story, Billy, but it's just another version of the code of silence. What the underworld reveres. It doesn't have anything to do with morality or justice or honor or even friendship. It's a simplistic perversion of all those things.'

'Whatever it is it don't make me a stool pigeon.'

'All that's wanted is information.'

'Maybe. Or maybe they want Morrie for something particular.'

'No, I don't think so.'

'How the hell do you know what they want, Martin?'

'Suit yourself in this, Billy. I was asked to put the question to you and I did.'

'I don't get it, a man like you running errands for the McCalls. I don't figure you for that.'

'What else can I tell you after I say I'm fond of Charlie, and I don't like kidnappers. I'm also part of that family.'

'Yeah. We're all part of that family.'

'I'll be around later to root for our money. Think about it.'

'What exactly did Patsy say?'

'He said to hang around Berman and listen. That's all he said.'

'That's all. Yeah.'

And Billy crossed Clinton toward the alley beside Nick's haberdashery, where Nick, Footers O'Brien, and Morrie Berman were talking. Martin walked up the other side of the street, past the Pruyn Library, and crossed to The Grand Theater when he saw the Laughton film on the marquee. He looked back at the library corner and remembered the death of youth: his cousin's suicide in the wagon. Sudden behavior and pervasive silence. But sometimes living men tell no tales either. Francis Phelan suddenly gone and still no word why. *The Beachcomber.* Martin hadn't told Billy that his father was back in town. Duplicity and the code of silence. Who was honored by this? What higher morality was Martin preserving by keeping Billy ignorant of a fact so potentially significant to him? We are all in a conspiracy against the next man. Duplicity. And Billy Phelan saw through you, Martin: errand boy for the McCalls. Duplicity at every turn. Melissa back in town to remind you of how deep it goes. Oh yes, Martin Daugherty, you are one duplicitous son of a bitch.

* * *

In the drugstore next to The Grand, Martin phoned Patsy McCall.

'Do you have any news, Patsy?'

'No news.'

'I made that contact we talked about, and it went just about the way I thought it would. He didn't like the idea. I don't think you can look for much information there.'

'What the hell's the matter with him?'

'He's just got a feeling about that kind of thing. Some people do.'

'That's all he's got a feeling for?'

'It gets sticky, Patsy. He's a good fellow, and he might well come up with something. He didn't say no entirely. But I thought you ought to know his reaction and maybe put somebody else on it if you think it's important.'

'I'll take care of it,' Patsy said curtly and hung up.

Martin called the *Times-Union* and got Emory. Yes, the lid was still on the Charlie story. 'Everybody went along,' Emory said, 'including Dunsbach. I seared his ass all right. He wouldn't touch the story now with rubber gloves.'

'Heroic, Em. I knew you could do it.'

'Have you smoked out any kidnappers yet?'

'You know I don't smoke, Em. What happened with the A.L.P.?'

'I don't give a damn about that piss-ant stuff when I've got a story like this. Here. Talk to Viglucci.'

Viglucci, the city editor, explained that some twelve hundred new voters had enrolled in the A.L.P., twice as many as necessary for Patsy McCall to control the young party. No, the desk hadn't reached Jake Berman, the phone constantly busy at the A.L.P. office. Martin volunteered to go there personally, being only two blocks away. Fine.

Jake Berman had been barely a specter all day for Martin, whose sympathy was all with the McCalls because of Charlie. But now Jake could surely use a little consolation. Martin had known Jake for years and liked him, a decent man, a lawyer for the poor, knew him when he was a city judge, appointed by McCall fiat as a sop to the Albany Jews. But that didn't last, for Jake refused to throw out a case against a gouging landlord, an untouchable who was a heavy contributor to the Democratic Party. Jake quit the bench and the party, and went back to practicing law.

In 1935, when the A.L.P. was founded to gain another line for Roosevelt's second run, Jake spearheaded the party locally and opened headquarters in his father's old tailor shop on Sheridan Avenue, just off North Pearl Street. Old Socialists and laboring men, who wanted nothing to do with the Democrats but liked F.D.R.'s New Deal, made the new party their own, and by 1936 the Albany branch had one hundred and eighty-four members. Patsy McCall tolerated it because it was a stepchild of the Democratic party, even though he had no use for Roosevelt, the snob son of a bitch. The Catholic Church grew restless with the New Party, however, as its ranks fattened with anti-Franco radicals and socialist intellectuals who spat on God. What's more, it promised the kind of growth that one day could be a power balance in local elections, and so Patsy decided it was time to pull the plug.

The word went out to the aldermen and ward leaders of the city's nineteen wards that some sixty voters in each ward should change their enrollment from Democrat to American Labor. As enrolled members, they would then be entitled to vote at A.L.P. meetings, and would vote as Patsy told them to. Jake Berman's few hundred regulars would be dwarfed by the influx, and Jake's chairmanship negated. In time, all in good time, Patsy's majority, of which Chickie Phelan was now one, would elect a new party chairman.

The garmentless tailor's dummy that had been in Berman's tailor shop for as long as Martin could remember was still visible behind the Lehman-for-Governor posters taped to the old store window. The shop had stood empty for several years after the death of old Ben Berman, a socialist since the turn of the century and a leader in the New York City garment industry's labor struggle until strikebreakers fractured his skull. He came to Albany to put his life and his head back together and eventually opened this shop, just off Pearl Street at the edge of an old Irish slum,

Sheridan Hollow, where Lackey Quinlan once advertised in the paper to rent a house with running water, and curious applicants found he had built his shack over a narrow spot in the old Canal Street creek. This was the running water, and in it Lackey kept his goose and his gander.

Ben Berman worked as a tailor in the neighborhood, though his clients came from all parts of the city, until he lost most of his eyesight and could no longer sew. He died soon after that, and then his son Jacob rented the shop to another tailor, who ran it for several years. But the new man was inferior to Ben Berman with the needle, and the trade fell away. It remained for the A.L.P. to reopen the shop, and now it looked as if its days were again numbered.

Martin pushed open the door, remembering when Ben Berman made suits and coats for his own father, those days when the Daughertys lived under the money tree. Martin could vividly recall Edward Daugherty standing in this room trying on a tan, speckled suit with knickers and a belt in the back, mottled buttons, and a brown, nonmatching vest. Martin mused again on how he had inherited none of his father's foppery, never owned a tailor-made suit or coat, lived off the rack, satisfied with ready-made. A woman Martin did not know was coming down the inside stairs as he entered. She looked about forty, a matron in style. She was weeping and her hat looked crooked to Martin.

'Jake upstairs?'

She nodded, sniffled, wiped an eye. Martin yearned to console her with gentle fondling.

'Can I help you?' he asked her.

She laughed once and shook her head, then went out. Martin climbed the old stairs and found Jake Berman leaning back in a swivel chair, hands behind head, feet propped up on an open rolltop desk. Jake had a thick gray mustache and wore his hair long, like a serious musician. The elbow was out of his gray sweater, and he was tieless. The desk dominated the room, two rooms really, with the adjoining wall knocked out. Folding chairs cluttered both rooms, and at a long table two men younger than Jake sat tallying numbers on pink pads. The phone on Jake's desk was off the hook.

'Why don't you answer your phone?' Martin asked.

'I'm too busy,' Jake said. He moved only his lips and eyes to say that. 'What can I do for you?'

'I heard the results.'

'You did. And did they surprise you?'

'Quite a heavy enrollment. I was told twelve hundred plus. Is that accurate?'

'Your information is as good as mine. Better. You get yours from McCall headquarters.'

'I got mine from the city desk.'

'Same thing really, isn't it, Martin?'

'I wouldn't say so. The McCalls do have some support there.'

'Some?'

'I for one don't see myself a total McCaller.'

'Yes, you write some risky things now and then, Martin. You're quite an independent-minded man in your way. But I didn't see you or anybody else reporting about the plan to take us over. Didn't anybody down on that reactionary rag know about it?'

'Did you?'

'I knew this morning,' said Jake. 'I knew when I saw it happening. Fat old Irishmen who loathe us, drunken bums from the gutter, little German hausfraus enrolling with us. Up until then, the subversion was a well-kept secret.'

Jake's face was battered, his eyes asymmetric, one lower than the other, his mustache trimmed too high on one side. In anger, his lower lip tightened to the left. His face was as off balance as his father's battered and dusty samovar, which sat behind him on a table, a fractured sculpture with spigot, one handle, and one leg broken. Another fractured face for Martin in a matter of hours: Charlie when Scotty died; Patsy and Matt this morning; and now Jake, victim of the McCalls. Interlocking trouble. Binding ironies. Martin felt sympathy for them all, had a fondness for them all, gave allegiance to none. Yet, now he was being accused, for the second time in half an hour, of being in league with the McCall machine. And was he not? Oh, duplicitous man, are you not?

'I came for a statement, Jake. Do you have one?'

'Very brief. May the McCalls be boiled in dead men's piss.'

A young man at the tabulating table, bald at twenty-five, threw down his pencil and stood up. 'And you can tell the Irish in this town to go fuck a duck.'

'That's two unprintable statements,' said Martin. 'Shall we try for three?'

'Always a joke, Martin. Everything is comic to you.'

'Some things are comic, Jake. When a man tells me with high seriousness to go fuck a duck, even though I'm only half Irish, I'm amused somewhere.'

The young man, in shirtsleeves, and with Ben Franklin spectacles poised halfway down his nose, came to the desk, hovering over Martin. 'It's the religion, isn't it?' he said. 'Political Jews stand as an affront to the McCalls and their priests, priests no better than the fascist-dog Catholics who kiss the boots of Franco and Mussolini.'

Martin made a squiggle on his notepad.

'Quote it about the fascists,' said the young man.

'Do you think the McCalls are fascists, Jake?' Martin asked.

'I know a Jew who's been with them almost since the beginning,' said Jake. 'He works for a few pennies more than he started for in nineteen twenty-two, sixteen years of penurious loyalty and he never asked for a raise, or threatened to quit over money. "If I do," he once said to me, "you know what they'll tell me? The same they told Levy, the accountant. Quit, then, you Jew fuck." He is a man in fear, a man without spirit.'

'People who don't promote Jews, are they fascists, or are they anti-Semites?'

'The same thing. The fascists exist because of all those good people, like those sheep who enrolled with us today, all full of passive hate, waiting for the catalyst to activate it.'

'Your point is clear, Jake, but I still want a statement.'

'Print this. That I'm not dead, not even defeated, that I'll take the party's case to court, and that we'll win. If ever the right to free elections was violated, then it was violated today in Albany with this farcical maneuver.'

'The McCalls own the courts, too,' said the young man. 'Even the Federal court.'

'There are honest judges. We'll find one,' Jake said.

'We won't yield to mob rule,' the young man said.

'He's right,' Jake said. 'We will not. You know an Irish mob threw my grandfather out a third-story window in New York during the Civil War. They were protesting against their great enemy back then, the niggers, but they killed a pious old Jew. He tried to reason with them, with the mob. He thought they would listen to reason, for, after all, he was an intelligent man and had nothing to do with the war, or the niggers. He was merely living upstairs over the draft office. Nevertheless, they threw him down onto the street and let him lie there twitching, dying, for hours. They wouldn't let anyone pick him up or even help him, and so he died, simply because he lived over the draft office. It was a moment of monstrous ethnic truth in American history, my friend, the persecuted Irish throwing a persecuted Jew out the window in protest against drafting Irishmen into the Union Army to help liberate the persecuted Negro.

'But the enormous irony hasn't led to wisdom, only to self-preservation and the awareness of the truth of mobs. My father told me that story after another mob set fire to paper bags on our front porch, and, when my father came out to stomp out the flames, the bags broke and human excrement squirted everywhere. A brilliant stroke by the mob. They were waiting with their portable flaming cross to watch my father dance on the fire and the shit. Fire and shit, my friend, fire and shit. Needless to say, we moved soon thereafter.'

'The Klan's an old friend of mine, too, Jake,' Martin said. 'They burned a cross in front of my house and fired a shot through our front window because of what I wrote in support of Al Smith. You can't blame the Klan on the Irish. Maybe the Irish were crazy, but they were also used as cannon fodder in the Civil War. I could match grandfathers with you. One of mine was killed at Antietam, fighting for the niggers.'

Jake held a letter opener in his hand like a knife. He poked the point of it lightly at the exposed desk top. Then his arm went rigid. 'Goddamn it, Martin, this is a stinking, lousy existence. Goddamn its stink! Goddamn all of it!' And with sudden force he drove the point of the letter opener into the desk top. The point stuck but the blade broke and pierced the muscle of his thumb.

'Perfect,' he said, and held his hand in front of his face and watched it bleed. The young man ran to the bathroom for a towel. He wrapped the wound tightly as Jake slumped in his chair.

'Violence solves it all,' Jake said. 'I no longer feel the need to say anything.'

'We'll talk another night,' Martin said.

'I won't be less bitter.'

'Maybe less bloody.'

'And unbowed.'

'There's something else, Jake, and you ought to know. It'll be in the paper tonight. Your son, Morrie, is named as a possible intermediary in a kidnapping.'

'Repeat that, Martin.'

'Bindy McCall's son, Charlie, was kidnapped this morning and the ransom demand is a quarter of a million. The McCalls are publishing a list of names in a simple code, names of men they view as potential go-betweens for the kidnappers to pick from. Morrie is one of twelve.'

'God is just,' said Jake's young aide. 'The McCalls are now getting theirs back.'

'Stupid, stupid to say such a thing,' Jake snapped. 'Know when to be angry.'

'I just saw Morrie,' Martin said, 'getting ready to go into a card game.'

'Naturally,' said Jake.

'I may see him later. Do you have any message?'

'We no longer talk. I have three daughters, all gold, and I have Morris, a lead slug.'

Martin suddenly pictured Jake with a flowing beard, knife in hand on Mount Moriah, cutting out the heart of his son.

'I just had a vision of you holding that letter opener,' Martin said to Jake. 'You look very much like an engraving of Abraham I've looked at for years in the family Bible. Your hair, your forehead.'

'Abraham with the blade.'

'And Isaac beneath it,' said Martin. He could not bring himself to mention the dissection of Isaac. 'The likeness of you to that drawing of Abraham is amazing.'

As he said this Martin was withholding; for he now had a clear memory of the biblical engraving and it wasn't like Jake at all. Abraham's was a face of weakness, a face full of faith and anguish, but no bitterness, no defiance. And the knife did not touch Isaac. Abraham's beard then disappeared in the vision. Where he gripped the sacrificial knife, part of a finger was missing. Isaac bore the face of a goat. The vision changed. The goat became a bawling infant, then a bleating lamb. Martin shut his eyes to stop the pictures. He looked at the samovar.

'Isaac,' Jake was saying. 'God loves the Isaacs of the world. But he wouldn't have bothered to ask Abraham to sacrifice a son as worthless as my Morris.'

'Now you even know what God asks,' Martin said.

'I withdraw the remark.'

With his gaze, Martin restored the samovar, new leg, new handle, new spigot. Steam came from it once again. He looked up to see the 1936 poster: Roosevelt, the Working Man's President. Out of the spigot came the hot blood of centuries.

7

Bump Oliver was a dapper little guy with a new haircut who played cards with his hat on. Billy met him when he sat down at the table in Nick Levine's cellar, just under the electric meter and kitty-corner from the old asbestos coal furnace which smudged up the cellar air but didn't heat it enough so you could take off your suit coat. New man on Broadway, Nick said of Bump when he introduced him to Billy; no more than that and who needs to know more?

And yet after Bump had dealt twice, Billy did want to know more. Because he sensed a cheater. Why? Don't ask Billy to be precise about such things. He has been listening to cheater stories for ten years, has even seen some in action and found out about it later, to his chagrin. He has watched Ace Reilly, a would-be cheater, practicing his second-card deal for hours in front of a mirror. Billy even tried that one himself to see how it went, but didn't like it, didn't have the patience or the vocation for it. Because cheaters, you see, already know how it's going to end, and what the hell good is that? Also, Billy saw a cheater caught once: a salesman who played in Corky Ronan's clubroom on Van Woert Street, and when Corky saw he was using a shiner, he grabbed the cheater's hand and showed everybody how he wore it, a little bit of a mirror under a long fingernail. Joe Dembski reached over and punched the cheater on the side of the neck, and the others were ready to move in for their licks, but Corky said never mind that, just take his money and he won't come back, and they let the cheater go. Why? Well,

Corky's idea was that everybody's got a trade, and that's Billy's idea too, now.

So Billy has seen all this and has thought about it, and because he knows so well how things should be when everything is straight, he also thinks he knows when it's off center, even when it's only a cunt hair off. That's how sensitive Billy's apparatus is. Maybe it was the way Bump beveled the deck and crooked a finger around it, or maybe it was his eyes and the fact that he was new on Broadway. Whatever it was, even though Bump lost twelve straight hands, Billy didn't trust him.

The game was now five-card stud, quarter ante, no limit, and four flush beats a pair. The deal was walking and when it came to Bump, Billy gave him the full eyeball.

'Where you from, Bump?' he asked, just like a fellow who was looking for information.

'Troy,' Bump said. 'Albia. You know it?'

'Sure, I know it. Who the hell don't know Albia?'

'Well, I was asking. Lot of people know about Troy don't know Albia.'

'I know Albia, for chrissake. I know Albia.'

'That's terrific, really terrific. Congratulations.'

Bump looked at Billy; Billy looked at Bump. The others in the game looked at them both: dizzy-talking bastards. But Billy wanted the cheater thinking about something besides cheating, wanted him edgy. Billy smiled at Bump. Bump didn't smile at Billy. Good.

Billy drew deuce, four, eight and folded. He was ahead $21, which was nice. He'd sat down with about $315 and change, which included his original $170, $20 from Peg, $40 from Tod, another $20 from Red Tom, and $67 from the Harvey Hess Benevolent Association. All he'd spent was carfare and the drinks at Becker's. Roughly speaking he still needed about $455 to get straight with Martin, but he was winging it now, wasn't he, getting where he had to go? And was there ever any doubt? Don'tcha know Billy can always get a buck?

Morrie Berman won the hand with three nines. He was a bigger winner than Billy.

'Your luck's running,' Billy said to him.

'Yeah,' said Morrie. 'Money coming in, name in the paper.'

Billy had told him as soon as they met in front of Nick's that both their names were on the list. Morrie already knew. Max Rosen had called around supper to ask him to stay in town, keep himself on tap. Rosen was nice as pie, Morrie said. If you don't mind, Mr Berman. Naturally I don't mind, Mr Rosen, and if I can be of any help at all, just call me. What else do you tell a McCall flunky in a situation like this? Neither Billy nor Morrie mentioned the list to anybody else at Nick's. Billy listened carefully to what Morrie said. He didn't say a goddamn thing worth telling anybody.

'What's that about name in the paper?' Nick Levine asked. Nick was his own house player, cutting the game. Nick would cut a deuce out of a $40 pot. Nick also had a nose for gossip when it moved into his cellar.

'Aw nothin', just a thing,' Morrie said.

'What thing?'

'Forget it.'

'I'll get the paper.'

'That's it, get the paper.'

But Nick wasn't satisfied. He was a persistent little man with double-thick glasses and he owned more suits of clothes personally than anybody Billy knew, except maybe George Quinn. But then Nick owned a suit store and George didn't, and George looked a hell of a lot better in clothes than Nick. Some people don't know how to wear clothes.

Nick looked across the table at Morrie and gave him a long stare while all play stopped. 'They pull you in?'

'No, nothing like that,' Morrie said. 'Look, play cards. I'll tell you later.'

That satisfied Nick and he bet his kings.

Lemon Lewis was a pointy-headed bald man, which was how he got his nickname. Didn't have a hair on his body. Not even a goddamn eyelash. When Lemon, who worked for Bindy McCall, didn't say anything about Morrie's name in the paper, Billy knew he hadn't heard about the list. But Lemon wasn't that close to

Bindy any more, not since he overdid it with kickbacks when he handled the gambling patronage. Bindy demoted Lemon for his greed and put him to work on the odds board in the Monte Carlo. Man with the chalk, just another mug.

Lemon was alongside Bump and when the deal reached Lemon, Billy asked for a new deck. If Bump, who would deal next, had been marking cards, beveling them, nicking edges, waiting for his time to handle them again, then the new deck would wipe out his work. Coming at Lemon's deal, the request would also not point to Bump. But it did rattle Lemon, which was always nice.

'New deck, and you're winning?' Lemon said.

'Double my luck,' Billy said.

'You think maybe Lemon knows something?' Footers O'Brien asked, and everybody laughed but Lemon. No mechanic, Lemon. Last man in town you'd accuse of cheating. A hound dog around the rackets all his life and he never learned how the game was played.

'Lemon shuffles like my mother when she deals Go Fish to my ten-year-old nephew,' Billy said.

Lemon dealt the new cards, delivering aces wired to Billy.

'Ace bets,' said Lemon, and when Billy bet five dollars, Bump, Morrie, and Nick all folded. Footers, a retired vaudevillian who sang Jolson tunes at local ministrel shows, stayed with a king. Lemon stayed with a queen.

On the third card nobody improved. Billy drew an eight and bet again with the ace. Lemon raised and so Billy read him for queens wired, because Lemon rarely bluffed. Footers called with king and jack showing, so probably he had a pair too. Footers wouldn't chase a pair. Too good a player. But whatever either of them had, Billy had them beat.

On the fourth card, Billy paired the eights. Aces and eights now. Neither Lemon nor Footers looked like they improved. Very unlikely. Yet both called, even when Billy bet $20. We can beat your eights, Billy.

Footers's last card was a seven, which didn't help, and Lemon drew a spade, which gave him three spades up. The bet was still to Billy's eights, but before he could bet them, Lemon turned over his hole card and showed the four flush.

'Can you beat it, boys?' he asked, smiling sunbeams.

'Only with a stick,' Footers said, and he folded his jacks.

'I bet forty dollars,' Billy said.

His hand, showing, was ace, seven and the pair of eights.

'Well that's a hell of a how-do-you-do,' Lemon said. 'I turn my hand over and show you I got a four flush.'

'Yes, you did that. And then I bet you forty dollars. You want to play five cards open, that's okay by me. But, Lemon, my word to you is still four-oh.'

'You're bluffing, Phelan.'

'You could find out.'

'What do you think of a guy like this, Nick?' Lemon said.

'It's the game, Lemon. Who the hell ever told you to show your hole card before the bet?'

'He's bluffing. I know the sevens were all played. He's got a third eight? Aces,' Lemon said, now doing his private calculating out loud. 'Nick folded an ace, I got an ace. So you got the case ace? That's what you're telling me?'

'Forty dollars, Lemon.'

Lemon went to the sandwich table, bit a bologna sandwich, and drew a glass of beer. He came back and studied Billy's hand. Still ace, seven and the eights.

Billy sat with his arms folded. Keeping cool. But folks, he was really feeling the sweet pressure, and had been, all through the hand: rising, rising. And he keeps winning on top of that. It was so great he was almost ready to cream. Goddamn, life is fun, ain't it Billy? Win or lose, you're in the mix. He ran his fingers over the table's green felt, fingered his pile of quarters, flipped through his stack of bills while he waited for the Lemon squash. Goddamn, it's good.

Bump watched him with a squinty eye.

Footers was smiling as he chewed his cigar, his nickel Headline. The Great Footers. Nobody like him. Drinking pal of Billy's for years, always good for a touch. Footers knew how to survive, too.

Told Billy once how he came off a four-day drunk and woke up broke and dirty, needing a shave bad. Called in a neighbor's kid and gave him a nickel, the only cash Footers had. Sent him down to the Turk's grocery for a razor blade. The kid came back with it and Footers shaved. Then he washed and dried the blade and folded it back in its wrapper and called the kid again and told him, take this back to the Turk and tell him you didn't get it straight. Tell him Mr O'Brien didn't want a razor blade, he wanted a cigar. And the kid came back with the cigar.

Billy looked at Footers and laughed at the memory. Footers smiled and shook his head over the mousehole in Lemon's character. Five minutes had passed since Lemon turned up the hole card.

'Thirty seconds, Lemon,' Nick said. 'I give you thirty seconds and then you call it or the pot's over.'

Lemon sat down and bit the bologna. He looked Billy in the eye as his time ticked away.

'You said it too fast when you bet,' Lemon said with a mouthful. 'You probably got it.'

'I'll be glad to show you,' Billy said.

'Yeah, well you're good, you lucky bastard.'

'Ah,' said Billy, pulling in the pot at last. 'My mother thanks you, my sister thanks you, my nephew thanks you, and above all, Lemon, I, William Francis Irish Catholic Democrat Phelan, I too thank you.'

And Billy shoved his hole card face down into the discards.

Lemon sulked, but life went on. Bump Oliver dealt and Billy came up with kings wired. Very lovely. Also Billy heard for the first time the unmistakable whipsaw snap of a real mechanic at work dealing seconds. Billy watched Bump deal, admiringly. Billy appreciated talent wherever he saw it. Nobody else seemed to notice, but the whipsaw was as loud as a brass band to Billy's ear. It was not Billy's music, however. He did not mind the music cheaters made, so long as they didn't make it all over him. He caught Bump's eye, smiled, and then folded the kings.

'No thanks,' was all he said to Bump, but it was plenty. Bump stopped looking at Billy and folded his own hand after the next card. He played two more hands and dropped out of the game. The cheater lost money. Never took a nickel from anybody, thanks to doughty Billy. Nobody knew Bump was really a wicked fellow at heart. Nobody knew either, how Billy absolutely neutralized him.

Billy, you're a goddamned patent-leather wonder.

Martin arrived at the card game in time to see Lemon Lewis throw the deck across the room and hear Nick tell him, 'Pick 'em up or get out. Do it again, I don't want your action.' Lemon, the world's only loser, picked up the cards and sat down, bent his shiny bald head over a new hand and continued, sullenly, to lose. Billy looked like a winner to Martin, but Morrie Berman had the heavyweight stack of cash.

'You've been doing all right, then,' Martin said, pulling a chair up behind Billy.

'Seem to be doing fine.' Half a glass of beer sat beside Billy's winnings, his eyes at least six beers heavier than when Martin had last seen him.

'You coachin' this fella, Martin?' Nick said.

'Doesn't look to me as if he needs much coaching.'

'He's got the luck of the fuckin' Irish,' Lemon said.

'Be careful what you say about the Irish,' Footers said. 'There's Jews in this game.'

'So what? I'm a Jew.'

'You're not a Jew, Lemon. You're an asshole.'

'Up yours, too,' Lemon said, and he checked his hole card.

'Lemon, with repartee like that you belong on the stage,' Footers said, and he looked at his watch. 'And there's one leaving in ten minutes.'

'Play cards,' Nick said.

'The bet,' said Morrie, 'is eighty dollars.'

'Eighty,' Nick said.

Morrie smiled and looked nothing like Isaac. He had a theatrical quality Martin found derivative – a touch of Valentino, a bit of George Raft, but very like Ricardo Cortez: dark, slick, sleek-haired

Latin stud, as if Morrie had studied the type to energize his own image as a Broadway cocksmith and would-be gigolo, a heavy gambler, an engaging young pimp with one of the smartest whores on Broadway, name of Marsha. Marsha was still in business but had split with Morrie five years back and worked alone now. Pimping is enough to weight down a paternal brow, but Jake's imputation of lead sluggery implied a far broader absence of quality in Morrie, and Martin could not see it.

What he saw was Morrie's suavity, and an ominous reserve in that muscular smile which George Raft, at his most evil, could never have managed; for Raft was too intellectually soft, too ready for simple solutions. Morrie, like Cortez, and unlike the pliant, innocent Isaac, conveyed with that controlled smile that he understood thoroughly that life was shaped by will, wit, brains, a reverence for power, a sense of the comic; that things were never simple; and that the end of behavior was not action but comprehension on which to base action. George Raft, you are a champion, but how would you ever arrive at such a conclusion?

'K-K-K-Katy, he's bettin' me eighty,' sang Footers, and he folded. That left Nick, Billy, and Morrie with money to win. The pot fattened, and Nick cut it for the house.

The cellar door opened and a kid, twenty-two maybe, stepped in and was met by Nick's doorman, the hefty Bud Bradt, an All-Albany fullback for Philip Schuyler High in the late twenties. The players looked up, saw the kid getting the okay from Bud, and went back to their cards. Then the kid came down the eight steps, stood with his back to the door that led to Nick's furnace and coal bin, and, taking a small pistol from his sock, told the players: 'Okay, it's a holdup.'

'Cowboy,' Morrie said, and he reached for his cash.

'Don't touch that, mister,' the kid said. 'That's what I came for,' and he threw a cloth bag on top of the pot. 'Put your watches and rings in that.'

'This isn't a healthy thing to do in Albany, young man,' Footers said to him. 'They've got rules in this town.'

'Do what I say, Pop. Off with the jewelry and out with the

wallets. Empty your pockets and then move over against that wall.' He pointed with his small pistol toward the bologna sandwiches.

The kid looked barely twenty to Martin, if that. Yet here he was committed to an irrevocably bold act. Psychopathic? Suicidal? Early criminal? Breadwinner desperate for cash? An aberrant gesture in the young, in any case. The kid's shoulders were spotted with rain, a drizzle that had begun as Martin arrived. The kid wore a black fedora with brim down, and rubbers. A holdup man in shiny rubbers with large tongues that protected his shoelaces from the damp night. What's wrong with this picture?

'Come on, move,' the kid said, in a louder voice. And Martin felt his body readying to stand and obey, shed wallet, watch, and gold wedding band bought and inscribed in Galway: *Martin and Maire, Together.* Never another like that. Give it up? Well, there are priorities beyond the staunchest sentiment. And yet, and yet. Martin contained his impulse, for the other players still stared at the kid and his .22 target pistol. Gentlemen, do you realize that psychopaths snap under stress? Are you snapping, young crazy? Is blood in the cards tonight? Martin envisioned a bleeding corpus and trembled at the possibilities.

And then Billy reached for the kid's swag bag, picked it off the money pile, and threw it back at the gunny boy. Billy grabbed a fistful of cash from the pot and stuffed it into his coat. The kid stepped behind Bump Oliver's chair and shoved the pistol into the light. 'Hey,' he said to Billy, yelling. But Billy went back for a second handful of bills.

'That pea-shooter you got there wouldn't even poison me,' he said.

Martin's thought was: Billy's snapped; the kid will kill him. But the kid could not move, his response to Billy lost, perhaps, inside his rubbers. The kid's holding position deteriorated entirely with the arrival of a sucker punch to the back of his neck by Bud Bradt, a man of heft, yes, but also of stealth, who had been edging toward the kid from the rear and then made a sudden leap to deliver his massive dose of fist to the sucker spot, sending the kid sprawling over the empty chair, gun hand sliding through the money, gun clattering to the floor on the far side of the table. Lemon pulled the kid off the table, punched his face, and threw him to the floor. Then he and Morrie kicked the kid body in dual celebration of the vanquishing until Nick said, 'Shit, that's enough.' Bud Bradt took over, kicked the kid once more, and then lifted him by collar and leg up the stairs, a bleeding carcass.

'Don't leave him in my alley,' Nick said.

Bud Bradt came right back and Nick said, 'Where'd you put him?'

'In the gutter between two cars.'

'Good,' said Nick. 'Maybe they'll run over him.'

'I would guess,' said Martin, 'that that would look very like a murder to somebody. And that's not only illegal, it also requires explanations.'

'Yeah,' said Nick, crestfallen. 'Put him up on the sidewalk.'

Martin went outside with Bud in time to see the kid hoisting himself up from the gutter with the help of the bumper of a parked car. The kid drew up to full height, full pain, and a fully bloodied face. He looked toward the alley and saw Martin and Bud, and then, with strength rising up from the secret reservoir fear draws upon, he turned from them and ran with a punishing limp across Clinton Avenue, down Quackenbush Street, down toward the waterworks and the New York Central tracks, and was gone then, fitfully gone into the darkness.

'Didn't kick him enough,' Bud said. 'The son of a bitch can still run. But he'll think twice before he does that again.'

'Or shoot somebody first to make his point.'

'Yeah, there's that.'

Footers had come up behind them in time to see the kid limp into the blackness. 'I was in a crap game once,' Footers said, 'and a fellow went broke and put a pistol on the table to cover his bet. Five guys faded him.'

Martin saw the kid limping into the beginning of his manhood, victim of crazy need, but insufficient control of his craziness. Martin had been delighted to see the kid sucker-punched five minutes earlier, salvation of the Galway wedding band. Now he felt only compassion for a victim, lugubrious emotions having to do with pity at pain, foreboding over concussions, lungs punctured by broken ribs, internal ruptures, and other leaky avenues to death or lesser grievings. Victims, villains were interchangeable. Have it both ways, lads. Weep for Judas at the last gasp. We knew he'd come to the end of his rope. He couldn't beat the fate the Big Boy knew was on him, poor bastard.

'I don't know what the hell to do with this pot,' Nick was saying as they reentered the cellar. He was still picking quarters off the floor.

'Give it to Billy,' Morrie said. 'He deserves it.'

'You're a genuine hero,' Martin said to Billy. 'Like the quarterback who makes the touchdown with a broken leg. There's a heroic edge to such behavior. You think bullets don't kill the single-minded.'

'Weird day,' Billy said. 'I took a knife away from a looney in the Grand Lunch a few hours ago.'

The others stopped talking.

'This kid was poking near my belly,' and Billy showed them and told them about the coffee game.

'But you had a weapon in the coffee,' Martin said. 'Tonight you had nothing. You know a twenty-two slug can damage you just as permanently as five rounds from a machine gun. Or is your education lacking in this?'

'I didn't think like that,' Billy said. 'I just wasn't ready to hand over a night's work to that drippy little bastard. His gun didn't even look real. Looked like a handful of candy. Like one of them popguns my nephew has that shoots corks. Worst I'm gonna get is a cork in the ear, that's how it went. But the money counted, Martin. I owe people, and I was hot for that pot, too. I had kings and nines, ready to fill up.'

'Billy should get a chunk of that pot, Nick,' Morrie said.

'He got two handfuls,' Nick said.

'That was his own dough going back home,' Morrie said. 'What about the rest? And Bud ought to get something. Without them guys, I'd have personally lost one hell of a bundle.'

'Everybody oughta split the pot,' Lemon said. 'Nobody had a winning hand.'

'Especially you,' Footers said.

'You folded, Lemon, forget it,' Morrie said.

'Fuck you guys,' Lemon said.

'Why you gommy, stupid shit,' Morrie said. 'You might be dead if it wasn't for Billy and Bud. Your head is up your ass.'

'While it's up there, Lemon,' Footers said, 'see if you can see Judge Crater anywhere. He's been gone a long time.'

'The only three had the power in that last hand,' said Morrie, 'was Billy, me, and you, Nick. Everybody else was out of it. So it's a three-way split. I say Billy gets half my share and Bud the other half.'

'I got enough,' Billy said.

'I'll take it,' said Bud.

'It's about forty apiece, what's left, three ways. One-twenty and some silver here.' Nick counted out the split, forty to each, and pocketed his own share.

'You really keeping your whole forty, Nick?' Morrie asked, divvying his share between Billy and Bud. 'After what those boys did for you and your joint?'

'Whataya got in mind now?'

'The house buys them steaks at Becker's.'

'I don't fight that,' Billy said.

'I ate,' Nick said.

'So eat again, or send money.'

Nick snapped a five on the table to Morrie, who looked at it, looked at Nick, didn't pick it up. Nick peeled off another five.

'I give ten to the meal. Eat up. But is the game dead here? What the hell, everybody gonna eat? Nobody gonna play cards?'

'Dead for me,' Morrie said, picking up the fivers. And clearly, Billy and Martin were pointed elsewhere when Nick took a good look, and Footers was drawing himself another beer.

'I do believe I'll pass, Nick, me boy,' Footers said. 'That last one was a tough act to follow.'

'I'm still playing,' Lemon said, sitting alone at the table.

'You're playing with yourself,' Footers said. 'As usual.'

'Tomorrow night, nine-thirty,' Nick said. 'Same time, same station.'

'Steak time, boys,' Morrie said.

Billy found Nick's toilet and pissed before they left. While the old beer sudsed up in the bowl, he consolidated his cash. Out of the coat pocket came the handfuls of bills. He counted it all. Nice. He'd pulled more out of the pot than he put in. He wrapped it all around the rest of the wad. He still needed $275 to pay off Martin, his bankroll now up to $514.

It mounts up. No question about that. Put your mind to it and it mounts up.

8

No man who wore socks in Albany felt better in the nighttime than Billy Phelan, walking with a couple of pals along his own Broadway from Nick's card game to Union Station to get the papers, including the paper that was going to make him famous tonight. Maybe he feels so good that he's getting a little crazy about not being afraid. Martin was right. A .22 in the eye gives you a hell of a headache.

But now Billy looks around and sees this Broadway of his and knows he's not crazy, because he knows it all and it all makes sense. He has known it this way since 1913 when he was six and his father took him in the rowboat and they rowed down the middle of the street. The Hudson had backed up over its banks and they were rowing down to Keeler's Hotel to rescue his Uncle Peter, who had had a fight with Billy's grandmother and hadn't been home for a month and was caught now, stranded at the hotel with the big trunk he was taking to New York, leaving Albany to work in a Manhattan publishing house. But he could not carry the trunk on his back through two and three feet of water from Keeler's to the station. And so his brother, Francis, became the hero who would travel across the waters to the rescue. Francis put Billy in the boat at the station and right now Billy can see the spot where he stepped off the curb into that boat, where Steuben Street intersects Broadway. The water was up to the curb there, and toward State Street it became deeper and deeper.

Billy got into the boat, one of a dozen rowing around on

Broadway, and his father rowed them down the center of the street, down the canyon of buildings, wearing his cap and the heavy knit sweater with the collar that Billy remembers. Never a coat; a sweater and gloves always enough for that man. He rowed Billy half a block and then said: They'll fix this stuff one of these days.

I don't want them to fix it, Billy said.

They've got to, said his father, because they can't let this kind of thing go on.

Billy, sitting in the back of the boat like the captain, said, I hope they never fix it. Then they got the trunk and Uncle Peter, who sat with Billy on his lap, and the trunk standing up in the middle of the boat.

A damn shame, Uncle Peter said, to put up with this, but I suppose you like it, young fellow. And Billy said he liked it better than snow. They rowed to the station, where Uncle Peter got his train and went away.

Now 1913 was gone, too, but Billy was again gliding down Broadway in a craft of his own making, and he relished the sight. There was Albany's river of bright white lights, the lights on in the Famous Lunch, still open, and the dark, smoky reds of Brockley's and Becker's neon tubes, and the tubes also shaping the point over the door of the American Hotel, and the window of Louie's pool room lit up, where somebody was still getting some action, and the light on in the Waldorf restaurant, where the pimps worked out of and where you could get a baked apple right now if you needed one, and the lights of the Cadillac Cafeteria with the pretty great custard pie, and the lights on in the upper rooms of the Cadillac Hotel, where the Greek card game was going on and where Broadway Frances was probably turning a customer upside down and inside out, pretty, tough, busy, knobby lady and Billy's old friend, and the lights in the stairway to the Monte Carlo, where the action would go on until everybody ran out of money or steam, and the lights, too, in Chief Humphrey's private detective office, the Chief working late on somebody's busted marriage, and the light in Joe Mangione's rooms upstairs over his fruit store, and light in the back of Red's barbershop coming through a crack in the door, and Billy knew that Red and others were in there playing blackjack. And look there, too, buddy boy: The lights are on in Bill's Magic Shop, where Bill is staying late, hoping to sell a deck of cards or a pair of dice or a punch board or a magic wand to some nighthawk in search of transport, and the lights are on, too, in Bradt's drug store, where Billy does all his cundrum business.

The lights are on because it's not quite half past eleven on Broadway and some movies are still not out and plenty of people are waiting for the westbound train just now pulling into Union Station, bound for Cleveland and Chicago and carrying the New York papers. Lights are on in Gleason's Grill, which was a soda fountain before beer came back, and lights are shining in the other direction, up toward Orange Street and Little Harlem, like Broadway but only a block long, with the colored crap and card games going strong now, and the Hotel Taft doing its colored business on white sheets, and Prime and Ginsburg's candy store still open, with beer by the bottle and a game in the back and people talking politics there, McCall nigger politics, even at this hour, because that is where the power Democrats gather in Little Harlem.

There is Helen's Lunch, dark now, which feeds the colored hungry and Martha's colored bar all lit up and full of all-night wild music (Play it, Fatha), where Martha wets down the colored thirsty but not *just* the colored. Lights burn in the Carterer Mission, where the colored bums get the same treatment and food the white bums get; and in the colored rooming house run by Mrs Colored O'Mara, where Slopie Dodds has his rooms and where he keeps his crutches when he's wearing his leg.

There is light still in the triangular sign of the Railroad YMCA, keeping the lamp lit for the conductors and brakemen and engineers who terminate in Albany tonight and want a clean pillow. And next door a light is on in the Public Bath, closed now but where Billy watched his sister, Peg, learn to swim, ducked by Uncle Chick. Peg, older than Billy by eight years, was terrified when she went under. Billy was already a swimmer then, learned in the Basin and in the Hudson when Peg was afraid to go near it. Billy learned everything by himself, everything worth learning. He'd been swimming all that summer when his mother told him to stay away from the river. That August he climbed the Livingston Avenue railroad bridge and dove in – forty feet high, was it? – wearing a straw hat to protect his head. The next summer Billy dove off that trestle without the hat and came up with a fish in his mouth and a mermaid biting his big toe.

Look down Broadway.

Here comes a Pine Hills trolley, and here are the cars coming in to pick up the train people, and there are the Yellow cabs and the gypsies waiting for their long-distance action.

And here comes Mike the Wop ahead of all the passengers, Mike always one of the first off the train because he knows the kids are waiting. Thirty kids anyway. Oughta be in bed, you scurvy little rug-rats. But they know Mike is due.

Mike comes out wearing his candy butcher's apron full of change. He has no use for change because he is thick with folding money and bound for the action at the Monte Carlo, and after that he may contract for a bit of the old interrelatedness with Broadway Frances or one of her peers, but for now he is the God Almighty Hero of the Albany rug-rats who scream: Here he comes. And of course Mike sees them as soon as he moves across the concourse of the station, the great, glorious, New York Central monument to power, and, feeling perhaps as potent as Vanderbilt, Mike expansively lets his great, pasta-filled stomach precede him toward the door to Broadway.

He then pushes open the station's storm door and enters onto that segment of Broadway Billy and his friends are just now approaching from the north.

Billy pauses and says, Hey, Mike.

Mike turns and is distracted only momentarily from the performance at hand but does say, Eh, Billy, and turns back then to the rug-rats and spins out the change onto the sidewalk under the canopy: dollar, two, five, ten, twenty. Who knows how much change Mike the Wop strews before the rug-rats of Broadway? He gives, they receive. They scramble and pick it up, take it home, and buy the milk and beer.

A man, a grown man, a bum, a wino, a lost derelict from the sewers and gutters of elsewhere, passes and sees Mike's generosity and reaches down for a dime.

Get lost, bum, says Mike, and when the bum does not, Mike raises a foot and pushes the bum over, into the street, where he falls and rolls and is almost run over by a Yellow cab just leaving for Loudonville with a customer and four valises, and is also almost decapitated by the Number Four Pine Hills trolley.

The bum rises, walks on, the dime in his grip.

Mike supervises as the rug-rats clean up every visible nickel and penny, sift in the soft dirt of the gutters for dimes that rolled into the glop. And some will be back, scrounging at dawn for coins that eluded everyone last night. Now they take their cache and disentangle themselves from one another. They run, seethe into the night, and evaporate off Broadway.

Billy watches them go, watches, too, as Mike crosses the street to walk beneath the brightest of the bright lights, one of the many maestros of Broadway power, now heading into the center of the garden in search of other earthly delights.

The station was still alive with travelers, with the queers buzzing in and out of the men's room, and the night crowd hot for the papers. When Billy had bought the *Times-Union*, found the ad, decoded what they all knew was there to begin with, then Martin said to Morrie: 'I saw your father tonight and told him about this.'

'Heh,' said Morrie. 'What'd he say?'

'Ah, a few things.'

'Nothing good, bet your ass on that, the old son of a bitch.'

'It wasn't exactly flattering, but he was interested.'

'Who's that?' Billy asked, looking up from the newspaper.

'My old man,' Morrie said.

'He's a son of a bitch?'

'In spades.'

'What'd he do?'

'Nothing. He's just a son of a bitch. He always was.'

Well, you got an old man, is what Billy did not say out loud.

They stood in the rotunda, in front of the busy Union News stand with the belt-high stacks of Albany papers, the knee-high stacks of New York *News*es and *Daily Mirror*s, the ankle-high stacks of *Herald Trib*s and *Times*es and *Sun*s. Billy was translating Honey Curry's name from the code. E-d-w-a-r-d C-u-r-r-e-y. They spelled it wrong.

'Honey Curry,' Billy said. 'Where the hell is he these days?'

Martin passed on that, and Morrie said, 'Who knows where that son of a bitch is?'

Billy laughed out loud. 'Remember when they had the excursion. The Sheridan Avenue Gang. And Curry went wild and hit Healy, the cop, with a crock of butter and knocked him right off the boat and Healy goddamn near drowned. Curry lit out and wound up in Boston and Maloy met him there, downtown, and they're cuttin' it up and Curry's afraid of his shadow. Then a broad walks by, a hooker, and looks at Curry and says to him, Hi ya, honey, how ya doin'? and Curry grabs her with both hands and shoves her up against a tree and shakes the hell out of her. How come you know my name? he says to her.'

'That's Curry,' said Morrie.

'Where's Maloy? I hear he's in Jersey. Newark, is it?' Billy asked.

'Could be,' said Morrie.

'Goddamn,' Billy said. 'That's where I heard it.'

'What?'

'The rumor they were going to kidnap Bindy last summer. We were up in Tabby Bender's saloon. You and me. Remember?'

'No. When was that?' said Morrie.

'Goddamn it, don't anybody remember what I remember? We were sitting at the bar, you and me, and Maloy was with Curry, and Maloy asks if I heard about the Bindy kidnap thing and I didn't. We talked about it, Maloy and Curry shootin' the shit and comin' up to the bar for drinks. And then Maloy tells me, We're gonna take this joint. Now, you remember?'

'I remember *that*,' Morrie said. 'Screwballs.'

'Right,' said Billy. 'Maloy says, Get out now if you want; we're gonna clean him out. And I told him, I'm comfortable. Clean him out. Take the pictures off the walls. What the hell do I care? And you and me kept drinking.'

'Right,' Morrie said. 'We never moved.'

'Right, and they go out and they're gone ten minutes and back they come with handkerchiefs on their faces. Goddamn wouldn't of fooled my nephew, in the same suits and hats. And they cleaned out the whole damper, every nickel. And when they were gone, I said to George Kindlon, the bartender, Let's have a drink, George, and I pushed a fiver at him. I don't think I can change it, he said, and we all busted up because George didn't give a rat's ass, he didn't own the joint. It was Tabby's problem, not George's.'

'Right,' Morrie said, 'and George give us the drink free.'

'Yeah,' said Billy. 'But it was Maloy and Curry really got us the free drink.'

'That's it. Maloy and Curry bought that one,' and Morrie laughed.

'Son of a bitch,' Billy said.

'Right,' said Morrie.

Billy pictured Morrie kicking the holdup kid. Vicious mouth on him then, really vicious, yet likable even if he used to be a pimp. He had a good girl in Marsha. Marsha Witherspoon, what the hell kind of a name is that? Billy screwed her before she even went professional. She was a bum screw. Maybe that's why Morrie dumped her, couldn't make a buck with her. But he didn't take up any other whores. Morrie would always let Billy have twenty, even fifty if he needed it. Morrie was with Maloy the night Billy almost lost a match to Doc Fay two years ago. Billy played safe till his ass fell off to win that one, and when he won and had the cash, Morrie and Maloy came over and Maloy said, You didn't have to worry, Billy. If he'd of won the game, we'd of taken the fuckin' money away from him and give it to you anyway. Crazy Maloy. And Morrie was tickled when Maloy said that, and he told Billy, Billy, you couldn't have lost tonight even if you threw the match.

Morrie was two years older than Billy and he was a Jew and a smart Jew and Billy liked him. This was funny because Billy didn't like or even know that many Jews. But then Billy thought of Morrie as a gambler, not as a Jew. Morrie was a hustler who knew how to make a buck. He was all right. One of Billy's own kind.

While Billy, Martin, and Morrie ate midnight steaks in Becker's back room, tables for ladies but no ladies, George Quinn came in and found Billy, took him away from the table and whispered: 'You hear that Charlie McCall's been kidnapped?'

'I heard that, George.'

'Do you know your name's in the paper in some kind of mixed-up spelling?'

'I know that, too.'

'The cops were just at the house looking for you.'

'Me? What for?'

'They didn't say. Peg talked to them. She asked if you were in trouble and they said no, but that's all they'd tell her.'

'Who was it?'

'Bo Linder and somebody else in the car, maybe Jimmy Bergan. That's his partner.'

'You see Bo?'

'He came to the door and told Peg for you to call the detective office.'

'He didn't say why.'

'He said what I told you.'

'Right, George. Peg said you wanted to talk to me about a book.'

'There's a fellow named Muller works over in Huyck's mill and writes a hell of a good-sized book. I figured you might sit in while I talked to him about taking his layoff. Kind of break the ice a little. I don't know him at all.'

'All right, George, I'll do that. When you meeting him?'

'Tonight, one-thirty, quarter to two, when he gets off work. He's coming here.'

'I'll probably be here. If I go anyplace, I'll try to be back by then.'

'Are you in trouble, Billy? Did you get mixed up with something?'

'No, George. I really don't know what the hell they want.'

'You need money? Peg said you took a lickin' today.'

'I'm all right on that.'

'I can rustle up some if you need it. What do you need?'

'Don't worry about it, George. You need it yourself. I'll be all right. I just got lucky in a card game.'

'You're sure you're not in trouble?'

'If I was in trouble, I'd be the first to know.'

'All you got to do is ask, whatever it is. And I mean that, even on the money if you're in a jackpot. We'll find it.'

'You're a sweetheart, George. Have a drink, relax. I gotta finish my steak.'

'Isn't that Jake Berman's kid there?'

'Right, Morrie.'

'His name's in the paper, too.'

'Right.'

'Jake's father made me the first suit of clothes I ever had made.'

At the bar a man's voice said, 'That's right, I said I hope they don't catch them, whoever they are.'

The bar went quiet and Red Tom said, 'That's just about enough of that talk,' and he took the man's beer away. Billy recognized the talker, name of Rivera, spic like Angie's husband, a pimp. Red Tom poured Rivera's beer in the sink and shoved his change closer to him on the bar. 'I don't want your business,' Red Tom said. But Rivera wouldn't move. Red Tom came around the bar and grabbed his arm. Rivera resisted. Red Tom reached for the change and shoved it into his pocket. Then he lifted him with one arm, like a sack of garbage, lifted him off the bar stool and walked him out the door.

'The McCalls got everybody scared to do pee-pee,' Rivera said over his shoulder. 'They think they can treat people like dogs.'

'Who's that guy?' George Quinn asked.

'He's a bughouse pimp. Gotta be bugs,' Billy said.

Red Tom closed the front door and moved in behind the bar.

'That kind of talk stays out in the street,' he said to all in earshot, looking at no one in particular. He pointed twice toward the door with one finger. 'Out in the street,' he said.

When he'd finished his steak, Morrie Berman stood up and announced he was going off to get laid. Billy thought of tagging along with him but rejected the idea. He envisioned Angie in bed up at the Kenmore, waiting. He would go and see her. He was tired of gambling, tired of these people here. Maybe later he could come back and play some blackjack if the game was still running. Do that when he left Angie. If he left Angie. All right, he would see her, then leave her be and come down and play some blackjack. Billy still owed money. First things first.

'I got a date, Martin,' Billy said, pushing away from the table.

'That sounds healthful. Bon voyage.'

'I'll keep you posted on the bankroll. We're doing all right.'

'I know we are. You've decided not to go along with Patsy's suggestion?'

'I listened all night. He didn't say a goddamn thing.'

'What about the Bindy kidnap rumor? He doesn't seem to remember it, but you do. Isn't that odd?'

'That don't mean anything.'

'Are you sure?'

'Aaahh,' Billy said, and he waved off the possibility and went out onto Broadway and turned up Columbia Street, past the old Satin Slipper, a hot place when Butch McHale ran it during Prohibition and now cut up into furnished rooms. He crossed James Street and was halfway to North Pearl when the car pulled alongside him, Bo Linder at the wheel, Jimmy Bergan with him. Billy. Bo. Been looking for you. Oh yeah?

'Bindy wants to talk to you.'

'Bindy? About what?'

'You ask him that.'

'Where is he?'

'Up at Patsy's house.'

'Patsy who?'

'Patsy who my ass.'

'When's he want to see me?'

'Two hours ago.'

'If this's got something to do with Charlie, I don't know anything.'

'Tell Bindy that. Get in.'

'No thanks.'

'Get in, Billy.'

'You pulling me in? Charging me with something?'

'I can get particular.'

'I'm under arrest, I'll get in. Otherwise, I'll take a cab. I know where Patsy lives.'

'All right, take a cab. We'll follow so the driver don't get lost.'

Billy walked to Pearl Street and at the corner looked up at the Kenmore, maybe at Angie's room. She liked the front so she could look down and see people on Pearl Street after she and Billy had loved all possible juices out of one another. Billy didn't see Angie in any window. She'd be asleep now, wouldn't go on the town alone. Twelve-thirty now, hell of a time to visit the McCalls.

Two cabs stood in front of the Kenmore. Billy whistled and the front one made a U-turn and Billy got in. Bo Linder was idling at the corner, Bo the cop, a good kid when he was a kid. Good second baseman for The Little Potatoes, Hard to Peel. But what can you do with somebody who grows up to be a mean cop? Never was mean on second base. After he went on the force, Bo walked into Phil Slattery's joint and shot Phil's dog when it growled at him. Dog should've bit him on the ass.

'Conalee Street,' Billy told the cabbie.

Billy had never learned to pronounce Colonie Street the usual way. But people understood anyway. The driver moved north on Pearl Street, and Bo Linder swung out of Columbia Street and made it a parade.

9

Billy didn't hate Colonie Street entirely, for it would have meant hating his mother, his greatest friends, Toddy Dunn, for one, even his ancestors. It would have meant hating the city the Irish had claimed as their own from vantage points of streets like Colonie. It was the street where he was born and had lived until adolescence, when he went off to room by himself. It was the street his sister, Peg, left with their mother when Peg married George Quinn and took a bigger and newer house in the North End.

Billy told the taxi driver to leave him off at the corner of North Pearl, and he walked up the hill toward Patsy McCall's house. He passed the old Burns house, where the ancient Joe Burns always sat in the window, ten years in the window at least. Old Joe lived with his son, Kid, the sexton of St Joseph's Church for years until Father Mooney put him through undertakers' school; and next door to them the Dillons: Floyd, a conductor on the Central, who put Billy and Peg and their mother in a Pullman with only coach tickets when they went to New York to see the ocean for the first time. Across the street was the vacant lot where the Brothers School used to stand, and next to that the Daugherty house, gone, and then the other house: That house Billy did not now look at directly but saw always in his memory and hated, truly did hate that much of the old street.

And it was an old street even when Billy was born on it. It ran westward along the river flats from the Basin, that sheltered harbor that formed the mouth of the Erie Canal, and rose up the northernmost of the three steep ridges on which Albany was built: Arbor Hill. It rose for half a mile, crossed Ten Broeck, the street where the lumber barons had built their brownstones, and, still rising, ran another half mile westward to all but bump the Dudley Observatory, where scientific men of the city catalogued the stars (8241 measured and recorded for the International Catalogue as of 1883) from the top of the same hill on which Mike Mulvaney grazed and daily counted his two dozen goats.

The street took its name from The Colonie itself, that vast medieval demesne colonized in 1630 by an Amsterdam pearl merchant named Kiliaen Van Rensselaer, who was also known as the First Patroon, the absentee landlord who bought from five tribes of Indians some seven hundred thousand acres of land, twenty-four miles long and forty-eight miles wide, out of which a modest seven thousand acres would eventually be expropriated by the subsequent Yankee overlords to create the city of Albany.

Each power-wielding descendant of Van Rensselaer to assume the feudal mantle of the Patroonship during the next two centuries would maintain exploitative supremacy over thousands of farm renters on the enormous manor called, first, Rensselaerswyck, and later, The Colonie. Each Patroon would make his home in the Manor House, which rose handsomely out of a riverside meadow just north of the city on the bank of a stream that is still called Patroon Creek. Mickey McManus from Van Woert Street went rabbit hunting one day near The Patroon's creek and shot a cow. Few can now remember that meadow or even where the Manor House stood precisely. It closed forever in 1875, when the widow of the Last Patroon died there, and it was later moved to make room for the Delaware and Hudson railroad tracks, dismantled brick by brick and reassembled in Williamstown as a fraternity house.

But long before that, North Albany, where Billy Phelan and Martin Daughterty both now lived, and Arbor Hill, where the McCalls and Billy's aunts and uncles still lived, had been seeded in part with the homes of settlers who worked as servants and as farm and field hands for the Patroon. Billy Phelan's great-grandfather, Johnny Phelan, a notably belligerent under-sheriff, was given the safekeeping of the Manor House as his personal charge after four rebellious prisoners barricaded themselves in their cell at the penitentiary and, with a stolen keg of gunpowder, threatened to blow themselves up unless the food improved. Johnny Phelan sneaked a fire hose to the door of their cell, opened the door suddenly, and drenched their powder with a swift blast. Then he leaped over their barricade and clubbed them one by one into civility.

Martin Daugherty's grandmother, Hanorah Sweeney, had been the pastry cook in the Patroon's kitchen and was famed for her soda bread and fruitcakes, which, everyone said, always danced off their platters and onto the finicky palates of the Patroon and his table companions, among them the Prince of Wales, George Washington's grandnephew, and Sam Houston.

Arbor Hill and North Albany continued to grow as the railroads came in, along with the foundries, the stove works, the tobacco factory and the famous Lumber District, which started at the Basin and ran northward two and a half miles between the river and the canal. Processing Adirondack logs into lumber was Albany's biggest business at mid-century, and the city fathers proclaimed that Albany was now the white pine distribution center of the world.

The North End and Arbor Hill grew dense with the homes of lumber handlers, moulders, railroad men, and canalers, and in the winter, when the river and the canal froze, many of them cut ice, fifteen thousand men and boys cutting three million tons from the Hudson in six weeks at century's end.

They all clustered on streets such as Colonie to live among their own kind, and the solidarity became an obvious political asset. Not the first to notice this, but the first to ride it to local eminence, was the fat, bearded, Irish-born owner of the Beverwyck brewery, Michael Nolan, who in 1878 was elected mayor of the city. Coming only three years after the death of the Last Patroon's widow, this clearly signaled a climactic change in city rule: the Dutch and Yankees fading, the American Irish, with the help of Jesus, and by dint of numbering forty per cent of the city's population, waxing strong. And eight years ahead of Boston in putting an Irishman in City Hall.

Nolan had lived on Millionaire's Row, on the east side of Ten Broeck, two and a half blocks from Patsy McCall's home on Colonie Street. Patsy, who could have lived like a millionaire but didn't, was in the Irish descendance of political power from Nolan as surely as the Last Patroon had descended from the first; and was a descendant in style as well as power. When Nolan was elected, he swathed his brewery wagons and dray horses in red, white, and blue bunting and saw to it that Beverwyck beer was sold in every saloon in town. Nolan's example was not wasted on the McCalls. Gubernatorial hopeful Tom Dewey revealed that in October 1938, Stanwix, the McCall beer, was sold in 243 of the city's 249 taverns.

Billy Phelan knew the Patroon only as a dead word, Nolan not at all. But in the filtered regions of his cunning Irish brain, he knew the McCalls stood for power far beyond his capacity to imagine.

They were up from below. And when you're up, you let no man pull you down. You roll your wagons over the faces of the enemy.

And who is the enemy?

It's well you might ask.

Billy pushed the door bell.

Bindy McCall opened the door, smiled, and pulled Billy by the arm, gently, into the house, the first time Billy had entered Patsy's home. The front hall, leading upstairs and also into both front and back parlors, reminded Billy of the hated house across the street, probably built from the same blueprints.

Bindy held Billy's arm and led him into the front parlor with its thick oriental rug, its heavy drapes and drawn shades, where a scowling male ancestor of the McCalls looked down insistently on Billy: a powerful face above a neck stretched by a high collar and string tie, a face not unlike Patsy's, who sat beneath it at a card table, shirtless, reclining in his blue bathrobe in a leather armchair; pads and pencils on the table beside a telephone. An old player piano dominated the room, where Patsy no doubt played and sang the ditties he was famous for, 'Paddy McGinty's Goat,' for one.

Billy had heard him sing that at the Phoenix Club in the North End on a Sunday years ago when the political notables of North Albany turned out for an election rally. Billy went just to watch the spectacle and barely spoke to anyone, never said, Hello Patsy, as he could have, as thousands did whenever the great leader hove into range. Hello Patsy. Billy just listened and never forgot the song and later learned it himself: *Patrick McGinty, an Irishman of note, fell heir to a fortune and he bought himself a goat.*

A panorama of a Civil War battle, one of Patsy's well-known interests, hung in a gilded frame over the piano. A pair of brass donkeys as bookends, and with Dickens and Jefferson, a biography of Jim Jeffries, and canvasses of Fifth and Eighth Ward voters sandwiched between the butt ends of the animals, sat on top of the piano. On an old oak sofa across from Patsy sat a man Billy didn't know. Bindy introduced him as Max Rosen, Matt McCall's law partner.

'You're a tough man to find,' Bindy said. 'We've been looking for you.'

'I wasn't hiding. Just playing cards.'

'We heard about the holdup and what you did. You're a tough guy, Billy.'

'How'd you hear about it? It just happened.'

'Word gets around. We also heard what you did in the Grand Lunch with that crazy kid.'

'You heard that, too?'

'That, too,' Bindy said.

'Listen, Bin,' said Billy, 'I'm really sorry about Charlie.'

'Are you?'

'Sure I am. You got any word on him yet?'

'We got a little. That's why we wanted to talk to you.'

'Me? What've I got to do with anything?'

'Relax. You want a beer?'

'Sure, I'll have a beer with you, Bin.'

Bindy, shirtsleeves rolled above the elbow, soup stain on shirtfront, no tie, wearing eyeglasses and house slippers, looked like somebody else to Billy, not Bindy McCall, the dapper boss of the street. He looked tired, too, and Patsy the same. Patsy stared at Billy. Max Rosen, in his suit coat, tie up tight to a fresh collar, also stared. Billy in the middle, a new game. He was glad to see Bindy come back with the beer bottle and glass: Stanwix.

'I heard you took a beating today with the nags,' Bindy said, pouring Billy's beer.

'You hear what I had for breakfast?'

'No, but I could find out.'

'I ate alone, no witnesses.'

'There's other ways.'

'Yeah.' And Billy took a drink.

'You know where your old man is?' Patsy asked.

'My old man?'

'Yours.'

'No. I don't know.'

'I heard he was in town,' said Patsy.

'My father in Albany? Where?'

'I didn't hear that. Somebody saw him downtown today.'

'Goddamn,' Billy said.

'You wanna see him?' asked Patsy.

'Sure I wanna see him. I haven't saw him in twenty years. Twenty-two years.'

'I'll see if I can track him down.'

'That'd be terriffic, Mr McCall.'

'Call me Patsy.'

'Patsy. That's a terrific thing if you can do that.'

'Maybe you can do something for us.'

'Maybe I can.'

'You heard that kidnap rumor about me,' Bindy said, sitting on a folding chair across the card table from Patsy. The card table Billy worked at was in better shape.

'I heard that last summer.'

'From who?'

'Jesus, I don't remember, Bin. One of those things you hear at a bar when you're half in the bag, you don't remember. I didn't give it the time of day. Then I remembered it today.'

'And got hot at Louie Dugan for telling me about it.'

'I didn't expect to have it repeated.'

'We heard the same rumor last year and traced it to a couple of local fellows. And maybe, just maybe, that ties in to Charlie. Do you follow me?'

'I follow.'

'Neither of these fellows are in town and we don't know just where they are. But they got a friend who's in town, and that's why you're here.'

'I'm the friend?'

'No, you're a friend of the friend. The friend is Morrie Berman.'

The noise Billy made then was a noncommittal grunt. Maloy and Curry, Berman's pals. On the list, Curry.

'We understand you know Mr Berman well,' Max Rosen said.

'We play cards together.'

'We understand you know him better than that,' Rosen said.

'I know him a long time.'

'Yeah, yeah, we know all about it,' said Patsy, 'and we also know you didn't give Pop O'Rourke's man his ten dollars today.'

'I told Pop why.'

'We know what you told him,' said Patsy, 'and we know your brother-in-law, Georgie Quinn, is writing numbers and don't have the okay for the size books he's taking on.'

'Georgie talked to Pop about that, too.'

'And Pop told him he could write a little, but now he's backing the play himself. He's ambitious, your brother-in-law.'

'What is all this, Bindy? What are we talking about? You know the color of my shorts. What's it for?' Billy felt comfortable only with Bindy, but Bindy said nothing.

'Do you know the Berman family, Mr Phelan?' Max Rosen asked.

'I know Morrie's old man's in politics, that's all.'

'Do you like Morrie Berman?' Rosen asked.

'I like him like I like a lot of guys. I got nothing against him. He's the guy had the idea to buy me a steak tonight. Nice.'

'Do you like Charlie?' Patsy asked.

'Do I like him? Sure I like him. I grew up with him. Charlie was always a good friend of mine, and I don't say that just here. I bullshit nobody on this.'

Bindy poured more beer into Billy's glass and smiled at him.

'All right, Billy,' Bindy said, 'we figure we know your feelings. We wouldn't have okayed you for that Saratoga job if we didn't trust you. We know you a long time. And you remember after the Paul Whiteman thing, we gave you that other job, too.'

'The Chicago Club?'

'That's right.'

'I thought that came from Lemon Lewis. I didn't think you even knew about that.'

'We knew. We do Albany people.'

'Then it's two I owe you.'

'Just one,' Bindy said. 'We trusted you then, we trust you now. But that don't mean forever.'

'Who the hell am I not to trust? What do I know?'

'We don't know what you know,' Patsy said.

'It's what you might come to know in the next few days that's important,' Max Rosen said. 'We're interested in Mr Berman, in everything he says and does. Everything.'

'Morrie doesn't tell me secrets,' Billy said.

'We don't expect that,' said Max. 'If he's involved in the kidnapping, and we're by no means saying that he is, then he's hardly likely to talk about it at all. But you must know, Mr Phelan, that men sometimes betray themselves indirectly. They reveal what's on their mind merely by random comment. Berman might, for instance, mention the men involved in a context other than criminal. Do you follow me?'

'No.'

'You're not stupid,' Patsy said, an edge to his voice. He leaned forward in his chair and looked through Billy's head.

'Nobody ever said I was,' Billy said, looking back through Patsy's head.

'Billy,' said Bindy in a soothing tone, 'we're playing in every joint where we can get a bet down. I tell you one thing. Some people wouldn't even put it past Berman's old man to be in on this.'

'That's ridiculous,' Max Rosen said. 'Jake Berman isn't capable of such behavior. I've known him all my life.'

'I don't accuse him,' Bindy said, 'but he don't like us. I just make the point that we suspect everybody.'

'People might even suspect you, with your name in the paper,' Patsy said.

Billy snorted. 'Me?'

'People talk.'

'Don't pay attention if you hear that,' Bindy said. 'We know you're clean. We wanted you and Berman in the same boat. He don't know why you're on the list, but now you and him got that in common.'

'You think that'll make him talk to me?'

'It could. What'd he say tonight?'

'We played cards and he kicked the holdup guy a little. He said he talked to Mr Rosen here, and he said he didn't get along with his old man. We talked about a drink that we had one time.'

'Who did he talk about?' Bindy asked. 'Who?'

'Tabby Bender. George Kindlon, who tended bar for Tabby.'

'Who else?'

'That's all I remember.'

'Edward Curry is on the list. Did he mention him?'

'I mentioned Curry, that his name was spelled wrong. And I told a story about him.'

'What story?'

'About the whore in Boston called him honey and he asked her, How come you know my name. You think Curry's mixed up in this?'

'What did Berman say when you told the story?' Bindy asked.

'He laughed.'

'You didn't talk about nobody else? Nobody? Think.'

'I talked about a lot of things but not to Berman.'

'Did he say anything about Hubert Maloy?'

'No.'

Bindy leaned back in his chair and looked at Patsy. Billy looked at the brothers, from one to the other, and wondered how he would get out of the Maloy lie. He wondered why he'd even bothered to lie. It meant nothing. He saw the faces of strangers he'd known all his life staring him down. In between them, the face of the McCall ancestor was no longer scowling down from the wall but was only stern and knowing, a face flowing with power and knowledge in every line. There was a world of behavior in this room Billy did not grasp with the clarity he had in pool and poker, or at the crap table. Billy knew jazz and betting and booking horses and baseball. He knew how to stay at arm's length from the family and how to make out. He resisted knowing more than these things. If you knew what the McCalls knew, you'd be a politician. If you knew what George Quinn knew, you'd be a family man. They had their rewards but Billy did not covet them. Tie you up in knots, pin you down, put you in the box. He could learn anything, study it. He could have been in politics years ago. Who couldn't on Colonie Street? But he chose other ways of staying alive. There never was a politician Billy could really talk to, and never a hustler he couldn't.

'All right, Billy,' Bindy said, standing up. 'I think we've made our point. Call us any time.' He wrote two phone numbers on the pad and handed the sheet to Billy.

'You come up with anything that means something to Charlie,' Patsy said, 'you got one hell of a future in this town.'

'What if I don't run into Berman again?'

'You don't run into him, then you find him and stay with him,' Patsy said. 'If you need money for that, call us.'

'Berman's a big boy. He goes where he wants.'

'You're a big boy, too,' Patsy said.

'What Patsy says about your future,' Bindy said, 'that goes triple for me. For a starter we clear up your debt with Martin Daugherty. And you never worry about anything again. Your family the same.'

'What if Berman catches on? He's too smart to pump.'

'If you're sure he's on to it, drop it.'

'We'll get word to you.'

When Billy stood up, Max Rosen put a paternal hand on his

shoulder. 'Don't worry about anything, Mr Phelan. Do what you can. It's an unusual situation.'

'Yeah, all of that,' Billy said.

Bindy shook hands and Patsy gave him a nod, and then Billy was in the hallway looking at the bannister, pretty much like the one he used to slide down in the shithouse across the street until his Aunt Sate caught him and pulled his ear and sent him home. He went out the door and closed it behind him. He stood on the McCall stoop, looking up the street at the Dolan house, remembering the Dolan kid who was kidnapped off this street when Billy was little. An uncle did it. They found the kid in the Pine Bush, safe, and brought him home and put him in the window so everybody could see that he was all right. The kid was only four. Everybody wanted to hang the uncle, but he only went to jail.

Billy walked toward Pearl Street, heading back downtown. He remembered Georgie Fox, marked lousy for what he did to Daddy Big. All anybody on Broadway needed to hear was that Billy was finking on Morrie, and they'd put him in the same box with Georgie. Who'd trust him after that? Who'd tell him a secret? Who'd lend him a quarter? He wouldn't have a friend on the whole fucking street. It'd be the dead end of Billy's world, all he ever lived for, and the McCalls were asking him to risk that. Asking hell, telling him. Call us any time.

When he was halfway to Clinton Avenue, Bo Linder pulled up and asked if everything was all right. Billy said it was, and Bo said, 'That's good, Billy, now keep your nose clean.' And Billy just looked at the son of a bitch and finally nodded, not at all sure he knew how to do that any more.

When Billy got to Becker's and sat down in the booth beside him (across from Bart Muller), George Quinn was eating a ham sandwich and telling Muller of the old days when he ran dances in Baumann's Dancing Academy and hired King Jazz and his orchestra to play, and McEnelly's Singing Orchestra, and ran dances, too, up in Sacandaga Park and brought in Zita's orchestra, and danced himself at all of them, of course. 'They put pins in our heels for the prize waltz,' George said. 'Anybody bent the pin was out. I won many a prize up on my toes and I got the loving cups to prove it.'

'No need to prove it,' Muller said.

'We danced on the boat to Kingston sometimes, and the night boat to New York, but mostly we took the ferry from Maider Lane for a nickel and it went up to Al-Tro Park, Al-Tro Park on the Hudson; they even wrote a song about that place, and what a wonder of a place it was. Were you ever up there?'

'Many times,' Muller said.

'We'd take the boat back down to Maiden Lane, or sometimes we'd walk back downtown to save the nickel. One night, three fellows on the other side of the street kept up with me and Giddy O'Laughlin all the way to Clinton Avenue. We didn't know who they were till they crossed Broadway, and one was Legs Diamond. Somebody was gonna throw Legs off the roof of the Hendrick Hudson Hotel that night, but he gave 'em the slip.'

'Why are you talking about Legs Diamond?' Billy asked George.

'I'm not talking about Legs Diamond, I'm talking about going to dances. Bart lives in Rensselaer. We both went to dances at the pavilion out at Snyder's Lake.'

'George,' said Billy, 'did you come in here to reminisce or what?'

'We've just been cuttin' it up, me and Bart,' George said, 'and the business is on, anyway. I'm interested in Bart's book. I'm branching out and Bart knows that. He just took over the night-shift book over at Huyck's mill, and now he's looking for somebody to lay off with. Am I right, Bart?'

'That's right, George.'

'Then you made the deal,' Billy said.

'I guess we did,' said George.

'I'll give you a buzz on it,' Muller said. 'But I got to get home or the wife worries.'

'We'll talk on the phone, Bart,' George said. 'I was glad to meet you.'

'Mutual,' said Muller, and he nodded at Billy and left.

George sat back and finished his tea and wiped his lips with his white linen napkin and folded it carefully.

'I don't know what the hell that was all about,' Billy said. 'Why'd you want me here?'

'Just to break the ice.'

'Break the ice? There was no ice. You never shut up.'

'I didn't want to push too hard the first time. We'll iron out the details when he calls.'

'Calls? He's not gonna call. You made no impression on him. You didn't talk about money.'

'He didn't bring it up.'

'He came to see you, didn't he? Why the hell does he want to talk about Snyder's Lake, for chrissake? He's writing a book and he wants a layoff and he wants protection. You didn't give him a goddamn thing to make him think you even know what the hell a number is.'

'He knows.'

'He does like hell. How could he? You didn't talk about having the okay or that you got cash to guarantee his payoffs. You didn't say how late he could call in a play or tell him he wouldn't have to worry getting stuck with a number because you'll give him the last call and get rid of it for him. You didn't tell him doodley bejesus. George, what the hell are you doing in the rackets? You ought to be selling golf clubs.'

'Who died and left you so smart?'

'I'm not smart, George, or I'd be rich. But I hustle. You don't know how to hustle.'

'I'm not in debt up to my ass.'

'You ain't rich either. And let me tell you something else. You don't even have the okay.'

'Says who?'

'Says Patsy McCall. I was talking to him, and he says you never got the okay to back numbers. All you got the okay for was to lay off. Twenty per cent, no more.'

'Pop O'Rourke knows what I'm doing.'

'Patsy said Pop *didn't* know.'

'I'll call Pop in the morning. I'll straighten it out. How come you talked to Patsy?'

'It was about another thing.'

'Something about your name in the paper?'

'Something about that, yeah.'

'Oh, it's a secret. You got secrets with Patsy McCall. Excuse me, let me out. Your company is too rich for my blood.'

'Look, George, don't strain your juice. I don't keep secrets I don't have to keep. You know what's going on with Charlie McCall, and you ought to know by this time I'm on your side. For chrissake, don't you know that?'

'Mmmmmm,' said George.

'You don't *want* to know what I know, George. Believe me.'

'All right, Billy, but you got a nasty tongue.'

'Yeah. Have a drink. I buy.'

'No, I just had tea.'

'Have a drink, for chrissake. Do you good.'

'I don't want a drink. I'll take the nickel. What did Patsy say about me? Was he mad?'

'He didn't sound happy. He mentioned you by name.'

'I don't want to get in any jackpots with Patsy. I'll call Pop first thing in the morning. I never had a cross word with the McCalls all my life. I give fifteen dollars to John Kelleher for Patsy's first campaign as assessor and Kelleher only asked me for five.'

'You'll fix it. Probably you just got to pay more dues.'

'I'm not making anything yet. I'm losing money.'

'It's goin' around, that problem.'

'But I can't afford more.'

'You can't afford to stay in business?'

'Pop understands I'm not in the chips yet.'

'How does he understand that? You expect him to check your books?'

'No, I don't expect nothing like that.'

'Then how the hell does he know your action? All he knows is you're moving into heavier stuff. And you got to pay heavier dues for that. George, you been in this racket fifteen years, and you been in this town all your life. You know how it works.'

'I'll pay if Patsy said I got to pay. But Patsy understands a guy being down on his luck.'

'Don't cry the blues to them. Don't beg for anything. If they say pay, just pay and shut up about it.'

'I don't beg from anybody.'

'Tell 'em your story straight and don't weep no tears. I'm telling you be tough, George.'

'I know what I'm doing. I know how it works.'

'All right. You want that drink?'

'I'll take a rain check.'

George went out onto Broadway, and Billy went to the bar for a tall beer, thinking how George couldn't get off the dime. A banty rooster and don't underrate him when he fights. But he don't fight easy enough. Been around tough guys and politicians all his life and he don't know how to blow his nose right. But Billy has to admit George ain't doing bad for a fifty-year-old geezer. Got the house and Peg and a great kid in Danny. Billy's fifty, he'll be what? Alone? Racking balls like Daddy Big? On the chalk like Lemon Lewis? Nineteen years to find out.

'Your lady friend Angie called again, Billy,' Red Tom said, as he slid Billy a new, tall, free one. 'She says it's urgent.'

'I know her urgent.'

'And she says it's not what you think. Important, she says.'

'Important.'

'She sounded like she meant it.'

'I'll check her out, Tommy. Have one on me.'

'Save your money, Billy. Winter's coming.'

'Billy knows where the heat is.'

'Up in Angie's room?'

'Some there, yeah. Definitely some up there.'

10

I'll screw you as long as my equipment lasts, Billy once told Angie, but I won't marry you. She repeated the line for Billy after he rolled off her. He sat up, lit a cigarette, and then fixed a scotch with tap water. He put on his white boxer shorts, hiding the ragged scar on the left cheek of his behind. He got that when he was ten, sliding into a second base made from a flattened tin oil can. Almost made him half-assed. But Doc Lennon sewed it up after he poured two bottles of iodine into the slice, which still gives Billy the screaming meemies when he thinks about it. Then Billy's mother bathed the wound and fussed at it for weeks, and the teamwork let Billy grow up with a complete tail.

'Why you bringing that up now?' Billy asked. 'You thinking about marriage again?'

'I'm always thinking about marriage, with you.'

'Drop it, Ange. I'll never be any good in that husband racket.'

'And you couldn't, wouldn't marry a divorcee.'

'The hell with that stuff.'

'I'm only teasing, Billy. I love to tease you.'

Angie stood up and slipped back into her nightgown, sheer white silk with white lace trim where her cleavage would've been if she had any. She was a long, lean, dark-haired Latinesque girl of twenty-five who looked thirty when she talked because she was smart but who grew wispy with a turn of emotion and fled into the look of adolescence. She read sad poetry and went to sad movies in order to cry, for crying at trouble, she told Billy, was almost as good as weeping with love. There was so little love in the world, she said, that people needed substitutes. It's why lonely old people keep pets, she said. Billy was Angie's pet. I can't imagine anyone who didn't sometime want to do away with themselves because of love, she once said to Billy, for chrissake. Billy, she said, stroking him, tickling the back of his neck, if you ever died I'd make sure they put flowers on your grave forever, just like they do for Valentino. This, of course, is just what Billy needs.

But Angie was part of his life now, and had been since her husband slapped her around in the Clubhouse at Saratoga. Billy was watching from the bar when they started their screaming over the car keys. Give 'em to me, you bitch, he said. I haven't got 'em, Angie said. You got 'em, he said. You just wanna hang around here makin' moon eyes at all the studs. Billy was her only stud then, and when her husband was around, she never even gave Billy a nod. So she walked away from the son of a bitch when he said that, and he spun her around by the arm and slapped her twice. Billy wanted to hit him till his teeth fell out, but all he could do was watch. Angie took the whipping and didn't say a word, which beat the bastard. He slammed out of the Clubhouse and left their car in the lot and walked back to the hotel. And found the car keys in his own coat pocket when he was halfway there. Billy bought Angie a drink and smooched her on the cheek where she'd been hit and put her in a taxi and bet twenty on a horse named Smacker in the last race and it showed eight dollars.

Angie came to Albany every other month after that, for a weekend at least and sometimes a week. She'd call Billy and he'd see her and once in a while she'd give him money, which made him feel like a gigolo, but of course that wasn't what Billy was. He only took it when he needed it. Angie called Billy her little wheel of excitement. When I was a kid I used to sit on the stoop and wait for it to roll down the street to me, she said. But it never showed up till I met you.

Why'd ya marry that bum? Billy asked her once, and she said, Because he was like my father and I loved my father, but you're right, he is a bum, he's not like my father at all. He's a bum, he's a bum, and he's got his women, too. He came home one night with the smell of oral sex on his face. Angie never called him on it. She just packed a bag and came to Albany. But he was good in bed, Angie said, he was very good. Angie never told Billy he was very good in bed, but then he didn't hear any complaints out of her either. What got Billy about Angie was the way she was alone so much. Billy was almost never alone. I can stand being alone, Angie told him. Being with him is like being alone. It won't kill you.

Billy looked down on the lights of Pearl Street. No traffic.

'You got aspirin?' he asked Angie. 'I got a headache.'

'The closet shelf on the left, a small bag,' she said. 'Why have you got a headache? You never get headaches.'

'Whataya mean I never get headaches? Everybody gets headaches. How the hell do you know I never get headaches?'

'All right, you get headaches,' Angie said, and she fell back into bed and crossed her feet.

In the closet, Billy looked at her picture hat, black with two white flowers. Billy snatched the hat off the shelf and waved it at her. 'When you got a face like you got, you don't need any flowers on your hat.' He put the hat back on the shelf and felt for the aspirin and found them. Then he saw her black linen suit with the plaid scarf, and the gray wool suit with the darker gray silk lapels. Goddamn Angie knew how to dress. Like a model. Too goddamn smart. A college dame. Thinks like a man.

'You're too goddamn smart,' he said, as he went to the sink.

'What does that mean?'

'The hell with it.'

'Billy, come here. Come and sit down.'

'Gimme a rest.'

'Not that. Just come and sit.'

Billy washed his aspirin down and went and sat. She stroked his face and then dropped her hand and eyes and said, 'I've got something sad to tell you.'

'Your cat got run over.'

'Something like that. I had an abortion.'

'Yeah?'

'It was ours.'

Billy smoked a little and then looked at her. Her eyes were on him now.

'When?'

'About three weeks ago.'

'Why didn't you ring me in on it?'

'What would you have done?'

'I don't know. Helped you.'

'Helped get it done? A good Catholic boy like you?'

'I mean with your head. It must've been lousy for you.'

'You never want to know things like that. Anything that involves you. You really didn't want to know, did you?'

'Half of it's my kid.'

'Not a kid, a fetus. And it's gone. Nobody's now.'

'Goddamn it, I had a right to know.'

'You had a *right*?'

'You bet your ass. What the hell, I don't have a say in my own son?'

'Of course it was a boy. You're really classic, Billy.'

'Whatever the hell it was.'

Billy looked at his hand and saw the cigarette shaking. Goddamn ton of goddamn bricks. He'd wanted to talk about the Berman business and about his father being back in town. Angie had good sense. He wanted to ask her about money, maybe borrow some, but they got into the sack too fast. You can't ask for money after you've been in the sack with a woman. Now, with this business, he couldn't ask her anything. How do so many things happen all of a sudden? He thought of making nineteen straight passes at Slicky Joyce's in Mechanicville. Almost broke the Greek bankrolling the game. How do nineteen straight passes happen? He stubbed out his cigarette and walked across the room to put on his pants.

'Why are you putting on your pants?'

'I got chilly.'

'No. You're ashamed of the part of you that made me pregnant and now you want to cover yourself and hide.'

'You know everything about me. My headaches, why I put on

my pants. Goddamn it cut it *out*!' Billy screamed. 'You don't know the first goddamn thing that's going on with me. You think I'm a goddamn moron like your goddamn dummy husband?'

'All right, Billy. Don't get violent.'

'Violent? You kill my kid without even asking me about it. Who made you the butcher?'

'Don't get like this, Billy. I'm sorry I started it this way.'

'Started?'

'I'm pregnant.'

'Oh, Christ Jesus, what is this game?'

'I wanted to see if you wanted the baby.'

'Hell no, I don't want no baby.'

'So now it's different.'

Billy put on his shirt, unable to speak. He folded his tie and put it in the pocket of his coat, which hung on a black bentwood chair. He sat on the chair and stared at Angie.

'I can take care of it,' she said. 'I already slept with Joe when I found I had it, just so I could tell him it was his. But I'd never raise it with him. All he wants to raise is money. But I would keep it and give it all the nannies and private schools a kid'd ever need. The only thing it wouldn't have is a real father.'

She stood up. 'Or I could put it up for adoption.'

'No,' Billy said.

She came across the room and stroked his face. 'Or we could raise it together, somehow. Any way you wanted. I don't mean marriage. I'll go away and have it, and you can come and see us when you want to. The only problem is that if my husband figured it out, he'd probably have all three of us killed. But I don't care, do you?'

'No. Of course not. What the hell do I care?'

Billy walked away from her and sat in the armchair and looked at her standing there barefoot in front of him, the shadow of her crotch winking through the silk nightgown.

'Or you can claim it any time you want, and we could go off then. I've got plenty of my own money. I wouldn't need alimony.'

Billy shook his head. 'I don't buy it. All this shotgun stuff can go to hell.'

'Then you want me to get rid of it?'

'No, I don't want that. I think you oughta have it.'

'But you don't want anything to do with it?'

'I'll do something.'

'What?'

'I'll go see it.'

'Like a cocker spaniel? Why shouldn't I get rid of it?'

'By myself, I don't want to hurt nobody. If you do it, it's you and I can't say don't. I don't even want to know about it.'

'That's as far as you go?'

'If you have it, I'll say it's mine.'

'You'll do that?'

'I'll do that, yeah.'

'Even if Joe says he'll shoot you?'

'He shoots me, he's got big trouble.'

'I didn't expect this.'

'I'd do it for any kid. You let him into the action, he's got to know who his old man is.'

'It's for the kid, not me?'

'Maybe some is for you.'

'Birth certificate, baptism, that whole business?'

'Whatever you want.'

'I really didn't think you'd do this. You never committed yourself to me on anything. You never even answered my letters.'

'Letters? What the hell am I gonna do, write you letters and have you fix up my spelling?'

'I wouldn't do that. Oh God, I love you. You're such a life-bringer, Billy. You're the real man for me, but you're the wrong clay.'

'Clay?'

'You can't be molded. Sex won't do it and money won't. Even the idea of a kid wouldn't. But you did say you'd go along with me. That's really something.'

'What do you mean the *idea* of a kid?'

'There's no kid.'

She was rocking from foot to foot, half-twisting her body, playing with the ends of her hair.

'You did get rid of it.'

'I was never pregnant.' She smiled at Billy.

'Then what, what the hell, what?'

'I needed to know what you felt, Billy. You really think I'm dumb enough to let you knock me up? It's just that we never talk about things that really matter. This was the first time we ever talked about anything important that wasn't money or my goddamn husband. I know almost nothing about your life. All I know is I love you more now than I did when you walked in the door. I knew I wanted you even before I met you.'

Billy was shaking his head. 'Imagine that,' he said. 'You conned me right out of my jock.'

'Yes, I know.'

'What a sucker.'

'Yes, it was lovely. You were wonderful. Now will you take me out for a sandwich? I missed dinner waiting for you.'

'Sure. But first get busy with the douche bag. And I'm gonna watch. I'm not going through this noise again.'

'Ah, Romeo,' Angie said, massaging Billy's crotch.

11

Martin, thinking of his father, of Charlie Boy, of Noah, all spread-eagled on their beds, of Melissa spread-eagled naked in fatigue on the floor of her suite at the Hampton Hotel, failed to sleep. He faced downward and leftward into the pillow, a trick he played on the fluids of his brain that generally brought sleep, but not now. And so he faced upward, rightward. He closed his eyes, fixating on a point just above his nose, behind the frontal bone, trying to drive out thoughts as they appeared.

But this also failed, and he saw the lonely, driven figure entering the wholly darkened tunnel, so narrow no man could survive the train should it come roaring through before he reached the far exit. He would be crushed by the wheels or squeezed to juice and pulp against the wall. The figure reached the trestle that spanned the bottomless canyon and began to inch across it on hands and knees, fearful of falling, fearful the train would come from beyond the forest curve and bear down on him at mid-trestle. No chance then for backward flight, no chance to sidestep, only to hang from trestle's edge by fingertips. Would vertigo then claim him? Would his fingers hold him?

He sat up and lit the bedside lamp and began to count the ceiling panels again, eleven horizontal, twelve vertical. He multiplied. One hundred and thirty-two panels, including fragments. He counted the sides of the dresser, the number of edges on the six drawers: twenty-four. He counted the edges on the decorative trim on Mary Daugherty's closet. He totaled the edge count: two-seventy-eight.

He counted the edges on the ceiling molding. He counted the backs, fronts, and sides of books on his dresser. He lost track of the total.

He could never contain the numbers, nor did he want to. He usually counted sidewalk cracks when he walked, telephone poles when he drove. He remembered no totals except the eighteen steps to the city room, twelve to the upstairs of this house, and remembered these only after years of repetition. If he miscounted either staircase, he would recount carefully on the return trip. He once viewed the counting as a private way of demarcating his place in the world, numbering all boundaries, four counts to the edge of a drawer, four to the perimeter of a tile, an act of personal coherence. On the day he awoke and drawer edges were worth three, tile perimeters five, he would know the rules of his civilization had been superseded.

He switched off the lamp, closed his eyes, and found a staircase. He climbed it and at the turning saw the hag squirming on the wide step, caught in an enormous cobweb which covered all of her except her legs. Beneath her thighs, two dozen white baby shoes were in constant motion, being hatched.

I don't like what everybody is doing to me, she said.

The hag reached a hand out to Martin, who fled up the stairs in terror, a wisp of cobweb caught on his sleeve.

He plucked himself from the scene without moving and felt panic in his heartbeat. He said the Our Father, the Hail Mary, the Confiteor. Deliver us from evil. Blessed is the fruit of thy womb. *Mea maxima culpa.* He had not prayed in twenty-five years except for knee-jerk recitations at funerals, and did not now believe in these or any other prayers. Yet as he prayed, his pulse slowly slackened, his eyes stayed closed. And as he moved into sleep, he knew that despite his infidel ways, the remnants of tattered faith still had power over his mind.

He knew his mind had no interest in the genuineness of faith, that it fed on the imagery of any conflict that touched the deepest layers of his history. Years ago, he'd dreamed repeatedly of hexagons, rhomboids, and threes, and still had no idea why. He understood almost none of the fragmented pictures his mind created, but he knew now for the first time that it was possible to trick the apparatus. He had done it. He was moving into a peaceful sleep, his first since the departure of Peter. And as he did, he understood the message the images had sent him. He would go to Harmanus Bleecker Hall and watch Melissa impersonate his mother on stage. Then, all in good time, he would find a way to make love to Melissa again, in the way a one-legged man carves a crutch from the fallen tree that crushed his leg.

The fountain cherub, small boy in full pee, greeted Martin as he walked through the Hall's foyer. Psssss. *The Golden Bowlful*, by Henry Pease Lotz. Martin remembered seeing Bert Lytell here, the Barrymores and Mrs Fiske strutting on this cultural altar. He saw the young Jolson here, and the great Isadora, and when he was only thirteen he saw a play called *The Ten-Ton Door*, in which a man strapped to that huge door was exploded across the stage by a great blast, an epic moment.

'So you made it,' said Agnes, the hennaed gum chewer in the Hall's box office. 'We expected you last night.'

'I was up in Troy last night,' Martin said, 'walking the duck.'

'The duck?'

Martin smiled and looked at his ticket, B-108 center, and then he entered the Hall, a quarter century after the premiere that never was. Edward Sheldon's *Romance* premiered here in 1913 instead of *The Flaming Corsage*, and Sheldon's reputation blossomed. But when the priests and Grundys killed Edward Daugherty's play, calling it the work of a scandalous, vice-ridden man, they made Edward a pariah in the theater for years to come.

In 1928, a bad year for some, Melissa set out to convert the play to a talking picture in which she would star as the mistress, her long-standing dream. She wanted Von Stroheim to direct, appreciative of his sexual candor, but the studios found both the play and the scandal dated, and dated, too, Melissa, the idea of you as a young mistress.

Aging but undauntable, Melissa turned up then with something not so old: Edward Daugherty's journal from the years just before and just after the scandal, full of the drama and eroticism of the famous event, in case, chums, you can't find enough in the play. Still, no studio was interested, for Melissa was a fading emblem of a waning era, her voice adjudged too quirky for talkies, her imperious and litigious ways (when in doubt she sued) too much of a liability for the moguls.

And so *The Flaming Corsage* continued unproduced either as play or film until the Daugherty renaissance, which began with an obscure New York mounting of his 1902 work, *The Car Barns*. George Jean Nathan saw that production and wrote that here was a writer many cuts above Gillette, Belasco, Fitch, and others, more significantly Irish-American than Boucicault or Sheldon, for he is tapping deeper currents, and superior to any of the raffish Marxist didacticists currently cluttering up the boards. Was this neglected writer an American O'Casey or Pirandello? Another O'Neill? No, said Nathan, he's merely original, which serious men should find sufficient.

The Car Barns revival was followed by *The Masks of Pyramis*, Edward Daugherty's one venture into symbolism. It provoked a great public yawn and slowed the renaissance. *The Baron of Ten Broeck Street* followed within a year, a play with the capitalist as villain and tragic figure, the protagonist patterned after Katrina Daugherty's father, an Albany lumber baron. Reaction to the play was positive, but the renaissance might have halted there had not Melissa's need to see herself transfigured on stage been so unyielding.

Six more years would pass before *The Flaming Corsage* entered its new age. By then, three decades after its inspiration, it had become a wholly new play, its old sin now the stuff of myth, its antique realism now an exquisite parody of bitter love and foolish death. The New York production was a spectacular success. Melissa made her comeback, and Edward Daugherty strode into the dimension he had sought for a lifetime as an artist. But he strode with a partial mind. He beamed at the telling when Martin brought the news, but minutes later he had forgotten that he had ever written that play, or any other. What would please him most, he said, squirming in his leather armchair in the old house on Main Street, would be a hot cup of tea, son, with lemon if you'd be so kind, and a sugar cookie.

The theater was already two-thirds full and more were still arriving to see the famed beauty in the infamous play about Albany. Martin positioned himself at the head of an aisle, holding his battered hat in hand, standing out of the way as the playgoers seated themselves. Joe Morrissey nodded to him, ex-assemblyman, tight as a teacup, who lived near Sacred Heart; when the pastor asked him to donate his house to the nuns, old Joe sold the place immediately and moved out of the parish. And there, moving down front, Tip Mooney, the roofer, with the adopted daughter everybody chucklingly says is his mistress. Taboo. Ooo-ooo. The zest for it. And here, as the houselights dim, stands the fellow out for redemption. I'm just as big a sinner as you, Dad. Playboy of the North End, but keeping it in the family. Here to see everybody's favorite honeycomb, who, as Marlene, the reporter, wrote, is out to prove she can plumb the depths of the human heart with her acting, even as she keeps the human spirit all aglow with her dancing, and the human imagination fevered merely by her well-known sensual presence, etc.

The lights went all the way down, the curtain rose and the Daugherty living room on Colonie Street was magically reconstituted from thirty years past, even to the Edison phonograph and its cylinders, the Tiffany butterfly lamp from Van Heusen Charles, the Hudson River landscape on the far wall, and all the other meticulously copied details demanded by the author; for those possessions were inseparable from the woman who sits there among them: the simulated Katrina, remarkably reincarnated by Melissa in a blondish gray wig, unswept into a perfect Katrina crown, her glasses on, her lavender shawl over her legs as she sits in the black rocker, book open in her lap, hands crossed upon it.

'Where will you go?' she asks the young man standing by the bay window.

And the young man, in whom Martin does not recognize

anything of his disordered self of 1908, replies, 'Someplace where they don't snigger when my name is mentioned.'

'Will you go to Paris?'

'Perhaps. I don't know.'

'It must be dreary there without Baudelaire and Rimbaud.'

'They have that tower now.'

'Your father will want to know where you are.'

'Perhaps I'll go to Versailles and see where the king kept Marie Antoinette.'

'Yes, do that. Send your father a postcard.'

And Melissa put her book aside and stood up, sweeping her hand up behind her neck, tapping the wig, smoothing the rattled mind. The gesture was not Katrina's but Melissa's, which generated confusion in Martin. He felt impatient with the play, half fearful of seeing the development a few scenes hence when his father would enter with the awful dialogue of duplicity and defeat, to be met by the witty near-madness of Katrina.

Now the dialogue of mother and son moved the play on toward that moment, but Martin closed out all the talk and watched the silent movement of Melissa, not at all like Katrina, and remembered her in her voluptuary state, drenched in sweat, oozing his semen. The Olmecs built a monument of a sacred jaguar mating with a lustful woman. A male offspring of such a mating would have been half-jaguar, half-boy, a divine creature. The boy-animal of Martin's morning vision, perhaps? Is your mind telling you, Martin, that you're the divine progeny of a sacred mating? But which one? Your father's with your mother? Your father's with Melissa? Your own with Melissa?

The corruption he felt after his time with Melissa came back now with full power: the simoniac being paid off with venereal gifts. He stayed with her three days, she securing her purchase with a lust that soared beyond his own. That body, now walking across the stage, he saw walking the length of the sitting room in The Hampton to stand naked by the window and peer through the curtains at the movement on Broadway and State Street below. He stood beside her and with a compulsion grown weary, slid his hand between her thighs as a gesture. They looked down together, connected to the traffic of other men and women in transit toward and away from their lust. He would stay in the room with her another day, until she said, Now I want a woman. And then Martin went away.

Through the years since then he insisted he would never touch her sexually again. But perceiving now that a second infusion of pain distracts the brain and reduces the pain of the first and more grievous wound, he would, yes, make love to Melissa as soon as possible. He might ask her to wear the blond wig. That would appeal to her twist. He might even call her Katrina. She could call him Edward.

They would pretend it was 1887 and that this was a true wedding of sacred figures. He would tell her of the Olmecs, and of the divine progeny. He would tell her his dream of the divine animal at bedside and suggest that it was perhaps himself in a new stage of being. As they made their fierce and fraudulent love, they would become jaguar and lustful partner entwined. Both would know that a new Martin Daugherty would be the offspring of this divine mating.

The quest to love yourself is a moral quest.

How simple this psychic game is, once you know the rules.

12

All of a sudden Doc Fay was playing like a champ in Daddy Big's round robin. Billy had been ahead sixteen points and then old Doc ran twenty-six and left Billy nothing on the table. The Doc blew his streak on the last ball of a rack. Didn't leave himself in a position where he could sink it and also make the cue ball break the new rack. And so he called safe and sank the ball, and it was respotted at the peak of the new rack, the full rack now facing Billy.

The Doc also left the cue ball way up the table, snug against the back cushion. Toughest possible shot for Billy. Or anybody. Billy, natch, had to call another safe shot – make contact with a ball, and make sure one ball, any ball, also touched a cushion. If he failed to do this, it would be his third scratch in a row, and he'd lose fifteen points, plus a point for the lastest scratch. Billy did have the out of breaking the rack instead of playing safe, as a way of beating the third scratch. But when he looked at the full rack he couldn't bring himself to break it. It would seem cowardly. What's more, it'd set Doc up for another fat run, and they'd all know Billy Phelan would never do a thing like that.

He bent over the table and remembered bringing Danny into this pool room one afternoon. The kid stood up straight to shoot. Get your head down, put your eye at the level of the ball, Billy told him. How the hell can you see what you're hitting when you ain't even looking at it? Get that head down and stroke that cue, firm up your bridge, don't let them fingers wobble. The kid leaned over and sank a few. Great kid. Stay out of pool rooms, kid, or all you'll ever have is fun.

Billy tapped the cue ball gently. He was thrilled at how lightly he hit it. Just right. The ball moved slowly toward the rear right corner of the pack. It touched the pack and separated two balls. No ball touched a cushion.

Scratch.

Scratch number three, in a row.

Billy loses fifteen, plus one for this scratch.

Billy is down twenty-seven points and the Doc is hot. Billy doubts he could catch the Doc now even if he wanted to.

Billy hits the table with his fist, hits the floor with the heel of his cue and curses that last goddamn safe shot, thrilled.

Billy is acting. He has just begun to throw his first match.

The lights in the pool room went out just as the Doc lined up for the next shot. I'll get candles, said Daddy Big. Don't nobody touch them balls. Which balls are they, Daddy? Footers asked in a falsetto. Billy remembered Footers just before the lights went out, licking a green lollipop, and Harvey Hess, his thumbs stuck in his vest, nodding his approval at the Doctor burying Billy. Daddy Big liked that development too, the string of his change apron tight on his gut, like a tick tied in the middle. Behind Billy stood Morrie Berman, who was again backing Billy. Morrie had given Billy fifty to bet on himself with the Doc, and also took all side bets on his boy. Billy heard Morrie softly muttering unhhh, eeeng, every time the Doc sank one.

Maybe a hundred men were standing and sitting around the table when the lights went. Billy saw Martin come in late and stand at the back of the crowd, behind the chairs Daddy Big had set up. Daddy Big lit four candles. They flickered on the cigar counter, on the edge of a pool table covered with a tarpaulin, on a shelf near the toilet. Many of the men were smoking in the half-darkness, their cigars and cigarettes glowing and fading, their faces moving in and out of shadows. Here was the obscure collective power. What'll they do if I fink? Will I see my father? Some of the shadowy men left the room when the lights went out. Most of those with chairs stayed put, but then some of them, too, went down to the street, needing, in the absence of light, at least an open sky.

'Tough shot you had,' Morrie said to Billy.

'The toughest.'

'You'll pick up. You got what it takes.'

'That Doctor's hot as ten-cent pussy.'

'You'll take him.'

'Sure,' said Billy.

But he won't, or else how can he do what he's got to do, if he's got to do it? Wrong-Way Corrigan starts out for California and winds up in Ireland. I guess I got lost, he says, and people say, Yeah, oh yeah, he got lost. Ain't he some sweet son of a bitch?

13

Through the front window of Louie's, Martin saw that the lights were out on Broadway and in the station. He saluted Billy across the candlelight and went down to the street, which was dark in all directions. He walked to the corner of Columbia Street and looked up. Pearl Street was also dark, candles already dancing in two windows up the block. He walked back and into Becker's and headed for the phone, past customers drinking by the light of the old kerosene lamp that had sat on the back bar for years, unused. Now it illuminated Red Tom's mustache. The test of a real mustache is whether it can be seen from behind. Red Tom's therefore is not real.

The city desk told him that lights were out all over the city and parts of Colonie, Watervliet and Cohoes. All hospitals had been called an hour earlier and told a power failure was possible, and not to schedule any operations unless they had their own generators. Nursing homes were also alerted. But the power company said it hadn't made the calls. Who had? Nobody knew.

Martin went back to the bar and ordered a Grandad on ice and looked at the photo behind the bar. A new star shone on the chest of Scotty Streck, brighter than all others. In the kerosene lamplight the men in the photo moved backward in time. They were all smiling and all younger than their pictures. They were boys and young men under the shirt-sleeved, summer sun. None of them was dead or would ever die.

'Lights are out all over town,' Martin told Red Tom.

'Is that a fact? I was listening to the radio when they went. Dewey was on, talking about Albany.'

'Albany? What was he saying?'

'He mentioned Patsy, and that was all I heard.'

'Did he mention Charlie Boy?'

'Not that I heard.'

Martin gulped his drink and went outside. People were clustered under the canopy at the station, all cabs were gone, and a West Albany trolley was stalled between Maiden Lane and Steuben Street. Martin could see it in the headlights of cars. The night was a deep, moonless black, with only a few stars visible. It was as if rural darkness had descended upon the city. Faces were unrecognizable three feet away. Albany had never been so dark in Martin's memory. There were gas lamps in his boyhood, then the first few electric lights, now the power poles everywhere. But tonight was the lightless time in which highwaymen had performed, the dark night of the century gone, his father's childhood darkness on new streets cut out of the raw hills and the grassy flats. A woman with a bundle came by, half running toward Clinton Avenue, pursued by the night. Alongside Martin, a match flared and he turned to see Morrie Berman lighting a cigar.

'What news do you hear?'

'Only that they're out all over town.'

'I mean about the McCall kid. You fellows at the paper turn up any news?'

'I heard there was another ransom note.'

'Is that so?'

'Signed by Charlie Boy. I didn't see it, but from what I gather there'll be another go-between list in the paper tonight.'

'They didn't like us on the first list?'

'So it seems.'

'You hear anything else?'

Dark shapes moved in behind Morrie, and Martin withheld his answer. The shapes hovered.

'Let's take a walk,' Martin said and he took a step toward Steuben Street. Morrie stepped along and they moved south on Broadway, candles in the Waldorf, a bunch of men on the street in front of the Monte Carlo. They stepped around the men in the light of a passing auto. Martin did not want to speak until they had turned the corner onto Steuben. They passed Hagaman's Bakery and Joe's Bookshop on Steuben Street, where Martin knew his father's early novel, *The Mosquito Lovers*, and the volume of his collected plays were sitting in faded dust jackets in the window, and had been for months, ever since the success of *The Flaming Corsage*.

'So what's the secret?' Morrie asked.

'No secret, but I don't want to broadcast it. I know you're a friend of Maloy and the news is they're looking for him. And Curry.'

'Why tell me? They got a lot of friends.'

'You asked for news. They've both been out of town a week.'

'So that ties them in?'

'No, but even their families don't know where they are.'

'Hell, I saw Maloy two or three days ago on Broadway. They're apt to be anywhere. Maloy's crazy and Curry's a moron. But they wouldn't mix up in a thing like this, not in their own town.'

'Nevertheless, they're looking for them.'

'They'll turn up. What else do you hear?'

'The note said they'd starve Charlie Boy till the ransom was paid.'

'Tough stuff.'

'Very.'

Up toward Pearl Street, a window shattered and a burglar alarm rang and rang. Martin saw a silhouette running toward him and Morrie. The runner brushed Martin's elbow, stepping off the curb as they touched, but Martin could not see the face.

'Somebody did all right,' said Morrie. 'Ain't that a jewelry store there?'

'Right,' said Martin. 'Just about where Henry James's grandmother used to live.'

'Who?'

'An old-timer.'

And on the other corner, DeWitt Clinton lived. And across the street, Bret Harte was born. And up Columbia was one of Melville's homes, and on Clinton Square another. An old man had answered when Martin knocked on the door of the Columbia Street house and said, yeauh, he seemed to remember the name Melville but that was next door and they tore that house down and built a new one. Melville, he said. I heard he moved to Troy. Don't know what become of him after that.

Martin and Morrie neared Pearl Street, the glimmerings of light from the cars giving them a fragmented view of the broken window in Wilson's Jewelry Store. When they saw the window, they crossed Pearl. Martin looked down toward State and saw a torchlight parade coming north in support of the nomination of Millard Fillmore. The John G. Myers department store collapsed into itself, killing thirteen and making men bald from flying plaster dust. Henry James, suffused in the brilliance of a sunny summer morning, walked out of his grandmother's house, opened the front gate, and floated like a flowered balloon into ethereal regions. Martin walked in the phosphorescent footsteps of his father and his grandfather.

'Where the hell are we walking?' Morrie asked.

'Just around,' said Martin. 'You want to go back down?'

'I guess it's all right.'

They walked to Clinton Square, where two more trolleys were stalled on the bend. A siren screamed and stopped, back near Steuben and Pearl. Martin and Morrie, their eyes grown accustomed to the darkness, watched the shadowy action in front of the Palace Theater, hundreds waiting to go back inside and see the rest of *Boys' Town* with Spencer Tracy as Father Flanagan, the miracle man. There is no such thing as a bad boy.

'They got some kind of light in the Grand Lunch,' Morrie said. 'You want some coffee?'

'No, you go ahead. I want to watch the panic.'

'What panic?'

'There's got to be panic someplace with this much darkness.'

'Whatever you say. See you down below.'

In the Sudetenland only last week when Hitler arrived, at nightfall there was an epidemic of suicide.

In France in 1918, Martin had heard a man scream from the darkness beyond a farmhouse where a shell had just hit. Help me, oh God, oh heavenly God, help me, the man yelled, and then he wailed his pain. Martin nudged a corporal and they crawled toward the voice and found an American soldier pinned between two dead cows. The top cow was bloated from inhaling the explosion. Martin and the corporal could not move the bloated cow so they pulled the squeezed man by his arms, and the top half of him came away in their grip. He stopped screaming.

Martin crossed Pearl and went into the K. of C. and called the city desk by candlelight. Viglucci said there was still no explanation for the blackout, but up at Harmanus Bleecker Hall the audience had panicked when the lights went. People shoved one another and Tip Mooney was knocked down and trampled.

Punishment.

'This bum's a Cuban and so's one of the broads,' said Morrie as Billy and Martin followed him down two slate steps to the basement doorway beneath the high stoop. Morrie rapped and the pimp peered out in his puce shirt, his hair brilliantined, his shoes pointed and shiny, both ends of him gleaming in the harsh backlight. The lights of the city had come back on an hour earlier.

'Hey, Mo-ree,' the pimp said. 'Whatchou lookin' for?'

'Pussy,' said Morrie.

'You in the right place.'

The pimp, the same man Red Tom threw out of Becker's, had a face as pointy as his shoes and resembled Martin's long-snouted animal child. Why should the likes of him concretize a Daugherty abstraction? But why not? Ooze to ooze, slime to slime. Brothers under the sheets.

Two young women sat at the kitchen table drinking sarsaparilla out of jelly glasses. Knives, forks, glasses, and dishes sat in the sink. The stub of a candle stood in a pool of dry wax on a saucer. The pimp introduced the girls as Fela and Margie. Fela, obviously *La*

Cubana, was dark, with hair to her kidneys. Margie had carroty red hair, redder by blood weight than Mary Daugherty's crop. Both wore brassieres, Woolworth couture, a size too small, shorts to mid-thigh, with cuffs, and high heels.

'They got shorts on,' Morrie said. 'Last time I saw a whore in shorts was Mame Fay's.'

'I know Mame,' said the pimp. 'She's got influence up in Troy.'

'She used to recruit salesgirls in the grocery marts,' Billy said. 'She tried to hawk a friend of mine.'

'She'd give talks in the high schools if they let her,' said Morrie.

'Young stuff is what Mame likes,' Margie said.

'Yeah,' said Morrie, licking his lips.

'Talk is gettin' hot, *hombres.* Young stuff right in front of you. Who's ready?'

'Don't rush me,' said Morrie.

Billy pulled up a chair between Fela and Margie and looked them over. Martin felt a thirst rising.

'You have any beer?'

'Twenty-five cents, *hombre*.'

'I'm a sport,' said Martin, and the pimp cracked a quart of Stanwix.

'Those broads up at Mame's,' Morrie said, 'took their tops off when we come in. I'm the best, one of 'em says to us, so take me. If you're the best, says the other, how come your boyfriend screwed me? You? says the other. He'd screw a dead dog with the clap, but he wouldn't screw you. And then they went at it. Best whore fight I ever saw. Bit one another, blood all over the joint, one of their heads split open. Me and Maloy laughed our tits off.'

'We don't fight,' Margie said. 'We like one another.'

'That's nice,' said Morrie, and he put his hand inside her brassiere. 'Soft.' He laughed, found a chair, and sat down.

'Maloy,' said Billy. 'What the hell is he doing in Newark?'

'Who said he was in Newark?' Morrie asked.

'I thought you did.'

'He ain't in Newark.'

'Where is he?'

'He's someplace else.'

'How do you know he ain't in Newark. I heard he was in Newark.'

'What the hell'd he be in Newark for?'

'Why not Newark?'

'He don't know nobody in Newark.'

'This is a famous guy,' the pimp told the girls, putting his hand on Morrie's shoulder. 'His name's in the paper this morning. They say that's all about the kidnapping, right Mo-ree?'

'Billy's name's in there, too.'

'Very big men in Albany if the McCalls put your name in there,' said the pimp.

'You don't like the McCalls,' Billy said. 'They threw you out of Becker's for bad-mouthing them.'

'I never like them,' said the pimp. 'They make me a janitor at the public bath, then fire me.'

'What'd they do that for?'

'For nothing. A little thing. Look at the ladies and pull the old rope. They catch me and tell me I'm all finish. Little thing like that.'

'It ain't against the law to pull your rope,' Morrie said. 'It's against the law to get caught.'

'It sure ain't against the law here,' Margie said.

'Yeah, you boys come here to talk or screw?' Fela the *Cubana* said.

'Screw,' said Morrie, 'and you got it, lady. Let's go.' He stood up and tongued her ear and she knocked a jelly glass off the table. He took her down the hallway and into a bedroom.

'Hey, Mo-ree,' said the pimp, 'she's the best blow-job in town.' Then he told Martin and Billy: 'Margie's good too.'

'Is that right?' Billy asked Margie. 'Are you good?'

'I ain't had a complaint all week.'

Billy washed a glass in the sink with soap and water and poured himself a beer. The pimp came over to Martin.

'What do you like, Mister? Little blow from the best?'

'I'm just along for the ride. I'll stay with the drink.'

Martin washed a glass and poured a beer. He stared at the door of the broom closet, then opened the door and saw the notebook for *The Flaming Corsage* hanging from a nail on a short piece of cord. It was inscribed on the cover: *To my beloved son, who played a whore's trick on his father.* Martin closed the closet door and sipped his beer, which tasted like the juice of rotted lemons. He spat into the sink.

Martin dried his mouth and studied Margie, who removed her brassiere for him. Her nipples lay at the bottom of the curves, projecting somewhat obliquely. Martin considered the nipple fetishists of history. Plutarch, Spinoza, Schubert, Cardinal Wolsey. The doorbells of ecstasy, Curzio Malaparte called them. Billy reached across the table and lifted one of Margie's breasts. People preparing for sexual conflict. The pimp slavered and picked his nose with his thumb.

How had Martin's father prepared for sex? On spindly legs, he stood in his shorts in his bedroom, reading Blake on the dresser top. The shorts seemed unusually long. Perhaps he had short thighs. He looked sexually disinterested, but that was unquestionably deceptive. His teeth carried stains from pipe-smoking. He had a recurring ingrown toenail, clipped with a V, a protruding bone on the right elbow from an old fracture. These things were antisexual.

How would Martin's son ever know anything of his own sexuality? Gone to the priests at thirteen, blanketed with repressive prayer and sacramental censure. How could the tigers of chastity be wiser than the horses of coition?

Ten years ago, a phone call had come for Martin after he'd completed a sexual romp with his wife. The caller, a Boston lawyer, had heard that the notebook of *The Flaming Corsage* was in Martin's possession. Was that true?

Yes.

Was it for sale, or would it be preserved in the trove of Daugherty papers?

The latter, of course.

Well, you may take my name and address, and should you change your mind I want you to know that I will pay a handsome price for that notebook. Like the play made from it, it has a deep significance for my client.

What significance is that?

My client, said the lawyer, was your father's mistress.

'All right,' Morrie said, emerging from the bedroom. 'Little bit of all right.'

'That was quick,' Billy said. 'You like it?'

'Short but sweet,' Morrie said. 'How much?'

'Buck and a half,' said the pimp.

Morrie snapped a dollar off his roll and fished for the fifty cents. Margie put on her brassiere. Fela picked up the sarsaparilla bottle and looked for a glass.

'Only a buck and a half?' Billy said.

'That's all,' said the pimp.

'It must be some great stuff for a buck and a half.'

'Go try it.'

Fela tipped up the bottle and gargled with sarsaparilla. She spat it into the sink and eyed Billy. The pimp took Morrie's dollar and change. Martin opened the broom closet and found a dust pan hanging from a nail.

'How the hell can it be any good for a buck and a half?' Billy asked.

'Hey, I ought to know,' said the pimp with a rattish smile of cuspids. 'She's my sister.'

Billy hit him on the chin. The pimp sped backward and knocked over a chair, shook his head and leaped at Billy's throat. Billy shook him off, and the pimp reached for the butcher knife in the sink, but Martin reached it first and threw it out the open window into the alley. Billy hit the pimp again, a graze of the head, but the pimp found Billy's throat again and held on. Martin pulled at the pimp as the whores scrambled away from the table. Morrie pushed past Martin and bashed the pimp with the sarsaparilla bottle. The pimp slid to the floor and lay still.

The whores came out of the bedroom carrying their dresses and handbags.

'He looks dead,' Billy said.

'Who gives a goddamn?' Morrie said, and he tipped over the kitchen table, opened the dish closet and threw the dishes on the floor. Billy tipped over the garbage pail and threw a chair at the kitchen window. The whores went out the back door.

'Son of a bitch, pimping for his own sister,' said Billy.

'She wasn't bad,' said Morrie as he swept the contents of the refrigerator onto the floor. 'She's got nice teeth.'

Martin salvaged a new cold bottle of Stanwix and poured himself a glass. He opened the broom closet so Morrie could empty it. Billy went into the bedroom where Morrie had been with Fela and tore up the bed clothes, then kicked the foot-board until the bed fell apart. On the bedside table stood a metal lamp of a nautical F.D.R. at the wheel of the Ship of State, standing above the caption: 'Our Leader.' Billy threw the lamp through the bedroom window. Martin straightened up two kitchen chairs, sat on one and used the other as a table for his beer, which no longer tasted like rotten lemons. Billy came back and nudged the inert pimp with his foot.

'I think you killed him,' he said to Morrie.

'No,' said Martin. 'He moved his fingers.'

'He's all right then,' Morrie said. 'You ain't dead if you can move your fingers.'

'I knew a guy couldn't move his toes,' Billy said, winded but calming. 'His feet turned to stone. First his feet then the rest of him. Only guy I ever knew whose feet turned to stone and then the rest of him.'

Transgressors of good fame are punished for their deeds, was what occurred to Martin. He stood up and opened his fly, then urinated on the pimp's feet. Simoniacs among us.

'What'd you make of Morrie's answer about Maloy?' Billy asked.

'I thought he was evasive,' Martin said.

'I think he's lying.'

'Why would he lie?'

'You tell me,' Billy said. 'Must be he doesn't want Maloy connected to Newark.'

'Maybe he's not connected.'

'No. He was lying. I saw it in his face.'

They listened to the dismal blues Slopie Dodds was making at the piano. Martin squinted in the dim light of Martha's Place, where they'd come for a nightcap after leaving Morrie. The smoke was dense in the low-ceilinged bar, which was full of Negroes. There were four white men in the place, Martin and Billy, a stranger at the far end of the bar, and Daddy Big, a nightly Negrophile after he reached his drunken beyond. Daddy was oblivious now of everything except hustling Martha, a handsome tan woman in her forties with shoulder-length conked hair, small lips, and a gold-capped canine tooth. Martha was not about to be hustled, but Daddy Big did not accept this, steeped as he was in his professional wisdom that everybody is hustleable once you find the weak spot.

Slopie ended his blues and, as Martha moved to another customer, Daddy Big swung around on his stool and said, 'Play me the white man's song, Slopie.' Slopie grinned and trilled an intro, a ricky-tick throwback, and Daddy Big sang from his barstool the song he said he had learned from a jail-house nigger who'd sung it in World War One: *I don't care what it costs, I'll suffer all the loss. It's worth twice the money just to be the boss. 'Cause I got a white man workin' for me now*. The song merged with 'The Broadway Rag,' into which Slopie passed without comment. Daddy Big opened his arms to the room and said as the ragtime bounced off the walls, 'I love all niggers.' Looking then to the black faces for reciprocation and getting none, he discovered Billy at the corner table, near the neon-lighted window.

'What're you doing here, Phelan?' he asked. 'You ain't a nigger.' The words were crooked with whiskey.

'I'm an Irish Catholic,' Billy said. 'Same thing to some people.'

A few who heard this smiled. Daddy Big hurled himself off the barstool and staggered toward Billy, stopping his own forward motion by grabbing the back of a chair with both hands.

'You got your tail whipped tonight.'

'Doc was hot,' Billy said. 'A good player got hot.'

'Bet your ass he's a good player. Bet your ass. He'll whip you every time out.'

'Then why didn't he whip me the last two matches we played?'

'He'll whip you from now on. He's got your number. All you know how to shoot is safe and you blew that tonight. You ain't got nothin' left, if you ever had anything.' Daddy waved his left hand in front of his face like a man shooing flies. He lurched for the door with one word: 'Bum,' and went out cross-footed, leaving the door ajar. Martin closed it as Daddy Big careened in the direction of Union Station.

'He's got a mean mouth,' Martin said.

'Yeah,' said Billy. 'He's a prick now. Prison got him twisted. But he used to be a nice guy, and at pool he was a champ. Nobody in Albany could beat him. I learned a whole lot watching him sucker chumps who thought they knew something about the game.'

The white man from the end of the bar stopped beside Billy. 'That guy talks like he wants to wind up dead in the alley. He keeps that up in here, he'll get what he's after.'

'He's a cousin of the McCalls,' Billy told the man. 'Nobody'll touch him.'

'Is that so?' The man was chastened. 'I didn't know that.'

'That pimp,' Billy said to Martin when the stranger left, 'I don't know why he didn't stay down. I hit him right on the button. They used to stay down when I hit 'em like that.'

'Do you suppose he'll try to get even?'

'He'd get worse. You don't come back at Morrie.'

'Then you think Morrie's dangerous?'

'Anybody pals around with Maloy and Curry's dangerous.' Billy thought about that. 'But I like Morrie,' he said. 'And I like Maloy. Curry's nuts, but Morrie's all right. He saved my ass there.'

Slopie finished his ragtime number, a tour de force that won applause. Billy signaled to Martha to buy Slopie a drink.

'Can I tell you something, Martin?'

'Anything.'

'Positively on the q.t.'

'Do you trust me?'

'Yeah, I do. For a straight guy, you know a lot. Why'd you piss on that guy's feet?'

'He seemed worth that kind of attention. I don't meet too many like that. What did you want to tell me?'

'I threw that match tonight.'

'Hey,' said Martin. 'What for?'

'So I wouldn't owe Berman.'

'I don't think I follow that.'

'He lent me fifty to bet on myself. If I win, then I got money through him, right? But if I lose, I owe him nothing. I already give him back the fifty and we were even. Then the son of a bitch saves my ass.'

'So you were going to talk to Patsy about him then?'

'I don't know.'

'I could tell them what you want to say. I don't have your qualms.'

'They'd know I pumped him and then didn't tell them.'

'Then tell them.'

'But that puts me full on the tit. Bindy and Patsy paying my debts. Paying you. Me on the tit like Daddy Big. That bastard calls me a bum, but he'd chew catshit if Bindy said it was strawberries.'

The stranger who said Daddy Big wanted to die came back into Martha's. 'Somebody better call an ambulance,' he said. 'That drunk guy is outside bleedin' all over the street.'

Martha went for the phone, and Billy and Martin ran down the block. Daddy Big lay on his back, his face bloodied badly, staring at the black sky with bugged eyes and puffed cheeks, his skin purple where it wasn't smeared with blood. Two of his front teeth were bent inward and the faint squeal of a terrified mouse came out of his mouth. Billy rolled him face down and with two fingers pulled out his upper plate, then grabbed him around the waist with both arms and lifted him, head down, to release the vomit in his throat. Billy sat down on the sidewalk, knees up, and held Daddy across his lap, face down, tail in the air. Billy slapped his back and pressed both knees into his stomach until his vomiting stopped. Daddy looked up.

'You son of a bitch,' Billy said. 'Are you all right?'

'Blllgggggggghhh,' Daddy said, gasping.

'Then get your ass up.'

Billy rolled him off his lap, stood up and pulled the drunken Daddy to his feet. Customers from Martha's stood behind the two men, along with half a dozen passersby. Billy leaned Daddy against the wall of the Railroad Y.M.C.A. and Martha blotted his face with a wet towel, revealing a split forehead and a badly scraped nose, cheek, and chin. A prowl car arrived and two patrolmen helped Daddy into the back seat.

'Where'll you take him?' Martin asked.

'Home. He does this regular,' one policeman said.

'You should have him looked at up at the emergency room. He might have aspirated. Inhaled some vomit.'

'Nngggggnnnhhh,' said Daddy Big.

The policeman frowned at Martin and got behind the wheel.

'He don't have any teeth,' Billy said. Billy found the teeth on the edge of the curb, where a dog was licking the vomit. Billy reached in through the car window and put the teeth in Daddy Big's shirt pocket. As the crowd moved back toward Martha's, Martin saw another car pull up behind the police car, Poop Powell at the wheel.

'Hey, Phelan,' Poop called, and both Billy and Martin then saw Bindy McCall in the front seat alongside Poop. Martin patted Billy gently on the shoulder.

'You do lead a full life, Billy,' he said.

Martin sat in Martha's window looking at Billy standing in the middle of Broadway, his back to traffic, talking into Bindy's window. The neon sign, which spelled Martha's name backward, gave off a humming, crackling sound, flaming gas contained, controlled. Martin drank his beer and considered the combustibility of men. Billy on fire going through the emotions of whoring for

Bindy when he understood nothing about how it was done. It was not done out of need. It rose out of the talent for assuming the position before whore-mongers. Billy lacked such talent. He was so innocent of whoring he could worry over lead slugs.

Slopie played 'Lullaby of Broadway,' a seductive tune. Slopie was now playing in a world never meant to be, a world he couldn't have imagined when he had both his legs and Bessie on his arm. Yet, he'd arrived here in Martha's, where Billy and Martin had also arrived. The music brought back *Gold Diggers* of some year gone. Winnie Shaw singing and dancing the 'Lullaby.' Come and dance, said the hoofers, cajoling her, and she danced with them through all those early mornings. Broadway Baby couldn't sleep till break of dawn, and so she danced, but fled them finally. Please let me rest, she pleaded from her balcony refuge. Dick Powell kissed her through the balcony door, all the hoofers pleading, beckoning. Dance with us, Baby. And they pushed open the door. She backed away from them, back, back, and ooooh, over the railing she went. There goes Broadway Baby, falling, poor Baby, falling, falling, and gone. Good night, Baby.

Spud, the paper boy, came into Martha's with a stack of *Times-Union*s under his right arm, glasses sliding down his nose, cap on, his car running outside behind Bindy's, with doors open, hundreds more papers on the back seat.

'Paper,' Martin said. He gave Spud the nickel and turned to the classifieds, found the second code ad. Footers O'Brien was the top name, then Benny Goldberg, who wrote a big numbers book in Albany and whose brother was shot in his Schenectady roadhouse for having five jacks in a house deck. Martin lost patience translating the names in the dim light and turned to the front page. No story on Charlie Boy, but the Vatican was probing a new sale of indulgences in the U.S. And across the top a promotion headline screamed: 'Coming Sunday in the *Times-Union:* How and Why We Piss.'

Billy went straight to the men's room when he came back into Martha's and washed off Daddy Big's stink. Then he ordered a double scotch and sat down.

'So I told him about Newark,' he said.

'You did? Was he pleased?'

'He wanted more, but I told him straight. I can't do this no more, Bin. I ain't cut out to be a squealer.'

'Did he accept that?'

'I don't think so.'

'Why don't you think so?'

'Because he says to me, All right, hotshot, you're all by yourself, and he rolls up the window.'

14

Martin, ducking his head, entered the city room at pristine morning. Across the freshly oiled floor, free now from the sea of used paper, shinbone high, that would cover it nine or ten hours hence, he walked softly, playing the intruder, hoping to catch a rat in action. The room was empty except for the clacking, which never deterred the *Times-Union*'s rats. It was their lullaby. They got to be a size, came along a pipe from out back, and ran over the heads of the working stiffs. Benson Hunt, the rewrite man, the star, moved his desk back two feet and never took off his hat again after a three-pounder lost its footing on the pipe and tumbled into his lap. Benson screamed and tipped himself over, breaking a pint of gin in his coat. Martin had no such worries, for no pipes traversed the space over his desk, and he never packed gin. But he too wore his hat to keep his scalp free of the fine rain of lead filings that filtered through the porous ceiling from the composing room overhead.

Martin paused at the sports desk to read a final edition with the story on the blackout. Some sort of sabotage, perhaps, went one theory; though the power company and the police had no culprits. The darkness blacked out, through most of Albany County, the speech by Thomas E. Dewey, aaaahhh, largely an attack on the McCall machine. Sublime. The speech was reported separately. Political monopoly in Albany. Vicious mess of corruption in the shadow of the Capitol. Vice not fit to discuss on the radio. Politics for profit. Packed grand juries. Tax assessments used to punish enemies. Vote fraud rampant.

The arrest only today of several men, one for registering twenty-one times.

Martin clicked on the drop light over his own desk and prepared to write a column for the Sunday paper, his first since the kidnapping. In the days since Charlie Boy had been taken, Martin stayed busy chronicling the event as he came to know it, for use when the story finally did break. He had filled his regular space in the paper with extra columns he kept in overset for just such distracted times.

Now he wrote about Billy's two-ninety-nine game and about Scotty dropping dead. Without malice toward Scotty, he discussed the hex, and Billy's response to it. He viewed Billy as a strong man, indifferent to luck, a gamester who accepted the rules and played by them, but who also played above them. He wrote of Billy's disdain of money and viewed Billy as a healthy man without need for artifice or mysticism, a serious fellow who put play in its proper place: an adjunct to breathing and eating.

By comparison, Martin wrote, I find myself an embarrassed ecclesiarch, a foolish believer in luck, fate, magicians, and divine animals. It would serve me right if I died and went to heaven and found out it was a storefront run by Hungarian palm readers. In the meantime, he concluded, I aspire to the condition of Billy Phelan, and will try to be done mollycoddling my personal spooks.

It took him half an hour to write the column. He put it in the overnight folder in a drawer of the city desk, ready for noontime scrutiny by Matt Viglucci, the city editor.

In his mailbox, he found a letter on Ten Eyck Hotel stationery, delivered by hand. Dearest Martin, I missed you at the theater. Do come and call. We have so much to talk about and I have a 'gift' for you. Yours always, Melissa.

A gift, oh yes. Another ticket to lotus land? Or was there mystery lurking in those quotation marks? What son eats the body of his father in the womb of his mother? The priest, of course, devouring the host in the Holy Church. But what son is it that eats the body of his father's sin in the womb of his father's mistress? Suggested answer: the plenary self-indulger.

Paper rustled behind him as he stood amid the clackety lullaby. He turned noiselessly to see a large, relaxed rat walking across the scatter of early editions and old wire copy left by the nightside on top of the copy desk. The rat stopped at a paste pot on the desk and nibbled at the hardened outer crust. The pot moved, the rat inched forward, and then, with dexterous forefeet, it lifted the dauber an inch and pushed its own nose into the center of the pot, into the cool, fresh, soft, sweet stickiness of the paste.

Breakfast.

Martin counted eighteen steps going out of the building and waved at Rory Walsh, the early man in the sports department, schoolboy football specialist coming out of Steve White's twenty-four-hour bar. Old man Ridley stood in front of his newsroom, burning yesterday's policy slips in the gutter. The window seats of the Capitol Hotel restaurant, reserved for *T-U* folk, were empty. Martin's stomach rolled at the thought of the lobster tail special, three for fifty-five cents. He stopped at Green's stationery store and bought wrapping paper, ribbon, and a card for the present he would give Melissa, tit for tat. The horseroom upstairs over Green's was already open for business. Across the street, Keeler's tempted, as always, and his stomach rolled again. He had slept badly and left the house without waking Mary, without eating. Should he indulge? He did.

Perhaps his decision was colored by his having eaten here in 1928 with Melissa, two breakfasts and one dinner in three days, the only times they left the hotel room, fortifying their bodies with what he considered the equal of the best food on earth, reconstituting themselves for the return to their bed of second-generation concubinage.

He now ordered eggs Benedict, hard rolls and salt sticks, iced butter, marmalade, hashed browns, steaming coffee in the silver pot. A grumpy Jewish waiter in black jacket and long white apron, shuffling on flat feet, served the meal impeccably. Two thirty-five with tip. Gorgeous. He felt stylish, and buoyed by nostalgia. Ready for the lady.

She was registered in a twelfth-floor suite, and he approached it along the carpeted hallway, certain he would rouse her from sleep. He knocked loudly four times before she opened the door, each rap an explosion in the silent corridor.

'I came for my gift,' he said.

'You fool. Why didn't you call? Haven't you any thought for a lady's condition at such an hour?'

'Your condition looks fetchingly normal to me. Dressed for bed.'

'I must look wretched.'

She left the door open and crossed the suite's sitting room, barefoot in a white calf-length negligee, and disappeared into the bedroom. Martin entered and the door swung closed. He put his hat on the coffee table and sat in the love seat. An etching of a step-gabled Dutch house hung on one wall, a Maxfield Parrish print on another wall – *Daybreak*, everybody's favorite picture fifteen years ago. The naked nymph bent over the reclining beauty waking from sleep, the mountain lake and the trees of Arcadia framing the morning confrontation, the brightening sky dappling the mountains and lighting incipient joy. Beneath it on the sideboard Martin saw his father's notebook. It lay flat, a ledger eighteen inches long with canvas and leather cover and binding, and bearing the India ink marking his father had made to identify it by date.

Here was a contrast of low and high art by master achievers: Parrish setting out to entrap popular taste, Edward Daugherty laboring with the death throes of his soul to produce a play that reflected his supreme independence of the crowd. The ledger contained the notation of the history of a masterpiece as well as the revelations of a notorious disgrace. *Daybreak*, with all its dynamic symmetry, made Martin want to throttle Parrish for foisting on the millions the notion that life was tidy, life was golden. Still, the hint of Lesbos had its place on any wall of Melissa's suite, as Edward and Martin Daugherty both knew.

Looking at the ledger, it occurred to him to take it and leave. He had often mused on burglary as a means of retrieving it. He turned his eyes from it only because Melissa re-entered the room in a baby blue satin robe and matching pompommed mules. She had brushed her silvering chestnut hair, colored the cream of her cheeks with a subtle touch of rouge, lifted her eyes from sleep with pale green eye shadow, and powdered away the gleam of her shining morning brow. Her beauty, though controlled by chemistry, was a miracle at forty-nine, given the terror of personal and professional oblivion with which she had lived most of the last decade. Even her wrinkles were now seemly, allowing her to relinquish at last that girlish beauty with which she had lived far too long, keeping her on the cover of *Photoplay*, but sabotaging all her efforts to become a serious actress. For who could believe an anguished spirit lurked behind a face as elegant and proud of itself as Melissa's? No one could, until her role as the cloistered Marina (Katrina) of *The Flaming Corsage* forced a reappraisal of her talent by the critics: Here is a totally new Melissa Spencer . . . acts as if born to the stage . . . confounds critics who said her voice would fail in talkies . . . most fully articulated female presence on the Broadway stage this year, etc.

She went straight to the telephone and ordered breakfast for two: cantaloupe, camembert, croissants, and champagne. Of course. Then she flounced into an armchair across from Martin, framed by *Daybreak* and a cut-glass vase full of white roses opening to the morning with the shining sublimity of their final blooming, only hours left in their life.

'Are you well?' she asked.

'I may be recuperating, but I'm not sure.'

'That sounds dreadful, as if you're living in some awful sanitarium.'

'That's not far off. I've been on a morose spiritual jag for years, and it's worse these past few days.'

'Is it your father? How is he?'

'It's that, but it's not that simple. And he's quite senile but otherwise healthy. It's my son going off to the priesthood, and it's a friend just kidnapped by hoodlums.'

'A kidnapping! How fascinating!'

'Oh, Christ, Melissa.'

'Well, isn't it fascinating?'

'Everything isn't fascinating. Some things are serious.'

'Oh, poo.'

'Tell me about you. I suspect you're well. I read your notices.'

'It is rather a ducky time.'

'You look very fit. For anything.'

'Don't be forward now, lovey. It's much too early.'

'I've known you, my dear, to throw away the clock.'

'Me? Not me, Martin. You must be remembering one of your casual women.'

'I could've sworn it was you. That week the taboos came tumbling down. The Hampton, was it?'

'Don't be awful now. Don't. I get shivery about that. Tell me about the play. Did you like it?'

'You were quite splendid. But then you're always quite splendid. And I did find that wig becoming.'

'Did I look like her to you? I did try.'

'At times. But she was never quite as sensually animated as you played her.'

'She must have had her moments.'

'I think,' said Martin, and he pictured his mother coming down the back stoop naked, walking past the small garbage pail, wearing only her sunbonnet hat and her white shoes and carrying her calico handbag, 'that all she ever had was her repressions.' Walking into the waiting arms of Francis Phelan? Did they ever make love after that intimacy?

'So sad,' said Melissa.

'Very sad. But that's not one of your problems, I've noticed.'

'Avoiding things never made any sense to me, none whatever.'

'You've done it all.'

'I wouldn't go as far as to say that, lovey.'

'But it must be difficult to surprise you.' Martin resented her use of 'lovey.' It sounded vaguely cockney, and insufficiently intimate for what they'd had together.

'Surprises are always welcome,' said Melissa, 'but they're only the interest on the principal, and it's the principal I'm most fond of.'

'I have a bit of a surprise for you,' Martin said.

'How delicious,' said Melissa. 'When do I get it?'

'Don't be forward now.'

When breakfast came she insisted he sit on the sofa as they had at the Hampton, and she dropped pieces of melon into his mouth, a scene, he presumed, she had copied from a Valentino or Gilbert film. She lifted champagne to his lips, gave him wafer-thin slices of camembert and croissant, and more and more champagne. He thought he had eaten his fill at Keeler's, but satiation too has its limitations, and he accepted all that she offered.

He kissed her when both their mouths were full, shared his champagne with her. He kissed her again when their mouths were empty, stroking the breast of her robe lightly. And then he leaned away.

'What is this gift you have for me?' he said.

'Can't you guess?'

'I've imagined a thing or two.'

'I hope you didn't see it,' she said, rising from the sofa and crossing the room. She held up the ledger, giving him a full view of the cover with another of his father's date markings: February 1908 to April 1909.

'I didn't mean to leave it here in full view, but you caught me unawares, coming in like that. You didn't see it before, did you?'

'No, no, I didn't. You say you're returning it?'

'It's yours,' she said, coming toward him with it. 'I took all I needed for my memoirs.'

'I thought you wanted it for the film.'

'It's not necessary now. They have more than enough in the play, if they really want to do it. They don't deserve any more than that. So it's yours.'

'Then I must return your money.'

'Of course you must *not*. *Absolutely* you must not.'

He had charged her eight hundred dollars for the ledger, an arbitrary price from nowhere, for how could he possibly have set a true dollar value on one of his father's notebooks? He'd said eight hundred for reasons no more explicable than his dream of rhomboids. An odd figure, she said. Oddness, he told her, is my profession.

They had been talking then on the roof garden of the Hampton, where she had taken a suite while she found a way to take possession of the ledger, whose contents she had, at moments, watched being written. The Albany sky was the darkest of blues, swept by millions of stars, the moon silvering the river and the rooftops of buildings on the Rensselaer side. From where Martin and Melissa sat, the Yacht Club, the night boat landing, the Dunn bridge, and much of lower Broadway were blocked from view by a tall, ghostly structure with window openings but no windows, with an unfinished, jagged, and roofless top. This was the 'Spite Building,' built by a bitter cleric who felt the Hampton had wronged him. And when the hotel opened its roof garden to enormous crowds, the cleric erected this uninhabitable tower of vengeance. It fronted on Beaver Street and nestled back to back with the hotel, and it rose, finally, above the glamorous rooftop cafe, blocking the view and insulting the lofty crowds with its crude bricks and its grotesque eyeless sockets, where squads of verminous pigeons roosted.

Martin and Melissa dined and danced and drank together, abandoning the Hampton roof eventually for the privacy of Melissa's suite. And when the morning came, Martin walked the few blocks to the newspaper, took the ledger from the bottom drawer of his desk, where he'd put it the day before, and brought it back to Melissa. In return he accepted the mysterious eight hundred, and also accepted two and a half more days of lascivious riches from this calculating, venal, and voluptuous incarnation of his psychic downfall.

Melissa now placed the ledger on his lap and sat beside him. He opened it to a page from 1908 and read the words written in his father's upright script, which looked like a wheat field on a windless day.

The hero will not be a writer. Profession left vague? No.

He will be Irish-American foundry owner who came up hard way in commerce, through opportunity and hard work, well educated, from family whose social pretensions were wiped out by influx of '49. Marries daughter of aristocratic Dutch-English family (any near-autobiographical data must be transformed) and secret life of failed marriage is revealed. Wife's aspirations for money and position, not for themselves but out of halcyon yearning, become clear; and these are ineradicable and dementing. Sexually dutiful but her wound in Delavan Hotel fire eradicates even that; early traumas only suggested, yet evident. Eventually she retreats, marriage begins to wither.

Martin turned the pages well forward, stopped, smiled, and read out loud: '"Clarissa. Valley of veneration. Cave of nuances. Isosceles jungle. Lair of the snake. Grave of the stalker."' He paused to look at her.

'I know that page by heart,' she said.

'"Grave of the stalker,"' Martin said. 'He could be a silly man. I see an erected Hawkshaw. Tell me. Did you ever go round the clock with him for three days as you did with me?'

'That's a very impertinent question. Do you really think I'd tell you?'

'I thought one day you might compare notes on us. I fantasized your reply.'

'And naturally you win that contest.'

'I didn't think of it as a contest. More a contrast of styles.'

'Let me say, and end it here, that exuberance runs in your family.'

'Up exuberance,' he said, and drank his champagne.

She refilled his glass and raised hers.

'And here,' she said, 'a toast to my gifts.'

'And rare and splendid they are. Up your gifts.'

'I was speaking of my gifts to you.'

'Gifts, you say. Is there more than one?' And he touched the ledger.

'One more.'

'Which one is that?'

'The one and only,' she said, and stood up before him and opened her robe to reveal no negligee, only that indelibly remembered torso, with its somewhat graying isosceles jungle trimmed and shaved with supreme care in the contour of a heart.

'It's a bit late in the year,' she said, 'but will you be my valentine?'

Martin opened his belt, the front buttons of his trousers, the three buttons of the shorts he'd put on clean this morning, and presented to her the second generation stalker, full grown now, oh yes, wrapped in white tissue paper, tied with green ribbon, and tagged with a small card bearing the greeting: Happy Anniversary.

As he made love to Melissa he studied that portion of her neck and breast where his mother had been scarred by the point of a flaming, flying stick in the fire that killed fifteen people, most of them Irish servant girls. Melissa bore no such marks. Her mark was her face, and he kissed it lavishly, loathing both himself and her, loving her with passionate confusion, pitying her the gift of such a face, for it had been her torment. What man could ever think he alone possessed a beauty so famed, so excessive. Who could own Botticelli's Primavera?

His mother's scar had been a white oval with a scalloped circumference where the stitching had drawn her wound together. He closed his eyes as he kissed Melissa, and behind him the white scar grew by itself, a floating ovoid that became witness to his act. The scar swelled, and Martin thought of the flaming ball of tow that had marked the elder Henry James, playing in Albany Academy park, the park on which Katrina's Elk Street home fronted. The young James, then only thirteen, had been flying hot-air balloons, which rose skyward when the flaming tow balls were placed beneath them. One James balloon ascended from the park and when the flaming tow ball fell to earth, someone kicked it and arced it into the hayloft of a livery stable across Washington Avenue. The conscientious James ran to the stable to put out the fire, but his pants leg had been splashed by turpentine from soaking the tow, and it ignited like the tail of a comet. The burns led to amputation, creating a mystic philosopher from an incipient outdoorsman, and changing the future of American culture. Serendipitous movement from Edward to Melissa to Henry to Martin. Bright flaming people in a roundelay of accidental life that alters the world.

The scar grew behind Martin, its center becoming the most brilliant of all possible whites. Martin saw to it that the animal-child was seated on the chair beside the hotel bed in a typical spectator's position.

The animal-child watched the cleansing siege of the taboo, unaware the maternal flame was flirting blindly with his presence. The divine figure saw too late the advent of love's flaming embrace, and he ignited with a rasping, crackling brilliance. He tried to scream but the sound caught in his immaterial throat, and he was suddenly ashes, a spume of sooty flakes flying upward. To heaven? To hell?

Martin ejaculated with an onrush of benediction.

Aware that Melissa had been shorted on the significance of the moment, Martin manipulated her vigorously into a writhing, low-level ecstasy. This, she sadly admitted, was the only estate she could inhabit since her hysterectomy four years before. When her ovaries were taken from her, something else went with them. Oh, she could approach climax, almost peak. But there was a point beyond which nothing would take her. She had tried. Oh, how she had tried. Poor little one. And now she gave what could be given, took what must be taken. Her explanation sounded vaguely biblical to Martin, as if she read Saint Augustine hopefully every time the nuances flooded her cave.

Yet Martin could not escape the notion that his presence here at this altar of hand-me-down flesh was in some way therapistic, that he was expected to remantle the wings of Melissa's passion, that his time with her a decade ago had been as maleficent for her as it had for him, that she was searching in his flaming ashes for a new display of her own lost fireworks. They're not really *all* gone, are they, Daddy?

He rubbed, oh, how he rubbed. She tried, oh, how she tried.

But when she exploded it was only with exhaustion, to save her heart's wearying ventricle.

They dressed and rested and poured new champagne, and Melissa ate a piece of melon standing up. Martin sat on the sofa trying to understand the meaning of what he had just gone through. He was unable to grasp the significance of so many people suddenly webbed in the same small compass of events. He dismissed coincidence as a mindless explanation of anything. Was it his mind discovering patterns that had always existed but that he, in his self-absorption, had never noticed? But how? He was a fairly perceptive man. More than that, he was foresightful. Even now he had the impulse to call the newspaper, for what reason he did not know. Emory would not be in yet, and he had no reason to speak with anyone else.

He went to Melissa's bedroom and sat on the rumpled bed, still damp with drops of love and loathing, and asked the hotel operator to ring the *Times-Union*. When Madge, the crone, answered, all he could think to ask was whether anyone had left him a message. 'Yes,' said Madge, 'some bozo named Franny Phelan called. He's in jail and wants you to bail him out.'

Martin went back to the couch.

'Did you ever hear my father speak of having a gift of foresight, or anything comparable?' he asked Melissa.

'I remember he was superstitious,' she said. 'He used to throw salt over his shoulder when it spilled and he had a lucky pair of pants. They were green with small checks. I can still see them. He almost never wore them except when he needed money, and he swore that when he put them on, money started to trickle in. We were standing in the middle of Fourteenth Street one afternoon and he was wearing a blue suit and he didn't have enough money to buy our lunch at Luchow's. "Nobody knows I need money," he said. "How could they? I don't have my green pants on." We went to his rooms and he put the pants on, and the next day he got a bank draft in the mail for eleven hundred dollars from a producer.'

Martin felt a lazy rapture come over him looking at Melissa, the golden bird of paradise. Yet, he resented the intimacy such a story reflected, and the pain it caused his mother in her grave. It was the first time he'd ever heard of clairvoyance in anyone else in the family. But Martin quickly decided his father, through telepathy with the producer, learned of the money on the way and put on the green pants as a way of turning the vision into something magical but not quite serious. It was not the same gift as his own. No.

'You're going now, aren't you?' Melissa said.

'I had a call at the paper. An old neighbor of mine's in jail and wants my help.'

'I could tell by your face you were going to leave me.'

'What is it? Do you want to talk? I don't have to go right this minute.'

'I don't see you in ten years and you pop in and use me like a Klondike whore.'

'Use you? Klondike?' Martin's fingers still ached from the reciprocal friction.

'You drink my champagne and eat my food and exploit my body and leave me alone with my energy. You use me.' She hurled a croissant at him. It missed him and bounced off a lampshade.

'You crazy bitch,' he said. 'You're as crazy as my mother.'

He pulled her robe off her shoulders, pinning her arms to her side. Then he dragged her to the floor and undid his trousers.

How do I use thee? Let me count the ways. As a sacred vessel to be violated. As a thief of Holy Writ. As the transcendent trinity: Melissa-Katrina-Marina, which my father discovered and loved; which I now love. As my father immortalized them all, like the figures on the Grecian urn, so do I now perceive them in all their lambent lunacy. Seeing with my father's eyes and knowing how he was victimized by glory and self-absorption, I now forgive the man his exorbitant expectations, his indifference, his absence. Once forgiven, it is a short walk to forgive myself for failing to penetrate such passionate complexity as his. Forgiving myself, I can again begin to love myself. All this, thanks to the use of the fair Melissa.

As he pronged the dying fire, Martin sensed the presence of his parents in the room, not as flaming balls of tow this time, but as a happy couple, holding hands and watching him do diddle with Melissa for them, just as he had once done proud piddle for them in his personal pot. Clearly, they saw him as the redeemer of all their misalliances, the conqueror of incoherence, the spirit of synthesis in an anarchic family. Martin, in the consanguineous saddle, was their link with love past and future, a figure of generational communion, the father of a son en route to the priesthood, the functioning father of the senile Edward. More than that he had, here, obviously become his own father. He was Edward, son of Emmett Daugherty, father of Martin Daugherty, grandfather of Peter Daugherty, and progenitor of the unchartable Daugherty line to come. Lost son of a lost father, he was now fatherhood incarnate.

Perceiving this, he spent himself in Melissa's ravine of purification.

'You are my yum-yum,' she said to him, wholly flattened, the corners of her mouth yanked downward by unseen powers at the center of the earth. She stroked the fluids at the center of herself and sucked the mixture off her middle finger, evoking in Martin a ten-year-old memory of the same act performed at the Hampton. Moved profoundly both by the act and the memory, he loathed himself for his own psychic mendacity, for trying to persuade himself he had other than venereal reasons for jingling everybody's favorite triangle.

Hypocrite!

Lecher!

My boy!

15

Billy found Martin in the news coop of police headquarters playing knock rummy with Ned Curtin, the *Times-Union*'s police reporter. Martin saw Billy and nodded. Then he drew a card and knocked. Ned Curtin slid a dime to him across the desk.

'How come he called you?' Billy said when Martin came out to meet him. They walked together up the stairs, Billy still smelling the pine disinfectant he always associated with this building. Billy had been here only once, five years ago, for dealing cards on Orange Street. He'd been hired by a punk who said he had Bindy's okay to run the game, but didn't, so they pulled everybody in and held them an hour here and then let the players go. But they kept the punk, who had to pay up and do a night in jail.

'I saw him Thursday down in Spanish George's,' Martin said, 'and I told him to call me if he needed anything.'

'You didn't tell me you saw him.'

'He didn't want me to. When you see him, you'll know why.'

'Why'd you call me now?'

'It'll be in the paper tonight, or maybe even this afternoon, who he is and used to be. You had to know before that.'

They sat down on a long, wooden bench in the empty courtroom. A white-haired man in shirtsleeves came in from the room behind the judge's bench and sniffed at them, then went out again.

'Did you ever know why he left home?' Billy asked.

'I know the gossip. He drank, then the baby died. The one fed the other.'

'I was nine.'

'Do you remember him well? You could at nine.'

'I don't know if I remember his face from seeing it, or from the picture. There's one home in a box of snapshots, about nineteen fifteen, the year before he left. He's standing on our old stoop on Colonie Street.'

'He was all done with baseball then. I can remember how he looked. He doesn't look like that any more.'

With a magnifying glass, Billy had studied how his father wore his sweater, the same one he wore in the rowboat, and maybe the same cap. He studied the cut of his jaw, the shape of his eyes, and his smile, the lips open and twisted a little to the left. It was a good smile, a strong smile. But Billy's mother said it was a weak thing to leave us and drink so much. A man shouldn't be weak like that, she said. But, oh my, how he cried, she said. How we all cried.

'Here,' said Martin, nudging Billy. Through an open door they saw men entering the hallway behind the courtroom. One guard in blue shirt and policeman's cap walked ahead of the prisoner, and one behind him. Billy was not prepared for this sight. It was Pete the Tramp without a hat, without the spiky mustache, without the comedy. When tramps came to the house and asked for a meal, Billy's mother always fed them, and gave them coffee with milk. Now he knew why. Billy and Martin followed the procession. The tramp dragged his feet, slouched, shuffled on fallen arches, or maybe on stumps with toes frozen and gone. Billy kept his father's dirty gray hair in sight. He did not remember hair on his father, he remembered a cap.

The white-haired man who had sniffed at them turned from the large ledger in which he was writing. Billy remembered seeing the man only last month at Foley's pit in Troy, handling fighting cocks for Patsy McCall. His name was Kelly and he was a hell of a handler.

'What's this?' Kelly said, pen in hand.

'Bail. Francis Phelan,' said the first policeman.

'Ah, you're the one,' Kelly said, putting down his pen and sticking out his right hand to Francis. 'Congratulations. Twenty-one, was it?' And everyone laughed.

'So they say,' Francis said.

Billy saw his father's smile and recognized the curve of the lips, but the teeth were brown in front, and there were no teeth at all behind them. The mouth was a dark cavity. The smile was dead.

'Somebody got bail money?' Kelly asked.

'Here,' said Billy, and he weaved his way through the men. He counted out four hundred dollars and Kelly took it to the next room and put it in a box in the open safe. Billy looked at his father and received a stare of indifference.

'You a bail bondsman? I don't remember you,' Kelly said, his pen poised over the receipt book.

'No,' Billy said. 'Family.'

Kelly handed Billy a receipt, and one of the policemen gave Francis a small white envelope with his belongings. Then both guards left the corridor. Billy, Martin, and Francis stood looking at one another until Martin said, 'Let's go,' and led the way out the door. He stopped at the top of the stairs.

'Martin, thanks for fixing it up,' Francis said.

'Not at all. I told you to call me.'

'You know a lawyer who'll take me on?'

'I do. Marcus Gorman, the best in town. I already talked to him.'

Francis looked at Billy and nodded his head. 'You're Billy, ain't you?'

'Yeah,' said Billy.

'Thanks for that dough.'

'My pleasure.'

Francis nodded again. 'How you been?'

'Not bad,' Billy said. 'How about yourself?'

'Well, I ain't in jail.' And Francis cackled a throaty laugh, showing his brown teeth and the cavity of his mouth, and fell into a cough that twisted his whole body.

Billy offered him a Camel.

He took it.

They went down the stairs and out the front door onto Eagle Street, confronting a golden October afternoon, the bright sun warming the day with Indian summer's final passion. Men were walking the street in shirtsleeves, and women's dresses still had the look of August about them. The black mood that had fallen on Billy when he first saw his father faded into a new and more hopeful coloration under a sky so full of white, woolly clouds.

The bail almost wiped out Billy's bankroll, but he still had sixty-two dollars and change. It was enough to get the old man a new outfit: shoes, suit, shirt, and tie. Make him look like an American citizen again.

When Martin told Billy about the bail, Billy had immediately said, I got it, I'll go for it. I know it's your money, Martin, but I'll get more. I don't want that money, Martin had said. Forget I ever won that bet. No, I don't forget that, Billy said. What do you do when you lose? You pay.

'I gotta get something in my stomach,' Francis said. 'I ain't et in two days.'

'Didn't they feed you out there in the can?' Billy asked.

'Nothin'd stay down. I still ain't right.'

'We can go home. I'll call Peg at the office and have her whip up a meal. She cooks good.'

'No,' Francis said. 'No thanks, no. No.'

'Then what do you want?' asked Billy.

'Garlic soup,' Francis said. 'You know an Italian place? They always got garlic.'

'Garlic soup?'

'Lombardo's,' Martin said. 'First-rate place.'

'I don't want no meal,' said Francis. 'Just garlic soup. Fixes up the stomach. A Mexican bum taught me that in Texas.'

'They'll make whatever you want at Lombardo's,' said Martin. 'But listen, I've got appointments. I'll leave you all to solve the garlic problem.'

'No, stick around,' Francis said.

'I've got work to do, Fran.'

'Nah, nah, nah,' said Francis and he grabbed Martin's arm and started to walk with him. 'Nah, nah. Stick around a while. It ain't gonna kill you to be seen with an old bum.'

'Some of my best friends are bums,' said Martin. 'The newspaper specializes in them.'

'So stick around, stick around.'

Billy followed the two men as they all walked down Eagle Street, his father's slouch not so pronounced now, but his shuffle clearly the gimp's gait, left leg dragging. Billy remembered somebody in the family saying Francis was lame, very lame, when he came back to Albany in thirty-five. Whatever it was, he's still got a little of it.

They turned down Hudson Avenue and walked toward the Italian neighborhood, through the farmers' market with its half a hundred trucks, and a scattering of horses and wagons. This had been the city produce market since the days before Francis was born, when everything here was horses and wagons. Billy was maybe six or seven when he gripped his father's hand as they walked among the animals here, smelling the fresh and decaying produce, the fresh and decaying manure, a fluid stench Billy remembered now as clearly as he'd remembered the pine disinfectant. They walked past a spavined animal in its traces, chomping at the feed bag, mashing its leavings with its hind feet, and Billy looked at his father's right hand, the back of it bulging with blue veins and scars Billy did not remember. Then he saw the first two joints were gone from the first finger. Billy pictured them curving around the hand-sewn and soap-rubbed seams of a baseball when his father was instructing him in the ways of an outcurve.

'What happened to your finger?' Billy asked. They were three abreast and he was beside his father.

'What finger?'

'The one that ain't there.'

'Oh, that. Some wine bum went nuts and chopped it off. Tried to cut my feet off with a cleaver, but all he got was a piece of the finger.'

'Why'd he come after you?'

'He wanted my shoes. I had good-lookin' shoes on and he didn't have none.'

'What'd you do to him?'

'I think he went in the river. Somebody told me that.'

'When was all this?'

'Hell, I don't know. Ten, twelve years ago. Colorado, I think. Or maybe Idaho.'

'You got around some.'

'Yowsah. Trains go everywhere.'

'Lunch is on me,' Billy said.

'Okay by me, Bill.'

Bill. That didn't sound right to Billy. People who didn't know him called him Bill. But that's the way it is. He don't know me at all. It then occurred to Billy that he'd known for a day and a half that his father was in town and that he'd made no effort to find him. No effort. None.

'I was never here,' Francis said when they walked into the bar of Lombardo's restaurant. 'How long's it been here?'

'Must be twenty years,' Martin said. 'You shouldn't stay away so long.'

'Got great Italian roast beef, best in town,' Billy said.

'No beef, just soup,' Francis said.

They sat in a booth in the bar area, Martin seating himself first, Francis sliding in beside him. At the bar, three young men with black hair and pure white shirts were talking to the bartender. The bar mirror was spotless, and so were the white floor tiles. Only thing old man Lombardo don't have in the joint is dirt. Billy, in his gray gabardine, new last month, and a fresh silk shirt, felt clean to the skin. His father looked dirtier now than he had on the street.

Francis told the chubby waitress the way to make the soup. Boil two garlic cloves in water for five minutes. That's all? No salt, no oregano? No, nothing but the garlic, said Francis.

'You want something to drink?' the waitress asked.

'A double scotch,' Billy said.

'I'll have a glass of port,' said Martin.

'In that case, muscatel, large,' said Francis.

Martin gave Francis the phone number of Marcus Gorman and explained why the best trial lawyer in town might take his case: because the McCalls, up against the wall from the Dewey attack, would be looking for scapegoats, and who'd care if a drifter and runaway husband took the fall? And Gorman would take any case that needled the McCalls, because they had dumped him as their candidate for Congress after a photo of him vacationing in Europe with Legs Diamond appeared in the local papers.

'The McCall people still owe me money,' Francis said. 'I could pay the lawyer something. I only collected fifty of the hundred and five I got coming.'

'Hundred and five,' Billy said. 'That ain't a bad day's work at the polls.'

'I didn't work the whole day,' Francis said.

'I doubt they'll pay you that,' Martin said. 'They'll be afraid of a setup now.'

'If they don't, I'll sing to the troopers and take some of them two-bit sonsabitches to jail with me.'

'So we both got our problems with the McCalls,' Billy said.

'What's your problem?'

'Did you know Bindy's son, Charlie, was snatched?'

'I heard that out in jail.'

'So Bindy and Patsy want me to shadow a guy they think might be mixed up in it. Spy on him, pump him, then tell them what he says.'

'What's wrong with that?'

'The guy's a friend of mine.'

'Yeah, Bill, but don't forget the McCalls got the power. You do a favor for a guy in power, chances are he'll do you one back. That's why I think they won't do nothin' to me after what I done for them.'

'I look at it different,' Billy said.

'Did anybody hit on you, or anything like that?'

'Not yet, but I'm waiting.'

The waitress brought the drinks and Francis drank half of his wine in one draught. He motioned to her for another and fished in his pocket for the white envelope. He took a crisp five dollar bill from it and put it on the table.

'Not a chance,' Billy said. 'I told you this was on me.'

'You said lunch.'

'That's everything.'

Francis held the fiver up. 'The troopers found I had ten of these and they said, How come a bum like you has fifty bucks in new bills? They was old ones, I said. I just sent 'em out to the Chink's to get 'em washed and ironed.' He laughed and showed his cavity.

'You didn't ask about my mother,' Billy said.

'No, I didn't. How is she?'

'She's fine.'

'Good.'

'You didn't ask about my sister, either.'

'No. How is *she?*'

'She's fine.'

'I'm glad they're all right.'

'You really don't give a shit about them, or me either, do you?'

'Keep it cool now, Billy,' Martin said.

'I'm not anybody you know any more,' Francis said. 'It ain't personal. I always liked the family.'

'That's why you left us?'

'I been leavin' home ever since I was a kid. Martin knows some of that. And I woulda been long gone even before that if only they'da let me. I wanted to go west and work on the railroad but Ma always said the railroad killed my father. He was a boss gandy dancer, and an engine knocked him fifty feet. But what the hell, he couldn'ta been payin' attention. Maybe he was gettin' deef, I don't know. You can't blame the railroad if a man backs his ass into a steam engine. But Ma did and wouldn't let me go.'

'Did you hate my mother?'

'Hate her? No. I liked her fine. She was a great girl. We had good times, good years. But I was one of them guys never shoulda got married. And after I dropped the kid, I knew nobody'd ever forgive me, that it was gonna be hell from then on. So I ran.'

'You dropped Gerald? I never knew that.'

'No?'

'No. Whataya mean dropped?'

'You didn't know?'

'I told you I didn't.'

'Somebody knew.'

'Peg never knew it, either. Nobody knows it.'

'Somebody knows it. Your mother knows it.'

'The hell she does.'

'She saw it happen.'

'She saw it? She never told none of us if she did.'

'Nobody?'

'Not even me and Peg, I'm telling you.'

'She musta told somebody. Her brother, or her screwball sisters.'

'They all talked about you and still do, but nobody ever mentioned that, and they don't keep secrets.'

'That's the goddamn truth.'

Francis drank the rest of his wine. When the waitress set a new glass in front of him, he immediately drank half of that and stared at the empty seat beside Billy.

'She never told,' he said. 'Imagine that.' He glugged more wine as tears came to his eyes. 'She was a great girl. She was always a great girl.' Tears fell off his chin into the muscatel.

'Why don't you come home and see her?' Billy said. 'Whatever you did, she forgave you for it a long time ago.'

'I can't,' Francis said and finished the wine. 'You tell her I'll come back some day when I can do something for her. And for your sister. And you, too.'

'Do what?'

'I don't know. Something. Maybe I'll come by of a Sunday and bring a turkey.'

'Who the fuck wants a turkey?' Billy said.

'Yeah,' said Francis. 'Who does?'

'Come on home and see them, even if you don't stay. That's something you can do. Never mind the turkey.'

'No, Bill, I can't do that. You don't understand that I can't do it. Not now. Not yet.'

'You better do it soon. You ain't gonna live forever, the way you look.'

'I'll do it one of these days. I promise you that.'

'Why should I believe your promises?'

'No reason you should, I guess.'

Francis shoved the empty wine glass away and pushed himself sideways out of the booth.

'I gotta get outa here. Tell her I don't want the soup. I gotta get me down to George's and get the rest of my money.'

'You're goin'?' Billy said. 'You're leavin'?'

'Gotta keep movin'. My bones don't know nothin' about sittin' still.'

'You'll get in touch with Gorman yourself, then?' Martin said.

'I'll do that,' Francis said. 'Righty so.'

'That bail money,' Billy said. 'Don't worry about it. You wanna skip, just skip and forget it. It don't mean anything to me.'

'I ain't figurin' to skip,' Francis said. 'But okay, thanks.'

'It doesn't make any sense to skip,' Martin said. 'You won't do any time with Gorman taking your case. Nobody wants to go to court with him. He turns them all into clowns.'

'I'll remember that,' Francis said. 'Now I gotta move. You understand, Martin.'

'I was gonna buy you some new clothes,' Billy said.

'Hell, they'd just get dirtied up, the way I bounce around. These clothes ain't so bad.'

When he got no response to that, he took a step toward the door and stopped. 'You tell the folks I said hello and that I'm glad they're feelin' good.'

'I'll pass the word,' Billy said.

'Wish you'd let me pay for the drinks. I got the cash.' He was halfway into another step and didn't know where to put his hands. He held them in front of his stomach.

Billy just stared at him. Martin spoke up.

'No need for that, Fran. Billy said it was his treat.'

'Well, I enjoyed it,' Francis said. 'Be seein' ya around.'

'Around,' Billy said.

Billy and Martin sipped their drinks and said nothing.

'He thinks it's all right to fink,' Billy said finally, staring at the empty seat.

'I heard what he said.'

'He's nothin' like I thought he'd be.'

'Who could be, Billy?'

'How could he tell me to rat on a friend?'

'He doesn't understand your situation. He knows better. When he got in trouble in the trolley strike . . . you know about that?'

'He killed a guy.'

'Not too many knew, and it never got in the papers who did it. Three of us helped him look for round stones that morning. Patsy McCall, your Uncle Chick, and myself. We were twelve, fourteen, like that, and your father was seven or eight years older and on strike. But we hated the scabs as much as he did and we all had stones of our own. Any one of us might have done what he did, but your father had that ball-player's arm. He had the fastest throw from third to first I ever saw, and I include Heine Groh. We were down on Broadway in front of the Railroad Y, standing at the back of the crowd. People collected there because they thought the strike talks were going on in the Traction Company building across the street.

'Just then the scabs and the soldiers came along with a trolley and tried to drive it straight through that crowd. It was a bad mistake. There were hundreds ready for them, women too. The women were warriors in the street during that strike. Well, the crowd trapped the trolley between two fires and it couldn't move either way, and that's when the stones flew. Everybody was throwing them, and then Francis threw his. It flew out of his fist like a bullet and caught the scab driver on the head. People turned to see who threw it, but your father was already on the run down Broadway and around the corner of Columbia toward the tracks. The soldiers fired on the crowd, and I saw two men hit. We ran then, too, nobody chasing us, and we saw Francis way off and followed him, and when he saw it was us, he waited. We all thought somebody must've seen him make the throw, so we started running again and went up to the filtration plant in North Albany, about three miles. Your grandfather, Iron Joe Farrell, was caretaker up there then, and he hid Francis in a room full of sinks and test tubes for two hours.

'We all hung around the place while Iron Joe went back up to Broadway and hitched a ride downtown to find out what was up. He learned from a cop he knew that the soldiers were looking for a young man wearing a cap. The cops didn't care about catching your father, of course. They were all with the strikers. But the Traction Company bosses forced them into a manhunt, and so we all knew your father couldn't go back to Colonie Street for a while. Chick went home and packed your father a suitcase and brought it back. Francis said he might head west to play ball somewhere, and if he got a job in a few months, he'd write and tell us.

'He cried then. We all did, over the way he had to go, especially Chick, who worshipped your father. Even Patsy cried a little bit. I remember he wiped his eyes dry with a trainman's blue handkerchief. And then your father walked across the tracks and hopped a slow freight going north to Troy, which was the wrong direction, but that's what he did. And Iron Joe said solemnly that none of us should ever say what we knew, and he told us to go home.

'On the way home, Chick said we should take a blood oath not to talk. Patsy and I said that was okay with us but we didn't know where to get the blood. Patsy wanted to steal a kid from old man Bailey's herd, but Chick said that was against the Seventh Commandment and he suggested Bid Finnerty's one-eyed cat, which everybody on Colonie Street hated as a hoodoo anyway. It took us an hour to find the cat, and then Patsy coaxed it with a fish head and brained it with a billy club so it'd lay still. Chick sliced it open and pulled out its heart and made the sign of the cross in blood on the palms of each of our hands. And I made the oath. We swear by the heart of Bid Finnerty's cat that we won't say what we know about Francis Phelan as long as we live, and that we won't wash this sacrificial blood off our hands until it's time to eat supper.

'The blood was all gone in half an hour, the way we sweated that day. As far as I know, none of us ever said anything until your father came back to town by himself months later, when the baseball season was over in Dayton. He called my father from out there to find out whether it was safe for him to come home to Colonie Street. And it was. And he came home and stayed fifteen years.'

'Yeah,' Billy said. 'He stayed until he killed somebody else.'

16

When Martin reached the paper, he found that Patsy McCall had left three messages since noontime. Martin called immediately and Patsy said he didn't want to go near the newspaper but would pick Martin up by the post office dock on Dean Street in ten minutes. His tone admitted of no other possibility for Martin.

Patsy showed up alone, driving his Packard, and when Martin got in, Patsy gunned the car northward on Quay Street and into Erie Boulevard, a little-traveled dirt road that paralleled the old Erie Canal bed, long since filled in. Patsy said nothing. The road bumped along toward the old filtration plant and led Martin to the vision of Francis running, and to echoes of long-dead voices of old North End canalers and lumber handlers. Immigrants looked out forlornly from the canal boats as they headed west, refused entrance to Albany in the cholera days.

Patsy pulled the car to the side of the road in a desolate spot near the Albany Paper Works. Along the flats in the distance Martin could see the tar-paper shacks hoboes had built. Did Francis have a reservation in one?

'They picked Berman as go-between,' Patsy said.

During the morning, Morrie had sent word to Bindy through Lemon Lewis that a letter had been left for him at Nick Levine's haberdashery. 'We got Charlie Boy and we want you to negotiate,' it said. 'If you agree to do this, go to State and Broadway at one o'clock today and buy a bag of peanuts at Coulson's. Cross the street and sit on a bench in the Plaza facing Broadway and feed the pigeons for fifteen minutes.' The letter was signed 'Nero' and also bore Charlie McCall's signature.

Almost simultaneously Patsy received a letter in his mailbox at the main post office on Broadway, the third letter since the kidnapping. 'We want the cash pronto and we are treating your boy nice but we can end that if you don't get the cash pronto. We know all about you people and we don't care about your kind so don't be funny about this.' It was also signed 'Nero' and countersigned by Charlie.

'You're not surprised they picked Berman?' Martin said.

'Not a bit,' said Patsy. 'I always thought the son of a bitch was in it.'

'But why suspect him out of everybody else?'

'It's an Albany bunch did this, I'll bet my tailbone on that and so will Bindy. They know too much about the whole scene. Berman's always been tied in with the worst of the local hoodlums – Maloy, the Curry brothers, Mickey Fink, Joe the Polack. We know them all, and they'd need Morrie because he's smarter than any of them.'

'Me, Patsy. What am I doing here?'

'Morrie's playing cute. He says he really doesn't want to do this thing but he will as a favor. He wants somebody there when they deliver Charlie, a witness who'll take some of the weight off his story. He asked me to pick somebody and when I gave him four or five names, he picked yours. He thinks you're straight.'

'What do I do?'

'Go with him. Do what he says and what they tell you to do. If he's their man, you're ours. And take care of Charlie when you get to him.'

'When does this happen?'

'Now. Morrie's waiting for me up in the Washington Park lake house. Can you do it?'

'You'll have to tell Mary something to put her mind at ease. And clue Emory in somehow.'

'Here's a couple of hundred for lunch money. And put this

in your pocket, too.' And Patsy handed Martin a snub-nosed thirty-eight with a fold of money.

'I wouldn't want to use a gun.'

'It won't hurt to take it.'

Patsy then drove north on Erie Boulevard to Erie Street and turned on it toward Broadway, past the car barns Edward Daugherty had written about. Scabs clung to the frame of a trolley as it rocketed through the gauntlet of stone throwers. Across Erie Street from the barns the old wooden Sacred Heart Church once stood, long gone now, Father Maguire on horseback with his whip, his church plagued by pigs and chickens. God be good to Charlie Boy, and all the sick and simple, and all the unhappy dead in Purgatory, and Mama and Papa.

Patsy drove up Broadway through North Albany and up Lawn Avenue to Wolfert's Roost, where the tony Irish played golf. Martin took Peter there one day and the boy fired a hole in one on a par three and thought he'd learned the secret of the game. The car sped along Northern Boulevard, through a rush of memories now for Martin, who considered that on this day, or another very soon, he might be dead. All the history in his head would disappear, the way his father's history was fading into whiteness.

Patsy drove over Northern Boulevard and into Washington Park, past the statues of Robert Burns and Moses, and up to the gingerbread yellow-brick lake house. Patsy parked and Martin got out of the car and stared at a stunning sight: a maple tree shedding its yellow leaves in a steady, floating rain. The leaves fell softly and brilliantly into a perfect yellow circle, hundreds of them constantly in the air, an act of miraculous shedding of the past while it was still golden. The tree was ancient, maybe as old as the park, or older. Martin had walked through the park with his father an age ago. Young people with sleds rolled in the snow and embraced and kissed behind bushes glittering with icy lace. Young people rode together in the summer in open carriages. They held hands and walked around the spectacular Moses fountain. Martin's father stood at the edge of these visions, watching. This is no country for old men, his father said. I prefer, said Edward Daugherty, to be with the poet, a golden bird on a golden bough, singing of what is past.

The land was a cemetery before it was a park. To prepare the park, men dug up the old bones and carted them to new cemeteries north of the city.

'Come on, let's move,' Patsy said to Martin.

Martin touched the pistol in his pocket and took a final look at the yellow rain of leaves, a sunburst of golden symmetry. On a day such as this, God rescued Isaac from his father's faith.

Morrie Berman, looking sharp in a gray fedora and blue pinstripe suit, sat alone on a bench inside the desolate lake house, legs spread, elbows on knees, blowing smoke rings at the tile floor. He stood up and stepped on his cigarette when Patsy came through the door. Patsy shook his hand and said, 'I brought our friend.' Then Martin too shook Morrie's hand, enriching with a quantum leap his comprehension of duplicity.

'They just said a heavy no to the twenty,' Morrie told Patsy. 'I got the message just before I came up here.'

'What else did they say?'

'They think you're trying to chisel them. They called you a muzzler and said they want at least seventy-five.'

'I got everything here the family can scrape together,' Patsy said, tapping the black leatherette suitcase he carried in his left hand. 'Matt just came back from New York with the last five and now there's forty here. And that's all there is, Morrie, that's all there is. I don't even have enough left for a shave. Morrie, you know we wouldn't chisel on Charlie's life. You got to make them know that.'

'I'll do my level best, Patsy.'

'I know you will, Morrie. You're one in a thousand to do this for us.'

Patsy handed Morrie the suitcase. 'Count it, make sure.'

Morrie opened the suitcase and riffled swiftly, without counting, through the wrapped tens and twenties, then closed it.

'What about their letters?'

Patsy took a white envelope from his inside pocket and handed it to Morrie.

'One more thing. How do I account for all this cash if I get stopped?'

Pat took the envelope back from Morrie and wrote on it: 'To whom it may concern. Morris Berman is carrying this money on a business errand for me. To confirm this, call me collect at one of these telephones.' And he wrote the numbers of his home and his camp in the Helderberg Mountains, and then signed it. Patrick Joseph McCall.

'Is there anything special I need to know?' Martin asked.

'Morrie will tell you everything,' Patsy said. 'Just do what needs doing.'

'They didn't like it you were a newspaperman,' Morrie said, 'but I convinced them you were okay.'

'Do we need my car?' Martin asked.

'We drive mine,' said Morrie.

'You tell them we want that boy back safe,' Patsy said.

Morrie smiled and Patsy embraced him.

'They'll know if I'm followed,' Morrie said.

'You won't be followed.'

And then the three men went out of the lake house, one behind the other. Indian file. The truculent Mohawks once walked this same patch of earth. The Mohawks were so feared that one brave could strike terror into a dozen from another tribe. When the six tribes met to talk of land on Long Island ceded to the white man in exchange for guns and wampum, the lone Mohawk delegate asked whose decision it had been to cede the land. The Long Island chief said it was his. The Mohawk then stood up from his place in the tribal circle, scalped the chief, and left the meeting, a gesture which called the validity of the land transaction into some question.

In 1921, when Martin walked through the park with his father, they talked of Martin's novel in progress. Martin had just returned from Europe, where he had written about the war. His articles had been published chiefly in the Albany press by Martin H. Glynn, and several of his longer pieces were printed in *The Atlantic* and *Scribner's* and the North American Review, which had once printed the writing of his father. Certain editors regarded Martin as a writer of notable talent and encouraged him to challenge it. Accordingly, he wrote two-thirds of a novel about reincarnation.

He traced the story of the soul of the Roman soldier who diced for Christ's cloak, and who was subsequently to live as an Alexandrian fishwife, a cooper in Constantinople, a roving gypsy queen, a French dentist, the inventor of a spring popularized by Swiss watchmakers in the late seventeenth century, a disgraced monk in Brittany, a bailiff in Chiswick, an Irish sailor in the American Fenian movement, and finally a twentieth-century Mexican trollop who marries into the high society of Watervliet.

'You have excellent language at your disposal, and a talent for the bizarre,' said the elder Daugherty, 'but the book is foolish and will be judged the work of a silly dilettante. My advice is to throw it away and refrain from writing until you have something to say. A novel, Martin, is not a book of jokes.'

As a retort, Martin told his father of a former schoolmate, Howie McMahon, who was obsessed with the fate of the oiler in Crane's open boat. Howie taught it to his students at Albany State Teachers College, wrote of it, spoke frequently of it to Martin. My struggle, Howie said, has no more meaning than the life of the oiler with his lifeless head bobbing in the surf after such a monumental struggle to survive. The oiler lived and died to reveal to me the meaning of his life: that life has no meaning. And Howie McMahon, Martin told his father, on a Sunday morning while the family was at high mass, hanged himself from a ceiling hook in the coal bin of his cellar.

'My response to the ravings of a lunatic like your friend,' said Edward Daugherty, 'is that whether he knows it or not, his life has a meaning that is instructive, if only to illuminate the impenetrability of God's will. Nothing is without purpose in this world.'

Martin plucked a crimson leaf from a maple tree and tore it into small pieces.

'That leaf,' said the elder writer, 'was created to make my point.'

17

By late afternoon on Saturday, the Albany newspaper and wire service editors decided they could no longer withhold news of the kidnapping from the world, and they told this to Patsy McCall. He said he understood but had no further comment. At seven o'clock Saturday night, sixty-three hours after Charlie had been taken, his story was told in print for the first time. Headlines seemed not to have been so fat and febrile since the Roosevelt landslide.

The nation's press sent its luminaries of the word to Albany to pursue the story: Jack Lait, Meyer Berger, James Kilgallen, and Damon Runyon among many, forcing comparisons with the 1931 killing of Legs Diamond in an Albany rooming house, the last time America had cast such a fascinated eye on the underside of Albany life.

Shortly after nine-thirty Saturday night, Billy bought one of the last of the *Times-Union* extras, an early edition of the Sunday paper, at the Union Station newsstand. The story of the kidnapping carried Martin's byline. Billy read his own name in the story. No mention was made of any intermediary having been chosen, and no member of the McCall family would speak for publication.

The confirming source for all information was the district attorney, Dick Maloney, who complained that neither he nor the police could convince the McCalls to cooperate with their investigation. Governor Herbert Lehman suggested a reward for the capture of the kidnappers but Patsy told the governor, no, this is between us and them.

Billy folded the newspaper, shoved it into his coat pocket and crossed Broadway to Becker's. The bar was busy, but he found a spot and caught Red Tom's eye. Red Tom nodded but made no move to come near him. 'A beer, Tom,' Billy finally said, and Red Tom nodded again, drew a beer, and placed it in front of Billy.

'Only one, Billy.'

'What do you mean, only one?'

Red Tom put up his hands, palms out, and said nothing. A stranger at the bar looked Billy over, and Red Tom walked away. Billy sipped his beer and waited for enlightenment. When the stranger left the bar, Red Tom came down to Billy and whispered: 'Gus don't want your business.'

'Why not?'

'I don't know. What'd you do to him?'

'Nothing. I haven't saw Gus in weeks to talk to. And I don't owe him a nickel.'

'Tell Billy Phelan we don't want his business is his exact words,' said Red Tom. 'Why not? I says to him. Because he's no good, he says. Wait a minute, I says to him, Billy is all right, he's a good friend of mine. Okay, you open up your own place and serve him. Here he don't get served, do you get my meaning? I get his meaning. I can't serve you, Billy, and I don't know why. Do you know?'

'Maybe I know,' Billy said.

'We're friends, Billy, but I got to work.'

'I know that. I don't blame you for anything.'

'If I did own the joint, nobody'd keep you out.'

Billy managed a small smile and finished his beer. 'Have you seen Martin tonight?'

'Not yet. He must be on the story.'

'I'll catch you later, Tommy.'

And Billy went out of Becker's, feeling a door close on his life when the outside door clicked behind him. He stood looking around Broadway, which was at its Saturday night brightest, bustling with the traffic of cars and people, the usual bunch thickened by the showgoers and nightclubbers.

Not wanted in Becker's? That's like a ball game with no home plate.

Billy walked down Broadway and up the stairs into the Monte Carlo. The horse room was dark but the bird cage, the crap table, and two roulette wheels were all busy, and in the back Billy saw lights on in the card room. He stepped to the crap table, where Marty Mitchell was on the stick and Bill Shea, who ran the Monte Carlo for Bindy, was watching the play. Billy didn't know the shooter, who was trying to make a six. He made it, and then threw an eleven. He doubled his bet to forty dollars and threw a seven. 'That's five passes,' somebody whispered, and Billy pulled out the exchequer, sixty-two dollars, and put twenty on the come line.

'That twenty is dead,' Bill Shea said, and the game stopped.

'What's the problem?' Billy said as the stickman nudged the twenty off the line and back toward Billy.

'No problem,' Shea said. 'Your money's no good here, Phelan.'

'Since when?'

'Since now. And you're not wanted on the premises.'

'Is this Bindy's orders?'

'I wouldn't know that. Now, be a good fellow and take your money and get out.'

Billy put the twenty around the rest of his cash and backed away from the table under the silent eyes of the players. As he went out the door, the game resumed and the stickman called: 'Seven again.' Billy walked slowly down to the street.

He found the same response in three more Broadway bars, in Louie's pool room and at Nick Levine's card game. Nick, like Red Tom, apologized. No one gave Billy a reason for turning him away. In Martha's, he sat at the bar and she poured him a double scotch and then told him he'd been marked lousy.

'It was Bindy, I know that much,' Billy said. 'When did you hear about it?'

'This afternoon,' Martha said.

'How?'

'Mulligan, the ward leader, called me. Said you might be mixed up in the kidnapping and to give you the treatment. I said, I got no argument with Billy, and he said, You don't do what I ask, your taxes go through the roof. So bottoms up, honey, and find someplace else to drink.'

'That's a lie about the kidnapping. They wanted me to inform on somebody and I wouldn't. That's what it's about.'

'Don't make no difference to me what it's about. Them taxes are what this place is about all of a sudden. They go through the roof, Martha goes back on the street, and Martha's too old for that.'

'I'm not your problem, Martha. Don't worry.'

'You hear about Louie?'

'Louie?'

'Louie Dugan. He died about two this afternoon. Cop who took him to the hospital last night came by and took a statement. I liked that crazy old man. He was mean as a goose but I liked him.'

'What'd he die of?'

'Stuff he swallowed in his lungs, the cop says. Drink up, Billy. Don't make me no trouble.'

'I'll catch you later, Martha.'

'Not till things is straight. Then you catch me all you like.'

Billy called Angie at the Kenmore, and while he waited for her room to ring he decided to ask her: How'd you like some fingerprints on your buns? But what he really wanted was to talk to her. Her phone never rang. The operator said she'd checked out and left no message. He went up to the Kenmore anyway and found the bar was out of bounds for him. Wally Stanton, a bartender, said the word came from Poop Powell, not Mulligan. Bindy had a whole team on the street fencing Billy out. Broadway gone, now Pearl Street.

He walked up Pearl toward Clinton Avenue and stopped in front of Moe Cohen's old jewelry store. Now the store was a meat market and Moe was meat, too; hired three punks to get himself killed, gave them five grand in diamonds and two hundred in promised cash. They shot him in the head and all it give him was a headache, and he says, Do something else, I'm dying of cancer and heart trouble, hurry, and they let him have it in the wrist and then in the shoulder and hit him with seven shots before they got one through the eye to do the trick. When they checked his pants for the two hundred, all they found was twenty-eight cents. The bum robbed us. They all went to jail, but nobody could figure out why Moe wanted to die. He didn't have cancer or heart trouble, he had something else.

My father has something else, is what Billy thought.

He thought of Moe among the sausages and turned around and headed toward South Pearl Street. Clinton Avenue would be fenced off by Bindy, too, but he probably wouldn't bother with State Street or South Pearl. That wasn't Billy's territory. Billy might even get a game on Green Street. Dealers didn't know him very well there. But the Cronins ran Green Street for Bindy and they knew Billy and they'd get the word around sooner or later. It'd be a game of recognition. Anybody know Billy Phelan? Throw the bum out. What it came down to was Billy could go anyplace they didn't recognize him, anyplace he'd never been before. Or he could leave town. Or hire some of those fellows like Moe. Or go off the Hawk Street viaduct like Georgie the Syph.

No.

All his life Billy had put himself into trouble just to get himself out of it. Independent Billy. Now, you dumb bastard, you're so independent you can't even get inside to get warm, and it's getting chilly. Night air, like watching the last games of the Albany baseball season. Up high in Hawkins Stadium and the wind starts to whizz a little and you came in early when it was warm and now you're freezing your ass only the game ain't over.

Tommy Dyke's Club Petite? No. Bob Parr's Klub Eagle? No. Packy Delaney's Parody Club? No. Big Charlie's? No. Ames O'Brien's place? No.

Billy didn't want to think about his problem in solitude. He wanted to watch something while he was thinking.

The University Club? Dopey B-girls. Club Frolics? The emcee stinks.

Hey. The Tally Ho on Hudson Avenue. Billy knew the Hawaiian dancer. She was Jewish. And the comic was Moonlight Brady. Billy went to St Joseph's school with him. He turned off Pearl toward the Tally Ho.

Billy ordered a triple scotch and kept his hat on. The place was jammed, no elbowroom at the bar. The lights were dim while the adagio dancers did their stuff. When the lights went up Billy looked at the half-naked-lady mural among the champagne glasses and bubbles on the wall. Some singer did a medley of Irish songs, for what? It ain't Saint Patrick's Day. The shamrocks are growing on Broadway. Oh yeah. And the Hudson looks like the Shannon. Right. Betty Rubin, the Hawaiian dancer, had fattened up since Billy last saw her and since Billy likes 'em thin, he'll keep his distance and check out the toe dancer.

Billy had been chain smoking for an hour and the tip of his tongue was complaining. He wanted to punish himself for his independence. He could punish himself by going to Bindy and apologizing. Yes, you may kiss my foot. He'd already punished himself by throwing the pool match to the Doc.

Moonlight Brady came on and told a joke about Kelly, who got drunk and fell into an open grave and when he woke up he thought it was Judgment Day and that an Irishman was the first man up. He sang a song: Don't throw a brick at your father, you may live to regret it one day.

Billy's brain was speeding from the scotch, speeding and going sideways. Moonlight came out to the bar when the show ended, a chunky man with a face like a meat pie. All ears and no nose so's you'd notice and built like a fire plug. Billy bought him a drink to have someone to talk to. He would not apologize to Bindy, he decided, but what else he would do was not clear.

'I saw your story in the paper,' Moonlight told him.

'What story?'

And Moonlight told him about Martin's column on the two-ninety-nine game and the hex. Billy took the paper out of his pocket and found the column and tried to read it but the light was bad.

'I bowled two-ninety-nine and two-ninety-seven back to back about six years ago,' Moonlight said.

'Is that so?'

'Damndest thing. I was in Baltimore and just got red hot.'

Billy smiled and bought Moonlight another drink. He was the greatest liar Billy ever knew. You wouldn't trust him if he just came out of Purgatory. He dove into Lake George one day and found two corpses. He put a rope around his chest and swam across Crooked Lake pulling three girls in a row-boat. He was sitting at a table with Texas Guinan and Billy Rose the night Rose wrote the words to 'Happy Days and Lonely Nights.' He gave Bix Beiderbecke's old trumpet to Clara Bow, and she was such a Bix fan she went to the men's room with Moonlight and he screwed her on the sink. He pimped once for John Barrymore in Miami and got him two broads and a dog. He took care of a stable of polo ponies for Big Bill Dwyer, the rum-runner. Billy's line on Moonlight was that some guys can't even lay in bed straight.

Morrie Berman was probably one of those guys. What if he was in on the kidnap? They took Charlie Boy's world away from him and maybe they'll even kill him. When Billy's father was gone for a year, his Uncle Chick told him he might never come back and that Billy would pretty soon forget his father and develop all sorts of substitutes, because that was how it went in life. Chick was trying to be kind to Billy with that advice. Chick wasn't as bad as the rest of them. And did Billy develop substitutes for his father? Well, he learned how to gamble. He got to know Broadway.

He wanted to see his father and ask him again to come home.

If there was a burlesque show in town he'd go to it.

He watched Betty Rubin, who was beginning to look good.

Billy hated the sons of bitches who closed the town to him, including Red Tom, you prick. Why don't you yell at them that it ain't right to do such a thing?

He would not test out any more places. He would do something else.

Tough as Clancy's nuts.

And to think, Billy, that you were afraid they'd mark you lousy if you finked.

'Oh yeah, I forgot,' Moonlight Brady said. 'I saw your father's name in the paper. That vote business. Funny as a ham sandwich on raisin bread.'

'That's in the paper, too?'

'Same paper. They mentioned how he played ball so I knew it was him.'

'Where's your father now, Moonlight?'

'He died ten years ago. Left me a quarter of a million he made on the stock market, every nickel he had, and I went through it in eighteen months. But it was a hell of an eighteen months. What a guy he was.'

Billy laughed at that. It was one of Moonlight's wilder, more unbelievable lies, but it had what it takes, and Billy's laughter grew and grew. It took on storm proportions. He coughed and tears came to his eyes. He hit the bar with his hand to emphasize the power of the mirth that was on him, and he took out his handkerchief to wipe his eyes.

'What got him?' the barman asked.

'I did,' Moonlight said, 'but I don't know how.' Moonlight was doing his best to keep smiling. 'If the line is that funny, I oughta use it in the act,' he said to Billy.

'Oh absolutely, Moonlight, absolutely,' Billy said. 'Use that one in the act. You gotta use that one in the act.'

Billy walked down Green Street and looked at the whorehouses with their awnings, the sign. They were houses that used to be homes for Irish families like his own. Chinks on the street now, and second-hand clothing stores and the grocery where George used to write numbers upstairs. Bucket-of-blood joints and guinea pool rooms where the garlic smell makes you miscue. Bill Shea lives on Green Street, the son of a bitch. Billy brought him home one night in a cab, sick drunk from Becker's, and he forgets that and says my twenty is dead.

Billy walked into a telephone pole.

Really in the guinea section now. Billy went with a guinea for two years. Teresa. Terrific Teresa. A torch singer. 'Along

Came Bill,' she'd sing when he showed up. She wanted to get married, too.

Angie, you bitch, where are you when I need you?

Would Billy marry Angie? 'Frivolous Sal.' Peculiar gal.

Angie got Billy thinking about marriage, all right, and now he thinks of Peg and George and the house they've got, and Danny. They can't fence you out of your own house. They can't fence you away from your kid.

His father fenced himself out of the house because he thought they were ready to fence *him* out.

Billy can hear a mandolin being played in a second-floor apartment and he can taste the dago red. He got drunk once on dago red with Red the Barber, dago red and mandolins, and he went out like a light and woke up the next day and lit a cigarette and was drunk all over again. So he don't drink dago red no more.

After he crossed Madison Avenue, the bum traffic picked up. He turned on Bleecker Street toward Spanish George's. It was moving toward eleven o'clock. Hello, Bill.

The stench of Spanish George's hit Billy in the face when he walked through the door, the door's glass panel covered with grating on both sides. A dozen bums and a woman were huddled around five round wooden tables, three of the bums asleep, or dead. The stench of their breath, their filth, their shitty drawers, the old puke on their coats and shirtfronts, rose up into Billy's nose like sewer gas.

George was behind the bar in his sombrero, propped against the wall on the back legs of a wooden chair. Billy ordered a scotch, and George delivered it in a shot glass. Billy tossed it off and asked for another.

'You know anybody named Francis Phelan?' he asked George.

George eyed him and touched the handle of his six gun.

'You ain't a copper. I know coppers. Who are you?'

'I'm a relative. The guy's my father.'

'Whoosa guy you want?'

'Francis Phelan.'

'I don't know nobody that name.'

Billy ordered another scotch and took it to the only empty table in the room. The floor beneath his feet had been chewed up long ago by old horses' hooves and wagon wheels. It looked like the faces in the room, old men with splintered skin. The wagons of the old days had rolled over them, too, many times. Most of them seemed beyond middle age, though one with a trimmed mustache looked in his thirties. Yet he was a bum, no matter what he did to his mustache. His eyes were bummy and so were his clothes. He was at the table next to Billy and he stank of old sweat, like Billy's locker at the K. of C. gym. Billy was in the Waldorf one night, and an old drunk was raving on about his life. Not a bum, just an old man on a drunk, and he looked clean. He got Billy's eye and told him, Son, have B.O. and they'll never forget you.

Unforgettable stench of right now. They oughta bottle the air in this joint and sell it for stink bombs.

The man with the mustache saw Billy looking at him.

'You fuck around with me,' the man said, 'I'll cut your head off.' The man could barely lift his glass. Billy laughed out loud and other men took notice of him. He could lick any four of them at once. But if they got him down, they'd all kick him to death. Billy saw that the men had no interest in him beyond the noise he made when he laughed.

The woman at the far table was drinking beer and sitting upright and seemed the soberest one in the room, soberer than Billy. Old bat. Fat gut and spindle legs, but her face wasn't so bad. She wore a beret off to the left and smoked a cigarette and stared out the front window, which was also covered with grating. Bums like to put their hands through windows. And their heads.

The man next to the woman lay with his face on the table. He moved an arm, and Billy noticed the coat and remembered the twill. Billy went across the room and stood beside the woman and stared down at his father. The old man's mouth was open and his lips were pushed to one side so that Billy could see part way into the black cavity that had once been the smile of smiles.

'I don't want any,' the woman said.

'What?'

'Whatever it is you're gonna ask.'

'Conalee Street.'

'I don't want any.'

'Neither do I.'

'Go way and leave me alone. I don't want any.'

'Is he all right?'

'Go way.'

'Is he all right? I asked a polite question.'

'He's all right if he ain't dead.'

Billy grabbed a handful of her blouse and coat just below the neck and lifted her halfway to her feet.

'Holy Mother of God, you're as crazy as two bastards.'

'Is he hurt?'

'No, he's passed out, and he'll probably be out for hours.'

'How do you know that?'

'Because he drank whiskey. He had money and he drank whiskey till he fell over. He never drinks whiskey. Who the hell are you?'

'I'm a relative. Who are you?'

'I'm his wife.'

'His wife?'

'You got very good hearing.'

'His wife?'

'For nine years.'

Billy let go of her coat and slumped into an empty chair beside her.

When he told his mother he'd met him he made sure Peg was in the room. They sat in the breakfast nook, just the three of them, George still working. Billy was looking out at the dog in the back yard, and he told them all that had happened and how he wouldn't come home. The response of the women bewildered Billy. His mother smiled and nodded her head. Peg's mouth was tight, the way it gets when she fights. They listened to it all. He didn't say anything about Gerald just then. Just the bail and the turkey and the money he had and the way he looked and the change Billy saw from the photograph. I'm goddamn glad you didn't bring him home, Peg said. I don't ever want to see him again. Let him stay where he is and rot for all of me. And Ma said, No, the poor man, the poor, poor man, what an awful life he's had. Think of what a life he could've had here with us and how awful it must've been for him as a tramp. But neither of them said they were sorry he didn't come home. They think of him like he was some bum down the block.

So Billy told them then about Gerald, and Peg couldn't believe it, couldn't believe Ma hadn't told us, and Ma cried because of that and because your father didn't mean it, and how he apologized to her and she accepted his apology, but she was numb then, and he took her numbness for hatred, and he went away. But she wouldn't hold an accident against a man as good as Francis was and who loved the children so and was only weak, for you can hate the weakness but not the man. Oh, we're all so weak in our own ways, and none of us want to be hated for that or killed for that. He suffered more than poor little Gerald, who never suffered at all, any more than the innocents who were slaughtered suffered the way Our Lord suffered. Your father was only a man who didn't know how to help himself and didn't know better. I kept it from you both because I didn't want you to hate him more than you did. You couldn't know how it was, because he loved Gerald the way he loved both of you, and he picked him up the way he'd picked you up a thousand times. Only this time the diaper wasn't pinned right, and that was my fault, and Gerald slipped out of it, and your father stood there with the diaper in his hand, and Gerald was already dead with a broken neck, I'm sure of that, the way his little head was. I'm sure he never suffered more than a pinprick of pain and then he went to heaven because he was baptized, and I thanked God for that in the same minute I knew he was gone. Your father knelt over him and tried to pick him up, but I said, Don't, it might be his back and we shouldn't move him, and we both knelt there looking at him and trying to see if he was breathing, and finally we both knew he wasn't, and your father fell over on the floor and cried, oh, how he cried, how that man cried. And I cried for him as well as for Gerald, because I knew he'd never get over this as long as he lived. Gerald was gone but your father would have to live with it, and so we held one another and in a minute or so I covered him with a blanket and went up the street for Doctor Lynch and told him I put him on the table to change his diaper and then he rolled off and I never knew he could move so much. He believed me and put accidental death on the record, and it surely was that, even though your father was drinking when it happened, which I know is the reason he went away. But he wasn't drunk the way he got to be in the days after that, when he never saw a sober minute. He had just come home after the car barns and a few jars at the saloon, and he wasn't no different from the way he was a thousand other nights, except what he did was different, and that made him a dead man his whole life. He's the one now that's got to forgive himself, not me, not us. I knew you'd never forgive him because you didn't understand such things and how much he loved you and Gerald and loved me in his way, and it was a funny way, I admit that, since he kept going off to play baseball. But he always came back. When he went this time I said to myself, He'll never come into this house again, and he never did, and when we moved here to North Pearl, I used to think, If he does come back he'll go to Colonie Street and never find us, but then I knew he would if he wanted to. He'd find us if he had to.

Sweet Jesus, I never thought he'd come back and haunt you both with it, and that's why I'm telling you this. Because when a good man dies, it's reason to weep, and he died that day and we wept and he went away and buried himself and he's dead now, dead and can't be resurrected. So don't hate him and don't worry him, and try to understand that not everything that happens on this earth has a reason behind it that we can find in the prayer book. Not even the priests have answers for things like this. It's a mystery we can't solve any more than we can solve the meaning of the stars. Let the man be, for the love of the sweet infant Jesus, let the man be.

* * *

Billy stared at the woman next to him and smiled.

'What's your name?'

'Helen.'

'Do you have any money, Helen?'

'There's a few dollars left of what he had. We'll get a room with that when he wakes up.'

Billy took out his money, fifty-seven dollars, and pressed it into Helen's hand.

'Now you can get a room, or get as drunk as he is if you like. Tell him Billy was here to say hello.'

Billy tossed the newspaper on the table.

'And tell him he can read all about me and him both in the paper. This paper.'

'Who are you?'

'I told you. I'm Billy.'

'Billy. You're the boy.'

'Boy, my ass. I'm a goddamn man-eating tiger.'

He stood up and patted Helen on the beret.

'Good night, Helen,' he said. 'Have a good time.'

'God bless your generosity.'

'Generosity can go piss up a rainpipe,' Billy said, and he started to laugh. The laugh storm again. The coughing, the tears of mirth. He moved toward Spanish George's door, laughing and telling the old bums who watched him: 'Generosity can go piss up two rainpipes for all I give a good goddamn.'

He halted in the doorway.

'Anybody here like to disagree with me?'

'You fuck with me,' said the bum with the trimmed mustache, 'I'll cut your head off.'

'Now you're talkin',' Billy said. 'Now you're talkin'.'

18

Billy could go anywhere now, anywhere in town. He was broke. All the way broke.

He began to run, loping across a vacant lot, where a man was warming himself by a bonfire. It had grown chillier. No place for that fellow to go.

Billy could always get a buck. But where now?

He padded down Madison Avenue to Broadway, where the ramp to the Dunn bridge began. Tommy Kane's garage, where George got his car fixed. He turned up Broadway, still running, putting distance between him and the drunken dead. He wasn't even winded when he reached the Plaza and the D&H building. But he stopped running at Coulson's and went inside for a later edition of the *Times-Union*. The front page was different, but the kidnapping news was the same. He turned to Martin's column and read about himself. A gamester who accepts the rules and plays by them, but who also plays above them. Billy doesn't care about money. A healthy man without need for artifice or mysticism.

What the hell was Martin talking about? Whose rules? And what the hell was that about money? How can anybody not care about money? Who gets along without it? Martin is half crazy, a spooky bird. What is that stuff about mysticism? I still believe in God. I still go to the front.

He folded the paper and went out and crossed State Street and walked north on Broadway past Van Heusen Charles, which always reminded him of the goddamn house on Colonie Street, where they bought their junk. And Cottrell and Leonard and the mannequins in the window. Two bums broke that window one night, drunked up on zodiac juice, everybody's bar dregs, beer, whiskey, wine, that old Lumberg kept in a can and then bottled and sold to the John bums for six bucks a gallon. When the cops caught up with the bums, one of them was dead and the other was screwing the mannequin through a hole cut in its crotch.

Jimmy-Joe's shoeshine stand. Jimmy-Joe told his customers he shined Al Smith's shoes once, and Jack Dempsey's. Everybody's a sucker for big names. Bindy McCall. I kissed Bindy McCall's foot. Suckers.

Broadway was slowing down at one o'clock, all the trains in except the Montreal Limited. Traffic down to nothing, shows all let out. Bill's Magic Shop in darkness. Billy was sweating slightly and breathing heavily. Get the blood pounding and sober up. But he was still drunk as a stewbum, and reeling. Scuse me.

'Where the hell you walkin'?' said Mike the Wop coming out of Brockley's.

'Hey, Mike.'

'That you, Billy?'

'Me.'

'Whataya know. You got yourself in trouble, I hear.'

'What do you hear?'

'That you got yourself in trouble and nobody'll take your action.'

'They'll get over it.'

'Didn't sound that way.'

'Hey, Mike, you got a double sawbuck? I need coffee money and cab fare.'

'Double sawbuck?'

'Don'tcha think I'm good for it?'

'You're a bad risk all of a sudden, Billy. You ain't got a connection. You can't even get a drink on this street.'

Mike pulled out his roll and crumpled a twenty and tossed it up in the air at Billy. Billy bobbled it and the bill fell to the sidewalk. He picked it up and said nothing. Mike grunted and walked up

Broadway and into Becker's. Billy walked toward Clinton Avenue, considering a western at the Grand Lunch. Martha's across the street. Martha's door opened, and Slopie Dodds came out wearing his leg. He saw Billy and crossed the street.

'Hey, man, how you makin' it?'

'I'm coastin', Slope.'

'You got a little grief, I hear.'

'Little bit.'

'How you fixed? You need anything?'

'I need a drink.'

'She don't want you over there.'

'I know all about that. That ain't the only place in town.'

'You ain't mixed up in that snatch, Billy. That ain't true.'

'It's bullshit, Slope.'

'I knew it was.'

'Hey, man. You got a double sawbuck?'

'Sure, I got it. I got fifty if you need it.'

'All right, twenty-five. That'll cover me.' And Slopie counted it out for Billy.

'Where's your bootlegger?' Billy asked.

'Spencer Street. You want a whole bottle?'

'Yeah. Let me make a visit first and we'll go up.'

'Fine with me. I'm done playin'.'

They walked back toward the station and Billy went into Becker's. The bar was crowded and Red Tom looked at Billy and shook his head sadly. Oh, Billy. But Billy asked for nothing. He saw Mike the Wop at the bar and went to him. He threw the twenty, still crumpled up, onto the bar in front of Mike and said, 'We're even.'

'You pay your debts fast,' Mike said.

'I pay guys like you fast,' Billy said, and he went out. Then with Slopie he walked up to Spencer Street.

The last time Billy needed action from a bootlegger was in Prohibition. And he'd never used a nigger bootlegger before. George had been a bootlegger for about three weeks. Made rye in the kitchen in a wash tub, and Billy peddled it for eight bucks a quart and kept four. Then George got the job writing nigger numbers and gave up the hooch, and a good thing, too, because his rye was moose piss.

The bootlegger was in one of the last houses, a dim light in a first-floor flat. Quarts and pints for five and three, a good price at this hour. The bootlegger was a woolly-headed grandpa, half asleep. Probably made a fortune before it went legal, and now the bottles catch dust. He went to the kitchen to get Billy some Johnnie Walker. Billy opened the bottle and drank and passed it to Slopie.

'Take it outside,' the old man said. 'This ain't no saloon.'

Billy and Slopie went down the stoop and stood on the sidewalk.

'Where you wanna go, Billy?'

'Go someplace and build a fire.'

'A fire? You crazy?'

'Gettin' chilly. Need a little heat.'

'Go over to my place if you like to warm up. I got some chairs. What the hell you want a fire for?'

'I wanna stay outside. You up for that?'

'Well, I give you a little while. Till my bones freeze over.'

'It ain't that cold. Have a drink,' and Billy upended the bottle.

'You in a big hurry to fall down tonight, Billy.'

'I got a hollow leg, Slope.'

'You gonna need it.'

Slopie took a swallow and they walked toward the river, crossed the D&H tracks, and headed toward the station on a dirt path under the brightest moon Billy ever looked at. Billy picked up wood as they walked, but a bit of kindling was all he found. They walked past the sidings where Ringling Brothers unloaded every year. Billy had brought Danny down here at four in the morning two years ago and they'd seen an elephant get off the train and walk up to Broadway.

'I'm a little cold, Billy. I ain't sure I'm ready for this.'

'Down by the river. There'll be some wood there.'

They walked toward the bridge, toward Quay Street, and looked at the Hudson. Just like the Shannon. Billy never swam down this far but he skated on it sometimes when it wasn't all buckled, or snowed over.

'Ever skate on the river, Slope?'

'Never owned no skates.'

On the riverbank, Billy found a crate somebody had dumped. He broke it up and made a pile on the flat edge of the bank. He wadded up the *Times-Union*, page by page, and stuck it between the boards. In the moonlight he saw the page with Martin's column and crumpled it. But then he uncrumpled it, folded it and put it in his inside coat pocket. He lit the papers, and then he and Slopie sat down on the flat sides of the crate and watched the fire compensate for the shortcomings of the moon.

'I hear Daddy Big kicked it,' Billy said.

'What I hear.'

'What a way to go.'

'You did what you could, Billy. He'da been dead in the gutter on Broadway, wasn't for you.'

'I didn't even like the son of a bitch.'

'He was a sorry man. Never knew how to do nothin' he wanted to do. He spit in your eye and think he's doin' you a favor.'

'He knew how to shoot pool.'

'Shootin' pool ain't how you get where you're goin'.'

'Goin'? Where you goin', Slope?'

'Goin' home outa here pretty quick and get some winks, wake up and cook a little, see my woman, play a little piano.'

'That where you started out for?'

'I never started out for nowhere. Just grifted and drifted all my life till I hit this town. Good old town.'

'How is it, bein' a nigger, Slope?'

'I kinda like it.'

'Goddamn good thing.'

'What, bein' a nigger?'

'No, that you like it.'

Billy passed the bottle and they drank and kept the fire going until a prowl car came by and put its searchlight on them.

'Everything all right here, girls?' one cop asked.

'Who you talkin' to, peckerhead?' Billy said. Slopie grabbed his arm and kept him from standing up. The cops studied the scene and then moved on. The fire and the moon lighted up the night, and Billy took another drink.

He woke up sick. Slopie was gone and Billy remembered him trying to talk Billy into going back to Broadway. But Billy just burned the rest of the crate to keep the fire going. He remembered watching the fire grow and then fade, remembered watching the night settle in again without heat, with even the light gone cold. The darkness enveloped him under the frigid moon, and he lay back on the grass and watched the sky and all them goddamn stars. The knowledge of what was valuable in his life eluded him, except that he valued Slopie now as much as he valued his mother, or Toddy. But Slopie was gone and Billy felt wholly alone for the first time in his life, aware that nothing and no one would save him from the coldness of the moon and the October river.

He heard whisperings on the water and thought they might be the spirits of all the poor bastards who had jumped off the bridge, calling to him to make the leap. He became afraid and listened for the voices to say something he could understand, but they remained only whisperings of words no man could understand at such a distance. They could be understood out on the water. He edged himself upward on the bank, away from the voices, and took a drink of whiskey. He was still drunk and he had a headache. He was out of focus in the world and yet he was more coherent than he had been since this whole business began. He knew precisely how it was before the kidnapping and how it was different now, and he didn't give a shit. You think Billy Phelan gives a shit about asskissers and phonies? Maybe they wanted Billy to run. Maybe they thought if he got shut out of a joint like Becker's, he'd pack his bag and hop a freight. But his old man did that, and all he got was drunk.

The fire was out, and so Billy must have slept a while. He felt an ember. Cold. Maybe he'd slept an hour.

What I learned about pool no longer applies.

What Daddy Big learned no longer applies.

He took a swig of the whiskey, looked at the bottle, still half full, and then flung it into the river.

He saw a train coming in over the Maiden Lane trestle and watched the moving lights. He stood up and saw mail trucks moving in the lights of the post office dock on Dean Street. Up on the hill, he could see lights in the Al Smith building, and street lights blazed across the river in Rensselaer. People all over town were alone in bed. So what the hell's the big deal about being alone in the dark? What's the big deal about being alone?

Billy saw the elephant going up toward Broadway, a man walking beside it, holding its ear with a long metal hook on a stick.

Billy brushed off the seat of his pants, which was damp from the earth. He went to touch the brim of his hat but he had no hat. He looked around but his hat was gone. The goddamn river spirits got it. What do they want with my hat? Well, keep it. That's all you're gonna get out of me, you dead bastards.

Billy knew he was going to puke. He kept walking and after a while he puked. Good. He wiped his mouth and his eyes with his handkerchief and straightened his tie. He brushed grass off the sleeves of his coat, then took the coat off and brushed its back and put it on again. He bent over and pulled up his silk socks.

He walked toward Broadway.

No money.

No hat.

No connection.

The street was bright and all but empty, a few lights, a few cars, two trainmen waiting for a bus in front of the station, carrying lunch pails.

The street was closed, not only to Billy.

Billy knew he'd lost something he didn't quite understand, but the onset of mystery thrilled him, just as it had when he threw the match to the Doc. It was the wonderment at how it would all turn out.

Something new going on here.

A different Broadway.

He walked into the station and went to the men's room. He washed his face and hands and combed his hair. The tie was fine. He inspected his suit, his tan glen plaid, for grass and dirt, and he shined the toes of his shoes with toilet paper. He pissed, shat, and spit and went out and bought the New York *News* and *Mirror* with his last half a buck. Forty cents left in the world. He looked at the papers and saw Charlie Boy's picture on page one of each. The news of the day is Charlie McCall. A nice kid, raised like a hothouse flower. He folded the papers and put them in his coat pocket. In the morning, he'd read Winchell and Sullivan and Dan Parker and Nick Kenny and Moon Mullins.

He would have an orange for breakfast to make his mouth feel good.

He went out of the station and climbed into a parked Yellow cab. He rode it to North Albany, to Jack Foy's Blackout on Erie Street and Broadway, and told the cabbie to wait. Jack hadn't heard the news about Billy yet and so Billy hit him for a deuce and paid the cabbie and then hoisted two cold beers to cool his throat. He knew Jack Foy all his life and liked him. When the word came down from Pop O'Rourke, Jack would not let him inside the joint.

Erie Street'd be as dead as Broadway downtown.

The word would spread and every joint in town would be dead.

Billy drank up and walked across Broadway and up through Sacred Heart Park to North Pearl Street, which was deserted, silent at four in the morning. He walked up Pearl, Joe Keefe sleeping, Pop O'Rourke sleeping, Henny Hart sleeping, Babe McClay sleeping.

He was in front of his house when he heard what he heard. First came the quiet snap, then almost simultaneously the streetlight exploded behind him like a cherry bomb, and he ran like a goddamn antelope for the porch.

He crouched behind the solid railing of the porch and listened for new shooting, but the street was already reenveloped by silence. Still crouching, he leaped for the door to the vestibule and, with key at the ready, he opened the inside door and crawled into the living room. He locked the door and peered over the radio, out a front window, then out a dining room and a kitchen window, without moving any curtains, but he saw nothing. He heard movement upstairs and went toward it.

The door to the attic stairway was ajar.

Peg was in bed, but no George. Danny was in bed.

Billy went back to the attic door and climbed the stairs. The upper door to the attic was also ajar. He opened it all the way.

'Hello,' he said. Who the hell to?

He smelled dust and old cloth and mothballs. He waited for noise but heard nothing. He went in and pulled the string of the ceiling light and stood in the midst of family clutter that belonged mostly to a child. Boxing gloves and bag, fire engine and steam locomotive, a stack of games, toy animals, skis, two sleds, a collection of matchcovers, a large pile of funny books, a smaller pile of pulps – *Doc Savage*, *The Shadow*, *The Spider*. On a rack in transparent bags hung George's World War uniform, his satin-lapeled tux, a dozen old suits, and, unbagged, a blue woolen bathrobe full of moth holes. Peg's old windup Victrola sat alongside a dusty stack of records, half of which Billy had bought her, or boosted. There was the fake Christmas tree wrapped in a sheet, and the ornament boxes, and a dozen of Peg's hatboxes.

The front window was open. Two inches.

Under it Billy found a flashlight and a copy of *The Spider Strikes*, a pulp Billy remembered buying five years ago, anyway. Richard Wentworth, the polo-playing playboy, is secretly The Spider, avenger of wrong. More than just the law, more dangerous than the underworld. Hated, wanted, feared by both. Alone and desperate, he wages deadly one-man war against the supercriminal whose long-planned crime coup will snuff a thousand lives! Can The Spider prevent this slaughter of innocents?

When he put the magazine back on the floor, Billy found an empty BB package.

He put the light out and went downstairs and met Peg coming out of her bedroom, pushing her arm into her bathrobe.

'What's going on? I heard walking upstairs.'

'Is that all you heard?'

'What is it?'

'Somebody shot out the street light out in front.'

'Shot it out?'

Billy showed her the BB package.

'The Spider carries the most powerful air pistol there is.'

'Oh,' she said.

They went into the room of Daniel Quinn, and Billy snapped on the wall switch, lighting two yellow bulbs in the ceiling fixture. The boy pulled the covers off his face and looked at them. Billy held up the BB package.

'Did you shoot out the streetlight?' Peg asked.

The boy nodded.

'Why?'

'I wanted it dark so when Billy came home the police wouldn't see him. I didn't know it was you, Billy. I thought you'd have your hat on.'

'The police were here tonight,' Peg said. 'He was very impressed.'

'What'd they want?'

'I don't know. They didn't come in. They just stopped out front and shone their searchlight in the front window. We had all the lights out, because George got a call they were coming to see him.'

'Him? What the hell they want with him?'

'Nobody knows.'

'Were they looking for me, too?'

'Only George, from what we heard. But they never came in.'

'Where is George?'

'He went out for a while.' She turned her head away from her son and winked at Billy.

Billy went to Danny's bedside and poked a finger in his ear.

'Thanks for the protection, kid, but you scared the bejesus out of me. I thought I was bushwhacked.'

Daniel Quinn reciprocated the remark with a smile.

'You got a hell of an aim with that pistol. That's gotta be twenty-five yards, anyway.'

'I had to hit it thirty-two times before it busted.'

'An eye like that, you'll make a hell of a dart shooter.'

Daniel Quinn reciprocated that remark with another smile.

Billy went to bed after he poured himself a glass of milk. Peg told him George had gone to Troy to stay at the Hendrick Hudson Hotel under the name of Martin Dwyer and would stay there until someone called him and said it was all right to come home. Billy pulled up the covers and thought of taking a trip to Miami or New York, if this was how it was going to be. But where would the money come from? Clean out the kid's bank account? He's been saving since he was in first grade. Probably got fifty by this time. Hock George's golf clubs for train fare?

Billy had a vision of wheat pouring into a grain elevator.

He saw Angie in bed with his twins.

When Billy was a kid he had no attic, no pile of toys, no books. He didn't want books. Billy played on the street. But now Billy has a trunk in this attic with his old spikes and glove in it, and old shirts, and pictures Teresa took of him in his bathing suit out at Crystal Lake. What the hell, it's his attic.

The kid was protecting himself and his mother. George was gone and Billy wasn't home. The kid must've felt he was alone.

Billy thought of the carton of tuna fish Toddy won at a church raffle and how he took a taxi and left the tuna on Billy's stoop because Toddy never ate fish.

Billy thought of all the times he'd been suckered. In high school, it was a blonde who said she would and then didn't after it took him two days to find somebody who'd sell him cundrums. Plenty of bums stiffed him on horse bets, but then Pope McNally, a friend of Billy's all his life, welshed on a fifty-dollar phone bet and said he'd never made it. And that whole Colonie Street bunch. Presents at Christmas and your birthday, and in between you couldn't get a glass of water out of any of them. You think you know how it is with some people, but you don't know. Billy thought he knew Broadway.

He listened to the night and heard a gassy bird waking up. The light of Sunday morning was just entering the sky, turning his window from black to dark blue at the bottom. The house was silent and his brain was entering a moment of superficial peace. He began to dream of tall buildings and thousands of dice and Kayo and Moon Mullins and their Uncle Willie all up in a palm tree, a scene which had great significance for the exhausted man, a significance which, as he reached for it, faded into the region where answers never come easy.

And then Billy slept.

19

Free the children. The phrase commanded the attention of Martin's head the way a war slogan might. Stop the fascists.

Charlie McCall was the child uppermost in his thought, but he kept receiving images of Peter as a priest in a long, black cassock, blessing the world. He'd be good at that. Free Peter. Let him bless anybody he wants to bless.

It was three o'clock Monday morning and Martin was sitting alone in Morrie's DeSoto in an empty lot on Hudson Street in Greenwich Village, Patsy's loaded pistol in his right coat pocket. Hudson Street was deserted, and in the forty minutes he'd been sitting here, only two cars had passed.

This was the finale. Perhaps.

With Morrie, he'd left Albany and driven to Red Hook and then onto the Taconic Parkway. They stopped at the second gas station on the parkway and waited half an hour by the pay phone for a call. The caller told them to go to the Harding Hotel on 54th and Broadway in Manhattan, check in, and wait for another call. They did. They listened to 'The Shadow' on the radio, and dance music by Richard Himber and the orchestra, and ordered coffee and sandwiches sent up. They played blackjack for a nickel and Martin won four dollars. Jimmie Fiddler was bringing them news of Hollywood when the phone rang and Morrie was given a circuitous route to deliver the money. Change cabs here and then there, take a bus, take two more cabs, get out at this place and wait to be picked up. Morrie was gone two hours and came back with the money.

'They threw it at me,' he said. 'They looked at it once and saw right away it was marked.'

Martin called Patsy, who took two hours to call back. Go to a Wall Street bank on Sunday morning and the manager will give you new, unmarked money. Martin and Morrie slept and in the morning went together to the bank. They were watched, they later learned, by New York detectives, and also by the kidnappers, whose car Morrie recognized. With the new money, Morrie set off again on a new route given in another call. He was back at noon and said they took the money and would call with directions on where to get Charlie.

Martin and Morrie ate in the room and slept some more and exhausted all card games and the radio. Martin ordered a bottle of sherry, which Morrie would not drink. Martin sipped it and grew inquisitive.

'Why did they pick you, Morrie?'

'They know my rep.'

'You know them?'

'Never saw any of them before.'

'What's your rep?'

'I hung around with guys like them a few years back, tough guys who died with their shoes on. And I did a little time for impersonating a Federal officer during Prohibition. I even fooled Jack Diamond with that one. Our boys had the truck half loaded with his booze when he caught on.'

'What'd he do?'

'He congratulated me, with a pistol in his hand. I knew him later and he bought me a drink.'

'Were you a street kid?'

'Yeah. My old man wanted me to study politics, but I always knew politics was for chumps.'

'The McCalls do all right with it.'

'What they do ain't politics.'

'What would you call it?'

'They got a goddamn Roman empire. They own all the people, they own the churches, they even own most of the Jews in town.'

'They don't own your father.'

'No. What'd he tell you when you talked to him?'

'I already gave you that rundown. He said you two didn't get along, but he gets along with your sisters.'

'When my mother died, they worked like slaves around the house for him. But he was never there when I was a kid. He worked two jobs and went to college nights. I had to find a way to amuse myself.'

'You believe in luck, Morrie?'

'You ever know a gambler who didn't?'

'How's your luck?'

'It's runnin'.'

'How's Charlie's luck?'

'He's all right.'

'You saw him?'

'They told me.'

'And you believe them?'

'Those fellas wouldn't lie.'

To free the children it is necessary to rupture the conspiracy against them. We are all in conspiracy against the children. Fathers, mothers, teachers, priests, bankers, politicians, gods, and prophets. For Abraham of the upraised knife, prototypical fascist father, Isaac was only a means to an enhanced status as a believer. Go fuck yourself with your knife, Abe.

When Martin was eight, he watched his mother watching Brother William chastising fourth graders with a ruler. She watched it for two days from the back parlor and then opened her window and yelled into the open window of the Brothers School: If you strike any more of those children, I'm coming in after you. Brother William closed the window of his classroom and resumed his whipping.

She went out the front door and Martin followed her. She went down the stoop empty-handed and up the stoop of the school and down the corridor into the classroom opposite the Daugherty back parlor. She went directly to the Brother, yanked the ruler out of his hand, and hit him on his bald head with it. She slapped him on the ear with her left hand and slapped his right shoulder and arm with the ruler. He backed away from her, but she pursued him, and he ran. She ran after him and caught him at a door and hit him again on his bald head and drew blood. Brother William opened the chapel door and ran across the altar and escaped. Katrina Daugherty went back to the classroom and told the boys: Go home and tell your parents what happened here. The student who was being whipped when she came in stopped to thank her. Thank you, mum, he said, and half genuflected.

The last time Martin went to Hibernian Hall for Saint Patrick's Day a woman danced for an hour with her mongoloid son, who was wearing a green derby on his enormous head. When the music stopped, the boy bayed like a hound.

The call about Charlie came at midnight. Go to Hudson Street near the meat market with your friend and park in the empty lot. Your friend stays in the car. You walk to Fourteenth Street and Sixth Avenue and get a cab and go such and such a route. You should be back in maybe an hour with the property.

Martin felt the need to walk. He got out of Morrie's car and crossed the empty lot. He looked across the street at a car and saw its back window being lowered. Resting on the window as it rolled downward were the double barrels of a shotgun. Martin felt the useless weight of Patsy's pistol in his pocket, and he walked back to the DeSoto.

At four-fifteen a taxi pulled up to the lot and stopped. When two men got out, the shotgun car screeched off in the direction of the Battery. Martin opened the back door of the DeSoto and helped Charlie Boy to climb in and sit down. Martin snapped on the interior light and saw Charlie's face was covered with insect bites. The perimeter of his mouth was dotted with a rash where adhesive tape had been. He reeked of whiskey, which Morrie said the kidnappers used to revive him from the stupor into which he had sunk.

'Are you hurt anyplace?' Martin asked him. 'This is Martin Daugherty, Charlie. Are you hurt?'

'Martin. No. They treated me all right.'

'He's hungry,' Morrie said. 'He wants a corned beef sandwich. He said he's been thinking about a corned beef sandwich for three days.'

'Is my father with you, Martin?'

'He's in Albany waiting for you. Your mother, too. And Patsy. Your whole family.'

'It's good to see you fellows.'

'Charlie,' said Martin, 'the whole world's waiting for you to go home.'

'They hit me on the head and then kept me tied to a bed.'

'Is your head all right?'

'One of them put ice cubes on the bump. I want to call up home.'

'Were they tough on you?' Morrie asked.

'They fed me and one of them even went out and got me a couple of bottles of ale. But after I'd eat, they'd tie me down again. My legs don't work right.'

Martin's vision of his own life was at times hateful. Then a new fact would enter and he would see that it was not his life itself that was hateful but only his temporary vision of it. The problem rests in being freed from the omnipotence of thought, he decided. The avenue of my liberation may well lie in the overthrow of my logic. Not until Charlie Boy was kidnapped did Patsy and Bindy think of electrifying the windows of their homes. Given the benign nature of most evenings on Colonie Street, there is a logic to living with nonelectrified windows. But, of course, it is a dangerously bizarre logic.

'It's time to move,' Martin said, and he put out the car light and sat alongside Charlie Boy in the back seat. Morrie took the wheel and moved the DeSoto out of darkness onto the West Side Highway. It now seemed they were all safe and that no one would die. History would continue.

'Stop at the first place that looks like it's got a telephone,' said Martin, to whom the expedition now belonged.

We move north on the Henry Hudson Parkway.

When we free the children we also drown Narcissus in his pool.

On the day after Charlie Boy returned home, Honey Curry was shot dead in Newark during a gun battle with police, Hubert Maloy was wounded, and ten thousand dollars of ransom money, identifiable by the serial numbers of the bills as recorded by the Wall Street bank, was found in their pockets.

When Charlie Boy was returned to Patsy McCall's cabin in the Helderberg Mountains, Morrie Berman and Martin Daugherty became instant celebrities. The press tracked them everywhere, and even Damon Runyon sought out Martin to interview him on the climactic moments on Hudson Street.

'Martin Daugherty,' wrote Runyon, 'climbs out of the DeSoto with the aim of stretching his legs. But he does not get very far with his stretching before he is greeted by a double-breasted hello from a sawed-off shotgun peeking out of the window of a parked car. Being respectful of double-breasted hellos of such size and shape, Martin Daugherty goes back where he comes from and ponders the curious ways kidnappers have of taking out insurance on their investments.'

Eight hours after Charlie Boy's return, the Albany police arrested Morrie Berman at the ticket office in Union Station, just after he had purchased a ticket to Providence. He was taken to the McCall camp for interrogation, and, Martin later learned, dunked in Patsy's new swimming pool, which was partly filled for the occasion, until he revealed the kidnappers' names. Curry and Maloy were among the names he disclosed, along with the nicknames of four hoodlums from New Jersey and Rhode Island.

The Newark shootout proved not to be the result of Morrie's disclosures, for no amount of dunking could have forced him to reveal a fact he did not know. He thought Maloy and Curry had gone to Providence. Maloy, under interrogation on what he erroneously thought was his death bed, said his flight with Curry from Greenwich Village to Newark was his own decision. He was tired and did not want to drive all the way to Rhode Island at such an hour.

None of the kidnappers had been in Newark before, during, or after the kidnapping. None of them had any way of knowing that the hangouts of criminals in that city had been under the most intensive surveillance for several days.

* * *

When Martin heard of Billy's status as a pariah on Broadway, he wrote a column about it, telling the full story, including how Berman saved Billy's life in a brawl, and wondering: 'Is betrayal what Billy should have done for Berman by way of saying thank you?' He argued that Billy's information on Newark, and only Billy's information, brought Maloy and Curry to justice and saved the McCalls ten thousand dollars. Yet even this was not a betrayal of Berman, for Berman had told Billy the truth about Newark: Maloy was not there, and had no plans to go there.

'Though I doubt he believes it,' Martin wrote, 'Billy knew Maloy would go to Newark at some point. He knew this intuitively, his insight as much touched with magic, or spiritual penetration of the future, as was any utterance of the biblical prophets which time has proved true. Billy Phelan is not only the true hero of this whole sordid business, he is an ontological hero as well.

'Is it the policy of the McCall brothers to reward their benefactors with punishment and ostracism? Is this how the fabled McCalls gained and kept power in this city of churches for seventeen years? Does their exalted omnipotence in this city now have a life of its own, independent of the values for which so many men have struggled so long in this country? If the McCalls are the forthright men I've always known them to be, they will recognize that what is being done to Billy Phelan is not only the grossest kind of tyranny over the individual, but also a very smelly bag of very small potatoes.'

Emory Jones refused to print the column.

'If you think I'm going to get my ass into a buzz saw by taking on the McCalls over a two-bit pool hustler,' he explained, 'you're a certifiable lunatic.'

Martin considered his alternatives.

He could resign indignantly, the way Heywood Broun had quit *The World* over the Sacco-Vanzetti business. But this was not in character for Martin, and he did like his job.

He could send the column in the mail to Patsy or Bindy, or handcarry it to them and argue the case in person. Possible.

He could put it in the drawer and forget about it and recognize that children must free themselves. True, but no.

The condition of being a powerless Albany Irishman ate holes in his forbearance. Piss-ant martyr to the rapine culture, to the hypocritical handshakers, the priest suckups, the nigger-hating cops, the lace-curtain Grundys and the cut-glass banker-thieves who marked his city lousy. Are you from Albany? Yes. How can you stand it? I was there once and it's the asshole of the northeast. One of the ten bottom places of the earth.

Was it possible to escape the stereotypes and be proud of being an Albany Irishman?

Martin awoke late one morning, hung over and late for a doctor's appointment. He dressed and rushed and when he stripped for the examination by the doctor, a stranger, he could smell the stink of his own undershirt. He yearned to apologize, to explain that he was not one of the unwashed. Sorry I stink, Doc, but I had no time to change. I got up late because I was drunk last night. Oh yes.

The quest to love yourself is also an absurd quest.

Martin called Patsy and told him he was wrong in what he was doing to Billy.

'I am like hell,' said Patsy, and he hung up in Martin's ear.

Mary Daugherty agreed with Patsy McCall.

She sat in the Daugherty living room, reading in the evening paper the latest story on the kidnap gang. When Martin raised the issue of Billy Phelan by way of making polite conversation, she dropped the paper in her lap and looked at him through the top of her bifocals, her gaze defining him as a booster for the anti-Christ.

'The boy is evil,' she said. 'Only an evil person would refuse to help bring back young Charles from the clutches of demons.'

'But Billy gave them the information that caught the demons,' Martin said.

'He didn't know what he was doing.'

'Of course he knew. He knew he was informing, which was why he refused to inform any further.'

'Let him go to hell with his evil friends.'

'Your tone lacks charity.'

'Charity begins at home,' said Mary, 'and I feel first for young Charles, my own flesh and blood, and for his father and his uncles. Better men never drew breath.'

Martin silently charted the difference between his wife and Melissa. Michelangelo and Hieronymus Bosch, Saint Theresa and Sally Rand. In the sweetness of her latter-day bovinity, Mary Daugherty swathed herself in immaculate conceptions and divine pleasure. And with recourse to such wonders, who has need of soiled visions? Life is clean if you keep it clean. Hire the priests to sweep up and there will be no disease. Joan of Arc and Joan Crawford. Hell hath no fury like a zealous virgin.

'What are we having for dinner?' Martin inquired.

Martin decided to send the column to Damon Runyon, for the recent edict from Hearst on Runyon was still fresh in his mind. Runyon was now the oriflamme of the Hearst newspapers, and yet editors across the country were cutting and shaving his column regularly. 'Run Runyon uncut,' came the word from The Chief when he heard what was happening.

'If you find a way to get this piece into print,' Martin wrote Runyon, 'I will try to find it in my heart to forgive you for those four bum tips you gave me at Saratoga in August.'

And so, on a morning a week after he wrote it, Martin's defense of Billy Phelan appeared in Runyon's column in full, with a preface reminding his readers who Martin was, and suggesting that if he only gambled as well as he wrote, he would very soon make Nick the Greek look like a second-class sausage salesman.

The day it appeared in the *Times-Union*, the word went out to Broadway: Billy Phelan is all right. Don't give him any more grief.

Red Tom called Billy with the news and Billy called George Quinn at the Hendrick Hudson Hotel in Troy and told him to come home.

And Martin Daugherty bought himself six new sets of underwear.

* * *

Martin visited his father in the nursing home the afternoon the Runyon column appeared. His purpose was to read the old man a letter from Peter. Martin found his father sitting in a wheelchair with a retractable side table, having lunch. His hair had been combed but he needed a shave, his white whiskers sticking out of his chin like bleached grass waiting for the pure white lawnmower.

'Papa,' he said, 'how are you feeling?'

'Glmbvvvvv,' said the old man, his mouth full of potatoes.

By his eyes, by the movement of his hands over the bread, by the controlled hoisting of the fork to his mouth, Martin perceived that the old man was clear-headed, as clear-headed as he would ever again be.

'Did I tell you I had lunch with Henry James?' the old man said, when he had swallowed the potatoes.

'No, Papa, when was that?'

'Nineteen-oh-three, I think. He and I had just published some of our work in the *North American Review*, and the editor dropped me a note saying James was coming to America and wanted to talk to me. He was interested in Elk Street. His aunt had lived there when she married Martin Van Buren's son, and he wanted news of the Coopers and the Pruyns and others. I had written about life on Elk Street and he remembered the street fondly, even though he loathed Albany. We had lunch at Delmonico's and he had turtle soup. He talked about nothing but his varicose veins. An eccentric man.'

'Mary and I had a letter from Peter,' Martin said.

'Peter?'

'Your grandson.'

'Oh yes.'

'He's gone off to become a priest.'

'Has he?'

'He likes the idea of being good.'

'Quite a novel pursuit.'

'It is. He thinks of Saint Francis as his hero.'

'Saint Francis. A noble fellow but rather seedy.'

'The boy is out of my hands, at any rate. Somebody else will shape him from now on.'

'I hope it's not the Christian Brothers. Your mother was very distrustful of the Christian Brothers.'

'It's the Franciscans.'

'Well they're grotesque but they have the advantage of not being bellicose.'

'How is the food these days, Papa?'

'It's fine but I long for some duck. Your mother was always very fond of duck *à l'orange*. She could never cook it. She could never cook anything very well.'

'Melissa was in town this week.'

'Melissa was in town?'

'She appeared in your play.'

'Which play?'

'*The Flaming Corsage*.'

'Melissa appeared in *The Flaming Corsage?*'

'At Harmanus Bleecker Hall. It was quite a success. Well attended, good reviews, and quite a handsome production. I saw it, of course.'

'What was Melissa's last name?'

'Spencer.'

'Ah yes. Melissa Spencer. Quite a nice girl. Well rounded. She could command the attention of an entire dinner table.'

'She asked for you.'

'Did she?'

'She's writing her memoirs. I presume you'll figure in them somewhere.'

'Will I? How so?'

'I couldn't say. I'll get a copy as soon as they're published.'

'I remember her profile. She had a nose like Madame Albani. Exactly like Madame Albani. I remarked on that frequently. I was there the night Albani came to Albany and sang at the Music Hall on South Pearl Street. In 'eighty-three it was. She drew the largest crowd they ever had there. Did you know she lived in Arbor Hill for a time? She played the organ at St Joseph's Church. She always denied she was named for Albany, but she wouldn't have used the name if she hadn't had a fondness for the city.'

'Papa, you're full of stories today.'

'Am I? I didn't realize.'

'Would you like to hear Peter's letter?'

'Peter who?'

'Your grandson.'

'Oh, by all means.'

'I won't read it all, it's full of trivial detail about his trip, but at the end he says this: "Please tell Grandpa that I already miss him and that I am going to pray every day for his good health. I look forward to the day when I will be able to lay my anointed hands on his head in priestly blessing so that he may have the benefit, in the next, of my vocation. I know that you, Papa, and Grandpa, too, have been worldly men. But for me, I am committed to the way of the Cross. 'Live in the world but be no part of it,' is what I have been instructed and I will try with all my heart and soul to follow that guidance. I love you and Mother and bless you all and long for the time when next we meet. Your loving son, Peter."'

'Who wrote that?' the old man asked.

'Peter.'

'Peter who?'

'Peter Daugherty.'

'He's full of medieval bullshit.'

'Yes, I'm afraid he is.'

'It's a nice letter, however.'

'The sentiment is real.'

'What was his name?'

'Peter Daugherty.'

'Daugherty. That's the same name as mine.'

'Yes, it is. Quite a coincidence.'

'The Irish always wrote good letters. If they could write.'

Martin's view of his meeting with his father was this: that all sons are Isaac, all fathers are Abraham, and that all Isaacs become Abrahams if they work at it long enough.

He decided: We are only as possible as what happened to us yesterday. We all change as we move.

20

Billy Phelan came into Becker's at early evening wearing a new hat and a double-breasted gray topcoat. The fall winds howled outside as the door swung closed behind him. He walked to the middle of the bar and stood between Footers O'Brien and Martin Daugherty.

'The magician is among us,' Footers said.

'I couldn've done without that line, Martin,' Billy said.

'Magic is magic,' said Martin. 'Let's call things by their rightful names.'

'What're you drinking, Billy?' Red Tom asked.

'You still sellin' scotch?'

'Most days.'

'A small one, with water.'

'On the house,' Red Tom said, setting the drink down in front of Billy.

'Times certainly do change,' Billy said.

'Hey, Billy,' Footers said, 'there's a hustler upstairs looking for fish. Why don't you go give him a game?'

'I'm resting,' Billy said. 'Too much action all at once gives you the hives. Who's running the pool room now?'

'Nobody yet,' Footers said. 'Just the helpers Daddy had. Did you hear? They had to take up a collection to pay the undertaker. Bindy bought the coffin, but that still left a hundred and ten due. All they got was seventy-five.'

'Who passed the hat?' Billy asked.

'Gus. Lemon. I scraped up a few bucks for the old bastard. Let this be a lesson to us all. He who lives by the tit shall die by the tit.'

Gus Becker came out of the kitchen and saw Billy.

'So the renegade hero returns.'

'The door was open.'

'Give the man a drink on me, Tom,' Gus said.

'I already did.'

'Then give him another one.'

'I don't need free booze, Gus. I got money.'

'Don't hold it against us, Bill,' Gus said. 'When the word comes down, the word comes down. You understand.'

'Sure, Gus. You got your business to think of. Your wife and kids. Your insurance policies.'

'Don't be difficult, Bill. There was no other way.'

'I understand that, Gus. I really understand that now.'

'That a new hat, Billy?' Red Tom asked. 'It looks like a new hat.'

'It's a new hat. The river spirits got my old one.'

'The river spirits?' Martin said.

'He's over the edge,' said Footers. 'You started this, Martin.'

'You wouldn't want to explain that, Billy?' said Martin.

'No,' Billy said.

'In that case,' Martin said, 'did you hear that Jake Berman raised two thousand dollars to have Marcus Gorman defend Morrie? It'll be in the paper tonight, without mentioning the fee, of course.'

'I thought old Jake didn't like Morrie.'

'He doesn't.'

'Yeah. What star is that up there?' Billy said. 'The one in the back row. That's new.'

'That's Curry,' Red Tom said.

'Curry? I didn't know he was in that picture. I must've looked at it five thousand times, I never saw him.'

'It's him. He hung in here a lot in those days.'

Curry was a gen-u-ine crazy,' Footers said. 'I saw him and another guy steal a billy club away from a sleeping cop one night over in the station. But the billy club wasn't enough so they took the cop's pants and left the poor sucker in the middle of the station in his long underwear.'

'And Daddy's got his star, too,' Billy said. 'That's three in a couple of weeks.'

'They go,' Red Tom said.

Billy looked at the picture and thought about the three dead. They all died doing what they had to do. Billy could have died, could have jumped into the river to earn his star. But he didn't have to do that. There were other things Billy had to do. Going through the shit was one of them. If Billy had died that night, he'd have died a sucker. But the sucker got wised up and he ain't anywheres near heaven yet. They are buying you drinks now, Billy, because the word is new, but they'll remember you're not to be trusted. You're a renegade, Billy. Gus said so. You got the mark on you now.

Lemon Lewis came in the front door with red cheeks. Never looked healthier.

'Cold as a witch's tit out there,' Lemon said.

'Don't talk about witches,' Footers said. 'The magician is here.'

'What magician?'

'Don't you ever read the papers, Lemon?'

'Oh, you mean Phelan. Aaaaah. So they let you back in, eh, hotshot?'

'They just did it to make you feel good, Lemon,' Billy said.

'Hey, Phelan,' said Lemon, 'that card game at Nick's that night of the holdup. Did you really have that ace in the hole?'

All Billy could do was chuckle.

'You'll never know, will you, Lemon?'

'You ready for another?' Red Tom asked Billy. 'You got a free one coming from Gus.'

'Tell him to give it to the starving Armenians. Footers, what about that guy looking for fish. You ready to back me till I figure him out? Fifty, say?'

'How does twenty-five grab you?' Footers said.

'In a pinch I'll take twenty-five,' Billy said.

Billy drank his scotch and said, 'Come on, Martin, maybe we'll get even yet.'

And with Footers beside him, and Martin trailing with an amused smile, Billy went out into the early freeze that was just settling on Broadway and made a right turn into the warmth of the stairs to Louie's pool room, a place where even serious men sometimes go to seek the meaning of magical webs, mystical coin, golden birds, and other artifacts of the only cosmos in town.

IRONWEED

This book is for four good men:

Bill Segarra, Tom Smith,
Harry Staley, and Frank Trippett.

Tall Ironweed is a member of the Sunflower Family (Asteraceae). It has a tall erect stem and bears deep purple-blue flower heads in loose terminal clusters. Its leaves are long and thin and pointed, their lower surfaces downy. Its fruit is seed-like, with a double set of purplish bristles. It flowers from August to October in damp, rich soil from New York south to Georgia, west to Louisiana, north to Missouri, Illinois and Michigan. The name refers to the toughness of the stem.

– Adapted from The Audubon Society's
Field Guide to North American Wildflowers

To course o'er better waters now hoists sail the little bark of my wit, leaving behind her a sea so cruel.

– Dante, *Purgatorio*

1

Riding up the winding road of Saint Agnes Cemetery in the back of the rattling old truck, Francis Phelan became aware that the dead, even more than the living, settled down in neighborhoods. The truck was suddenly surrounded by fields of monuments and cenotaphs of kindred design and striking size, all guarding the privileged dead. But the truck moved on and the limits of mere privilege became visible, for here now came the acres of truly prestigious death: illustrious men and women, captains of life without their diamonds, furs, carriages, and limousines, but buried in pomp and glory, vaulted in great tombs built like heavenly safe deposit boxes, or parts of the Acropolis. And ah yes, here too, inevitably, came the flowing masses, row upon row of them under simple headstones and simpler crosses. Here was the neighborhood of the Phelans.

Francis's mother twitched nervously in her grave as the truck carried him nearer to her; and Francis's father lit his pipe, smiled at his wife's discomfort, and looked out from his own bit of sod to catch a glimpse of how much his son had changed since the train accident.

Francis's father smoked roots of grass that died in the periodic droughts afflicting the cemetery. He stored the root essence in his pockets until it was brittle to the touch, then pulverized it between his fingers and packed his pipe. Francis's mother wove crosses from the dead dandelions and other deep-rooted weeds; careful to preserve their fullest length, she wove them while they were still in the green stage of death, then ate them with an insatiable revulsion.

'Look at that tomb,' Francis said to his companion. 'Ain't that somethin'? That's Arthur T. Grogan. I saw him around Albany when I was a kid. He owned all the electricity in town.'

'He ain't got much of it now,' Rudy said.

'Don't bet on it,' Francis said. 'Them kind of guys hang on to a good thing.'

The advancing dust of Arthur T. Grogan, restless in its simulated Parthenon, grew luminous from Francis's memory of a vital day long gone. The truck rolled on up the hill.

FARRELL, said one roadside gravestone. KENNEDY, said another. DAUGHERTY, MCILHENNY, BRUNELLE, MCDONALD, MALONE, DWYER, and WALSH, said others. PHELAN, said two small ones.

Francis saw the pair of Phelan stones and turned his eyes elsewhere, fearful that his infant son, Gerald, might be under one of them. He had not confronted Gerald directly since the day he let the child slip out of its diaper. He would not confront him now. He avoided the Phelan headstones on the presumptive grounds that they belonged to another family entirely. And he was correct. These graves held two brawny young Phelan brothers, canalers both, and both skewered by the same whiskey bottle in 1884, dumped into the Erie Canal in front of The Black Rag Saloon in Watervliet, and then pushed under and drowned with a long stick. The brothers looked at Francis's clothes, his ragged brown twill suit jacket, black baggy pants, and filthy fireman's blue shirt, and felt a kinship with him that owed nothing to blood ties. His shoes were as worn as the brogans they both had been wearing on the last day of their lives. The brothers read also in Francis's face the familiar scars of alcoholic desolation, which both had developed in their graves. For both had been deeply drunk and vulnerable when the cutthroat Muggins killed them in tandem and took all their money: forty-eight cents. We died for pennies, the brothers said in their silent, dead-drunken way to Francis, who bounced past them in the back of the truck, staring at the emboldening white clouds that clotted the sky so richly at midmorning. From the heat of the sun Francis felt a flow of juices in his body, which he interpreted as a gift of strength from the sky.

'A little chilly,' he said, 'but it's gonna be a nice day.'

'If it don't puke,' said Rudy.

'You goddamn cuckoo bird, you don't talk about the weather that way. You got a nice day, take it. Why you wanna talk about the sky pukin' on us?'

'My mother was a full-blooded Cherokee,' Rudy said.

'You're a liar. Your old lady was a Mex, that's why you got them high cheekbones. Indian I don't buy.'

'She come off the reservation in Skokie, Illinois, went down to Chicago, and got a job sellin' peanuts at Wrigley Field.'

'They ain't got any Indians in Illinois. I never seen one damn Indian all the time I was out there.'

'They keep to themselves,' Rudy said.

The truck passed the last inhabited section of the cemetery and moved toward a hill where raw earth was being loosened by five men with pickaxes and shovels. The driver parked and unhitched the tailgate, and Francis and Rudy leaped down. The two then joined the other five in loading the truck with the fresh dirt. Rudy mumbled aloud as he shoveled: 'I'm workin' it out.'

'What the hell you workin' out now?' Francis asked.

'The worms,' Rudy said. 'How many worms you get in a truckload of dirt.'

'You countin' 'em?'

'Hundred and eight so far,' said Rudy.

'Dizzy bedbug,' said Francis.

When the truck was fully loaded Francis and Rudy climbed atop the dirt and the driver rode them to a slope where a score of graves of the freshly dead sent up the smell of sweet putrescence, the incense of unearned mortality and interrupted dreams. The driver, who seemed inured to such odors, parked as close to the new graves as possible and Rudy and Francis then carried shovelfuls of dirt to the dead while the driver dozed in the truck. Some of the dead had been buried two or three months, and yet their coffins were still burrowing deeper into the rain-softened earth. The gravid weight of the days they had lived was now seeking its equivalent level in firstborn death, creating a rectangular hollow on the surface of each grave. Some of the coffins seemed to be on their way to middle earth. None of the graves were yet marked with headstones, but a few were decorated with an American flag on a small stick, or bunches of faded cloth flowers in clay pots. Rudy and Francis filled in one hollow, then another. Dead gladiolas, still vaguely yellow in their brown stage of death, drooped in a basket at the head of the grave of Louis (Daddy Big) Dugan, the Albany pool hustler who had died only a week or so ago from inhaling his own vomit. Daddy Big, trying futilely to memorize anew the fading memories of how he used to apply topspin and reverse English to the cue ball, recognized Franny Phelan, even though he had not seen him in twenty years.

'I wonder who's under this one,' Francis said.

'Probably some Catholic,' Rudy said.

'Of course it's some Catholic, you birdbrain, it's a Catholic cemetery.'

'They let Protestants in sometimes,' Rudy said.

'They do like hell.'

'Sometimes they let Jews in too. And Indians.'

Daddy Big remembered the shape of Franny's mouth from the first day he saw him playing ball for Albany at Chadwick Park. Daddy Big sat down front in the bleachers behind the third-base line and watched Franny on the hot corner, watched him climb into the bleachers after a foul pop fly that would have hit Daddy Big right in the chest if Franny hadn't stood on his own ear to make the catch. Daddy Big saw Franny smile after making it, and even though his teeth were almost gone now, Franny smiled that same familiar way as he scattered fresh dirt on Daddy Big's grave.

Your son Billy saved my life, Daddy Big told Francis. Turned me upside down and kept me from chokin' to death on the street when I got sick. I died anyway, later. But it was nice of him, and I wish I could take back some of the lousy things I said to him.

And let me personally give you a piece of advice. Never inhale your own vomit.

Francis did not need Daddy Big's advice. He did not get sick from alcohol the way Daddy Big had. Francis knew how to drink. He drank all the time and he did not vomit. He drank anything that contained alcohol, anything, and he could always walk, and he could talk as well as any man alive about what was on his mind. Alcohol did put Francis to sleep, finally, but on his own terms. When he'd had enough and everybody else was passed out, he'd just put his head down and curl up like an old dog, then put his hands between his legs to protect what was left of the jewels, and he'd cork off. After a little sleep he'd wake up and go out for more drink. That's how he did it when he was drinking. Now he wasn't drinking. He hadn't had a drink for two days and he felt a little bit of all right. Strong, even. He'd stopped drinking because he'd run out of money, and that coincided with Helen not feeling all that terrific and Francis wanting to take care of her. Also he had wanted to be sober when he went to court for registering twenty-one times to vote. He went to court but not to trial. His attorney, Marcus Gorman, a wizard, found a mistake in the date on the papers that detailed the charges against Francis, and the case was thrown out. Marcus charged people five hundred dollars usually, but he only charged Francis fifty because Martin Daugherty, the newspaper columnist, one of Francis's old neighbors, asked him to go easy. Francis didn't even have the fifty when it came time to pay. He'd drunk it all up. Yet Marcus demanded it.

'But I ain't got it,' Francis said.

'Then go to work and get it,' said Marcus. 'I get paid for what I do.'

'Nobody'll put me to work,' Francis said. 'I'm a bum.'

'I'll get you some day work up at the cemetery,' Marcus said.

And he did. Marcus played bridge with the bishop and knew all the Catholic hotshots. Some hotshot ran Saint Agnes Cemetery in Menands. Francis slept in the weeds on Dongan Avenue below the bridge and woke up about seven o'clock this morning, then went up to the mission on Madison Avenue to get coffee. Helen wasn't there. She was truly gone. He didn't know where she was and nobody had seen her. They said she'd been hanging around the mission last night, but then went away. Francis had fought with her earlier over money and she just walked off someplace, who the hell knows where?

Francis had coffee and bread with the bums who'd dried out, and other bums passin' through, and the preacher there watchin' everybody and playin' grabass with their souls. Never mind my soul, was Francis's line. Just pass the coffee. Then he stood out front killin' time and pickin' his teeth with a matchbook cover. And here came Rudy.

Rudy was sober too for a change and his gray hair was combed and trimmed. His mustache was clipped and he wore white suede shoes, even though it was October, what the hell, he's just a bum, and a white shirt, and a crease in his pants. Francis, no lace in one of his shoes, hair matted and uncut, smelling his own body stink and ashamed of it for the first time in memory, felt deprived.

'You lookin' good there, bum,' Francis said.

'I been in the hospital.'

'What for?'

'Cancer.'

'No shit. Cancer?'

'He says to me you're gonna die in six months. I says I'm gonna wine myself to death. He says it don't make any difference if you wined or dined, you're goin'. Goin' out of this world with a cancer. The stomach, it's like pits, you know what I mean? I said I'd like to make it to fifty. The doc says you'll never make it. I said all right, what's the difference?'

'Too bad, grandma. You got a jug?'

'I got a dollar.'

'Jesus, we're in business,' Francis said.

But then he remembered his debt to Marcus Gorman.

'Listen, bum,' he said, 'you wanna go to work with me and make a few bucks? We can get a couple of jugs and a flop tonight. Gonna be cold. Look at that sky.'

'Work where?'

'The cemetery. Shovelin' dirt.'

'The cemetery. Why not? I oughta get used to it. What're they payin'?'

'Who the hell knows?'

'I mean they payin' money, or they give you a free grave when you croak?'

'If it ain't money, forget it,' Francis said. 'I ain't shovelin' out my own grave.'

They walked from downtown Albany to the cemetery in Menands, six miles or more. Francis felt healthy and he liked it. It's too bad he didn't feel healthy when he drank. He felt good then but not healthy, especially not in the morning, or when he woke up in the middle of the night, say. Sometimes he felt dead. His head, his throat, his stomach: he needed to get them all straight with a drink, or maybe it'd take two, because if he didn't, his brain would overheat trying to fix things and his eyes would blow out. Jeez it's tough when you need that drink and your throat's like an open sore and it's four in the morning and the wine's gone and no place open and you got no money or nobody to bum from, even if there was a place open. That's tough, pal. Tough.

Rudy and Francis walked up Broadway and when they got to Colonie Street Francis felt a pull to turn up and take a look at the house where he was born, where his goddamned brothers and sisters still lived. He'd done that in 1935 when it looked possible, when his mother finally died. And what did it get him? A kick in the ass is what it got him. Let the joint fall down and bury them all before I look at it again, was his thought. Let it rot. Let the bugs eat it.

In the cemetery, Kathryn Phelan, sensing the militance in her son's mood, grew restless at the idea that death was about to change for her. With a furtive burst of energy she wove another cross from the shallow-rooted weeds above her and quickly swallowed it, but was disappointed by the taste. Weeds appealed to Kathryn Phelan in direct ratio to the length of their roots. The longer the weed, the more revulsive the cross.

Francis and Rudy kept walking north on Broadway, Francis's

right shoe flapping, its counter rubbing wickedly against his heel. He favored the foot until he found a length of twine on the sidewalk in front of Frankie Leikheim's plumbing shop. Frankie Leikheim. A little kid when Francis was a big kid and now he's got his own plumbing shop and what have you got, Francis? You got a piece of twine for a shoelace. You don't need shoelaces for walking short distances, but on the bum without them you could ruin your feet for weeks. You figured you had all the calluses anybody'd ever need for the road, but then you come across a different pair of shoes and they start you out with a brand-new set of blisters. Then they make the blisters bleed and you have to stop walking almost till they scab over so's you can get to work on another callus.

The twine didn't fit into the eyelets of the shoe. Francis untwined it from itself and threaded half its thickness through enough of the eyelets to make it lace. He pulled up his sock, barely a sock anymore, holes in the heel, the toe, the sole, gotta get new ones. He cushioned his raw spot as best he could with the sock, then tightened the new lace, gently, so the shoe wouldn't flop. And he walked on toward the cemetery.

'There's seven deadly sins,' Rudy said.

'Deadly? What do you mean deadly?' Francis said.

'I mean daily,' Rudy said. 'Every day.'

'There's only one sin as far as I'm concerned,' Francis said.

'There's prejudice.'

'Oh yeah. Prejudice. Yes.'

'There's envy.'

'Envy. Yeah, yup. That's one.'

'There's lust.'

'Lust, right. Always liked that one.'

'Cowardice.'

'Who's a coward?'

'Cowardice.'

'I don't know what you mean. That word I don't know.'

'Cowardice,' Rudy said.

'I don't like the coward word. What're you sayin' about coward?'

'A coward. He'll cower up. You know what a coward is? He'll run.'

'No, that word I don't know. Francis is no coward. He'll fight anybody. Listen, you know what I like?'

'What do you like?'

'Honesty,' Francis said.

'That's another one,' Rudy said.

At Shaker Road they walked up to North Pearl Street and headed north on Pearl. Where they live now. They'd painted Sacred Heart Church since he last saw it, and across the street School 20 had new tennis courts. Whole lot of houses here he never saw, new since '16. This is the block they live in. What Billy said. When Francis last walked this street it wasn't much more than a cow pasture. Old man Rooney's cows would break the fence and roam loose, dirtyin' the streets and sidewalks. You got to put a stop to this, Judge Ronan told Rooney. What is it you want me to do, Rooney asked the judge, put diapers on 'em?

They walked on to the end of North Pearl Street, where it entered Menands, and turned down to where it linked with Broadway. They walked past the place where the old Bull's Head Tavern used to be. Francis was a kid when he saw Gus Ruhlan come out of the corner in bare knuckles. The bum he was fighting stuck out a hand to shake, Gus give him a shot and that was all she wrote. Katie bar the door. Too wet to plow. Honesty. They walked past Hawkins Stadium, hell of a big place now, about where Chadwick Park was when Francis played ball. He remembered when it was a pasture. Hit a ball right and it'd roll forever, right into the weeds. Bow-Wow Buckley'd be after it and he'd find it right away, a wizard. Bow-Wow kept half a dozen spare balls in the weeds for emergencies like that. Then he'd throw the runner out at third on a sure home run and he'd brag about his fielding. Honesty. Bow-Wow is dead. Worked on an ice wagon and punched his own horse and it stomped him, was that it? Nah. That's nuts. Who'd punch a horse?

'Hey,' Rudy said, 'wasn't you with a woman the other night I saw you?'

'What woman?'

'I don't know. Helen. Yeah, you called her Helen.'

'Helen. You can't keep track of where she is.'

'What'd she do, run off with a banker?'

'She didn't run off.'

'Then where is she?'

'Who knows? She comes, she goes. I don't keep tabs.'

'You got a million of 'em.'

'More where she came from.'

'They're all crazy to meet you.'

'My socks is what gets 'em.'

Francis lifted his trousers to reveal his socks, one green, one blue.

'A reg'lar man about town,' Rudy said.

Francis dropped his pantlegs and walked on, and Rudy said, 'Hey, what the hell was all that about the man from Mars last night? Everybody was talkin' about it at the hospital. You hear about that stuff on the radio?'

'Oh yeah. They landed.'

'Who?'

'The Martians.'

'Where'd they land?'

'Someplace in Jersey.'

'What happened?'

'They didn't like it no more'n I did.'

'No joke,' Rudy said. 'I heard people saw them Martians comin' and ran outa town, jumped outa windows, everything like that.'

'Good,' Francis said. 'What they oughta do. Anybody sees a Martian oughta jump out two windows.'

'You don't take things serious,' Rudy said. 'You have a whatayacallit, a frivolous way about you.'

'A frivolous way? A frivolous way?'

'That's what I said. A frivolous way.'

'What the hell's that mean? You been readin' again, you crazy kraut? I told you cuckoos like you shouldn't go around readin', callin' people frivolous.'

'That ain't no insult. Frivolous is a good word. A nice word.'

'Never mind words, there's the cemetery.' And Francis pointed to the entrance-road gates. 'I just thought of somethin'.'

'What?'

'That cemetery's full of gravestones.'

'Right.'

'I never knew a bum yet had a gravestone.'

They walked up the long entrance road from Broadway to the cemetery proper. Francis sweet-talked the woman at the gatehouse and mentioned Marcus Gorman and introduced Rudy as a good worker like himself, ready to work. She said the truck'd be along and to just wait easy. Then he and Rudy rode up in the back of the truck and got busy with the dirt.

They rested when they'd filled in all the hollows of the graves, and by then the truck driver was nowhere to be found. So they sat there and looked down the hill toward Broadway and over toward the hills of Rensselaer and Troy on the other side of the Hudson, the coke plant spewing palpable smoke from its great chimney at the far end of the Menands bridge. Francis decided this would be a fine place to be buried. The hill had a nice flow to it that carried you down the grass and out onto the river, and then across the water and up through the trees on the far shore to the top of the hills, all in one swoop. Being dead here would situate a man in place and time. It would give a man neighbors, even some of them really old folks, like those antique dead ones at the foot of the lawn: Tobias Banion, Elisha Skinner, Elsie Whipple, all crumbling under their limestone headstones from which the snows, sands, and acids of reduction were slowly removing their names. But what did the perpetuation of names matter? Ah well, there were those for whom death, like life, would always be a burden of eminence. The progeny of those growing nameless at the foot of the hill were ensured a more durable memory. Their new, and heavier, marble stones higher up on the slope had been cut doubly deep so their names would remain visible for an eternity, at least.

And then there was Arthur T. Grogan.

The Grogan Parthenon reminded Francis of something, but he

could not say what. He stared at it and wondered, apart from its size, what it signified. He knew nothing of the Acropolis, and little more about Grogan except that he was a rich and powerful Albany Irishman whose name everybody used to know. Francis could not suppose that such massive marbling of old bones was a sweet conflation of ancient culture, modern coin, and self-apotheosizing. To him, the Grogan sepulcher was large enough to hold the bodies of dozens. And as this thought grazed his memory he envisioned the grave of Strawberry Bill Benson in Brooklyn. And that was it. Yes. Strawberry Bill had played left field for Toronto in ought eight when Francis played third, and when Francis hit the road in '16 after Gerald died, they bumped into each other at a crossroads near Newburgh and caught a freight south together.

Bill coughed and died a week after they reached the city, cursing his too-short life and swearing Francis to the task of following his body to the cemetery. 'I don't want to go out there all by myself,' Strawberry Bill said. He had no money, and so his coffin was a box of slapsided boards and a few dozen tenpenny nails, which Francis rode with to the burial plot. When the city driver and his helper left Bill's pile of wood sitting on top of some large planks and drove off, Francis stood by the box, letting Bill get used to the neighborhood. 'Not a bad place, old buddy. Couple of trees over there.' The sun then bloomed behind Francis, sending sunshine into an opening between two of the planks and lighting up a cavity below. The vision stunned Francis: a great empty chasm with a dozen other coffins of crude design, similar to Bill's, piled atop one another, some on their sides, one on its end. Enough earth had been dug away to accommodate thirty or forty more such crates of the dead. In a few weeks they'd all be stacked like cordwood, packaged cookies for the great maw. 'You ain't got no worries now, Bill,' Francis told his pal. 'Plenty of company down there. You'll be lucky you get any sleep at all with them goin's on.'

Francis did not want to be buried like Strawberry Bill, in a tenement grave. But he didn't want to rattle around in a marble temple the size of the public bath either.

'I wouldn't mind bein' buried right here,' Francis told Rudy.

'You from around here?'

'Used to be. Born here.'

'Your family here?'

'Some.'

'Who's that?'

'You keep askin' questions about me, I'm gonna give you a handful of answers.'

Francis recognized the hill where his family was buried, for it was just over from the sword-bearing guardian angel who stood on tiptoe atop three marble steps, guarding the grave of Toby, the dwarf who died heroically in the Delavan Hotel fire of '94. Old Ed Daugherty, the writer, bought that monument for Toby when it came out in the paper that Toby's grave had no marker. Toby's angel pointed down the hill toward Michael Phelan's grave and Francis found it with his gaze. His mother would be alongside the old man, probably with her back to him. Fishwife.

The sun that bloomed for Strawberry Bill had bloomed also on the day Michael Phelan was buried. Francis wept out of control that day, for he had been there when the train knocked Michael fifty feet in a fatal arc; and the memory tortured him. Francis was bringing him his hot lunch in the lunch pail, and when Michael saw Francis coming, he moved toward him. He safely passed the switch engine that was moving slowly on the far track, and then he turned his back, looked the way he'd just come, and walked backward, right into the path of the north-bound train whose approach noise was being blocked out by the switch engine's clatter. He flew and then fell in a broken pile, and Francis ran to him, the first at his side. Francis looked for a way to straighten the angular body but feared any move, and so he pulled off his own sweater and pillowed his father's head with it. So many people go crooked when they die.

A few of the track gang followed Michael home in the back of Johnny Cody's wagon. He lingered two weeks and then won great obituaries as the most popular track foreman, boss gandy dancer, on the New York Central line. The railroad gave all track workers on the Albany division the morning off to go to the funeral, and hundreds came to say so long to old Mike when he rode up here to live. Queen Mama ruled the house alone then, until she joined him in the grave. What I should do, Francis thought, is shovel open the grave, crawl down in there, and strangle her bones. He remembered the tears he cried when he stood alongside the open grave of his father and he realized then that one of these days there would be nobody alive to remember that he cried that morning, just as there is no proof now that anyone ever cried for Tobias or Elisha or Elsie at the foot of the hill. No trace of grief is left, abstractions taken first by the snows of reduction.

'It's okay with me if I don't have no headstone,' Francis said to Rudy, 'just so's I don't die alone.'

'You die before me I'll send out invites,' Rudy said.

Kathryn Phelan, suddenly aware her worthless son was accepting his own death, provided it arrived on a gregarious note, humphed and fumed her disapproval to her husband. But Michael Phelan was already following the line of his son's walk toward the plot beneath the box elder tree where Gerald was buried. It always amazed Michael that the living could move instinctually toward dead kin without foreknowledge of their location. Francis had never seen Gerald's grave, had not attended Gerald's funeral. His absence that day was the scandal of the resident population of Saint Agnes's. But here he was now, walking purposefully, and with a slight limp Michael had not seen before, closing the gap between father and son, between sudden death and enduring guilt. Michael signaled to his neighbors that an act of regeneration seemed to be in process, and the eyes of the dead, witnesses all to their own historical omissions, their own unbridgeable chasms in life gone, silently rooted for Francis as he walked up the slope toward the box elder. Rudy followed his pal at a respectful distance, aware that some event of moment was taking place. Hangdog, he observed.

In his grave, a cruciformed circle, Gerald watched the advent of his father and considered what action might be appropriate to their meeting. Should he absolve the man of all guilt, not for the dropping, for that was accidental, but for the abandonment of the family, for craven flight when the steadfast virtues were called for? Gerald's grave trembled with superb possibility. Denied speech in life, having died with only monosyllabic goos and gaahs in his vocabulary, Gerald possessed the gift of tongues in death. His ability to communicate and to understand was at the genius level among the dead. He could speak with any resident adult in any language, but more notable was his ability to understand the chattery squirrels and chipmunks, the silent signals of the ants and beetles, and the slithy semaphores of the slugs and worms that moved above and through his earth. He could read the waning flow of energy in the leaves and berries as they fell from the box elder above him. And because his fate had been innocence and denial, Gerald had grown a protective web which deflected all moisture, all moles, rabbits, and other burrowing creatures. His web was woven of strands of vivid silver, an enveloping hammock of intricate, near-transparent weave. His body had not only been absolved of the need to decay, but in some respects – a full head of hair, for instance – it had grown to a completeness that was both natural and miraculous. Gerald rested in his infantile sublimity, exuding a high gloss induced by early death, his skin a radiant white-gold, his nails a silvery gray, his cluster of curls and large eyes perfectly matched in gleaming ebony. Swaddled in his grave, he was beyond capture by visual or verbal artistry. He was neither beautiful nor perfect to the beholder but rather an ineffably fabulous presence whose like was not to be found anywhere in the cemetery, and it abounded with dead innocents.

Francis found the grave without a search. He stood over it and reconstructed the moment when the child was slipping through his fingers into death. He prayed for a repeal of time so that he might hang himself in the coal bin before picking up the child to change his diaper. Denied that, he prayed for his son's eternal peace in the grave. It was true the boy had not suffered at all in his short life, and he had died too quickly of a cracked neckbone to have felt pain: a sudden twist and it was over. *Gerald Michael Phelan*, his gravestone said, *born April 13, 1916, died April 26, 1916. Born on the 13th, lived 13 days. An unlucky child who was much loved.*

Tears oozed from Francis's eyes, and when one of them fell onto his shoetop, he pitched forward onto the grave, clutching the grass, remembering the diaper in his grip. It had smelled of Gerald's pungent water, and when he squeezed it with his horrified right hand, a drop of the sacred fluid fell onto his shoetop. Twenty-two years gone, and Francis could now, in panoramic memory, see, hear, and feel every detail of that day, from the time he left the carbarns after work, to his talk about baseball with Bunt Dunn in King Brady's saloon, and even to the walk home with Cap Lawlor, who said Brady's beer was getting a heavy taste to it and Brady ought to clean his pipes, and that the Taylor kid next door to the Lawlors was passing green pinworms. His memory had begun returning forgotten images when it equated Arthur T. Grogan and Strawberry Bill, but now memory was as vivid as eyesight.

'I remember everything,' Francis told Gerald in the grave. 'It's the first time I tried to think of those things since you died. I had four beers after work that day. It wasn't because I was drunk that I dropped you. Four beers, and I didn't finish the fourth. Left it next to the pigs'-feet jar on Brady's bar so's I could walk home with Cap Lawlor. Billy was nine then. He knew you were gone before Peggy knew. She hadn't come home from choir practice yet. Your mother said two words, "Sweet Jesus," and then we both crouched down to snatch you up. But we both stopped in that crouch because of the looks of you. Billy come in then and saw you. "Why is Gerald crooked?" he says. You know, I saw Billy a week or so ago and the kid looks good. He wanted to buy me new clothes. Bailed me outa jail and even give me a wad of cash. We talked about you. He says your mother never blamed me for dropping you. Never told a soul in twenty-two years it was me let you fall. Is that some woman or isn't it? I remember the linoleum you fell on was yellow with red squares. You suppose now that I can remember this stuff out in the open, I can finally start to forget it?'

Gerald, through an act of silent will, imposed on his father the pressing obligation to perform his final acts of expiation for abandoning the family. You will not know, the child silently said, what these acts are until you have performed them all. And after you have performed them you will not understand that they were expiatory any more than you have understood all the other expiation that has kept you in such prolonged humiliation. Then, when these final acts are complete, you will stop trying to die because of me.

Francis stopped crying and tried to suck a small piece of bread out from between the last two molars in his all but toothless mouth. He made a slurping sound with his tongue, and when he did, a squirrel scratching the earth for food to store up for the winter spiraled up the box elder in sudden fright. Francis took this as a signal to conclude his visit and he turned his gaze toward the sky. A vast stand of white fleece, brutally bright, moved south to north in the eastern vault of the heavens, a rush of splendid wool to warm the day. The breeze had grown temperate and the sun was rising to the noonday pitch. Francis was no longer chilly.

'Hey bum,' he called to Rudy. 'Let's find that truck driver.'

'Whatayou been up to?' Rudy asked. 'You know somebody buried up there?'

'A little kid I used to know.'

'A kid? What'd he do, die young?'

'Pretty young.'

'What happened to him?'

'He fell.'

'He fell where?'

'He fell on the floor.'

'Hell, I fall on the floor about twice a day and I ain't dead.'

'That's what you think,' Francis said.

2.

They rode the Albany–Troy–via–Watervliet bus downtown from the cemetery. Francis told Rudy: 'Spend a dime, ya bum,' and they stepped up into the flat-faced, red-and-cream window box on wheels, streamline in design but without the spark of electric life, without the rocking-horse comfort, or the flair, or the verve, of the vanishing trolley. Francis remembered trolleys as intimately as he remembered the shape of his father's face, for he had seen them at loving closeness through all his early years. Trolleys dominated his life the way trains had dominated his father's. He had worked on them at the North Albany carbarns for years, could take them apart in the dark. He'd even killed a man over them in 1901 during the trolley strike. Terrific machines, but now they're goin'.

'Where we headed?' Rudy asked.

'What do you care where we're headed? You got an appointment? You got tickets for the opera?'

'No, I just like to know where I'm goin'.'

'You ain't knowed where you was goin' for twenty years.'

'You got somethin' there,' Rudy said.

'We're goin' to the mission, see what's happenin', see if anybody knows where Helen is.'

'What's Helen's name?'

'Helen.'

'I mean her other name.'

'Whatayou want to know for?'

'I like to know people's names.'

'She ain't got only one name.'

'Okay, you don't want to tell me, it's all right.'

'You goddamn right it's all right.'

'We gonna eat at the mission? I'm hungry.'

'We could eat, why not? We're sober, so he'll let us in, the bastard. I ate there the other night, had a bowl of soup because I was starvin'. But god it was sour. Them dried-out bums that live there, they sit down and eat like fuckin' pigs, and everything that's left they throw in the pot and give it to you. Slop.'

'He puts out a good meal, though.'

'He does in a pig's ass.'

'Wonderful.'

'Pig's ass. And he won't feed you till you listen to him preach. I watch the old bums sittin' there and I wonder about them. What are you all doin', sittin' through his bullshit? But they's all tired and old, they's all drunks. They don't believe in nothin'. They's just hungry.'

'I believe in somethin',' Rudy said. 'I'm a Catholic.'

'Well so am I. What the hell has that got to do with it?'

The bus rolled south on Broadway following the old trolley tracks, down through Menands and into North Albany, past Simmons Machine, the Albany Felt Mill, the Bond Bakery, the Eastern Tablet Company, the Albany Paper Works. And then the bus stopped at North Third Street to pick up a passenger and Francis looked out the window at the old neighborhood he could not avoid seeing. He saw where North Street began and then sloped down toward the canal bed, the lumber district, the flats, the river. Brady's saloon was still on the corner. Was Brady alive? Pretty good pitcher. Played ball for Boston in 1912, same year Francis was with Washington. And when the King quit the game he opened the saloon. Two big-leaguers from Albany and they both wind up on the same street. Nick's delicatessen, new to Francis, was next to Brady's, and in front of it children in false faces – a clown, a spook, a monster – were playing hopscotch. One child hopped in and out of chalked squares, and Francis remembered it was Halloween, when spooks made house calls and the dead walked abroad.

'I used to live down at the foot of that street,' Francis told Rudy, and then wondered why he'd bothered. He had no desire to tell Rudy anything intimate about his life. Yet working next to the simpleton all day, throwing dirt on dead people in erratic rhythm with him, had generated a bond that Francis found strange. Rudy, a friend for about two weeks, now seemed to Francis a fellow traveler on a journey to a nameless destination in another country. He was simple, hopeless and lost, as lost as Francis himself, though somewhat younger, dying of cancer, afloat in ignorance, weighted with stupidity, inane, sheeplike, and given to fits of weeping over his lostness; and yet there was something in him that buoyed Francis's spirit. They were both questing for the behavior that was proper to their station and their unutterable dreams. They both knew intimately the etiquette, the taboos, the protocol of bums. By their talk to each other they understood that they shared a belief in the brotherhood of the desolate; yet in the scars of their eyes they confirmed that no such fraternity had ever existed, that the only brotherhood they belonged to was the one that asked that enduring question: How do I get through the next twenty minutes? They feared drys, cops, jailers, bosses, moralists, crazies, truth-tellers, and one another. They loved storytellers, liars, whores, fighters, singers, collie dogs that wagged their tails, and generous bandits. Rudy, thought Francis: he's just a bum, but who ain't?

'You live there a long time?' Rudy asked.

'Eighteen years,' Francis said. 'The old lock was just down from my house.'

'What kind of lock?'

'On the Erie Canal, you goddamn dimwit. I could throw a stone from my stoop twenty feet over the other side of the canal.'

'I never saw the canal, but I seen the river.'

'The river was a little ways further over. Still is. The lumber district's gone and all that's left is the flats where they filled the canal in. Jungle town been built up on 'em right down there. I stayed there one night last week with an old bo, a pal of mine. Tracks run right past it, same tracks I went west on out to Dayton to play ball. I hit .387 that year.'

'What year was that?'

''Oh-one.'

'I was five years old,' Rudy said.

'How old are you now, about eight?'

They passed the old carbarns at Erie Street, all full of buses. Buildings a different color, and more of 'em, but it looks a lot like it looked in '16. The trolley full of scabs and soldiers left this barn that day in '01 and rocketed arrogantly down Broadway, the street supine and yielding all the way to downtown. But then at Columbia and Broadway the street changed its pose: it became volatile with the rage of strikers and their women, who trapped the car at that corner between two blazing bedsheets which Francis helped to light on the overhead electric wire. Soldiers on horses guarded the trolley; troops with rifles rode on it. But every scabby-souled one of them was trapped between pillars of fire when Francis pulled back, wound up his educated right arm, and let fly that smooth round stone the weight of a baseball, and brained the scab working as the trolley conductor. The troops saw more stones coming and fired back at the mob, hitting two men who fell in fatal slumps; but not Francis, who ran down to the railroad tracks and then north along them till his lungs blew out. He pitched forward into a ditch and waited about nine years to see if they were on his tail, and they weren't, but his brother Chick and his buddies Patsy McCall and Martin Daugherty were; and when the three of them reached his ditch they all ran north, up past the lumberyards in the district, and found refuge with Iron Joe Farrell, Francis's father-in-law, who bossed the filtration plant that made Hudson River water drinkable for Albany folk. And after a while, when he knew for sure he couldn't stay around Albany because the scab was surely dead, Francis hopped a train going north, for he couldn't get a westbound without going back down into that wild city. But it was all right. He went north and then he walked awhile and found his way to some westbound tracks, and went west on them, all the way west to Dayton, O-hi-o.

That scab was the first man Francis Phelan ever killed. His name was Harold Allen and he was a single man from Worcester,

Massachusetts, a member of the IOOF, of Scotch-Irish stock, twenty-nine years old, two years of college, veteran of the Spanish-American War who had seen no combat, an itinerant house painter who found work in Albany as a strikebreaker and who was now sitting across the aisle of the bus from Francis, dressed in a long black coat and a motorman's cap.

Why did you kill me? was the question Harold Allen's eyes put to Francis.

'Didn't mean to kill you,' Francis said.

Was that why you threw that stone the size of a potato and broke open my skull? My brains flowed out and I died.

'You deserved what you got. Scabs get what they ask for. I was right in what I did.'

Then you feel no remorse at all.

'You bastards takin' our jobs, what kind of man is that, keeps a man from feedin' his family?'

Odd logic coming from a man who abandoned his own family not only that summer but every spring and summer thereafter, when baseball season started. And didn't you finally abandon them permanently in 1916? The way I understand it, you haven't even been home for a visit in twenty-two years.

'There are reasons. That stone. The soldiers would've shot me. And I had to play ball – it's what I did. Then I dropped my baby son and he died and I couldn't face that.'

A coward, he'll run.

'Francis is no coward. He had his reasons and they were goddamn good ones.'

You have no serious arguments to justify what you did.

'I got arguments,' Francis yelled, 'I got arguments.'

'Whatayou got arguments about?' Rudy asked.

'Down there,' Francis said, pointing toward the tracks beyond the carbarns, 'I was in this boxcar and didn't know where I was goin' except north, but it seemed I was safe. It wasn't movin' very fast or else I couldn't of got into it. I'm lookin' out, and up there ahead I see this young fella runnin' like hell, runnin' like I'd just run, and I see two guys chasin' him, and one of them two doin' the chasin' looks like a cop and he's shootin'. Stoppin' and shootin'. But this fella keeps runnin', and we're gettin' to him when I see another one right behind him. They're both headin' for the train, and I peek around the door, careful so's I don't got me shot, and I see the first one grab hold of a ladder on one of the cars, and he's up, he's up, and they're still shootin,' and then damn if we don't cross that road just about the time the second fella gets to the car I'm ridin' in, and he yells up to me: Help me, help me, and they're shootin' like sonsabitches at him and sure as hell I help him, they're gonna shoot at me too.'

'What'd you do?' Rudy asked.

'I slid on my belly over to the edge of the car, givin' them shooters a thin target, and I give that fella a hand, and he's grabbin' at it, almost grabbin' it, and I'm almost gettin' a full purchase on him, and then whango bango, they shoot him right in the back and that's all she wrote. Katie bar the door. Too wet to plow. He's all done, that fella, and I roll around back in the car and don't find out till we get to Whitehall, when the other fella drops into my boxcar, that they both was prisoners and they was on their way to the county jail in Albany. But then there was this big trolley strike with shootin' and stuff because some guy threw a stone and killed a scab. And that got this mob of people in the street all mixed up and crazy and they was runnin' every which way and the deputies guardin' these two boys got a little careless and so off went the boys. They run and hid awhile and then lit out and run some more, about three miles or so, same as me, and them deputies picked up on 'em and kept right after them all the way. They never did get that first fella. He went to Dayton with me, 'preciated what I tried to do for his buddy and even stole two chickens when we laid over in some switchyards somewheres and got us a fine meal. We cooked it up right in the boxcar. He was a murderer, that fella. Strangled some lady in Selkirk and couldn't say why he done it. The one that got shot in the back, he was a horse thief.'

'I guess you been mixed up in a lot of violence,' Rudy said.

'If it draws blood or breaks heads,' said Francis, 'I know how it tastes.'

The horse thief was named Aldo Campione, an immigrant from the town of Teramo in the Abruzzi. He'd come to America to seek his fortune and found work building the Barge Canal. But as a country soul he was distracted by an equine opportunity in the town of Coeymans, was promptly caught, jailed, transported to Albany for trial, and shot in the back escaping. His lesson to Francis was this: that life is full of caprice and missed connections, that thievery is wrong, especially if you get caught, that even Italians cannot outrun bullets, that a proffered hand in a moment of need is a beautiful thing. All this Francis knew well enough, and so the truest lesson of Aldo Campione resided not in intellected fact but in spectacle; for Francis can still remember Aldo's face as it came toward him. It looked like his own, which is perhaps why Francis put himself in jeopardy: to save his own face with his own hand. On came Aldo toward the open boxcar door. Out went the hand of Francis Phelan. It touched the curved fingers of Aldo's right hand. Francis's fingers curved and pulled. And there was tension. Tension! On came Aldo yielding to that tension, on and on and lift! Leap! Pull, Francis, pull! And then up, yes up! The grip was solid. The man was in the air, flying toward safety on the great right hand of Francis Phelan. And then whango bango and he let go. Whango bango and he's down, and he's rolling, and he's dead. Katie bar the door.

When the bus stopped at the corner of Broadway and Columbia Street, the corner where that infamous trolley was caught between flaming bedsheets, Aldo Campione boarded. He was clad in a white flannel suit, white shirt, and white necktie, and his hair was slicked down with brilliantine. Francis knew instantly that this was not the white of innocence but of humility. The man had been of low birth, low estate, and committed a low crime that had earned him the lowliest of deaths in the dust. Over there on the other side they must've give him a new suit. And here he came down the aisle and stopped at the seats where Rudy and Francis sat. He reached out his hand in a gesture to Francis that was ambiguous. It might have been a simple Abruzzian greeting. Or was it a threat, or a warning? It might have been an offer of belated gratitude, or even a show of compassion for a man like Francis who had lived long (for him), suffered much, and was inching toward death. It might have been a gesture of grace, urging, or even welcoming Francis into the next. And at this thought, Francis, who had raised his hand to meet Aldo's, withdrew it.

'I ain't shakin' hands with no dead horse thief,' he said.

'I ain't no horse thief,' Rudy said.

'Well you look like one,' Francis said.

By then the bus was at Madison Avenue and Broadway, and Rudy and Francis stepped out into the frosty darkness of six o'clock on the final night of October 1938, the unruly night when grace is always in short supply, and the old and the new dead walk abroad in this land.

In the dust and sand of a grassless vacant lot beside the Mission of Holy Redemption, a human form lay prostrate under a lighted mission window. The sprawl of the figure arrested Francis's movement when he and Rudy saw it. Bodies in alleys, bodies in gutters, bodies anywhere, were part of his eternal landscape: a physical litany of the dead. This one belonged to a woman who seemed to be doing the dead man's float in the dust: face down, arms forward, legs spread.

'Hey,' Rudy said as they stopped. 'That's Sandra.'

'Sandra who?' said Francis.

'Sandra There-ain't-no-more. She's only got one name, like Helen. She's an Eskimo.'

'You dizzy bastard. Everybody's an Eskimo or a Cherokee.'

'No, that's the straight poop. She used to work up in Alaska when they were buildin' roads.'

'She dead?'

Rudy bent down, picked up Sandra's hand and held it. Sandra pulled it away from him.

'No,' Rudy said, 'she ain't dead.'

'Then you better get up outa there, Sandra,' Francis said, 'or the dogs'll eat your ass off.'

Sandra didn't move. Her hair streamed out of her inertness,

long, yellow-white wisps floating in the dust, her faded and filthy cotton housedress twisted above the back of her knees, revealing stockings so full of holes and runs that they had lost their integrity as stockings. Over her dress she wore two sweaters, both stained and tattered. She lacked a left shoe. Rudy bent over and tapped her on the shoulder.

'Hey Sandra, it's me, Rudy. You know me?'

'Hnnn,' said Sandra.

'You all right? You sick or anything, or just drunk?'

'Dnnn,' said Sandra.

'She's just drunk,' Rudy said, standing up. 'She can't hold it no more. She falls over.'

'She'll freeze there and the dogs'll come along and eat her ass off,' Francis said.

'What dogs?' Rudy asked.

'The dogs, the dogs. Ain't you seen them?'

'I don't see too many dogs. I like cats. I see a lotta cats.'

'If she's drunk she can't go inside the mission,' Francis said.

'That's right,' said Rudy. 'She comes in drunk, he kicks her right out. He hates drunk women more'n he hates us.'

'Why the hell's he preachin' if he don't preach to people that need it?'

'Drunks don't need it,' Rudy said. 'How'd you like to preach to a room full of bums like her?'

'She a bum or just on a heavy drunk?'

'She's a bum.'

'She looks like a bum.'

'She's been a bum all her life.'

'No,' said Francis. 'Nobody's a bum all their life. She hada been somethin' once.'

'She was a whore before she was a bum.'

'And what about before she was a whore?'

'I don't know,' Rudy said. 'She just talks about whorin' in Alaska. Before that I guess she was just a little kid.'

'Then that's somethin'. A little kid's somethin' that ain't a bum or a whore.'

Francis saw Sandra's missing shoe in the shadows and retrieved it. He set it beside her left foot, then squatted and spoke into her left ear.

'You gonna freeze here tonight, you know that? Gonna be frost, freezin' weather. Could even snow. You hear? You oughta get yourself inside someplace outa the cold. Look, I slept the last two nights in the weeds and it was awful cold, but tonight's colder already than it was either of them nights. My hands is half froze and I only been walkin' two blocks. Sandra? You hear what I'm sayin'? If I got you a cup of hot soup would you drink it? Could you? You don't look like you could but maybe you could. Get a little hot soup in, you don't freeze so fast. Or maybe you wanna freeze tonight, maybe that's why you're layin' in the goddamn dust. You don't even have any weeds to keep the wind outa your ears. I like them deep weeds when I sleep outside. You want some soup?'

Sandra turned her head and with one eye looked up at Francis. 'Who you?'

'I'm just a bum,' Francis said. 'But I'm sober and I can get you some soup.'

'Get me a drink?'

'No, I ain't got money for that.'

'Then soup.'

'You wanna stand up?'

'No. I'll wait here.'

'You're gettin' all dusty.'

'That's good.'

'Whatever you say,' Francis said, standing up. 'But watch out for them dogs.'

She whimpered as Rudy and Francis left the lot. The night sky was black as a bat and the wind was bringing ice to the world. Francis admitted the futility of preaching to Sandra. Who could preach to Francis in the weeds? But that don't make it right that she can't go inside to get warm. Just because you're drunk don't mean you ain't cold.

'Just because you're drunk don't mean you ain't cold,' he said to Rudy.

'Right,' said Rudy. 'Who said that?'

'I said that, you ape.'

'I ain't no ape.'

'Well you look like one.'

From the mission came sounds made by an amateur organist of fervent aggression, and of several voices raised in praise of good old Jesus, where'd we all be without him? The voices belonged to the Reverend Chester, and to half a dozen men in shirt sleeves who sat in the front rows of the chapel area's folding chairs. Reverend Chester, a gargantuan man with a clubfoot, wild white hair, and a face flushed permanently years ago by a whiskey condition all his own, stood behind the lectern looking out at maybe forty men and one woman.

Helen.

Francis saw her as he entered, saw her gray beret pulled off to the left, recognized her old black coat. She held no hymnal as the others did, but sat with arms folded in defiant resistance to the possibility of redemption by any Methodist like Chester; for Helen was a Catholic. And any redemption that came her way had better be through her church, the true church, the only church.

'Jesus,' the preacher and his shirt-sleeved loyalists sang, 'the name that charms our fears, That bids our sorrows cease, 'Tis music in the sinners' ears, 'Tis life and health and peace . . .'

The remaining seven eighths of Reverend Chester's congregation, men hiding inside their overcoats, hats in their laps if they had hats, their faces grimed and whiskered and woebegone, remained mute, or gave the lyrics a perfunctory mumble, or nodded already in sleep. The song continued: '. . . He breaks the power of canceled sin, He sets the prisoner free; His blood can make the foulest clean, His blood availed for me.'

Well not me, Francis said to his unavailed-for self, and he smelled his own uncanceled stink again, aware that it had intensified since morning. The sweat of a workday, the sourness of dried earth on his hands and clothes, the putrid perfume of the cemetery air with its pretension to windblown purity, all this lay in foul encrustation atop the private pestilence of his being. When he threw himself onto Gerald's grave, the uprush of a polluted life all but asphyxiated him.

'Hear him, ye deaf; his praise, ye dumb, Your loosened tongues employ; Ye blind, behold your Savior come; and leap, ye lame, for joy.'

The lame and the halt put their hymnals down joylessly, and Reverend Chester leaned over his lectern to look at tonight's collection. Among them, as always, were good men and straight, men honestly without work, victims of a society ravaged by avarice, sloth, stupidity, and a God made wrathful by Babylonian excesses. Such men were merely the transients in the mission, and to them a preacher could only wish luck, send prayer, and provide a meal for the long road ahead. The true targets of the preacher were the others: the dipsos, the deadbeats, the wetbrains, and the loonies, who needed more than luck. What they needed was a structured way, a mentor and guide through the hells and purgatories of their days. Bringing the word, the light, was a great struggle today, for the decline of belief was rampant and the anti-Christ was on the rise. It was prophesied in Matthew and in Revelation that there would be less and less reverence for the Bible, greater lawlessness, depravity, and self-indulgence. The world, the light, the song, they would all die soon, for without doubt we were witnessing the advent of end times.

'Lost,' said the preacher, and he waited for the word to resound in the sanctums of their damaged brains. 'Oh lost, lost forever. Men and women lost, hopeless. Who will save you from your sloth? Who will give you a ride on the turnpike to salvation? Jesus will! Jesus delivers!'

The preacher screamed the word *delivers* and woke up half the congregation. Rudy, on the nod, flared into wakefulness with a wild swing of the left arm that knocked the hymnal out of Francis's grip. The book fell to the floor with a splat that brought Reverend Chester eye-to-eye with Francis. Francis nodded and the preacher gave him a firm and flinty smile in return.

The preacher then took the beatitudes for his theme. Blessed are the poor in spirit, for theirs is the kingdom of heaven. Blessed are the meek, for they shall inherit the earth. Blessed are they that mourn, for they shall be comforted.

'Oh yes, you men of skid row, brethren on the poor streets of the one eternal city we all dwell in, do not grieve that your spirit is low. Do not fear the world because you are of a meek and gentle nature. Do not feel that your mournful tears are in vain, for these things are the keys to the kingdom of God.'

The men went swiftly back to sleep and Francis resolved he would wash the stink of the dead off his face and hands and hit Chester up for a new pair of socks. Chester was happiest when he was passing out socks to dried-out drunks. Feed the hungry, clothe the sober.

'Are you ready for peace of mind and heart?' the preacher asked. 'Is there a man here tonight who wants a different life? God says: Come unto me. Will you take him at his word? Will you stand up now? Come to the front, kneel, and we will talk. Do this now and be saved. Now. Now. Now!'

No one moved.

'Then amen, brothers,' said the preacher testily, and he left the lectern.

'Hot goddamn,' Francis said to Rudy. 'Now we get at that soup.'

Then began the rush of men to table, the pouring of coffee, ladling of soup, cutting of bread by the mission's zealous volunteers. Francis sought out Pee Wee, a good old soul who managed the mission for Chester, and he asked him for a cup of soup for Sandra.

'She oughta be let in,' Francis said. 'She's gonna freeze out there.'

'She was in before,' Pee Wee said. 'He wouldn't let her stay. She was really shot, and you know him on that. He won't mind on the soup, but just for the hell of it, don't say where it's going.'

'Secret soup,' Francis said.

He took the soup out the back door, pulling Rudy along with him, and crossed the vacant lot to where Sandra lay as before. Rudy rolled her onto her back and sat her up, and Francis put the soup under her nose.

'Soup,' he said.

'Gazoop,' Sandra said.

'Have it.' Francis put the cup to her lips and tipped the soup at her mouth. It dribbled down her chin. She swallowed none.

'She don't want it,' Rudy said.

'She wants it,' Francis said. 'She's just pissed it ain't wine.'

He tried again and Sandra swallowed a little.

'When I was sleepin' inside just now,' Rudy said, 'I remembered Sandra wanted to be a nurse. Or used to be a nurse. That right, Sandra?'

'No,' Sandra said.

'No, what? Wanted to be a nurse or was a nurse?'

'Doctor,' Sandra said.

'She wanted to be a doctor,' Francis said, tipping in more soup.

'No,' Sandra said, pushing the soup away. Francis put the cup down and slipped her ratty shoe onto her left foot. He lifted her, a feather, carried her to the wall of the mission, and propped her into a sitting position, her back against the building, somewhat out of the wind. With his bare hand he wiped the masking dust from her face. He raised the soup and gave her another swallow.

'Doctor wanted me to be a nursie,' she said.

'But you didn't want it,' Francis said.

'Did. But he died.'

'Ah,' said Francis. 'Love?'

'Love,' said Sandra.

Inside the mission, Francis handed the cup back to Pee Wee, who emptied it into the sink.

'She all right?' Pee Wee asked.

'Terrific,' Francis said.

'The ambulance won't even pick her up anymore,' Pee Wee said. 'Not unless she's bleedin' to death.'

Francis nodded and went to the bathroom, where he washed Sandra's dust and his own stink off his hands. Then he washed his face and his neck and his ears; and when he was finished he washed them all again. He sloshed water around in his mouth and brushed his teeth with his left index finger. He wet his hair and combed it with nine fingers and dried himself with a damp towel that was tied to the wall. Some men were already leaving by the time he picked up his soup and bread and sat down beside Helen.

'Where you been hidin'?' he asked her.

'A fat lot you care where anybody is or isn't. I could be dead in the street three times over and you wouldn't know a thing about it.'

'How the hell could I when you walk off like a crazy woman, yellin' and stompin'.'

'Who wouldn't be crazy around you, spending every penny we get. You go out of your mind, Francis.'

'I got some money.'

'How much?'

'Six bucks.'

'Where'd you get it?'

'I worked all the damn day in the cemetery, fillin' up graves. Worked hard.'

'Francis, you did?'

'I mean all day.'

'That's wonderful. And you're sober. And you're eating.'

'Ain't drinkin' no wine either. I ain't even smokin'.'

'Oh that's so lovely. I'm very proud of my good boy.'

Francis scarfed up the soup, and Helen smiled and sipped the last of her coffee. More than half the men were gone from table now, Rudy still eating with a partial mind across from Francis. Pee Wee and his plangently compassionate volunteers picked up dishes and carried them to the kitchen. The preacher finished his coffee and strode over to Francis.

'Glad to see you staying straight,' the preacher said.

'Okay,' said Francis.

'And how are you, little lady?' he asked Helen.

'I'm perfectly delightful,' Helen said.

'I believe I've got a job for you if you want it, Francis,' the preacher said.

'I worked today up at the cemetery.'

'Splendid.'

'Shovelin' dirt ain't my idea of that much of a job.'

'Maybe this one is better. Old Rosskam the ragman came here today looking for a helper. I've sent him men from time to time and I thought of you. If you're serious about quitting the hooch you might put a decent penny together.'

'Ragman,' Francis said. 'Doin' what, exactly?'

'Going house to house on the wagon. Rosskam himself buys the rags and bottles, old metal, junk, papers, no garbage. Carts it himself too, but he's getting on and needs another strong back.'

'Where's he at?'

'Green Street, below the bridge.'

'I'll go see him and I 'preciate it. Tell you what else I'd 'preciate's a pair of socks, if you can spare 'em. Ones I got are all rotted out.'

'What size?'

'Tens. But I'll take nines, or twelves.'

'I'll get you some tens. And keep up the good work, Franny. Nice to see you're doing well too, little lady.'

'I'm doing very well,' Helen said. 'Very exceptionally well.' When he walked away she said: 'He says it's nice I'm doing well. I'm doing just fine, and I don't need him to tell me I'm doing well.'

'Don't fight him,' Francis said. 'He's givin' me some socks.'

'We gonna get them jugs?' Rudy asked Francis. 'Go somewheres and get a flop?'

'Jugs?' said Helen.

'That's what I said this mornin',' Francis said. 'No, no jugs.'

'With six dollars we could get a room and get our suitcase back,' Helen said.

'I can't spend all six,' Francis said. 'I gotta give some to the lawyer. I figure I'll give him a deuce. After all, he got me the job and I owe him fifty.'

'Where do you plan to sleep?' Helen asked.

'Where'd you sleep last night?'

'I found a place.'

'Finny's car?'

'No, not Finny's car. I won't stay there anymore, you know that. I will absolutely not stay in that car another night.'

'Then where'd you go?'

'Where did *you* sleep?'

'I slept in the weeds,' Francis said.

'Well I found a bed.'

'Where, goddamn it, where?'

'Up at Jack's.'

'I thought you didn't like Jack anymore, or Clara either.'

'They're not my favorite people, but they gave me a bed when I needed one.'

'Somethin' to be said for that,' Francis said.

Pee Wee came over with a second cup of coffee and sat across from Helen. Pee Wee was bald and fat and chewed cigars all day long without lighting them. He had cut hair in his younger days, but when his wife cleaned out their bank account, poisoned Pee Wee's dog, and ran away with the barber whom Pee Wee, by dint of hard work and superior tonsorial talent, had put out of business, Pee Wee started drinking and wound up on the bum. Yet he carried his comb and scissors everywhere to prove his talent was not just a bum's fantasy, and gave haircuts to other bums for fifteen cents, sometimes a nickel. He still gave haircuts, free now, at the mission.

When Francis came back to Albany in 1935, he met Pee Wee for the first time and they stayed drunk together for a month. When Francis turned up in Albany only weeks back to register for the Democrats at five dollars a shot, he met Pee Wee again. Francis registered to vote twenty-one times before the state troopers caught up with him and made him an Albany political celebrity. The pols had paid him fifty by then and still owed him fifty-five more that he'd probably never see. Pee Wee was off the juice when Francis met him the second time, and was full of energy, running the mission for Chester. Pee Wee was peaceful now, no longer the singing gin-drinker he used to be. Francis still felt good things about him, but now thought of him as an emotional cripple, dry, yeah, but at what cost?

'You see who's playin' over at The Gilded Cage?' Pee Wee asked Francis.

'I don't read the papers.'

'Oscar Reo.'

'You mean our Oscar?'

'The same.'

'What's he doin'?'

'Singin' bartender. How's that for a comedown?'

'Oscar Reo who used to be on the radio?' Helen asked.

'That's the fella,' said Pee Wee. 'He blew the big time on booze, but he dried out and tends bar now. At least he's livin', even if it ain't what it was.'

'Pee Wee and me pitched a drunk with him in New York. Two, three days, wasn't it, Pee?'

'Mighta been a week,' Pee Wee said. 'None of us was up to keepin' track. But he sang a million tunes and played piano everyplace they had one. Most musical drunk I ever see.'

'I used to sing his songs,' Helen said. '"Hindustan Lover" and "Georgie Is My Apple Pie" and another one, a grand ballad, "Under the Peach Trees with You." He wrote wonderful, happy songs and I sang them all when I was singing.'

'I didn't know you sang,' Pee Wee said.

'Well I most certainly sang, and played piano very well too. I was getting a classical education in music until my father died. I was at Vassar.'

'Albert Einstein went to Vassar,' Rudy said.

'You goofy bastard,' said Francis.

'Went there to make a speech. I read it in the papers.'

'He could have,' Helen said. 'Everybody speaks at Vassar. It just happens to be one of the three best schools in the world.'

'We oughta go over and see old Oscar,' Francis said.

'Not me,' said Pee Wee.

'No,' said Helen.

'What no?' Francis said. 'You afraid we'd all get drunked up if we stopped in to say hello?'

'I'm not afraid of that.'

'Then let's go see him. He's all right, Oscar.'

'Think he'll remember you?' Pee Wee said.

'Maybe. I remember him.'

'So do I.'

'Then let's go.'

'I wouldn't drink anything,' Pee Wee said. 'I ain't been in a bar in two years.'

'They got ginger ale. You allowed to drink ginger ale?'

'I hope it's not expensive,' Helen said.

'Just what you drink,' Pee Wee said. 'About usual.'

'Is it snooty?'

'It's a joint, old-timey, but it pulls in the slummers. That's half the trade.'

Reverend Chester stepped lively across the room and thrust at Francis a pair of gray woolen socks, his mouth a crescent of pleasure and his great chest heaving with beneficence.

'Try these for size,' he said.

'I thank ya for 'em,' said Francis.

'They're good and warm.'

'Just what I need. Nothin' left of mine.'

'It's fine that you're off the drink. You've got a strong look about you today.'

'Just a false face for Halloween.'

'Don't run yourself down. Have faith.'

The door to the mission opened and a slim young man in bifocals and a blue topcoat two sizes small for him, his carroty hair a field of cowlicks, stood in its frame. He held the doorknob with one hand and stood directly under the inside ceiling light, casting no shadow.

'Shut the door,' Pee Wee yelled, and the young man stepped in and shut it. He stood looking at all in the mission, his face a cracked plate, his eyes panicked and rabbity.

'That's it for him,' Pee Wee said.

The preacher strode to the door and stood inches from the young man, studying him, sniffing him.

'You're drunk,' the preacher said.

'I only had a couple.'

'Oh no. You're in the beyond.'

'Honest,' said the young man. 'Two bottles of beer.'

'Where did you get the money for beer?'

'A fella paid me what he owed me.'

'You panhandled it.'

'No.'

'You're a bum.'

'I just had a drink, Reverend.'

'Get your things together. I told you I wouldn't put up with this a third time. Arthur, get his bags.'

Pee Wee stood up from the table and climbed the stairs to the rooms where the resident handful lived while they sorted out their lives. The preacher had invited Francis to stay if he could get the hooch out of his system. He would then have a clean bed, clean clothes, three squares, and a warm room with Jesus in it for as long as it took him to answer the question: What next? Pee Wee held the house record: eight months in the joint, and managing it after three, such was his zeal for abstention. No booze, no smoking upstairs (for drunks are fire hazards), carry your share of the work load, and then rise you must, rise you will, into the brilliant embrace of the just God. The kitchen volunteers stopped their work and came forward with solemnized pity to watch the eviction of oen of their promising young men. Pee Wee came down with a suitcase and set it by the door.

'Give us a cigarette, Pee,' the young man said.

'Don't have any.'

'Well roll one.'

'I said I don't have any tobacco.'

'Oh.'

'You'll have to leave now, Little Red,' the preacher said.

Helen stood up and came over to Little Red and put a cigarette in his hand. He took it and said nothing. Helen struck a match and lit it for him, then sat back down.

'I don't have anyplace to go,' Little Red said, blowing smoke past the preacher.

'You should have thought of that before you started drinking. You are a contumacious young man.'

'I got noplace to put that bag. And I got a pencil and paper upstairs.'

'Leave it here. Come and get your pencil and paper when you get that poison out of your system and you can talk sense about yourself.'

'My pants are in there.'

'They'll be all right. Nobody here will touch your pants.'

'Can I have a cup of coffee?'

'If you found money for beer, you can find money for coffee.'

'Where can I go?'

'I couldn't begin to imagine. Come back sober and you may have some food. Now get a move on.'

Little Red grabbed the doorknob, opened the door, and took a step. Then he stepped back in and pointed at his suitcase.

'I got cigarettes there,' he said.

'Then get your cigarettes.'

Little Red undid the belt that held the suitcase together and rummaged for a pack of Camels. He rebuckled the belt and stood up.

'If I come back tomorrow . . .'

'We'll see about tomorrow,' said the preacher, who grabbed the doorknob himself and pulled it to as he ushered Little Red out into the night.

'Don't lose my pants,' Little Red called through the glass of the closing door.

Francis, wearing his new socks, was first out of the mission, first to cast an anxious glance around the corner of the building at Sandra, who sat propped where he had left her, her eyes sewn as tightly closed by the darkness as the eyes of a diurnal bird. Francis touched her firmly with a finger and she moved, but without opening her eyes. He looked up at the full moon, a silver cinder illuminating this night for bleeding women and frothing madmen, and which warmed him with the enormous shadow it thrust forward in his own path. When Sandra moved he leaned over and put the back of his hand against her cheek and felt the ice of her flesh.

'You got an old blanket or some old rags, any old bum's coat to throw over her?' he asked Pee Wee, who stood in the shadows considering the encounter.

'I could get something,' Pee Wee said, and he loosened his keys and opened the door of the darkened mission: all lights off save the kitchen, which would remain bright until eleven, lockout time. Pee Wee opened the door and entered as Rudy, Helen, and Francis huddled around Sandra, watching her breathe. Francis had watched two dozen people suspire into death, all of them bums except for his father, and Gerald.

'Maybe if we cut her throat the ambulance'd take her,' Francis said.

'She doesn't want an ambulance,' Helen said. 'She wants to sleep it all away. I'll bet she doesn't even feel cold.'

'She's a cake of ice.'

Sandra moved, turning her head toward the voices but without opening her eyes. 'You got no wine?' she asked.

'No wine, honey,' Helen said.

Pee Wee came out with a stone-gray rag that might once have been a blanket and wrapped its rough doubleness around Sandra. He tucked it into the neck of her sweater, and with one end formed a cowl behind her head, giving her the look of a monastic beggar in sackcloth.

'I don't want to look at her no more,' Francis said, and he walked east on Madison, the deepening chill aggravating his limp. Helen and Pee Wee fell in behind him, and Rudy after that.

'You ever know her, Pee Wee?' Francis asked. 'I mean when she was in shape?'

'Sure. Everybody knew her. You took your turn. Then she got to givin' love parties, is what she called 'em, but she'd turn mean, first love you up and then bite you bad. Half-ruined enough guys so only strangers'd go with her. Then she stopped that and hung out with one bum name of Freddy and they specialized in one another about a year till he went somewheres and she didn't.'

'Nobody suffers like a lover left behind,' Helen said.

'Well that's a crock,' Francis said. 'Lots suffer ain't ever been in love even once.'

'They don't suffer like those who have,' said Helen.

'Yeah. Where's this joint, Pee Wee, Green Street?'

'Right. Couple of blocks. Where the old Gayety Theater used to be.'

'I used to go there. Watch them ladies' ankles and can-canny crotches.'

'Be nice, Francis,' Helen said.

'I'm nice. I'm the nicest thing you'll see all week.'

Goblins came at them on Green Street, hooded spooks, a Charlie Chaplin in whiteface, with derby, cane, and tash, and a girl wearing an enormous old bonnet with a full-sized bird on top of it.

'They gonna get us!' Francis said. 'Look out!' He threw his arms in the air and shook himself in a fearful dance. The children laughed and spooked boo at him.

'Gee it's a nice night,' Helen said. 'Cold but nice and clear, isn't it, Fran?'

'It's nice,' Francis said. 'It's all nice.'

The Gilded Cage door opened into the old Gayety lobby, now the back end of a saloon that mimicked and mocked the Bowery pubs of forty years gone. Francis stood looking toward a pair of monumental, half-wrapped breasts that heaved beneath a hennaed wig and scarlet lips. The owner of these spectacular possessions was delivering outward from an elevated platform a song of anguish in the city: *You would not insult me, sir, if Jack were only here,* in a voice so devoid of musical quality that it mocked its own mockery.

'She's terrible,' Helen said. 'Awful.'

'She ain't that good,' Francis said.

They stepped across a floor strewn with sawdust, lit by ancient chandeliers and sconces, all electric now, toward a long walnut bar with a shining brass bar rail and three gleaming spittoons. Behind the half-busy bar a man with high collar, string tie, and arm garters drew schooners of beer from a tap, and at tables of no significant location sat men and women Francis recognized: whores, bums, barflies. Among them, at other tables, sat men in business suits, and women with fox scarves and flyaway hats, whose presence was such that their tables this night were landmarks of social significance merely because they were sitting at them. Thus, The Gilded Cage was a museum of unnatural sociality, and the smile of the barman welcomed Francis, Helen, and Rudy, bums all, and Pee Wee, their clean-shirted friend, to the tableau.

'Table, folks?'

'Not while there's a bar rail,' Francis said.

'Step up, brother. What's your quaff?'

'Ginger ale,' said Pee Wee.

'I believe I'll have the same,' said Helen.

'That beer looks tantalizin',' Francis said.

'You said you wouldn't drink,' Helen said.

'I said wine.'

The barman slid a schooner with a high collar across the bar to Francis and looked to Rudy, who ordered the same. The piano player struck up a medley of 'She May Have Seen Better Days' and 'My Sweetheart's the Man in the Moon' and urged those in the audience who knew the lyrics to join in song.

'You look like a friend of mine,' Francis told the barman, drilling him with a smile and a stare. The barman, with a full head of silver waves and an eloquent white mustache, stared back long enough to ignite a memory. He looked from Francis to Pee Wee, who was also smiling.

'I think I know you two turks,' the barman said.

'You thinkin' right,' Francis said, 'except the last time I seen you, you wasn't sportin' that pussy-tickler.'

The barman stroked his silvery lip. 'You guys got me drunk in New York.'

'You got us drunk in every bar on Third Avenue,' Pee Wee said.

The barman stuck out his hand to Francis.

'Francis Phelan,' said Francis, 'and this here is Rudy the Kraut. He's all right but he's nuts.'

'My kind of fella,' Oscar said.

'Pee Wee Packer,' Pee Wee said with his hand out.

'I remember,' said Oscar.

'And this is Helen,' said Francis. 'She hangs out with me, but damned if I know why.'

'Oscar Reo's what I still go by, folks, and I really do remember you boys. But I don't drink anymore.'

'Hey, me neither,' said Pee Wee.

'I ain't turned it off yet,' Francis said. 'I'm waitin' till I retire.'

'He retired forty years ago,' Pee Wee said.

'That ain't true. I worked all day today. Gettin' rich. How you like my new duds?'

'You're a sport,' Oscar said. 'Can't tell you from those swells over there.'

'Swells and bums, there ain't no difference,' Francis said.

'Except swells like to look like swells,' Oscar said, 'and bums like to look like bums. Am I right?'

'You're a smart fella,' Francis said.

'You still singin', Oscar?' Pee Wee asked.

'For my supper.'

'Well goddamn it,' Francis said, 'give us a tune.'

'Since you're so polite about it,' Oscar said. And he turned to the piano man and said: '"Sixteen"'; and instantly there came from the piano the strains of 'Sweet Sixteen.'

'Oh that's a wonderful song,' Helen said. 'I remember you singing that on the radio.'

'How durable of you, my dear.'

Oscar sang into the bar microphone and, with great resonance and no discernible loss of control from his years with the drink, he turned time back to the age of the village green. The voice was as commonplace to an American ear as Jolson's, or Morton

Downey's; and even Francis, who rarely listened to the radio, or ever had a radio to listen to in either the early or the modern age, remembered its pitch and its tremolo from the New York binge, when this voice by itself was a chorale of continuous joy for all in earshot, or so it seemed to Francis at a distance of years. And further, the attention that the bums, the swells, the waiters, were giving the man, proved that this drunk was not dead, not dying, but living an epilogue to a notable life. And yet, and yet . . . here he was, disguised behind a mustache, another cripple, his ancient, weary eyes revealing to Francis the scars of a blood brother, a man for whom life had been a promise unkept in spite of great success, a promise now and forever unkeepable. The man was singing a song that had grown old not from time but from wear. The song is frayed. The song is worn out.

The insight raised in Francis a compulsion to confess his every transgression of natural, moral, or civil law; to relentlessly examine and expose every flaw of his own character, however minor. What was it, Oscar, that did you in? Would you like to tell us all about it? Do you know? It wasn't Gerald who did *me*. It wasn't drink and it wasn't baseball and it wasn't really Mama. What was it that went bust, Oscar, and how come nobody ever found out how to fix it for us?

When Oscar segued perfectly into a second song, his talent seemed awesome to Francis, and the irrelevance of talent to Oscar's broken life even more of a mystery. How does somebody get this good and why doesn't it mean anything? Francis considered his own talent on the ball field of a hazy, sunlit yesterday: how he could follow the line of the ball from every crack of the bat, zap after it like a chicken hawk after a chick, how he would stroke and pocket its speed no matter whether it was lined at him or sizzled erratically toward him through the grass. He would stroke it with the predatory curve of his glove and begin with his right hand even then, whether he was running or falling, to reach into that leather pocket, spear the chick with his educated talons, and whip it across to first or second base, or wherever it needed to go and you're out, man, you're out. No ball player anywhere moved his body any better than Franny Phelan, a damn fieldin' machine, fastest ever was.

Francis remembered the color and shape of his glove, its odor of oil and sweat and leather, and he wondered if Annie had kept it. Apart from his memory and a couple of clippings, it would be all that remained of a spent career that had blossomed and then peaked in the big leagues far too long after the best years were gone, but which brought with the peaking the promise that some belated and over-due glory was possible, that somewhere there was a hosannah to be cried in the name of Francis Phelan, one of the best sonsabitches ever to kick a toe into third base.

Oscar's voice quavered with beastly loss on a climactic line of the song: Blinding tears falling as he thinks of his lost pearl, broken heart calling, oh yes, calling, dear old girl. Francis turned to Helen and saw her crying splendid, cathartic tears: Helen, with the image of inexpungeable sorrow in her cortex, with a lifelong devotion to forlorn love, was weeping richly for all the pearls lost since love's old sweet song first was sung.

'Oh that was so beautiful, so beautiful,' Helen said to Oscar when he rejoined them at the beer spigot. 'That's absolutely one of my all-time favorites. I used to sing it myself.'

'A singer?' said Oscar. 'Where was that?'

'Oh everywhere. Concerts, the radio. I used to sing on the air every night, but that was an age ago.'

'You should do us a tune.'

'Oh never,' said Helen.

'Customers sing here all the time,' Oscar said.

'No, no,' said Helen, 'the way I look.'

'You look as good as anybody here,' Francis said.

'I could never,' said Helen. But she was readying herself to do what she could never, pushing her hair behind her ear, straightening her collar, smoothing her much more than ample front.

'What'll it be?' Oscar said. 'Joe knows 'em all.'

'Let me think awhile.'

Francis saw that Aldo Campione was sitting at a table at the far end of the room and had someone with him. That son of a bitch is following me, is what Francis thought. He fixed his glance on the table and saw Aldo move his hand in an ambiguous gesture. What are you telling me, dead man, and who's that with you? Aldo wore a white flower in the lapel of his white flannel suitcoat, a new addition since the bus. Goddamn dead people travelin' in packs, buyin' flowers. Francis studied the other man without recognition and felt the urge to walk over and take a closer look. But what if nobody's sittin' there? What if nobody sees these bozos but me? The flower girl came along with a full tray of white gardenias.

'Buy a flower, sir?' she asked Francis.

'Why not? How much?'

'Just a quarter.'

'Give us one.'

He fished a quarter out of his pants and pinned the gardenia on Helen's lapel with a pin the girl handed him. 'It's been a while since I bought you flowers,' he said. 'You gonna sing up there for us, you gotta put on the dog a little.'

Helen leaned over and kissed Francis on the mouth, which always made him blush when she did it in public. She was always a first-rate heller between the sheets, when there was sheets, when there was somethin' to do between them.

'Francis always bought me flowers,' she said. 'He'd get money and first thing he'd do was buy me a dozen roses, or a white orchid even. He didn't care what he did with the money as long as I got my flowers first. You did that for me, didn't you, Fran?'

'Sure did,' said Francis, but he could not remember buying an orchid, didn't know what orchids looked like.

'We were lovebirds,' Helen said to Oscar, who was smiling at the spectacle of bum love at his bar. 'We had a beautiful apartment up on Hamilton Street. We had all the dishes anybody'd ever need. We had a sofa and a big bed and sheets and pillowcases. There wasn't anything we didn't have, isn't that right, Fran?'

'That's right,' Francis said, trying to remember the place.

'We had flowerpots full of geraniums that we kept alive all winter long. Francis loved geraniums. And we had an icebox crammed full of food. We ate so well, both of us had to go on a diet. That was such a wonderful time.'

'When was that?' Pee Wee asked. 'I didn't know you ever stayed anyplace that long.'

'What long?'

'I don't know. Months musta been if you had an apartment.'

'I was here awhile, six weeks maybe, once.'

'Oh we had it much longer than that,' Helen said.

'Helen knows,' Francis said. 'She remembers. I can't call one day different from another.'

'It was the drink,' Helen said. 'Francis wouldn't stop drinking and then we couldn't pay the rent and we had to give up our pillowcases and our dishes. It was Haviland china, the very best you could buy. When you buy, buy the best, my father taught me. We had solid mahogany chairs and my beautiful upright piano my brother had been keeping. He didn't want to give it up, it was so nice, but it was mine. Paderewski played on it once when he was in Albany in nineteen-oh-nine. I sang all my songs on it.'

'She played pretty fancy piano,' Francis said. 'That's no joke. Why don't you sing us a song, Helen?'

'Oh I guess I will.'

'What's your pleasure?' Oscar asked.

'I don't know. "In the Good Old Summertime," maybe.'

'Right time to sing it,' Francis said, 'now that we're freezin' our ass out there.'

'On second thought,' said Helen, 'I want to sing one for Francis for buying me that flower. Does your friend know "He's Me Pal," or "My Man"?'

'You hear that, Joe?'

'I hear,' said Joe the piano man, and he played a few bars of the chorus of 'He's Me Pal' as Helen smiled and stood and walked to the stage with an aplomb and grace befitting her reentry into the world of music, the world she should never have left, oh why ever did you leave it, Helen? She climbed the three steps to the platform, drawn upward by familiar chords that now seemed to her to have always evoked joy, chords not from this one song but from an era of songs, thirty, forty years of songs that celebrated the splendors of love, and loyalty, and friendship, and family, and country, and the natural world. Frivolous Sal was a wild sort of devil, but wasn't she dead on the level too? Mary was a great pal, heaven-sent on Christmas morning, and love lingers on for her. The new-mown hay, the silvery moon, the home fires burning, these were sanctuaries of Helen's spirit, songs whose like she had sung from her earliest days, songs that endured for her as long as the classics she had committed to memory so indelibly in her youth, for they spoke to her, not abstractly of the aesthetic peaks of the art she had once hoped to master, but directly, simply, about the everyday currency of the heart and soul. The pale moon will shine on the twining of our hearts. My heart is stolen, lover dear, so please don't let us part. Oh love, sweet love, oh burning love – the songs told her – you are mine, I am yours, forever and a day. You spoiled the girl I used to be, my hope has gone away. Send me away with a smile, but remember: you're turning off the sunshine of my life.

Love.

A flood tide of pity rose in Helen's breast. Francis, oh sad man, was her last great love, but he wasn't her only one. Helen has had a lifetime of sadnesses with her lovers. Her first true love kept her in his fierce embrace for years, but then he loosened that embrace and let her slide down and down until the hope within her died. Hopeless Helen, that's who she was when she met Francis. And as she stepped up to the microphone on the stage of The Gilded Cage, hearing the piano behind her, Helen was a living explosion of unbearable memory and indomitable joy.

And she wasn't a bit nervous either, thank you, for she was a professional who had never let the public intimidate her when she sang in a church, or at musicales, or at weddings, or at Woolworth's when she sold song sheets, or even on the radio with that audience all over the city every night. Oscar Reo, you're not the only one who sang for Americans over the airwaves. Helen had her day and she isn't a bit nervous.

But she is . . . all right, yes, she is . . . a girl enveloped by private confusion, for she feels the rising of joy and sorrow simultaneously and she cannot say whether one or the other will take her over during the next few moments.

'What's Helen's last name?' Oscar asked.

'Archer,' Francis said. 'Helen Archer.'

'Hey,' said Rudy, 'how come you told me she didn't have a last name?'

'Because it don't matter what anybody tells you,' Francis said. 'Now shut up and listen.'

'A real old-time trouper now,' said Oscar into the bar mike, 'will give us a song or two for your pleasure, lovely Miss Helen Archer.'

And then Helen, still wearing that black rag of a coat rather than expose the even more tattered blouse and skirt that she wore beneath it, standing on her spindle legs with her tumorous belly butting the metal stand of the microphone and giving her the look of a woman five months pregnant, casting boldly before the audience this image of womanly disaster and fully aware of the dimensions of this image, Helen then tugged stylishly at her beret, adjusting it forward over one eye. She gripped the microphone with a sureness that postponed her disaster, at least until the end of this tune, and sang then 'He's Me Pal,' a ditty really, short and snappy, sang it with exuberance and wit, with a tilt of the head, a roll of the eyes, a twist of the wrist that suggested the proud virtues. Sure, he's dead tough, she sang, but his love ain't no bluff. Wouldn't he share his last dollar with her? Hey, no millionaire will ever grab Helen. She'd rather have her pal with his fifteen a week. Oh Francis, if you only made just fifteen a week.

If you only.

The applause was full and long and gave Helen strength to begin 'My Man,' Fanny Brice's wonderful torch, and Helen Morgan's too. Two Helens. Oh Helen, you were on the radio, but where did it take you? What fate was it that kept you from the great heights that were yours by right of talent and education? You were born to be a star, so many said it. But it was others who went on to the heights and you were left behind to grow bitter. How you learned to envy those who rose when you did not, those who never deserved it, had no talent, no training. There was Carla, from high school, who could not even carry a tune but who made a movie with Eddie Cantor, and there was Edna, ever so briefly from Woolworth's, who sang in a Broadway show by Cole Porter because she learned how to wiggle her fanny. But ah, sweetness was Helen's, for Carla went off a cliff in an automobile, and Edna sliced her wrists and bled her life away in her lover's bathtub, and Helen laughed last. Helen is singing on a stage this very minute and just listen to the voice she's left with after all her troubles. Look at those well-dressed people out there hanging on her every note.

Helen closed her eyes and felt tears forcing their way out and could not say whether she was blissfully happy or fatally sad. At some point it all came together and didn't make much difference anyway, for sad or happy, happy or sad, life didn't change for Helen. Oh, her man, how much she loves you. You can't imagine. Poor girl, all despair now. If she went away she'd come back on her knees. Some day. She's yours. Forevermore.

Oh thunder! Thunderous applause! And the elegant people are standing for Helen, when last did that happen? More, more, more, they yell, and she is crying so desperately now for happiness, or is it for loss, that it makes Francis and Pee Wee cry too. And even though people are calling for more, more, more, Helen steps delicately back down the three platform steps and walks proudly over to Francis with her head in the air and her face impossibly wet, and she kisses him on the cheek so all will know that this is the man she was talking about, in case you didn't notice when we came in together. This is the man.

By god that was great, Francis says. You're better'n anybody.

Helen, says Oscar, that was first-rate. You want a singing job here, you come round tomorrow and I'll see the boss puts you on the payroll. That's a grand voice you've got there, lady. A grand voice.

Oh thank you all, says Helen, thank you all so very kindly. It is so pleasant to be appreciated for your God-given talent and for your excellent training and for your natural presence.

Oh I do thank you, and I shall come again to sing for you, you may be sure.

Helen closed her eyes and felt tears beginning to force their way out and could not say whether she was blissfully happy or devastatingly sad. Some odd-looking people were applauding politely, but others were staring at her with sullen faces. If they're sullen, then obviously they didn't think much of your renditions, Helen. Helen steps delicately back down the three steps, comes over to Francis, and keeps her head erect as he leans over and pecks her cheek.

'Mighty nice, old gal,' he says.

'Not bad at all,' Oscar says. 'You'll have to do it again sometime.'

Helen closed her eyes and felt tears forcing their way out and knew life didn't change. If she went away she'd come back on her knees. It is so pleasant to be appreciated.

Helen, you are like a blackbird, when the sun comes out for a little while. Helen, you are like a blackbird made sassy by the sun. But what will happen to you when the sun goes down again?

I do thank you.

And I shall come again to sing for you.

Oh sassy blackbird! Oh!

3

Rudy left them to flop someplace, half-drunk on six beers, and Francis, Helen, and Pee Wee walked back along Green Street to Madison and then west toward the mission. Walk Pee Wee home and go get a room at Palombo's Hotel, get warm, stretch out, rest them bones. Because Francis and Helen had money: five dollars and seventy-five cents. Two of it Helen had left from what Francis gave her last night; plus three-seventy-five out of his cemetery wages, for he spent little in The Gilded Cage, Oscar buying twice as many drinks as he took money for.

The city had grown quiet at midnight and the moon was as white as early snow. A few cars moved slowly on Pearl Street but otherwise the streets were silent. Francis turned up his suitcoat collar and shoved his hands into his pants pockets. Alongside the mission the moon illuminated Sandra, who sat where they had left her. They stopped to look at her condition. Francis squatted and shook her.

'You sobered up yet, lady?'

Sandra answered him with an enveloping silence. Francis pushed the cowl off her face and in the vivid moonlight saw the toothmarks on her nose and cheek and chin. He shook his head to clear the vision, then saw that one of her fingers and the flesh between forefinger and thumb on her left hand had been chewed.

'The dogs got her.'

He looked across the street and saw a red-eyed mongrel waiting in the half-lit corner of an alley and he charged after it, picking up a stone as he went. The cur fled down the alley as Francis turned his ankle on a raised sidewalk brick and sprawled on the pavement. He picked himself up, he now bloodied too by the cur, and sucked the dirt out of the cuts.

As he crossed the street, goblins came up from Broadway, ragged and masked, and danced around Helen. Pee Wee, bending over Sandra, straightened up as the goblin dance gained in ferocity.

'Jam and jelly, big fat belly,' the goblins yelled at Helen. And when she drew herself inward they only intensified the chant.

'Hey you kids,' Francis yelled. 'Let her alone.'

But they danced on and a skull goblin poked Helen in the stomach with a stick. As she swung at the skull with her hand, another goblin grabbed her purse and then all scattered.

'Little bastards, devils,' Helen cried, running after them. And Francis and Pee Wee too joined the chase, pounding through the night, no longer sure which one wore the skull mask. The goblins ran down alleys, around corners, and fled beyond capture.

Francis turned back to Helen, who was far behind him. She was weeping, gasping, doubled over in a spasm of loss.

'Sonsabitches,' Francis said.

'Oh the money,' Helen said, 'the money.'

'They hurt you with that stick?'

'I don't think so.'

'That money ain't nothin'. Get more tomorrow.'

'It was.'

'Was what?'

'There was fifteen dollars in there besides the other.'

'Fifteen? Where'd you get fifteen dollars?'

'Your son Billy gave it to me. The night he found us at Spanish George's. You were passed out and he gave us forty-five dollars, all the cash he had. I gave you thirty and kept the fifteen.'

'I went through that pocketbook. I didn't see it.'

'I pinned it inside the lining so you wouldn't drink it up. I wanted our suitcase back. I wanted our room for a week so I could rest.'

'Goddamn it, woman, now we ain't got a penny. You and your sneaky goddamn ways.'

Pee Wee came back from the chase empty-handed.

'Some tough kids around here,' he said. 'You okay, Helen?'

'Fine, just fine.'

'You're not hurt?'

'Not anyplace you could see.'

'Sandra,' Pee Wee said. 'She's dead.'

'She's more than that,' Francis said. 'She's partly chewed away.'

'We'll take her inside so they don't eat no more of her,' Pee Wee said. 'I'll call the police.'

'You think it's all right to bring her inside?' Francis asked. 'She's still got all that poison in her system.'

Pee Wee said nothing and opened the mission door. Francis picked Sandra up from the dust and carried her inside. He put her down on an old church bench against the wall and covered her face with the scratchy blanket that had become her final gift from the world.

'If I had my rosary I'd say it for her,' Helen said, sitting on a chair beside the bench and looking at Sandra's corpse. 'But it was in my purse. I've carried that rosary for twenty years.'

'I'll check the vacant lots and the garbage cans in the mornin',' Francis said. 'It'll turn up.'

'I'll bet Sandra prayed to die,' Helen said.

'Hey,' said Francis.

'I would if I was her. Her life wasn't human anymore.'

Helen looked at the clock: twelve-ten. Pee Wee was calling the police.

'Today's a holy day of obligation,' she said. 'It's All Saints' Day.'

'Yup,' said Francis.

'I want to go to church in the morning.'

'All right, go to church.'

'I will. I want to hear mass.'

'Hear it. That's tomorrow. What are we gonna do tonight? Where the hell am I gonna put you?'

'You could stay here,' Pee Wee said. 'All the beds are full but you can sleep down here on a bench.'

'No,' Helen said. 'I'd rather not do that. We can go up to Jack's. He told me I could come back if I wanted.'

'Jack said that?' Francis asked.

'Those were his words.'

'Then let's shag ass. Jack's all right. Clara's a crazy bitch but I like Jack. Always did. You sure he said that?'

'"Come back anytime," he said as I was going out the door.'

'All right. Then we'll move along, old buddy,' Francis said to Pee Wee. 'You'll figure it out with Sandra?'

'I'll do the rest,' Pee Wee said.

'You know her last name?'

'No. Never heard it.'

'Don't make much difference now.'

'Never did,' Pee Wee said.

Francis and Helen walked up Pearl Street toward State, the absolute center of the city's life for two centuries. One trolley car climbed State Street's violent incline and another came toward them, rocking south on Pearl. A man stepped out of the Waldorf Restaurant and covered his throat with his coat collar, shivered once, and walked on. The cold had numbed Francis's fingertips, frost was blooming on the roofs of parked cars, and the night-walkers exhaled dancing plumes of vapor. From a man-hole in the middle of State Street steam rose and vanished. Francis imagined the subterranean element at the source of this: a huge human head with pipes screwed into its ears, steam rising from a festering skull wound.

Aldo Campione, walking on the opposite side of North Pearl from Francis and Helen, raised his right hand in the same ambiguous gesture Francis had witnessed at the bar. As Francis speculated on the meaning, the man who had been sitting with Aldo stepped out of the shadows into a streetlight's glow, and Aldo's gesture then became clear: it introduced Francis to Dick Doolan, the bum who tried to cut off Francis's feet with a meat cleaver.

'I went to the kid's grave today,' Francis said.

'What kid?'

'Gerald.'

'Oh, you did?' she said. 'Then that was the first time, wasn't it? It must've been.'

'Right.'

'You're thinking about him these days. You mentioned him last week.'

'I never stop thinkin' about him.'

'What's gotten into you?'

Francis saw the street that lay before him: Pearl Street, the central vessel of this city, city once his, city lost. The commerce along with its walls jarred him: so much new, stores gone out of business he never even heard of. Some things remained: Whitney's, Myers', the old First Church, which rose over Clinton Square, the Pruyn Library. As he walked, the cobblestones turned to granite, houses became stores, life aged, died, renewed itself, and a vision of what had been and what might have been intersected in an eye that could not really remember one or interpret the other. What would you give never to have left, Francis?

'I said, what's got into you?'

'Nothin's got into me. I'm just thinkin' about a bunch of stuff. This old street. I used to own this street, once upon a time.'

'You should've sold it when you had the chance.'

'Money. I ain't talkin' about money.'

'I didn't think you were. That was a funny.'

'Wasn't much funny. I said I saw Gerald's grave. I talked to him.'

'Talked? How did you talk?'

'Stood and talked to the damn grass. Maybe I'm gettin' nutsy as Rudy. He can't hold his pants up, they fall over his shoes.'

'You're not nutsy, Francis. It's because you're here. We shouldn't be here. We should go someplace else.'

'Right. That's where we oughta go. Else.'

'Don't drink any more tonight.'

'Listen here. Don't you nag my ass.'

'I want you straight, please. I want you straight.'

'I'm the straightest thing you'll see all week. I am so straight. I'm the straightest thing you'll sweek. The thing that happened on the other side of the street. The thing that happened was Billy told me stuff about Annie. I never told you that. Billy told me stuff about Annie, how she never told I dropped him.'

'Never told who, the police?'

'Never nobody. Never a damn soul. Not Billy, not Peg, not her brother, not her sisters. Ain't that the somethin'est thing you ever heard? I can't see a woman goin' through that stuff and not tellin' nobody about it.'

'You've got a lot to say about those people.'

'Not much to say.'

'Maybe you ought to go see them.'

'No, that wouldn't do no good.'

'You'd get it out of your system.'

'What out of my system?'

'Whatever it is that's in there.'

'Never mind about my system. How come you wouldn't stay at the mission when you got an invite?'

'I don't want their charity.'

'You ate their soup.'

'I did not. All I had was coffee. Anyway, I don't like Chester. He doesn't like Catholics.'

'Catholics don't like Methodists. What the hell, that's even. And I don't see any Catholic missions down here. I ain't had any Catholic soup lately.'

'I won't do it and that's that.'

'So freeze your ass someplace. Your flower's froze already.'

'Let it freeze.'

'You sang a song at least.'

'Yes I did. I sang while Sandra was dying.'

'She'da died no matter. Her time was up.'

'No, I don't believe that. That's fatalism. I believe we die when we can't stand it anymore. I believe we stand as much as we can and then we die when we can, and Sandra decided she could die.'

'I don't fight that. Die when you can. That's as good a sayin' as there is.'

'I'm glad we agree on something,' Helen said.

'We get along all right. You ain't a bad sort.'

'You're all right too.'

'We're both all right,' Francis said, 'and we ain't got a damn penny and noplace to flop. We on the bum. Let's get the hell up to Jack's before he puts the lights out on us.'

Helen slipped her arm inside Francis's. Across the street Aldo Campione and Dick Doolan, who in the latter years of his life was known as Rowdy Dick, kept silent pace.

Helen pulled her arm away from Francis and tightened her collar around her neck, then hugged herself and buried her hands in her armpits.

'I'm chilled to my bones,' she said.

'It's chilly, all right.'

'I mean a real chill, a deep chill.'

Francis put his arm around her and walked her up the steps of Jack's house. It stood on the east side of Ten Broeck Street, a three-block street in Arbor Hill named for a Revolutionary War hero and noted in the 1870s and 1880s as the place where a dozen of the city's arriviste lumber barons lived, all in a row, in competitive luxury. For their homes the barons built handsome brownstones, most of them now cut into apartments like Jack's, or into furnished rooms.

The downstairs door to Jack's opened without a key. Helen and Francis climbed the broad walnut staircase, still vaguely elegant despite the threadbare carpet, and Francis knocked. Jack opened the door and looked out with the expression of an ominous crustacean. With one hand he held the door ajar, with the other he gripped the jamb.

'Hey Jack,' Francis said, 'we come to see ya. How's chances for a bum gettin' a drink?'

Jack opened the door wider to look beyond Francis and when he saw Helen he let his arm fall and backed into the apartment. Kate

Smith came at them, piped out of a small phonograph through the speaker of the radio. The Carolina moon was shining on somebody waiting for Kate. Beside the phonograph sat Clara, balancing herself on a chamber pot, propped on all sides with purple throw pillows, giving her the look of being astride a great animal. A red bedspread covered her legs, but it had fallen away at one side, revealing the outside of her naked left thigh, visible to the buttocks. A bottle of white fluid sat on the table by the phonograph, and on a smaller table on her other side a swinging rack cradled a gallon of muscatel, tiltable for pouring. Helen walked over to Clara and stood by her.

'Golly it's cold for this time of year, and they're calling for snow. Just feel my hands.'

'This happens to be my home,' Clara said hoarsely, 'and I ain't about to feel your hands, or your head either. I don't see any snow.'

'Have a drink,' Jack said to Francis.

'Sure,' Francis said. 'I had a bowl of soup about six o'clock but it went right through me. I'm gonna have to eat somethin' soon.'

'I don't care whether you eat or not,' Jack said.

Jack went to the kitchen and Francis asked Clara: 'You feelin' better?'

'No.'

'She's got the runs,' Helen said.

'I'll tell people what I got,' Clara said.

'She lost her husband this week,' Jack said, returning with two empty tumblers. He tilted the jug and half-filled both.

'How'd you find out?' Helen said.

'I saw it in the paper today,' Clara said.

'I took her to the funeral this morning,' Jack said. 'We got a cab and went to the funeral home. They didn't even call her.'

'He didn't look any different than when I married him.'

'No kiddin',' Francis said.

'Outside of his hair was snow-white, that's all.'

'Her kids were there,' Jack said.

'The snots,' Clara said.

'Sometimes I wonder what if I run off or dropped dead,' Francis said. 'Helen'd probably go crazy.'

'Why if you dropped dead she'd bury you before you started stinkin',' Jack said. 'That's all'd happen.'

'What a heart you have,' Francis said.

'You gotta bury your dead,' Jack said.

'That's a rule of the Catholic church,' said Helen.

'I'm not talkin' about the Catholic church,' Francis said.

'Anyway, now she's a single girl,' Jack said, 'I'm gonna find out what Clara's gonna do.'

'I'm gonna go right on livin' normal,' Clara said.

'Normal is somethin',' Francis said. 'What the hell is normal anyway, is what I'd like to know. Normal is cold. Goddamn it's cold tonight. My fingers. I rubbed myself to see if I was livin'. You know, I wanna ask you one question.'

'No,' Clara said.

'You said no. Whataya mean no?'

'What's he gonna ask?' Jack said. 'Find out what he's gonna ask.'

Clara waited.

'How's everythin' been goin'?' Francis asked.

Clara lifted the bottle of white fluid from the phonograph table, where the Kate Smith record was scratching in its final groove, and drank. She shook her head as it went down, and the greasy, uncombed stringlets of her hair leaped like whips. Her eyes hung low in their sockets, a pair of collapsing moons. She recapped the bottle and then swigged her muscatel to drive out the taste. She dragged on her cigarette, then coughed and spat venomously into a wadded handkerchief she held in her fist.

'Things ain't been goin' too good for Clara,' Jack said, turning off the phonograph.

'I'm still trottin',' Clara said.

'Well you look pretty good for a sick lady,' Francis said. 'Look as good as usual to me.'

Clara smiled over the rim of her wineglass at Francis.

'Nobody,' said Helen, 'asked how things are going for me, but I'll tell you. They're going just wonderful. Just wonderful.'

'She's drunker than hell,' Francis said.

'Oh I'm loaded to the gills,' Helen said, giggling. 'I can hardly walk.'

'You ain't drunk even a nickel's worth,' Jack said. 'Franny's the drunk one. You're hopeless, right, Franny?'

'Helen'll never amount to nothin' if she stays with me,' Francis said.

'I always thought you were an intelligent man,' Jack said, and he swallowed half his wine, 'but you can't be, you can't be.'

'You could be mistaken,' Helen said.

'Keep out of it,' Francis told her, and he hooked a thumb at her, facing Jack. 'There's enough right there to put you in the loony bin, just worryin' about where she's gonna live, where she's gonna stay.'

'I think you could be a charmin' man,' Jack said, 'if you'd only get straight. You could have twenty dollars in your pocket at all times, make fifty, seventy-five a week, have a beautiful apartment with everything you want in it, all you want to drink, once you get straight.'

'I worked today up at the cemetery,' Francis said.

'Steady work?' asked Jack.

'Just today. Tomorrow I gotta see a fella needs some liftin' done. The old back's still tough enough.'

'You keep workin' you'll have fifty in your pocket.'

'I had fifty, I'd spend it on her,' Francis said. 'Or buy a pair of shoes. Other pair wore out and Harry over at the old clothes joint give 'em to me for a quarter. He seen me half barefoot and says, Francis you can't go around like that, and he give me these. But they don't fit right and I only got one of 'em laced. Twine there in the other one. I got a shoestring in my pocket but ain't put it in yet.'

'You mean you got the shoelace and you didn't put it in the shoe?' Clara asked.

'I got it in my pocket,' Francis said.

'Then put it in the shoe.'

'I think it's in this pocket here. You know where it is, Helen?'

'Don't ask me.'

'Look and see,' Clara said.

'She wants me to put a shoestring in my shoe,' Francis said.

'Right,' said Clara.

Francis stopped fumbling in his pocket and let his hands fall away.

'I'm renegin',' he said.

'You're what?' Clara asked.

'I'm renegin' and I don't like to do that.'

Francis put down his wine, walked to the bathroom, and sat on the toilet, cover down, trying to understand why he'd lied about a shoestring. He smelled the odor that came up from his fetid crotch and stood up then and dropped his trousers. He stepped out of them, then pulled off his shorts and threw them in the sink. He lifted the toilet cover and sat on the seat, and with Jack's soap and handfuls of water from the bowl, he washed his genitals and buttocks, and all their encrusted orifices, crevices, and secret folds. He rinsed himself, relathered, and rinsed again. He dried himself with one of Jack's towels, picked his shorts out of the sink, and mopped the floor with them where he had splashed water. Then he filled the sink with hot water and soaked the shorts. He soaped them and they separated into two pieces in his hands. He let the water out of the sink, wrung the shorts, and put them in his coat pocket. He opened the door a crack and called out: 'Hey, Jack,' and when Jack came, Francis hid his nakedness with a towel.

'Jack, old buddy, you got an old pair of shorts? Any old pair. Mine just ripped all to hell.'

'I'll go look.'

'Could I borry the use of your razor?'

'Help yourself.'

Jack came back with the shorts and Francis put them on. Then, as Francis soaped his beard, Aldo Campione and Rowdy Dick Doolan entered the bathroom. Rowdy Dick, dapper in a three-piece blue-serge suit and a pearl-gray cap, sat on the toilet, cover down. Aldo made himself comfortable on the rim of the tub, his gardenia unintimidated by the chill of the evening. Jack's razor wouldn't cut Francis's three-day beard, and so he rinsed off the lather, soaked his face again in hot water, and relathered. While Francis rubbed the soap deeply into his beard, Rowdy Dick studied him but could remember nothing of Francis's face. This was to be expected, for when last seen, it was night in Chicago, under a bridge not far from the railyards, and five men were sharing the wealth in 1930, a lean year. On the wall of the abutment above the five, as one of them had pointed out, a former resident of the space had inscribed a poem:

Poor little lamb,
He wakes up in the morning,
His fleece all cold.
He knows what's coming.
Say, little lamb,
We'll go on the bummer this summer.
We'll sit in the shade
And drink lemonade,
The world'll be on the hummer.

Rowdy Dick remembered this poem as well as he remembered the laughter of his sister, Mary, who was striped dead, sleigh riding, under the rails of a horse-drawn sleigh; as clearly as he remembered the plaintive, dying frown of his brother, Ted, who perished from a congenital hole in the heart. They had been three until then, living with an uncle because their parents had died, one by one, and left them alone. And then there was Dick, truly alone, who grew up tough, worked the docks, and then found an easier home in the Tenderloin, breaking the faces of nasty drunks, oily pickpockets, and fat titty-pinchers. But that didn't last either. Nothing lasted for Rowdy Dick, and he went on the bum and wound up under the bridge with Francis Phelan and three other now-faceless men. What he did remember of

Francis was his hand, which now held a razor that stroked the soapy cheek.

What Francis remembered was talking about baseball that famous night. He'd begun by reliving indelible memories of his childhood as a way of explaining, at leisurely pace since none of them had anyplace to go, the generation of his drive to become a third baseman. He had been, he was saying, a boy playing among men, witnessing their talents, their peculiarities, their capacity to dive for a grounder, smash a line drive, catch a fly – all with the very ease of breath itself. They had played in the Van Woert Street polo grounds (Mulvaney's goat pasture) and there were a heroic dozen and a half of them who came two or three evenings a week, some weeks, after work to practice; men in their late twenties and early thirties, reconstituting the game that had enraptured them in their teens. There was Andy Heffern, tall, thin, saturnine, the lunger who would die at Saranac, who could pitch but never run, and who played with a long-fingered glove that had no padding whatever in the pocket, only a wisp of leather that stood between the speed of the ball and Andy's most durable palm. There was Windy Evans, who played outfield in his cap, spikes, and jock, and who caught the ball behind his back, long flies he would outrun by twenty minutes, and then plop would go that dilatory fly ball into the peach basket of his glove; and Windy would leap and beam and tell the world: There's only a few of us left! And Red Cooley, the shortstop who was the pepper of Francis's ancient imagination, and who never stopped the chatter, who leaped at every ground ball as if it were the brass ring to heaven, and who, with his short-fingered glove, wanted for nothing to be judged the world's greatest living ball player, if only it hadn't been for the homegrown deference that kept him a prisoner of Arbor Hill for the rest of his limited life.

These reminiscences by Francis evoked from Rowdy Dick an envy that surpassed reason. Why should any man be so gifted not only with so much pleasurable history but also with a gift of gab that could mesmerize a quintet of bums around a fire under a bridge? Why were there no words that would unlock what lay festering in the heart of Rowdy Dick Doolan, who needed so desperately to express what he could never even know needed expression?

Well, the grand question went unanswered, and the magic words went undiscovered. For Rowdy Dick took vengeful focus on the shoes of the voluble Francis, which were both the most desirable and, except for the burning sticks and boards in the fire, the most visible objects under that Chicago bridge. And Rowdy Dick reached inside his shirt, where he kept the small meat cleaver he had carried ever since Colorado, and slid it out of its carrying case, which he had fashioned from cardboard, oilcloth, and string; and he told Francis then: I'm gonna cut your goddamn feet off; explaining this at first and instant lunge, but explaining, even then, rather too soon for achievement, for the reflexes of Francis were not so rubbery then as they might be now in Jack's bathroom. They were full of fiber and acid and cannonade; and before Rowdy Dick, who had drunk too much of the homemade hooch he had bought, unquestionably too cheaply for sanity, earlier in the day, could make restitution for his impetuosity, Francis deflected the cleaver, which was aimed no longer at his feet but at his head, losing in the process two thirds of a right index finger and an estimated one eighth of an inch of flesh from the approximate center of his nose. He bled then in a wild careen, and with diminished hand knocking the cleaver from Rowdy Dick's grip, he took hold of that same Rowdy Dick by pantleg and armpit and swung him, oh wrathful lambs, against the abutment where the poem was inscribed, swung him as a battering ram might be swung, and cracked Rowdy Dick's skull from left parietal to the squamous area of the occipital, rendering him bloody, insensible, leaking, and instantly dead.

What Francis recalled of this unmanageable situation was the compulsion to flight, the most familiar notion, after the desire not to aspire, that he had ever entertained. And after searching, as swiftly as he knew how, for his lost digital joints, and after concluding that they had flown too deeply into the dust and the weeds ever to be retrieved again by any hand of any man, and after pausing also, ever so briefly, for a reconnoitering, not of what might be recoverable of the nose but of what might be visually memorable because of its separation into parts, Francis began to run, and in so doing, reconstituted a condition that was as pleasurable to his being as it was natural: the running of bases after the crack of the bat, the running from accusation, the running from the calumny of men and women, the running from family, from bondage, from destitution of spirit through ritualistic straightenings, the running, finally, in a quest for pure flight as a fulfilling mannerism of the spirit.

He found his way to a freight yard, found there an empty boxcar with open door, and so entered into yet another departure from completion: the true and total story of his life thus far. It was South Bend before he got to a hospital, where the intern asked him: Where's the finger? And Francis said: In the weeds. And how about the nose? Where's that piece of the nose? If you'd only brought me that piece of the nose, we might be able to put it back together and you wouldn't even know it was gone.

All things had ceased to bleed by then, and so Francis was free once again from those deadly forces that so frequently sought to sever the line of his life.

He had stanched the flow of his wound.

He had stood staunchly irresolute in the face of capricious and adverse fate.

He had, oh wondrous man, stanched death its very self.

Francis dried his face with the towel, buttoned up his shirt, and put on his coat and trousers. He nodded an apology to Rowdy Dick for having taken his life and included in the nod the hope that Dick would understand it hadn't been intentional. Rowdy Dick smiled and doffed his cap, creating an eruption of brilliance around his dome. Francis could see the line of Dick's cranial fracture running through his hair like a gleaming river, and Francis understood that Rowdy Dick was in heaven, or so close to it that he was taking on the properties of an angel of the Lord. Dick put his cap on again and even the cap exuded a glow, like the sun striving to break through a pale, gray cloud. 'Yes,' said Francis, 'I'm sorry I broke your head so bad, but I hope you remember I had my reasons,' and he held up to Rowdy Dick his truncated finger. 'You know, you can't be a priest when you got a finger missin'. Can't say mass with a hand like this. Can't throw a baseball either.' He rubbed the bump in his nose with the stump of a finger. 'Kind of a bump there, but what the hell. Doc put a big bandage on it, and it got itchy, so I ripped it off. Went back when it got infected, and the doc says, You shouldn'ta took off that bandage, because now I got to scrape it out and you'll have an even bigger bump there. I'da had a bump anyway. What the hell, little bump like that don't look too bad, does it? I ain't complainin'. I don't hold no grudges more'n five years.'

'You all right in there, Francis?' Helen called. 'Who are you talking to?'

Francis waved to Rowdy Dick, understanding that some debts of violence had been settled, but he remained full of the awareness of rampant martyrdom surrounding him: martyrs to wrath, to booze, to failure, to loss, to hostile weather. Aldo Campione gestured at Francis, suggesting that while there may be some inconsistency about it, prayers were occasionally answerable, a revelation that did very little to improve Francis's state of mind, for there had never been a time since childhood when he knew what to pray for.

'Hey bum,' he said to Jack when he stepped out of the bathroom, 'how about a bum gettin' a drink?'

'He ain't no bum,' Clara said.

'Goddamn it, I know he ain't,' Francis said. 'He's a hell of a man. A workin' man.'

'How come you shaved?' Helen asked.

'Gettin' itchy. Four days and them whiskers grow back inside again.'

'It sure improves how you look,' Clara said.

'That's the truth,' said Jack.

'I knew Francis was handsome,' Clara said, 'but this is the first time I ever saw you clean shaved.'

'I was thinkin' about how many old bums I know died in the weeds. Wake up covered with snow and some of 'em layin' there dead as hell, froze stiff. Some get up and walk away from it. I did myself. But them others are gone for good. You ever know a guy named Rowdy Dick Doolan in your travels?'

'Never did,' Jack said.

'There was another guy, Pocono Pete, he died in Denver, froze like a brick. And Poocher Felton, he bought it in Detroit, pissed his pants and froze tight to the sidewalk. And a crazy bird they called Ward Six, no other name. They found him with a red icicle growin' out of his nose. All them old guys, never had nothin', never knew nothin', stupid, thievin', crazy. Foxy Phil Tooker, a skinny little runt, he froze all scrunched up, knees under his chin. 'Stead of straightenin' him out, they buried him in half a coffin. Lorda mercy, them geezers. I bet they all of 'em, dyin' like that, I bet they all wind up in heaven, if they ever got such a place.'

'I believe when you're dead you go in the ground and that's the end of it,' Jack said. 'Heaven never made no sensicality to me whatsoever.'

'You wouldn't get in anyhow,' Helen said. 'They've got your reservations someplace else.'

'Then I'm with him,' Clara said. 'Who'd want to be in heaven with all them nuns? God what a bore.'

Francis knew Clara less than three weeks, but he could see the curve of her life: sexy kid likes the rewards, goes pro, gets restless, marries and makes kids, chucks that, pro again, sickens, but really sick, gettin' old, gettin' ugly, locks onto Jack, turns monster. But she's got most of her teeth, not bad; and that hair: you get her to a beauty shop and give her a marcel, it'd be all right; put her in new duds, high heels and silk stockin's; and hey, look at them titties, and that leg: the skin's clear on it.

Clara saw Francis studying her and gave him a wink. 'I knew a fella once, looked a lot like you. I had the hots for him.'

'I'll bet you did,' Helen said.

'He loved what I gave him.'

'Clara never lacked for boyfriends,' Jack said. 'I'm a lucky man. But she's pretty sick. That's why you can't stay. She eats a lot of toast.'

'Oh I could make some toast,' Helen said, standing up from her chair. 'Would you like that?'

'If I feel like eatin' I'll make my own toast,' Clara said. 'And I'm gettin' ready to go to bed. Make sure you lock the door when you go out.'

Jack grabbed Francis by the arm and pulled him toward the kitchen, but not before Francis readjusted his vision of Clara sitting in the middle of her shit machine, sending up a silent reek from her ruined guts and their sewerage.

When Jack and Francis came back into the living room Francis was smoking one of Jack's cigarettes. He dropped it as he reached for the wine, and Helen groaned.

'Everything fallin' on the floor,' Francis said. 'I don't blame you for throwin' these bums out if they can't behave respectable.'

'It's gettin' late for me,' Jack said. 'I used to get by on two, three hours' sleep, but no more.'

'I ain't stayed here in how long now?' Francis asked. 'Two weeks, ain't it?'

'Oh come on, Francis,' Clara said. 'You were here not four days ago. And Helen last night. And last Sunday you were here.'

'Sunday we left,' Helen said.

'I flopped here two nights, wasn't it?' Francis said.

'Six,' Jack said. 'Like a week.'

'I beg to differ with you,' Helen said.

'It was over a week,' Jack said.

'I know different,' said Helen.

'From Monday to Sunday.'

'Oh no.'

'It's a little mixed up,' Francis said.

'He's got a lot of things mixed up,' Helen said. 'I hope you don't get your food mixed up like that down at the diner.'

'No,' Jack said.

'You know, you're very insultin',' Francis said to Helen.

'It was a week,' Jack said.

'You're a liar,' Helen said.

'Don't call me a liar because I know so.'

'Haven't you got any brains at all?' Francis said. 'You supposed to be a college woman, you supposed to be this and that.'

'I am a college woman.'

'You know what I thought,' Jack said, 'was for you to stay here, Franny, till you get work, till you pick up a little bankroll. You don't have to give me nothin'.'

'Shake hands on it,' Helen said.

'I don't know about the proposition now,' Jack said.

'Because I'm a bum,' Francis said.

'No, I wouldn't put it that way.' Jack poured more wine for Francis.

'I knew he didn't mean it,' Helen said.

'I'm gonna tell you,' Francis said. 'I always thought a lot of Clara.'

'You're drunk, Francis,' Helen screamed, standing up again. 'Stay drunk for the rest of your life. I'm leaving you, Francis. You're crazy. All you want is to guzzle wine. You're insane!'

'What'd I say?' Francis asked. 'I said I liked Clara.'

'Nothin' wrong about that,' Jack said.

'I don't mind about that,' Helen said, sitting down.

'I don't know what to do with that woman,' Francis said.

'Do you even know if you're staying here tonight?' Helen asked.

'No, he's not,' Jack said. 'Take him with you when you go.'

'We're going,' Helen said.

'Clara's too sick, Francis,' said Jack.

Francis sipped his wine, put it on the table, and struck a tap dancer's pose.

'How you like these new duds of mine, Clara? You didn't tell me how swell I look, all dressed up.'

'You look sharp,' Clara said.

'You can't keep up with Francis.'

'Don't waste your time, Francis,' Helen said.

'You're getting very hostile, you know that? Listen, you want to sleep with me in the weeds tonight?'

'I never slept in the weeds,' Helen said.

'Never?' asked Clara.

'No, never,' said Helen.

'Oh yes,' Francis said. 'She slept in the coaches with me, and the fields.'

'Never. You made that up, Francis.'

'We been through the valley together,' Francis said.

'Maybe you have,' said Helen. 'I've never gone that far down and I don't intend to go that far down.'

'It ain't far to go. She slept in Finny's car night before last.'

'That's the last time. If it came to that, I'd get in touch with my people.'

'You really ought to get in touch with them, dearie,' said Clara.

'My people are very high class. My brother is a very well-to-do lawyer but I don't like to ask him for anything.'

'Sometimes you have to,' Jack said. 'You oughta move in with him.'

'Then Francis'd be out. No, I've got Francis. We'd get married tomorrow if only he could get a divorce, wouldn't we, Fran.'

'That's right, honey.'

'We battle sometimes, but only when he drinks. Then he goes haywire.'

'You oughta get straight, Franny,' Jack said. 'You could have twenty bucks in your pocket at all times. They need men like you. You could have everything you want. A new Victrola like that one right there. That's a honey.'

'I had all that shit,' Francis said.

'It's late,' Clara said.

'Yeah, people,' said Jack. 'Gotta hit the hay.'

'Fix me a sandwich, will ya?' Francis asked. 'To take out.'

'No,' Clara said.

Helen rose, screaming, and started for Clara. 'You forget when you were hungry.'

'Sit down and shut up,' Francis said.

'I won't shut up. I remember when she came to my place years ago, begging for food. I know her a long time. I'm honest in what I know.'

'I never begged,' said Clara.

'He only asked for a sandwich,' said Helen.

'I'm gonna give him a sandwich,' Jack said.

'Jack don't want you to come back again,' Francis said to Helen.

'I don't want to ever come back again,' Helen said.

'He asked for a sandwich,' Jack said, 'I'll give him a sandwich.'

'I knew you would,' Francis told him.

'Damn right I'll give you a sandwich.'

'Damn right,' Francis said, 'and I knew it.'

'I don't want to be bothered,' Clara said.

'Sharp cheese. You like sharp cheese?'

'My favorite,' Francis said.

Jack went to the kitchen and came back into a silent room with a sandwich wrapped in waxed paper. Francis took it and put it in his coat. Helen stood in the doorway.

'Good night, pal,' Francis said to Jack.

'Best of luck,' Jack said.

'See you around,' Francis said to Clara.

'Toodle-oo,' said Clara.

On the street, Francis felt the urge to run. Ten Broeck Street, in the direction they were walking, inclined downward toward Clinton Avenue, and he felt the gravitational fall driving him into a trot that would leave her behind to solve her own needs. The night seemed colder than before, and clearer too, the moon higher in its sterile solitude. North Pearl Street was deserted, no cars, no people at this hour, one-forty-five by the great clock on the First Church. They had walked three blocks without speaking and now they were heading back toward where they had begun, toward the South End, the mission, the weeds.

'Where the hell you gonna sleep now?' Francis asked.

'I can't be sure, but I wouldn't stay there if they gave me silk sheets and mink pillows. I remember her when she was whoring and always broke. Now she's so high and mighty. I had to speak my piece.'

'You didn't accomplish anything.'

'Did Jack really say that they don't want me anymore?'

'Right. But they asked me to stay. Clara thinks you're a temptation to Jack. The way I figure, if I give her some attention she won't worry about you, but you're so goddamn boisterous. Here. Have a piece of sandwich.'

'It'd choke me.'

'It won't choke you. You'll be glad for it.'

'I'm not a phony.'

'I'm not a phony either.'

'You're not, eh?'

'You know what I'll do?' He grabbed her collar and her throat and screamed into her eyes. 'I'll knock you right across that goddamn street! You don't bullshit me one time. Be a goddamn woman! That's the reason you can't flop with nobody. I can go up there right now and sleep. Jack said I could stay.'

'He did not.'

'He certainly did. But they don't want you. I asked for a sandwich. Did I get it?'

'You're really stupendous and colossal.'

'Listen' – and he still held her by the collar – 'you squint your eyes at me and I'll knock you over that goddamn automobile. You been a pain in the ass to me for nine years. They don't want you because you're a pain in the ass.'

Headlights moved north on Pearl Street, coming toward them, and Francis let go of her. She did not move, but stared at him.

'You got some goddamn eyes, you know?' He was screaming. 'I'll black 'em for you. You're a horse's ass! You know what I'll do? I'll rip that fuckin' coat off and put you in rags.'

She did not move her body or her eyes.

'I'm gonna eat this sandwich. Whole hunk of cheese.'

'I don't want it.'

'By god I do. I'll be hungry tomorrow. It won't choke me. I'm thankful for everything.'

'You're a perfect saint.'

'Listen. Straighten up or I'm gonna kill you.'

'I won't eat it. It's rat food.'

'I'm gonna kill you!' Francis screamed. 'Goddamn it, you hear what I said? Don't drive me insane. Be a goddamn woman and go the fuck to bed somewhere.'

They walked, not quite together, toward Madison Avenue, south again on South Pearl, retracing their steps. Francis brushed Helen's arm and she moved away from him.

'You gonna stay at the mission with Pee Wee?'

'No.'

'Then you gonna stay with me?'

'I'm going to call my brother.'

'Good. Call him. Call him a couple of times.'

'I'll have him meet me someplace.'

'Where you gonna get the nickel to make the call?'

'That's my business. God, Francis, you were all right till you started on the wine. Wine, wine, wine.'

'I'll get some cardboard. We'll go to that old building.'

'The police keep raiding that place. I don't want to go to jail. I don't know why you didn't stay with Jack and Clara since you were so welcome.'

'You're a woman for abuse.'

They walked east on Madison, past the mission. Helen did not look in. When they reached Green Street she stopped.

'I'm going down below,' she said.

'Who you kiddin'?' Francis said. 'You got noplace to go. You'll be knocked on the head.'

'That wouldn't be the worst ever happened to me.'

'We got to find something. Can't leave a dog out like this.'

'Shows you what kind of people they are up there.'

'Stay with me.'

'No, Francis. You're crazy.'

He grabbed the hair at the back of her head, then held her whole head in both hands.

'You're gonna hit me,' she said.

'I won't hit ya, babe. I love ya some. Are ya awful cold?'

'I don't think I've been warm once in two days.'

Francis let go of her and took off his suitcoat and put it around her shoulders.

'No, it's too cold for you to do that,' she said. 'I've got this coat. You can't be in just a shirt.'

'What the hell's the difference. Coat ain't no protection.'

She handed him back the coat. 'I'm going,' she said.

'Don't walk away from me,' Francis said. 'You'll be lost in the world.'

But she walked away. And Francis leaned against the light pole on the corner, lit the cigarette Jack had given him, fingered the dollar bill Jack had slipped him in the kitchen, ate what was left of the cheese sandwich, and then threw his old undershorts down the sewer.

Helen walked down Green Street to a vacant lot, where she saw a fire in an oil drum. From across the street she could see five coloreds around the fire, men and women. On an old sofa in the weeds just beyond the drum, she saw a white woman lying underneath a colored man. She walked back to where Francis waited.

'I couldn't stay outside tonight,' she said. 'I'd die.'

Francis nodded and they walked to Finny's car, a 1930 black Oldsmobile, dead and wheelless in an alley off John Street. Two men were asleep in it, Finny in the front passenger seat.

'I don't know that man in back,' Helen said.

'Yeah you do,' said Francis. 'That's Little Red from the mission. He won't bother you. If he does I'll pull out his tongue.'

'I don't want to get in there, Francis.'

'It's warm, anyhow. Cold in them weeds, honey, awful cold. You walk the streets alone, they'll pinch you quicker'n hell.'

'You get in the back.'

'No. No room in there for the likes of me. Legs're too long.'

'Where will you go?'

'I'll find me some of them tall weeds, get outa the wind.'

'Are you coming back?'

'Sure, I'll be back. You get a good sleep and I'll see you here or up at the mission in the ayem.'

'I don't want to stay here.'

'You got to, babe. It's what there is.'

Francis opened the passenger door and shook Finny.

'Hey bum. Move over. You got a visitor.'

Finny opened his eyes, heavy with wine. Little Red was snoring.

'Who the hell are you?' Finny said.

'It's Francis. Move over and let Helen in.'

'Francis.' Finny raised his head.

'I'll get you a jug tomorrow for this, old buddy,' Francis said. 'She's gotta get in outa this weather.'

'Yeah,' said Finny.

'Never mind yeah, just move your ass over and let her sit. She can't sleep behind that wheel, condition her stomach's in.'

'Unnngghh,' said Finny, and he slid behind the wheel.

Helen sat on the front seat, dangling her legs out of the car. Francis stroked her cheek with three fingertips and then let his hand fall. She lifted her legs inside.

'You don't have to be scared,' Francis said.

'I'm not scared,' Helen said. 'Not that.'

'Finny won't let nothin' happen to you. I'll kill the son of a bitch if he does.'

'She knows,' Finny said. 'She's been here before.'

'Sure,' said Francis. 'Nothing can happen to you.'

'No.'

'See you in the mornin'.'

'Sure.'

'Keep the faith,' Francis said.

And he closed the car door.

He walked with an empty soul toward the north star, magnetized by an impulse to redirect his destiny. He had slept in the weeds of a South End vacant lot too many times. He would do it no more. Because he needed to confront the ragman in the morning, he would not chance arrest by crawling into a corner of one of the old houses on lower Broadway where the cops swept through periodically with their mindless net. What difference did it make whether four or six or eight lost men slept under a roof and out of the wind in a house with broken stairs and holes in the floors you could fall through to death, a house that for five or maybe ten years had been inhabited only by pigeons? What difference?

He walked north on Broadway, past Steamboat Square, where as a child he'd boarded the riverboats for outings to Troy, or Kingston, or picnics on Lagoon Island. He passed the D & H building and Billy Barnes's Albany *Evening Journal*, a building his simpleminded brother Tommy had helped build in 1913. He walked up to Maiden Lane and Broadway, where Keeler's Hotel used to be, and where his brother Peter sometimes spent the night when he was on the outs with Mama. But Keeler's burned the year after Francis ran away and now it was a bunch of stores. Francis had rowed down Broadway to the hotel, Billy in the rowboat with him, in 1913 when the river rose away the hell and gone up and flooded half of downtown. The kid loved it. Said he liked it better'n sleigh ridin'. Gone. What the hell ain't gone? Well, me. Yeah, me. Ain't a whole hell of a lot of me left, but I ain't gone entirely. Be god-diddley-damned if I'm gonna roll over and die.

Francis walked half an hour due north from downtown, right into North Albany. At Main Street he turned east toward the river, down Main Street's little incline past the McGraw house, then past the Greenes', the only coloreds in all North Albany in the old days, past the Daugherty house, where Martin still lived, no lights on, and past the old Wheelbarrow, Iron Joe Farrell's old saloon, all boarded up now, where Francis learned how to drink, where he watched cockfights in the back room, and where he first spoke to Annie Farrell.

He walked toward the flats, where the canal used to be, long gone and the ditch filled in. The lock was gone and the lockhouse too, and the towpath all grown over. Yet incredibly, as he neared North Street, he saw a structure he recognized. Son of a bitch. Welt the Tin's barn, still standing. Who'd believe it? Could Welt the Tin be livin'? Not likely. Too dumb to live so long. Was it in use? Still a barn? Looks like a barn. But who keeps horses now?

The barn was a shell, with a vast hole in the far end of the roof where moonlight poured cold fire onto the ancient splintered floor. Bats flew in balletic arcs around the streetlamp outside, the last lamp on North Street; and the ghosts of mules and horses snorted and stomped for Francis. He scuffed at the floorboards himself and found them solid. He touched them and found them dry. One barn door canted on one hinge, and Francis calculated that if he could move the door a few feet to sleep in its lee, he would be protected from the wind on three sides. No moonlight leaked through the roof above this corner, the same corner where Welt the Tin had hung his rakes and pitchforks, all in a row between spaced nails.

Francis would reclaim this corner, restore all rakes and pitchforks, return for the night the face of Welt the Tin as it had been, reinvest himself with serendipitous memories of a lost age. On a far shelf in the moonlight he saw a pile of papers and a cardboard box. He spread the papers in his chosen corner, ripped the box at its seams, and lay down on the flattened pile.

He had lived not seventy-five feet from where he now lay.

Seventy-five feet from this spot, Gerald Phelan died on the 26th of April, 1916.

In Finny's car Helen would probably be pulling off Finny, or taking him in her mouth. Finny would be unequal to intercourse, and Helen would be too fat for a toss in the front seat. Helen would be equal to any such task. He knew, though she had never told him, that she once had to fuck two strangers to be able to sleep in peace. Francis accepted this cuckoldry as readily as he accepted the onus of pulling the blanket off Clara and penetrating whatever dimensions of reek necessary to gain access to a bed. Fornication was standard survival currency everywhere, was it not?

Maybe I won't survive tonight after all, Francis thought as he folded his hands between his thighs. He drew his knees up toward his chest, not quite so high as Foxy Phil Tooker's, and considered the death he had caused in this life, and was perhaps causing still. Helen is dying and Francis is perhaps the principal agent of hastening her death, even as his whole being tonight has been directed to keeping her from freezing in the dust like Sandra. I don't want to die before you do, Helen, is what Francis thought. You'll be like a little kid in the world without me.

He thought of his father flying through the air and knew the old man was in heaven. The good leave us behind to think about the deeds they did. His mother would be in purgatory, probably for goddamn ever. She wasn't evil enough for hell, shrew of shrews that she was, denier of life. But he couldn't see her ever getting a foot into heaven either, if they ever got such a place.

The new and frigid air of November lay on Francis like a blanket of glass. Its weight rendered him motionless and brought peace to his body, and the stillness brought a cessation of anguish to his brain. In a dream he was only just beginning to enter, horns and mountains rose up out of the earth, the horns – ethereal, trumpets – sounding with a virtuosity equal to the perilousness of the crags and cornices of the mountainous pathways. Francis recognized the song the trumpets played and he floated with its melody. Then, yielding not without trepidation to its coded urgency, he ascended bodily into the exalted reaches of the world where the song had been composed so long ago. And he slept.

4

Francis stood in the junkyard driveway, looking for old Rosskam. Gray clouds that looked like two flying piles of dirty socks blew swiftly past the early-morning sun, the world shimmered in a sudden blast of incandescence, and Francis blinked. His eyes roved over a cemetery of dead things: rusted-out gas stoves, broken wood stoves, dead iceboxes, and bicycles with twisted wheels. A mountain of worn-out rubber tires cast its shadow on a vast plain of rusty pipes, children's wagons, toasters, automobile fenders. A three-sided shed half a block long sheltered a mountain range of cardboard, paper, and rags.

Francis stepped into this castoff world and walked toward a wooden shack, small and tilted, with a swayback horse hitched to a four-wheeled wooden wagon in front of it. Beyond the wagon a small mountain of wagon wheels rose alongside a sprawling scatter of pans, cans, irons, pots, and kettles, and a sea of metal fragments that no longer had names.

Francis saw probably Rosskam, framed in the shack's only window, watching him approach. Francis pushed open the door and confronted the man, who was short, filthy, and sixtyish, a figure of visible sinew, moon-faced, bald, and broad-chested, with fingers like the roots of an oak tree.

'Howdy,' Francis said.

'Yeah,' said Rosskam.

'Preacher said you was lookin' for a strong back.'

'It could be. You got one, maybe?'

'Stronger than some.'

'You can pick up an anvil?'

'You collectin' anvils, are you?'

'Collect everything.'

'Show me the anvil.'

'Ain't got one.'

'Then I'd play hell pickin' it up.'

'How about the barrel. You can pick that up?'

He pointed to an oil drum, half full of wood scraps and junk metal. Francis wrapped his arms around it and lifted it, with difficulty.

'Where'd you like it put?'

'Right where you got it off.'

'You pick up stuff like this yourself?' Francis asked.

Rosskam stood and lifted the drum without noticeable strain, then held it aloft.

'You got to be in mighty fair shape, heftin' that,' said Francis. 'That's one heavy item.'

'You call this heavy?' Rosskam said, and he heaved the drum upward and set its bottom edge on his right shoulder. Then he let it slide to chest level, hugged it, and set it down.

'I do a lifetime of lifting,' he said.

'I see that clear. You own this whole shebang here?'

'All. You still want to work?'

'What are you payin'?'

'Seven dollar. And work till dark.'

'Seven. That ain't much for back work.'

'Some might even bite at it.'

'It's worth eight or nine.'

'You got better, take it. People feed families all week on seven dollar.'

'Seven-fifty.'

'Seven.'

'All right, what the hell's the difference?'

'Get up the wagon.'

Two minutes in the moving wagon told Francis his tail-bone

would be grieving by day's end, if it lasted that long. The wagon bounced over the granite blocks and the trolley tracks, and the men rode side by side in silence through the bright streets of morning. Francis was glad for the sunshine, and felt rich seeing the people of his old city rising for work, opening stores and markets, moving out into a day of substance and profit. Clearheadedness always brought optimism to Francis; a long ride on a freight when there was nothing to drink made way for new visions of survival, and sometimes he even went out and looked for work. But even as he felt rich, he felt dead. He had not found Helen and he had to find her. Helen was lost again. The woman makes a goddamn career out of being lost. Probably went to mass someplace. But why didn't she come back to the mission for coffee, and for Francis? Why the hell should Helen always make Francis feel dead?

Then he remembered the story about Billy in the paper and he brightened. Pee Wee read it first and gave it to him. It was a story about Francis's son Billy, written by Martin Daugherty, the newspaperman, who long ago lived next door to the Phelans on Colonie Street. It was the story of Billy getting mixed up in the kidnapping of the nephew of Patsy McCall, the boss of Albany's political machine. They got the nephew back safely, but Billy was in the middle because he wouldn't inform on a suspected kidnapper. And there was Martin's column defending Billy, calling Patsy McCall a very smelly bag of very small potatoes for being rotten to Billy.

'So how do you like it?' Rosskam said.

'Like what?' said Francis.

'Sex business,' Rosskam said. 'Women stuff.'

'I don't think much about it anymore.'

'You bums, you do a lot of dirty stuff up the heinie, am I right?'

'Some like it that way. Not me.'

'How do you like it?'

'I don't even like it anymore, I'll tell you the truth. I'm over the hill.'

'A man like you? How old? Fifty-five? Sixty-two?'

'Fifty-eight,' said Francis.

'Seventy-one here,' said Rosskam. 'I go over no hills. Four, five times a night I get it in with the old woman. And in the daylight, you never know.'

'What's the daylight?'

'Women. They ask for it. You go house to house, you get offers. This is not a new thing in the world.'

'I never went house to house,' Francis said.

'Half my life I go house to house,' said Rosskam, 'and I know how it is. You get offers.'

'You probably get a lot of clap, too.'

'Twice all my life. You use the medicine, it goes away. Those ladies, they don't do it so often to get disease. Hungry is what they got, not clap.'

'They bring you up to bed in your old clothes?'

'In the cellar. They love it down the cellar. On the woodpile. In the coal. On top the newspapers. They follow me down the stairs and bend over the papers to show me their bubbies, or they up their skirts on the stairs ahead of me, showing other things. Best I ever got lately was on top of four ash cans. Very noisy, but some woman. The things she said you wouldn't repeat. Hot, hotsy, oh my. This morning we pay her a visit, up on Arbor Hill. You wait in the wagon. It don't take long, if you don't mind.'

'Why should I mind? It's your wagon, you're the boss.'

'That's right. I am the boss.'

They rode up to Northern Boulevard and started down Third Street, all downhill so as not to kill the horse. House by house they went, carting out old clocks and smashed radios, papers always, two boxes of broken-backed books on gardening, a banjo with a broken neck, cans, old hats, rags.

'Here,' old Rosskam said when they reached the hot lady's house. 'If you like, watch by the cellar window. She likes lookers and I don't mind it.'

Francis shook his head and sat alone on the wagon, staring down Third Street. He could have reconstructed this street from memory. Childhood, young manhood were passed on the streets of Arbor

Hill, girls discovering they had urges, boys capitalizing on this discovery. In the alleyways the gang watched women undress, and one night they watched the naked foreplay of Mr and Mrs Ryan until they put out the light. Joey Kilmartin whacked off during that show. The old memory aroused Francis sexually. Did he want a woman? No. Helen? No, no. He wanted to watch the Ryans again, getting ready to go at it. He climbed down from the wagon and walked into the alley of the house where Rosskam's hot lady lived. He walked softly, listening, and he heard groaning, inaudible words, and the sound of metal fatigue. He crouched down and peered in the cellar window at the back of the house, and there they were on the ash cans, Rosskam's pants hanging from his shoes, on top of a lady with her dress up to her neck. When Francis brought the scene into focus, he could hear their words.

'Oh boyoboy,' Rosskam was saying, 'oh boyoboy.'

'Hey I love it,' said the hot lady. 'Do I love it? Do I love it?'

'You love it,' said Rosskam. 'Oh boyoboy.'

'Gimme that stick,' said the hot lady. 'Gimme it, gimme it, gimme, gimme, gimme that stick.'

'Oh take it,' said Rosskam. 'Oh take it.'

'Oh gimme it,' said the hot lady. 'I'm a hot slut. Gimme it.'

'Oh boyoboy,' said Rosskam.

The hot lady saw Francis at the window and waved to him. Francis stood up and went back to the wagon, conjuring memories against his will. Bums screwing in box-cars, women gang-banged in the weeds, a girl of eight raped, and then the rapist kicked half to death by other bums and rolled out of the moving train. He saw the army of women he had known: women upside down, women naked, women with their skirts up, their legs open, their mouths open, women in heat, women sweating and grunting under and over him, women professing love, desire, joy, pain, need. Helen.

He met Helen at a New York bar, and when they found out they were both from Albany, love took a turn toward the sun. He kissed her and she tongued him. He stroked her body, which was old even then, but vital and full and without the tumor, and they confessed a fiery yearning for each other. Francis hesitated to carry it through, for he had been off women eight months, having finally and with much discomfort rid himself of the crabs and a relentless, pusy drip. Yet the presence of Helen's flaming body kept driving away his dread of disease, and finally, when he saw they were going to be together for much more than a one-nighter, he told her: I wouldn't touch ya, babe. Not till I got me a checkup. She told him to wear a sheath but he said he hated them goddamn things. Get us a blood test, that's what we'll do, he told her, and they pooled their money and went to the hospital and both got a clean bill and then took a room and made love till they wore out. Love, you are my member rubbed raw. Love, you are an unstoppable fire. You burn me, love. I am singed, blackened. Love, I am ashes.

The wagon rolled on and Francis realized it was heading for Colonie Street, where he was born and raised, where his brothers and sisters still lived. The wagon wheels squeaked as they moved and the junk in the back rattled and bounced, announcing the prodigal's return. Francis saw the house where he grew up, still the same colors, brown and tan, the vacant lot next to it grown tall with weeds where the Daugherty house and the Brothers' School had stood until they burned.

He saw his mother and father alight from their honeymoon carriage in front of the house and, with arms entwined, climb the front stoop. Michael Phelan wore his trainman's overalls and looked as he had the moment before the speeding train struck him. Kathryn Phelan, in her wedding dress, looked as she had when she hit Francis with an open hand and sent him sprawling backward into the china closet.

'Stop here a minute, will you?' Francis said to Rosskam, who had uttered no words since ascending from his cellar of passion.

'Stop?' Rosskam said, and he reined the horse.

The newlyweds stepped across the threshold and into the house. They climbed the front stairs to the bedroom they would share for all the years of their marriage, the room that now was also their shared grave, a spatial duality as reasonable to Francis as the concurrence of this moment both in the immediate present of his fifty-eighth year of life and in the year before he was born: that year of sacramental consummation, 1879. The room had about it the familiarity of his young lifetime. The oak bed and the two oak dressers were as rooted to their positions in the room as the trees that shaded the edge of the Phelan burial plot. The room was redolent of the blend of maternal and paternal odors, which separated themselves when Francis buried his face deeply in either of the personal pillows, or opened a drawer full of private garments, or inhaled the odor of burned tobacco in a cold pipe, say, or the fragrance of a cake of Pears' soap, kept in a drawer as a sachet.

In their room Michael Phelan embraced his new wife of fifty-nine years and ran a finger down the crevice of her breasts; and Francis saw his mother-to-be shudder with what he assumed was the first abhorrent touch of love. Because he was the firstborn, Francis's room was next to theirs, and so he had heard their nocturnal rumblings for years; and he well knew how she perennially resisted her husband. When Michael would finally overcome her, either by force of will or by threatening to take their case to the priest, Francis would hear her gurgles of resentment, her moans of anguish, her eternal arguments about the sinfulness of all but generative couplings. For she hated the fact that people even knew that she had committed intercourse in order to have children, a chagrin that was endlessly satisfying to Francis all his life.

Now, as her husband lifted her chemise over her head, the virginal mother of six recoiled with what Francis recognized for the first time to be spiritually induced terror, as visible in her eyes in 1879 as it was in the grave. Her skin was as fresh and pink as the taffeta lining of her coffin, but she was, in her youthfully rosy bloom, as lifeless as the spun silk of her magenta burial dress. She has been dead all her life, Francis thought, and for the first time in years he felt pity for this woman, who had been spayed by self-neutered nuns and self-gelded priests. As she yielded her fresh body to her new husband out of obligation, Francis felt the iron maiden of induced chastity piercing her everywhere, tightening with the years until all sensuality was strangulated and her body was as bloodless and cold as a granite angel.

She closed her eyes and fell back on the wedding bed like a corpse, ready to receive the thrust, and the old man's impeccable blood shot into her aged vessel with a passionate burst that set her writhing with the life of newly conceived death. Francis watched this primal pool of his own soulish body squirm into burgeoning matter, saw it change and grow with the speed of light until it was the size of an infant, saw it then yanked roughly out of the maternal cavern by his father, who straightened him, slapped him into being, and swiftly molded him into a bestial weed. The body sprouted to wildly matured growth and stood fully clad at last in the very clothes Francis was now wearing. He recognized the toothless mouth, the absent finger joints, the bump on the nose, the mortal slouch of this newborn shade, and he knew then that he would be this decayed self he had been so long in becoming, through all the endless years of his death.

'Giddap,' said Rosskam to his horse, and the old nag clomped on down the hill of Colonie Street.

'Raaaa-aaaaaags,' screamed Rosskam. 'Raaaa-aaaaaags.' The scream was a two-noted song, C and B-flat, or maybe F and E-flat. And from a window across the street from the Phelan house, a woman's head appeared.

'Goooo-ooooooo,' she called in two-noted answer. 'Raaaag-maaan.'

Rosskam pulled to a halt in front of the alley alongside her house.

'On the back porch,' she said. 'Papers and a washtub and some old clothes.'

Rosskam braked his wagon and climbed down.

'Well?' he said to Francis.

'I don't want to go in,' Francis said. 'I know her.'

'So what's that?'

'I don't want her to see me. Mrs Dillon. Her husband's a railroad man. I know them all my life. My family lives, in that house over there. I was born up the street. I don't want people on this block to see me looking like a bum.'

'But you're a bum.'

'Me and you know that, but they don't. I'll cart anything, I'll cart it all the next time you stop. But not on this street. You understand?'

'Sensitive bum. I got a sensitive bum working for me.'

While Rosskam went for the junk alone, Francis stared across the street and saw his mother in housedress and apron surreptitiously throwing salt on the roots of the young maple tree that grew in the Daugherty yard but had the temerity to drop twigs, leaves, and pods onto the Phelan tomato plants and flowers. Kathryn Phelan told her near-namesake, Katrina Daugherty, that the tree's droppings and shade were unwelcome at the Phelans'. Katrina trimmed what she could of the tree's low branches and asked Francis, a neighborhood handyman at seventeen, to help her trim the higher ones; and he did: climbed aloft and sawed living arms off the vigorous young tree. But for every branch cut, new life sprouted elsewhere, and the tree thickened to a lushness unlike that of any other tree on Arbor Hill, infuriating Kathryn Phelan, who increased her dosage of salt on the roots, which waxed and grew under and beyond the wooden fence and surfaced ever more brazenly on Phelan property.

Why do you want to kill the tree, Mama? Francis asked.

And his mother said it was because the tree had no right insinuating itself into other people's yards. If we want a tree in the yard we'll plant our own, she said, and threw more salt. Some leaves withered on the tree and one branch died entirely. But the salting failed, for Francis saw the tree now, twice its old size, a giant thing in the world, rising high out of the weeds and toward the sun from what used to be the Daugherty yard.

On this high noon in 1938, under the sun's full brilliance, the tree restored itself to its half size of forty-one years past, a July morning in 1897 when Francis was sitting on a middle branch, sawing the end off a branch above him. He heard the back door of the Daughertys' new house open and close, and he looked down from his perch to see Katrina Daugherty, carrying her small shopping bag, wearing a gray sun hat, gray satin evening slippers, and nothing else. She descended the five steps of the back piazza and strode toward the new barn, where the Daugherty landau and horse were kept.

'Mrs Daugherty?' Francis called out, and he leaped down from the tree. 'Are you all right?'

'I'm going downtown, Francis,' she said.

'Shouldn't you put something on? Some clothes?'

'Clothes?' she said. She looked down at her naked self and then cocked her head and widened her eyes into quizzical rigidity.

'Mrs Daugherty,' Francis said, but she gave no response, nor did she move. From the piazza railing that he was building, Francis lifted a piece of forest-green canvas he would eventually install as an awning on a side window, and wrapped the naked woman in it, picking her up in his arms then, and carrying her into her house. He sat her on the sofa in the back parlor and, as the canvas slid slowly away from her shoulders, he searched the house for a garment and found a housecoat hanging behind the pantry door. He stood her up and shoved her arms into the housecoat, tied its belt at her waist, covering her body fully, and undid the chin ribbon that held her hat. Then he sat her down again on the sofa.

He found a bottle of Scotch whiskey in a cabinet and poured her an inch in a goblet from the china closet, held it to her lips, and cajoled her into tasting it. Whiskey is magic and will cure all your troubles. Katrina sipped it and smiled and said, 'Thank you, Francis. You are very thoughtful,' her eyes no longer wide, the glaze gone from them, her rigidity banished, and the softness of her face and body restored.

'Are you feeling better?' he asked her.

'I'm fine, fine indeed. And how are *you*, Francis?'

'Do you want me to go and get your husband?'

'My husband? My husband is in New York City, and rather difficult to reach, I'm afraid. What did you want with my husband?'

'Someone in your family you'd like me to get, maybe? You seem to be having some kind of spell.'

'Spell? What do you mean, spell?'

'Outside. In the back.'

'The back?'

'You came out without any clothes on, and then you went stiff.'

'Now really, Francis, do you think you should be so familiar?'

'I put that housecoat on you. I carried you indoors.'

'You carried me?'

'Wrapped in canvas. That there.' And he pointed to the canvas on the floor in front of the sofa. Katrina stared at the canvas, put her hand inside the fold of her housecoat, and felt her naked breast. In her face, when she again looked up at him, Francis saw lunar majesty, a chilling fusion of beauty and desolation. At the far end of the front parlor, observing all from behind a chair, Francis saw also the forehead and eyes of Katrina Daugherty's nine-year-old son, Martin.

A month passed, and on a day when Francis was doing finishing work on the doors of the Daugherty carriage barn, Katrina called out to him from the back porch and beckoned him into the house, then to the back parlor, where she sat again on the same sofa, wearing a long yellow afternoon frock with a soft collar. She looked like a sunbeam to Francis as she motioned him into a chair across from the sofa.

'May I make you some tea, Francis?'

'No, ma'am.'

'Would you care for one of my husband's cigars?'

'No, ma'am. I don't use 'em.'

'Have you none of the minor vices? Do you perhaps drink whiskey?'

'I've had a bit but the most I drink of is ale.'

'Do you think I'm mad, Francis?'

'Mad? How do you mean that?'

'Mad. Mad as the Red Queen. Peculiar. Crazy, if you like. Do you think Katrina is crazy?'

'No, ma'am.'

'Not even after my spell?'

'I just took it as a spell. A spell don't have to be crazy.'

'Of course you're correct, Francis. I am not crazy. With whom have you talked about that day's happenings?'

'No one, ma'am.'

'No one? Not even your family?'

'No, ma'am, no one.'

'I sensed you hadn't. May I ask why?'

Francis dropped his eyes, spoke to his lap. 'Could be, people wouldn't understand. Might figure it the wrong way.'

'How wrong?'

'Might figure they was some goin's on. People with no clothes isn't what you'd call reg'lar business.'

'You mean people would make something up? Conjure an imaginary relationship between us?'

'Might be they would. Most times they don't need that much to start their yappin'.'

'So you've been protecting us from scandal with your silence.'

'Yes, ma'am.'

'Would you please not call me ma'am. It makes you sound like a servant. Call me Katrina.'

'I couldn't do that.'

'Why couldn't you?'

'It's more familiar than I oughta get.'

'But it's my name. Hundreds of people call me Katrina.'

Francis nodded and let the word sit on his tongue. He tried it out silently, then shook his head. 'I can't get it out,' he said, and he smiled.

'Say it. Say Katrina.'

'Katrina.'

'So there, you've gotten it out. Say it again.'

'Katrina.'

'Fine. Now say: May I help you, Katrina?'

'May I help you, Katrina?'

'Splendid. Now I want never to be called anything else again. I insist. And I shall call you Francis. That is how we were designated at birth and our baptisms reaffirmed it. Friends should dispense with formality, and you, who have saved me from scandal, you, Francis, are most certainly my friend.'

From the perspective of his perch on the junk wagon Francis could see that Katrina was not only the rarest bird in his life, but very likely the rarest bird ever to nest on Colonie Street. She brought to this street of working-class Irish a posture of elegance that had instantly earned her glares of envy and hostility from the neighbors. But within a year of residence in her new house (a scaled-down copy of the Elk Street mansion in which she had been born and nurtured like a tropical orchid, and where she had lived until she married Edward Daugherty, the writer, whose work and words, whose speech and race, were anathema to Katrina's father, and who, as a compromise for his bride, built the replica that would maintain her in her cocoon, but built it in a neighborhood where he would never be an outlander, and built it lavishly until he ran out of capital and was forced to hire neighborhood help, such as Francis, to finish it), her charm and generosity, her absence of pretension, and her abundance of the human virtues transformed most of her neighbors' hostility into fond attention and admiration.

Her appearance, when she first set foot in the house next door to his, stunned Francis; her blond hair swept upward into a soft wreath, her eyes a dark and shining brown, the stately curves and fullness of her body carried so regally, her large, irregular teeth only making her beauty more singular. This goddess, who had walked naked across his life, and whom he had carried in his arms, now sat on the sofa and with eyes wide upon him she leaned forward and posed the question: 'Are you in love with anyone?'

'No, m – no. I'm too young.'

Katrina laughed and Francis blushed.

'You are such a handsome boy. You must have many girls in love with you.'

'No,' said Francis. 'I never been good with girls.'

'Why ever not?'

'I don't tell 'em what they want to hear. I ain't big with talk.'

'Not all girls want you to talk to them.'

'Ones I know do. Do you like me? How much? Do you like me better'n Joan? Stuff like that. I got no time for stuff like that.'

'Do you dream of women?'

'Sometimes.'

'Have you ever dreamt of me?'

'Once.'

'Was it pleasant?'

'Not all that much.'

'Oh my. What was it?'

'You couldn't close your eyes. You just kept lookin' and never blinked. It got scary.'

'I understand the dream perfectly. You know, a great poet once said that love enters through the eyes. One must be careful not to see too much. One must curb one's appetites. The world is much too beautiful for most of us. It can destroy us with its beauty. Have you ever seen anyone faint?'

'Faint? No.'

'No, what?'

'No, Katrina.'

'Then I shall faint for you, dear Francis.'

She stood up, walked to the center of the room, looked directly at Francis, closed her eyes, and collapsed on the rug, her right hip hitting the floor first and she then falling backward, right arm outstretched over her head, her face toward the parlor's east wall. Francis stood up and looked down at her.

'You did that pretty good,' he said.

She did not move.

'You can get up now,' he said.

But still she did not move. He reached down and took her left hand in his and tugged gently. She did not move. He took both her hands and tugged. She did not move voluntarily, nor did she open her eyes. He pulled her to a sitting position but she remained limp, with closed eyes. He lifted her off the floor in his arms and put her on the sofa. When he sat her down she opened her eyes and sat fully erect. Francis still had one arm on her back.

'My mother taught me that,' Katrina said. 'She said it was useful in strained social situations. I performed it once in a pageant and won great applause.'

'You did it good,' Francis said.

'I can do a cataleptic fit quite well also.'

'I don't know what that is.'

'It's when you stop yourself in a certain position and do not move. Like this.'

And suddenly she was rigid and wide-eyed, unblinking.

A week after that, Katrina passed by Mulvaney's pasture on Van Woert Street, where Francis was playing baseball, a pickup game. She stood on the turf, just in from the street, across the diamond from where Francis danced and chattered as the third-base pepper pot. When he saw her he stopped chattering. That inning he had no fielding chances. The next inning he did not come to bat. She watched through three innings until she saw him catch a line drive and then tag a runner for a double play; saw him also hit a long fly to the outfield that went for two bases. When he reached second base on the run, she walked home to Colonie Street.

She called him to lunch the day he installed the new awnings. After the first day she always chose a time to talk with him when her husband was elsewhere and her son in school. She served lobster *gratiné*, asparagus with hollandaise, and Blanc de Blancs. Only the asparagus, without sauce, had Francis ever tasted before. She served it at the dining-room table, without a word, then sat across from him and ate in silence, he following her lead.

'I like this,' he finally said.

'Do you? Do you like the wine?'

'Not very much.'

'You will learn to like it. It is exquisite.'

'If you say so.'

'Have you had any more dreams of me?'

'One. I can't tell it.'

'But you must.'

'It's crazy.'

'Dreams must be. Katrina is not crazy. Say: May I help you, Katrina?'

'May I help you, Katrina?'

'You may help me by telling me your dream.'

'What it is, is you're a little bird, but you're just like you always are too, and a crow comes along and eats you up.'

'Who is the crow?'

'Just a crow. Crows always eat little birds.'

'You are protective of me, Francis.'

'I don't know.'

'What does your mother know of me? Does she know you and I have talked as friends?'

'I wouldn't tell her. I wouldn't tell her anything.'

'Good. Never tell your mother anything about me. She is your mother and I am Katrina. I will always be Katrina in your life. Do you know that? You will never know another like me. There can be no other like me.'

'I sure believe you're right.'

'Do you ever want to kiss me?'

'Always.'

'What else do you want to do with me?'

'I couldn't say.'

'You may say.'

'Not me. I'd goddamn die.'

When they had eaten, Katrina filled her own and Francis's wineglasses and set them on the octagonal marble-topped table in front of the sofa where she always sat; and he sat in what had now become his chair. He drank all of the wine and she refilled his glass as they talked of asparagus and lobster and she taught him the meaning of *gratiné*, and why a French word was used to describe a dish made in Albany from a lobster caught in Maine.

'Wondrous things come from France,' she said to him, and by this time he was at ease in the suffusion of wine and pleasure and possibility, and he gave her his fullest attention. 'Do you know Saint Anthony of Egypt, Francis? He is of your faith, a faith I cherish without embracing. I speak of him because of the way he was tempted with the flesh and I speak too of my poet, who frightens me because he sees what men should not see in women. He is dead these thirty years, my poet, but he sees through me still with his image of a caged woman ripping apart the body of a living rabbit with her teeth. Enough, says her keeper, you should not spend all you receive in one day, and he pulls the rabbit from her, letting some of its intestines dangle from her teeth. She remains hungry, with only a taste of what might nourish her. Oh, little Francis, my rabbit, you must not fear me. I shall not rip you to pieces and let your sweet intestines dangle from my teeth. Beautiful Francis of sweet excellence in many things, beautiful young man whom I covet, please do not speak ill of me. Do not say Katrina was made for the fire of *luxuria*, for you must understand that I am Anthony and am tempted by the devil with the sweetness of yourself in my house, in my kitchen, in my yard, in my tree of trees, sweet Francis who carried me naked in his arms.'

'I couldn't let you go out in the street with no clothes on,' Francis said. 'You'd get arrested.'

'I know you couldn't,' Katrina said. 'That's precisely why I did it. But what I do not know is what will be the consequence of it. I do not know what strengths I have to confront the temptations I bring into my life so willfully. I only know that I love in ten thousand directions and that I must not; for that is the lot of the harlot. My poet says that caged woman with the rabbit in her teeth is the true and awful image of this life, and not the woman moaning aloud her dirge of unattainable hopes . . . dead, so dead, how sad. Of course you must know I am not dead. I am merely a woman in self-imposed bondage to a splendid man, to a mannerism of life which he calls a sacrament and I call a magnificent prison. Anthony lived as a hermit, and I too have thought of this as a means of thwarting the enemy. But my husband worships me, and I him, and we equally worship our son of sons. You see, there has never been a magnificence of contact greater than that which exists within this house. We are a family of reverence, of achievement, of wounds sweetly healed. We yearn for the touch, the presence of each other. We cannot live without these things.

And yet you are here and I dream of you and long for the pleasures you cannot speak of to me, of joys beyond the imaginings of your young mind. I long for the pleasures of Mademoiselle Lancet, who pursued doctors as I pursue my young man of tender breath, my beautiful Adonis of Arbor Hill. The Mademoiselle cherished all her doctors did and were. The blood on their aprons was a badge of their achievement in the operating room, and she embraced it as I embrace your swan's throat with its necklace of dirt, the haunting pain of young ignorance in your eyes. Do you believe there is a God, Francis? Of course you do and so do I, and I believe he loves me and will cherish me in heaven, as I will cherish him. We shall be lovers. God made me in his image, and so why should I not believe that God too is an innocent monster, loving the likes of me, this seductress of children, this caged animal with blood and intestines in her teeth, embracing her own bloody aprons and then kneeling at the altar of all that is holy in the penitential pose of all hypocrites. Did you ever dream, Francis, when I called you out of our tree, that you would enter such a world as I inhabit? Would you kiss me if I closed my eyes? If I fainted would you undo the buttons of my dress to let me breathe easier?'

Katrina died in 1912 in the fire that began in the Brothers' School and then made the leap to the Daugherty house. Francis was absent from the city when she died, but he learned the news from a newspaper account and returned for her funeral. He did not see her in her coffin, which was closed to mourners. Smoke, not fire, killed her, just as the ashes and not the flames of her sensuality had finally smothered her desire; so Francis believed.

In the immediate years after her death, Katrina's grave in the Albany Rural Cemetery, where Protestants entered the underworld, grew wild with dandelions and became a curiosity to the manicurists of the cemetery's floral tapestry. In precisely the way Katrina and Francis had trimmed the maple tree, only to see it grow ever more luxuriant, so was it that the weeding of her burial plot led to an intensity of weed growth: as if the severing of a single root were cause for the birth of a hundred rootlings. Such was its growth that the grave, in the decade after her death, became an attraction for cemetery tourists, who marveled at the midspring yellowing of her final residence on earth. The vogue passed, though the flowers remain even today; and it is now an historical marvel that only the very old remember, or that the solitary wanderer discovers when rambling among the gravestones, and generally attributes to a freakish natural effusion.

'So,' said Rosskam, 'did you have a nice rest?'

'It ain't rest what I'm doin',' said Francis. 'You got all the stuff from back there?'

'All,' said Rosskam, throwing an armful of old clothes into the wagon. Francis looked them over, and a clean, soft-collared, white-on-white shirt, one sleeve half gone, caught his eye.

'That shirt,' he said. 'I'd like to buy it.' He reached into the wagon and lifted it from the pile. 'You take a quarter for it?'

Rosskam studied Francis as he might a striped blue toad.

'Take it out of my pay,' Francis said. 'Is it a deal?'

'For what is it a bum needs a clean shirt?'

'The one I got on stinks like a dead cat.'

'Tidy bum. Sensitive, tidy bum on my wagon.'

Katrina unwrapped the parcel on the dining-room table, took Francis by the hand, and pulled him up from his chair. She unbuttoned the buttons of his blue workshirt.

'Take that old thing off,' she said, and held the gift aloft, a white-on-white silk shirt whose like was as rare to Francis as the *fruits de mer* and Château Pontet-Canet he had just consumed.

When his torso was naked, Katrina stunned him with a kiss, and with an exploration of the whole of his back with her fingertips. He held her as he would a crystal vase, fearful not only of her fragility but of his own. When he could again see her lips, her eyes, the sanctified valley of her mouth, when she stood inches from him, her hands gripping his naked back, he cautiously brought his own fingers around to her face and neck. Emulating her, he explored the exposed regions of her shoulders and her throat, letting the natural curve of her collar guide him to the top button of her blouse. And then slowly, as if the dance of their fingers had been choreographed, hers crawled across her own chest, brushing past his, which were carefully at work at their gentlest of chores, and she pushed the encumbering chemise strap down over the fall of her left shoulder. His own fingers then repeated the act on her right shoulder and he trembled with pleasure, and sin, and with, even now, the still unthinkable possibilities that lay below and beneath the boundary line her fallen clothing demarcated.

'Do you like my scar?' she asked, and she lightly touched the oval white scar with a ragged pink periphery, just above the early slope of her left breast.

'I don't know,' Francis said. 'I don't know about likin' scars.'

'You are the only man besides my husband and Dr Fitzroy who has ever seen it. I can never again wear a low-necked dress. It is such an ugly thing that I do believe my poet would adore it. Does it offend you?'

'It's there. Part of you. That's okay by me. Anything you do, or got, it's okay by me.'

'My adorable Francis.'

'How'd you ever get a thing like that?'

'A burning stick flew through the air and pierced me cruelly during a fire. The Delavan Hotel fire.'

'Yeah. I heard you were in that. You're lucky you didn't get it in the neck.'

'Oh I'm a very lucky woman indeed,' Katrina said, and she leaned into him and held him again. And again they kissed.

He commanded his hands to move toward her breasts but they would not. They would only hold tight to their grip on her bare arms. Only when she moved her own fingers forward from the blades of his back toward the hollows of his arms did his own fingers dare move toward the hollows of hers. And only when she again inched back from him, letting her fingers tweeze and caress the precocious hair on his chest, did he permit his own fingers to savor the curving flow, the fleshy whiteness, the blooded fullness of her beautiful breasts, culminating his touch at their roseate tips, which were now being so cleverly cataleptic for him.

When Francis put the new shirt on and threw the old one into the back of Rosskam's wagon, he saw Katrina standing on her front steps, across the street, beckoning to him. She led him into a bedroom he had never seen and where a wall of flame engulfed her without destroying even the hem of her dress, the same dress she wore when she came to watch him play baseball on that summer day in 1897. He stood across the marriage bed from her, across a bridge of years of love and epochs of dream.

Never a woman like Katrina: who had forced him to model that shirt for her, then take it home so that someday she would see him walking along the street wearing it and relive this day; forced him first to find a hiding place for it outside his house while he schemed an excuse as to why a seventeen-year-old boy of the working classes should come to own a shirt that only sublime poets, or stage actors, or unthinkably wealthy lumber barons could afford. He invented the ruse of a bet: that he had played poker at a downtown sporting club with a man who ran out of dollars and put up his new shirt as collateral; and Francis had inspected the shirt, liked it, accepted the bet, and then won the hand with a full house.

His mother did not seem to believe the story. But neither did she connect the gift to Katrina. Yet she found ways to slander Katrina in Francis's presence, knowing that he had formed an allegiance, if not an affection, for not only a woman, but the woman who owned the inimical tree.

She is impudent, arrogant. (Wrong, said Francis.)

Slovenly, a poor housekeeper. (Go over and look, said Francis.)

Shows off by sitting in the window with a book. (Francis, knowing no way to defend a book, fumed silently and left the room.)

In the leaping windows of flame that engulfed Katrina and her bed, Francis saw naked bodies coupled in love, writhing in lascivious embrace, kissing in sweet agony. He saw himself and Katrina in a ravenous lunge that never was, and then in a blissful stroking that might have been, and then in a sublime fusion of desire that would always be.

Did they love? No, they never loved. They always loved. They knew a love that Katrina's poet would abuse and befoul. And they befouled their imaginations with a mutation of love that Katrina's poet would celebrate and consecrate. Love is always insufficient, always a lie. Love, you are the clean shirt of my soul. Stupid love, silly love.

Francis embraced Katrina and shot into her the impecable blood of his first love, and she yielded up not a being but a word: clemency. And the word swelled like the mercy of his swollen member as it rose to offer her the enduring, erubescent gift of retributive sin. And then this woman interposed herself in his life, hiding herself in the deepest center of the flames, smiling at him with all the lewd beauty of her dreams; and she awakened in him the urge for a love of his own, a love that belonged to no other man, a love he would never have to share with any man, or boy, like himself.

'Giddap,' Rosskam called out.

And the wagon rolled down the hill as the sun moved toward its apex, and the horse turned north off Colonie Street.

5

Tell me, pretty maiden, are there any more at home like you?
There are a few, kind sir, and dum-de-dum and dum-dum too.

So genteel, so quaint.

Helen hummed, staring at the wall in the light of the afternoon sun. In her kimono (only ten-cent-store silk, alas, but it did have a certain elegance, so much like the real thing no one would ever know; no one but Francis had ever seen her in it, or ever would; no one had seen her take it ever so cleverly off the rack in Woolworth's): in her kimono, and naked beneath it, she sank deeper into the old chair that was oozing away its stuffing; and she stared at the dusty swan in the painting with the cracked glass, swan with the lovely white neck, lovely white back: swan was, was.

Dah dah-dah,
Dah dah-de-dah-dah,
Dah dah-de-dah-dah,
Dah dah dah,

She sang. And the world changed.

Oh the lovely power of music to rejuvenate Helen. The melody returned her to that porcelain age when she aspired so loftily to a classical career. Her plan, her father's plan before it was hers, was for her to follow in her grandmother's footsteps, carry the family pride to lofty pinnacles: Vassar first, then the Paris Conservatory if she was truly as good as she seemed, then the concert world, then the entire world. If you love something well enough, Grandmother Archer told Helen when the weakness was upon her, you will die for it; for when we love with all our might, our silly little selves are already dead and we have no more fear of dying. Would you die for your music? Helen asked. And her grandmother said: I believe I already have. And in a month she was very unkindly cut down forever.

Swan was, was.

Helen's first death.

Her second came to her in a mathematics class at Vassar when she was a freshman of two months. Mrs Carmichael, who was pretty and young and wore high shoes and walked with a limp, came for Helen and brought her to the office. A visitor, said Mrs Carmichael, your uncle Andrew: who told Helen her father was ill,

And on the train up from Poughkeepsie changed that to dead,

And in the carriage going up State Street hill from the Albany depot added that the man had,

Incredibly,

Thrown himself off the Hawk Street viaduct.

Helen, confusing fear with grief, blocked all tears until two days after the funeral, when her mother told her that there will be no more Vassar for you, child; that Brian Archer killed himself because he had squandered his fortune; that what money remained would not be wasted in educating a foolish girl like Helen but would instead finance her brother Patrick's final year in Albany Law School; for a lawyer can save the family. And whatever could a classical pianist do for it?

Helen had been in the chair hours, it seemed, though she had no timepiece for such measurement. But it did seem an hour at least since crippled old Donovan came to the door and said: Helen, are you all right? You been in there all day. Don't you wanna eat something? I'm makin' some coffee, you want some? And Helen said: Oh thank you, old cripple, for remembering I still have a body now that I've all but forgotten it. And no, no thank you, no coffee, kind sir. Are there any more at home like you?

Freude, schöner Götterfunken,
Tochter aus Elysium!

The day had all but begun with music. She left Finny's car humming the 'Te Deum'; why, she could not say. But at six o'clock, when it was still dark and Finny and the other man were both snoring, it became the theme of her morning pathway. As she walked she considered the immediate future for herself and her twelve dollars, the final twelve dollars of her life capital, money she never intended to tell Francis about, money tucked safely in her brassiere.

Don't touch my breasts, Finny, they're too sore, she had said again and again, afraid he would feel the money. Finny acceded and explored her only between the thighs, trying mightily to ejaculate, and she, Lord have mercy on her, tried to help him. But Finny could not ejaculate, and he fell back in exhaustion and dry indifference and then slept, as Helen did not, could not; for sleep seemed to be a thing of the past.

What for weeks she had achieved in her time of rest was only an illustrated wakefulness that hovered at the edge of dream: angels rejoicing, multitudes kneeling before the Lamb, worms all, creating a great butterfly of angelic hair, Helen's joyous vision.

Why was Helen joyous in her sleeplessness? Because she was able to recede from evil love and bloodthirsty spiders. Because she had mastered the trick of escaping into music and the pleasures of memory. She pulled on her bloomers, slid sideways out of the car, and walked out into the burgeoning day, the morning star still visible in her night's vanishing sky. Venus, you are my lucky star.

Helen walked to the church with head bowed. She was picking her steps when the angel appeared (and she still in her kimono) and called out to her: *Drunk with fire, o heav'n-born Goddess, we invade thy haildom!*

How nice.

The church was Saint Anthony's, Saint Anthony of Padua, the wonder-working saint, hammer of heretics, ark of the testament, finder of lost articles, patron of the poor and of pregnant and barren women. It was the church where the Italians went to preserve their souls in a city where Italians were the niggers and micks of a new day. Helen usually went to the Cathedral of the Immaculate

Conception a few blocks up the hill, but her tumor felt so heavy, a great rock in her belly, that she chose Saint Anthony's, not such a climb, even if she did fear Italians. They looked so dark and dangerous. And she did not care much for their food, especially their garlic. And they seemed never to die. They eat olive oil all day long, Helen's mother had instructed her, and that's what does it; did you ever in all your life see a sick Italian?

The sound of the organ resonated out from the church before the mass began, and on the sidewalk Helen knew the day boded well for her, with such sanctified music greeting her at the dawning. There were three dozen people in the church, not many for a holy day of obligation. Not everybody feels obligations the way Helen feels them, but then again, it is only ten minutes to seven in the morning.

Helen walked all the way to the front and sat in the third pew of center-aisle left, in back of a man who looked like Walter Damrosch. The candle rack caught her eye and she rose and went to it and dropped in the two pennies she carried in her coat pocket, all the change she had. The organist was roaming free through Gregorian hymns as Helen lit a candle for Francis, offering up a Hail Mary so he would be given divine guidance with his problem. The poor man was so guilty.

Helen was giving help of her own to Francis now by staying away from him. She had made this decision while holding Finny's stubby, bloodless, and uncircumcised little penis in her hand. She would not go to the mission, would not meet Francis in the morning as planned. She would stay out of his life, for she understood that by depositing her once again with Finny, and knowing precisely what that would mean for her, Francis was willfully cuckolding himself, willfully debasing her, and, withal, separating them both from what still survived of their mutual love and esteem.

Why did Helen let Francis do this to them?

Well, she is subservient to Francis, and always has been. It was she who, by this very subservience, had perpetuated his relationship to her for most of their nine years together. How many times had she walked away from him? Scores upon scores. How many times, always knowing where he'd be, had she returned? The same scores, but minus one now.

The Walter Damrosch man studied her movements at the candle rack, just as she remembered Damrosch himself studying the score of the Ninth Symphony at Harmanus Bleecker Hall when she was sixteen. Listen to it carefully, her father had told her. It's what Debussy said: the magical blossoming of a tree whose leaves burst forth all at once. It was the first time, her father said, that the human voice ever entered into a symphonic creation. Perhaps, my Helen, you too will create a great musical work of art one day. One never knows the potential within any human breast.

A bell jingled as the priest and two altar boys emerged from the sacristy and the mass began. Helen, without her rosary to say, searched for something to read and found a *Follow the Mass* pamphlet on the pew in front of her. She read the ordinary of the mass until she came to the Lesson, in which John sees God's angel ascending from the rising of the sun, and God's angel sees four more angels, to whom it is given to hurt the earth and the sea; and God's angel tells those four bad ones: Hurt not the earth, nor the sea, nor the trees . . .

Helen closed the pamphlet.

Why would angels be sent to hurt the earth and the sea? She had never read that passage before that she could remember, but it was so dreadful. Angel of the earthquake, who splits the earth. Sargasso angel, who chokes the sea with weeds.

Helen could not bear to think such things, and so cast her eyes to others hearing the mass and saw a boy, perhaps nine, who might have been hers and Francis's if she'd had a child instead of a miscarriage, the only fertilization her womb had ever accepted. In front of the boy a kneeling woman with the palsy and twisted bones held on to the front of the pew with both her crooked hands. Calm her trembling, oh Lord, straighten her bones, Helen prayed. And then the priest read the gospel. Blessed are they who mourn, for they shall be comforted. Blessed are ye when they shall revile you, and persecute you, and speak all that is evil against you, untruly, for my sake: be glad and rejoice, for your reward is very great in heaven.

Rejoice. Yes.

> *Oh embrace now, all you millions,*
> *With one kiss for all the world.*

Helen could not stand through the entire gospel. A weakness came over her and she sat down. When mass ended she would try to put something in her stomach. A cup of coffee, a bite of toast.

Helen turned her head and counted the house, the church now more than a third full, a hundred and fifty maybe. They could not all be Italians, since one woman looked rather like Helen's mother, the imposing Mrs Mary Josephine Nurney Archer in her elegant black hat. Helen had that in common with Francis: both had mothers who despised them.

It was twenty-one years before Helen discovered, folded in a locked diary, the single sheet of paper that was her father's final will, never known to exist and written when he knew he was going to kill himself, leaving half the modest residue of his fortune to Helen, the other half to be divided equally between her mother and brother.

Helen read the will aloud to her mother, a paralytic then, nursed toward the grave for ten years by Helen alone, and received in return a maternal smile of triumph at having stolen Helen's future, stolen it so that mother and son might live like peahen and peacock, son grown now into a political lawyer noted for his ability to separate widows from their inheritances, and who always hangs up when Helen calls.

Helen never got even with you for what you, without understanding, did to her, Patrick. Not even you, who profited most from it, understood Mother's duplicitous thievery. But Helen did manage to get even with Mother; left her that very day and moved to New York City, leaving brother dear to do the final nursing, which he accomplished by putting the old cripple into what Helen likes to think of now as the poorhouse, actually the public nursing home, and having her last days paid for by Albany County.

Alone and unloved in the poorhouse.

Where did your plumage go, Mother?

But Helen. Dare you be so vindictive? Did you not have tailfeathers of your own once, however briefly, however long ago? Just look at yourself sitting there staring at the bed with its dirty sheets beckoning to you. Your delicacy resists those sheets, does it not? Not only because of their dirt but because you also resist lying on your back with nothing of beauty to respond to, only the cracked plaster and peeling ceiling paint; whereas by sitting in the chair you can at least look at Grandmother Swan, or even at the blue cardboard clock on the back of the door, which might help you to estimate the time of your life: WAKE ME AT: as if any client of this establishment ever had, or ever would, use such a sign, as if crippled Donovan would ever see it if they did use it, or seeing it, heed it. The clock said ten minutes to eleven. Pretentious.

When you sit at the edge of the bed in a room like this, and hold on to the unpolished brass of the bed, and look at those dirty sheets and the soft cocoons of dust in the corner, you have the powerful impulse to go to the bathroom, where you were just sick for more than half an hour, and wash yourself. No. You have the impulse to go to the genuine bath farther down the hall, with the bathtub where you so often swatted and drowned the cockroaches before you scrubbed that tub, scrub, scrub, scrub. You would walk down the hall to the bath in your Japanese kimono with your almond soap inside your pink bathtowel and the carpets would be thick and soft under the soft soles of your slippers, which you kept under the bed when you were a child; the slippers with the brown wool tassel on the top and the soft yellow lining like a kid glove, that came in the Whitney's box under the Christmas tree. Santa Claus shops at Whitney's.

When you really don't care anymore about Whitney's, or Santa Claus, or shoes, or feet, or even Francis, when that which you thought would last as long as breath itself has worn out and you are a woman like Helen, you hold tightly to the brass, as surely as you would walk down the hall in bare feet, or in shoes with one broken strap, walk on filthy, threadbare carpet and wash under your arms and between your old breasts with the washcloth to keep down the body odor, if you had anyone to keep down the odor for.

Of course Helen is putting on airs with this thought, being just like her mother, washing out the washcloth with the cold water, all there is, and only after washing the cloth twice would she dare to use it on her face. And then she would (yes, she would, can you imagine? can you remember?) dab herself all over with the Madame Pompadour body powder, and touch her ears with the Violet de Paris perfume, and give her hair sixty strokes that way, sixty strokes this way, and say to her image in the mirror that pretty is as pretty does. Arthur loved her pretty.

Helen saw a man who looked a little bit like Arthur, going bald the way he always was, when she was leaving Saint Anthony's Church after mass. It wasn't Arthur, because Arthur was dead, and good enough for him. When she was nineteen, in 1906, Helen went to work in Arthur's piano store, selling only sheet music at first, and then later demonstrating how elegant the tone of Arthur's pianos could be when properly played.

Look at her sitting there at the Chickering upright, playing 'Won't You Come Over to My House?' for that fashionable couple with no musical taste. Look at her there at the Steinway grand, playing a Bach suite for the handsome woman who knows her music. Look how both parties are buying pianos, thanks to magical Helen.

But then, one day when she is twenty-seven and her life is over, when she knows at last that she will never marry, and probably never go further with her music than the boundaries of the piano store, Helen thinks of Schubert, who never rose to be anything more than a children's music teacher, poor and sick, getting only fifteen or twenty cents for his songs, and dead at thirty-one; and on this awful day Helen sits down at Arthur's grand piano and plays 'Who Is Silvia?' and then plays all she can remember of the flight of the raven from *Die Winterreise*.

The Schubert blossom,

Born to bloom unseen,

Like Helen.

Did Arthur do that?

Well, he kept her a prisoner of his love on Tuesdays and Thursdays, when he closed early, and on Friday nights too, when he told his wife he was rehearsing with the Mendelssohn Club. There is Helen now, in that small room on High Street, behind the drawn curtains, sitting naked in bed while Arthur stands up and puts on his dressing gown, expostulating no longer on sex but now on the *Missa Solemnis*, or was it Schubert's lieder, or maybe the glorious Ninth, which Berlioz said was like the first rays of the rising sun in May?

It was really all three, and much, much more, and Helen listened adoringly to the wondrous Arthur as his semen flowed out of her, and she aspired exquisitely to embrace all the music ever played, or sung, or imagined.

In her nakedness on that continuing Tuesday and Thursday and unchanging Friday, Helen now sees the spoiled seed of a woman's barren dream: a seed that germinates and grows into a shapeless, windblown weed blossom of no value to anything, even its own species, for it produces no seed of its own; a mutation that grows only into the lovely day like all other wild things, and then withers, and perishes, and falls, and vanishes.

The Helen blossom.

One never knows the potential within the human breast.

One would never expect Arthur to abandon Helen for a younger woman, a tone-deaf secretary, a musical illiterate with a big bottom.

Stay on as long as you like, my love, Arthur told Helen; for there has never been a saleswoman as good as you.

Alas, poor Helen, loved for the wrong talent by angelic Arthur, to whom it was given to hurt Helen: who educated her body and soul and then sent them off to hell.

Helen walked from Saint Anthony's Church to South Pearl Street and headed north in search of a restaurant. She envisioned herself sitting at one of the small tables in the Primrose Tea Room on State Street, where they served petite watercress sandwiches, with crusts cut off, tea in Nippon cups and saucers, and tiny sugar cubes in a silver bowl with ever-so-delicate silver tongs.

But she settled for the Waldorf Cafeteria, where coffee was a nickel and buttered toast a dime. Discreetly, she took one of the dollar bills out of her brassiere and held it in her left fist inside her coat pocket. She let go of it only long enough to carry the coffee and toast to a table, and then she clutched it anew, a dollar with a fifteen-cent hole in it now. Eleven-eighty-five all she had left. She sweetened and creamed her coffee and sipped at it. She ate half a piece of toast and a bite of another and left the rest. She drank all the coffee, but food did not want to go down.

She paid her check and walked back out onto North Pearl, clutching her change, wondering about Francis and what she should do now. The air had a bite to it, in spite of the warming sun, driving her mind indoors. And so she walked toward the Pruyn Library, a haven. She sat at a table, shivering and hugging herself, warming slowly but deeply chilled. She dozed willfully, in flight to the sun coast where the white birds fly, and a white-haired librarian shook her awake and said: 'Madam, the rules do not allow sleeping in here,' and she placed a back issue of *Life* magazine in front of Helen, and from the next table picked up the morning *Times-Union* on a stick and gave it to her, adding: 'But you may stay as long as you like, my dear, if you choose to read.' The woman smiled at Helen through her pince-nez and Helen returned the smile. There are nice people in the world and sometimes you meet them. Sometimes.

Helen looked at *Life* and found a picture of a two-block-long line of men and women in dark overcoats and hats, their hands in their pockets against the cold of a St Louis day, waiting to pick up their relief checks. She saw a photo of Millie Smalls, a smiling Negro laundress who earned fifteen dollars a week and had just won $150,000 on her Irish Sweepstakes ticket.

Helen closed the magazine and looked at the newspaper. Fair and warmer, the weatherman said. He's a liar. Maybe up to fifty today, but yesterday it was thirty-two. Freezing. Helen shivered and thought of getting a room. Dewey leads Lehman in Crosley poll. Dr Benjamin Ross of Albany's Dudley Observatory says Martians can't attack earth, and adds: 'It is difficult to imagine a rocketship or space ship reaching earth. Earth is a very small target and in all probability a Martian space ship would miss it altogether.' Albany's Mayor Thacher denies false registration of 5,000 voters in 1936. Woman takes poison after son is killed trying to hop freight train.

Helen turned the page and found Martin Daugherty's story about Billy Phelan and the kidnapping. She read it and began to cry, not absorbing any of it, but knowing the family was taking Francis away from her. If Francis and Helen still had a house together, he would never leave her. Never. But they hadn't had a house since early 1930. Francis was working as a fixit man in the South End then, wearing a full beard so nobody'd know it was him, and calling himself Bill Benson. Then the fixit shop went out of business and Francis started drinking again. After a few months of no job, no chance of one, he left Helen alone. 'I ain't no good to you or anybody else,' he said to her during his crying jag just before he went away. 'Never amounted to nothin' and never will.'

How insightful, Francis. How absolutely prophetic of you to see that you would come to nothing, even in Helen's eyes. Francis is somewhere now, alone, and even Helen doesn't love him anymore. Doesn't. For everything about love is dead now, wasted by weariness. Helen doesn't love Francis romantically, for that faded years ago, a rose that bloomed just once and then died forever. And she doesn't love Francis as a companion, for he is always screaming at her and leaving her alone to be fingered by other men. And she certainly doesn't love him as a love thing, because he can't love that way anymore. He tried so hard for so long, harder and longer than you could ever imagine, Finny, but all it did was hurt Helen to see it. It didn't hurt Helen physically because that part of her is so big now, and so old, that nothing can ever hurt her there anymore.

Even when Francis was strong he could never reach all the way up, because she was deeper. She used to need something exceptionally big, bigger than Francis. She had that thought the first time, when she began playing with men after Arthur, who was so big, but she never got what she needed. Well, perhaps once. Who was that? Helen can't remember the face that went with the once. She can't remember anything now but how that night, that once, something in her was touched: a deep center no one had touched before, or has touched since. That was when she thought: This is why some girls become professionals, because it is so good, and there would always be somebody else, somebody new, to help you along.

But a girl like Helen could never really do a thing like that, couldn't just open herself to any man who came by with the price of another day. Does anyone think Helen was ever that kind of a girl?

Ode to Joy, please.

Freude, schöner Götterfunken,
Tochter aus Elysium!

Helen's stomach rumbled and she left the library to breathe deeply of the therapeutic morning air. As she walked down Clinton Avenue and then headed south on Broadway, a vague nausea rose in her and she stopped between two parked cars to hold on to a phone pole, ready to vomit. But the nausea passed and she walked on, past the railroad station, until the musical instruments in the window of the Modern Music Shop caught her attention. She let her eyes play over the banjos and ukuleles, the snare drum and the trombone, the trumpet and violin. Phonograph records stood on shelves, above the instruments: Benny Goodman, the Dorsey Brothers, Bing Crosby, John McCormack singing Schubert, Beethoven's 'Appassionata.'

She went into the store and looked at, and touched, the instruments. She looked at the rack of new song sheets: 'The Flat Foot Floogie,' 'My Heart Belongs to Daddy,' 'You Must Have Been a Beautiful Baby.' She walked to the counter and asked the young man with the slick brown hair: 'Do you have

Beethoven's Ninth Symphony?' She paused. 'And might I see that Schubert album in your window?'

'We do, and you may,' said the man, and he found them and handed them to her and pointed her to the booth where she could listen to the music in private.

She played the Schubert first, John McCormack inquiring: Who is Silvia? What is she? That all our swains commend her? . . . Is she as kind as she is fair? And then, though she absolutely loved McCormack, adored Schubert, she put them both aside for the fourth movement of the *Choral* Symphony.

> *Joy, thou spark from flame immortal,*
> *Daughter of Elysium!*

The words tumbled at Helen in the German and she converted them to her own joyful tongue.

> *He that's won a noble woman,*
> *Let him join our jubilee!*

Oh the rapture she felt. She grew dizzy at the sounds: the oboes, the bassoons, the voices, the grand march of the fugal theme. Scherzo. Molto vivace.

Helen swooned.

A young woman customer saw her fall and was at her side almost instantly. Helen came to with her head in the young woman's lap, the young clerk fanning her with a green record jacket. Beethoven, once green, green as a glade. The needle scratched in the record's end groove. The music had stopped, but not in Helen's brain. It rang out still, the first rays of the rising sun in May.

'How you feeling, ma'am,' the clerk asked.

Helen smiled, hearing flutes and violas.

'I think I'm all right. Will you help me up?'

'Rest a minute,' the girl said. 'Get your bearings first. Would you like a doctor?'

'No, no thank you. I know what it is. I'll be all right in a minute or two.'

But she knew now that she would have to get the room and get it immediately. She did not want to collapse crossing the street. She needed a place of her own, warm and dry, and with her belongings near her. The clerk and the young woman customer helped her to her feet and stood by as she settled herself again on the bench of the listening booth. When the young people were reassured that Helen was fully alert and probably not going to collapse again, they left her. And that's when she slipped the record of the fourth movement inside her coat, under her blouse, and let it rest on the slope of her tumor her doctor said was benign. But how could anything so big be benign? She pulled her coat around her as tightly as she could without cracking the record, said her thank yous to both her benefactors, and walked slowly out of the store.

Her bag was at Palombo's Hotel and she headed for there: all the way past Madison Avenue. Would she make it to the hotel without a collapse? Well, she did. She was exhausted but she found crippled old Donovan in his rickety rocker, and his spittoon at his feet, on the landing between the first and second floors, all there was of a lobby in this establishment. She said she wanted to redeem her bag and rent a room, the same room she and Francis always took whenever it was empty. And it was empty.

Six dollars to redeem the bag, old Donovan told her, and a dollar and a half for one night, or two-fifty for two nights running. Just one, Helen said, but then she thought: What if I don't die tonight? I will need it tomorrow too. And so she took the bargain rate, which left her with three dollars and thirty-five cents.

Old Donovan gave her the key to the second-floor room and went to the cellar for her suitcase.

'Ain't seen ya much,' Donovan said when he brought the bag to her room.

'We've been busy,' Helen said. 'Francis got a job.'

'A job? Ya don't say.'

'We're all quite organized now, you might describe it. It's just possible that we'll rent an apartment up on Hamilton Street.'

'You're back in the chips. Mighty good. Francis comin' in tonight?'

'He might be, and he might not be,' said Helen. 'It all depends on his work, and how busy he might or might not be.'

'I get it,' said Donovan.

She opened the suitcase and found the kimono and put it on. She went then to wash herself, but before she could wash she vomited; sat on the floor in front of the toilet bowl and vomited until there was nothing left to come up; and then she retched dryly for five minutes, finally taking sips of water so there would be something to bring up. And Francis thought she was just being contrary, refusing Jack's cheese sandwich.

Finally it passed, and she rinsed her mouth and her stinging eyes and did, oh yes, did wash herself, and then padded back along the threadbare carpet to her room, where she sat in the chair at the foot of the bed, staring at the swan and remembering nights in this room with Francis.

Clara, that cheap whore, rolled that nice young man in the brown suit and then came in here to hide. If you're gonna sleep with a man, sleep with him, Francis said. Be a goddamn woman. If you're gonna roll a man, roll him. But don't sleep with him and then roll him. Francis had such nice morals. Oh Clara, why in heaven's name do you come in here with your trouble? Haven't we got trouble enough of our own without you? All Clara got was fourteen dollars. But that is a lot.

Helen propped her Beethoven record against the pillow in the center of the bed and studied its perfection. Then she rummaged in the suitcase to see and touch all that was in it: another pair of bloomers, her rhinestone butterfly, her blue skirt with the rip in it, Francis's safety razor and his pen-knife, his old baseball clippings, his red shirt, and his left brown shoe, the right one lost; but one shoe's better than none, ain't it? was Francis's reasoning. Sandra lost a shoe but Francis found it for her. Francis was very thoughtful. Very everything. Very Catholic, though he pretended not to be. That was why Francis and Helen could never marry.

Wasn't it nice the way Helen and Francis put their religion in the way of marriage?

Wasn't that an excellent idea?

For really, Helen wanted to fly free in the same way Francis did. After Arthur she knew she would always want to be free, even if she had to suffer for it.

Arthur, Arthur, Helen no longer blames you for anything. She knows you were a man of frail allegiance in a way that Francis never was; knows too that she allowed you to hurt her.

Helen remembers Arthur's face and how relieved it was, how it smiled and wished her luck the day she said she was leaving to take a job playing piano for silent films and vaudeville acts. Moving along in the world willfully, that's what Helen was doing then (and now). A will to grace, if you would like to call it that, however elusive that grace has proven to be.

Was this willfulness a little deceit Helen was playing on herself?

Was she moving, instead, in response to impulses out of that deep center?

Why was it, really, that things never seemed to work out?

Why was Helen's life always turning into some back alley, like a wandering old cat?

What is Helen?

Who is Silvia, please?

Please?

Helen stands up and holds the brass. Helen's feet are like fine brass. She is not unpolished like the brass of this bed. Helen is the very polished person who is standing at the end of the end bed in the end room of the end hotel of the end city of the end.

And when a person like Helen comes to an ending of something, she grows nostalgic and sentimental. She has always appreciated the fine things in life: music, kind words, gentility, flowers, sunshine, and good men. People would feel sad if they knew what Helen's life might have been like had it gone in another direction than the one that brought her to this room.

People would perhaps even weep, possibly out of some hope

that women like Helen could go on living until they found themselves, righted themselves, discovered ever-unfolding joy instead of coming to lonely ends. People would perhaps feel that some particular thing went wrong somewhere and that if it had only gone right it wouldn't have brought a woman like Helen so low.

But that is the error; for there are no women like Helen.

Helen is no symbol of lost anything, wrong-road-taken kind of person, if-they-only-knew-then kind of person.

Helen is no pure instinct deranged, no monomaniacal yearning out of a deep center that wants everything, even the power to destroy itself.

Helen is no wandering cat in its ninth termination.

For since Helen was born, and so elegantly raised by her father, and so exquisitely self-developed, she has been making her own decisions based on rational thinking, reasonably current knowledge, intuition about limitations, and the usual instruction by friends, lovers, enemies, and others. Her head was never injured, and her brain, contrary to what some people might think, is not pickled. She did not miss reading the newspapers, although she has tapered off somewhat in recent years, for now all the news seems bad. She always listened to the radio and kept up on the latest in music. And in the winter in the library she read novels about women and love: Helen knows all about Lily Bart and Daisy Miller. Helen also cared for her appearance and kept her body clean. She washed her underthings regularly and wore earrings and dressed modestly and carried her rosary until they stole it. She did not sleep when sleep was not called for. She went through her life feeling: I really do believe I am doing the more-or-less right thing. I believe in God. I salute the flag. I wash my armpits and between my legs, and what if I did drink too much? Whose business is that? Who knows how much I didn't drink?

They never think of that sort of thing when they call a woman like Helen a drunken old douchebag. Why would anyone (like that nasty Little Red in the back of Finny's car) ever want to revile Helen that way? When she hears people say such things about her, Helen then plays the pretend game. She dissembles. Helen remembers that word even though Francis thinks she has forgotten her education. But she has not. She is not a drunk and not a whore. Her attitude is: I flew through my years and I never let a man use me for money. I went Dutch lots of times. I would let them buy the drinks but that's because it's the man's place to buy drink.

And when you're a woman like Helen who hasn't turned out to be a whore, who hasn't led anybody into sin . . . (Well, there were some young boys in her life occasionally, lonely in the bars like Helen so often was, but they seemed to know about sin already. Once.)

Once.

Was once a boy?

Yes, with a face like a priest.

Oh Helen, how blasphemous of you to have such a thought. Thank God you never loved up a priest. How would you ever explain that?

Because priests are good.

And so when Helen holds the brass, and looks at the clock that still says ten minutes to eleven, and thinks of slippers and music and the great butterfly and the white pebble with the hidden name, she has this passing thought for priests. For when you were raised like Helen was, you think of priests as holding the keys to the door of redemption. No matter how many sins you have committed (sands of the desert, salt of the sea), you are bound to come to the notion of absolution at the time of brass holding and clock watching, and to the remembering of how you even used to put Violet de Paris on your brassiere so that when he opened your dress to kiss you there, he wouldn't smell any sweat.

But priests, Helen, have nothing whatsoever to do with brassieres and kissing, and you should be ashamed to have put them all in the same thought. Helen does truly regret such a thought, but after all, it has been a most troubled time for her and her religion. And even though she prayed at mass this morning, and has prayed intermittently throughout the day ever since, even though she prayed in Finny's car last night, saying her Now I Lay Me Down to Sleeps when there was no sleep or chance of it, then the point is that, despite all prayer, Helen has no compulsion to confess her sins to gain absolution.

Helen has even come to the question of whether or not she is really a Catholic, and to what a Catholic really is these days. She thinks that, truly, she may not be one anymore. But if she isn't, she certainly isn't anything else either. She certainly isn't a Methodist, Mr Chester.

What brought her to this uncertainty is the accumulation of her sins, and if you must call them sins, then there is certainly quite an accumulation. But Helen prefers to call them decisions, which is why she has no compulsion to confess them. On the other hand, Helen wonders whether anyone is aware of how really good a life she lived. She never betrayed anybody, and that, in the end, is what counts most with her. She admits she is leaving Francis, but no one could call that a betrayal. One might, perhaps, call it an abdication, the way the King of England abdicated for the woman he loved. Helen is abdicating for the man she used to love so he can be as free as Helen wants him to be, as free as she always was in her own way, as free as the two of them were even when they were most perfectly locked together. Didn't Francis beg on the street for Helen when she was sick in '33? Why, he never begged even for himself before that. If Francis could become a beggar out of love, why can't Helen abdicate for the same reason?

Of course the relationships Helen had with Arthur and Francis were sinful in the eyes of some. And she admits that certain other liberties she has taken with the commandments of God and the Church might also loom large against her when the time of judgment comes (brass and clock, brass and clock). But even so, there will be no priests coming to see her, and she is surely not going out to see them. She is not going to declare to anyone for any reason that loving Francis was sinful when it was very probably – no, very certainly – the greatest thing in her life, greater, finally, than loving Arthur, for Arthur failed of honor.

And so when crippled Donovan knocks again at eleven o'clock

and asks if Helen needs anything, she says no, no thank you, old cripple, I don't need anything or anybody anymore. And old Donovan says: The night man's just comin' on, and so I'm headin' home. I'll be here in the mornin'. And Helen says: Thank you, Donovan, thank you ever so much for your concern, and for saying good night to me. And after he goes away from the door she lets go of the brass and thinks of Beethoven, Ode to Joy,

And hears the joyous multitudes advancing,

Dah dah-dah,

Dah dah-de-dah-dah,

And feels her legs turning to feathers and sees that her head is floating down to meet them as her body bends under the weight of so much joy,

Sees it floating ever so slowly

As the white bird glides over the water until it comes to rest on the Japanese kimono

That has fallen so quietly,

So softly,

Onto the grass where the moonlight grows.

6

First came the fire in a lower Broadway warehouse, near the old Fitzgibbon downtown ironworks. It rose in its own sphere, in an uprush into fire's own perfection, and great flames violated the sky. Then, as Francis and Rosskam halted behind trucks and cars, Rosskam's horse snorty and balky with elemental fear, the fire touched some store of thunder and the side of the warehouse blew out in a great rising cannon blossom of black smoke, which the wind carried toward them. Motorists rolled up their windows, but the vulnerable lights of Francis, Rosskam, and the horse smarted with evil fumes.

Ahead of them a policeman routed traffic into a U-turn and sent it back north. Rosskam cursed in a foreign language Francis didn't recognize. But that Rosskam was cursing was unmistakable. As they turned toward Madison Avenue, both men's faces were astream with stinging tears.

They were now pulling an empty wagon, fresh from dumping the day's first load of junk back at Rosskam's yard. Francis had lunched at the yard on an apple Rosskam gave him, and had changed into his new white-on-white shirt, throwing his old blue relic onto Rosskam's rag mountain. They had then set out on the day's second run, heading for the deep South End of the city, until the fire turned them around at three o'clock.

Rosskam turned up Pearl Street and the wagon rolled along into North Albany, the smoke still rising into the heavens below and behind them. Rosskam called out his double-noted ragman's dirge and caught the attention of a few cluttered housewives. From the backyard of an old house near Emmett Street, Francis hauled out a wheelless wheelbarrow with a rust hole through its bottom. As he heaved it upward into the wagon, the odor of fire still in his nostrils, he confronted Fiddler Quain, sitting on an upended metal chamber pot that had been shot full of holes by some backyard marksman.

The Fiddler, erstwhile motorman, now wearing a tan tweed suit, brown polka-dot bow tie, and sailor straw hat, smiled coherently at Francis for the first time since that day on Broadway in 1901 when they both ignited the kerosene-soaked sheets that trapped the strikebreaking trolley car.

When a soldier split the Fiddler's skull with a rifle butt, the sympathetic mob spirited him away to safety before he could be arrested. But the blow left the man mindless for a dozen years, cared for by his spinster sister, Martha. Martyred herself by his wound, Martha paraded the Fiddler through the streets of North Albany, a heroic vegetable, so the neighbors could see the true consequences of the smartypants trolley strike.

Francis offered to be a bearer at the Fiddler's funeral in 1913, but Martha rejected him; for she believed it was Francis's firebrand style that had seduced the Fiddler into violence that fated morning. Your hands have done enough damage, she told Francis. You'll not touch my brother's coffin.

Pay her no mind, the Fiddler told Francis from his perch on the riddled pot. I don't blame you for anything. Wasn't I ten years your elder? Couldn't I make up my own mind?

But then the Fiddler gave Francis a look that loosened a tide of bafflement, as he said solemnly: It's those traitorous hands of yours you'll have to forgive.

Francis brushed rust off his fingers and went behind the house for more dead metal. When he returned with an armload, the scab Harold Allen, wearing a black coat and a motorman's cap, was sitting with the Fiddler, who had his boater in his lap now. When Francis looked at the pair of them, Harold Allen doffed his cap. Both men's heads were laid open and bloody, but not bleeding, their unchanging wounds obviously healed over and as much a part of their aerial bodies as their eyes, which burned with an entropic passion common among murdered men.

Francis threw the old junk into the wagon and turned away. When he turned back to verify the images, two more men were sitting in the wheelless wheelbarrow. Francis could call neither of them by name, but he knew from the astonishment in the hollows of their eyes that they were the shopper and haberdasher, bystanders both, who had been killed by the soldiers' random retaliatory fire after Francis opened Harold Allen's skull with the smooth stone.

'I'm ready,' said Francis to Rosskam. 'You ready?'

'What's the big hurry-up?' Rosskam asked.

'Nothin' else to haul. Shouldn't we be movin'?'

'He's impatient too, this bum,' Rosskam said, and he climbed aboard the wagon.

Francis, feeling the eyes of the four shades on him, gave them all the back of his neck as the wagon rolled north on Pearl Street, Annie's street. Getting closer. He pulled up the collar of his coat against a new bite in the wind, the western sky graying with ominous clouds. It was almost three-thirty by the Nehi clock in the window of Elmer Rivenburgh's grocery. First day of early winter. If it rains tonight and we're outside, we freeze our ass once and for all.

He rubbed his hands together. Were they the enemies? How could a man's hands betray him? They were full of scars, calluses, split fingernails, ill-healed bones broken on other men's jaws, veins so bloated and blue they seemed on the verge of explosion. The hands were long-fingered, except where there was no finger, and now, with accreting age, the fingers had thickened, like the low-growing branches of a tree.

Traitors? How possible?

'You like your hands?' Francis asked Rosskam.

'*Like*, you say? Do I like my hands?'

'Yeah. You like 'em?'

Rosskam looked at his hands, looked at Francis, looked away.

'I mean it,' Francis said. 'I got the idea that my hands do things on their own, you know what I mean?'

'Not yet,' said Rosskam.

'They don't need me. They do what they goddamn please.'

'Ah ha,' said Rosskam. He looked again at his own gnarled hands and then again at Francis. 'Nutsy,' he said, and slapped the horse's rump with the reins. 'Giddap,' he added, changing the subject.

Francis remembered Skippy Maguire's left hand, that first summer away at Dayton. Skippy was Francis's roommate, a pitcher: tall and lefty, a man who strutted when he walked; and on the mound he shaped up like a king of the hill. Why, when he wanted to, Skippy could strut standin' still. But then his left hand split open, the fingers first and then the palm. He pampered the hand: greased it, sunned it, soaked it in Epsom salts and beer, but it wouldn't heal. And when the team manager got impatient, Skippy ignored the splits and pitched ten minutes in a practice session, which turned the ball red and tore the fingers and the palm into a handful of bloody pulp. The manager told Skippy he was stupid and took him and his useless hand off the payroll.

That night Skippy cursed the manager, got drunker than usual, started a fire in the coal stove even though it was August, and when it was roaring, reached in and picked up a handful of flaming coal. And he showed that goddamn Judas of a hand a thing or two. The doc had to cut off three fingers to save it.

Well, Francis may be a little nutsy to people like Rosskam, but he wouldn't do anything like Skippy did. Would he? He looked at his hands, connecting scars to memories. Rowdy Dick got the finger. The jagged scar behind the pinky . . . a violent thirst gave him that one, the night he punched out a liquor store window in Chinatown to get at a bottle of wine. In a fight on Eighth Avenue with a bum who wanted to screw Helen, Francis broke the first joint on his middle finger and it healed crookedly. And a wild man in Philadelphia out to steal Francis's hat bit off the tip of the left thumb.

But Francis got 'em. He avenged all scars, and he lived to remember every last one of them dickie birds too, most of 'em probably dead now, by their own hand maybe. Or the hand of Francis?

Rowdy Dick.

Harold Allen.

The latter name suddenly acted as a magical key to history for Francis. He sensed for the first time in his life the workings of something other than conscious will within himself: insight into a pattern, an overview of all the violence in his history, of how many had died or been maimed by his hand, or had died, like that nameless pair of astonished shades, as an indirect result of his violent ways. He limped now, would always limp with the metal plate in his left leg, because a man stole a bottle of orange soda from him. He found the man, a runt, and retrieved the soda. But the runt hit him with an ax handle and splintered the bone. And what did Francis do? Well the runt was too little to hit, so Francis shoved his face into the dirt and bit a piece out of the back of his neck.

There are things I never wanted to learn how to do, is one thought that came to Francis.

And there are things I did without needin' to learn.

And I never wanted to know about them either.

Francis's hands, as he looked at them now, seemed to be messengers from some outlaw corner of his psyche, artificers of some involuntary doom element in his life. He seemed now to have always been the family killer; for no one else he knew of in the family had ever lived as violently as he. And yet he had never sought that kind of life.

But you set out to kill *me*, Harold Allen said silently from the back of the wagon.

'No,' answered Francis without turning. 'Not kill anybody. Just do some damage, get even. Maybe bust a trolley window, cause a ruckus, stuff like that.'

But you knew, even that early in your career, how accurate your throw could be. You were proud of that talent. It was what you brought to the strike that day, and it was why you spent the morning hunting for stones the same weight as a baseball. You aimed at me to make yourself a hero.

'But not to kill you.'

Just to knock out an eye, was it?

Francis now remembered the upright body of Harold Allen on the trolley, indisputably a target. He remembered the coordination of vision with arm movement, of distance with snap of wrist. For a lifetime he had remembered precisely the way Harold Allen crumpled when the stone struck his forehead at the hairline. Francis had not heard, but had forever after imagined, the sound the stone (moving at maybe seventy miles an hour?) made when it hit Harold Allen's skull. It made the skull sound as hollow, as tough, and as explodable, he decided, as a watermelon hit with a baseball bat.

Francis considered the evil autonomy of his hands and wondered what Skippy Maguire, in his later years, had made of his own left hand's suicidal impulse. Why was it that suicide kept rising up in Francis's mind? Wake up in the weeds outside Pittsburgh, half frozen over, too cold to move, flaked out 'n' stiffer than a chunk of old iron, and you say to yourself: Francis, you don't ever want to put in another night, another mornin', like this one was. Time to go take a header off the bridge.

But after a while you stand up, wipe the frost out of your ear, go someplace to get warm, bum a nickel for coffee, and then start walkin' toward somewheres else that ain't near no bridge.

Francis did nto understand this flirtation with suicide, this flight from it. He did not know why he hadn't made the big leap the way Helen's old man had when he knew he was done in. Too busy, maybe, figurin' out the next half hour. No way for Francis ever to get a real good look past the sunset, for he's the kind of fella just kept runnin' when things went bust; never had the time to stop anyplace easy just to die.

But he never wanted to run off all that much either. Who'd have figured his mother would announce to the family at Thanksgiving dinner, just after Francis married Annie, that neither he nor his common little woman would ever be welcome in this house again? The old bat relented after two years and Francis was allowed visiting privileges. But he only went once, and not even inside the door then, for he found out that privileges didn't extend to most uncommon Annie at his side.

And so family contact on Colonie Street ended for Francis in a major way. He vacated the flat he'd rented nine doors up the block, moved to the North End to be near Annie's family, and never set foot again in the god-damned house until the old battle-ax (sad, twisted, wrong-headed, pitiable woman) died.

Departure.

Flight of a kind, the first.

Flight again, when he killed the scab.

Flight again, every summer until it was no longer possible, in order to assert the one talent that gave him full and powerful ease, that let him dance on the earth to the din of brass bands, raucous cheers, and the voluptuous approval of the crowd. Flight kept Francis sane during all those years, and don't ask him why. He loved living with Annie and the kids, loved his sister, Mary, and half-loved his brothers Peter and Chick and his moron brother, Tommy, too, who all came to visit him at his house when he was no longer welcome at theirs.

He loved and half-loved lots of things about Albany.

But then one day it's February again,
And it won't be long now till the snow gets gone again,
And the grass comes green again,
And then the dance music rises in Francis's brain,
And he longs to flee again,
And he flees.

A man stepped out of a small apartment house behind Sacred Heart Church and motioned to Rosskam, who reined the horse and climbed down to negotiate for new junk. Francis, on the wagon, watched a group of children coming out of School 20 and crossing the street. A woman whom Francis took to be their teacher stood a few steps into the intersection with raised hand to augment the stopping power of the red light, even though there were no automobiles in sight, only Rosskam's wagon, which was already standing still. The children, their secular school day ended, crossed like a column of ants into the custody of two nuns on the opposite corner, gliding black figures who would imbue the pliant young minds with God's holy truth: Blessed are the meek. Francis remembered Billy and Peg as children, similarly handed over from the old school to this same church for instruction in the ways of God, as if anybody could ever figure that one out.

At the thought of Billy and Peg, Francis trembled. He was only a block away from where they lived. And he knew the address now, from the newspaper. I'll come by of a Sunday and bring a turkey, Francis had told Billy when Billy first asked him to come home. And Billy's line was: Who the fuck wants a turkey? Yeah, who does? Francis answered then. But his answer now was: I sorta do.

Rosskam climbed back on the wagon, having made no deal with the man from the apartment house, who wanted garbage removed.

'Some people,' said Rosskam to the rear end of his horse, 'they don't know junk. It ain't garbage. And garbage, it ain't junk.'

The horse moved forward, every clip clop of its hooves tightening the bands around Francis's chest. How would he do it? What would he say? Nothing to say. Forget it. No, just knock at the door. Well, I'm home. Or maybe just: How's chances for a cupacoffee; see what that brings. Don't ask no favors or make no promises. Don't apologize. Don't cry. Make out it's just a visit. Get the news, pay respects, get gone.

But what about the turkey?

'I think I'm gonna get off the wagon up ahead a bit,' Francis told Rosskam, who looked at him with a squinty eye. 'Gettin' near the end of the day anyway, 'bout an hour or so left before it starts gettin' dark, ain't that right?' He looked up at the sky, gray but bright, with a vague hint of sun in the west.

'Quit before dark?' Rosskam said. 'You don't quit before dark.'

'Gotta see some people up ahead. Ain't seen 'em in a while.'

'So go.'

''Course I want my pay for what I done till now.'

'You didn't work the whole day. Come by tomorrow, I'll figure how much.'

'Worked most of the day. Seven hours, must be, no lunch.'

'Half a day you worked. Three hours yet before dark.'

'I worked more'n half a day. I worked more'n seven hours. I figure you can knock off a dollar. That'd be fair. I'll take six 'stead of seven, and a quarter out for the shirt. Five-seventy-five.'

'Half a day you work, you get half pay. Three-fifty.'

'No sir.'

'No? I am the boss.'

'That's right. You are the boss. And you're one strong fella too. But I ain't no dummy, and I know when I'm bein' skinned. And I want to tell you right now, Mr Rosskam, I'm mean as hell when I get riled up.' He held out his right hand for inspection. 'If you think I won't fight for what's mine, take a look. That hand's seen it all. I mean the worst. Dead men took their last ride on that hand. You get me?'

Rosskam reined the horse, braked the wagon, and looped the reins around a hook on the footboard. The wagon stood in the middle of the block, immediately across Pearl Street from the main entrance to the school. More children were exiting and moving in ragged columns toward the church. Blessed are the many meek. Rosskam studied Francis's hand, still outstretched, with digits gone, scars blazing, veins pounding, fingers curled in the vague beginnings of a fist.

'Threats,' he said. 'You make threats. I don't like threats. Five-twenty-five I pay, no more.'

'Five-seventy-five. I say five-seventy-five is what's fair. You gotta be fair in this life.'

From inside his shirt Rosskam pulled out a change purse which hung around his neck on a leather thong. He opened it and stripped off five singles, from a wad, counted them twice, and put them in Francis's outstretched hand, which turned its palm skyward to receive them. Then he added the seventy-five cents.

'A bum is a bum,' Rosskam said. 'I hire no more bums.'

'I thank ye,' Francis said, pocketing the cash.

'You I don't like,' Rosskam said.

'Well I sorta liked you,' Francis said. 'And I ain't really a bad sort once you get to know me.' He leaped off the wagon and saluted Rosskam, who pulled away without a word or a look, the wagon half full of junk, empty of shades.

Francis walked toward the house with a more pronounced limp than he'd experienced for weeks. The leg pained him, but not excessively. And yet he was unable to lift it from the sidewalk in a normal gait. He walked exceedingly slowly and to a passerby he would have seemed to be lifting the leg up from a sidewalk paved with glue. He could not see the house half a block away, only a gray porch he judged to be part of it. He paused, seeing a chubby middle-aged woman emerging from another house. When she was about to pass him he spoke.

'Excuse me, lady, but d'ya know where I could get me a nice little turkey?'

The woman looked at him with surprise, then terror, and retreated swiftly up her walkway and back into the house. Francis watched her with awe. Why, when he was sober, and wearing a new shirt, should he frighten a woman with a simple question? The door reopened and a shoeless bald man in an undershirt and trousers stood in the doorway.

'What did you ask my wife?' he said.

'I asked if she knew where I could get a turkey.'

'What for?'

'Well,' said Francis, and he paused, and scuffed one foot, 'my duck died.'

'Just keep movin', bud.'

'Gotcha,' Francis said, and he limped on.

He hailed a group of schoolboys crossing the street toward him and asked: 'Hey fellas, you know a meat market around here?'

'Yeah, Jerry's,' one said, 'up at Broadway and Lawn.'

Francis saluted the boy as the others stared. When Francis started to walk they all turned and ran ahead of him. He walked past the house without looking at it, his gait improving a bit. He would have to walk two blocks to the market, then two blocks back. Maybe they'd have a turkey for sale. Settle for a chicken? No.

By the time he reached Lawn Avenue he was walking well, and by Broadway his gait, for him, was normal. The floor of Jerry's meat market was bare wood, sprinkled with sawdust and extraordinarily clean. Shining white display cases with slanted and glimmering glass offered rows of splendid livers, kidneys, and bacon, provocative steaks and chops, and handsomely ground sausage and hamburg to Francis, the lone customer.

'Help you?' a white-aproned butcher asked. His hair was so black that his facial skin seemed bleached.

'Turkey,' Francis said. 'I'd like me a nice dead turkey.'

'It's the only kind we carry,' the butcher said. 'Nice and dead. How big?'

'How big they come?'

'So big you wouldn't believe it.'

'Gimme a try.'

'Twenty-five, twenty-eight pounds?'

'How much those big fellas sell for?'

'Depends on how much they weigh.'

'Right. How much a pound, then?'

'Forty-four cents.'

'Forty-four. Say forty.' He paused. 'You got maybe a twelve-pounder?'

The butcher entered the white meat locker and came out with a turkey in each hand. He weighed one, then another.

'Ten pounds here, and this is twelve and a half.'

'Give us that big guy,' Francis said, and he put the five singles and change on the white counter as the butcher wrapped the turkey in waxy white paper. The butcher left him twenty-five cents change on the counter.

'How's business, pal?' Francis asked.

'Slow. No money in the world.'

'They's money. You just gotta go get it. Lookit that five bucks I just give ye. I got me that this afternoon.'

'If I go out to get money, who'll mind the store?'

'Yeah,' said Francis, 'I s'pose some guys just gotta sit and wait. But it's a nice clean place you got to wait in.'

'Dirty butchers go out of business.'

'Keep the meat nice and clean, is what it is.'

'Right. Good advice for everybody. Enjoy your dead turkey.'

He walked down Broadway to King Brady's saloon and then stared down toward the foot of North Street, toward Welt the Tin's barn and the old lock, long gone, a daylight look at last. A few more houses stood on the street now, but it hadn't changed so awful much. He'd looked briefly at it from the bus, and again last night in the barn, but despite the changes time had made, his eyes now saw only the vision of what had been so long ago; and he gazed down on reconstituted time: two men walking up toward Broadway, one of them looking not unlike himself at twenty-one. He understood the cast of the street's incline as the young man stepped upward, and upward, and upward toward where Francis stood.

The turkey's coldness penetrated his coat, chilling his arm and his side. He switched the package to his other arm and walked up North Third Street toward their house. They'll figure I want 'em to cook the turkey, he thought. Just tell 'em: Here's a turkey, cook it up of a Sunday.

Kids came toward him on bikes. Leaves covered the sidewalks of Walter Street. His leg began to ache, his feet again in the glue. Goddamn legs got a life of their own too. He turned the corner, saw the front stoop, walked past it. He turned at the driveway and stopped at the side door just before the garage. He stared at the dotted white curtain behind the door's four small windowpanes, looked at the knob, at the aluminum milkbox. He'd stole a whole gang of milk outa boxes just like it. Bum. Killer. Thief. He touched the bell, heard the steps, watched the curtain being pulled aside, saw the eye, watched the door open an inch.

'Howdy,' he said.

'Yes?'

Her.

'Brought a turkey for ye.'

'A turkey?'

'Yep. Twelve-and-a-half-pounder.' He held it aloft with one hand.

'I don't understand.'

'I told Bill I'd come by of a Sunday and bring a turkey. It ain't Sunday but I come anyway.'

'Is that you, Fran?'

'It ain't one of them fellas from Mars.'

'Well my God. My God, my God.' She opened the door wide.

'How ya been, Annie? You're lookin' good.'

'Oh come in, come in.' She went up the five stairs ahead of him. Stairs to the left went into the cellar, where he thought he might first enter, carry out some of their throwaways to Rosskam's wagon before the made himself known. Now he was going into the house itself, closing the side door behind him. Up five stairs with Annie watching and into the kitchen, she backing away in front of him. She's staring. But she's smiling. All right.

'Billy told us he'd seen you,' she said. She stopped in the center of the kitchen and Francis stopped too. 'But he didn't think you'd ever come. My oh my, what a surprise. We saw the story about you in the paper.'

'Hope it didn't shame you none.'

'We all thought it was funny. Everybody in town thought it was funny, registering twenty times to vote.'

'Twenty-one.'

'Oh my, Fran. Oh my, what a surprise this is.'

'Here. Do somethin' with this critter. It's freezin' me up.'

'You didn't have to bring anything. And a turkey. What it must've cost you.'

'Iron Joe always used to tell me: Francis, don't come by empty-handed. Hit the bell with your elbow.'

She had store teeth in her mouth. Those beauties gone. Her hair was steel-gray, only a trace of the brown left, and her chin was caved in a little from the new teeth. But that smile was the same, that honest-to-god smile. She'd put on weight: bigger breasts, bigger hips; and her shoes turned over at the counters. Varicose veins through the stocking too, hands all red, stains on her apron. That's what housework does to a pretty kid like she was.

Like she was when she came into The Wheelbarrow.

The canalers' and lumbermen's saloon that Iron Joe ran at the foot of Main Street.

Prettiest kid in the North End. Folks always said that about pretty girls.

But she was.

Came in lookin' for Iron Joe,

And Francis, working up to it for two months,

Finally spoke to her.

Howdy, he'd said.

Two hours later they were sitting between two piles of boards in Kibbee's lumberyard with nobody to see them, holding hands and Francis saying goopy things he swore to himself he'd never say to anybody.

And then they kissed.

Not just then, but some hours or maybe even days later, Francis compared that kiss to Katrina's first, and found them as different as cats and dogs. Remembering them both now as he stood looking at Annie's mouth with its store teeth, he perceived that a kiss is as expressive of a way of life as is a smile, or a scarred hand. Kisses come up from below, or down from above. They come from the brain sometimes, sometimes from the heart, and sometimes just from the crotch. Kisses that taper off after a while come only from the heart and leave the taste of sweetness. Kisses that come from the brain tend to try to work things out inside other folks' mouths and don't hardly register. And kisses from the crotch and the brain put together, with maybe a little bit of heart, like Katrina's, well they are the kisses that can send you right around the bend for your whole life.

But then you get one like that first whizzer on Kibbee's lumber pile, one that come out of the brain and the heart and the crotch, and out of the hands on your hair, and out of those breasts that weren't all the way blown up yet, and out of the clutch them arms give you, and out of time itself, which keeps track of how long it can go on without you gettin' even slightly bored the way you got bored years later with kissin' almost anybody but Helen, and out of fingers (Katrina had fingers like that) that run themselves around and over your face and down your neck, and out of the grip you take on her shoulders, especially on them bones that come out of the middle of her back like angel wings, and out of them eyes that keep openin' and closin' to make sure that this is still goin' and still real and not just stuff you dream about and when you know it's real it's okay to close 'em again, and outa that tongue, holy shit, that tongue, you gotta ask where she learned that because nobody ever did that that good except Katrina who was married and with a kid and had a right to know, but Annie, goddamn, Annie, where'd you pick that up, or maybe you been gidzeyin' heavy on this lumber pile regular (No, no, no, I know you never, I always knew you never), and so it is natural with a woman like Annie that the kiss come out of every part of her body and more, outa that mouth with them new teeth Francis is now looking at, with the same lips he remembers and doesn't want to kiss anymore except in memory (though that could be subject to change), and he sees well beyond the mouth into a primal location in this woman's being, a location that evokes in him not only the memory of years but decades and even more, the memory of epochs, aeons, so that he is sure that no matter where he might have sat with a woman and felt this way, whether it was in some ancient cave or some bogside shanty, or on a North Albany lumber pile, he and she would both know that there was something in each of them that had to stop being one and become two, that had to swear that forever after there would never be another (and there never has been, quite), and that there would be allegiance and sovereignty and fidelity and other such tomfool horseshit that people destroy their heads with when what they are saying has nothing to do with time's forevers but everything to do with the simultaneous recognition of an eternal twain, well sir, then both of them, Francis and Annie, or the Francises and Annies of any age, would both know in that same instant that there was something between them that had to stop being two and become one.

Such was the significance of that kiss.

Francis and Annie married a month and a half later.

Katrina, I will love you forever.

However, something has come up.

'The turkey,' Annie said. 'You'll stay while I cook it.'

'No, that'd take one long time. You just have it when you want to. Sunday, whenever.'

'It wouldn't take too long to cook. A few hours is all. Are you going to run off so soon after being away so long?'

'I ain't runnin' off.'

'Good. Then let me get it into the oven right now. When Peg comes home we can peel potatoes and onions and Danny can go get some cranberries. A turkey. Imagine that. Rushing the season.'

'Who's Danny?'

'You don't know Danny. Naturally, you don't. He's Peg's boy. She married George Quinn. You know George, of course, and they have the boy. He's ten.'

'Ten.'

'In fourth grade and smart as a cracker.'

'Gerald, he'd be twenty-two now.'

'Yes, he would.'

'I saw his grave.'

'You did? When?'

'Yesterday. Got a day job up there and tracked him down and talked there awhile.'

'Talked?'

'Talked to Gerald. Told him how it was. Told him a bunch of stuff.'

'I'll bet he was glad to hear from you.'

'May be. Where's Bill?'

'Bill? Oh, you mean Billy. We call him Billy. He's taking a nap. He got himself in trouble with the politicians and he's feeling pretty low. The kidnapping. Patsy McCall's nephew was kidnapped. Bindy McCall's son. You must've read about it.'

'Yeah, I did, and Martin Daugherty run it down for me too, awhile back.'

'Martin wrote about Billy in the paper this morning.'

'I seen that too. Nice write-up. Martin says his father's still alive.'

'Edward. He is indeed, living down on Main Street. He lost his memory, poor man, but he's healthy. We see him walking with Martin from time to time. I'll go wake Billy and tell him you're here.'

'No, not yet. Talk a bit.'

'Talk. Yes, all right. Let's go in the living room.'

'Not me, not in these clothes. I just come off workin' on a junk wagon. I'd dirty up the joint somethin' fierce.'

'That doesn't matter at all. Not at all.'

'Right here's fine. Look out the window at the yard there. Nice yard. And a collie dog you got.'

'It is nice. Danny cuts the grass and the dog buries his bones all over it. There's a cat next door he chases up and down the fence.'

'The family changed a whole lot. I knew it would. How's your brother and sisters?'

'They're fine, I guess. Johnny never changes. He's a committeeman now for the Democrats. Josie got very fat and lost a lot of her hair. She wears a switch. And Minnie was married two years and her husband died. She's very lonely and lives in a rented room. But we all see one another.'

'Billy's doin' good.'

'He's a gambler and not a very good one. He's always broke.'

'He was good to me when I first seen him. He had money then. Bailed me outa jail, wanted to buy me a new suit of clothes. Then he give me a hefty wad of cash and acourse I blew it all. He's tough too, Billy. I liked him a whole lot. He told me you never said nothin' to him and Peg about me losin' hold of Gerald.'

'No, not until the other day.'

'You're some original kind of woman, Annie. Some original kind of woman.'

'Nothing to be gained talking about it. It was over and done with. Wasn't your fault any more than it was my fault. Wasn't anybody's fault.'

'No way I can thank you for that. That's something thanks don't even touch. That's something I don't even know –'

She waved him silent.

'Never mind that,' she said. 'It's over. Come, sit, tell me what finally made you come see us.'

He sat down on the backless bench in the breakfast nook and looked out the window, out past the geranium plant with two blossoms, out at the collie dog and the apple tree that grew in this yard but offered shade and blossoms and fruit to two other yards adjoining, out at the flower beds and the trim grass and the white wire fence that enclosed it all. So nice. He felt a great compulsion to confess all his transgressions in order to be equal to this niceness he had missed out on; and yet he felt a great torpor in his tongue, akin to what he had felt in his legs when he walked on the glue of the sidewalks. His brain, his body seemed to be in a drugged sleep that allowed perception without action. There was no way he could reveal all that had brought him here. It would have meant the recapitulation not only of all his sins but of all his fugitive and fallen dreams, all his random movement across the country and back, all his returns to this city only to leave again without ever coming to see her, them, without ever knowing why he didn't. It would have meant the anatomizing of his compulsive violence and his fear of justice, of his time with Helen, his present defection from Helen, his screwing so many women he really wanted nothing to do with, his drunken ways, his morning-after sicknesses, his sleeping in the weeds, his bumming money from strangers not because there was a depression but first to help Helen and then because it was easy: easier than working. Everything was easier than coming home, even reducing yourself to the level of social maggot, streetside slug.

But then he came home.

He is home now, isn't he?

And if he is, the question on the table is: Why is he?

'You might say it was Billy,' Francis said. 'But that don't really get it. Might as well ask the summer birds why they go all the way south and then come back north to the same old place.'

'Something must've caught you.'

'I say it was Billy gettin' me outa jail, goin' my bail, then invitin' me home when I thought I'd never get invited after what I did, and then findin' what you did, or didn't do is more like it, and not ever seein' Peg growin' up, and wantin' some of that. I says to Billy I want to come home when I can do something' for the folks, but he says just come home and see them and never mind the turkey, you can do that for them. And here I am. And the turkey too.'

'But something changed in you,' Annie said. 'It was the woman, wasn't it? Billy meeting her?'

'The woman.'

'Billy told me you had another wife. Helen, he said.'

'Not a wife. Never a wife. I only had one wife.'

Annie, her arms folded on the breakfast table across from him, almost smiled, which he took to be a sardonic response. But then she said: 'And I only had one husband. I only had one man.'

Which froze Francis's gizzard.

'That's what the religion does,' he said, when he could talk.

'It wasn't the religion.'

'Men must've come outa the trees after you, you were such a handsome woman.'

'They tried. But no man ever came near me. I wouldn't have it. I never even went to the pictures with anybody except neighbors, or the family.'

'I couldn'ta married again,' Francis said. 'There's some things you just can't do. But I did stay with Helen. That's the truth, all right. Nine years on and off. She's a good sort, but helpless as a baby. Can't find her way across the street if you don't take her by the hand. She nursed me when I was all the way down and sick as a pup. We got on all right. Damn good woman, I say that. Came from good folks. But she can't find her way across the damn street.'

Annie stared at him with a grim mouth and sorrowful eyes.

'Where is she now?'

'Somewheres, goddamned if I know. Downtown somewheres, I suppose. You can't keep track of her. She'll drop dead in the street one of these days, wanderin' around like she does.'

'She needs you.'

'Maybe so.'

'What do you need, Fran?'

'Me? Huh. Need a shoelace. All I got is a piece of twine in that shoe for two days.'

'Is that all you need?'

'I'm still standin'. Still able to do a day's work. Don't do it much, I admit that. Still got my memory, my memories. I remember you, Annie. That's an enrichin' thing. I remember Kibbee's lumber pile the first day I talked to you. You remember that?'

'Like it was this morning.'

'Old times.'

'Very old.'

'Jesus Christ, Annie, I missed everybody and everything, but I ain't worth a goddamn in the world and never was. Wait a minute. Let me finish. I can't finish. I can't even start. But there's somethin'. Somethin' to say about this. I got to get at it, get it out. I'm so goddamned sorry, and I know that don't cut nothin'. I know it's just a bunch of shitass words, excuse the expression. It's nothin' to what I did to you and the kids. I can't make it up. I knew five, six months after I left that it'd get worse and worse and no way ever to fix it, no way ever to go back. I'm just hangin' out now for a visit, that's all. Just visitin' to see you and say I hope things are okay. But I got other things goin' for me, and I don't know the way out of anything. All there is is this visit. I don't want nothin', Annie, and that's the honest-to-god truth, I don't want nothin' but the look of everybody. Just the look'll do me. Just the way things look out in that yard. It's a nice yard. It's a nice doggie. Damn, it's nice. There's plenty to say, plenty of stuff to say, explain, and such bullshit, excuse the expression again, but I ain't ready to say that stuff, I ain't ready to look at you while you listen to it, and I bet you ain't ready to hear it if you knew what I'd tell you.

Lousy stuff, Annie, lousy stuff. Just gimme a little time, gimme a sandwich too, I'm hungry as a damn bear. But listen, Annie, I never stopped lovin' you and the kids, and especially you, and that don't entitle me to nothin', and I don't want nothin' for sayin' it, but I went my whole life rememberin' things here that were like nothin' I ever saw anywhere in Georgia or Louisiana or Michigan, and I been all over, Annie, all over, and there ain't nothin' in the world like your elbows sittin' there on the table across from me, and that apron all full of stains. Goddamn, Annie. Goddamn. Kibbee's was just this mornin'. You're right about that. But it's old times too, and I ain't askin' for nothin' but a sandwich and a cupa tea. You still use the Irish breakfast tea?'

The talk that passed after what Francis said, and after the silence that followed it, was not important except as it moved the man and the woman closer together and physically apart, allowed her to make him a Swiss cheese sandwich and a pot of tea and begin dressing the turkey: salting, peppering, stuffing it with not quite stale enough bread but it'll have to do, rubbing it with butter and sprinkling it with summer savory, mixing onions in with the dressing, and turkey seasoning too from a small tin box with a red and yellow turkey on it, fitting the bird into a dish for which it seemed to have been groomed and killed to order, so perfect was the fit.

And too, the vagrant chitchat allowed Francis to stare out at the yard and watch the dog and become aware that the yard was beginning to function as the site of a visitation, although nothing in it except his expectation when he looked out at the grass lent credence to that possibility.

He stared and he knew that he was in the throes of flight, not outward this time but upward. He felt feathers growing from his back, knew soon he would soar to regions unimaginable, knew too that what had brought him home was not explicable without a year of talking, but a scenario nevertheless took shape in his mind: a pair of kings on a pair of trolley cars moving toward a single track, and the trolleys, when they meet at the junction, do not wreck each other but fuse into a single car inside which the kings rise up against each other in imperial intrigue, neither in control, each driving the car, a careening thing, wild, anarchic, dangerous to all else, and then Billy leaps aboard and grabs the power handle and the kings instantly yield control to the wizard.

He give me a Camel cigarette when I was coughin' my lungs up, Francis thought.

He knows what a man needs, Billy does.

Annie was setting the dining-room table with a white linen tablecloth, with the silver Iron Joe gave them for their wedding, and with china Francis did not recognize, when Daniel Quinn arrived home. The boy tossed his schoolbag in a corner of the dining room, then stopped in mid-motion when he saw Francis standing in the doorway to the kitchen.

'Hulooo,' Francis said to him.

'Danny, this is your grandfather,' Annie said. 'He just came to see us and he's staying for dinner.' Daniel stared at Francis's face and slowly extended his right hand. Francis shook it.

'Pleased to meet you,' Daniel said.

'The feeling's mutual, boy. You're a big lad for ten.'

'I'll be eleven in January.'

'You comin' from school, are ye?'

'From instructions, religion.'

'Oh, religion. I guess I just seen you crossin' the street and didn't even know it. Learn anything, did you?'

'Learned about today. All Saints' Day.'

'What about it?'

'It's a holy day. You have to go to church. It's the day we remember the martyrs who died for the faith and nobody knows their names.'

'Oh yeah,' Francis said. 'I remember them fellas.'

'What happened to your teeth?'

'Daniel.'

'My teeth,' Francis said. 'Me and them parted company, most of 'em. I got a few left.'

'Are you Grampa Phelan or Grampa Quinn?'

'Phelan,' Annie said. 'His name is Francis Aloysius Phelan.'

'Francis Aloysius, right,' said Francis with a chuckle. 'Long time since I heard that.'

'You're the ball player,' Danny said. 'The big-leaguer. You played with the Washington Senators.'

'Used to. Don't play anymore.'

'Billy says you taught him how to throw an inshoot.'

'He remembers that, does he?'

'Will you teach me?'

'You a pitcher, are ye?'

'Sometimes. I can throw a knuckle ball.'

'Change of pace. Hard to hit. You get a baseball, I'll show you how to hold it for an inshoot.' And Daniel ran into the kitchen, then the pantry, and emerged with a ball and glove, which he handed to Francis. The glove was much too small for Francis's hand but he put a few fingers inside it and held the ball in his right hand, studied its seams. Then he gripped it with his thumb and one and a half fingers.

'What happened to your finger?' Daniel asked.

'Me and it parted company too. Sort of an accident.'

'Does that make any difference throwing an inshoot?'

'Sure does, but not to me. I don't throw no more at all. Never was a pitcher, you know, but talked with plenty of 'em. Walter Johnson was my buddy. You know him? The Big Train?'

The boy shook his head.

'Don't matter. But he taught me how it was done and I ain't forgot. Put your first two fingers right on the seams, like this, and then you snap your wrist out, like this, and if you're a rightly – are you a righty?' – and the boy nodded – 'then the ball's gonna dance a little turnaround jig and head right inside at the batter's belly button, assumin', acourse, that he's a righty too. You followin' me?' And the boy nodded again. 'Now the trick is, you got to throw the opposite of the outcurve, which is like this.' And he snapped his wrist clockwise. 'You got to do it like this.' And he snapped his wrist counterclockwise again. Then he had the boy try it both ways and patted him on the back.

'That's how it's done,' he said. 'You get so's you can do it, the batter's gonna think you got a little animal inside that ball, flyin' it like an airplane.'

'Let's go outside and try it,' Daniel said. 'I'll get another glove.'

'Glove,' said Francis, and he turned to Annie. 'By some fluke you still got my old glove stuck away somewheres in the house? That possible, Annie?'

'There's a whole trunk of your things in the attic,' she said. 'It might be there.'

'It is,' Daniel said. 'I know it is. I saw it. I'll get it.'

'You will not,' Annie said. 'That trunk is none of your affair.'

'But I've already seen it. There's a pair of spikes too, and clothes and newspapers and old pictures.'

'All that,' Francis said to Annie. 'You saved it.'

'You had no business in that trunk,' Annie said.

'Billy and I looked at the pictures and the clippings one day,' Daniel said. 'Billy looked just as much as I did. He's in lots of 'em.' And he pointed at his grandfather.

'Maybe you'd want to have a look at what's there,' Annie said to Francis.

'Could be. Might find me a new shoelace.'

Annie led him up the stairs, Daniel already far ahead of them. They heard the boy saying: 'Get up, Billy, Grandpa's here'; and when they reached the second floor Billy was standing in the doorway of his room, in his robe and white socks, disheveled and only half awake.

'Hey, Billy. How you gettin' on?' Francis said.

'Hey,' said Billy. 'You made it.'

'Yep.'

'I woulda bet against it happenin'.'

'You'da lost. Brought a turkey too, like I said.'

'A turkey, yeah?'

'We're having it for dinner,' Annie said.

'I'm supposed to be downtown tonight,' Billy said. 'I just told Martin I'd meet him.'

'Call him back,' Annie said. 'He'll understand.'

'Red Tom Fitzsimmons and Martin both called to tell me things are all right again on Broadway. You know, I told you I had trouble with the McCalls,' Billy said to his father.

'I 'member.'

'I wouldn't do all they wanted and they marked me lousy. Couldn't gamble, couldn't even get a drink on Broadway.'

'I read that story Martin wrote,' Francis said. 'He called you a magician.'

'Martin's full of malarkey. I didn't do diddley. I just mentioned Newark to them and it turns out that's where they trapped some of the kidnap gang.'

'You did somethin', then,' Francis said. 'Mentionin' Newark was somethin'. Who'd you mention it to?'

'Bindy. But I didn't know those guys were in Newark or I wouldn't of said anything. I could never rat on anybody.'

'Then why'd you mention it?'

'I don't know.'

'That's how come you're a magician.'

'That's Martin's baloney. But he turned somebody's head around with it, 'cause I'm back in good odor with the pols, is how he put it on the phone. In other words, I don't stink to them no more.'

Francis smelled himself and knew he had to wash as soon as possible. The junk wagon's stink and the bummy odor of his old suitcoat was unbearable now that he was among these people. Dirty butchers go out of business.

'You can't go out now, Billy,' Annie said. 'Not with your father home and staying for dinner. We're going up in the attic to look at his things.'

'You like turkey?' Francis asked Billy.

'Who the hell don't like turkey, not to give you a short answer,' Billy said. He looked at his father. 'Listen, use my razor in the bathroom if you want to shave.'

'Don't be telling people what to do,' Annie said. 'Get dressed and come downstairs.'

And then Francis and Annie ascended the stairway to the attic.

When Francis opened the trunk lid the odor of lost time filled the attic air, a cloying reek of imprisoned flowers that unsettled the dust and fluttered the window shades. Francis felt drugged by the scent of the reconstituted past, and then stunned by his first look inside the trunk, for there, staring out from a photo, was his own face at age nineteen. The picture lay among rolled socks and a small American flag, a Washington Senators cap, a pile of newspaper clippings and other photos, all in a scatter on the trunk's tray. Francis stared up at himself from the bleachers in Chadwick Park on a day in 1899, his face unlined, his teeth all there, his collar open, his hair unruly in the afternoon's breeze. He lifted the picture for a closer look and saw himself among a group of men, tossing a baseball from bare right hand to gloved left hand. The flight of the ball had always made this photo mysterious to Francis, for the camera had caught the ball clutched in one hand and also in flight, arcing in a blur toward the glove. What the camera had caught was two instants in one: time separated and unified, the ball in two places at once, an eventuation as inexplicable as the Trinity itself. Francis now took the picture to be a Trinitarian talisman (a hand, a glove, a ball) for achieving the impossible: for he had always believed it impossible for him, ravaged man, failed human, to reenter history under this roof. Yet here he was in this aerie of reconstitutable time, touching untouchable artifacts of a self that did not yet know it was ruined, just as the ball, in its inanimate ignorance, did not know yet that it was going nowhere, was caught.

But the ball is really not yet caught, except by the camera, which has frozen only its situation in space.

And Francis is not yet ruined, except as an apparency in process.

The ball still flies.

Francis still lives to play another day.

Doesn't he?

The boy noticed the teeth. A man can get new teeth, store teeth. Annie got 'em.

Francis lifted the tray out of the trunk, revealing the spikes and the glove, which Daniel immediately grabbed, plus two suits of clothes, a pair of black oxfords and brown high-button shoes, maybe a dozen shirts and two dozen white collars, a stack of undershirts and shorts, a set of keys to long-forgotten locks, a razor strop and a hone, a shaving mug with an inch of soap in it, a shaving brush with bristles intact, seven straight razors in a case, each marked for a day of the week, socks, bow ties, suspenders, and a baseball, which Francis picked up and held out to Daniel.

'See that? See that name?'

The boy looked, shook his head. 'I can't read it.'

'Get it in the light, you'll read it. That's Ty Cobb. He signed that ball in 1911, the year he hit .420. A fella give it to me once and I always kept it. Mean guy, Cobb was, come in at me spikes up many a time. But you had to hand it to a man who played ball as good as he did. He was the best.'

'Better than Babe Ruth?'

'Better and tougher and meaner and faster. Couldn't hit home runs like the Babe, but he did everything else better. You like to have that ball with his name on it?'

'Sure I would, sure! Yeah! Who wouldn't?'

'Then it's yours. But you better look him up, and Walter Johnson too. Find out for yourself how good they were. Still kickin', too, what I hear about Cobb. He ain't dead yet either.'

'I remember that suit,' Annie said, lifting the sleeve of a gray herringbone coat. 'You wore it for dress-up.'

'Wonder if it'd still fit me,' Francis said, and stood up and held the pants to his waist and found out his legs had not grown any longer in the past twenty-two years.

'Take the suit downstairs,' Annie said. 'I'll sponge and press it.'

'Press it?' Francis said, and he chuckled. 'S'pose I could use a new outfit. Get rid of these rags.'

He then singled out a full wardrobe, down to the handkerchief, and piled it all on the floor in front of the trunk.

'I'd like to look at these again,' Annie said, lifting out the clippings and photos.

'Bring 'em down,' Francis said, closing the lid.

'I'll carry the glove,' Daniel said.

'And I'd like to borry the use of your bathroom,' Francis said. 'Take Billy up on that shave offer and try on some of these duds. I got me a shave last night but Billy thinks I oughta do it again.'

'Don't pay any attention to Billy,' Annie said. 'You look fine.'

She led him down the stairs and along a hallway where two rooms faced each other. She gestured at a bedroom where a single bed, a dresser, and a child's rolltop desk stood in quiet harmony.

'That's Danny's room,' she said. 'It's a nice big room and it gets the morning light.' She took a towel down from a linen closet shelf and handed it to Francis. 'Have a bath if you like.'

Francis locked the bathroom door and tried on the trousers, which fit if he didn't button the top button. Wear the suspenders with 'em. The coat was twenty years out of style and offended Francis's residual sense of aptness. But he decided to wear it anyway, for its odor of time was infinitely superior to the stink of bumdom that infested the coat on his back. He stripped and let the bathwater run. He inspected the shirt he took from the trunk, but rejected it in favor of the white-on-white from the junk wagon. He tried the laceless black oxfords, all broken in, and found that even with calluses his feet had not grown in twenty-two years either.

He stepped into the bath and slid slowly beneath its vapors. He trembled with the heat, with astonishment that he was indeed here, as snug in this steaming tub as was the turkey in its roasting pan. He felt blessed. He stared at the bathroom sink, which now had an aura of sanctity about it, its faucets sacred, its drainpipe holy, and he wondered whether everything was blessed at some point in its existence, and he concluded yes. Sweat rolled down his forehead and dripped off his nose into the bath, a confluence of ancient and modern waters. And as it did, a great sunburst entered the darkening skies, a radiance so sudden that it seemed like a bolt of lightning; yet its brilliance remained, as if some angel of beatific lucidity were hovering outside the bathroom window. So enduring was the light, so intense beyond even sundown's final gloryburst, that Francis raised himself up out of the tub and went to the window.

Below, in the yard, Aldo Campione, Fiddler Quain, Harold Allen, and Rowdy Dick Doolan were erecting a wooden structure that Francis was already able to recognize as bleachers.

He stepped back into the tub, soaped the long-handled brush, raised his left foot out of the water, scrubbed it clean, raised the right foot, scrubbed that.

Francis, that 1916 dude, came down the stairs in bow tie, white-on-white shirt, black laceless oxfords with a spit shine on them, the gray herringbone with lapels twenty-two years too narrow, with black silk socks and white silk boxer shorts, with his skin free of dirt everywhere, his hair washed twice, his fingernails cleaned, his left-over teeth brushed and the toothbrush washed with soap and dried and rehung, with no whiskers anymore, none, and his hair combed and rubbed with a dab of Vaseline so it'd stay in place, with a spring in his gait and a smile on his face; this Francis dude came down those stairs, yes, and stunned his family with his resurrectible good looks and stylish potential, and took their stares as applause.

And dance music rose in his brain.

'Holy Christ,' said Billy.

'My oh my,' said Annie.

'You look different,' Daniel said.

'I kinda needed a sprucin',' Francis said. 'Funny duds but I guess they'll do.'

They all pulled back then, even Daniel, aware they should not dwell on the transformation, for it made Francis's previous condition so lowly, so awful.

'Gotta dump these rags,' he said, and he lifted his bundle, tied with the arms of his old coat.

'Danny'll take them,' Annie said. 'Put them in the cellar,' she told the boy.

Francis sat down on a bench in the breakfast nook, across the table from Billy. Annie had spread the clips and photos on the table and he and Billy looked them over. Among the clips Francis found a yellowed envelope postmarked June 2, 1910, and addressed to Mr Francis Phelan, c/o Toronto Baseball Club, The Palmer House, Toronto, Ont. He opened it and read the letter inside, then pocketed it. Dinner advanced as Daniel and Annie peeled the potatoes at the sink. Billy, his hair combed slick, half a dude himself with open-collared starched white shirt, creased trousers, and pointy black shoes, was drinking from a quart bottle of Dobler beer and reading a clipping.

'I read these once,' Billy said. 'I never really knew how good you were. I heard stories and then one night down-town I heard a guy talking about you and he was ravin' that you were top-notch and I never knew just how good. I knew this stuff was there. I seen it when we first moved here, so I went up and looked. You were really a hell of a ball player.'

'Not bad,' Francis said. 'Coulda been worse.'

'These sportswriters liked you.'

'I did crazy things. I was good copy for them. And I had energy. Everybody likes energy.'

Billy offered Francis a glass of beer but Francis declined and took, instead, from Billy's pack, a Camel cigarette; and then he perused the clips that told of him stealing the show with his fielding, or going four-for-four and driving in the winning run, or getting himself in trouble: such as the day he held the runner on third by the belt, an old John McGraw trick, and when a fly ball was hit, the runner got ready to tag and head home after the catch but found he could not move and turned and screamed at Francis in protest, at which point Francis let go of the belt and the runner ran, but the throw arrived first and he was out at home.

Nifty.

But Francis was thrown out of the game.

'Would you like to go out and look at the yard?' Annie said, suddenly beside Francis.

'Sure. See the dog.'

'It's too bad the flowers are gone. We had so many flowers this year. Dahlias and snapdragons and pansies and asters. The asters lasted the longest.'

'You still got them geraniums right here.'

Annie nodded and put on her sweater and the two of them went out onto the back porch. The air was chilly and the light fading. She closed the door behind them and patted the dog, which barked twice at Francis and then accepted his presence. Annie went down the five steps to the yard, Francis and the dog following.

'Do you have a place to stay tonight, Fran?'

'Sure. Always got a place to stay.'

'Do you want to come home permanent?' she asked, not looking at him, walking a few steps ahead toward the fence. 'Is that why you've come to see us?'

'Nah, not much chance of that. I'd never fit in.'

'I thought you might've had that in mind.'

'I thought of it, I admit that. But I see it couldn't work, not after all these years.'

'It'd take some doing, I know that.'

'Take more than that.'

'Stranger things have happened.'

'Yeah? Name one.'

'You going to the cemetery and talking to Gerald. I think maybe that's the strangest thing I ever heard in all my days.'

'Wasn't strange. I just went and stood there and told him a bunch of stuff. It's nice where he is. It's pretty.'

'That's the family plot.'

'I know.'

'There's a grave there for you, right at the stone, and one for me, and two for the children next to that if they need them. Peg'll have her own plot with George and the boy, I imagine.'

'When did you do all that?' Francis asked.

'Oh years ago. I don't remember.'

'You bought me a grave after I run off.'

'I bought it for the family. You're part of the family.'

'There was long times I didn't think so.'

'Peg is very bitter about you staying away. I was too, for years and years, but that's all done with. I don't know why I'm not bitter anymore. I really don't. I called Peg and told her to get the cranberries and that you were here.'

'Me and the cranberries. Easin' the shock some.'

'I suppose.'

'I'll move along, then. I don't want no fights, rile up the family.'

'Nonsense. Stop it. You just talk to her. You've got to talk to her.'

'I can't say nothin' that means anything. I couldn't say a straight word to you.'

'I know what you said and what you didn't say. I know it's hard what you're doing.'

'It's a bunch of nothin'. I don't know why I do anything in this goddamn life.'

'You did something good coming home. It's something Danny'll always know about. And Billy. He was so glad to be able to help you, even though he'd never say it.'

'He got a bum out of jail.'

'You're so mean to yourself, Francis.'

'Hell, I'm mean to everybody and everything.'

The bleachers were all up, and men were filing silently into them and sitting down, right here in Annie's backyard, in front of God and the dog and all: Bill Corbin, who ran for sheriff in the nineties and got beat and turned Republican, and Perry Marsolais, who inherited a fortune from his mother and drank it up and ended up raking leaves for the city, and Iron Joe himself with his big mustache and big belly and big ruby stickpin, and Spiff Dwyer in his nifty pinched fedora, and young George Quinn and young Martin Daugherty, the batboys, and Martin's grandfather Emmett Daugherty, the wild Fenian who talked so fierce and splendid and put the radical light in Francis's eye with his stories of how moneymen used workers to get rich and treated the Irish like pigdog paddyniggers, and Patsy McCall, who grew up to run the city and was carrying his ball glove in his left hand, and some men Francis did not know even in 1899, for they were only hangers-on at the saloon, men who followed the doings of Iron Joe's Wheelbarrow Boys, and who came to the beer picnic this day to celebrate the Boys' winning the Albany-Troy League pennant.

They kept coming: forty-three men, four boys, and two mutts, ushered in by the Fiddler and his pals.

And there, between crazy Specky McManus in his derby and Jack Corbett in his vest and no collar, sat the runt, is it?

Is it now?

The runt with the piece out of his neck.

There's one in every crowd.

Francis closed his eyes to retch the vision out of his head, but when he opened them the bleachers still stood, the men seated as before. Only the light had changed, brighter now, and with it grew Francis's hatred of all fantasy, all insubstantiality. I am sick of you all, was his thought. I am sick of imagining what you became, what I might have become if I'd lived among you. I am sick of your melancholy histories, your sentimental pieties, your goddamned unchanging faces. I'd rather be dyin' in the weeds than standin' here lookin' at you pinin' away, like the dyin' Jesus pinin' for an end to it when he knew every stinkin' thing that was gonna happen not only to himself but to everybody around him, and to all those that wasn't even born yet. You ain't nothin' more than a photograph, you goddamn spooks. You ain't real and I ain't gonna be at your beck and call no more.

You're all dead, and if you ain't, you oughta be.

I'm the one is livin'. I'm the one puts you on the map.

You never knew no more about how things was than I did.

You'd never even be here in the damn yard if I didn't open that old trunk.

So get your ass gone!

'Hey Ma,' Billy yelled out the window. 'Peg's home.'

'We'll be right in,' Annie said. And when Billy closed the window she turned to Francis: 'You want to tell me anything, ask me anything, before we get in front of the others?'

'Annie, I got five million things to ask you, and ten million things to tell. I'd like to eat all the dirt in this yard for you, eat the weeds, eat the dog bones too, if you asked me.'

'I think you probably ate all that already,' she said.

And then they went up the back stoop together.

When Francis first saw his daughter bent over the stove, already in her flowered apron and basting the turkey, he thought: She is too dressed up to be doing that. She wore a wristwatch on one arm, a bracelet on the other, and two rings on her wedding ring finger. She wore high heels, silk stockings with the seams inside out, and a lavender dress that was never intended as a kitchen costume. Her dark-brown hair, cut short, was waved in a soft marcel, and she wore lipstick and a bit of rouge, and her nails were long and painted dark red. She was a few, maybe even more than a few, pounds overweight, and she was beautiful, and Francis was immeasurably happy at having sired her.

'How ya doin', Margaret?' Francis asked when she straightened up and looked at him.

'I'm doing fine,' she said, 'no thanks to you.'

'Yep,' said Francis, and he turned away from her and sat across from Billy in the nook.

'Give him a break,' Billy said. 'He just got here, for chrissake.'

'What break did he ever give me? Or you? Or any of us?'

'Aaahhh, blow it out your ear,' Billy said.

'I'm saying what is,' Peg said.

'Are you?' Annie asked. 'Are you so sure of what is?'

'I surely am. I'm not going to be a hypocrite and welcome him back with open arms after what he did. You don't just pop up one day with a turkey and all is forgiven.'

'I ain't expectin' to be forgiven,' Francis said. 'I'm way past that.'

'Oh? And just where are you now?'

'Nowhere.'

'Well that's no doubt very true. And if you're nowhere, why are you here? Why've you come back like a ghost we buried years ago to force a scrawny turkey on us? Is that your idea of restitution for letting us fend for ourselves for twenty-two years?'

'That's a twelve-and-a-half-pound turkey,' Annie said.

'Why leave your nowhere and come here, is what I want to know. This is somewhere. This is a home you didn't build.'

'I built you. Built Billy. Helped to.'

'I wish you never did.'

'Shut up, Peg,' Billy yelled. 'Rotten tongue of yours, shut it the hell UP!'

'He came to visit, that's all he did,' Annie said softly. 'I already asked him if he wanted to stay over and he said no. If he wanted to he surely could.'

'Oh?' said Peg. 'Then it's all decided?'

'Nothin' to decide,' Francis said. 'Like your mother says, I ain't stayin'. I'm movin' along.' He touched the salt and pepper shaker on the table in front of him, pushed the sugar bowl against the wall.

'You're moving on,' Peg said.

'Positively.'

'Fine.'

'That's it, that's enough!' Billy yelled, standing up from the bench. 'You got the feelin's of a goddamn rattlesnake.'

'Pardon me for having any feelings at all,' Peg said, and she left the kitchen, slamming the swinging door, which had been standing open, slamming it so hard that it swung, and swung, and swung, until it stopped.

'Tough lady,' Francis said.

'She's a creampuff,' Billy said. 'But she knows how to get her back up.'

'She'll calm down,' Annie said.

'I'm used to people screamin' at me,' Francis said. 'I got a hide like a hippo.'

'You need it in this joint,' Billy said.

'Where's the boy?' Francis asked. 'He hear all that?'

'He's out playin' with the ball and glove you gave him,' Billy said.

'I didn't give him the glove,' Francis said. 'I give him the ball with the Ty Cobb signature. That glove is yours. You wanna give it to him, it's okay by me. Ain't much of a glove compared to what they got these days. Danny's glove's twice the quality my glove ever was. But I always thought to myself: I'm givin' that old glove to Billy so's he'll have a touch of the big leagues somewhere in the house. That glove caught some mighty people. Line drive from Tris Speaker, taggin' out Cobb, runnin' Eddie Collins outa the baseline. Lotta that.'

Billy nodded and turned away from Francis. 'Okay,' he said, and then he jumped up from the bench and left the kitchen so the old man could not see (though he saw) that he was choked up.

'Grew up nice, Billy did,' Francis said. 'Couple of tough bozos you raised, Annie.'

'I wish they were tougher,' Annie said.

The yard, now ablaze with new light against a black sky, caught Francis's attention. Men and boys, and even dogs, were holding lighted candles, the dogs holding them in their mouths sideways. Specky McManus, as usual bein' different, wore his candle on top of his derby. It was a garden of acolytes setting fire to the very air, and then, while Francis watched, the acolytes erupted in song, but a song without sense, a chant to which Francis listened carefully but could make out not a word. It was an antisyllabic lyric they sang, like the sibilance of the wren's softest whistle, or the tree frog's tonsillar wheeze. It was clear to Francis as he watched this performance (watched it with awe, for it was transcending what he expected from dream, from reverie, even from Sneaky Pete hallucinations) that it was happening in an arena of his existence over which he had less control than he first imagined when Aldo Campione boarded the bus. The signals from this time lock were ominous, the spooks utterly without humor. And then, when he saw the runt (who knew he was being watched, who knew he didn't belong in this picture) putting the lighted end of the candle into the hole in the back of his neck, and when Francis recognized the chant of the acolytes at last as the 'Dies Irae,' he grew fearful. He closed his eyes and buried his head in his hands and he tried to remember the name of his first dog.

It was a collie.

Billy came back, clear-eyed, sat across from Francis, and offered him another smoke, which he took. Billy topped his own beer and drank and then said, 'George.'

'Oh my God,' Annie said. 'We forgot all about George.' And she went to the living room and called upstairs to Peg: 'You should call George and tell him he can come home.'

'Let her alone, I'll do it,' Billy called to his mother.

'What about George?' Francis asked.

'The cops were here one night lookin' for him,' Billy said. 'It was Patsy McCall puttin' pressure on the family because of me. George writes numbers and they were probably gonna book him for gamblin' even though he had the okay. So he laid low up in Troy, and the poor bastard's been alone for days. But if I'm clear, then so is he.'

'Some power the McCalls put together in this town.'

'They got it all. They ever pay you the money they owed you for registerin' all those times?'

'Paid me the fifty I told you about, owe me another fifty-five. I'll never see it.'

'You got it comin'.'

'Once it got in the papers they wouldn't touch it. Mixin' themselves up with bums. You heard Martin tell me that. They'd also be suspicious that I'd set them up. I wouldn't set nobody up. Nobody.'

'Then you got no cash.'

'I got a little.'

'How much?'

'I got some change. Cigarette money.'

'You blew what you had on the turkey.'

'That took a bit of it.'

Billy handed him a ten, folded in half. 'Put it in your pocket. You can't walk around broke.'

Francis took it and snorted. 'I been broke twenty-two years. But I thank ye, Billy. I'll make it up.'

'You already made it up.' And he went to the phone in the dining room to call George in Troy.

Annie came back to the kitchen and saw Francis looking at the Chadwick Park photo and looked over his shoulder. 'That's a handsome picture of you,' she said.

'Yeah,' said Francis. 'I was a good-lookin' devil.'

'Some thought so, some didn't,' Annie said. 'I forgot about this picture.'

'Oughta get it framed,' Francis said. 'Lot of North Enders in there. George and Martin as kids, and Patsy McCall too. And Iron Joe. Real good shot of Joe.'

'It surely is,' Annie said. 'How fat and healthy he looks.'

Billy came back and Annie put the photo on the table so that all three of them could look at it. They sat on the same bench with Francis in the middle and studied it, each singling out the men and boys they knew. Annie even knew one of the dogs.

'Oh that's a prize picture,' she said, and stood up. 'A prize picture.'

'Well, it's yours, so get it framed.'

'Mine? No, it's yours. It's baseball.'

'Nah, nah, George'd like it too.'

'Well I will frame it,' Annie said. 'I'll take it down-town and get it done up right.'

'Sure,' said Francis. 'Here. Here's ten dollars toward the frame.'

'Hey,' Billy said.

'No,' Francis said. 'You let me do it, Billy.'

Billy chuckled.

'I will not take any money,' Annie said. 'You put that back in your pocket.'

Billy laughed and hit the table with the palm of his hand. 'Now I know why you been broke twenty-two years. I know why we're all broke. It runs in the family.'

'We're not all broke,' Annie said. 'We pay our way. Don't be telling people we're broke. You're broke because you made some crazy horse bet. But *we're* not broke. We've had bad times but we can still pay the rent. And we've never gone hungry.'

'Peg's workin',' Francis said.

'A private secretary,' Annie said. 'To the owner of a tool company. She's very well liked.'

'She's beautiful,' Francis said. 'Kinda nasty when she puts her mind to it, but beautiful.'

'She shoulda been a model,' Billy said.

'She should not,' Annie said.

'Well she shoulda, goddamn it, she shoulda,' said Billy. 'They wanted her to model for Pepsodent toothpaste, but Mama wouldn't hear of it. Somebody over at church told her models were, you know, loose ladies. Get your picture taken, it turns you into a floozy.'

'That had nothing to do with it,' Annie said.

'Her teeth,' Billy said. 'She's got the most gorgeous teeth in North America. Better-lookin' teeth than Joan Crawford. What a smile! You ain't seen her smile yet, but that's a fantastic smile. Like Times Square is what it is. She coulda been on billboards coast to coast. We'd be hip-deep in toothpaste, and cash too. But no.' And he jerked a thumb at his mother.

'She had a job,' Annie said. 'She didn't need that. I never liked that fellow that wanted to sign her up.'

'He was all right,' Billy said. 'I checked him out. He was legitimate.'

'How could you know what he was?'

'How could I know anything? I'm a goddamn genius.'

'Clean up your mouth, genius. She would've had to go to New York for pictures.'

'And she'd of never come back, right?'

'Maybe she would, maybe she wouldn't.'

'Now you got it,' Billy said to his father. 'Mama likes to keep all the birds in the nest.'

'Can't say as I blame her,' Francis said.

'No,' Billy said.

'I never liked that fellow,' Annie said. 'That's what it really was. I didn't trust him.'

Nobody spoke.

'And she brought a paycheck home every week,' Annie said. 'Even when the tool company closed awhile, the owner put her to work as a cashier in a trading port he owned. Trading port and indoor golf. An enormous place. They almost brought Rudy Vallee there once. Peg got wonderful experience.'

Nobody spoke.

'Cigarette?' Billy asked Francis.

'Sure,' Francis said.

Annie stood up and went to the refrigerator in the pantry. She came back with the butter dish and put it on the dining-room table. Peg came through the swinging door, into the silence. She poked the potatoes with a fork, looked at the turkey, which was turning deep brown, and closed the oven door without basting it. She rummaged in the utensil drawer and found a can opener and punched it through a can of peas and put them in a pan to boil.

'Turkey smells real good,' Francis said to her.

'Uh-huh, I bought a plum pudding,' she said to all, showing them the can. She looked at her father. 'Mama said you used to like it for dessert on holidays.'

'I surely did. With that white sugar sauce. Mighty sweet.'

'The sauce recipe's on the label,' Annie said. 'Give it here and I'll make it.'

'I'll make it,' Peg said.

'It's nice you remembered that,' Francis said.

'It's no trouble,' Peg said. 'The pudding's already cooked. All you do is heat it up in the can.'

Francis studied her and saw the venom was gone from her eyes. This lady goes up and down like a thermometer. When she saw him studying her she smiled slightly, not a billboard smile, not a smile to make anybody rich in toothpaste, but there it was. What the hell, she's got a right. Up and down, up and down. She come by it naturally.

'I got a letter maybe you'd all like to hear while that stuff's cookin' up,' he said, and he took the yellowed envelope with a canceled two-cent stamp on it out of his inside coat pocket. On the back, written in his own hand, was: *First letter from Margaret.*

'I got this a few years back, quite a few,' he said, and from the envelope he took out three small trifolded sheets of yellowed lined paper. 'Come to me up in Canada in nineteen-ten, when I was with Toronto.' He unfolded the sheets and moved them into the best possible light at longest possible arm's length, and then he read:

'"Dear Poppy, I suppose you never think that you have a daughter that is waiting for a letter since you went away. I was so mad because you did not think of me that I was going to join the circus that was here last Friday. I am doing my lesson and there is an arithmetic example here that I cannot get. See if you can get it. I hope your leg is better and that you have good luck with the team. Do not run too much with your legs or you will have to be carried home. Mama and Billy are good. Mama has fourteen new little chickens out and she has two more hens sitting. There is a wild west circus coming the eighth. Won't you come home and see it? I am going to it. Billy is just going to bed and Mama is sitting on the bed watching me. Do not forget to answer this. I suppose you are having a lovely time. Do not let me find you with another girl or I will pull her hair. Yours truly, Peggy."'

'Isn't that funny,' Peg said, the fork still in her hand. 'I don't remember writing that.'

'Probably lots you don't remember about them days,' Francis said. 'You was only about eleven.'

'Where did you ever find it?'

'Up in the trunk. Been saved all these years up there. Only letter I ever saved.'

'Is that a fact?'

'It's a provable fact. All the papers I got in the world was in that trunk, except one other place I got a few more clips. But no letters noplace. It's a good old letter, I'd say.'

'I'd say so too,' Annie said. She and Billy were both staring at Peg.

'I remember Toronto in nineteen-ten,' Francis said. 'The game was full of crooks them days. Crooked umpire named Bates, one night it was deep dark but he wouldn't call the game. Folks was throwin' tomatoes and mudballs at him but he wouldn't call it 'cause we was winnin' and he was in with the other team. Pudge Howard was catchin' that night and he walks out and has a three-way confab on the mound with me and old Highpockets Wilson, who was pitchin'. Pudge comes back and squats behind the plate and Highpockets lets go a blazer and the ump calls it a ball, though nobody could see nothin' it was so dark. And Pudge turns to him and says: "You call that pitch a ball?" "I did," says the ump. "If that was a ball I'll eat it," says Pudge. "Then you better get eatin'," says the ump. And Pudge, he holds the ball up and takes a big bite out of it, 'cause it ain't no ball at all, it's a yellow apple I give High-pockets to throw. And of course that won us the game and the ump went down in history as Blindy Bates, who couldn't tell a baseball from a damn apple. Bates turned into a bookie after that. He was crooked at that too.'

'That's a great story,' Billy said. 'Funny stuff in them old days.'

'Funny stuff happenin' all the time,' Francis said.

Peg was suddenly tearful. She put the fork on the sink and went to her father, whose hands were folded on the table. She sat beside him and put her right hand on top of his.

After a while George Quinn came home from Troy, Annie served the turkey, and then the entire Phelan family sat down to dinner.

7

'I look like a bum, don't I?' Rudy said.

'You are a bum,' Francis said. 'But you're a pretty good bum if you wanna be.'

'You know why people call you a bum?'

'I can't understand why.'

'They feel better when they say it.'

'The truth ain't gonna hurt you,' Francis said. 'If you're a bum, you're a bum.'

'It hurt a lotta bums. Ain't many of the old ones left.'

'There's new ones comin' along,' Francis said.

'A lot of good men died. Good mechanics, machinists, lumberjacks.'

'Some of 'em ain't dead,' Francis said. 'You and me, we ain't dead.'

'They say there's no God,' Rudy said. 'But there must be a God. He protects bums. They get up out of the snow and they go up and get a drink. Look at you, brand-new clothes. But look at me. I'm only a bum. A no-good bum.'

'You ain't that bad,' Francis said. 'You're a bum, but you ain't that bad.'

They were walking down South Pearl Street toward Palombo's Hotel. It was ten-thirty, a clear night, full of stars but very cold: winter's harbinger. Francis had left the family just before ten o'clock and taken a bus downtown. He went straight to the mission before they locked it for the night, and found Pee Wee alone in the kitchen, drinking leftover coffee. Pee Wee said he hadn't seen, or heard from, Helen all day.

'But Rudy was in lookin' for you,' Pee Wee told Francis. 'He's either up at the railroad station gettin' warm or holed up in some old house down on Broadway. He says you'd know which one. But look, Francis, from what I hear, the cops been raidin' them old pots just about every night. Lotta guys usually eat here ain't been around and I figure they're all in jail. They must be repaintin' the place out there and need extra help.'

'I don't know why the hell they gotta do that,' Francis said. 'Bums don't hurt nobody.'

'Maybe it's just cops don't like bums no more.'

Francis checked out the old house first, for it was close to the mission. He stepped through its doorless entrance into a damp, deep-black stairwell. He waited until his eyes adjusted to the darkness and then he carefully climbed the stairs, stepping over bunches of crumpled newspaper and fallen plaster and a Negro who was curled up on the first landing. He stepped through broken glass, empty wine and soda bottles, cardboard boxes, human droppings. Streetlights illuminated stalagmites of pigeon leavings on a windowsill. Francis saw a second sleeping man curled up near the hole he heard a fellow named Michigan Mac fell through last week. Francis sidestepped the man and the hole and then found Rudy in a room by himself, lying on a slab of board away from the broken window, with a newspaper on his shoulder for a blanket.

'Hey bum,' Francis said, 'you lookin' for me?'

Rudy blinked and looked up from his slab.

'Who the hell you talkin' to?' Rudy said. 'What are you, some kinda G-man?'

'Get your ass up off the floor, you dizzy kraut.'

'Hey, is that you, Francis?'

'No, it's Buffalo Bill. I come up here lookin' for Indians.'

Rudy sat up and threw the newspaper off himself.

'Pee Wee says you was lookin' for me,' Francis said.

'I didn't have noplace to flop, no money, no jug, nobody around.

I had a jug but it ran out.' Rudy fell back on the slab and wept instant tears over his condition. 'I'll kill myself, I got the tendency,' he said. 'I'm last.'

'Hey,' Francis said. 'Get up. You ain't bright enough to kill yourself. You gotta fight. You gotta be tough. I can't even find Helen. You seen Helen anyplace? Think about that woman on the bum somewheres on a night like this. Jesus I feel sorry for her.'

'Where the wind don't blow,' Rudy said.

'Yeah. No wind. Let's go.'

'Go where?'

'Outa here. You stay here, you wind up in jail tonight. Pee Wee says they're cleanin' out all these joints.'

'Go to jail, at least it's warm. Get six months and be out in time for the flowers.'

'No jail for Francis. Francis is free and he's gonna stay free.'

They walked down the stairs and back to Madison because Francis decided Helen must have found money somewhere or else she'd have come looking for him. Maybe she called her brother and got a chunk. Or maybe she was holding out even more than she said. Canny old dame. And sooner or later, with dough, she'd hit Palombo's because of the suitcase.

'Where we goin'?'

'What the hell's the difference? Little walk'll keep your blood flowin'.'

'Where'd you get them clothes?'

'Found 'em.'

'Found 'em? Where'd you find 'em?'

'Up a tree.'

'A tree?'

'Yeah. A tree. Grew everything. Suits, shoes, bow ties.'

'You never tell me nothin' that's true.'

'Hell, it's all true,' Francis said. 'Every stinkin' damn thing you can think of is true.'

At Palombo's they met old man Donovan just getting ready to go off duty, making way for the night clerk. It was a little before eleven and he was putting the desk in order. Yes, he told Francis, Helen was here. Checked in late this morning. Yeah, sure she's all right. Looked right perky. Walked up them stairs lookin' the same as always. Took the room you always take.

'All right,' said Francis, and he took out the ten-dollar bill Billy gave him. 'You got change of this?' Donovan made change and then Francis handed him two dollars.

'You give her this in the mornin',' he said, 'and make sure she gets somethin' to eat. If I hear she didn't get it, I'll come back here and pull out all your teeth.'

'She'll get it,' Donovan said. 'I like Helen.'

'Check her out now,' Francis said. 'Don't tell her I'm here. Just see is she okay and does she need anything. Don't say I sent you or nothin' like that. Just check her out.'

So Donovan knocked on Helen's door at eleven o'clock and found out she needed nothing at all, and he came back and told Francis.

'You tell her in the mornin' I'll be around sometime during the day,' Francis said. 'And if she don't see me and she wants me, you tell her to leave me a message where she'll be. Leave it with Pee Wee down at the mission. You know Pee Wee?'

'I know the mission,' Donovan said.

'She claim the suitcase?' Francis asked.

'Claimed it and paid for two nights in the room.'

'She got money from home, all right,' Francis said. 'But you give her that deuce anyway.'

Francis and Rudy walked north on Pearl Street then, Francis keeping the pace brisk. In a shopwindow Francis saw three mannequins in formal dresses beckoning to him. He waved at them.

'Now where we goin'?' Rudy asked.

'The all-night bootlegger's,' Francis said. 'Get us a couple of jugs and then go get a flop and get some shut-eye.'

'Hey,' Rudy said. 'Now you're sayin' somethin' I wanna hear. Where'd you find all this money?'

'Up in a tree.'

'Same tree that grows bow ties?'

'Yep,' said Francis. 'Same tree.'

Francis bought two quarts of muscatel at the upstairs bootlegger's on Beaver Street and two pints of Green River whiskey.

'Rotgut,' he said when the bootlegger handed him the whiskey, 'but it does what it's supposed to do.'

Francis paid the bootlegger and pocketed the change: two dollars and thirty cents left. He gave a quart of the musky and a pint of the whiskey to Rudy and when they stepped outside the bootlegger's they both tipped up their wine.

And so Francis began to drink for the first time in a week.

The flop was run by a bottom-heavy old woman with piano legs, the widow of somebody named Fennessey, who had died so long ago nobody remembered his first name.

'Hey Ma,' Rudy said when she opened the door for them.

'My name's Mrs Fennessey,' she said. 'That's what I go by.'

'I knew that,' Rudy said.

'Then call me that. Only the niggers call me Ma.'

'All right, sweetheart,' Francis said. 'Anybody call you sweetheart? We want a couple of flops.'

She let them in and took their money, a dollar for two flops, and then led them upstairs to a large room that used to be two or three rooms but now, with the interior walls gone, was a dormitory with a dozen filthy cots, only one occupied by a sleeping form. The room was lit by what Francis judged to be a three-watt bulb.

'Hey,' he said, 'too much light in here. It'll blind us all.'

'Your friend don't like it here, he can go somewhere else,' Mrs Fennessey told Rudy.

'Who wouldn't like this joint?' Francis said, and he bounced on the cot next to the sleeping man.

'Hey bum,' he said, reaching over and shaking the sleeper. 'You want a drink?'

A man with enormous week-old scabs on his nose and forehead turned to face Francis.

'Hey,' said Francis. 'It's the Moose.'

'Yeah, it's me,' Moose said.

'Moose who?' asked Rudy.

'Moose what's the difference,' Francis said.

'Moose Backer,' Moose said.

'That there's Rudy,' Francis said. 'He's crazier than a cross-eyed bedbug, but he's all right.'

'You sharped up some since I seen you last,' Moose said to Francis. 'Even wearin' a tie. You bump into prosperity?'

'He found a tree that grows ten-dollar bills,' Rudy said.

Francis walked around the cot and handed Moose his wine. Moose took a swallow and nodded his thanks.

'Why'd you wake me up?' Moose asked.

'Woke you up to give you a drink.'

'It was dark when I went to sleep. Dark and cold.'

'Jesus Christ, I know. Fingers cold, toes cold. Cold in here right now. Here, have another drink and warm up. You want some whiskey? I got some of that too.'

'I'm all right. I got an edge. You got enough for yourself?'

'Have a drink, goddamn it. Don't be afraid to live.' And Moose took one glug of the Green River.

'I thought you was gonna trade pants with me,' Moose said.

'I was. Pair I had was practically new, but too small.'

'Where are they? You said they were thirty-eight, thirty-one, and that's just right.'

'You want these?'

'Sure,' said Moose.

'If I give 'em to you, then I ain't got no pants,' Francis said.

'I'll give you mine,' Moose said.

'Why you tradin' your new pants?' Rudy asked.

'That's right,' said Francis, standing up and looking at his own legs. 'Why am I? No, you ain't gonna get these. Fuck you, I need these pants. Don't tell me what I need. Go get your own pants.'

'I'll buy 'em,' Moose said. 'How much you want? I got another week's work sandin' floors.'

'Well shine 'em,' Francis said. 'They ain't for sale.'

'Sandin', not shinin'. I sand 'em. I don't shine 'em.'

'Don't holler at me,' Francis said. 'I'll crack your goddamn head and step on your brains. You're a tough man, is that it?'

'No,' said Moose. 'I ain't tough.'

'Well I'm tough,' Francis said. 'Screw around with me, you'll die younger'n I will.'

'Oh I'll die all right. I'm just as busted as that ceiling. I got TB.'

'Oh God bless you,' Francis said, sitting down. 'I'm sorry.'

'It's in the knee.'

'I didn't know you had it. I'm sorry. I'm sorry anybody's got TB.'

'It's in the knee.'

'Well cut your leg off.'

'That's what they wanted to do.'

'So cut it off.'

'No, I wouldn't let them do that.'

'I got a stomach cancer,' Rudy said.

'Yeah,' said Moose. 'Everybody's got one of them.'

'Anybody gonna come to my funeral?' Rudy asked.

'Probably ain't nothin' wrong with you work won't cure,' Moose said.

'That's right,' Francis said to Rudy. 'Why don't you go get a job?' He pointed out the window at the street. 'Look at 'em out there. Everybody out there's workin'.'

'You're crazier than he is,' Moose said. 'Ain't no jobs anyplace. Where you been?'

'There's taxis. There goes a taxi.'

'Yeah, there's taxis,' Moose said. 'So what?'

'Can you drive?' Francis asked Rudy.

'I drove my ex-wife crazy,' Rudy said.

'Good. What you're supposed to do. Drive 'em nuts is right.'

In the corner of the room Francis saw three long-skirted women who became four who became three and then four again. Their faces were familiar but he could call none of them by name. Their ages changed when their number changed: now twenty, now sixty, now thirty, now fifty, never childish, never aged. At the house Annie would now be trying to sleep, but probably no more prepared for it than Francis was, no more capable of closing the day than Francis was. Helen would be out of it, whipped all to hell by fatigue and worry. Damn worrywart is what she is. But not Annie. Annie, she don't worry. Annie knows how to live. Peg, she'll be awake too, why not? Why should she sleep when nobody else can? They'll all be up, you bet. Francis give 'em a show they ain't gonna forget in a hurry.

He showed 'em what a man can do.

A man ain't afraid of goin' back.

Goddamn spooks, they follow you everywheres but they don't matter. You stand up to 'em is all. And you do what you gotta do.

Sandra joined the women of three, the women of four, in the far corner. Francis gave me soup, she told them. He carried me out of the wind and put my shoe on me. They became the women of five.

'Where the wind don't blow,' Rudy sang. 'I wanna go where the wind don't blow, where there ain't no snow.'

Francis saw Katrina's face among the five that became four that became three.

Finny and Little Red came into the flop, and just behind them a third figure Francis did not recognize immediately. Then he saw it was Old Shoes.

'Hey, we got company, Moose,' Francis said.

'Is that Finny?' Moose asked. 'Looks like him.'

'That's the man,' Francis said. Finny stood by the foot of Francis's cot, very drunk and wobbling, trying to see who was talking about him.

'You son of a bitch,' Moose said, leaning on one elbow.

'Which son of a bitch you talkin' to?' Francis asked.

'Finny. He used to work for Spanish George. Liked to use the blackjack on drunks when they got noisy.'

'Is that true, Finny?' Francis asked. 'You liked to sap the boys?'

'Arrrggghhh,' said Finny, and he lurched off toward a cot down the row from Francis.

'He was one mean bastard,' Moose said. 'He hit me once.'

'Hurt you?'

'Hurt like hell. I had a headache three weeks.'

'Somebody burned up Finny's car,' Little Red announced. 'He went out for somethin' to eat, and he came back, it was on fire. He thinks the cops did it.'

'Why are the cops burnin' up cars?' Rudy asked.

'Cops're goin' crazy,' Little Red said. 'They're pickin' up everybody. American Legion's behind it, that's what I heard.'

'Them lard-ass bastards,' Francis said. 'They been after my ass all my life.'

'Legionnaires and cops,' said Little Red. 'That's why we come in here.'

'You think you're safe here?' Francis asked.

'Safer than on the street.'

'Cops'd never come up here if they wanted to get you, right?' Francis said.

'They wouldn't know I was here,' Little Red said.

'Whataya think this is, the Waldorf-Astoria? You think that old bitch downstairs don't tell the cops who's here and who ain't when they want to know?'

'Maybe it wasn't the cops burned up the car,' Moose said. 'Finny's got plenty of enemies. If I knew he owned one, I'da burned it up myself. The son of a bitch beat up on us all, but now he's on the street. Now we got him in the alley.'

'You hear that, Finny?' Francis called out. 'They gonna get your ass good. They got you in the alley with all the other bums.'

'Ngggggghhhh,' said Finny.

'Finny's all right,' Little Red said. 'Leave him alone.'

'You givin' orders here at the Waldorf-Astoria, is that it?' Francis asked.

'Who the hell are you?' Little Red asked.

'I'm a fella ready to stomp all over your head and squish it like a grape, you try to tell me what to do.'

'Yeah,' said Little Red, and he moved toward the cot beside Finny.

'I knew it was you soon as I come in,' Old Shoes said, coming over to the foot of Francis's cot. 'I could tell that foghorn voice of yours anyplace.'

'Old Shoes,' Francis said. 'Old Shoes Gilligan.'

'That's right. You got a pretty good memory. The wine ain't got you yet.'

'Old Shoes Gilligan, a grand old soul, got a cast-iron belly and a brass asshole.'

'Not cast-iron anymore,' Old Shoes said. 'I got an ulcer. I quit drinkin' two years ago.'

'Then what the hell you doin' here?'

'Just came by to see the boys, see what was happenin'.'

'You hangin' out with Finny and that redheaded wise-ass?'

'Who you callin' a wiseass?' Little Red said.

'I'm callin' you wiseass, wiseass,' Francis said.

'You got a big mouth,' Little Red said.

'I got a foot's even bigger and I'm gonna shove it right up your nose, you keep bein' nasty to me when I'm tryna be polite.'

'Cool off, Francis,' Old Shoes said. 'What's your story? You're lookin' pretty good.'

'I'm gettin' rich,' Francis said. 'Got me a gang of new clothes, couple of jugs, money in the pocket.'

'You're gettin' up in the world,' Old Shoes said.

'Yeah, but what the hell you doin' here if you ain't drinkin' is what I don't figure.'

'I just told you. I'm passin' through and got curious about the old joints.'

'You workin'?'

'Got a steady job down in Jersey. Even got an apartment and a car. A car, Francis. You believe that? Me with a car? Not a new car, but a good car. A Hudson two-door. You want a ride?'

'A ride? Me?'

'Sure, why not?'

'Now?'

'Don't matter to me. I'm just sightseein'. I'm not sleepin' up here. Wouldn't sleep here anyway. Bedbugs'd follow me all the way back to Jersey.'

'This bum here,' Francis explained to Rudy, 'I saved from dyin' in the street. Used to fall down drunk three, four times a night, like he was top-heavy.'

'That's right,' Old Shoes said. 'Broke my face five or six times, just like his.' And he gestured at Moose. 'But I don't do that no more. I hit three nuthouses and then I quit. I been off the bum three years and dry for two. You wanna go for that ride, Francis? Only thing is, no bottle. The wife'd smell it and I'd catch hell.'

'You got a wife too?' Francis said.

'You got a car and a wife and a house and a job?' Rudy asked. He sat up on his cot and studied this interloper.

'That's Rudy,' Francis said. 'Rudy Tooty. He's thinkin' about killin' himself.'

'I know the feelin',' Old Shoes said. 'Me and Francis we needed a drink somethin' awful one mornin'. We walked all over town but we couldn't score, snow comin' through our shoes, and it's four below zero. Finally we sold our blood and drank the money. I passed out and woke up still needin' a drink awful bad, and not a penny and no chance for one, couldn't even sell any more blood, and I wanted to die and I mean die. Die.'

'Where there ain't no snow,' Rudy sang. 'Where the handouts grow on bushes and you sleep out every night.'

'You wanna go for a ride?' Old Shoes asked Rudy.

'Oh the buzzin' of the bees in the cigarette trees, by the soda water fountains,' Rudy sang. Then he smiled at Old Shoes, took a swallow of wine, and fell back on his cot.

'Man wants to go for a ride and can't get no takers,' Francis said. 'Might as well call it a day, Shoes, stretch out and rest them bones.'

'Naaah, I guess I'll be movin' on.'

'One evenin' as the sun went down, and the jungle fires were burnin',' Rudy sang, 'Down the track came a hobo hikin', and said, Boys, I am not turnin'.'

'Shut up that singin',' Little Red said. 'I'm tryna sleep.'

'I'm gonna mess up his face,' Francis said and stood up.

'No fights,' Moose said. 'She'll kick us the hell out or call the cops on us.'

'That'll be the day I get kicked out of a joint like this,' Francis said. 'This is pigswill. I lived in better pigswill than this goddamn pigswill.'

'Where I come from –' Old Shoes began.

'I don't give a goddamn where you come from,' Francis said.

'Goddamn you, I come from Texas.'

'Name a city, then.'

'Galveston.'

'Behave yourself,' Francis said, 'or I'll knock you down. I'm a tough son of a bitch. Tougher than that bum Finny. Licked twelve men at once.'

'You're drunk,' Old Shoes said.

'Yeah,' said Francis. 'My mind's goin'.'

'It went there. Rattlesnake got you.'

'Rattlesnake, my ass. Rattlesnake is nothin'.'

'Cottonmouth?'

'Oh, cottonmouth rattler. Yeah. That's somethin'. Jesus, this is a nice subject. Who wants to talk about snakes? Talk about bums is more like it. A bum is a bum. Helen's got me on the bum. Son of a bitch, she won't go home, won't straighten up.'

'Helen did the hula down in Hon-oh-loo-loo,' Rudy sang.

'Shut your stupid mouth,' Francis said to Rudy.

'People don't like me,' Rudy said.

'Singin' there, wavin' your arms, talkin' about Helen.'

'I can't escape myself.'

'That's what I'm talkin' about,' Francis said.

'I tried it before.'

'I know, but you can't do it, so you might as well live with it.'

'I like to be condemned,' Rudy said.

'No, don't be condemned,' Francis told him.

'I like to be condemned.'

'Never be condemned.'

'I like to be condemned because I know I done wrong in my life.'

'You never done wrong,' Francis said.

'All you screwballs down there, shut up,' yelled Little Red, sitting up on his cot. Francis instantly stood up and ran down the aisle. He was running when he lunged and grazed Little Red's lips with his knuckles.

'I'm gonna mess you up,' Francis said.

Little Red rolled with the blow and fell off the cot. Francis ran around the cot and kicked him in the stomach. Little Red groaned and rolled and Francis kicked him in the side. Little Red rolled under Finny's cot, away from Francis's feet. Francis followed him and was ready to drive a black laceless oxford deep into his face, but then he stopped. Rudy, Moose, and Old Shoes were all standing up, watching.

'When I knew Francis he was strong as a bull,' Old Shoes said.

'Knocked a house down by myself,' Francis said, walking back to his cot. 'Didn't need no wreckin' ball.' He picked up the quart of wine and gestured with it. Moose lay back down on his cot and Rudy on his. Old Shoes sat on the cot next to Francis. Little Red licked his bleeding lip and lay quietly on the floor under the cot where Finny was supine and snoring. The faces of all the women Francis had ever known changed with kaleidoscopic swiftness from one to the other to the other on the three female figures in the far corner. The trio sat on straight-backed chairs, witnesses all to the whole fabric of Francis's life. His mother was crocheting a Home Sweet Home sampler while Katrina measured off a bolt of new cloth and Helen snipped the ragged threads. Then they all became Annie.

'When they throw dirt in my face, nobody can walk up and sell me short, that's what I worry about,' Francis said. 'I'll suffer in hell, if they ever got such a place, but I still got muscles and blood and I'm gonna live it out. I never saw a bum yet said anything against Francis. They better not, goddamn 'em. All them sufferin' bastards, all them poor souls waitin' for heaven, walkin' around with the snow flyin', stayin' in empty houses, pants fallin' off 'em. When I leave this earth I wanna leave it with a blessing to everybody. Francis never hurt nobody.'

'The mockin'birds'll sing when you die,' Old Shoes said.

'Let 'em. Let 'em sing. People tell me: Get off the bum. And I had a chance. I had a good mind but now it's all flaked out, like a heavin' line on a canal boat, back and forth, back and forth. You get whipped around so much, everything comes to a standstill, even a nail. You drive it so far and it comes to a stop. Keep hittin' it and the head'll break off.'

'That's a true thing,' Moose said.

'On the Big Rock Candy Mountain,' Rudy sang, 'the cops got wooden legs.' He stood up and waved his wine in a gesture imitative of Francis; then he rocked back and forth as he sang, strongly and on key: 'The bulldogs all got rubber teeth, and the hens lay soft-boiled eggs. The boxcars all are empty and the sun shines every day. I wanna go where there ain't no snow, where the sleet don't fall and the wind don't blow, on the Big Rock Candy Mountain.'

Old Shoes stood up and made ready to leave. 'Nobody wants a ride?' he said.

'All right, goddamn it,' Francis said. 'Whataya say, Rudy? Let's get outa this pigswill. Get outa this stink and go where I can breathe. The weeds is better than this pigswill.'

'So long, friend,' Moose said. 'Thanks for the wine.'

'You bet, pal, and God bless your knee. Tough as nails, that's what Francis is.'

'I believe that,' Moose said.

'Where we goin'?' Rudy asked.

'Go up to the jungle and see a friend of mine. You wanna give us a lift to the jungle?' Francis asked Old Shoes. 'Up in the North End. You know where that is?'

'No, but you do.'

'Gonna be cold,' Rudy said.

'They got a fire,' Francis said. 'Cold's better than this bughouse.'

'By the lemonade springs, where the bluebird sings,' Rudy sang.

'That's the place,' Francis said.

As Old Shoes' car moved north on Erie Boulevard, where the Erie Canal used to flow, Francis remembered Emmett Daugherty's face: rugged and flushed beneath wavy gray hair, a strong, pointed nose truly giving him the look of the Divine Warrior, which is how Francis would always remember him, an Irishman who never drank more than enough, a serious and witty man of control and high purpose, and with an unkillable faith in God and the laboring man. Francis had sat with him on the slate step in front of Iron Joe's Wheelbarrow and listened to his endless talk of the days when he and the country were young, when the riverboats brought the greenhorns up the Hudson from the Irish ships. When the cholera was in the air, the greenhorns would be taken off the steamboats at Albany and sent west on canal boats, for the city's elders had charged the government with keeping the pestilential foreigners out of the city.

Emmett rode up from New York after he got off the death ship from Cork, and at the Albany basin he saw his brother Owen waving frantically to him. Owen followed the boat to the North Albany lock, ran along the towpath yelling advice to Emmett, giving him family news, telling him to get off the boat as soon as they'd let him, then to write saying where he was so Owen could send him money to come back to Albany by stagecoach. But it was days before Emmett got off that particular packet boat, got off in a place whose name he never learned, and the authorities there too kept the newcomers westering, under duress.

By the time Emmett reached Buffalo he had decided not to return to such an inhospitable city as Albany, and he moved on to Ohio, where he found work building streets, and then with the railroads, and in time went all the way west on the rails and became a labor organizer, and eventually a leader of the Clann na Gael, and lived to see the Irish in control of Albany, and to tell his stories and inspire Francis Phelan to throw the stone that changed the course of life, even for people not yet born.

That vision of the packet moving up the canal and Owen running alongside it telling Emmett about his children was as real to Francis, though it happened four decades before he was born, as was Old Shoes' car, in which he was now bouncing ever northward toward the precise place where the separation took place. He all but cried at the way the Daugherty brothers were being separated by the goddamned government, just as he was now being separated from Billy and the others. And by what? What and who were again separating Francis from those people after he'd found them? It was a force whose name did not matter, if it had a name, but whose effect was devastating. Emmett Daugherty had placed blame on no man, not on the cholera inspectors or even the city's elders. He knew a larger fate had moved him westward and shaped in him all that he was to become; and that moving and shaping was what Francis now understood, for he perceived the fugitive thrust that had come to be so much a part of his own spirit. And so he found it entirely reasonable that he and Emmett should be fused in a single person: the character of the hero of the play written by Emmett's son, Edward Daugherty the playwright: Edward (husband of Katrina, father of Martin), who wrote *The Car Barns*, the tale of how Emmett radicalized Francis by telling his own story of separation and growth, by inspiring Francis to identify the enemy and target him with a stone. And just as Emmett truly did return home from the west as a labor hero, so also did the playright conjure an image of Francis returning home as underground hero for what that stone of his had done.

For a time Francis believed everything Edward Daugherty had written about him: liberator of the strikers from the capitalist beggars who owned the trolleys, just as Emmett had helped Paddy-with-a-shovel straighten his back and climb up out of his ditch in another age. The playwright saw them both as Divine Warriors, sparked by the socialistic gods who understood the historical Irish need for aid from on high, for without it (so spoke Emmett, the golden-tongued organizer of the play), 'how else would we rid ourselves of those Tory swine, the true and unconquerable devils of all history?'

The stone had (had it not?) precipitated the firing by the soldiers and the killing of the pair of bystanders. And without that, without the death of Harold Allen, the strike might have continued, for the scabs were being imported in great numbers from Brooklyn, greenhorn Irish the likes of Emmett on the packet boat, some of them defecting instantly from the strike when they saw what it was, others bewildered and lost, lied to by men who hired them for railroad work in Philadelphia, then duped them into scabbery, terror, even death. There were even strikers from other cities working as scabs, soulless men who rode the strike trains here and took these Albany men's jobs, as other scabs were taking theirs. And all of that might have continued had not Francis thrown the first stone. He was the principal hero in a strike that created heroes by the dozen. And because he was, he lived all his life with guilt over the deaths of the three men, unable to see any other force at work in the world that day beyond his own right hand. He could not accept, though he knew it to be true, that other significant stones had flown that day, that the soldiers' fusillade at the bystanders had less to do with Harold Allen's death than it did with the possibility of the soldiers' own, for their firing had followed not upon the release of the stone by Francis but only after the mob's full barrage had flown at the trolley. And then Francis, having seen nothing but his own act and what appeared to be its instant consequences, had fled into heroism and been suffused further, through the written word of Edward Daugherty, with the hero's most splendid guilt.

But now, with those events so deeply dead and buried, with his own guilt having so little really to do with it, he saw the strike as simply the insanity of the Irish, poor against poor, a race, a class divided against itself. He saw Harold Allen trying to survive the day and the night at a moment when the frenzied mob had turned against him, just as Francis himself had often had to survive hostility in his flight through strange cities, just as he had always had to survive his own worst instincts. For Francis knew now that he was at war with himself, his private factions mutually bellicose, and if he was ever to survive, it would be with the help not of any socialistic god but with a clear head and a steady eye for the truth; for the guilt he felt was not worth the dying. It served nothing except nature's insatiable craving for blood. The trick was to live, to beat the bastards, survive the mob and that fateful chaos, and show them all what a man can do to set things right, once he sets his mind to it.

Poor Harold Allen.

'I forgive the son of a bitch,' Francis said.

'Who's that?' Old Shoes asked. Rudy lay all but blotto across the backseat, holding the whiskey and wine bottles upright on his chest with both tops open in violation of Old Shoes' dictum that they stay closed, and not spilling a drop of either.

'Guy I killed. Guy named Allen.'

'You killed a guy?'

'More'n one.'

'Accidental, was it?'

'No. I tried to get that one guy, Allen. He was takin' my job.'

'That's a good reason.'

'Maybe, maybe not. Maybe he was just doin' what he had to do.'

'Baloney,' Old Shoes said. 'That's what everybody does, good, bad, and lousy. Burglars, murderers.'

And Francis fell quiet, sinking into yet another truth requiring handling.

The jungle was maybe seven years old, three years old, a month old, days old. It was an ashpit, a graveyard, and a fugitive city. It stood among wild sumac bushes and river foliage, all fallen dead now from the early frost. It was a haphazard upthrust of tarpaper shacks, lean-tos, and impromptu constructions describable by no known nomenclature. It was a city of essential transiency and would-be permanency, a resort of those for whom motion was either anathema or pointless or impossible. Cripples lived here, and natives of this town who had lost their homes, and people who had come here at journey's end to accept whatever disaster was going to happen next. The jungle, a visual manifestation of the malaise of the age and the nation, covered the equivalent of two or more square city blocks between the tracks and the river, just east of the old carbarns and the empty building that once housed Iron Joe's saloon.

Francis's friend in the jungle was a man in his sixties named Andy, who had admitted to Francis in the boxcar in which they both traveled to Albany that people used to call him Andy Which One, a name that derived from his inability, until he was nearly twenty, to tell his left hand from his right, a challenge he still faced in certain stressful moments. Francis found Andy Which One instantly sympathetic, shared the wealth of cigarettes and food he was carrying, and thought instantly of him again when Annie handed him two turkey sandwiches and Peg slipped him a hefty slice of plum pudding, all three items wrapped in waxed paper and intact now in the pockets of his 1916 suitcoat.

But Francis had not seriously thought of sharing the food with Andy until Rudy had begun singing of the jungle. On top of that, Francis almost suffocated seeing his own early venom and self-destructive arrogance reembodied in Little Red, and the conjunction of events impelled him to quit the flop and seek out something he could value; for above all now, Francis needed to believe in simple solutions. And Andy Which One, a man confused by the names of his own hands, but who survived to dwell in the city of useless penitence and be grateful for it, seemed to Francis a creature worthy of scrutiny. Francis found him easily when Old Shoes parked the car on the dirt road that bordered the jungle. He roused Andy from shallow sleep in front of a fading fire, and handed him the whiskey bottle.

'Have a drink, pal. Lubricate your soul.'

'Hey, old Francis. How you makin' out there, buddy?'

'Puttin' one foot in front of the other and hopin' they go somewheres,' Francis said. 'The hotel open here? I brought a couple of bums along with me. Old Shoes here, he says he ain't a bum no more, but that's just what he says. And Rudy the Cootie, a good ol' fella.'

'Hey,' said Andy, 'just settle in. Musta known you was comin'. Fire's still goin', and the stars are out. Little chilly in this joint. Lemme turn up the heat.'

They all sat down around the fire while Andy stoked it with twigs and scraps of lumber, and soon the flames were trying to climb to those reaches of the sky that are the domain of all fire. The flames gave vivid life to the cold night, and the men warmed their hands by them.

A figure hovered behind Andy and when he felt its presence he turned and welcomed Michigan Mac to the primal scene.

'Glad to meet ya,' Francis said to Mac. 'I heard you fell through a hole the other night.'

'Coulda broke my neck,' Mac said.

'Did you break it?' Francis asked.

'If I'da broke my neck I'd be dead.'

'Oh, so you're livin', is that it? You ain't dead?'

'Who's this guy?' Mac asked Andy.

'He's an all-right guy I met on the train,' Andy said.

'We're all all right,' Francis said. 'I never met a bum I didn't like.'

'Will Rogers said that,' Rudy said.

'He did like hell,' Francis said. 'I said it.'

'All I know. That's what he said. All I know is what I read in the newspapers,' Rudy said.

'I didn't know you could read,' said Francis.

'James Watt invented the steam engine,' Rudy said. 'And he was only twenty-nine years old.'

'He was a wizard,' Francis said.

'Right. Charles Darwin was a very great man, master of botany. Died in nineteen-thirty-six.'

'What's he talkin' about?' Mac asked.

'He ain't talkin' about nothin',' Francis said. 'He's just talkin'.'

'Sir Isaac Newton. You know what he did with the apple?'

'I know that one,' Old Shoes said. 'He discovered gravity.'

'Right. You know when that was? Nineteen-thirty-six. He was born of two midwives.'

'You got a pretty good background on these wizards,' Francis said.

'God loves a thief,' Rudy said. 'I'm a thief.'

'We're all thieves,' Francis said. 'What'd you steal?'

'I stole my wife's heart,' Rudy said.

'What'd you do with it?'

'I gave it back. Wasn't worth keepin'. You know where the Milky Way is?'

'Up there somewheres,' Francis said, looking up at the sky, which was as full of stars as he'd ever seen it.

'Damn, I'm hungry,' Michigan Mac said.

'Here,' said Andy. 'Have a bite.' And from a coat pocket he took a large raw onion.

'That's an onion,' Mac said.

'Another wizard,' Francis said.

Mac took the onion and looked at it, then handed it back to Andy, who took a bite out of it and put it back in his pocket.

'Got it at a grocery,' Andy said. 'Mister, I told the guy, I'm starvin', I gotta have somethin'. And he gave me two onions.'

'You had money,' Mac said. 'I told ya, get a loaf of bread, but you got a pint of wine.'

'Can't have wine and bread too,' Andy said. 'What are you, a Frenchman?'

'You wanna buy food and drink,' said Francis, 'you oughta get a job.'

'I caddied all last week,' Mac said, 'but that don't pay, that shit. You slide down them hills. Them golf guys got spikes on their shoes. Then they tell ya: Go to work, ya bum. I like to, but I can't. Get five, six bucks and get on the next train. I'm no bum, I'm a hobo.'

'You movin' around too much,' Francis said. 'That's why you fell through that hole.'

'Yeah,' said Mac, 'but I ain't goin' back to that joint. I hear the cops are pickin' the boys outa there every night. That pot is hot. Travel on, Avalon.'

'Cops were here tonight earlier, shinin' their lights,' Andy said. 'But they didn't pick up anybody.'

Rudy raised up his head and looked over all the faces in front of the fire. Then he looked skyward and talked to the stars. 'On the outskirts,' he said, 'I'm a restless person, a traveler.'

They passed the wine among them and Andy restoked the fire with wood he had stored in his lean-to. Francis thought of Billy getting dressed up in his suit, topcoat, and hat, and standing before Francis for inspection. You like the hat? he asked. I like it, Francis said. It's got style. Lost the other one, Billy said. First time I ever wore this one. It look all right? It looks mighty stylish, Francis said. All right, gotta get downtown, Billy said. Sure, said Francis. We'll see you again, Billy said. No doubt about it, Francis said. You hangin' around Albany or movin' on? Billy asked. Couldn't say for sure, said Francis. Lotta things that need figurin' out. Always is, said Billy, and then they shook hands and said no more words to each other.

When he himself left an hour and a little bit later, Francis shook hands also with George Quinn, a quirky little guy as dapper as always, who told bad jokes (Let's all eat tomatoes and catch up) that made everybody laugh, and Peg threw her arms around her father and kissed him on the cheek, which was a million-dollar kiss, all right, all right, and then Annie said when she took his hand in both of hers: You must come again. Sure, said Francis. No, said Annie, I mean that you must come so that we can talk about the things you ought to know, things about the children and about the family. There's a cot we could set up in Danny's room if you wanted to stay over next time. And then she kissed him ever so lightly on the lips.

'Hey Mac,' Francis said, 'you really hungry or you just mouthin' off for somethin' to say?'

'I'm hungry,' Mac said. 'I ain't et since noon. Goin' on thirteen, fourteen hours, whatever it is.'

'Here,' Francis said, unwrapping one of his turkey sandwiches and handing Mac a half, 'take a bite, take a couple of bites, but don't eat it all.'

'Hey all right,' Mac said.

'I told you he was a good fella,' Andy said.

'You want a bite of sandwich?' Francis asked Andy.

'I got enough with the onion,' Andy said. 'But the guy in the piano box over there, he was askin' around for something awhile back. He's got a baby there.'

'A baby?'

'Baby and a wife.'

Francis snatched the remnants of the sandwich away from Michigan Mac and groped his way in the firelight night to the piano box. A small fire was burning in front of it and a man was sitting cross-legged, warming himself.

'I hear you got a kid here,' Francis said to the man, who looked up at Francis suspiciously, then nodded and gestured at the box. Francis could see the shadow of a woman curled around what looked to be the shadow of a swaddled infant.

'Got some stuff here I can't use,' Francis said, and he handed the man the full sandwich and the remnant of the second one. 'Sweet stuff too,' he said and gave the man the plum pudding. The man accepted the gifts with an upturned face that revealed the incredulity of a man struck by lightning in the rainless desert; and his benefactor was gone before he could even acknowledge the gift. Francis rejoined the circle at Andy's fire, entering into silence. He saw that all but Rudy, whose head was on his chest, were staring at him.

'Give him some food, did ya?' Andy asked.

'Yeah. Nice fella. I ate me a bellyful tonight. How old's the kid?'

'Twelve weeks, the guy said.'

Francis nodded. 'I had a kid. Name of Gerald. He was only thirteen days old when he fell and broke his neck and died.'

'Jeez, that's tough,' Andy said.

'You never talked about that,' Old Shoes said.

'No, because it was me that dropped him. Picked him up with the diaper and he slid out of it.'

'Goddamn,' said Old Shoes.

'I couldn't handle it. That's why I run off and left the family. Then I bumped into one of my other kids last week and he tells me the wife never told nobody I did that. Guy drops a kid and it dies and the mother don't tell a damn soul what happened. I can't figure that out. Woman keeps a secret like that for twenty-two years, protectin' a bum like me.'

'You can't figure women,' Michigan Mac said. 'My old lady used to peddle her tail all day long and then come home and tell me I was the only man ever touched her. I come in the house one day and found her bangin' two guys at once, first I knew what was happenin'.'

'I ain't talkin' about that,' Francis said. 'I'm talkin' about a woman who's a real woman. I ain't talkin' about no trashbarrel whore.'

'My wife was very good-lookin', though,' Mac said. 'And she had a terrific personality.'

'Yeah,' said Francis. 'And it was all in her ass.'

Rudy raised up his head and looked at the wine bottle in his hand. He held it up to the light.

'What makes a man a drunk?' he asked.

'Wine,' Old Shoes said. 'What you got in your hand.'

'You ever hear about the bears and the mulberry juice?' Rudy asked. 'Mulberries fermented inside their stomachs.'

'That so?' said Old Shoes. 'I thought they fermented before they got inside.'

'Nope. Not with bears,' Rudy said.

'What happened to the bears and the juice?' Mac asked.

'They all got stiff and wound up with hangovers,' Rudy said, and he laughed and laughed. Then he turned the wine bottle upside down and licked the drops that flowed onto his tongue. He tossed the bottle alongside the other two empties, his own whiskey bottle and Francis's wine that had been passed around.

'Jeez,' Rudy said. 'We got nothin' to drink. We on the bum.'

In the distance the men could hear the faint hum of automobile engines, and then the closing of car doors.

Francis's confession seemed wasted. Mentioning Gerald to strangers for the first time was a mistake because nobody took it seriously. And it did not diminish his own guilt but merely cheapened the utterance, made it as commonplace as Rudy's brainless chatter about bears and wizards. Francis concluded he had made yet another wrong decision, another in a long line. He concluded that he was not capable of making a right decision, that he was as wrongheaded a man as ever lived. He felt certain now that he would never attain the balance that allowed so many other men to live peaceful, nonviolent, nonfugitive lives, lives that spawned at least a modicum of happiness in old age.

He had no insights into how he differed in this from other men. He knew he was somehow stronger, more given to violence, more in love with the fugitive dance, but this was all so for reasons that had nothing to do with intent. All right, he had wanted to hurt Harold Allen, but that was so very long ago. Could anyone in possession of Francis's perspective on himself believe that he was responsible for Rowdy Dick, or the hole in the runt's neck, or the bruises on Little Red, or the scars on other men long forgotten or long buried?

Francis was now certain only that he could never arrive at any conclusions about himself that had their origin in reason. But neither did he believe himself incapable of thought. He believed he was a creature of unknown and unknowable qualities, a man in whom there would never be an equanimity of both impulsive and premeditated action. Yet after every admission that he was a lost and distorted soul, Francis asserted his own private wisdom and purpose: he had fled the folks because he was too profane a being to live among them; he had humbled himself willfully through the years to counter a fearful pride in his own ability to manufacture the glory from which grace would flow. What he was was, yes, a warrior, protecting a belief that no man could ever articulate, especially himself; but somehow it involved protecting saints from sinners, protecting the living from the dead. And a warrior, he was certain, was not a victim. Never a victim.

In the deepest part of himself that could draw an unutterable conclusion, he told himself: My guilt is all that I have left. If I lose it, I have stood for nothing, done nothing, been nothing.

And he raised his head to see the phalanx of men in Legionnaires' caps advancing into the firelight with baseball bats in their hands.

The men in caps entered the jungle with a fervid purpose, knocking down everything that stood, without a word. They caved in empty shacks and toppled lean-tos that the weight of weather and time had already all but collapsed. One man who saw them coming left his lean-to and ran, calling out one word: 'Raiders!' and rousing some jungle people, who picked up their belongings and fled behind the leader of the pack. The first collapsed shacks were already burning when the men around Andy's fire became aware that raiders were approaching.

'What the hell's doin'?' Rudy asked. 'Why's everybody gettin' up? Where you goin', Francis?'

'Get on your feet, stupid,' Francis said, and Rudy got up.

'What the hell did I get myself into?' Old Shoes said, and he backed away from the fire, keeping the advancing raiders in sight. They were half a football field away but Michigan Mac was already in heavy retreat, bent double like a scythe as he ran for the river.

The raiders moved forward with their devastation clubs and one of them flattened a lean-to with two blows. A man following them poured gasoline on the ruins and then threw a match on top of it all. The raiders were twenty yards from Andy's lean-to by then, with Andy, Rudy, and Francis still immobilized, watching the spectacle with disbelieving eyes.

'We better move it,' Andy said.

'You got anything in that lean-to worth savin'?' Francis asked.

'Only thing I own that's worth anything's my skin, and I got that with me.'

The three men moved slowly back from the raiders, who were clearly intent on destroying everything that stood. Francis looked at the piano box as he moved past it and saw it was empty.

'Who are they?' Rudy asked Francis. 'Why they doin' this?'

But no one answered.

Half a dozen lean-tos and shacks were ablaze, and one had ignited a tall, leafless tree, whose flames were reaching high into the heavens, far above the level of the burning shacks. In the wild firelight Francis saw one raider smashing a shack, from which a groggy man emerged on hands and knees. The raider hit the crawling man across the buttocks with a half swing of the bat until the man stood up. The raider poked him yet again and the man broke into a limping run. The fire that rose from the running man's shack illuminated the raider's smile.

Francis, Rudy, and Andy turned to run then too, convinced at last that demons were abroad in the night. But as they turned they confronted a pair of raiders moving toward them from their left flank.

'Filthy bums,' one raider said, and swung his bat at Andy, who stepped deftly out of range, ran off, and was swallowed up by the night. The raider reversed his swing and caught the wobbling Rudy just above neck level, and Rudy yelped and went down. Francis leaped on the man and tore the bat from him, then scrambled away and turned to face both raiders, who were advancing toward him with a hatred on their faces as anonymous and deadly as the exposed fangs of rabid dogs. The raider with the bat raised it above his own head and struck a vertical blow at Francis, which Francis sidestepped as easily as he once went to his left for a fast grounder. Simultaneously he stepped forward, as into a wide pitch, and swung his own bat at the man who had struck Rudy. Francis connected with a stroke that would have sent any pitch over any center-field fence in any ball park anywhere, and he clearly heard and truly felt bones crack in the man's back. He watched with all but orgasmic pleasure as the breathless man twisted grotesquely and fell without a sound.

The second attacker charged Francis and knocked him down,

not with his bat but with the weight and force of his moving body. The two rolled over and over, Francis finally separating himself from the man by a glancing blow to the throat. But the man was tough and very agile, fully on his feet when Francis was still on his knees, and he was raising his arms for a horizontal swing when Francis brought his own bat full circle and smashed the man's left leg at knee level. The knee collapsed inward, a hinge reversed, and the raider toppled crookedly with a long howl of pain.

Francis lifted Rudy, who was mumbling incoherent sounds, and threw him over his shoulder. He ran, as best he could, toward the dark woods along the river, and then moved south along the shore toward the city. He stopped in tall weeds, all brown and dead, and lay prone, with Rudy beside him, to catch his breath. No one was following. He looked back at the jungle through the barren trees and saw it aflame in widening measure. The moon and the stars shone on the river, a placid sea of glass beside the sprawling, angry fire.

Francis found he was bleeding from the cheek and he went to the river and soaked his handkerchief and rinsed off the blood. He drank deeply of the river, which was icy and shocking and sweet. He blotted the wound, found it still bleeding, and pressed it with the handkerchief to stanch it.

'Who were they?' Rudy asked when he returned.

'They're the guys on the other team,' Francis said. 'They don't like us filthy bums.'

'You ain't filthy,' Rudy said hoarsely. 'You got a new suit.'

'Never mind my suit, how's your head?'

'I don't know. Like nothin' I ever felt before.' Francis touched the back of Rudy's skull. It wasn't bleeding but there was one hell of a lump there.

'Can you walk?'

'I don't know. Where's Old Shoes and his car?'

'Gone, I guess. I think that car is hot. I think he stole it. He used to do that for a livin'. That and peddle his ass.'

Francis helped Rudy to his feet, but Rudy could not stand alone, nor could he put one foot in front of the other. Francis lifted him back on his shoulder and headed south. He had Memorial Hospital in mind, the old Homeopathic Hospital on North Pearl Street, downtown. It was a long way, but there wasn't no other place in the middle of the damn night. And walking was the only way. You wait for a damn bus or a trolley at this hour, Rudy'd be dead in the gutter.

Francis carried him first on one shoulder, then on the other, and finally piggyback when he found Rudy had some use of both arms and could hold on. He carried him along the river road to stay away from cruising police cars, and then down along the tracks and up to Broadway and then Pearl. He carried him up the hospital steps and into the emergency room, which was small and bright and clean and empty of patients. A nurse wheeled a stretcher away from one wall when she saw him coming, and helped Rudy to slide off Francis's back and stretch out.

'He got hit in the head,' Francis said. 'He can't walk.'

'What happened?' the nurse asked, inspecting Rudy's eyes.

'Some guy down on Madison Avenue went nuts and hit him with a brick. You got a doctor can help him?'

'We'll get a doctor. He's been drinking.'

'That ain't his problem. He's got a stomach cancer too, but what ails him right now is his head. He got rocked all to hell, I'm tellin' you, and it wasn't none of his fault.'

The nurse went to the phone and dialed and talked softly.

'How you makin' it, pal?' Francis asked.

Rudy smiled and gave Francis a glazed look and said nothing. Francis patted him on the shoulder and sat down on a chair beside him to rest. He saw his own image in the mirror door of a cabinet against the wall. His bow tie was all cockeyed and his shirt and coat were spattered with blood where he had dripped before he knew he was cut. His face was smudged and his clothes were covered with dirt. He straightened the tie and brushed off a bit of the dirt.

After a second phone call and a conversation that Francis was about to interrupt to tell her to get goddamn busy with Rudy, the nurse came back. She took Rudy's pulse, went for a stethoscope, and listened to his heart. Then she told Francis Rudy was dead.

Francis stood up and looked at his friend's face and saw the smile still there. Where the wind don't blow.

'What was his name?' the nurse asked. She picked up a pencil and a hospital form on a clipboard.

Francis could only stare into Rudy's glassy-eyed smile. Isaac Newton of the apple was born of two midwives.

'Sir, what was his name?' the nurse said.

'Name was Rudy.'

'Rudy what?'

'Rudy Newton,' Francis said. 'He knew where the Milky Way was.'

It would be three-fifteen by the clock on the First Church when Francis headed south toward Palombo's Hotel to get out of the cold, to stretch out with Helen and try to think about what had happened and what he should do about it. He would walk past Palombo's night man on the landing, salute him, and climb the stairs to the room he and Helen always shared in this dump. Looking at the hallway dirt and the ratty carpet as he walked down the hall, he would remind himself that this was luxury for him and Helen. He would see the light coming out from under the door, but he would knock anyway to make sure he had Helen's room. When he got no answer he would open the door and discover Helen on the floor in her kimono.

He would enter the room and close the door and stand looking at her for a long time. Her hair would be loose, and fanned out, and pretty.

He would, after a while, think of lifting her onto the bed, but decide there was no point in that, for she looked right and comfortable just as she was. She looked as if she were sleeping.

He would sit in the chair looking at her for an amount of time he later would not be able to calculate, and he would decide that he had made a right decision in not moving her.

For she was not crooked.

He would look in the open suitcase and would find his old clippings and put them in his inside coat pocket. He would find his razor and his penknife and Helen's rhinestone butterfly, and he would put these in his coat pockets also. In her coat hanging in the closet he would find her three dollars and thirty-five cents and he would put that in his pants pocket, still wondering where she got it. He would remember the two dollars he left for her and that she would never get now, nor would he, and he would think of it as a tip for old Donovan. Helen says thank you.

He would then sit on the bed and look at Helen from a different angle. He would be able to see her eyes were closed and he would remember how vividly green they were in life, those gorgeous emeralds. He would hear the women talking together behind him as he tried to peer beyond Helen's sheltered eyes.

Too late now, the women would say. Too late now to see any deeper into Helen's soul. But he would continue to stare, mindful of the phonograph record propped against the pillow; and he would know the song she'd bought, or stole. It would be 'Bye Bye Blackbird,' which she loved so much, and he would hear the women singing it softly as he stared at the fiercely glistening scars on Helen's soul, fresh and livid scars whitening among the old, the soul already purging itself of all wounds of the world, flaming with the green fires of hope, but keeping their integrity too as welts of insight into the deepest secrets of Satan.

Francis, this twofold creature, now an old man in a mortal slouch, now again a fledgling bird of uncertain wing, would sing along softly with the women: Here I go, singin' low, the song revealing to him that he was not looking into Helen's soul at all but only into his own repetitive and fallible memory. He knew that right now both Rudy and Helen had far more insight into his being than he himself ever had, or would have, into either of theirs.

The dead, they got all the eyes.

He would follow the thread of his life backward to a point well in advance of the dying of Helen and would come to a vision of her in this same Japanese kimono, lying beside him after they had made sweet love, and she saying to him: All I want in the world is to have my name put back among the family.

And Francis would then stand up and vow that he would one

day hunt up Helen's grave, no matter where they put her, and would place a stone on top of it with her name carved deeply in its face. The stone would say: *Helen Marie Archer, a great soul.*

Francis would remember then that when great souls were being extinguished, the forces of darkness walked abroad in the world, filling it with lightning and strife and fire. And he would realize that he should pray for the safety of Helen's soul, since that was the only way he could now help her. But because his vision of the next world was not of the court of heaven where the legion of souls in grace venerate the Holy Worm, but rather of a foul mist above a hole in the ground where the earth itself purges away the stench of life's rot, Francis saw a question burning brightly in the air: How should this man pray?

He would think about this for another incalculably long moment and decide finally there was no way for him to pray: not for Helen, not even for himself.

He would then reach down and touch Helen on the top of the head and stroke her skull the way a father strokes the soft fontanel of his newborn child, stroke her gently so as not to disturb the flowing fall of her hair.

Because it was so pretty.

Then he would walk out of Helen's room, leaving the light burning. He would walk down the hall to the landing, salute the night clerk, who would be dozing in his chair, and then he would reenter the cold and living darkness of the night.

By dawn he would be on a Delaware & Hudson freight heading south toward the lemonade springs. He would be squatting in the middle of the empty car with the door partway open, sitting a little out of the wind. He would be watching the stars, whose fire seemed so unquenchable only a few hours before, now vanishing from an awakening sky that was between a rose and a violet in its early hue.

It would be impossible for him to close his eyes, and so he would think of all the things he might now do. He would then decide that he could not choose among all the possibilities that were his. By now he was sure only that he lived in a world where events decided themselves, and that all a man could do was to stay one jump into their mystery.

He had a vision of Gerald swaddled in the silvery web of his grave, and then the vision faded like the stars and he could not even remember the color of the child's hair. He saw all the women who became three, and then their impossible coherence also faded and he saw only the glorious mouth of Katrina speaking words that were little more than silent shapes; and he knew then that he was leaving behind more than a city and a lifetime of corpses. He was also leaving behind even his vivid memory of the scars on Helen's soul.

Strawberry Bill climbed into the car when the train slowed to take on water, and he looked pretty good for a bum that died coughin'. He was all duded up in a blue seersucker suit, straw hat, and shoes the color of a new baseball.

'You never looked that good while you was livin',' Francis said to him. 'You done well for yourself over there.'

Everybody gets an Italian tailor when he checks in, Bill said. But say, pal, what're you runnin' from this time?

'Same old crowd,' Francis said. 'The cops.'

Ain't no such things as cops, said Bill.

'Maybe they ain't none of 'em got to heaven yet, but they been pesterin' hell outa me down here.'

No cops chasin' you, pal.

'You got the poop?'

Would I kid a fella like you?

Francis smiled and began to hum Rudy's song about the place where the bluebird sings. He took the final swallow of Green River whiskey, which tasted sweet and cold to him now. And he thought of Annie's attic.

That's the place, Bill told him. They got a cot over in the corner, near your old trunk.

'I saw it,' said Francis.

Francis walked to the doorway of the freight car and threw the empty whiskey bottle at the moon, an outshoot fading away into the rising sun. The bottle and the moon made music like a soulful banjo when they moved through the heavens, divine harmonies that impelled Francis to leap off the train and seek sanctuary under the holy Phelan eaves.

'You hear that music?' Francis said.

Music? said Bill. Can't say as I do.

'Banjo music. Mighty sweet banjo. That empty whiskey bottle's what's makin' it. The whiskey bottle and the moon.'

If you say so, said Bill.

Francis listened again to the moon and his bottle and heard it clearer than ever. When you heard that music you didn't have to lay there no more. You could get right up off'n that old cot and walk over to the back window of the attic and watch Jake Becker lettin' his pigeons loose. They flew up and around the whole damn neighborhood, round and round, flew in a big circle and got themselves all worked up, and then old Jake, he'd give 'em the whistle and they'd come back to the cages. Damnedest thing.

'What can I make you for lunch?' Annie asked him.

'I ain't fussy. Turkey sandwich'd do me fine.'

'You want tea again?'

'I always want that tea,' said Francis.

He was careful not to sit by the window, where he could be seen when he watched the pigeons or when, at the other end of the attic, he looked out at the children playing football in the school athletic field.

'You'll be all right if they don't see you,' Annie said to him. She changed the sheets on the cot twice a week and made tan curtains for the windows and bought a pair of black drapes so he could close them at night and read the paper.

It was no longer necessary for him to read. His mind was devoid of ideas. If an idea entered, it would rest in the mind like the morning dew on an open field of stone. The morning sun would obliterate the dew and only its effect on the stone would remain. The stone needs no such effect.

The point was, would they ever know it was Francis who had broken that fellow's back with the bat? For the blow, indeed, had killed the murdering bastard. Were they looking for him? Were they pretending not to look for him? In his trunk he found his old warm-up sweater and he wore that with the collar turned up to shield his face. He also found George Quinn's overseas cap, which gave him a military air. He would have earned stripes, medals in the military. Regimentation always held great fascination for him. No one would ever think of looking for him wearing George's overseas cap. It was unlikely.

'Do you like Jell-O, Fran?' Annie asked him. 'I can't remember ever making Jell-O for you. I don't remember if they had Jell-O back then.'

If they were on to him, well that's all she wrote. Katie bar the door. Too wet to plow. He'd head where it was warm, where he would never again have to run from men or weather.

The empyrean, which is not spatial at all, does not move and has no poles. It girds, with light and love, the primum mobile, the utmost and swiftest of the material heavens. Angels are manifested in the primum mobile.

But if they weren't on to him, then he'd mention it to Annie someday (she already had the thought, he could tell that) about setting up the cot down in Danny's room, when things got to be absolutely right, and straight.

That room of Danny's had some space to it.

And it got the morning light too.

It was a mighty nice little room.

VERY OLD BONES

This book is dedicated to the Hard Core (they know who they are), and to certain revered and not-so-revered ancestors of the author (they don't know who they are, for they are dead; but they'd know if they ever got their hands on this book).

Any one who has common sense will remember that the bewilderments of the eyes are of two kinds, and arise from two causes, either from coming out of the light or from going into the light . . . and he who remembers this when he sees any one whose vision is perplexed and weak, will not be too ready to laugh; he will first ask whether that soul of man has come out of the brighter life, and is unable to see because unaccustomed to the dark, or having turned from darkness to the day is dazzled by excess of light.

– Plato
The Republic

Book One

1

It is Saturday, July twenty-sixth, 1958, the sun will rise in about twenty-five minutes, the air is still, and even the birds are not yet awake on Colonie Street. There is no traffic on North Pearl Street, half a block to the east, except for the occasional auto, police prowl car, or the Second Avenue bus marking its hourly trail. A moment ago fire sirens sounded on upper Arbor Hill, to the west, their wail carrying down on the silent air, interrupting the dreams of the two sleeping occupants of this house, Peter Phelan, a seventy-one-year-old artist, and his putative son, Orson Purcell, a thirty-four-year-old bastard.

'Orson,' Peter called out, 'where are those sirens?'

'Not around here,' I said.

'Good.'

He knew as well as I that the sirens weren't close. His hearing was excellent. But he was reassuring himself that in case of fire Orson was standing by; for I was now the organizer of his life (not his art; he was in full command of that), the putative son having become father to the putative father. His health was precarious, a serious heart condition that might take him out at any instant; and so he abdicated all responsibility for survival and gave himself utterly to his work. I could now hear him moving, sitting up on the side of the bed in his boxer shorts, reaching for the light and for his cane, shoving his feet into his slippers, readying himself to enter his studio and, by the first light of new morning, address his work-in-progress, a large painting he called *The Burial*.

I knew my sleep was at an end on this day, and as I brought myself into consciousness I recapitulated what I could remember of my vanishing dream: Peter in a gymnasium where a team of doctors had just operated on him and were off to the right conferring about the results, while the patient lay on the operating table, only half there. The operation had consisted of sawing parts off Peter, the several cuts made at the hip line (his arthritic hips were his enemy), as steaks are cut off a loin. These steaks lay in a pile at the end of Peter's table. He was in some pain and chattering to me in an unintelligible language. I reattached the most recent cut of steak to his lower extremity, and it fit perfectly in its former location. But when I let go of it it fell back atop its fellows. Peter did not seem to notice either my effort or its failure.

'Are you going to have coffee, Orson?' he called out from his room. In other words, are you going to make my breakfast?

'I am,' I said. 'Couple of minutes.' And I snapped on the light and sat up from the bed, naked, sweating in the grotesque heat of the morning. I put on a light robe and slippers and went down the front stairs and retrieved the morning *Times-Union* from the front porch. Eisenhower sending marines into Lebanon for mid-east crisis. Thunderstorms expected today. Rockefeller front runner for Republican nomination for Governor.

I put the paper on the dining-room table, filled the percolator, put out coffee cups and bread plates, and began plotting the day ahead, a day of significance to the family that had occupied this house since the last century. We would be gathering, the surviving Phelans and I, at the request of Peter, who was obeying a patriarchal whim that he hoped would redirect everybody's life. My principal unfinished task, apart from ridding the house of clutter, was to inveigle my cousin Billy to attend the gathering here, a place he loathed.

I first came here in 1934 for a funeral. Peter passed me off as the son of his landlady, Claire Purcell (which I was and am), whom he had never brought to this house even for tea, though he had been living with her then in Greenwich Village for more than fifteen years. I liked Albany, liked the relatives, especially my Aunt Molly, who became my nurse after I went crazy for the second time, and I liked Billy, who always tried to tell the truth about himself, a dangerous but admirable trait. I went to college in Albany before and after the war and came here for dinner now and again, slowly getting to know this ancestral place and its inhabitants: the Phelans and the McIlhennys, their loves, their work, their disasters.

I came to see how disaster does not always enter the house with thunder, high winds, and a splitting of the earth. Sometimes it burrows under the foundation and, like a field mouse on tiptoe, and at its own deliberate speed, gnaws away the entire substructure. One needs time to see this happening, of course, and eventually I had plenty of that.

Colonie Street in Arbor Hill was the neighborhood where these people had implanted their lives in the last century. The first Phelans arrived from Ireland in the 1820s to finish digging the Erie Canal and by mid-century were laborers, lumbermen, railroad men, and homemakers of modestly expanding means. The McIlhennys came in the late 1870s, poor as turkeys and twice as wild.

Michael Phelan inherited twenty-one thousand dollars upon the death of his father, a junior partner in a lumber mill, and in 1879 Michael built this house for his bride, Kathryn McIlhenny, creating what then seemed a landmark mansion (it was hardly that) on a nearly empty block: two parlors, a dining room, and seven bedrooms, those bedrooms an anticipatory act of notable faith and irony, for, after several years of marriage, Kathryn began behaving like an all-but-frigid woman. In spite of this, the pair filled the bedrooms with four sons and three daughters, the seven coming to represent, in my mind, Michael Phelan's warm-blooded perseverance in the embrace of ice.

The siblings were Peter and Molly; the long-absent Francis; the elder sister, Sarah; the dead sister, Julia; the failed priest, Chick; and the holy moron, Tommy. Peter had fled the house in the spring of 1913, vowing never to live here again. But the family insinuated itself back into his life after a death in the family, and he came home to care for the remnant kin, Molly and Tommy.

Peter's pencil sketches of his parents and siblings (but none of his putative son) populated the walls of the downstairs rooms in places Peter thought appropriate: Francis in his baseball uniform when he played for Washington, hanging beside the china closet, the scene of a major crisis in his life; Julia in her bathing costume, standing in the ankle-deep ocean at Atlantic City, where her mother took her to spend two months of the summer of 1909, hoping to hasten her recovery from rheumatic fever with sea air, this sketch hanging over the player piano; Sarah, without pince-nez, in high-necked white blouse, looking not pretty, for that wasn't possible for the willfully plain Sarah, but with an appealing benevolence that Peter saw in her, this sketch hanging on the east wall of the front parlor, close to the bric-a-brac Sarah had accumulated through the years, the only non-practical gifts the family ever gave her; for her horizon of pleasure in anything but the pragmatic was extremely limited. Molly hung in the back parlor also, with one foot on the running board of her new 1937 Dodge, looking very avant-garde for that year.

Peter sketched Chick at sixteen, in the black suit, Panama hat, and priestly collar he wore in the seminary, and hung the sketch in the front hallway, next to the autographed photo of Bishop T. M. A. Burke, former pastor of St Joseph's, whose sermon in 1900, on the fortieth anniversary of the church, inspired the fourteen-year-old Chick to devote his already pious life unreservedly to God. The parental sketches hung between the two windows of the dining room: Kathryn in the laundry of St Peter's Hospital on Broadway, which she worked in as a girl, then supervised for three years until the birth of Peter, after which she never worked; and Michael in his coveralls, at trackside with his gandy dancers, and with the same engine that killed him sitting benignly on the tracks behind him.

Only Tommy's sketch was upstairs (Peter did numerous self-portraits but hung none of them), hanging in his old room, which I occupied when I moved in to take care of Peter. Tommy is moon-faced and young and has already gone bald in the sketch, and his mouth is screwed rightward in a smile that makes him look both happy and brainless at the same time. Sarah was Tommy's caretaker, and though Tommy went to work every day as a sweeper in the North Albany (water) Filtration Plant, a major achievement in coherence for Tom, Sarah viewed it otherwise. She had a theme: 'Oh God let me outlive Tommy, for he can't survive alone.' But then she died and Tommy didn't, and Peter became his brother's keeper.

This was in the fall of 1954 and Peter was nearly destitute, a recurring condition; and so he welcomed a place to live rent-free. He moved up from Greenwich Village and settled back into the homestead. His old bedroom fronted on Colonie Street and, because its three bay windows offered the best light in the house, he turned it into his studio. He took down all the drapes, curtains, and dark green shades with which his mother and Sarah had kept out the light of the world for so long, and by so doing he let in not only the sunshine but also the nonplussed gazes of Arbor Hill rubbernecks who went out of their way to watch crazy old Peter Phelan, artist without a shirt, standing morning and afternoon with his expansive back to the open windows, forever dabbing paint onto his great canvases. Not like it used to be, the Phelan place.

When I moved into Tommy's room I swept out the cobwebs and dingbats, took off the old Tommy bedclothes, heavy with dust, and discovered the Tommy treasure under the bed: dozens of packages just as they'd been when he'd bought them at Whitney's and Myers' and other Downtown stores where he spent his wages. I opened one box and found white kid gloves, size four, petite, lovely, brand new in white tissue paper; opened another and found a beige slip with lace bodice; opened a third, a fourth, found pink panties, a pink brassiere.

'He gave them away to ladies,' Peter told me. 'He did that all his life until he ran out of ladies.'

Did you buy on spec, Tom, you old dog? Did you then walk the town till you found the hand, the bodice, the thighs that fit the garment?

– *Excuse me, ma'am, but I bought you a little gift.*

– *A gift, for me? Who are you? I don't know you.*

– *That's all right, ma'am, you don't have to know me.*

And you tip your cap and move on, leaving the woman holding the bra.

'The three Foley sisters up the street,' Peter said. 'They were his ladies before the war.' And I tried to imagine what they gave Tommy in return for his gifts. Did they model the garment? Give him a bit of stocking, a bit of white thigh? Could he have handled more? Whatever the Foley sights, they were not unfamiliar sights to many men in Arbor Hill, or so Peter said. But then one day Tommy's Tommy-love went unrequited by all Foleys – the sap bereft – and the gifts piled up under the bed.

I began to create this memoir five years ago among the pines and hemlocks of a summer hotel on the shore of Saratoga Lake, not knowing what its design would be. It began as a work of memory, passed through stages of fantasy, and emerged, I hope, as an act of the imagination. Freud wrote of imaginative artists that they could, through artistic illusion, produce emotional effects that seemed real, and so, he said, they could justly be compared to magicians.

Never mind art or justice, but I am a bit of a magician, having been exposed to the wisdom of the hand, the innocence of the eye, at an early age: when my mother was an assistant to Manfredo the Magnificent, a mediocre illusionist in the age of vaudeville. But I also learned magic by studying Peter Phelan, for, while Manfredo played tricks on the gullible, fantasy-ridden public, Peter pursued freedom from cheap illusion and untrustworthy instincts by trying for a lifetime to find magic in what was real in the world and in his heart, ultimately reaching a depth of the self that others rarely achieve. I tried this myself, went through my theatrical double break-downs in Germany and Manhattan in the process, and have now produced this cautionary tale of diseased self-contemplation – my own and others'.

I've often used my talent as a magician, that is as a card manipulator, to entertain, but only rarely for personal gain. The first time I did that I was finishing my bachelor's degree at Albany State after the war and found myself welcome at the tables of Fobie McManus's blackout poker game on Sheridan Avenue.

Fobie was a mean-spirited erstwhile burglar who ran a saloon that catered chiefly to newspaper people. He furnished them with drink and warmth until closing, then offered them the solace of dollar-limit poker until dawn. I was working weekends as a nightside rewrite man on the *Times-Union*, trying to pay my tuition. But the wages were puny and I would've quit if I hadn't discovered Fobie's game.

It was peopled with printers, reporters, and copy editors who fancied themselves gamesters of a high order. But there was only one minor-league thief (he hid cards) among them, a few anal retentives who nurtured their secret straights with confessional glee, and an assortment of barflies whose beer intake spurred them to ever greater mismanagement of their hands.

I was light-years beyond them all in handling both the deck and myself, for I had learned from Manfredo that a magician is also an actor; and so I considered my financial gain from those ink-stained wretches to be fair exchange for a thespian's risky performance. Some nights I chose to lose heavily at the outset, though good luck would usually stalk my later play. On occasions I might even drop thirty dollars on the night to prove my vulnerability, but by so doing was then free at the next sitting to fleece again those good- and well-tempered suckers. Thus did I move ever closer to my degree in education.

I interrupted my college career to enlist in the army in 1942, when I turned eighteen, gained a lieutenancy, and in '44 I landed at Normandy with replacement troops after the heroes and martyrs had taken the high ground as well as the beach. I was seldom in danger from then on but could not let go of the universal fantasy that death was a land mine ten steps ahead. I walked the wrong way to die, it turned out, and after the war I went back to Albany to finish my degree in three years instead of four. After graduation, instead of teaching, I found a job with the Manhattan publishing house where my father had worked as an illustrator.

Idiotically, I'd stayed in the reserve after the war, so when Korea erupted I turned into a retread. We started at Fort Benning, creating an infantry division from scratch. The Captain who had been assigned to establish the Public Information Office, the division's press section, liked my record: precocious scholar, sometime newsman, editor of books, working on a book of my own, and, on top of it all, a line officer in the big war. What can I say?

We went to Germany instead of Korea, the first troops to go back to Europe since the war, and we headquartered in the Drake *Kaserne*, a comfortable old Nazi Wehrmacht barracks outside Frankfurt, which brings me to Giselle, my somewhat excruciating wife, and the cause of my using my talent with cards for the second time in my life to enhance my net worth.

The enlisted men of our PIO section were throwing a Christmas party that year (it was 1951) and invited the Captain and me to stop by for a bit of wassail. I was already there when the Captain arrived with this remarkable beauty on his arm. They'd have a drink, then go to dinner; that was their plan. The men had hired a belly dancer named Eva to elevate the lust factor at the party and she was dancing when the Captain and Giselle arrived. The troops were yelling at Eva to remove garments, but she wouldn't even lower a strap. She did a few extra bumps, but that didn't cut the mustard with the boys, and half a dozen of them backed her into a corner. Because of who knows what reason, Giselle spoke up.

'Leave her alone,' she said. 'I'll take over.'

The Captain looked stricken as Giselle picked up a high stool from a corner and carried it to the center of the room. All eyes went to her as she sat on the stool with her hands in her lap, evaluating her audience. Then she undid the two top buttons of her blouse, revealing a contour – the quartering of a small moon. She lifted one leg, pointed her toe, her instep arched inside her elegant black pump, the heel of her other shoe hooked over the stool's bottom rung. One up, one down. The upward motion of her right leg moved her skirt a bit above the knee. She swept the room with her eyes, engaging everyone like a seductive angel: madonna of the high perch.

The swine who had been attacking Eva suddenly realized that Giselle's panorama seemed to be accessible. They didn't even notice Eva backing off to a corner, snatching up her coat, and running out the door.

The swine grunted when Giselle brought her right leg back and hooked her shoe on the highest rung, her skirt going higher still. Oh how they grunted, those swine. They were all in uniform, their Ike jackets swinging loose. They jostled each other to solidify their positions. They knew, as others jostled *them*, that their turf nearest Giselle had become valuable. They could have rented it out.

One of them leaped into a crouch, inches away from Giselle's knee, and he stared up the central boulevard of her shadow. But no one dared to touch her, for they intuited that vantage was all they would ever get, and the jostling grew stronger.

They moved in an ellipse, the ones with a clear view of the boulevard being the first to be shoved out of the vista.

Shoved out of the vista, imagine it.

Poor swine.

But they ran around the ellipse, got back into line, and shoved on. 'Keep it moving' was the unspoken motto, and on they shoved, those in the best position always trying to retain the turf. But they'd lose it to the needy, then circle back again.

Giselle started to sing, in French, 'Quand Madelon.'

'*Et chacun lui raconte une histoire, une histoire à sa façon . . .*' she sang.

Then she moved her blouse to the right and exposed more of that region. My impulse was to photograph her from a low angle, but when I told her this later she said she'd have considered it rape. She touched her breast lightly and I thought, 'Phantom queen as art object.'

'*La Madelon*,' Giselle sang, '*pour nous n'est pas sévère*.'

The swine kept moving round and round, like the old ploy of running from one end of the photo to the other in the days when the camera panned so slowly you could put yourself into the photo twice. I see those piggies still, moving in their everlasting ellipse – that piggy-go-round – shouldering one another, hunkering down as they moved to their left for a better view of that boulevard, lowering themselves, debasing all romance, groveling to Giselle's secrets with bend of knee and squint of eye.

I still can't blame them.

And what *did* the swine see? Quite amazing to talk about it afterward. One saw wildflowers – black-eyed Susans. Another said she wore a garment. Yet another no. A sergeant who'd been in the Fourth Armored during the war said he saw a landscape strewn with crosses and corpses, the reason why the war was fought.

And then she gave one final rising of the knee, stood up, and put herself back together. Slowly the troops started to applaud, and it grew and grew.

'More, more,' they called out, but Giselle only buttoned the last button, threw them a kiss, and returned to the Captain's side. The troops shook the Captain's hand, congratulated him on his taste in women, and when he went for their coats I asked Giselle her name but she wouldn't tell me. Then the Captain came and said, 'All right, Giselle, let's go.'

'Ah, Giselle,' I said.

It took me only a few days to track her to the office where she worked as a translator for diplomats and army bureaucrats.

'I've come to rescue you from old men,' I told her.

'I knew you would,' she said with a foxy smile.

But she resisted me, and professed fidelity to the Captain, who, though twice-and-a-half her age and going to fat, was flush with money from his black-market adventures in coffee and cigarettes.

'Can you take me to Paris for the weekend as he does?' she asked me. 'Can you fly me to the Riviera?'

'How direct the mercenary heart,' I said. 'I understand your point. I suspect we are much alike.'

But the truth was that I never valued money except when I had none. And Giselle's hedonist remarks were a façade to keep me at bay. You see she was already starting to love me.

Each day I sent her a yellow rose – yellow the color of age, cowardice, jaundice, jealousy, gold, and her own radiant hair. In a week the flowers softened her telephone voice, in two weeks she agreed to dinner, and in three to a Heidelberg weekend, which was the first stop on my road to dementia.

We stayed at a small pension and left it only for meals. Otherwise we inhabited the bed. She put all of her intimate arenas on display and let me do with them what I pleased, with a single exception: I could enter none of them with my principal entering device.

I had never been more excited by a woman's body, though I know the relative fraudulence of memory in such matters. Denial of entry was of small consequence to a man of my imagination, given the beatific pot of flesh to which I had access in every other way. Giselle said she was fearful of pregnancy, of disease, of sin, even of vice, can you imagine? But I know she was actually testing my capacity to tolerate her tantalizing. I've known exhibitionistic women, several, but none with the raw, artistic talent for exposure that Giselle demonstrated in Heidelberg. This was my initiation into the heavenly tortures of Giselle-love.

In the days that followed, she and I moved together in a delirium, I sick with love. When I was away from her I fell into what I came to think of as the coma of the quotidian, my imagination dead to everything except the vision of her face, her yellow hair, and the beige, angelical beauty of her sex, though that describes only the look of it, not the non-angelical uses to which she put it.

One understands addiction, obsession. It begins as the lunacy of whim, or desire, but ends as the madness of need, or essence. I could not be without her, and so all my waking movements were the orchestration of our next meeting.

I bought her gifts: Hummel dolls, a cuckoo clock, a Chanel suit, Italian shoes, cultured pearls (I could not afford diamonds). I bought her books. She'd never heard of Kafka, or Christopher Marlowe, or Philip Marlowe, for she was a visual animal, fascinated by art and photography, the twin provinces of her mother, who ran an art gallery in Paris.

I bought her a camera, took her to Versailles, Mont St. Michel, and other spectacles for the eye, took her to Omaha Beach and tried to explain to her some of the war and my puny part in it. She'd lived in Paris the entire war and saw no fighting, only occupation, during which her father had been executed by the Nazis. Her mother, a paragon of independence and survival, raised this very willful daughter.

There was much more, but, to get to the point, Giselle-love broke me. I ran through my paychecks and small savings account, and got a bit of money from my mother. But I soon went through it all, and it was out of the question to ask Peter for money. He never had any.

Then I remembered Walt Popp, captain of Special Services, mentioning a game of poker. That was a month after I met Giselle, the days when I had no time for any other game but her. Now I tracked down Popp at the officers' club and bought him a drink.

'I thought you were getting a poker game together,' I said.

'I did ask a few guys. Are you ready?'

'I could use a little action.'

'I thought you had this beauty, this cover-girl type.'

'Hanging out with you mugs, I'll appreciate her even more.'

'I'll round up a crowd for Friday night,' Popp said.

So I practiced. There'd never been a time I hadn't, really. Manfredo's wisdom was that once you lose your touch it will never come back with quite the same delicacy. Any talent must be husbanded or else we diminish in the breach; and so I spent two hours a week, maybe three, handling the cards, cutting them for aces, dealing seconds, bottoms, reading the deck when I shuffled. I practiced in bed, in the latrine, anytime I was alone. Almost nobody after Fobie's knew about me and cards. My magic was still in my hat.

Popp told the Captain there'd be a game and I'd be playing, and the Captain brought it up the next day in the office.

'Cards? You mean you aren't seeing Giselle any more?'

'Matter of fact I am,' I said.

'I don't see her any more.'

'Is that so?'

'You damn well know it's so.'

'I don't follow you around, Captain.'

'You follow Giselle around.'

'I wouldn't deny it.'

'She likes 'em young.'

'She's young.' She was twenty.

'I miss her,' he said.

'I'd miss her too.'

'You took her away from me.'

'That's not how it happens. People do what they want.'

'She liked me.'

'We all like you, Captain.'

'You do good work, Orson. It's a good *thing* you do good work.'

'I try not to disappoint.'

'That's smart. Never disappoint. What time is the game?'

'Seven o'clock.'

'I'll see you across the table,' he said.

It sounded like an invitation to a duel.

'Is the coffee ready, Orson?' my father called.

'It is,' I said. 'Come on down.'

I heard him shuffling toward the stairs in his slippers, and I remembered when as a child I shat in one of his slippers, a moment of my precocious psychosis. It is a thief's traditional trick to shit in the victim's lair, and I had been a thief of vision – of my father's and mother's private life. The occasion was an argument over love. Whose property was Claire Purcell? Was she owned body and soul by Peter, her live-in lover, or was she the intimate assistant to Manfredo the Magnificent?

I awoke in the middle of the night to find my father home after a two-week absence, heard his voice, moved toward it comprehending no words, closed on the parental bedroom to see my naked father standing over my supine, naked mother, and hear him say: 'Why don't you take your cunt back to Manfredo and have him give you another one?'

I, at the age of eight, had never heard the word 'cunt' uttered other than once in schoolboy talk: Why do they call it a cunt? . . . You ever see one? . . . Yeah . . . Well, then, what else would you call it? Nor did I understand the import of the phrase 'another one,' until time had passed and I had dwelled sufficiently on the overheard words to conclude that my father had been talking about me, the only *one* there was: Orson Purcell, son without siblings (living or dead) of Claire Purcell-never-Phelan. I was 'son,' 'sonny,' 'Orse,' and 'Orsy-Horsey' to Peter Phelan, the only father I'd ever known. But when I at last understood the meaning of his assault on my mother (I soon began to use the term 'father' in an ambiguous way, and eventually abandoned it), then it occurred to me that bastardy might be an enduring theme of my life. I grew angry at Peter for not (*if* not) being my father, grew angry also at Manfredo, who was unacceptable as a father.

This latter anger prevailed after I entered a dressing room of the Palace Theater in Albany, just after Manfredo had finished his act on stage. There sat Mother on the dressing-room vanity, naked legs akimbo. There stood Manfredo in top hat, tux jacket, and pants around ankles, thrusting his magic wand into her rabbit, and giving moon to all visitors who did not know they were not wanted, just as the magic couple did not realize that they had not locked the door until after the Orse was gone.

Orson the adventurer, Orson the thief of vision. I waited a week before making the assault on my father's slipper (I should have shat in Manfredo's hat) as an ultimate gesture of rebellion against his verbal cruelty. My mother rejected my act of solidarity with her, terming it loathsome, and my father, whose anger with Claire had abated, took off his belt and said, 'Now I'm going to whip you until you bleed,' and did. I then brooded myself into a dream of being attacked by crocodiles and, while pulling myself out of the water, of being consumed by the crocs up to the neck, my head floating away to live a disembodied life of its own.

That, more or less, is the truth of my head.

Peter finally reached the bottom of the stairs and shuffled toward the dining room.

'I never thought my bones would turn into my enemy,' he said with a great wheezing sound. 'Skeletons are not to be trusted.'

He sat at the dining-room table and I put the toast and butter on the table and poured his and my coffee.

'Are you going to go to work?' I asked him.

'I have no alternative.'

'You could take it easy. Take the day off. It's a special day, isn't it?'

'That's like cheating at solitaire. Who gets cheated?'

'Are you nearing the end of this painting?'

'There's distance to go, but there's even more to do after this one.'

'You always talk about dying but you don't behave like a dying man.'

'As soon as you behave like a dying man, you're dead.'

'You're a man with a mission.'

'A man with curiosity. I come from a long line of failed and sinful flesh, and there's a darkness in it I want to see.'

'Speaking of sin,' I said, 'isn't today the day that Adelaide comes to give you your therapy?'

'You have an abrasive tongue in your head this morning.'

'I just want to make sure I'm here to let her in.'

'You're a thoughtful boy, Orson.'

'I used to be a boy,' I said.

We looked at the window at the beginning of the day, a grudging gray light, no sunbeam to color it brilliant.

'They say it's going to rain,' I said.

'They always say that,' said Peter. 'And they're always right.'

2

Those who do the great heroic work of being human never work solely from experience. My father, for instance, could never have painted his *Malachi Suite*, that remarkable body of paintings and sketches that made him famous, without having projected himself into the lives of the people who had lived and died so absurdly, so tragically, in the days before and after his own birth. I am not implying here that *any* historical reconstruction is heroic, but rather that imaginative work of the first rank must come about through its creator's subordination of the self, and also from the absorption into that self of what has gone on beyond or before its own existence.

Clearly there is no way to absorb the history of even one other being wholly into oneself; but the continuity of the spirit relies on an imagination like my father's, which makes the long-dead world, with a fine suddenness, as Keats put it, fly back to us with its joys and its terrors and its wisdom. Keats invented the term 'negative capability' to define what he saw in the true poetical character: a quality of being that 'has no self – it is everything and nothing . . . it enjoys light and shade; it lives in gusto, be it foul or fair, high or low . . .' The poet should be able to throw his soul into any person, or object, that he confronts, and then speak out of that person, or object. 'When I am in a room with people,' wrote Keats, 'if I ever am free from speculating on creations of my own brain . . . the identity of every one in the room begins to press upon me [so] that I am in a very little time annihilated . . .'

I speak with some authority when I say that it is a major struggle for anyone to annihilate his or her own ego, to cure the disease of self-contemplation, for as you will see there is ample attention paid to myself in this memoir. But I believe it could not be otherwise, for only through what I was, and became, could the family be made visible, to me, to anyone. And so I invoke Keats, without any claim to art of my own, both to drain myself of myself, and to project myself into realms of the family where I have no credentials for being, but am there even so; for I do know the people in this memoir, know where and how they lived, or live still.

I know, for instance, what is going on in the Quinn house on North Pearl Street in North Albany this morning at a little past five o'clock. Two sleeping men are nearly naked, and three sleeping women are ritually modest in their shorty summer nightgowns. In each of three bedrooms a crucifix hangs on a nail over the sleepers' beds and, in a luminous print looking down at Peg and George Quinn in their double bed, the Christ exposes his sacred heart, that heart encircled by tongues of fire.

The house normally rouses itself from slumber at seven o'clock, except on Sunday, when late rising is the rule. As the milkman sets foot on the front stoop next door at this crepuscular hour, that house's resident chow disturbs all light sleepers here with his murderous bark from the back yard. Under the quietest of circumstances it is not easy to achieve sleep on this infernal morning, but after the chow's bark, George Quinn, vigorous still at seventy-one, raises himself on one elbow, rolls himself onto his wife's body, and then, with high comfort and the expertise that comes with practiced affection, he rides the lovely beast of love.

Dead heat was saturating the room, the sheet and pillowcases under the two bodies soaked from the long and humid night, no breeze at all coming in the fully opened window, no leaf moving on the trees of North Pearl Street; nor was any cross-ventilation possible, for the bedroom door was closed now in these moments of hot waking love, all nightclothes strewn on the floor beside the bed, the top sheet kicked away.

As they moved in their naked heat toward mutual climax the

door creaked open, its faint crack a thunderclap to both lovers. George knelt abruptly up from his wife's soft and sodden body, grabbed for his pajama bottoms as Peg felt for the lost topsheet to cover herself; and the door creaked again, the gap between its edge and its jamb widening, the hall light striping the room with a sliver of brilliance, then a board's width; and there, in the foot-wide opening, appeared Annie Phelan's face, ghostly inquisitor with flowing white hair, her face growing larger and more visible as she pushed the door open and stared into the bedroom of interrupted love.

'What is it, Mama?' Peg asked.

Behind the door George was stepping into his pajamas, and Peg, with the use of one deft arm, the other holding the found sheet in front of her breasts, was threading herself into her nightgown.

'What time is it, Margaret?' Annie asked.

'It's too early,' said Peg. 'Go back to bed.'

'We have to make the coffee and set the table.'

'Later, Mama. It isn't even five-thirty yet. Nobody's up except you.'

From his darkened bedroom Billy Phelan inquired: 'Is Ma all right?'

'She's all right,' Peg said. 'She's just off schedule again.'

Billy raised his head, flipped his pillow to put the wet side down, and tried to go back to sleep, thinking of how he used to work the window in Morty Pappas's horseroom, but no more.

Standing in the doorway of the third bedroom, where she and Annie Phelan slept in twin beds, Agnes Dempsey, wearing a pink knee-length nightgown, and yawning and scratching her head with both hands, said to Peg, 'I didn't hear her get up, she doesn't have her slippers on'; and then to Annie Phelan: 'What kind of an Irishman are you that you don't put your slippers on when you walk around the house?'

'Oh you shut up,' Annie said.

'Go in and get your slippers if you want to walk around.'

Annie went into the bedroom. 'The bitch,' she muttered. 'The bitch.'

'I heard you,' Agnes said.

'You did not,' said Annie.

'I could stay up and make the coffee,' Agnes said.

'No, it's too early,' said Peg. 'She'd stay up too, and then we'd never get her back on schedule.'

'You go to bed,' said Agnes. 'I'll keep her in the room. I'll put the chair in front of the door.'

George was already back in bed, eyes closed and trying for sleep as Peg lay on her back beside him and hoisted her nightgown to thigh level to let her legs breathe. Her interrupted climax would probably nag her at odd moments for the rest of the day, but she wouldn't dispel that now with her own touch. She wondered when the day of no more climaxes would arrive, wondered whether it would be her failure or George's. How long before George was as senile as Mama? When was Mama's last orgasm? When did she last feel Poppy's hand on her? Peg had no memory of anything sexual in Annie's life, never caught them at it the way Danny caught her and George up at the lake. We thought he was swimming for the afternoon, but in he came, George doing great, and me on the verge. He opens the door with the key and we both look at him. 'I didn't know you were sleeping,' he says, and out he goes, and that's that for that.

Peg charted the day to come: office till noon, the boss, and Basil, probably. Work will be light, all their attention on the strike vote in the shop this morning. I hope there's no fights. Then Roger. He wants to drive me down to Peter's luncheon. It'd be easy to go along with Roger. He has a way about him, and funny too. Smart and funny and so young. It's so silly. The important thing is to turn George around.

'Are you asleep, George?'

'Nobody can sleep in this stuff. It's like sleeping in pea soup.'

'We have to buy this house.'

'We do like hell.'

'Think about it, damn it all, *think about it!* Where could we *ever again* find this much space for that kind of money?'

'Who needs all this space? Danny's not home any more.'

'He comes home sometimes. And we still have Mama.'

'Yeah, and we also got Agnes. Jesus Christ.'

'She's a big help.'

'She's also another mouth.'

'If she wasn't here we'd have to pay *somebody* to watch Mama, unless *you* want to stay home and do it.'

'Why can't Billy take care of his own mother?'

'Billy can't do that sort of thing. And he wouldn't. The personal things, I mean.'

'You always got an answer,' George said.

'So do you. And the answer's always no.'

Peg pushed herself up from the bed, pulled off her nightgown, thrust herself into a cotton robe, and strode briskly to the bathroom, leaving the bedroom door ajar. The hall light would fall directly into George's eyes. Good. George stood up, walked to the door and closed it, sat back on the bed, and looked at his dim reflection in the dresser mirror.

'You're gonna die in the poorhouse of bullshit and other people's generosity,' he said to himself.

In her chair by the parlor window Annie Phelan monitored the passing of neighbors, sipping her first cup of tea of the day from the wheeled serving table, popping white grapes into her mouth, chewing them with great vigor, coming to an end of chewing, organizing her lips and tongue, and then spitting the grape seeds onto the oriental rug.

Billy, in the kitchen breakfast nook, was reading the baseball results (the Red Sox and the Albany Senators had both lost) in the morning *Times-Union*, his right leg stretched kitchenward, its plaster ankle cast covered by the leg of his navy-blue Palm Beach trousers, the toes of his shoeless foot covered by half a white sock, his hickory cane standing in the corner of the nook next to a paper bag containing his right shoe.

Agnes Dempsey, practical nurse and Billy's special friend, who'd been a now-and-then overnight guest for years, and who became a full-time live-in member of the household a year ago April, when

Annie's feebleness and vagueness were becoming a family problem, Agnes Dempsey at forty stood at the counter by the sink, breaking soft-boiled eggs into coffee cups with broken handles.

Peg, dressed perfectly, as usual, in high heels and blue flowered dress, stood at the gas stove pouring a cup of coffee, the only breakfast she would allow herself, except for one bite of Billy's toast, she in such a high-energized condition that we must intuit some private frenzy in her yet to be revealed.

Agnes brought Annie her breakfast before serving anyone else, stirred up the eggs with a teaspoon, topped them off with a touch of butter, salt, and pepper, then set them in front of Annie along with two pieces of toast. Annie looked at the eggs.

'They got bugs,' she said.

'What's got bugs?'

'Those things. Get the bugs off.'

'That's not bugs, Annie. That's pepper.'

Annie tried to shove the pepper to one side with a spoon.

'I don't eat bugs,' she said.

'That's a new one,' Agnes said when she set Billy's eggs in front of him on the oilcloth-covered table. 'She thinks pepper is bugs.'

'Then don't give her any pepper,' Billy said.

'Well, naturally,' said Agnes, and Peg saw a pout in Agnes's lips and knew it had more than pepper in it. They all ate in silence until Agnes said, 'I've got to get a room someplace.'

'You don't have to go noplace,' Billy said.

'Well, I do, and you know I do.'

'Let's not create a crisis,' Peg said.

'I'm not creating a crisis,' Agnes said. 'I'm saying I've got to get out of here. Father McDevitt said it, not me. But I've been thinking the same thing.'

'Then why didn't you ever say anything?' said Billy.

'Because I didn't know how to say it.'

'Well, you've said it now,' said Peg. 'Do you mean it, or is this just a little low-level blackmail?'

'What's that mean, blackmail?'

'Agnes,' said Peg, 'go on with your tale of woe.'

'I'm saying only what the Father said. That we can't go on living this way, because it doesn't look moral.'

'Very little in this life looks moral to me,' Peg said. 'When are you leaving?'

'She's not leaving,' Billy said. 'Who'll take care of Ma?'

'We can't let Ma interfere with Agnes's new moral look,' Peg said.

'You heard the Father,' Agnes said. '"How long have you been here, my dear?" "A little over a year, Father." I felt like I was in confession. "You did that? How many times did you do it, dear?" They always want the arithmetic.'

'I'm surprised the Vatican hasn't sent in a team of investigators to get to the bottom of this,' Peg said.

'Whataya talkin' about, *this*?' Billy said. 'There's nothin' goin' on.'

'Then you don't have anything to worry about,' said Peg.

'Worry? Why should I worry?'

'You shouldn't,' Peg said. 'You're clean.'

'Look, I know what you're gettin' at,' Billy said, 'and I'm not gettin' married, so change the subject.'

'Changed. When do you move out, Ag?'

'"We don't want to give scandal," the priest says. What does he think we do here?'

'He imagines what you do,' said Peg. 'It probably keeps him peppy. What else did he say?'

'He says we have to create the sacrament.'

'What sacrament?' Billy said.

'I don't think he meant baptism,' said Peg. 'Do you?'

'I don't know what's he mean sacrament,' Billy insisted.

'No more profane love in the afternoon, maybe? Make it sacred?'

'You'd better watch what you say,' Agnes said.

'You better organize this act you've got going here,' Peg said. 'And you too,' she said to Billy. 'I really don't give a rap what the priest says, or the bishop either. This is our house and we do what we like in it. But I think you ought to make a decision about your own lives for a change. I've got to get to work.' She bolted her coffee and stood up.

'I'll call about supper,' she told Agnes. 'I've got that luncheon with Peter and Orson. The lawyer's picking me up and I suppose the whole gang will be there. I want to go down early and help with the lunch.'

'We've got a roasting chicken and lamb chops,' Agnes said.

'Better be careful about lamb chops,' George Quinn said, coming through the swinging door into the kitchen. 'That's why Annie had her stroke. Always showin' off eatin' lamb-chop fat.'

'I'm going where there's no lamb chops,' Peg said. She gave George a quick kiss and went out.

The phone rang and George, the closest to it, answered: 'Hello there, who's calling this early? . . . Who? . . . Oh, yeah . . . Well, no, Peg's gone to work. Any message? . . . Yeah, Billy's right here,' and he handed Billy the phone with the words, 'It's Orson, that floo-doo.'

'What's the prospect, Orson?' Billy said into the phone.

'I need to get out of this goddamn house,' I said. 'What are you up to?'

'I gotta go to the doctor's.'

'When?'

'This morning.'

'I'll take you,' I said.

'What's your problem down there?' Billy asked.

'It's a big day today. I need to get out from under for a while.'

'So come have breakfast and we'll go down to Sport Schindler's for an eye-opener. I gotta meet a guy there owes me money.'

'Always a pleasant prospect,' I said. 'I'll see you in five minutes.'

'You can't get here sooner?'

George Quinn sprinkled a teaspoon of sugar on his eggs, his tie tied tight on his lightly starched collar on this day that was headed into the high nineties: sartorial propriety, impervious to weather.

'So how's the numbers business, George?' I asked as I sat across the breakfast table from him and Billy.

'It don't exist,' George said.

'What?'

'Where you been, Orson?' Billy said. 'George has been out of business for a year.'

'I thought that was temporary,' I said.

'A few of the big boys went to work by phone after it all closed down. But not me,' George said.

'I blame Dewey for starting it,' Billy said. 'That son of a bitch, what the hell's the town gonna do without numbers? Without Broadway.'

'Broadway? Broadway's not gone.'

'It ain't gone,' Billy said, 'but it ain't got no life to it. You can't get arrested on Broadway any more. Town is tough as Clancy's nuts. Even if you get a bet down you don't know the payoff. No phone line with the information any more. You gotta wait for tomorrow's newspaper. I blame Kefauver.'

'Forget I asked,' I said. 'Tell me about the house, George. Peg says you may buy this place after all these years.'

'Peg said that?'

'She said you might cash an insurance policy. Seven grand for this house sounds like the bargain of the century.'

'Not buyin',' George said.

'It's fifteen hundred down,' Billy said.

'Fifteen hundred down the bowl,' George said. 'Who's got money to buy houses when you're seventy-one years old? I'm not waitin' for my ship to come in. It's not comin' and I know it.'

'What're you gonna do, move?' I asked.

'Yeah. We'll find a place.'

'Probably not at this rent,' Billy said.

'Then we'll pay what it takes,' George said.

'Why not put that into owning the house?' I said. 'It'd make more sense.'

'I'm not buyin' a house!' George yelled, standing up from the table. 'Has everybody got that? No house. Period.'

'You ready to go, Orson?' Billy asked softly, reaching for his cane.

'I guess I'm ready. I haven't had any coffee but I guess I'm ready.'

'Let him have his coffee,' Agnes said.

'I don't know if I'll make it for dinner,' George said to Agnes. 'Depends on when the picnic ends.'

'Picnic? I thought it was a political meeting,' Agnes said.

'It's a political picnic.'

'What's not political in this town?' Billy said.

'Buyin' a house,' George said.

Agnes collected Annie's breakfast dishes and her untouched eggs and put them on the counter by the sink, gave Peg's African violets by the windowsill of the nook their weekly watering, then sat across from me to finish her second cup of coffee. As she sat, Billy rose up on his cane.

'I gotta do a wee-wee before we leave,' he said.

'Good,' I said. 'Time to worry is when you can't.'

'Stop that talk,' Agnes said.

I stared at her and decided she was a looker. Lucky Billy. Agnes had bottled blond hair, the color of which she changed whimsically, or maybe it was seasonally. She'd put on a few pounds since I'd last seen her, but she could handle them. She looked crisp and fresh in a red-and-white-check house dress with a box neck and two-inch straps over bare shoulders.

'I couldn't butt in on that conversation about the house,' Agnes said, 'but I'd be glad to give a hand with the down payment. I've got some dollars tucked away.'

'That's real nice, Agnes,' I said. 'Did you tell Peg?'

'Nobody yet. I'm just sayin' it now 'cause it occurred to me. But if Billy hears he'll think I'm proposin'.'

'Have you done that before?'

'Twenty times, how about. But he can't see himself married. He's been single too long.'

'Everybody's single till they marry.'

'Billy'd be single even *after* he got married, *if* he ever got married, which I don't think.'

'He loves you, though,' I said. 'Anybody can see that.'

'Sure. But what's he done for me lately?'

'Maybe you ought to go out together more often, be alone. I know you're in a lot with the family, taking care of Annie.'

'We go to the movies once a week, and dinner after. But you're right. We should. I also got another obligation, a patient. An old man I sit with one night a week. And another night I take piano.'

'How long you been taking?'

'Twenty-four years.'

'You must be good.'

'I'm terrible. Maybe I'll be good some day, but I don't practice enough.'

'It's hard without a piano.'

'Yeah. But I get a thrill playing the teacher's. I always do a half-hour alone, before and after the lesson. And once or twice a week I play in the church basement in the afternoons. It fills me up, excites me. You know how it is when you feel young and you know you still got a lot to learn, and it's gonna be good?'

'You're a graceful person, Agnes.'

'Yeah, well, George shouldn't be afraid of lettin' people do him a favor. That down payment's not a whole lot of money, really. But I heard him tell Peg, "They don't give loans to people like me."'

'What's he mean, "people like me"?'

'He doesn't know about credit,' Agnes said. 'He's got no credit anyplace. He paid cash all his life, even for cars. Doesn't wanna owe anybody a nickel. He thinks credit's bad news.'

'So's not having a place to live.'

'He said he'd live in a ditch before he bought a house.'

'He's batty.'

'Could be. Wouldn't be a first in this family.' She looked up at me. 'I didn't mean that personally,' she said.

Billy expected to have his cast removed but that didn't happen.

After Doc McDonald read the X-rays he decided the cast should stay in place another three weeks at least, and so Billy had to carry his right shoe around in a paper bag the rest of the day. We were in my car, Danny Quinn's old 1952 Chev that I'd bought from Peg. Billy mentioned an eye-opener at Sport Schindler's, but it was only ten-fifteen, and that's a little early for my eye.

'You been to the filtration plant since they started that dig?' I asked Billy.

'I ain't been there in years. My grandfather used to run that joint.'

'I know, and Tommy was the sweeper. You see in the paper about the bones they found?'

'Yeah, you think they're still there?'

'It's worth a look.'

The old plant, which had changed the health of Albany in 1899, was being torn down. The chronic 'Albany sore throat' of the nineteenth century had been attributed to inadequate filtering of Hudson River water. But after the North Albany plant opened, the sore throats faded. Still, river water was a periodic liability until the late 1920s, when the politicians dammed up two creeks in the Helderberg Mountains and solved all city water troubles forever. The filtration plant relaxed into a standby item, then a useless relic. Now it stood in the way of a superhighway's course and so it was time to knock it down.

Construction workers had found bones in their dig, near the mouth of the Staatskill, the creek that ran eastward from Albany's western plateau and had long ago been buried in a pipe under North Pearl Street and Broadway. When the dig reached the glacial ledge where the creek made its last leap into the Hudson River, half a dozen huge bones were found. Workers didn't inform the public until they also found two tusks, after which a geologist and biologist were summoned. No conclusions had been reported in the morning paper but everybody in town was saying elephants.

I drove down the hill from the doctor's office and into North Albany. When I reached Pearl Street Billy said 'Go down Main Street. I want to see what it looks like.'

Billy's grandfather Joe Farrell (they called him Iron Joe because two men broke their knuckles on his jaw) had lived at the bottom of Main Street, and also had run a saloon, The Wheelbarrow, next to his home. The house was gone but the saloon building still stood, a sign on it noting the headquarters of a truckers' union. Trucking companies had replaced the lumber yards as the commerce along Erie Boulevard, the filled-in bed of the old canal.

'I wouldn't know the place,' Billy said. 'I never get down here any more.' He'd been born and raised on Main Street.

'Lot of memories here for you,' I said.

'I knew how many trees grew in those lots over there. I knew how many steps it took to get from Broadway to the bottom of the hill. The lock house on the canal was right there.' And he pointed toward open space. 'Iron Joe carried me on his shoulder over the bridge to the other side of the lock.'

Implicit but unspoken in Billy's memory was that this was the street his father fled after dropping his infant son and causing his death. I was close to Billy, but I'd never heard him mention that. He and I are first cousins, sons of most peculiar brothers, I the unacknowledged bastard of Peter Phelan, Billy the abandoned son of Francis Phelan, both fathers flawed to the soul, both in their errant ways worth as much as most martyrs.

Billy was still looking at where his house had been when I turned onto the road that led to the filtration plant. It was busy with heavy equipment for the dig; also a police car was parked crossways in the road. A policeman got out of the car and raised his hand to stop us. Billy knew him, Doggie Murphy.

'Hey, Dog,' Billy said. 'We came to see the elephants.'

'Can't go through, Billy.'

'What's goin' on?'

'They found bones.'

'I know they found bones. I read the paper.'

'No, other bones. Human bones.'

'Oh yeah?'

'So nobody comes or goes till the coroner gets here.'

'Whose bones are they?'

'Somebody who don't need 'em any more,' Doggie said.

And so I swung the car around and headed for Sport Schindler's, where I would have my eye opened whether it needed it or not. Sport was pushing sixty, a retired boxer who had run this saloon for thirty-five years, keeping a continuity that dated to the last century. The place had a pressed-tin ceiling, a long mahogany bar with brass rail, shuffleboard, dart board, and years of venerable grime on the walls. Apart from the grime it was also unusually clean for a saloon, and a haven for the aging population of Broadway. A poster at one end of the bar showed two sixtyish, wrinkled, white-haired naked women, both seated with hands covering their laps, both wearing glasses, both with an enduring shapeliness and a splendid lack of sag. Centered over the back bar was the mounted head of a cow, shot in Lamb's lot by Winker Wilson, who thought it was a rabbit.

Billy had lived for years in the night world of Broadway, where Schindler's was a historic monument. But times were changing now with the press of urban renewal by squares and straights who had no use at all for Billy's vanishing turf. Also, the open horserooms of Albany had moved underground when the racing-information phone line was shut off by pressure from the Governor, and the only action available now was by personal phone call or handbook. Bookies, to avoid being past-posted, paid off only on the race results in tomorrow's newspaper. What the hell kind of a town is it when a man can't walk in off the street and bet a horse?

Sport Schindler's looked like an orthopedic ward when we settled in. Billy sat at the end of the bar, his right foot in his plaster cast partially covered by white sock and trouser cuff, his hickory cane dangling from the edge of the bar. Up the bar was a man whose complete right leg was in a cast elevated on another stool, a pair of crutches leaning against the bar beside him.

Billy earned his cast riding in a car whose windshield somebody hit with a rock, scaring hell out of the driver, who drove into a tree. Billy broke his ankle putting on the brakes in the back seat. 'You ain't safe noplace in this world,' Billy concluded.

The man with the crutches was Morty Pappas, a Greek bookie

who had been a casualty of the state-police crackdown on horserooms. Instead of booking on the sneak, Morty took his bankroll and flew to Reno with a stripper named Lulu, a dangerous decision, for Lulu was the most favored body of Buffalo Johnny Rizzo, the man who ran the only nightclub strip show in town. Morty came back to Albany six months after he left, flush with money from a streak of luck at the gaming tables, but minus Lulu and her body. Rizzo welcomed Morty back by shooting him in the leg, a bum shot, since he was aiming at Morty's crotch. Rizzo went to jail without bail, the shooting being his third felony charge in four years. But it had come out in the morning paper that by court order he was permitted bail; and so Buffalo Johnny was back in circulation.

Billy was offering Morty even money that the bones found up at the filtration plant were not elephant bones, Billy's argument based in his expressed belief that they never let elephants hang around Albany.

'Whataya mean they never let 'em hang around,' Morty said. 'Who's gonna tell an elephant he can't hang around?'

'You want the bet or don't you?' Billy asked.

'They found tusks with the bones.'

'That don't mean nothin',' Billy said.

'Who else got tusks outside of elephants?'

'Joey Doyle and his sister.'

'You're so sure gimme two to one,' said Morty.

'Six to five is all I go.'

'You're right and the newspaper's wrong, is that it?'

'What I'm sayin' is six to five.'

'You got a bet,' said Morty, and Billy looked at me and winked.

I couldn't figure out why Billy was so hot to bet against elephants, but neither could I bet against Billy, for I was his kinsman in more ways than one. Someone once remarked that Billy had lived a wastrel's useless life, which struck me as a point of view benightedly shrouded in uplift. I always found this world of Broadway to be the playground of that part of the soul that is impervious to any form of improvement not associated with chance, and relentlessly hostile to any conventional goad toward success and heaven. I remember years ago standing with Billy and Sport Schindler as a Fourth of July parade went past Sport's place on Broadway. A stranger beside us, seeing a Boy Scout troop stepping along, remarked, 'What a fine bunch of boys.' Sport took his cigar out of his mouth to offer his counterpoint: 'Another generation of stool pigeons,' he said.

That was years ago, and now here I was again with Sport and Billy and their friends, and those Scouts had grown up to become the lawyers, bankers, and politicians who had forced Sport to sell his saloon so they could level the block and transform it into somebody else's money. The Monte Carlo gaming rooms were gone, another victim of the crackdown: end of the wheel-and-birdcage era on Broadway; Louie's pool room was empty, only Louie's name left on the grimy windows; Red the barber had moved uptown and so you couldn't even get shaved on the street any more; couldn't buy a deck of cards either, Bill's Magic Shop having given way to a ladies' hat store. A ladies' hat store. Can you believe it, Billy?

Also Becker's Tavern had changed hands in the early fifties, and after that nobody paid any attention to the photographic mural behind the bar, mural of two hundred and two shirtsleeved men at a 1932 clambake. Nobody worried any more about pasting stars on the chests of those men after they died, the way old man Becker used to. One by one the stars had gone up on those chests through the years; then sometimes a star would fall and be carried off by the sweeper. Stars fell and fell, but they didn't rise any more, and so now the dead and the quick were a collage of uncertain fates. Hey, no star on his chest, but ain't he dead? Who knows? Who gives a goddamn? Put a star on him, why not? Put a star on Becker's.

One by one we move along and the club as we know it slowly dissolves, not to be reconstituted. 'Broadway never sleeps,' Sport always said, but now it did. It slept in the memories of people like him and Billy, men who wandered around the old turf as if it wasn't really old, as if a brand-new crap table might descend from the sky at any minute – and then, to the music of lightning bolt and thunder clap, the dice would roll again.

But no. No lightning. No thunder. No dice. Just the memory of time gone, and the vision of the vanishing space where the winners and losers, the grifters and suckers, had so vividly filled the air with yesterday's action.

'They want me to get married,' Billy said to me.

'Who does?'

'Peg. The priest. Agnes.'

'What's the priest say?'

'He says we're givin' scandal with Agnes livin' in. She's been with us a year maybe.'

'Then you're already married, basically.'

'Nah. She's got her own room. She's a roomer.'

'Ah, I get it,' I said.

'"Doesn't look moral," the priest says.'

'Well he's half right, if you worry about that sort of thing.'

'I don't worry. They worry.'

'What's Peg say?'

'Peg says she doesn't give a damn whether I marry the girl or not. But yeah, she wants it too. It'd get the priest off her back.'

'So get married, then,' I said. 'You like the girl?'

'She's great, but how the hell can I get married? I'm fifty-one years old and I don't have a nickel and don't know where to get one. I scrounge a little, deal now and then, but I haven't had steady work since Morty closed the horseroom. And the chiselin' bastard owes me back wages and two horse bets.'

'How much?'

'About a grand. Little less, maybe.'

'That's a lot.'

'He said he went dry, couldn't pay off, said he'd pay me later. But then he went off with Lulu and now he's runnin' a floatin' card game and he don't listen. I oughta cut his heart out, but it's even money he don't have one.'

Billy stopped talking, stopped looking me in the eye. Then, with his voice in a low register and on the verge of a tremolo, he said,

'You know, Orson, I never could hold a job. I never knew how to do nothin'. I couldn't even stay in the army. I got eye trouble and they sent me home after eight months. The horseroom was the longest steady job I ever had.'

'Something'll turn up,' I said.

'Yeah? Where? I could always get a buck around Broadway but now there ain't no Broadway.'

Yeah.

Put a star on Billy's Broadway.

I drank the beer Billy bought me, drank it in silent communion with his unexpected confession. Billy – who had been inhaling money for years in bowling alleys, pool rooms, and card games – was he unemployable? Was he really a man who 'never knew how to do nothin''? It's true Billy found straight jobs laughable, that he left as many as he was fired from, once even calling the foreman of a machine-shop paint gang a moron for presiding over such labor. Liberated by such words, Billy invariably wended his way back to the cocoon of Broadway, within whose bounds existed the only truly usable form of life; or so Billy liked to believe.

I was making a decision about telling him my own tribulations when the door opened and Buffalo Johnny Rizzo walked in, a fashion plate in blue seersucker suit and white Panama hat with a band that matched his suit. He stood in the doorway, hands in his coat pockets, looked us all over, opened his coat and took a pistol from his belt, then fired two shots at his most favored target: Morty Pappas's crotch, which was forked east toward Broadway, from whence Johnny was just arriving.

Billy saw it all happening and so did I, but Billy acted, lifting his cane from its dangle on bar's edge into a vivid upthrust and sending Johnny's pistol flying, but not before Johnny got off two shots. Morty fell from his bar stool with a crumpling plaster thud, his crotch intact but one bullet hitting his good leg, and the other lodging in the neck of the stuffed cow over the back bar, victim yet again of inept shooters.

Sport quickly retrieved the flown pistol and Johnny just as quickly moved toward the aging Sport to get it back and try again for Morty's gender. Billy and I both stepped between the two men, and Sport, still a formidable figure with the arms and fists of the light heavyweight he had once been, said only, 'Better get outa here, John.'

Buffalo Johnny, his failed plan sinking him into the throes of social wisdom, looked then at the fallen and bleeding Morty; and he smiled.

'Boom-boom, fucker,' he said. 'Boom-boom. Boom-boom.'

And then he went out onto Broadway.

Except for Billy and me, the customers at Sport's saloon exited with sudden purpose after Buffalo Johnny left the premises. Sport drew new beers for us as we gave aid and comfort to Morty Pappas in his hour of pain. Sport then called an ambulance and together Billy and I organized Morty on the floor, propping him with an overcoat someone had left on a hook during the winter. Sport made a pressure pack on the wound with a clean bar towel.

'So, ya bastard, ya saved my life,' Morty said to Billy between grimaces of agony.

'Yeah,' said Billy. 'I figure you're dead you'll never pay me what you owe me.'

'You oughta pay him,' Sport said, putting a new beer in Morty's grip.

'I'll pay him all right,' and Morty put down the beer and reached for his wallet, a hurtful move. 'What do I owe you?'

'You know what you owe me,' Billy said.

'Six hundred,' Morty said.

'That's wages. Plus the bets, three eighty, that's nine eighty.'

Morty fumbled with his wallet, took out his cash. 'Here. It's all I got with me,' he said. He yelped with new pain when he moved. Billy took the money, counted it.

'Count it,' said Morty.

'I'm countin'.'

'Four hundred, am I right?'

'Three sixty, three eighty, four.'

'That wacky bastard Rizzo,' Morty said. 'They'll lock him up now. Put him in a fucking dungeon.'

'If they find him,' said Sport.

'He's too stupid to hide out,' Morty said. 'Stupidest man I ever know. He ain't got the brains God gave a banana.'

'He knows somethin',' Sport said. 'He knows how to shoot you in the leg.'

'How was his broad?' Billy asked.

'She wasn't his broad.'

'He thought she was.'

'She was hot,' Morty said. 'Hot for everybody. Gimme his gun.'

'Whataya gonna do with it?' Sport asked.

'Give it to the cops.'

'I didn't call the cops,' Sport said.

'They'll turn up at the hospital.'

'Cops'll want witnesses,' Billy said. 'You got any?'

'You saw,' Morty said.

'Who, me?' Billy said.

'Who's your friend there?' Morty said, looking at me.

'I never saw him before,' Billy said.

'What's your name, bud?'

'Bud,' I said.

'All I can remember is my money,' Billy said.

'I was out in the kitchen when it happened,' Sport said.

'You bastards.'

'Pay the man, Morty,' Sport said.

'I got no more cash,' Morty said. 'You come to the game, Billy, I'll back you for what I owe you.' He turned to Sport. 'He comes to the game I'll back him for what I owe him.'

'You on the level?' asked Billy.

'Would I lie at a time like this?'

'You only lie when you move your lips. Where you playin'?'

'Tuesday eight o'clock, Win Castle's house.'

'Win Castle, the insurance guy?'

'He asked me to run a game for him. He likes to play but he needs players. You play pretty good.'

'You'll back me?' Billy asked.

'Up to what I owe you,' Morty said.

'Here's the ambulance,' Sport said.

After they packed Morty off to the hospital I told Billy, 'You get me into that card game and I'll make sure you get your money from Morty.' Then I explained my talent with cards to him, the first time I ever told anybody about it. Giselle knew I gambled but she didn't know there was no risk involved, that I could cut aces and deal anybody anything. I told Billy how I'd practiced for months in front of the mirror until I could no longer see myself dealing seconds, or bottom cards, and that now it was second nature. Billy was mesmerized. He never expected this out of me.

'They shoot guys they catch doin' that,' Billy said.

'They shoot guys anyway. Haven't you noticed?'

'You really good? You know I can spot cheaters.'

'Come over to the house I'll show you. I can't show you in public.'

When we got to Colonie Street Billy was vigorously aloof, refused to look at anything in the parlor in a way that would give the thing significance. He came here only when he was obliged to, and left as soon as possible. Now he let his gaze fall on the chandeliers, and sketches, and ancestor paintings, the framed old photos, dried flowers, the bric-a-brac on the mantel, the ancient furniture, the threadbare rugs, and the rest of the antique elegance, and it was all dead to him. He sat in the leather chair by the window where Peter always sat to watch the traffic on Colonie Street, took a sip of the beer I gave him, and then I told him, 'You look like your father.'

'They always told me that,' he said.

'I met him just once, in 1934, when your grandmother died. I have some old photos of him upstairs. He's in a baseball uniform, playing with Chattanooga in the Southern League.'

'He managed that team,' Billy said.

'I know. You want to see the pictures?'

'It don't matter,' Billy said. 'I know what he looked like.'

'He looks very young. My father did a sketch from one of them, a good sketch. In the dining room.'

'Never mind that stuff. Your father wouldn't let him in this joint when he came home in '34.'

'That's not how it was,' I said.

'Just get the cards,' said Billy, and I knew we'd come back to Francis before long. Billy was intimidated by the house, by the memories of his father's exile from it after his marriage to Annie Farrell, and by his inexact knowledge of Francis's peculiar visit here when Kathryn died. But here he was, on deck for the family luncheon with the lawyer that would take place in another hour or so. My father, when we organized this luncheon, thought it essential that Billy be present to hear whatever was going to be said, even if he didn't care about any of it.

The gathering had to do with money, but Peter was tight-lipped about specifics. He knew he was seriously ill and he was putting what was left of his life in order, the way I had put his *Malachi Suite* in order (with the Leica I'd given Giselle in Germany, and which she gave back to me when I undertook the job), numbering and photographing the hundreds of sketches, watercolors, and oils that my father was obsessively creating, and which had sprawled chaotically in all the upstairs rooms until I put everything into categories.

Peter did not consider the *Malachi Suite* finished, and I wasn't sure he ever would. Two days ago he had asked me to hang one of the oils over the dining-room table, the first time he'd exhibited any of the work anywhere in the house outside his studio. It was the painting he called *Banishing the Demons*, and it showed Malachi and his co-conspirator, Crip Devlin, shooing invisible demons out of Malachi's cottage, with five others, including a woman in bed, as terrorized witnesses. It is a mysterious and eerie painting, but Peter gave me no explanation of why he wanted it on the dining-room wall.

'Where's your old man now?' Billy asked me.

'Upstairs sleeping,' I said. 'He gets up at dawn, works till he drops, then goes back to bed.'

'Another screwball in the family.'

'Without a doubt. You gettin' hungry?'

'In a while.'

'We'll have lunch. Molly is bringing food, and Giselle's due in on the noon train. You never met Giselle, did you?'

'I heard about her. I seen that stuff she did about your father in a magazine.'

'She'll be here. So will Peg.'

'What's happening?'

'A get-together.'

'I'll get outa your hair,' Billy said.

'Not at all. You stick around. You should be here.'

'Who says I should?'

'I do.'

'You wanna show me your card tricks, is that it?'

'Right,' I said, and I found the cards in a cabinet and we went to the dining-room table, site of two notable crises in the life of Billy's father; and I wondered if Billy knew anything about the day Francis fell into the china closet. Billy took a long look at the sketch Peter had done of Francis and then we sat down with the cards. When I started to shuffle the deck I realized Billy was the only man I trusted totally in this life. After he confessed to me that he never knew how to do nothin', I felt bonded to him, and to his father, in a way that seemed new to me; and as I performed for him with the cards, I knew I was going to tell him about my nosedive in Germany. I dealt us both a hand of blackjack.

'Was that straight or seconds?' I asked him.

'Seconds?'

'Wrong.' And I turned up the cards to show him the ordinary cards I'd dealt. Then I dealt again, asked again.

'Straight,' he said.

'Wrong again,' and I showed him the ace and king I'd dealt myself.

'You're good,' he said. 'I can't see anything.'

'The best ones you never see.'

'Why you doin' this shit? You got a brain. You don't hafta cheat cards.'

'You're right, Billy,' I said. 'I don't have to cheat at cards. But it's a talent I acquired early, the way you learned how to play pool when you were in short pants. We tend to use our talents, don't we? We also tend to follow our demons. We'll do anything to gain a little power over life, since none of us know our limits until we're challenged – and that's when the strangeness begins.'

Billy just stared at me. He didn't know what I was getting at, but he'd understand. He was uneducated, but he was smart as hell.

'There I was,' I said, 'a little kid backstage, watching Manfredo organize his magic, putting birds in the hat, rabbits in the armpit, cards up both sleeves. He was a whiz, and I wanted to know his secrets. He'd shoo me away so he could be alone with my mother, but I'd insist on another trick, more know-how, and he'd always give in to get rid of me. By the time I was seven I was learning the key-and-lock trick, and by nine I could deal seconds and read the marked decks Manfredo used in his act. He even taught me how to palm cup-poker dice, control two out of five dice in your hand, but I never liked the game.

'Cards were my game and look where they led me. You knew I'd gotten into trouble in Germany, but you didn't know I was part of an international currency scam, did you?' Billy looked at me as if he'd never seen me before. I was rising in his esteem: more of a screwball than he thought.

'It all started with an army card game I played in,' I said, 'first to finance my love affair with Giselle, and then to support our marriage, all of which led me to conclude that there are no rules; that anything can develop out of anything, chaos out of conjugality, madness out of magic . . .'

3

I'll talk now about that game and its consequences, because that's where things started going down. My fellow players were the Captain, Walt Popp (we played at his apartment), Archie Bell, a warrant officer with the worst body odor I'd ever smelled, Herm Jelke, a nasty second-lieutenant runt with a Clark Gable mustache that made him look like a wax dummy, and my kid cousin, Dan Quinn, Peg and George's son, who had written about poker as a sports writer and for which reason the Captain, considering him an expert, invited him.

I'd gotten Quinn into our section after he'd finished basic training in a heavy-weapons company. He was a corporal, the only enlisted man in the poker game, and he played well and honestly and had a good time and lost. I didn't want him playing at all, but there he was.

I won money regularly for months, not a great deal, but enough to handle my scaled-down plan for keeping Giselle dazzled. She and I focused on the restaurants of Frankfurt, all of them within range of my military wages, even the Bruckenkeller and the outdoor café with violins at the Frankfurter Hof. We took day trips to Wiesbaden and Bad Nauheim for the baths and the Spielbanks, where we swam, bathed in steam, and spectated at the roulette and baccarat. We wandered the ruins of Frankfurt and took pictures of each other standing in the rubble of the opera house, or in somebody's exploded parlor, or on the altar of a church with no roof, or in Goethe's bedroom, or trying to find Schopenhauer's old digs in Sachenhausen. I recounted Schopenhauer's argument for Giselle: that the body is the objectification of the will. Tooth and penis, eye and vagina, were all created by the needs of the soul, no? Well, maybe. But Schopenhauer loathed women and called his white poodle Atma, the Soul of the World. I told Giselle she was the soul of my world, vividly isolating life for me: golden hair with violin, perfect knees crossed for wild arousal as taxi moves along Hauptwache. Phantom queen as art object. Clearly an existence such as hers was not happenstance. Clearly some arcane will had divined this glorious object in order to reflect what will demanded beauty must become. Schopenhauer had a point.

'I love the way you talk to me,' she said.

In these rapturous days she and I came to understand each other ever more intimately, finding where our intensities lurked, how soon boredom enveloped us, and why. Her goal, she said, was freedom, and she felt free with me.

'I think I want to be with you from now on,' she said.

I took kindly to this idea.

'Life traps you,' she said. 'It trapped my father when the Gestapo shot him for hiding two Jews. But they didn't kill him; they just shot him and left him there in the courtyard, and he became an invalid and made my mother his bedside prisoner for three years, until he finally died.'

'You don't want to be a prisoner,' I said.

'I think not.'

'Did you love your father?'

'Tremendously. But it was pitiful how my mother withered. My brothers took her gallery away from her in 1948. She had Picassos, Van Goghs, Mirós she'd kept hidden all during the war years and she wouldn't sell them. My brothers couldn't stand that money being there, inaccessible to them.'

'You didn't want the money?'

'I wanted my mother to keep everything, but they got the paintings away from her and sold them. And then she died too. A prisoner with no money.'

'But she loved your father.'

'I suppose she did.'

'Then she was a willing prisoner.'

'I couldn't say. She did her duty, as you military people say.'

I vowed not to become a prisoner. I vowed not to let Giselle become one. I vowed I would have money enough for us to live idyllic lives of love and freedom. I vowed to keep her with me now and tomorrow; always now, always tomorrow. That was my best-laid plan, and the reason I again became a poker player.

I preferred five players to six or seven, for I handled the cards more often. I told my fellow gamesters how great a player I was, how I knew cards. I told them how Nick the Greek, by the third card in a five-card-stud game, could call everybody's hole card, and that I was Nick's spiritual disciple. I intimidated them, and I became the one to beat. When I lost they were buoyant at the braggart's fall. That was my method, of course, putting their money where my mouth was.

I didn't mind keelhauling Popp, who could afford it, or Jelke, who was a schmuck, but I trod lightly with the Captain when I nailed him ('With all due respect for your rank and position, Captain, I must raise you thirty dollars'), for he was angry enough at me already and I didn't want to be sent down to a line company. I had to keep an eye on Quinn's earnestness, and watch over Archie too, but Arch was a sap gambler who didn't mind losing.

The game went on for months and slowly I built a bankroll to finance my addiction to Giselle's joys. We played for scrip, the dollar-equivalent currency the army had used since 1946, but sometimes players used German marks, at the legal rate of four marks to the dollar. The Captain often played with marks, for he was getting fat from his black-market deals. His sisters in Bridgeport sent him huge cartons of tea, coffee, cocoa, and cigarettes, and he'd sell it all to Germans at quadruple his investment. I'd done a bit of that too, but it smacked of grocery clerking, and so I concentrated on the game and sold my scrip winnings for the street price of five marks to the dollar, a modest profit, but the way to go as long as Giselle and I were cultivating rapture on the German economy.

And then Italy loomed, for I'd proposed to Giselle and told her we'd honeymoon in Venice. To do this right I needed dollars, not marks, and I mentioned during the game that because of stateside publicity on military black marketeering, the army was hovering over us all, their gumshoes noting who exchanged how many marks for how many dollars in excess of our monthly wages. I wondered out loud where to change marks for bucks outside army channels.

'I know somebody,' Archie said. 'Not a very savory character.'

'Who is he?' asked the Captain before I could ask.

Archie said his street name was Meister Geld, and that he could be reached through the Rhineland Bar, off Kaiserstrasse near the Hauptbahnhof, an arena of whores, beer halls, and black marketeers. But, said Arch, if you're in uniform they won't let you in. I was ready for that. The uniform was required everywhere in Germany but I'd picked up civilian clothes for traveling, and had also bought a cheap blue German suit, a chalk-stripe double-breasted with ridiculously wide lapels. I'd bought it one size too small so whenever I put it on I ceased looking American and could pass for a working-class German. The suit seemed just right for living anonymously, or hanging out in an off-limits bar, which is what the Rhineland was.

Six years after the surrender Germany remained treacherous, full of entropic hatred. Some of the hate eventually found outlets: packs of GIs breaking fascist heads during binges of vengeance; GIs found face down in the gutter with two broken arms, or floating in the river with a knife in the back, or a slit throat. Too many killings and maimings took place in or near the Rhineland, a watering hole for unreconstructed Nazis, so the MPs put it off limits. A weathered sign in English was tacked to the door of the club:

Dear Mr G.I. Sorry but you cannot come in.
Tonight is open only to club members.

The Manager

I went in and ordered a schnapps and sat across from a chesty, frizzy-haired woman I took to be a whore. She smiled at me and I smiled back and shook my head no. When the bartender brought my drink I asked him about Meister Geld and he said, '*Nicht verstehen.*' I repeated the question in French and invoked Archie Bell as my contact, but the barman still didn't get me. The woman came to my table and asked in French what I wanted and when I told her she said the barman didn't know anybody by that name but she did, and then in English asked, 'What you want with Meister Geld?'

'It has to do with money,' I told her.

She made a phone call and came back and said she would take me to him. I drank my schnapps and we went out. It was April in Frankfurt, a sunny day with a bit of a nip to it, and I made a mental note to buy a lighter-weight German suit for the summer.

'You speak bad French,' the woman said, taking my arm. 'Why not speak you English to the man?'

'I didn't want him to know I was American.'

'But you look like American, speak German like American, have American haircut. The man said polite, please leave, American.'

I shrugged and wondered was my disguise also transparent to the MPs? I walked with the young woman, who, erect, had a provocative shape and sprightly gait. The phrase 'abundantly frolicsome' occurred to me. I asked her how long she'd been a whore and she said she'd worked as a mechanic for the Luftwaffe during the war, now repaired auto engines, and only sometimes worked as a whore.

'Where are we going?' I asked her.

'It does not matter,' she said. 'He follow us where we go.'

'Who does?'

'Meister Geld. He always look to people before he meets. We go here,' and she pointed to a café with a window full of seven-layer chocolate cakes, cream tarts, glazed Apfelkuchen, and other ambrosial wonders. She said she loved sweet food and then ordered two kinds of chocolate cake. She was rosencheeked, a characteristic in many German women that I took to be seasonal, or perhaps dietetic. Her face, with very modest makeup, was a map of sensuality, her eyes wizened with what I construed to be sexual wisdom. Her tight sweater covered only unencumbered natural uplift. Was there a reason beyond money that she became a whore?

'Only money,' she said. 'For money I used to carry a piece of carpet so when I lay down in the ruins to fuck my boys I would not tear my clothes. I made much money but later I am unhappy that I will die in disgrace. Now I want to live only old and please self, so I eat sweet cake. I hungry now. In war days I only sometimes hungry, sometimes whore. Now I always hungry, always whore. Now I live to eat.'

I nodded and asked when Meister Geld was coming. She looked in my eye and said, 'I know you do not want me, but I always pay for cake.'

She opened her blouse and presented her naked breasts to my gaze. They were abundant and firm, underlined below by a long, jagged horizontal scar on her stomach. 'Gift from lover,' she said, touching the scar. She closed her blouse and stood up.

'I know nobody with name Meister Geld,' she said. 'It is silly name.' Then she left the café.

What was I to make of that? Conned out of two pieces of cake by a sugar whore? Was that all there was to it? I paid the check, and as I left the café, thinking about my next move, a black Mercedes pulled alongside me; and from the rear seat came a greeting.

'Good afternoon, Lieutenant. I have your tidings from Archie Bell,' this in very good English from a man in a dark blue leather coat, and a dark suit of color and cut not unlike the suit on my back. The man was corpulent, with the red beard of a Viking warrior. I judged him to be forty.

'Meister Geld?' I asked, and when he smiled and opened the car door I got in beside him.

In my hierarchy of personal demons at the time of the fall, Meister Geld holds a position of eminence. He had been wounded by the weather in December, 1941, on the day the Russians stopped Hitler at Stalingrad. Forty-two degrees below zero, and his left foot froze into the similitude of marble; a frozen foot as good as a bullet in the chest. He ran barefoot in the snow to gain circulation, then stole a felt shoe from a Russian soldier who lay dead in the street, needless of the shod life. He did not steal the Russian's right shoe but kept his own, a piece of cracked leather. His foot of marble recovered in the felt, but his right foot congealed and died inside the sodden leather. Also a hole in his glove cost him his right thumb.

The Meister told me all this when he saw me staring at that peculiar ersatz thumb: an unlikely length of glove-covered hard rubber, tied with a finger-threading thong. And, in the shoe where the front half of his foot used to be, a piece of toe-shaped wood. Why had the Meister not understood his thumb was freezing? Why had he not stolen the Russian's right shoe along with the left? Look to the minor devils of war for answers.

My simple task, to change two thousand marks for dollars, was achieved in the first moments of talking, the Meister excavating from a vast interior coat pocket a leather bag thick with banknotes, and giving me the going street rate of exchange.

'A formidable amount of marks, Lieutenant,' the Meister said. 'You have been saving your pfennigs.'

'Some belong to an associate of mine,' I said.

'Archie Bell?'

'No. Archie handles his own.'

'So you not only deal in money, you are also a courier for others. And out of uniform. You have the air of the adventurer about you, Lieutenant.'

The thought pleased me. I began to think of myself as Orson-at-large, Orson-on-the-town. Other than manipulating cards and a few black-market cigarette sales, I had done very little in life that could be construed as illegal. My moral stance on cards was that it was a survival tactic; also I gave back as much as I stole, although not always to the same citizens. I knew I was an adept, a figure of reasonable power in an unreasonable world, flush now with money, love awaiting at the other end of a taxi ride, Europe at my doorstep, needful only of a weekend or three-day pass to know the glories of civilized empire, including the empires of love, lust, beauty, and freedom (temporal for the moment, but longitude will develop; all things wait on the man who embraces the muse of freedom). And now, as I rode in the Mercedes with an underworld figure of notable dimension, I moved into a realm of possibility that included illegalities permissible to The Man Who Is, always stopping short of what might be considered serious criminality, of course. No need to venture *that* far into a new career.

Meister Geld took me to a small movie theater where we stood in the back and watched a scene from a German melodrama in black and white: A woman in a kitchen backs away from a threatening man and reaches for a knife. Close on the knife, as man of menace, undeterred, comes toward her. She thrusts. Close on knife entering his stomach. He crumples. She backs away, runs out of house. Close on man, dead. He opens eyes, removes knife from his stomach, no wound visible, rises, puts knife in sink, no blood visible on it, opens cabinet, takes down whiskey, pours self a drink, drinks, looks toward door, smiles.

The Meister grew bored and climbed the stairs to a second-floor office beside the windowed projection booth, the office similarly windowed to give access to the screen. The office was cluttered with German movie posters and photographs of naked women. The Meister hung his coat upon a hook, sat in his leather chair, and asked: 'Do you like to travel, Lieutenant? May I call you Orson?'

'Travel pleases me. Orson is my name.'

'One may make a great deal of money by traveling, especially if one is an American officer like yourself.'

'I'm in the mood for money,' I said.

'From the black market?'

'Everybody does it.'

'The army frowns on it.'

'But they do very little to discourage it, especially among officers. My partner in this deal is another officer.'

'I can't tell you how it pleases me to hear this,' said the Meister. 'I sense an alliance of substance.'

In agreeing to travel for the Meister, I perceived a change in my attitude toward myself and others. Clearly, I thought and acted faster and with more resolution than other men, knew what others would think before they thought it, knew, for instance, when I caught the Captain biting his nails, and he then guiltily hid his hands, that he was behaving like a recidivist thumbsucker, which is to say an autoeroticist. How swift the demon Orson – or is it Oreson-Whoreson? – faster by a whisker than old Freud devoid.

As he listened, the Meister unfolded the tale of his childhood in the war, early soldierhood in the Wehrmacht, surviving the bombings of Frankfurt, aiding in their aftermath (his half a foot then only a stump), putting out fires, carrying wounded to belowground shelters. The boy into man became the peddler who could get anybody anything at a price by the time he was twenty-three. He crossed into the British, French, and Russian zones during the early occupation years with great ease and casualness, owning papers of four nations, fluent in five tongues, and with a sixth sense for survival.

He stole an artificial leg from the hospital where he recuperated, sold the leg to an amputee for two hundred cigarettes, bartered the cigarettes for a live pig, traded the pig to a butcher who supplied the mayor of Darmstadt in exchange for the loan of a Leica and a roll of film, bided his time until he had secretly photographed an American lieutenant colonel in bed with three Fräuleins and a Doberman pinscher, blackmailed the colonel into lending him his automobile, drove to the officers' quarters and cleaned out another colonel's vast hoard of medicine, chocolate, uniforms, military insignia, and whiskey, imposed these gifts on a black marketeer known as the King of Mannheim, and earned himself the right to deal in currency for the King, which was his goal from the outset.

The Meister carried a pistol, which was visible in the crotch of his left arm, and as he dropped references to this killing, that murder attempt, I grew wary of getting thick with his mission, which I had yet to understand. But as he unraveled the operation, I again grew comfortable, because I would be dealing with *legitimate* life: buying money at banks, using legitimate dollars that I could easily have come by legally. I lost my fear and entered into the brilliance of a solvent future, one in which I would crown Giselle the queen of all fortune, and where we would reign as sovereigns of a post-military life in the *haut monde*.

The Meister's method was a complex cycle of money in motion. On the street he sold marks to Americans for scrip, turned the scrip into greenbacks through a network of American army associates (like myself) by legal means, buying money orders, for instance; then sent me and others to Switzerland with the greenbacks, where we bought German marks at considerably less than their value in the American sector of Germany. Back in Frankfurt we'd take our cut, and the Meister would then sell the marks for scrip at a profit, turn the scrip into greenbacks, and off we'd go again to Switzerland on our moneycycle.

The danger was minimal. Military personnel underwent baggage inspection at the American zone's exit points, but I had educated luggage and also the inspection of officers was usually perfunctory, for officers are honest – except the Captain, who was a grand thief in his heart, a petty thief in his skin. It was he who owned half the marks I first changed with the Meister, and it was he who saw dollar signs in his dreams after I told him of the Meister's scheme.

What can I say of international currency violation? Not much more than that it's the rape of the system. The Swiss have been fucking the rest of the world with their secret vaults for generations. What the Meister and I did was to join the game.

It would have taken me years to get rich on this arrangement, but I did finance my marriage and honeymoon, did fulfill the vision of Venice as altar and nuptial bed – Giselle and I afloat on the Grand Canal, stroked along in our gondola of desire, knowing that today is tomorrow, and tomorrow is forever, and that we will be in ecstasy, we will be rich and free, and we will manifest our own destiny forever; and not only will we never die, we will not even grow old. That's what I told Giselle the night before we returned to Germany and I was arrested by the Military Police.

* * *

They interrogated me for two days, then let me go but confined me to quarters, not as a total prisoner, but restricted to one room and the grounds at headquarters *Kaserne*, where the MPs were billeted. They escorted me to chow and kept checking to see that I hadn't gone off. Being a married officer, I'd had my own apartment in an army housing project close to the center of the city, but I could no longer live there.

They knew that two other officers were involved with the scam – my boss, the Captain, and Warrant Officer Archie Bell. They transferred Archie to Korea but sent the Captain to cushy London, which led me to believe that the Captain was the informer in the case. Vengeance is my estimate of his motive, since I took Giselle away from him. The police must have known he was dealing, confronted him, and he ratted. And there I was, an upstanding citizen, suddenly thrust among outcasts, thrown into an underworld role for which I had small talent and less stomach.

Right after they checked on me I dressed and left the *Kaserne*, walked past the guard at the gate and took his salute, then caught a taxi to my apartment, where I changed into my German suit. Giselle was at work and I decided not to leave her a note. I've always quested after mystery, and as I studied myself in the mirror I realized that the Orson of the past was gone forever. I took all the cash I had in the drawer, slicked my hair with Vaseline, put on the leather coat I'd bought in emulation of Meister Geld, and stepped out into the Teutonic darkness.

I went looking for the Meister, my first stop being his movie theater. The usher said he'd never heard of anybody named Meister Geld and I realized then that I didn't know the man's real name, or if he had one. The usher grew impatient and said if I wanted to go inside I'd have to buy a ticket, and I did.

A military hanging was in process in the film. A much-decorated warrior wearing his uniform and medals ascends to the gallows, and disdains the hood that covers a hanged man's death gasp. Hangman loops rope around his neck, man proudly strokes his medals, and hangman weeps as trapdoor springs. Close on face of hanged man: tongue out, eyes all but exploded. Hold on face as eyes return to normal, tongue recedes into mouth. View on military guards weeping as they look at hanging man. Close on hanged man, dead and smiling. His eyes suddenly open, his smile widens, and he laughs.

I went up the stairs toward the office by the projection booth. It was as I remembered, but empty: no movie posters, no naked women, no furniture, telephone, or rug. Meister the Magnificent had made himself disappear. The usher came in behind me, said I shouldn't be up here, and ushered me out into the night. I circled several blocks, looking for the Meister's car, my peregrinations bringing me eventually to the only other place where I knew to look for him, the Rhineland Bar. It was busy with a mix of men and women, whores and pimps, and I sought my main connection, the sugar whore, but without success. I wanted to see her again expose her scar, the validity of which I had begun to doubt. Was it pasted on? Tattooed? Drawn? Would it run during sex, or come off on your stomach? Would *you* then be scarred?

Sitting with a whore who was not as attractive as my sugar whore was a corporal from Seventh Army who had worked as a courier for the Meister. All I knew him by was Bosco, which may or may not have been his name. And when I had this thought I realized how very little I knew about any of my co-conspirators. I'd met Bosco in Switzerland, where the Meister had sent him with greenbacks – to deliver to me – for the purchase of German marks, the Meister reasoning that I was the more suave, more cosmopolitan figure to deal with bankers.

Bosco, now in civilian clothes, looked like a character out of the funny sheets of my childhood, Wash Tubbs. He was short with glasses and wiry black curls all over his head. I found him a mix of regular-army rube and bright, wily skuldugger. We'd had drinks on two occasions and talked of the Meister, about whom Bosco was mysterious but portentous. What I took home from him was that the Meister not only dabbled in the black market, the currency conduit, and the flesh exchange, but Bosco also hinted vaguely at the more exalted intrigue of politics. And that implied politics. Was the Meister an agent? A double agent? A provocateur? A hired political killer? I couldn't say. But that's how the imagination went.

I went over to Tubbs-Bosco and greeted him with a question: '*Zigarette, bitte?*' He smiled, proffered a Lucky Strike, and asked me to sit down beside his whore, whom I glanced at with a certain shock to the system, for she looked very like my Aunt Molly, one of the grand people of the universe. I squinted at her, disbelieving my eyes, and saw she looked not like Molly at all but really like Juliette Levinsky, a blond Jewess of great beauty who was the love of my life for a year or more, and yet this woman was not a blonde; and when I looked at her from another angle she resembled neither Molly nor Juliette. Clearly this face required further scrutiny.

'Have you seen the Meister?' I asked Bosco.

'Not since before the fall,' he said.

'Which fall is that?' I asked.

'Fall? Fall? What do you mean fall?' he asked.

'I mean fall. It's what *you* said. Whose fall? What fall are you talking about?'

'That's my question,' he said.

'The Meister,' I said. 'Where is he?'

'I wish I knew the answer to that,' Bosco said.

'When did you see him last?'

'Last week. We had a meal together. We both had *Heilbutt vom Rost, mit Toast.*'

'What do I care what you ate? Where is he? He's no longer at the theater.'

'He sold the theater,' Bosco said.

'*Heilbutt vom Rost* is my favorite German dish,' I said. 'I had it on Good Friday, with *Krauterbutter.*'

'The Captain threw you in, of course. You knew that.'

'I suppose I did,' I said.

'I'd have him killed, if I were you,' said Bosco.

'That's extreme,' I said. 'Not my way. I admit I considered it, however.'

'The Captain's in London,' Bosco said. 'Living it up at the

Strand and the Ritz, dining out at the Connaught and Brown's Hotel, shopping on Savile Row, screwing all the girls in Soho. And you call yourself a spy?'

'I never call myself a spy,' I said.

I looked at the whore. She looked like my third-grade teacher, who used to rub herself against the edge of the desk while lecturing us. A beautiful woman. A tall redhead with long blond hair. She was smitten with me. Followed my career all through grammar school. No one quite like her, the sweet little dolly.

'*Heilbutt vom Rost* I could go for right now,' I said.

'I can get it for you half price,' Bosco said.

'Where's Geld?' I asked.

'Geld is where you find him,' Bosco said. 'In the Russian zone by this time, I'd venture.'

'You always said he was a double agent.'

'No, I merely suggested that he was a provocateur-killer with a finger in every political honeycomb in Europe. Even his toenails are illegal. He's a great man. He's entitled to finger anything or anybody he pleases. You know who the greatest man in the world is?'

'Of course,' I said. 'Harry Truman. For dropping the bomb on Hiroshima. I never thought so many were undoable.'

'And the second-greatest man in the world?'

'The pilot who bombed Hiroshima. Think of the night sweats and headaches he's had to put up with ever since.'

'In my opinion,' Bosco said, 'there's only one war, with intermissions.'

'That's how it should be,' I said. 'Let me tell you the greatest bunch of men I ever came across. The glory brigades who landed at Normandy on D Day, pissy with fear, climbing that fucking cliff into the path of those fortified Nazi cocksuckers, soaked to the soul in blood, brine, sand, and shit, choking with putrescible courage and moving ahead into the goddamn vortex of exploding death. Who's got balls? Those guys had *cojones* big as combat boots. I arrived two weeks after Normandy, a goddamn latecomer, a slacker, a shitassed mewling little yellowbelly, and I got separated from my outfit for three days with no food or water and then I saw a Nazi, a fat fucking killer of women and children and newborn baby Jews, an asswipe shitface murdering swine of a fucking Nazi prick, and I got him in my sights and shot him through the nose. Then somebody shot at me. It was dusk. I couldn't see where the shot came from, but obviously he had a *Kamerad* on his flank, and so I went back into my cave, my earthworks, and laid low. Four days without food by this time, and we piss and moan when we miss a meal. I crawled as far into my earthworks as earth would allow and I heard someone up there walking around calling, "Here, doggie, come on, nice little doggie," all this with a kraut accent, of course, thinking I'd fall for the old dog-biscuit offer. He probably didn't even have a dog biscuit. Then it grew silent and I went dead out, probably slept two more days. It might've been a month. Who knows how long, or how well, or how deeply, or how significantly, or how richly, or how comfortably we sleep when we're fucking asleep? We're asleep, aren't we? So how the hell are we supposed to know how well, or how deeply, and so on? But to get to the point – are you with me?'

'Dogfood,' said Bosco.

'Good,' I said. 'So I came up from the earthworks, crawling out like some goddamn creature of the substructure, some toad of the underground river, some snake of the primeval slime, some cockroach from the cooling ooze of creation. I came up and looked out into the sky and saw it was fucking dawn or fucking twilight, what you will. Another fucking crepuscular moment, let's call it. And I said to myself, it's going to be all fucking right in half an hour. But *what* was going to be all right?'

'There's a question on the floor,' Bosco said.

'Exactly,' I said. 'What is it?'

'Crepuscularity,' he said.

'Of course. So I surveyed the scene as best I could and saw that the Nazi I'd shot through the nose was still there in the distance. I had a perfect vision of how he'd fallen, how his helmet went up on the right ear, how the blood coursed down his ex-nose into his mouth, et cetera. I listened for any telltale sign of that sly fucker with the goddamned dog biscuits and I stayed put but made demarcative notations in my brain of what lay between that Nazi son of a bitch and myself, what approximate distance I had to traverse, for I had already decided, with a form of self-defense made known to me by every cell in my body, that if I did not eat within several minutes I would die.

'I have no stomach for death, especially my own, and so I calculated the hectares, the rods, and the metrical leftovers between the Nazi and me, and I slithered on my belly like a lizard up from the putrid slush, the foul paste, the vomitous phlegm of a slop-jar swamp, and in time I reached my target, of whose freshness I was assured, unless I had been asleep for several days. I took his helmet off, cut off his head and let it roll, sliced his clothing, ripped him up the middle and cut a split steak off his stomach, turned him over and cut two chops off his buttocks, stuck him in the gizzard and ripped him sideways just so he'd remember me, slithered back to my cave with the steak and chops in his helmet, waited till dark, sealed up the cave so no fire would be seen, cut out a chimney for the smoke, then dined on filet of Nazi, chops on the Rhine, and lived to tell the tale.'

The whore looked me in the eye.

'You made steak and chops out of a German soldier?' she inquired.

'Where'd you ever get an idea like that?' I asked her.

'You just said it.'

'I wasn't talking to you. Whores should be fucked but not heard.'

She signaled to a man at the bar who was a perfect double of the hanged man in the film I'd just seen. Clearly there is a problem of identity here, I thought, as four of the men at the bar (one looking incredibly like the Captain) moved toward our booth and separated me from Bosco and the blond whore forever.

The hanged man came for me, while the other three converged on Bosco. We all went down as they stomped and punched us, then dragged us to our feet with the intention, I presume, of taking us elsewhere to cut our throats. But the hanged man could not resist punching me one more time while one of his fellows held me. Incredibly, I wrenched myself loose, though not in time to escape the punch, which sent me reeling backward toward the front door of the bar.

'You Nazi carbuncle,' I said to the hanged man, and the thought came to me then of how well I used the language, and that if I pursued the writing life seriously I might become as successful in one art form as my father had been in another. The sugar whore came into the bar as I was reeling toward the door and when she saw me falling she let me fall, then took me by the arm and raised me up. This interrupted my beating and I gathered my wits and kicked the hanged man in the vicinity of the scrotum, causing him what I'd estimate to be moderate pain. While two thugs dragged Bosco toward the back room, I grabbed the sugar whore by the hand, thinking how our visions, even in dreams, define us, how we are products of the unfathomable unknown, how, for instance, I knew that my sugar whore was not a whore at all but a transpositional figure – Joan of Arc, Kateri Tekakwitha, St Teresa of Avila – sent to ferry me out of danger; and, knowing this, I realized how superior I was to all in this barroom, how few people in the world could have such a beatific vision in this situation, and I pitied the crowd of them as I grabbed the whore by the wrist and ran with her out into the night streets of Frankfurt, where we would romp as lovers should, I, a prince of this darkness, about to embrace the saintly and virginal lark.

'Will they come after us?' I asked the whore.

'There is time and chance in all things,' she said.

When she said that, I could not resist putting my hand under her blouse to touch the scar I had seen, if it was a scar. I felt the ridges of it, let my fingers move upward between her mounds, touch her tips.

'Not here, not now, my darling,' she said, her voice a chorus of holy venereal rhapsodies.

We walked on dark streets, in time coming to the banks of the Main River. On an embankment where grass grew amid the rubble, a figure dressed as a bat knelt over a supine blond woman whom

I recognized as the librarian I unrequitedly loved for two years during adolescence. What retribution, I thought. How cruelly the Godhead dispenses justice. The librarian was bleeding from several orifices.

'Don't look,' my sugar whore said, and so I kissed her opulent mouth and put my hand under her skirt, stroking the naked thigh, the tender curve of her posterior puffs.

'Not here, not now, my darling,' she said.

I began to see the pattern: Bosco in the pay of the Meister, who was in the pay of Archie Bell of G-2, the main connection to army intelligence, Archie's cover blown by my arrest and so he is shipped to Korea to bide his time for subsequent return; and the Meister moves to the Russian zone, where he is at home, and will now be viewed as a fugitive from the very structure to which he still gives allegiance; though naturally he is a double-bladed allegiant, without pride, without pity, the pluperfect hypocrite with yet a third face toward any allegiance that offers him the solace of money, or pudenda. There he will sit, accumulating slaves in his icecap of Slavic disorder, a Pharaoh, a Buddha, a slavering three-headed Cerberus, lackey to the gluttonous, glutinous garbagemasters of east and west, the accumulators, the suppurating spawn of cold-war politics, putrid fiscality, and ravenous libido.

'Not here, not now, my darling,' said my sweet whore of this magical night as I raised her blouse for a bit of a suck.

We walked hand in hand toward the riverbank and both of us pointed to the same thing in the same instant. There, bobbing on the surface of the water, moving slowly with the current, came Bosco-Tubbs, minus his glasses, his head rotating as it bobbed, and for a moment I thought of leaping in and saving the man from drowning. But then, when he bobbed sideways, I perceived clearly that his head was connected to no body, only skull flesh, with livid neck fractions dangling free, and I knew it was pointless to effect a rescue. He was too far gone.

'Not here, not now, my darling,' said my honeypot, pushing my hand away from the concatenation of her thighs.

'May we go somewhere, then,' I asked, 'and spend a gentle hour together?'

'We can go where my pimp lives,' she said. 'Would you like that?'

'Is it far?' I asked.

'About ten miles,' she said.

'That's a long walk,' I said.

'We could take the *Strassenbahn.* You take the number four and then transfer to the number six, then take the yellow bus and transfer to the red bus, and there you are.'

'It would be easier if we drove,' I said, and with my Swiss knife I slit the canvas top of an old Mercedes convertible parked in front of us, hotwired it as a detective had taught me when I was covering the police beat, and away we went into the rosy-fingered dawn, moving out of fucking crepuscularity at last.

4

It was about an hour before dawn when I called Giselle to tell her I'd stolen a German policeman's car and was with a whore named Gisela at a place called Fritz's Garden of Eden. I said I'd fallen in love with the whore because her name was the German correlative of Giselle. I think this miffed Giselle, but she nevertheless got out of bed and dressed, and as she was going out the door she thought of her camera.

I'd given her that Leica thirty-five-millimeter with wide-angle lens, filters, light meter, the works, infecting her with light and shadow. She had moved well beyond the usual touristy snaps of me at the Köln Cathedral, or the Wurzburg Castle, and had come to think of the camera as her Gift of Eyes, the catalyst for her decision to seek out the images that lurk on the dark side of the soul. She was beginning to verify her life through the lens of her camera, while I, of a different order, was pursuing validation through hallucination, which some have thought to be demonic; and I suppose I have courted the demonic now and again.

I once told Giselle she was the essence of the esemplastic act, for as she was giving me the curl of her tongue at that moment, she would pause to speak love words to me in three languages. That spurred me to lecture her on unity, a Greek derivation. 'There is no shortage of unity but much of it is simulated,' I began. 'The one from the many is no more probable than many from the one. Only sea life propagates in solitude. But here, behold the esemplastic! . . . the unity of twain – I speaking, you comprehending, I delivering, you receiving, I the supplicant, you the benefactor, I me, you thee (I was within her at that moment), and yet we are loving in a way that is neither past, present, nor future, but only conditional: a time zone that is eternally renewable, in flux with mystery, always elusive, and may not even exist.'

She didn't know what I was talking about, but here I was, back in that elusive time zone at Fritz's Garden of Eden, melting with the heat of love and penance when she arrived. I was standing on what passed for a bar in this hovel of depravity, holding a glass of red wine, in shirtsleeves, delivering a singsong harangue to my audience, and biting myself on the right hand. Giselle wondered: Is he really biting himself?

'Jesus was the new Adam, and I report to you that I am the new Jesus,' I proclaimed, and then bit myself just below the right shoulder, and everybody laughed. A stain spread on my sleeve as I talked. Giselle thought it was a wine stain.

'Jesus descended into hell, and what did he find? He found my wonderful, lascivious mother, my saintly, incestuous father. He found all of you here, this carnival of panders and half-naked whores, scavenger cripples, easy killers, and poxy blind men. He found you burglars and dope fiends, you crutch thieves and condom salesmen, you paralytic beggars and syphilitic hags, all doomed and damned to this malignant pigmire for an eternity of endless and timeless sin.'

The audience hooted and whistled its approval of my sermon (Giselle took a photo of them) and I laughed wildly and bit myself on the palm of my left hand, then dripped blood from my thumb into my wineglass (Giselle took another photo, sending the carnival into a new eruption of applause). What she had thought to be wine was obviously my blood, and so she moved closer to where I could see her, and when she came into view I stopped my harangue. I snatched up my coat, jumped down from the bar, sucking my hand and balancing my wine, and I kissed Giselle on the mouth with my bloody lips. She backed off from me and raised her camera.

'I want you to see yourself as you are tonight,' she said to me, and I opened both palms outward to show her where I had invested myself with the stigmata of the new Jesus.

'We must leave,' I said to her. 'They all want to kill me for my coat and suit. And they'll kill both of us for your camera.'

'Where is your whore?' she asked me.

'She's working, over there,' I said, and I pointed to the table where my Gisela was fellating the handless wrist of a one-eyed beggar whose good hand was somewhere inside her blouse.

Giselle rapidly snapped photos of this, and of the entire mob, as the rabble eyed us and whispered. I broke my wineglass on the floor as we retreated, insuring that at least the barefoot and shoeless freaks would think twice before following us. We fled Fritz's Garden, leaped into the stolen Mercedes, and I then drove through the dark streets and woodlands of Frankfurt, zigzagging at wild speed, turning on two wheels (or so it felt) into a place that seemed to be a wall and certain death but was an alley, as I saw, though Giselle didn't, and she chose to scream.

'Let me out!' she yelled, and I slowed the car.

'Are you bored?' I asked.

'I find death boring. Why should I die because my husband wants to? I find it boring.'

'You certainly have style, Giselle, to think about death when we're out for a joy ride.'

I reached behind the driver's seat and found a small package, then deftly, with one hand, unwrapped it to reveal four bratwurst afloat in mustard, and I offered the mess to Giselle. She set it on her lap and I then found my bag of *Brötchen*, and while holding the steering wheel with my knee, I split *a Brötchen*, stuffed a bratwurst into its crevice, hot-dog style, and handed it to her.

'Is this today food?' she asked.

'As I recall.'

'How long since you bought this?'

'Time means nothing to me.'

'It means everything to bratwurst.'

'Trust me.'

'Are you in your right mind?'

'No, nor have I ever been. My life is a tissue of delirious memory.'

'What do you remember?'

'Peculiar things. The Captain's hypocritical face when we met at MP headquarters after my arrest. The smell of my father's whiskey-and-tobacco breath when I was twelve. The desire to raise a handlebar mustache like my father's. The spasms of bliss that always punctuate the onset of love with you. Why do you ask?'

'I was curious about your saintly incestuous father.'

'Did I speak of my saintly incestuous father?'

'You did.'

'I can't account for it. May I take off your clothing?'

'It remains to be seen.'

'I would stop the car, of course.'

'That would improve our chances of not dying a hideous death.'

I stopped the car and went for the back of her neck, running one hand under her hair and with the other seeking blouse buttons. She pushed me away and got out and I instantly broke into a fit of sobbing. The sobs choked me, my body twisted, my face fell into the bratwurst, and I made the noises a man makes when he knows that the sorrows of the world are his alone.

Giselle came round to my side of the car and opened my door, tugged me up and out. I stopped sobbing, rubbed the mustard off my face, and she and I walked together on strange streets, she silent, I smiling with what came to be known as my zombie joy. Giselle didn't know where to take me. I'd been a fugitive now for two days and she feared premature contact with the military. My wounds, though not serious to look at, were a problem; for she envisioned the Military Police ignoring them and throwing me into a cell where I'd molder in my zombie coma, oblivious to the venomous impact my own morbid bites might be having on my body.

'You bit yourself, Orson,' she said to me.

'Bit yourself,' I said.

'Our mouths are full of poison,' she said.

'Yes. Pyorrhea. Gingivitis.'

'What if you bit your own hand and infused the pyorrhea into your fingers?'

The thought gave me pause. I stopped walking and looked at my hand.

'Pestilential saliva,' I said.

'Exactly.'

'Bronchial methanes, colonic phosgenes. Can they become agents of involuntary suicide?'

'I think you're getting the idea,' she said.

The perception raised my spirits and Giselle decided to call Quinn, who would be getting ready for reveille, the sun now breaking through the final moments of the night. Quinn had access to a Jeep and had contacts with German newspapermen who would know where to get me treated. I liked Quinn and trusted him, which certainly proves something. I didn't know he'd been in love with Giselle since the night she performed on the high stool at the Christmas party. Quinn went to dinner with us now and again and I saw that Giselle found him appealingly innocent.

Quinn did know a doctor, an ex-medical officer in the Wehrmacht who had a small general practice in the suburb of Bonames. He treated my five bite wounds and then we went back to our apartment, where Giselle bathed me, washed the pomade out of my hair, and dressed me in my uniform so I would surrender as a soldier, not a madman. I was contrite at the surrender, but in a moment of messianic candor I told the officer of the day I had been to hell and back and was now prepared to redeem the world's sins, including his.

They put me in tight security and limited my visitors to Giselle and an army psychiatrist, Dr Tannen, who saw the condition I was in and transferred me to an army hospital. It became clear I was not fit to stand court martial.

'The man seems to have had a psychotic episode, but I would not say he's psychotic,' the doctor told Giselle in my presence, as if I didn't exist. 'He is living in the very real world of his second self, where there is always an answer to every riddle. He believes he is a bastard, an unwanted child. He was seriously neglected by mother and father, though he exudes love for them both. He is so insecure that he requires a façade to reduce his anxieties to manageable size; and so every waking moment is an exercise in mendacity, including self-delusion. He has found no career direction, and has completed nothing of significance to himself. He left the publishing world, rejects teaching and journalism, loathes the army, and rues the inertia that allowed him to be called back to active duty. He sees nothing worth doing, including completing the last contorted sentence of his unfinished book, which now ends on a high note of suspense with a comma. He is a man for whom money means nothing, but who has wrapped himself inside a cocoon of such hubris that he centers his life at the apex of the *haut monde*, as he calls it, a world for which there is no equivalent in reality, at least not without much more money than he possesses. Seated beside him at this apex is you, my dear, his goddess of the unattainable moon. He never quite believes you are really his wife, and so, when he reaches out to impose love upon you and you push him away, his moon explodes, and he drops into near catatonia, his so-called zombie condition.'

I nodded my agreement, which amused Giselle and also the doctor, who continued: 'To finance his life with you in the *haut monde*, he thrust himself into the petty criminality that now threatens his freedom. Further, after his arrest, and being simultaneously abandoned by his mentor in corruption, Meister Geld, a man about whom he knows almost nothing, he is once again the bereft bastard, without parent, without salvation. He is the unredeemable, loath-some, fear-ridden orphan of the storm, living in the shadow of an achieved father, crippled, he thinks, by the genes of unknown ancestors, and now with a future that holds only degradation, possibly of a lifelong order. And so he descended into a neurotic abyss, and resurrected from it in the guise of a blasphemous new Jesus, the only saviour available in this profane world he now inhabits. The army would be as mad as he is to put him on trial in this condition.'

The army, citing my illness and my sterling war record, moved me toward a medical discharge. Dr Tannen also announced that his tour of army duty was at an end, and that he was returning to private practice in Manhattan. This news plunged me into a new depression.

As I slowly came out of it, I was released from the hospital, and at the sunny lunch hour of the third day I told Giselle I wanted to go to the Künstler Klause to dance. It was the first time I'd expressed interest in doing anything since my collapse. The dismissal of the charges buoyed my spirit, but the impending loss of my therapist weighed on me. Giselle asked him if he would take me as a patient back in Manhattan, and he said of course. She then made the private decision to send me home alone.

Eva the belly dancer was one of the Künstler Klause's attractions, along with a magician and a four-piece band – trumpet, drums, violin, and accordion. The club was cheap glitz with a marine decor. Fishnets adorned with anchors, marlin, and mermaids formed the backdrop for the small stage and modest dance floor. The waiter lit the table candle when we sat down, and as we listened to the music I became intensely happy. The club's crowd was mostly Germans, with a few GIs. Quinn came in while the band played.

'I didn't know you were coming,' I said to him.

'I asked him,' Giselle said. 'I thought we'd celebrate your first night out.'

'That's a fine idea,' I said.

'I'd like some wine,' Quinn said to the waiter. 'Moselle.'

'Moselle all around,' I said and I took a fifty-mark note out of my pocket.

'Put your money away,' Quinn said.

Quinn looked very young. He had large even teeth and a handsome, crooked smile that gave him a knowing look.

'I saved the good news for our party,' Giselle said.

'What good news?' I asked.

'Quinn started it,' she said. 'He sent my photographs to *Paris Match* and they bought them. Isn't that something?'

'That's quite something,' I said. 'What photographs?'

'The photos of you at Fritz's Garden, you and all those freaks. The editors said they hadn't seen anything like this out of Germany since the early thirties. Isn't that remarkable?'

'Photos of me?' I said.

'No one could recognize you,' she said. 'You were biting yourself. *Paris Match* is using four pictures and they have an assignment for me in Berlin.'

I said nothing.

'I did very little,' Quinn said. 'I just put her in touch with the editors. The pictures sold themselves. Not only that, the magazine's art director knew Giselle's mother very well.'

'She knew everybody in art,' Giselle said.

'So Giselle comes by her talent naturally,' Quinn said.

'She's a natural, all right,' I said, and I heard that my voice had gone flat.

Eva the belly dancer came on, dancing close to the ringside tables so men could stuff money into her belt, which rode well below the belly.

'I remember her,' I said when I saw Eva. 'People insulted her at the Christmas party.' I took my fifty marks out of my pocket again and tucked it into Eva's belt, just under the navel.

'Orson,' Giselle said, grabbing the bill as Eva spun away from us, 'you can't afford to give money away.'

'We have to pay for insulting the girl.'

'I already paid,' Giselle said. 'Remember?'

'Ah,' I said.

'I remember,' said Quinn.

We didn't speak until Eva had finished her dance and the magician came on. He gave his patter in German and then did a few simple tricks with handkerchiefs and flowers. Boring. He lit a cigarette and made it disappear to his left, then picked it out of his right pocket, smoked it, threw it, lit, from hand to hand, and smoked it again.

'That's a fake cigarette,' I said. 'It's not lit. Watch what he does with it.'

The magician put the cigarette inside his shirt collar, against his neck.

'He gets rid of the real cigarette right away and holds its smoke in his mouth to use for the fake one,' I explained.

'You know all the tricks,' Giselle said.

The magician had relaxed me and I asked Giselle to dance. We danced well, like old times.

'I'm sorry I'm sick,' I said.

'You're not sick. Things just got to be too much.'

'I'll come out of it.'

'Dr. Tannen thinks he can help you. He said he'd continue treating you.'

'How? By mail?'

'You could go to New York.'

'*I* could.'

'Yes, you.'

'Not you?'

'One of us has to work. I've got another six months in my contract with the government. And now there's the photo assignment in Berlin, and I really want that.'

'So. You go your way, I'll go mine.'

'Wrong, wrong, wrong. I'll come to New York to stay in six months' time.'

I let my arm fall and walked back to the table and drank my wine. 'I have no place to live in New York,' I said.

'I called your father yesterday and again this morning. He has space in his apartment. He also called your old publisher and they'll give you free-lance editing work.'

That widened my smile. 'My father,' I said. 'My father, my father, my father. I could sleep on my father's couch anytime. I could sleep on his couch or I could sleep in his bathtub, in his sink. He'd give me his bed, two beds. Two beds and a couch. Three beds, two tubs, and six couches. Take your choice, boy, the sky's the limit, anything you want. Dad. My dad. Symbiotic, that's what we are. He's the symbi, I'm the otic, together we're a great team. It's just like this place, look around you. Ever see a more homey, more beautiful place? Look at those fishnets, listen to that music, straight from the angels, straight from the fish. And Eva, what a beauty. I thinks she wants to fuck me. Why don't we go back and tell her it's okay? She's such a sweetheart, nobody like her in Germany. Like my mother, a great dancer. Like my father, a great dancer. Dance is the thing, the ticket, the flow, the flood. Dance is manse and pants and ants in your prance. High kicking, watch those shanks and pasterns, folks, watch those hocks and fetlocks. Nothing like mothers and fathers dancing together, nothing like fucking beautiful women who love you and dance so well while they're doing it, wishing it, wishing will make it so, wish you were here, it is true if you think it is, true love, it's true, it's blue, it's you, it's moo moo *mulieribus in aeternitatem*, *ein Prosit*, *ein Prosit*, Herr Ober, more Moselle, more Moselle, more Moselle . . .'

And on I went until Giselle leaned over and kissed me with her Judas kiss. Then she and Quinn took me home. Dr Tannen came the next afternoon and the way to New York was arranged, the charges against me buried in the army's dead-case file, my troop ship awaiting. Quinn and Giselle took the train with me to Bremerhaven and we had a fine time while I said my farewells to Germany. We ate in the first-class dining car, ordered champagne to toast our reunion in six months, and the beginning of our new lives. I put Quinn in charge of Giselle, told him to report anyone who tried to move in on her while I was away. Quinn and I shook hands on it. On the way back to Frankfurt I have no doubt that Quinn, being in charge of Giselle, bought a first-class sleeper for their trip.

Book Two

1

When Kathryn Phelan died in her sleep of oblivion on December 9, 1934, her son and my father, Peter, after twenty-one years of part-time exile from his mother's influence, was at the brink of the success to which his exile had led him. The Greenwich Village gallery that had paid him seventy-five dollars for every painting he created during his first two years in New York, and which doubled that amount after he returned from the Great War, decided that the time for Peter's elevation into the stratosphere of artistic repute and solvency was at hand, and so its owners gave over all their wall space to an exclusive showing of his work. Peter's mother would neither know, nor, if she had known, care, whether Peter ever lifted a paintbrush. But her death, and his one-man show, were benchmarks of liberation for this son and erstwhile artist manqué.

Peter moved to the Village in 1913 after a fight with Kathryn and his sister Sarah over the Daugherty family. Until 1912 the Daughertys had lived in the house next door to the Phelan homestead on Colonie Street; but that year the Daugherty house burned and its only occupant of the moment, Katrina Daugherty, died on the sidewalk in her husband's arms, victim of smoke, anguish, and a prolonged marital emptiness.

One year later, on the anniversary of Katrina's death, her husband, Edward, an established playwright, would celebrate her by staging the play in which their idyllic marriage and blatant infidelities were dissected. This play, *The Flaming Corsage*, would run for two nights on the stage of Albany's premier theater, Harmanus Bleecker Hall, and would be assaulted unto death by critics, and by civil and ecclesiastical authorities, as a menace to the purity of the community. During this fated year the playwright would thus not only lose his wife, and see his lifetime accumulation of papers and unpublished plays incinerated, but would also find his career halted, and his voice silenced at the peak of its eloquence.

Edward Daugherty would recover from this assault, but my father would not, quite. Exposed for a decade and a half to the chorale of vitriol directed against Edward and Katrina Daugherty by his mother and sister – 'a family of filth . . . an evil man . . . a low woman . . . a vile slut . . . a corrupter of innocents' – Peter at long last counterattacked, defending Katrina, whom he had coveted as long as he could remember, as a splendid woman, whatever her peccadilloes, and the exemplary mother of his closest friend, Martin Daugherty; also defending Edward as a genuine artist and the only real writer Albany had produced in the new century, this latter defense being as much an expression of the passion for art that lay within Peter's own heart as it was empathy for a friend. Peter stood up from the dining-room table, which gave a view onto the ashes and embers of the Daugherty house, and told his sister she would shrivel from the vinegar in her veins, told his mother she was a wicked-tongued bigot whose poisoned thought came up from the cellars of hell, and told both that he would listen to them not a minute longer.

He climbed the stairs to his bedroom, pulled his steamer trunk out from the attic crawlspace, packed it (as he had planned to do five years earlier, when a similar impulse to escape was on him), filled it with art implements, shirts, socks, and umbrage, hoisted the trunk onto his shoulder, and then in the midst of a rainstorm that would not only drench him to his underwear and the brink of pneumonia, but would precipitate the worst flood in Albany's modern history, walked twelve blocks to Keeler's Hotel for Men Only, at Maiden Lane and Broadway, and there slept his first night of freedom from the matriarchal whipsong.

The next morning his brother Francis, with his son, Billy, came for Peter in a rowboat, and they rowed up the two-foot-deep river that Broadway had become, to Union Station, where Peter boarded the New York train. By prearrangement he settled in at the apartment of Edward Daugherty on MacDougal Street in Greenwich Village, those quarters not used by Edward during the year that he had stayed in Albany to stage his play, and now the temporary home of Edward's son, Martin. It was Martin who had convinced Peter that his future lay here among the artists, writers, political rebels, free-thinkers, unshockable women, and assorted social misfits and fugitives who were amorphously shaping Manhattan's new bohemian order.

Peter found work illustrating reprints of children's editions of James Fenimore Cooper, Jack London, and Mark Twain novels, and used a corner of the Daugherty kitchen to set up his easel to begin anew the work of his life. But it would be a year before he was able to think of himself as a genuine member of the bohemian brigade; for he was incapable of fully representing himself, even to himself, as an artist, that word too imperious for his provincially crippled soul. And so he ate, drank, and worshipped with the Village's Irish working class, into whose midst the bohemians were relentlessly intruding.

These Irish, who looked so very like his neighbors on Arbor Hill in Albany, but were so very unlike them in speech, formed the core of subjects for Peter's early paintings. He sketched people, if they'd let him, then grew brassy enough to carry his sketch pad to the saloon or the park and sketched what he saw, whether the subjects liked it or not. From hundreds of sketches his imagination would let one, then another, single themselves out for delineation in oil, his theme always being: this is evidence that yesterday did exist; this is what yesterday looked like.

One early choice was the face of Claire Purcell, a nineteen-year-old beauty from Brooklyn with a cascade of dark red hair, brown eyes, and milk-white skin, who resembled he knew not whom, but someone; and her curiosity about his sketch of her feeding pigeons in Washington Square on a spring morning in 1914 began the relationship that would dominate both their lives and lead to the erratic romance that would be interrupted first by the Great War (Peter enlisted in 1917, became a wagoner with the 304th Ammunition Train, ferried shells and bullets to troops in the Argonne, was hit at St-Mihiel by shrapnel which dislodged his helmet, ripped his gas mask in two, and knocked him into a shell hole from which he was eventually carried to the hospital and evacuated back to New York, the episode earning him a disability pension, two medals, and frontal semi-baldness from the gas), and interrupted the second time by my birth out of wedlock in 1924. Claire gave me her own name, Purcell, first name Orson, for Peter would neither marry her nor allow his own name to be given to me, uncertain as he was of the source of my conception.

The man Peter suspected of siring me was Rico Luca, a vaudeville magician known to audiences as Manfredo the Magnificent, who had hired Claire to be his assistant (known to audiences as The Beautiful Belinda) in 1923, two years after Peter moved into the boarding house on Waverly Place run by Claire's widowed mother. Peter and Claire pursued their romance in separate bedrooms until Claire's mother died and they then moved in together, marriage always a subject only for future discussion; for would not marriage negate the freedom that Peter had come to the city to find?

A decade of life amid the pagan romps of *la vie bohème* had conditioned him to think of fidelity as an abstraction out of his past, and yet he practiced it, and expected it from Claire without ever speaking of it. Then, when travel to the vaudeville houses of the eastern seaboard became part of Claire's life as well as the means of support for the boarding house that no longer accepted boarders, and whose upkeep and mortgage were beyond Peter's income, Peter entered into fits of jealousy. He was certain that a woman as comely as Claire, whose body clad in tights was a cause for whistles and hoots from any audience, would be unable to fend off forever the advances of the handsome Manfredo and the stage-door lotharios Peter imagined waiting for her at every whistle stop.

When she announced her pregnancy, Peter broke silence on fidelity and suggested Manfredo as just as likely a parent as himself. Claire first wept at the accusation, then grew furious when Peter persisted, and at last retreated into silence and a separate bedroom; and so the subject was tabled. Jealousy only fattened Peter's passion for Claire, and after some days she acceded to it. In this way they continued their lives until my birth, the cloud of bastardy always hovering even after I grew to resemble childhood tintypes of Peter (and even of his brother Francis), and even though Martin Daugherty insisted Peter had no worries, for clearly I had been made in the Phelan image. Without legal or moral ties, without faith in itself, this anomalous, double-named family persisted, jealousy, wounded love, and fear of error (in Peter) being the bonding elements of a tie that would not break.

Kathryn Phelan died in her sleep, presumably of a stroke, this, her second shock, coming on opening-night-minus-two of Peter's one-man show. For the next several days The Beautiful Belinda would be prancing on the boards somewhere in Boston, and therefore it was decided that I should stay in New York rather than travel with my mother, artistic revelation being more valuable to my young life than backstage privilege. But then arose Peter's dilemma: since the one-man show and its opening could not be canceled on behalf of a corpse, so long-standing had its planning been, would the artist, then, present himself among his works and bask in whatever glory accrues to such presence, or would he return to Colonie Street to bask in the cold exudation of a dead mother?

Several months after his breach with Kathryn and Sarah in 1913, Peter had returned to the house for fortnightly overnight visits, and also contributed to the support of the family with pittances that increased as his ability to sell paintings improved. The healing of the breach with the family had come so soon after the separation that Peter perceived that rancor was never the cause of the break, but merely the ruse by which he had gained momentum to pursue his art; and in perceiving this he understood that, even in aspiration, art is a way of gaining some measure of control over life.

And so, really, the dilemma's solution was foregone; for kinship maintained the major share of control over Peter's life, and his art, in the end, could only bear witness to this. He would go home.

2

Because of the pre-sale of two of his paintings Peter left Manhattan with four hundred dollars in his pocket, the most money he had ever held in his hand. The dawning of this realization spurred him to show the money to me when we settled into our seats on the Lake Shore Limited out of Grand Central Station.

'Four hundred dollars there, boy,' he said. 'Feast your eyes. The sky's the limit on this trip.'

I took the money into my own hand, counted it (fifties and twenties), tapped it on my knee to even its edges as I would a pack of cards, folded it, felt its thickness and heft.

'It's nice,' I said. 'What are you going to buy with it?'

'I'm going to buy the light of the world and bring it home,' Peter said.

'Where's the light of the world?' I asked.

'I'm not sure,' Peter said, 'we'll have to go shopping.'

I smelled the money, then gave it back to Peter, and we watched the streets of New York whiz by our window.

Peter had small alternative to bringing me with him to the wake, for my mother would be away through the weekend, and there was no one to leave me with (I was ten) except an untrustworthy neighbor. And though the poison thought of bastardy never stopped giving pain to Peter's gizzard, he was also coming to the conclusion that he really might, after all, be my father; and what sort of father would that be if he kept me apart from the blood kin I had never met, especially if he allowed me to miss out on the ultimate silencing of the whipsong?

And so he had packed my bag, and we rode in a taxi from the Village to Grand Central Station, my first taxi, and walked across the heavenly vaulted concourse of the station with its luminous artificial sky that bathed me in awe and wonder. We rode the train north out of the city and along the banks of the great Hudson, monitored the grandness of its waters and natural wonders, and emerged into another vast and dwarfing room, Albany's Union Station, this entire experience creating in my mind a vision of the American way that I would carry throughout my life: capitalism as a room full of rivers and mountains through which you rode in great comfort in the vehicle of your choice, your pockets bulging with money: an acute form of happiness.

Peter, holding me by the hand, walked out of the station and with evident purpose strode two blocks down Broadway from Union Station to the Van Heusen, Charles store (next door to where Keeler's Hotel for Men Only had been until it burned in 1919), the store a source of elegance and social amenity for many years, the place you went when you didn't know the difference between a butter knife and a fish knife (and you had better learn if you wanted your marriage to remain socially solvent), and where Peter suspected he would find the light he meant to bring home to Colonie Street.

He found the familiar face of Rance Redmond, who had been selling silver and china and vases and linens in this store for thirty years, and Peter told him precisely what he wanted: three chandeliers of similar, non-matching styles, plus sufficient wiring to bring power to them from the street; and an electrician to install them.

Rance Redmond, his pince-nez spectacles pressed into use to guide Peter's glance aloft to the broad display of suspended chandeliers, ceiling fixtures, and wall sconces, pointed out the new designs: chrome and milky glass globes of the Art Deco mode; clear glass etched with roses in the Art Nouveau mode; one-time gas chandeliers with a hanging bowl, pendant gasoliers transformed to electroliers.

'No, no gas, not even a memory of gas,' Peter said. 'We're finished with gas.' And he chose the milky Art Deco because it seemed the most modern and also reminded him of Claire's skin in the sunlight, and chose two others that seemed compatible with the first: the Claire fixture to give light in the front parlor, the second for the back parlor, the third for the dining room.

Jotting down their prices in his sales book, Rance Redmond spoke without raising his glance. 'I can have these delivered by the middle of next week.'

'No, I need them today or it's no sale,' Peter said.

'Today?' said Rance, his pince-nez falling to the end of their ribbon. 'That's not possible.'

'How long would it take to put them in a box?' Peter asked.

'Ten, fifteen minutes, I suppose,' said Rance.

'How long would it take to put them in the back of one of your trucks?'

'But that's it, the trucks are busy.'

'Then put them in a taxi,' Peter said. 'I'll pay the fare.'

'Well, I suppose we could do . . .'

'And an electrician. There's no power in the house. It's still lit by gaslight.'

'Is that right?'

'No, it's not right, but that's how it is, and that's why I want an electrician. Have you got one?'

'I don't know. And there's the power company. You can't just . . .'

'I'll pay the electrician extra. I'll call the power company myself.'

Rance's pince-nez had gone on, off, and on again, a manic measure of his fluster at such impetuousity in these sedate showrooms, but he handed Peter the telephone and then, clutching the sales slip that totaled more than one hundred and ninety dollars for the three fixtures, the largest sale he had made all week, Rance retreated to the store's artisan quarters to search out an electrician, and found one who approved of extra money; found also a taxi, into whose trunk and front seat two chandelier boxes were placed while Peter and I clambered into the rear seat with the third box. The taxi then led the way to Colonie Street, the electrician following in his truck with as much wire as any imagination could reasonably measure, and the two vehicles parked in front of the Phelan house. The power company's man would arrive within two hours.

Only with the death of his mother was Peter now able to challenge the light on Colonie Street. It was fitting that she died in early December, for on these days the exterior world matched the pale gray and sunless interior of the house, night coming on almost as a relief from the daytime sky that hovered over the city like a shroud. Peter remembered his own mood always being depressingly bleak during this time of year, days getting shorter, and darker; and not until January's false spring would the season of desperation begin to fade with the fading of this miasmic light.

He had not known he would buy the chandeliers until he showed me the money on the train; but he knew then that he could buy them and would, for at long last it was time. He knew also that Sarah would fight him on the matter and that Molly and Chick would join him in overriding her objections. But Mama's grip on the past had been released finally, she having been as dark-willed as the biddy of story who refused an indoor, running-water toilet saying, I wouldn't have one of them filthy things in the house, and equally adamantly Kathryn refused electric current as being diabolical; and so the children rarely brought visitors home, so shamed were they that their house, its clutter, its mood, even the odor of its air, had slowly become a museum of everybody else's rejected past.

With my help, Peter carried the Claire chandelier up the front stoop, opened the door with his key, and entered with the call, 'Peter is here.' He and I then carried the boxes into the front parlor as the electrician hauled his gear and wire into the house. Chairs and side tables, including Peter's leather armchair, footstool, pipe stand, and ash tray, had been moved from in front of the parlor's bay window, the designated area for coffin and corpse, though no corpse had occupied it for thirty-nine years, not since Peter's father waked here after stepping backward into the path of a slow-moving locomotive in 1895. Peter cut the twine on one box, put his hand inside, then turned to see his sisters, Sarah and Molly, in the doorway watching him.

'What are you doing?' Sarah asked. 'What is that box? Who is this boy, and that man there?'

'The man is our electrician. The boy is my landlady's son, Orson. Orson Purcell. Say hello to Sarah and Molly, Orson. My sisters.'

I saw two women who seemed at first to be twins, so alike was their dress: long-sleeved, high-necked white blouses, full dark skirts well below the knee, hair done in the same style: upswept into a soft crown, pinned in a bun at the back of the neck. But in glancing from one to the other I saw nothing else in their faces that matched: Sarah, with dark hair going gray, small round spectacles, hazel eyes very close together, long nose, pursed mouth, cheeks on the verge of sinking: here was plainness; and Molly, the same hazel eyes, but a longer, more finely pointed nose, finer symmetry and greater breadth to the eyes and mouth, and a fullness to the lips, and her hair still a pure, burnished yellow: here was beauty.

'How do you do,' I said. 'I'm pleased to meet you.'

'And we you,' said Molly.

'He speaks well,' said Sarah.

'His mother is very bright,' Peter said, 'and he and I do our share of talking, don't we, Orson?'

I nodded and smiled and looked at my father, who seemed so utterly unlike his sisters. There he stood, hand inside the chandelier box, still in his slouch hat and all-weather raincoat, his hair halfway down his neck and as unkempt as his handlebar mustache, his black corduroy shirt and twisted brown tie hanging like the end of a noose, the totality of his clothing, seen in the context of this house, a uniform of rebellion.

Everything I remember from this room on the day the light of the world arrived, had a fragility to it, the Queen Anne table, the china tea set, the French Antique sofa and love seat, the dragonfly lamps, the Louis Quinze chairs that seemed incapable of supporting adults. And the room was dustless: wood and vases and figurines and even the white marble bust of a beautiful woman on her five-foot pedestal (Peter had given it to Julia on her eighteenth birthday) scrubbed and shining, all tables oiled, all brass polished, all floors waxed, all things gleaming, even in that rationed fragment of gray December light that was allowed entry past the mauve drapes.

'What is in that box?' Sarah asked.

Peter, squatting, his right hand still in the box's mysterious interior, suddenly lifted the chandelier into freedom (like a magician, I could say), and with his other hand pulled away the tissue paper that surrounded it, then held it aloft. Presto!

'*Fiat lux!*' Peter said.

'What?'

'Light,' said Peter. 'Electric light. To replace that monstrosity.' And he gestured toward the pendant gasolier on the parlor ceiling. 'That ugly thing's been here since before Cleveland was President. Light. New light in this house, Sarah.'

'We don't want it,' said Sarah.

'How well I know *that*, dear sister. But we *shall* have light on the corpse of our mother, light unlike any that ever found its way into this arcane cave of gloom.'

'I love it,' said Molly. 'It's so pretty. Look at it, Sarah, look how it shines.'

'Wait till you see it lit,' Peter said.

'If you put it up I'll have it taken down as soon as you leave,' Sarah said.

'And if you do that,' said Peter, 'I shall come home with a club and break every piece of your beloved pottery, glassware, and bric-a-brac. Believe me, Sarah, I am serious.'

'You're a villain,' she said, and she walked into the hallway and up the front stairs.

'Don't mind,' Molly said. 'I'll take care of her.' And she walked to Peter and kissed his cheek, studied the chandelier which with his right arm Peter still held half aloft. She touched the shining chrome rims around the bottom of the globes, touched the ball-shaped switches under each globe.

'Isn't it beautiful,' said Molly.

'It's all of that,' Peter said. 'It will give us pleasure. It will banish our shame at being the leftover household. It will put a sheen on your beautiful hair, my sweet sister, and it will satisfy my craving to be done with gloom and come home to respectable radiance.'

I looked at the light around me for the first time in my life. Never had I considered it a topic worth conflict, or enthusiasm. Light was; and that was that. What more could you ask of it? It was bright or it was dim. You saw in it or you didn't see. If you didn't then it was dark. But now came revelation: that there were gradations, brightness to be measured not only in volume but in value. More brightness was better. Amazing.

The doorbell sounded, a pull-bell ding-dong. Molly answered the bell and accepted from the delivery man a small basket of white and purple flowers, brought them to the back parlor, and set them atop the player piano (which had replaced the Chickering upright that Julia Phelan played until she died; and music in this house died with her until Peter exchanged the Chickering for the player and bought piano rolls of the same songs Julia had played since they were children together).

'I know they're from Mame Bayly,' Molly said. 'She's always the first flowers at every wake, always a day early. By the time we get to the cemetery they'll be brown and wilted.'

The electrician had decided that the emergency installation of the chandeliers could be done only by running wire along the ceiling and through the outer wall to the nearest power pole and Peter said fine, run it anyplace you like, just get the power in here; and took off his coat and hat at last, and with his own tool chest began undoing the gasolier and capping the pipe that carried its gas. Since the death of his father Peter had been the master mechanic of the family, even in absentia, consulted via telephone on every plumbing and structural crisis, consulted when the back porch railing fell off, consulted on retarring the roof and on installing storm windows when the price of gas escalated in 1921.

I explored the downstairs rooms, finding photographs of my father when he was a youth (wearing a high collar and a short tie; he never dressed like that any more), and photos of the women I'd just seen, but as girls in bathing suits (with their mother, was it? mother in black long-sleeved high-necked beachwear that came to her shoetop), and I saw a cut-glass dish full of apples and oranges and grapes on the dining-room table and a photo of twenty men posing beside a locomotive, and over the piano a photo of a woman who looked like the beautiful Molly but more beautiful still, and younger, with her hair parted in the middle, and when Peter saw me looking at it he said, 'That's my sister Julia, Orse,' and he whispered in my ear, 'Don't tell anybody, but she was my love, my favorite,' and he said Julia had played the piano. He opened the seat of the piano bench and took out a scroll of paper titled 'In the Shade of the Old Apple Tree.'

'She played this one all the time. We both loved it.'

He opened a sliding door on the piano's upright front and inserted the roll, then sat at the piano and pumped its two pedals with his feet, and the roll moved as I watched with wonderment. Paper that makes music? Then Peter stood up and sat me in his place and told me to put my feet on the pedals and press, first left, then right, and I did and saw the paper move, and then I heard music, saw the keys on the piano depress themselves, and I said, 'It's magic!'

'Not quite,' said Peter, and I kept pumping and then my feet weakened, as did the song, and Peter said, 'Faster, kid, keep a steady rhythm,' and after a while the jerkiness went out of the song and out of my feet and the piano made beautiful music again and Peter sang along.

> I can hear the dull buzz of the bee
> In the blossom that you gave to me,
> With a heart that is true,
> I'll be waiting for you
> In the shade of the old apple tree.

'Are you insane? Are you out of your mind?'

It was Sarah, back with her black mood, black skirt, fierce voice, and I stopped my feet and Peter said, 'For chrissake, Sarah, I'm invoking Julia. Don't you think she has a right to be here today? Are you going to keep this wake all to yourself?' And Sarah again could not answer, and fled to the kitchen, slamming the door behind her.

'Continue, Orse,' Peter said, and, as I moved my feet, music again rose in the rooms where light and death were on the way.

The phone rang in the back parlor and Molly came down the stairs two at a time to answer it, then reported to all auditors that it was Ben Owens, the undertaker, and that he'd be here within the hour; which meant that Mama Kathryn would be returning to the front parlor to be observed in her death rigors, powdered and coiffed as she rarely had been in life; and to me it meant a question mark, for this was my entrance into the world of death.

Again the doorbell sounded and I placed myself in the angular hallway that ran from front door to back parlor, hiding behind wicker filigree decked with clusters of china, people in breeches and wigs and hoopskirts, and dogs and cats with flat bottoms, and then I saw a man with a happy and perfectly round face beneath a bald dome take a cigar out of his mouth and say to Peter, 'I got your mother here.'

And Peter said, 'Bring her in, she's welcome,' and from the smiles that followed this exchange and from all the smiles and music and ongoing electrification, I would take home from this day my first impression of death: that it was an occasion for music, levity, light, and love.

'How've you been, Ben?' Peter asked.

'If I was any better,' said Ben, looking for a place to rid himself of the half-inch ash on his cigar, 'I'd call the doctor to find out what ailed me.'

'In the window,' Peter said. And Ben swung his portly self toward the street and motioned to the four men standing at the back end of the hearse, and home came Kathryn Phelan, her last visitation in the flesh. Just ahead of her came another man with the catafalque, a four-wheeled accordionesque platform which stretched to meet the space, and upon which Kathryn and her mahogany coffin came to rest, the coffin's closed cover gleaming in the sunlight (no electricity yet).

The onlookers now included Ben Owens, Molly, Sarah, Peter, me, and the electrician, who was on a ladder in the middle of the room installing the Claire chandelier, and who said, 'Do you want this thing workin' tonight?' and Peter said, 'We do,' and the electrician said, 'Well, then, I ain't movin' offa here,' and Peter said, 'There's no reason you should. Make yourself at home up there,' and so they moved the coffin around his ladder and the advent of the light proceeded as planned.

The family then retreated to the back parlor as Peter closed the sliding doors between the two parlors and waved a go-ahead sign to Ben Owens. And then the tableau that I would carry with me created itself: Peter sitting at the piano, Sarah standing by the kitchen door off the back parlor with folded arms, Molly settling into the armless horsehair ladies' chair beside the piano and staring at Peter as he pumped up the music. I, sensing tension and trying desperately to make myself disappear, retreated to a far corner of the back parlor where I could observe the expanse of tradition and sibling relationships manifested in objects and body postures, and listen to love manifested in music, and perceive, I knew not how, the ineffable element that seeped under the closed parlor doors when the coffin was opened; all this fixing forever in me the image of life extended beyond death, and fixing too the precise moment of the advent of the light.

The electricity would insinuate itself from the power line on the outside pole, through the front wall, across the ceiling, and into the chandelier at the electrician's touch, and the onset of the light would startle Ben Owens so that the comb he was using to touch up Kathryn Phelan's hair would fly out of his hand and into a shadowy area behind the coffin, and Ben would say, 'Cripes, what was that?'

And light would seep under the sliding doors to be greeted by Peter's remark: 'It's here,' and the apple-tree song would end as light began.

The sliding doors would open onto the new tableau of undertaker, electrician, siblings, and myself, all of us staring at the corpse that was so regally resplendent in high-necked magenta burial gown and pink-taffeta-lined coffin, and Mame Bayly's flowers would give sweet fragrance to Kathryn Phelan's final performance – her first under the bright lights – on this very old stage.

3

Chick Phelan took a half-day off from his job as a linotypist in the *Times-Union*'s composing room for this first night of the wake, the night the family and a few select friends would have the corpse all to themselves. He brought home four bottles of Schenley's whiskey and a box of White Owl cigars for the wakegoers, and announced his partial list of bearers for the funeral: the McIlhenny brothers, Dave and Gerry, nephews of Kathryn recently off the boat from County Monaghan; Martin Daugherty, Barney Dillon from across the street, and two more to be recruited at the wake.

Food began to arrive. Betty Simmons sent her teenage son over with a turkey and stuffing; the Ryan sisters baked a ham and made their famous potato salad and delivered it themselves but didn't come in, would wait for the wake's second night, when friends called. Flowers came: six baskets at once, one from George and Peg Quinn and family, plus the pillow of red roses from the Phelan children, with the word 'Mama' in gold letters on a ribbon. When the deliveryman handed Peter the last basket of flowers and went back down the stoop to his truck, a figure came limping across the street and stood at the bottom step, hands in pockets, fedora at a rakish tilt, clothes old and grimed, and this man looked upward into Peter's eyes.

'I'll be a son of a bitch,' Peter said.

'Ya always have been,' the man said with a small smile.

Peter put the flowers aside and extended his hand. 'Come on in,' he said, and the man came up the three steps, wiped the soles of his shoes on the doormat, and stepped inside, gripping Peter in a strong handshake. Peter closed the door, holding the man's shoulder, and walked him down the hallway to the back parlor where Molly was giving a last-minute dusting to the furniture.

'Say hello to your brother, Moll,' Peter said, and she turned and looked and gaped and dropped the feather duster, and then ran four steps and threw her arms around the man and said 'Fran,' and looked at him again and cried and kissed him and cried some more. 'Fran, Fran. We thought you were dead.'

'Maybe I am,' Francis Phelan said.

He looked toward the front parlor and saw the corpse of his mother in her final silence. He stared at her.

'Go on in,' Molly said. 'Go in and see her.'

'I'll get to it,' Francis said, and he continued to stare.

'I'll tell the others you're here,' Molly said and she went toward the back stairs.

'How'd you find out?' Peter asked.

Francis broke his stare and looked at Peter. 'I was in a lunch-room down in Hudson. Been stayin' down there all fall, pickin' apples, fixin' up trucks for the owner, and this fella next to me gets up and leaves the Albany newspaper. I never do read a damn newspaper, but I pick this one up and turn the page and there's the obit. I look at it and I figure right off this fella left that paper so's I could see that, and I say to myself, Francis, maybe it's time to go back and see people, and I took the next train that come by.'

Francis turned back toward the coffin and Peter read the look on his face: The bitch is dead . . . lower away. Francis's honesty in the teeth of unpleasant truth was galling to Peter; always had been. Hypocrisy is a sometime virtue, but then again fraudulence can stifle, even smother. Hadn't Peter's stifling of his own anger cost him years of bondage to this woman, this house?

'What's goin' through your head?' Peter asked.

'I was just thinkin' how much she missed by bein' the way she was,' Francis said. 'She didn't really know nothin' about how to live.'

'Of course you're the expert on that,' Peter said. 'You're a walking example.'

Francis nodded, looked down at his ragged attire, his shoes with even the uppers falling apart.

'Ain't sayin' I ever figured out how it was done, but I still know more'n she did. I got nothin' against her any more. She done what she hadda do all her life, and somethin' gotta be said for that. I just never bought it, and neither did you.'

'Things got better when I moved to New York,' Peter said.

'That's what I mean,' Francis said. He looked again at his mother, nodded once, that's that, then turned his back to her.

Molly came in carrying two of the six flower baskets from the front hall. She set them on the floor near the head of the coffin.

'Everybody'll be right down,' Molly said.

'Who's everybody?' said Francis.

'Sarah and Tommy and Chick. They're all home. Tommy's a bit confused.'

'That figures,' said Francis.

Francis saw me edge into the room and sit in an empty chair. 'Who's the kid?' he asked.

'That's the boy,' said Peter. 'I mean the son of my landlady. Orson, say hello to a brother of mine, Francis.'

'How do you do, sir,' I said.

'I don't know how I do sometimes, kid. Nice t' meet ya.' And Francis shook my hand. He looked at his own hands then. 'Can I wash up a bit?' he said, and he rubbed his palms together. 'Kitchen'd be fine. Still where it used to be?'

'Go upstairs, use the bathroom,' Molly said.

'No need,' said Francis, and he moved to the kitchen, shoved his coat sleeves upward and soaped his hands with a bar of tan common soap. Molly watched him from the kitchen doorway, handed him a towel.

'Have you had lunch?' she asked.

''bout a week ago,' Francis said.

'I'll set the table,' she said. 'There's cold chicken, and Sarah's biscuits.'

'Sounds mighty good,' Francis said.

He walked to the dining room to take his old place, his back to the famous china closet, facing the window on the yard where Katrina's house had stood before it burned. Now only tall brown stickweeds inhabited the vacant lot where the house had been.

'You're limping,' Molly said.

'Bumped my leg a few days ago, but it's gettin' better.'

'Let me look at it.'

'Nah, it's fine. Nothin' to see, just a black-and-blue mark.'

But the leg was more than black and blue. It was a massive infection whose pain had grown, subsided, grown again. Francis had bathed and bandaged it when he could, but the last bandage had come off during his climb onto the train up from Hudson, and he threw the soiled cloth out the freight-car door after he'd settled in. The wound was a legacy from being hit with a club by a flophouse bouncer, and what seemed like a trivial gash turned into an ulceration six inches in length with a purplish center, a gouge from which pus oozed, scaly white skin flaked and peeled, and flesh vanished. Francis now saw the wound as an insurance policy against life. When times got worse, as they seemed to be doing, he would cultivate the pus, the pain, the purplish-white crust of poison. What's a little pain when it leads to the significant exit?

He heard steps on the back stairs, turned to see the feet of his brother Tommy, unmistakable canal boats in soiled white work socks, and behind him brother Chick, wearing galluses on a collarless shirt, a mile-wide smile on his face as he ogled Francis from midstairs.

'Hey, you old bastard,' Chick said. 'How you doin'?' Chick came down the final two steps, pushed Tommy aside, grabbed Francis's hand, threw an arm around his shoulder, slapped his back. 'You old bastard,' Chick said. 'Where you been?'

'How you, old Chickie pie? You're fat as a pregged-up porker.'

'I can't believe this, Francis, I can't believe it. We give up on you years ago. Never thought I'd see your mug in this house again.'

'I thought the same thing.'

'Franny? Franny?' Tommy stood at Francis's elbow, squinting, focusing. 'Franny?'

'Tommy. Howsa boy? Eh? Howsa boy, old Tom-Tom?'

'Franny?'

'It's me, Tom. It's me. You remember me?'

'Sure I remember, Franny. How's things, Franny?'

'Things is like they are, Tom boy.' Francis stood and wrapped his arms around Tommy's shoulders, then kissed him on the cheek. 'You old horse's ass.'

Tommy smiled.

'Horse's ass. Franny. You shouldn't call me a horse's ass.'

'Why not?' Francis said. 'Where'd a horse be without his ass? Think about it.'

'Horse's ass,' said Tommy in a whisper to Molly. 'Franny called me a horse's ass.'

Francis patted Tommy's right cheek and the room glowed with laughter, and the generosity of abuse.

Peter Phelan looked at his brother and saw himself as he wished he'd been but could never be. He saw a man who pursued his own direction freely, even if it led to the gutter and the grave. Francis was a wreck of a man, a lost soul on a dead-end street, yet in him was no deference to the awful finality of his condition. He did not seem to notice it. Nor did he defer to anything else, not the dead mother, or the need to spruce up for the family, or Tommy's softness. And not Peter. Especially not Peter.

'So what's with you, Fran?' Chick asked. 'You gonna hang around or are you gonna disappear again?'

'Couldn't quite say,' Francis said. 'Just came to see the family.'

'Will you see Annie and the children?' Molly asked. 'Peg sent flowers, you know. I'm sure she and George and Annie will be coming.'

'Don't know about that,' Francis said. 'Don't know what tomorrow'll bring. If I'm here and they come I guess I'll see them.'

Francis had been gone from Albany since 1916, a fugitive from wife and children after his infant son, Gerald, fell and died while

Francis was changing his diaper. But Francis had been gone from *this* family long before that: from the early days of his marriage to Annie Farrell. No, even before that.

Peter watched Francis chew a chicken leg, saw the lineaments of face, the geometry of gesture that had not significantly changed since childhood. The way he wiped his mouth with his knuckle was the same as when he'd sat in that seat and eaten cold chicken fifty years ago. Nobody ever changes: a truth Peter had embraced with reluctance. Did anybody really *progress*, or was it illusory? (Wasn't the illusion of change another opiate of believers? Carrot and stick, keep 'em movin'.) Certainly it was illusory in art. After twenty-one years Peter has a one-man show whose meaning he fails to comprehend. Perhaps, he concedes, it has no meaning, and I'll always be viewed as a pygmy among men.

But he can claim credit for having brought the light to Colonie Street. Top that, brother. There is serious merit in bringing the light. The better to see you with, *mon frère*. Peter: the voyeur still, where Francis is concerned; and then Peter called up Francis's last days as an intimate member of this household. That was in '98, and Francis was eighteen. They were at the table, Mama and all the children sitting then where they are now (Mama's chair empty now), Sarah then sitting where Papa had sat, for she had become Little Mother, that status her legacy from Papa, who, on his deathbed after the train accident in '95, grasped her hand and said to all in the room, 'I don't care who gets married as long as Sarah stays home with her mother.' Sarah was twelve then. And hadn't she done admirably well what her father asked in the thirty-nine years since his death? Oh hadn't she?

They were finishing supper that night in '98 when Francis carried his plate to the kitchen and announced that he had to go over and work for Mrs Daugherty, painting all her interior doors, windows, woodwork, two weeks of evening work at least. Francis then went out the back door and over the fence into the Daugherty back yard. Peter remembered the look on his face as he went: nothing betrayed, no hint that he was off on another mortally sinful expedition into the house of lust.

Lust thrives in the summertime. 'Outdoor fucking weather,' is how Peter heard Francis phrase it one day in front of Lenahan's grocery with half a dozen other boys, all Peter's elders. Peter did not think Francis had ever experienced any full-scale fucking, outdoors or in. Francis wouldn't risk that, Peter reasoned, wouldn't chance the damnation of his immortal soul for all eternity for the sake of 'getting his end wet,' another indelible phrase out of Francis. But Peter had gone through his childhood underestimating Francis, misjudging what he would and wouldn't do. Also Peter perceived in Katrina Daugherty a sensual streak possessed by no other woman he had ever known, loved her face and her hair and her body (body so perfectly designed with the proper arcs and upheavals, body he tried to imagine naked so he could draw it and possess its replica long before he'd ever given a thought to a career as an artist).

And so he waited until summer darkness enveloped Colonie Street, then left the baseball field, where after-supper sport was winding down, and fled across gulley and yard to the apple tree whose upper branches gave sanctuary and vantage to a voyeur seeking to verify the secrets of life and lust among the Daughertys. He had once watched Katrina and her husband, who were unaware that the trees had eyes, half disrobe each other, then walk all but naked up the stairs and out of his sight.

For the past three nights he had watched Katrina alone, or Katrina following Francis around the house, sitting by him while he painted, talking, always talking, never touching or kissing or disrobing, nothing, in sum, that would hold truly serious interest for a spy. But his reading of Francis – that this formidable brother would not be spending his nights painting if all that it availed him was money; that he had to have another motive to keep him from the baseball games that went on three blocks away every night of the summer that was not ruined by rain – kept the spy twined among the branches of the apple tree, waiting for the inevitable.

When it came Peter was not expecting its suddenness, even less so what came with it. His eye found Francis on a ladder, painting the window molding in an upstairs bedroom, saw Katrina's silhouette in the next room, visible through translucent curtains and moving with a purpose he could not define, saw her then with full clarity when she entered the room where Francis was, this room curtainless to receive the new paint.

Peter was close enough to throw an apple and hit Francis on the ladder, yet was certain he was concealed by the lush leafing of the tree, certain also that on this moonless night his profound purpose was served: the cultivation of an internal excitement like nothing he had ever known. The excitement came not only when he saw Francis and Katrina together (even if they only talked), but more so when she was wandering through the house and talking to herself, or reading a book as she walked, which, irrationally, excited him most: knowing she was oblivious of him and even of her present moment, seeing her transported as much by a book as he was by her solitary grace.

She came to the window, wrapped in a yellow robe, and with a matching ribbon holding her hair at the back of her neck, and looked out at the night, at Peter, seeing only shadows, and the lights next door, seeing nowhere near as much as Peter could see with his night eyes. She stood by the window and spoke (to him, he tried to believe), said clearly, 'For thou alone, like virtue and truth, art best in nakedness . . .

'Francis,' she then said.

'Yes, Katrina.'

'Thy virgin's girdle now untie . . .'

'What's that, ma'am?'

And she undid the cloth rope that bound her robe about her waist, opened the robe and then let it fall, then undid her ribbon so that her hair fell loose on her shoulders, and Peter for the first time saw her perfect nakedness, thinking: this can't be a dream, this must not be a dream, and then she turned her back to him and presented herself to Francis. The branches of the tree moved and Peter looked down in a fit of fright to see Sarah climbing toward him.

'I've been watching you,' she whispered. 'What are you looking at?'

'Shhhhh,' said Peter, for Sarah's whisper rang through the night like the bells of St Joseph's Church, and he was sure the naked woman had heard.

But she had not. Katrina pursued her plan, embracing Francis about the knees as he stood on the ladder. Sarah, agile as a monkey, was now beside Peter in the crotch of a branch, and so he could not look at what his eyes wanted so desperately to see. But Sarah could look, staring with her usual inquisition at her brother and the naked Katrina, and so Peter rejoined the vision, watching her take her arms from around Francis's legs and stare up at him as he came down the ladder, then (Sarah unable to restrain a gasp) seeing him kiss her and embrace her naked body. Sarah climbed down the tree then with greater speed than she had climbed up it. She ran off, not toward home but rather, Peter would later learn, toward the church, to seek out the priest and confess in the parish house what she had seen, confessing not her own sin but Francis's, as if his sin were *her* damnation as well as his own.

Peter did not leave the tree and knew Sarah would fault him for this; but he was fearful that this might be his only chance for years to come to witness what it was that people did to each other when they were naked. He saw Katrina unbutton Francis's shirt, then unbuckle his belt, saw her walk again to the window to show her full self to Peter, lean over and pick up her robe and then spread it on the floor, lie on it on her back as Francis, now naked, stood over her, then knelt astraddle her, then finally leaned his full self forward and on top of her into a prolonged kiss.

And thus did Peter Phelan, age eleven, witness with the eye of an artist-to-be the rubrics of profane love. He knew too, for the first time, a nocturnal emission that was not the involuntary product of his dreams; and when that happened to him he began the careful, soundless climb down from the tree, shamed by his spying and the wetness of his underwear (more afraid now of having to explain that wetness than of having to give good reason for peering at people from a tree), and regretting even as his feet touched the ground that he had not continued to watch until there was nothing more to see. He thought of his brother as a figure of awesome courage and achievement – courting damnation by conquering the body of the most beautiful woman in the world – but he also sensed, even in the callowness of his newborn pubescence, that, however much he admired Francis, he would never be able to forgive him for doing this before his eyes. Never.

Sarah had been watching Peter for two days before she decided to follow him to the apple tree. She had seen the oddness of his behavior, erratic, skulking in places he had no reason to be (such as the back yard, looking over the Daugherty fence), and in time she put it together as Peter's secret mission. He was, after all, only a child. But what the child led her to was the shock of her life.

In the infinite judicial wisdom of her Little Motherhood, Sarah, now fifteen, called a meeting of the witnesses and the accused in order to define the future. Clearly capital punishment for Francis was what the heavens screamed aloud for; but Sarah was no vessel for that. All she could do was elevate sin to communal knowledge, spoken of openly in the presence of the sinner (sinners, to be sure, for Peter was not without culpability). So she summoned them to the front steps of St Joseph's and, wearing the mantilla that the old Spanish nun had given her in school as a prize for her essay on chastity ('the virtue without which even good works are dead'), Sarah defined the terms under which she would allow her brothers to continue living in the same house with her and her mother, and the sainted moron Tommy, and the hapless Chick, and the good sisters, Molly and Julia (who, Sarah knew, had chastity problems of their own, but she chose not to raise them here), and the terms were these: That Francis would confess that he had been living in the occasion of sin by working for Mrs Daugherty, whose behavior we must somehow reveal without being vulgar. We can never tell our mother that you put your hands on her naked body, how could you do such an awful thing?

'Listen,' Francis said, 'don't knock it till you tried it,' whereupon Sarah ran up the stairs into the church and did not talk to either brother for three days, after which time she raised the issue at the dinner table.

'Mama,' Sarah said to all assembled siblings, 'Francis has something to tell you.'

'No I don't,' Francis said.

'You'll tell her or I will,' Sarah said.

'I got nothin' to say,' Francis said.

'Then Peter will tell,' Sarah said.

'Not me,' Peter said.

'Will somebody tell me what this is about?' Kathryn Phelan asked. Her other children, Chick, Julia, Molly, and Tommy, looked bewildered at their mother's question.

'It's what Francis is doing,' Sarah said. But she could say no more.

'Sarah doesn't think I oughta work for Katrina,' Francis said. 'I think Sarah oughta mind her own business.'

'Why *not* work for her?' Kathryn asked.

'There's more than work going on over there,' Sarah said.

'And what might that mean?'

'Are you going to tell her?' Sarah asked Francis.

Francis stared into Sarah's eyes, his face crimson, his mouth a line of rage.

'Well?' said Kathryn.

'She put her arms around him,' Sarah said.

'What does that mean?'

'It doesn't mean anything,' Francis said.

'Why did she do that?'

'She likes the way I work,' Francis said.

'He's lying,' Sarah said.

'How do you know?' Kathryn asked. 'Did you see her do this?'

'Yes, and so did Peter.'

'I don't know what I saw,' Peter said.

'Don't lie,' Sarah said.

'Everybody's a liar but Sarah,' Peter said.

'What were you doing watching over there?' Kathryn asked Sarah.

'I followed Peter. He's the one who was watching.'

'You're a lousy rat, Sarah,' Peter said. 'A real lousy rat.'

'Never mind name-calling. I want to know what went on. What is she talking about, Francis?'

'Nothin'. I work for her, that's all. She's a nice person.'

'She was naked,' Sarah said.

'Naked!' Kathryn said, and she stood up and grabbed Francis by the ear. 'What've you been doing, young man?'

Francis stood and jerked his head out of his mother's grip. 'I walked into her room when she was dressin',' he said. 'It was a mistake.'

'He's lying again,' Sarah said. 'He was painting and she took her robe off and was naked and then she threw her arms around him and he did the same thing to her.'

'Is that true?' Kathryn asked, her face inches from Francis.

'She's a little crazy sometimes,' Francis said. 'She does funny things.'

'Taking her clothes off in front of you? You consider that funny?'

'She doesn't know what she's doin' sometimes. But she's really all right.'

'He put his arms around her and they kissed for a long time,' Sarah said.

'You bitch,' Francis said. 'You stinkin' little sister bitch.'

Kathryn swung her left hand upward and caught Francis under the jaw. The blow knocked him off balance and he fell into the china closet, smashing its glass door, shattering plates, cups, glasses, then falling in a bleeding heap on the floor.

4

Thirty-six years gone and here he is back again, Peter thought, and there is the china closet, and here we all are (Sarah will come down from her room eventually; she will have to face the reality of his return), and here minus Julia are the non-conspirators, Molly, Chick, Tom-Tom, Orson, the added starter, about the same age I was when all this happened, and Francis, who is no more repentant today of whatever sin than he was when Mama knocked him down with her left hook.

'I thought Sarah was comin' down,' Francis said.

'She'll be down,' Molly said. 'She's getting dressed for tonight.'

'You look pretty, Moll. Real, real pretty. You got a beau? Somebody sweet on you?'

Molly put her eyes down to her plate. 'Not really,' she said.

'How about Sarah? She didn't marry, did she?'

'No,' said Molly.

'I ran into Floyd Wagner down in Baltimore. I'm on my way to Georgia and old Floyd, he's a cop now, was gonna arrest me. Then he seen who I was and instead of arrestin' me he bought me a beer and we cut it up about the old days. He said he went out a few times with Sarah.'

'That's so,' said Molly. 'Sarah broke it off.'

'So Floyd said.'

'Never mind about Floyd Wagner,' said Sarah, descending the back stairs into the room. She was in total mourning, even to the black combs that held her hair, her dress a high-necked, ankle-length replica of the recurring dress that Kathryn Phelan had worn most of her life, always made by the perfect, homemade dressmaker, Sarah. It was less a mourning garment than a maternal uniform – black cotton in the summer, black wool in winter – that asserted that unbelievable resistance to anything that smacked of vanity, though not even that: of lightness, of elevation. Her children and relatives had tried to sway her with gifts of floral-patterned dresses, colored skirts and blouses, but the gifts remained in boxes for years until finally Kathryn gave them to the Little Sisters of the Poor.

Francis looked at Sarah and retreated in time. Here was the mother incarnate in Sarah, now fifty-one, a willful duplicate; and Francis remembered that Sarah had even wanted to call herself Sate when they were young, because people called their mother Kate; but Mama would have none of that. Sarah would be Sarah, which was no hindrance at all to emulation, as this presence now proved; uncanny resemblance, even to the combing and parting of the hair and the black-and-white cameo brooch that Kathryn always wore at her throat.

'Hello, Sarah,' Francis said. 'How you been?'

'Fine, thank you.'

'Good. That's good.'

'Sarah looks like Mama,' Tommy said.

'I noticed that,' Francis said.

'So you're back,' Sarah said to Francis. 'You're looking well.'

'Is that so?' Francis said. 'I wouldn'ta said so.'

'Francis can be a bearer,' Chick said. 'I just thought of that. Then we only need one more.'

'Francis won't be here,' Sarah said. 'Francis isn't staying.'

'What?' said Peter.

'He's not staying,' Sarah said. 'He's not a part of this family and hasn't been for over thirty years. Feed him if you like, but that's all he gets out of us.'

'Sarah,' Molly said, 'that's wrong.'

'No,' said Sarah, 'nothing wrong except that he's back among us and I won't have it. Not on the day my mother is waking.'

'Right,' Francis said. 'I seen her wakin'. I seen her dead, and now I see her again, not dead at all. Nothin' changed here since I left the first time, and now I remember why I left. Sarah's got a way of joggin' your memory.'

'Sarah doesn't run this house,' Peter said.

'Right,' Chick said. 'Absolutely right. Sarah don't run nobody.'

'It's okay,' Francis said. 'Not a thing anybody's gotta worry about. I'm a travelin' man, and that's all I am. Never counted on anything more than seein' she was really dead. I figure, she's dead, I'm free. Know what I mean, Chickie pie?'

'No.'

'What's gone's gone, and I figure, good riddance. She wanted *me* dead is the way I figure it. Ain't that right, Sarah?'

'You were dead for years. You're dead now. Why don't you go live in the cemetery?'

'You know, you turned out just right, Sarah,' Francis said. 'Just like I knew you would. You ain't got a speck o' the real goods in you. You ain't got one little bit of Papa. You got it all from the other side of the family, all from that Malachi crowd. You're somebody they oughta cut up and figure out, 'cause you ain't hardly human, Sarah.'

'You're a tramp, Francis. You were a tramp when you were a child. You and your Katrina.'

Francis turned his eyes from Sarah and faced Peter, who could not take his eyes from Francis. Francis smiled, a man in control of his life. Oh yes.

'She remembers Katrina, Pete. Got a memory like a elephant, this sister of ours. You remember Katrina too?'

'Everybody remembers Katrina,' Peter said.

'Unforgettable lady,' Francis said.

'Don't bring that old filth back in here,' Sarah said.

'Filth,' Francis said, 'that's Sarah's favorite word. Where you'd be without filth I can't even figure, Sarah. You and filth – some double play. Old Floyd Wagner told me how you and him talked about filth all them years ago.'

'Make him leave,' Sarah said to the entire table.

'Floyd said the last time he saw Sarah . . .'

'Never mind anything Floyd Wagner said,' Sarah said.

'Sarah, let him talk,' Peter said.

'What about Floyd Wagner?' Chick asked.

'Old Floyd. He came to see Sarah one night and she threatened to stab him with a pair of scissors.'

'What?' Molly said.

'It's a lie,' Sarah said.

'Floyd said she was afraid he might kiss her and start doin' other filthy stuff, so she snatched up the scissors and told him to keep his distance or she'd stab him in the belly.'

'Oh, you foul thing,' Sarah said, and she pushed her chair back and walked to the living room.

'Floyd swears it,' Francis said (and in the front parlor Sarah, standing beside the corpse of her mother, covered her ears with both hands to fend off Francis's words).

'Floyd said he never did get to kiss Sarah, and after the scissors business he sorta lost interest.'

'I think we can change the subject,' Peter said.

'Suits me,' Francis said.

All eating, all talk at the table stopped. The front door bell changed the mood and, as Molly went to answer it, Chick said, 'That's probably Joe Mahar. He said he'd come early.' And Chick too left the table.

Francis drank the last of his tea, popped his last crust of bread into his mouth, and smiled at Peter. 'Always great to come back home,' he said.

'I got to go to the bathroom,' Tommy said, and he went up the back stairs.

'Just you and me, Pete,' Francis said, ignoring my presence.

Francis saw Molly, Sarah, and Chick talking to a priest in the living room and he could recognize Joe Mahar, whose name he could never have brought to mind if Chick hadn't mentioned it, but he knew he was the boy who had gone into the seminary with Chick out of high school. Joe had obviously carried it off, but poor Chickie pie came home after three years (the first year

Francis played for Chattanooga, blessin' himself every time he came to bat, and them rednecks yellin', 'Kill the Irishman,' but he kept on blessin' even though he didn't buy that holy stuff no more), and Chick's return plunged Mama into the weeping depths of secularity. No priests in the Phelan family, alas. Mama never to know the glory of having mothered a vicar of Christ.

'I see you got a new ceilin' light,' Francis said, looking at the new fixture.

'Installed this afternoon,' Peter said. 'How do you like it?'

'Nice and ritzy. Who picked it out, you?'

'Orson and I did, didn't we, Orse?' And I nodded.

'You still doin' newspaper work?'

'No, I make my living as an artist, such as it is.'

'Artist. By God that's a new one. Artist. What kind of artist?'

'A painter.'

'That's good,' Francis said. 'I like paintin's. My most favorite saloon had a paintin' back of the bar. Only reason I hung out there was to look at it. Eased my mind, you know what I mean?'

'What was it?'

'Birds, mostly,' Francis said. 'Birds and a naked woman. Reminded me of Katrina.' Francis winked at Peter.

Peter laughed, shook his head at Francis's philistinism. But it was an involuntary and unjustified response, and he knew it; knew that if Francis had set his mind to it he could have been an artist, or a writer, or a master mechanic. Anything Francis wanted he could have had. But of course he never wanted anything. Artist of the open road. Hero of Whitmanesque America: I hear America singing – about naked ladies.

'Peter,' Molly called, 'Father Joe wants to know about the funeral mass. Just for a minute. He'll be right back, Fran.'

Francis nodded at Molly, sweet sister, as Peter went to the front parlor. Francis looked at me and smiled. Alone at the table of his youth, made a hemispheric sweep of the room. No need to look behind him at the china closet. He knew what that looked like. He saw only one thing in the room that surprised him: the picture of the family taken at Papa's forty-fifth birthday party at Saratoga

Lake, where they had a camp that summer, the summer of the year Papa died. There was Francis at fifteen and Tommy as a baby. Francis would not approach it, not look closely at what was then; better off without any vision of a past that had led to these days of isolation from both past and future. Gone. Stay gone. Die. Go live in the cemetery.

Francis got up and saw that only I was looking at him. He made a silent shushing motion to me, then found his hat and coat on the hallway wall hooks, where Molly had hung them. He went through the kitchen and out the back door into the yard, and I followed him. We both looked at the dead automobile in the carriage barn, a 1923 Essex, up on blocks.

'That your car, kid?' he asked me.

'No sir. I'm not old enough to own a car.'

'Good,' he said. 'No point in ownin' that one anyway. Ain't worth nothin'.'

Then he smiled, threw me a so-long wave, and walked out of the alley and down Colonie Street, heading toward the railroad tracks, his home away from home.

I watched him limp toward the street and knew he was going away, perhaps forever, which was precocious of me to think that, and which saddened me. He was an imposing figure of a man, even with his dirty clothes. His heavy-duty smile made you like his looks, and like him, even though he was beat up, and kind of old.

Now, reconstituting that moment twenty-four years later, I remember that my sadness at the loss of his presence was the first time I was certain that my father really was Peter, and that I really did belong in this family. I had seen something in the man's face that resembled what I saw in my own face in the mirror: a kindred intangible, something lurking in the eyes, and in that smile, and in the tilt of the head – nothing you could say was genetic, but something you knew you wanted to acknowledge because it was valuable when you saw it, even though you couldn't say what it was. And you didn't want to lose it.

Francis turned at the front of the house and walked out of my sight, and so I then went and sat in the old car. As if to fill the void, a girl my own age entered the alley with a small black mongrel at her heel and came toward the carriage barn. She looked up into the car's front window and saw me pretending to drive.

'Do you know how to make that thing go?' the girl asked.

'I'm not sure,' I said.

'Then you shouldn't be up there. You could have an accident.'

'This car can't move,' I said. 'It's on blocks.'

The girl looked at the blocks and said, 'Oh, I see.' And then she opened the door and slid in alongside me. She was obviously a waif, her hair a stringy mess, her plaid jacket held at the throat with a safety pin, her feet in buttonless high-button shoes long out of fashion. But what overrode all things forlorn about her was her eyes: large and black beneath black brows and focused on me with an intensity that I now know was in excess of what her years should allow. This made me uneasy.

'Is that your dog?' I asked.

'He belongs to all of us.'

'All of who? Who are you? What are you doing here?'

'I was sent here,' she said.

'Who sent you?'

'My people. They want me to find something valuable and bring it back.'

'Valuable how?'

'I don't know yet. They didn't tell me.'

'Then how do you know where to look?'

'I don't know where to look. I don't know anything about this place. Would you like to help me?'

'Help you look for something you don't know what it is or where it might be?'

'Yes.'

I was befuddled, and while I thought about how ridiculous this girl was I saw Molly come out the back door.

'Orson,' she called out, 'did you see Francis?'

'Yes, ma'am,' I said, sticking my head out the car window. 'He went out the alley and down the street.'

Peter came out then, shoving his arms into his coat, and, when Molly told him what I had said, he too went toward the street.

'I have to go now,' I said to the girl.

'I'll go with you,' she said, and she left the Essex and followed me, as I was following Peter, the mongrel keeping pace behind us. When I reached the street I saw Peter already at the corner, looking in all directions, then heading toward Downtown on the run. I jogged and the girl jogged beside me.

'Are you looking for the man in the hat and the old clothes?' the girl asked.

'Yes, how did you know?'

'He didn't go that way,' she said, pointing toward Peter. 'He went straight ahead.' And she gestured toward the river.

I stopped and wondered whether the girl was lying, or knew something.

'He was limping,' she said.

'All right,' I said and I resumed jogging toward the river, wondering what I would do or say if I found Francis when Peter was not around. At least I could say Peter was looking for him, and Molly too.

We ran past an old hospital, empty now, with posters pasted haphazardly on its walls advertising the O. C. Tucker Shows, a carnival with high divers, games, rides, a fortune-teller, a freak show, dancers galore. On another wall I saw a minstrel-show poster of a man in blackface, and yet another of Fredric March in *Death Takes a Holiday*.

'That's where I live,' the dark-eyed girl said.

'In that empty building?'

'No, in the carnival.'

'Where is it now, around here?'

'Down that street,' the girl said, but she did not change her direction to go toward the carnival, if it was there, which I doubted, for this wasn't the right weather for carnivals or circuses. It was too cold for outdoor shows, and it was probably going to snow. I was not cold, because I was running. But I knew when I stopped I would feel chilled beneath my sweat.

'I think he went down there,' the girl said, and she ran ahead of me and down a dead-end street, beyond which lay the river flats at the edge of the old Lumber District. To this day I cannot give a cogent reason why I followed this girl, trusted her to lead me to a stranger she had seen only once, if that. But I felt that the child should not be resisted if I wanted to find Francis.

'How do you know he came this way?' I asked.

'I saw him,' the girl said.

'You couldn't have seen him down here.'

'That's what you say,' the girl said.

'I think you're a little crazy,' I said, to which the girl did not reply.

We left the paved streets of the city and ran on a dirt path toward the railroad tracks, across fields of weeds and trash, and I saw in the distance half a dozen shacks that hoboes had built, saw people moving near them. Then I saw eight freight cars on a siding, with more people sitting by fires, cooking something.

'That's where I live,' the girl said, and Orson saw the lettering painted on the cars: O. C. Tucker Shows.

'You live on the tracks?'

'We're waiting for a steam engine to take us south,' the girl said. 'We have to bribe the railroad men.'

I understood nothing about this girl. We ran in silence and then I saw Francis, walking on the flats with his limp. And how he had gotten this far walking at that speed was a mystery. Perhaps the girl and I had run in a roundabout circle to get here, though I doubted it.

'There he is,' I said, and I stopped running.

'You see?' the girl said.

We were uphill from Francis, fifty feet from him, on a slope covered with trees and high weeds, and I then chose to hide myself and watch Francis as he walked north along the tracks, his limp worse than when I last observed him. I felt myself in the presence of hidden meaning (was that what the dark-eyed girl was looking for?) both in my decision to hide, and in the vision that lay before me; and I shivered with the chill of comprehension that something woeful could happen that would mark me. In the presence of malevolence I understood that this is what you feel like before the woeful thing happens. I turned to the girl and saw her petting a kitten, stroking its head with her long, dirty fingernails. Her dog was nowhere to be seen. From the pocket of her jacket a naked doll with only one leg protruded.

'Where did the cat come from?' I asked, and I realized I was whispering.

'He found me,' the girl said.

'And the doll?'

'It was in the car that's up on blocks.'

'Then it doesn't belong to you.'

'No, it's yours,' she said.

'I don't own any dolls,' I said.

'It's yours because I give it to you,' the girl said, and she handed me the one-legged doll, which I assumed had belonged to Molly, or Sarah, or maybe the long-gone Julia. I put the doll on the ground and looked at Francis, who had stopped walking and was staring up the empty track, nothing to be seen. I felt the chill I knew would come. I heard noise to my right, someone walking, and turned to see Peter not thirty feet away, standing still and mostly concealed by bushes, looking toward Francis, who was standing beside the tracks. Peter, the dark-eyed child, and I now formed Francis's silent audience in the weeds.

Francis is a peasant, Peter thought. He is a polar bear. He can live in the snow. He is a walker, look at him walk with that game leg. What did you do to your leg, Francis? Francis is a buzzard, feeding on the dead. Francis is a man who never lost his looks, though he is in terrible condition. You cannot lose the shape of your face unless you lose all your flesh, or stretch it with fat, like Chick. Look at the way Francis wears his hat. In destitution he exudes style. He walks along the gray gravel of the track bed. He casts his shadow on the silverbrown tracks. He walks past a track signal light whose color I cannot see. The weeds where he walks are dun, are fawn, are raw umber, khaki, walnut, bronze, and copper. The sky is the color of lead, soon to be the color of mice. Bosch, *The Landloper*. Look, he sits on the switch box. He raises the leg of his trousers that are the color of lampblack gone to smoke, and he studies the wound that makes him limp. Not in my line of sight. He nods and decides that his leg has improved, though it pains him. He wipes sweat from his forehead, or is it an itch? He puts his hat on again, stands and walks, stops. Why walk? He will have to run when the train comes. I can see him running with his gimp gait, clever enough to grab the step-iron of the ladder and hoist himself aloft with arm strength alone, perhaps help from a push with the good leg, and up he goes, off he goes to the future in the noplace village of his nowhere world. Away we go, Francis, away we go, swinging from the rope on the hill, flying down into the mud pond. Do not miss the water or you will break your bones. I never missed. Francis taught me how not to miss. Can he see me now? He cannot, yet he can teach me still. The tracks converge in a distant fusion I cannot see from here, but I see them narrowing, darkening as they go, see the yellow lights of a lumber yard still busy, lights of a house so solitary, lights of a burnt-ocher fire (other fires toward the city, carny fire probably fake like everything about carnies), and I see you, Francis, in your termination, the end of family tie, the beginning of nothing. You will carry on, Francis. You will find a way not to die in the midst of your nothingness. You will feel the triumph of the spirit as you leave us in the dust of your memory, obliterating us as you go toward oblivion and the bottom of the jug. Be of good cheer, Francis. Wondrous drunkenness lurks in your future. You will recover from the awfulness of your finality and you will go on to the heights of the degraded imagination, always conjuring yet another rung on which to hoist yourself to new depths. Francis, in your suite of mice and dun, in the majority of your umberness, in the psychotic melancholy of your spirit, I salute you as my brother in the death of our history. You more than I knew how to murder it. You more than I knew how to arrive at the future. In solitude you are victorious, you son of a bitch, you son of a bitch, will you never give me peace? Son-of-a-bitch brother, why is it you do not die?

* * *

Francis put his foot on the track and felt the train before he could see it, or hear it. You goddamn leg, you rotted on me. Let *them* rot. Why'd it have to be me? Why not? Not a time to go for the religion. Sin and punishment, all that shit. Don't clutter your head, Francis. This is tricky. You don't want to miss. One time and we're on the way. Hey, boys, I'm goin' for a ride. You'd think a guy'd get an invite to at least sleep over after how the fuck many years. Too many to count. Don't bother. But they give you a chicken leg, and don't let the door hit you in the ass on the way out. Woulda seen Annie if this'd worked, if there was a place to stay and go slow, do a visit and get the lay of the land, don't push it too fast, but you can't goddamn go home lookin' like this, goddamn bum and filthy, got a chicken leg in his belly and that's all he's got. And lookin' out the window at Katrina. Jesus, lady, you don't go away easy, do you? Like a life you lived afore you was alive. A way of lookin' at women that keeps you on the edge of the goddamn furnace, dangerous, them women, God bless all of 'em, and I don't leave out none, all welcome here. Welcome, ladies, welcome. Anything I can do for you while you wait? Spurt up a couple of kids? How'd ya like that, Helen? You can't have no kids. And Bessie, you were some bundle, I'll tell the world, wouldn't of been the same world without that month, or was it a week? Who gives a barrel of shit? Not Francis. Francis knows there's no . . . I see it. I got a minute. A minute? Less? Step lively, Mr Francis, 'cause the time is now. Chicken leg here you go wherever the hell you're goin', chicken leg step lively step

When Papa died, Peter thought, there was Francis with him. Francis had everything.

When Papa died he stepped onto the track backwards and didn't know the engine

When Papa died he took my hand and said to me, 'Fear Christ.'

When Papa died

Francis is stepping onto the track

I scream.

* * *

Peter heard Orson yell and saw him running toward the track yelling a scream that had no words and he saw Francis turn and look not toward him not seeing him running toward the train and saw Francis stop look toward the train as if he and it were making no sound as if he were a figure in a dream where nobody hears what you most desperately want to say as if you were a nonexistent nothing nowhere and he even so steps off the track bed and looks toward you with a surprise in his eye and the train goes by and you can stop all that yelling now, Orson.

Not dead yet, Francis said silently, and he stepped off the track bed and out of the path of the fast freight, and said aloud, 'Fuck that nonsense,' and heard the screaming then and turned to it, saw the boy and Peter both coming toward him, both. They been watchin', the two of them, that's a pair, the boy can't even talk, just there.

'Are you all right?' Peter asked.

'I ain't been all right in ten years,' Francis said. 'Whatcha doin' down here, keepin' an eye on me?'

'You left.'

'You figured that out.'

'You left the house.'

'You been watchin'. You both been watchin'.'

'No,' I said.

'No,' Peter said.

'Did ya have a good time?' Francis asked. 'How'd I do?'

Only now has it begun to snow

Only now

I remember backing away mumbling scream, I did scream as soon as, and I saw the cat with its front left leg bleeding and the naked doll with both its legs gone now and the dark-eyed child gone

snow now

now snow

Book Three

1

The solidification of my father's reputation prior to this present hour, the summer of 1958, followed the exhibition of the six canvases and many sketches he made during the years 1936–1939, the ostensible subject of these works being the near suicide of Francis as witnessed by the artist, by the cruel waif from the carnival, and by myself.

In the wake of the aborted suicide, Peter fell into an artistic silence that persisted for much of 1935. I judge it to have been induced by his guilt over not confronting Francis when he first saw him beside the tracks, but instead waiting for the train he thought would carry the man away – and thus would Peter have been done with a pesky brother.

But again Francis confounded his sibling, stepped onto the track bed, then stepped off again, a game of perilous hopscotch if there ever was one. And what this did was derange Peter for more than a year, the greatest thing that had happened to him as an artist up to that time.

Artists, of course, use their guilt, their madness, their sexual energy, and anything else that comes their way, to advance the creation of new art. Peter had fared modestly in his one-man show in that winter of 1934, realizing some dollars, plus an enhanced (but still marginal) reputation, and proving to the gallery owners that, although he was perhaps not Matisse, he was worth wall space. But Peter, given this green light, immediately stopped painting, and no one could get him to say why. It all looks crystalline now in retrospect, but it was probably mysterious even to him for a time. His artistic cycle, as I came to perceive it, was this: profound guilt and remorse, followed by delight with the remorse, for it created the mood for art; self-loathing that followed being delighted by remorse; boredom with self-loathing; rumination about self-destruction as an escape from self-loathing; resurgence of boredom when self-destruction is rejected; and resumption of art to be done with boredom, art again being the doorway into the emotional life, the only life that mattered to him as an artist.

He began by objectifying, in segments, the scene as it had been, or as he had transformed it in his memory, revealing all that I saw, even to the cat, the legless doll, and especially the waif, which surprised me. She disappeared after I screamed at Francis, but Peter had already seen her in the weeds, and drew her peering out at the tracks like a vigilant demon, which is how I thought of her in subsequent years.

In one canvas he drew the scene from the perspective of Francis, leaving out the tracks, but including the lumber mill, the switch box, even the Phelan house, which he placed on a hill several blocks to the east and transformed into a place of dark and solitudinous dilapidation. He used the light of dusk, which was when the whole event took place, but he also painted Francis in bright sunlight, a way I never saw him. He painted the carnival boxcars in the background of one work, its people minimally developed, but busy with violence, copulation, voyeurism, and domestic acts around an open fire, none of which I had observed.

Peter learned about Francis's leg wound from me (it was years before we knew how he'd gotten it), for I had seen it at the house when, sitting alone at the table, he wrapped a napkin around it, then tied it with a piece of string he took from his pocket; and I saw it again clearly when he sat on the switch box and raised his pant leg to examine his lease on death, so to speak. Peter created one picture in which only that ghastly leg exists on a realistic plane (precisely the repulsive purplish-and-white scaliness as I had related it to him), vividly detailed in drybrush watercolor. The rest of the scene – the body of the leg's owner, the sky, the tracks – he rendered with a few pencil strokes and a smear of color. The leg in that drawing appeared to be a separate being, an autonomous entity. It did belong to a body, but further specifics of that body remained for other drawings to reveal.

I'm speaking now about the sketches Peter drew (he liked to quote Ingres that drawing included three-quarters of the content of a painting, that it contained everything but the hue), to some of which he added watercolor, most of them in pen or pencil or charcoal, depending on the tool at hand when the impulse came to conjure yet another response to the event. Peter did forty-nine sketches for the three paintings, which may seem sizable, but is really a parsimonious figure when one compares it to the hundreds of sketches he did for the Malachi paintings.

The Itinerant series, as the Francis paintings came to be called, was the realization of Peter's new artistic credo: profligacy in the service of certitude. He came to believe that he could and would paint for decades to come, and that there was no such thing as too much prefatory creation to any given work. But he did not behave in any way that supported his new flirtation with infinity. When he removed himself into silence he also began to ignore his personal life. He grew further estranged from Claire, remote from me (which I didn't understand; and I felt myself guilty for having done something I had perhaps not understood, or did not know I'd done; but I had *not* done anything except witness his fratricidal behavior), his personal hygiene deteriorated to the level of the most unwashed of those bohemians in whose midst he lived; his work as an illustrator, more in demand than ever, became loathsome to him, and he did less and less of it until his income was zero, and in this latter action he achieved a secondary goal: to so impoverish himself that he would henceforth be of no help whatever to Claire in supporting the house.

He was slowly converting himself into a replica of Francis at trackside: man without goal, home, family, or money, with only his wits to keep him alive. This was art imitating life, artist imitating man who lives or dies, who cares? Art be damned. Useless art. Pointless art. Now is the time to live or perish.

In this way Peter moved forward, trying to discover how the phantasm of death is visually framed in this life.

Peter concealed his *Itinerant* series for two years after he completed it, his first manifestation of that reclusive temperament that would continue for another two decades, and sold only three unrelated oil portraits (commissioned) to support himself. His year of silence had obviously fed his imagination, and led to the creative explosion he could no longer keep to himself. Critics who subsequently wrote about these paintings gave Peter his first leg up to fame, finding in them the originality he'd long sought, and either ignoring his earlier work or relegating it to the status of preparatory effort. They did not yet see that all six paintings had their subliminal inspiration in one late masterwork by Hieronymus Bosch, even to the name: *The Peddler*, or *The Tramp*, or *The Landloper*, or *The Prodigal Son*, as the Bosch work was variously called.

I doubt seriously Peter ever knew all the parallels the Bosch would have to his own work, his own family. He was not derivative, always argued against emulating the Impressionists who had so moved the American artistic world in the Armory Show in that year of his arrival in Greenwich Village, 1913. He resisted also the thrust of the Surrealists, who dominated the direction of art in the 1930s and 1940s. Peter used all these schools in his own way, never fitting any categories; yet the critics, after *The Itinerant* series, linked him to proletarian realists and Depression agitators, all of whom he might admire in principle, but would loathe in the particular for their politically partisan cheerleading.

An Interview with Peter Phelan
by Orson Purcell

O: These *Itinerant* paintings, they're all about your brother Francis, are they not?

P: No. They're not about anybody.

O: Who is the tramp figure in the paintings?

P: He's anybody, nobody.

O: How can you tell me this when you and I were watching as Francis stepped onto the tracks and then off?

P: Artistically I never saw that.

O: You're clearly lying, even to yourself.

P: All art is a lie.

O: Is your life a lie as well?

P: More often than not.

O: With the success of this art do you consider yourself an arrived man, a famous artist?

P: I will never arrive, but I'm famous with my friends.

O: Who would they be?

P: They're all dead. Their names no longer matter.

O: What motivated you to paint *The Itinerant* series?

P: The paintings, as they took shape.

O: The paintings inspired themselves?

P: That's how it happens. There is nothing and then there is a painting.

O: But things happen to make you arrive at a certain subject matter.

P: No. Nothing happens ever. There is no subject matter until the painting exists.

O: You are putting the egg before the chicken. What makes the egg?

P: The artist. He is an egg factory. He needs no chickens.

O: No guilt or envy or enmity or smoldering hatred or fratricidal impulse ever inspires art?

P: I know nothing of any of that.

O: You talk as if you have no internal life, as if only an empty canvas exists on which you, mindless vessel, an automated brush, shape the present. This is the school of unconscious art, is it not?

P: You see this painting here? That's a shoulder bone. This is a chest bone.

O: Whose bones are they?

P: Anybody's. Nobody's.

O: Why did you paint them?

P: Because they emerged.

O: Then they are your bones.

P: Quite possibly.

O: Just as *The Itinerant*, if not Francis, is then you?

P: I wouldn't deny it.

O: What else wouldn't you deny? Paternity, perhaps?

P: What?

O: I say paternity?

P: What?

O: I suggest that all your work and hence all your life is a parody of that subconscious you so revere. I suggest you cannot even take that deepest part of yourself seriously, that you have trouble acknowledging your status as a human being, as well as the status of your son, whom you treat as one of your works of art, disclaiming responsibility for him, allowing him to float free in the universe, devoid even of the right to the intentional fallacy. Your stance suggests you did not even intend him as quantitatively as one of your paintings, and so he remains a happenstance of history. Tell me if I am close.

P: Art is the ideation of an emotion.

O: Do I qualify as a work of art?

P: Art is the ineffable quotient of the work, the element that emerges when the work is done, that does not itself exist in the spatial qualities of the finished painting. Art has no subject matter.

O: Then neither do I.

P: Art is a received conception.

O: I am here, therefore I was conceived.

P: The conception of art has no logic and means nothing.

O: What does mean anything?

P: Art, as it exists.

O: What does art do after it exists?

P: It represents, it symbolizes, it expresses. Art is impact.

O: On whom? On what?

P: On the universe.

O: I doubt it.

P: Doubt is an impaction.

O: As a work of art I doubt myself, my conception, my creation.

P: A theory and its opposite may coexist in the same mind. The unavowed is the companion of mystery.

O: And mystery is the secret of art and paternity.

P: As you like it. As you like it.

2

I was home from Germany five and a half months in March of 1953 when I visited with my mother for the first time in four years. We talked on the phone from time to time but she consistently put off any meeting. She was no longer Claire Purcell. She now called herself Belinda Love (not legally) and said at last she'd meet me, under the clock in the Biltmore Hotel, because she saw that happen once in a movie.

I arranged my one outing of the week for that day, a visit to the publishing house for which I was editing and tidying up the erotic memoirs of Meriwether Macbeth, an extroverted and pseudonymous bohemian writer and sometime actor who was having a renascent vogue as a result of having been murdered. This was an assignment that seemed doable to me, first because it was the story of a real life lived in Greenwich Village, my environment of the moment; and further because Peter had known Macbeth personally in the 1920s and loathed his acting, his writing, his ideas, his presence, and his odor.

I brought in the heavily edited and rewritten segments of Macbeth's manuscript to my editorial boss, then walked the several blocks to the Biltmore, where I settled onto a bench from which I could monitor all who organized their futures under the clock.

I spotted my mother as soon as she appeared in the lobby, and saw that she looked remarkably like herself of five years gone. She was fifty-eight, looked forty-five, and exuded (with long, scarlet fingernails, spike heels, pillbox hat, wasp waist that was visible beneath her open, form-fitting coat) the aura of World War Two, the era when her independence had reached its apogee, the time of her final separation from Peter, and of her entrance into a solo career as singer and mistress of ceremonies, first in local Albany nightclubs, then with traveling USO shows, and, after the war, in a 52nd Street jazz club where she sang with the resident Dixieland group, her looks and her legs equally as important as her voice, and, ultimately, more interesting. As she walked across the lobby she drew the stares of the bell captain and his minions, then turned the heads of two men waiting to check in. Nearing retirement age and still a dazzler. Mother.

'Hello, darling boy,' she said when we embraced beneath the clock, 'are you still my darling?'

'Of course, Mother.'

'Are you well?'

'I wouldn't go that far.'

'Your letters were dreadful. You sounded positively wretched. So discontented, so – what can I say? – scattered.'

'Scattered is a good word. I'm nothing if not that.'

'Whatever happened to you?'

'I went out of my mind.'

'Just like your father.'

She signaled to the maître d' of the Palm Court and we were seated under a chandelier, amid the potted plants, the tourists, and the cocktail-hour habitués. She ordered a Manhattan on the rocks, I an orange juice, my alcohol intake at zero level as a way of not compounding my confusion.

'When was Peter out of his mind?' Orson asked.

'Ever since I've known him. And I was out of my mind when I took up with the man. I thought he'd have committed suicide by this time. Miraculous he hasn't.'

'Why would he commit suicide?'

'I certainly would have if I were him. The man is daft. Bats in his hat.'

'He's painting well.'

'Yes. He does that. Does he have any money?'

'Not really.'

'Of course not. How are you living?'

'Frugally. I'm editing a book for a publisher, and my wife is working.'

'Oh yes, and how is she? The dear thing, she couldn't bring herself to join us?'

'She's in Germany.'

'There now, a wife who gets around. Something I always wanted to do.'

'I remember you got around in vaudeville.'

'The east coast. I never went to Europe until the war.'

'What are you doing now, Mother? Are you singing?'

'Good Lord, no. I'm running a talent agency.'

'For singers?'

'Singers, jugglers, magicians, dancers.'

'Strippers?'

'One stripper.'

'Tell me her name?'

'Why do you want to know?'

'So if I see her I'll think of you.'

'I don't think I like that reason.'

'She's your client.'

'I was never a stripper.'

'You came close with some of your costumes.'

'If you're going to attack me I'll leave.'

'I don't want you to leave. It's taken five months to get you here.'

'I've been traveling.'

'It's all right. We mustn't dwell on maternal neglect. Tell me something important. How sure are you that my father is really my father?'

'Absolutely sure.'

'Manfredo had nothing to do with me?'

'Nothing.'

'He had something to do with you.'

'In a moment of weakness. You shouldn't have seen that.'

'Where is he now? Do you still see him?'

'Not for fifteen years or more. He has palsy and can't do his stage act any more. He does card tricks at veterans' hospitals.'

'Peter thinks Manfredo was the one. Nothing convinces him otherwise.'

'It's his way, to be difficult.'

'He really is consistent about it.'

'I gave up trying to persuade him when you were a baby. Doesn't he see how much you look like him? It's quite uncanny, the resemblance.'

'His sister Molly tells him the same thing, but he refuses to believe.'

'It's rotten that he still does this to you. And you've grown so handsome since I saw you last. Has he told you about all his women, how he even brought them home? He thought every man I knew was my lover, so that's the way *he* behaved. A severe case of over-compensation if there ever was one. Is he still the king of tarts?'

'He sees several women. I don't think they're tarts.'

'Take a closer look.'

'It's difficult getting close to him. I never even know what to call him. I've spent my whole life not calling him Dad. I don't think he'd answer if I ever did call him that, or Pa, or Papa. I never call him anything.'

'It's so depressing. The Phelans are crazed people. They always have been.'

'No more so than the rest of the world.'

'Oh yes. There's a history of madmen in their past.'

'You're making that up.'

'Get your father to tell you about his Uncle Malachi.'

'I've heard him mentioned, but not with any specifics. They don't like to dredge him up.'

'Of course not. He was certifiable.'

'What did he do?'

'I'm not sure. But I know it wasn't good for anybody's health. Ask your father.'

She finished her Manhattan and touched a napkin to her lips, and I saw in her face beauty in decline, the artful makeup not quite camouflaging the furrows in her cheeks that I couldn't remember seeing five years ago. She pushed her glass away and reached for her purse.

'I must dash, darling. I have a dinner party.'

'You're such a butterfly, Mother. I didn't even get to ask what I wanted to ask you.'

'Ask away.'

'It's awkward.'

'You can ask me anything.'

'All right, anything. Can I move in with you? Temporarily. Peter works all hours of the day and night and I can't sleep. It's rather a small apartment.'

'Yes it is.'

'It truly is cramped.'

'I'm sure.'

'What do you think?'

'Oh darling, I don't think so. I have any number of people coming through all the time. Friends, clients. You'd hate it.'

'Probably so.'

'You're far better off with your father.'

'Perhaps that's true.'

'Do you have money?'

'I can cover the drinks.'

She placed on the table, in front of me, a folded one-hundred-dollar bill she had been holding in her hand.

'Buy yourself a shirt. Something stylish.'

She stood up, leaned over, and kissed me on the cheek.

'And do get some rest,' she said. 'You look worn out. Call me some night and we'll have dinner.'

Dearest Moonflake,

I write you from the dregs of my father's teapot. We live together in an armed camp, tea leaves and silence being our weapons of choice. Neither of us drink any more, he out of fear that the rivers of hooch he has already drunk have given his muse cirrhosis, I because the jigsaw puzzle that is my life becomes increasingly difficult to solve when several pieces of the puzzle are invisible. You, for instance. It is coming onto six months, your contract is up, and when are you coming back?

I cheer your early photographic success from this remote bleacher seat, slowly gnawing away my own pericardium. I miss you with every inch of that bloody sack and all it contains. I live in a world without love, without affection, without joy. I have taken to sleeping for twenty-four-hour stretches whenever I can manage it, so as to lose a day and bring the time of your arrival closer. The job affords me small pleasure, but it does fill the hours with reading that does not remind me of my own inability to write. The author I'm editing is a micturator of language, a thirsty, leaky puppy whose saving quality is his cautionary, unstated message to me never to write out of the ego; in exalting himself he wets the bed, the floor, the ceiling below.

I finally visited with Mother Belinda this week. We met for a drink and I examined her being and found her in full, late-blooming flower, not that she hadn't bloomed in earlier seasons, but now she has the advantage of looking as young as she was in the previous blossom, quite an achievement for the old girl. She is utterly without guilt concerning her abandoned child and husband. She thinks him mad, and though I would also like to judge him so, I cannot; and she thinks me 'scattered,' which I suppose is how I appear to those unable to perceive any purpose in my chaos. There is purpose, of course . . .

It was at this point, while pacing the room and considering how to value my chaos on paper, that I went downstairs to the mailbox and found Giselle's letter. It was brief: 'Dearest Orson, I'm arriving at Idlewild Tuesday at 3 p.m. on Air France. Please meet me with love. *Life* magazine wants me to work for them. Thrilling?'

The letter was six days in arriving, and so I had only one day to make the apartment livable. My stomach was suddenly full of acid, my head ached, I was weary to the point of collapse, and relentlessly sleepy.

I began moving things, carrying a three-foot standing file of Peter's finished and unfinished canvases out of my bedroom and into his studio, which may once have been a living room. Tubes of paint, boxes of tubes, jars of old brushes, boxes of jars, table sculptures, easels, palettes, rolls of canvas, and half-made frames had also spilled into my room from the studio. Whatever the artist used or created eventually found its way into every corner and closet, onto every table and shelf in the four-room apartment. He threw away nothing.

I swept the floor, washed dirty dishes, hid dirty laundry, stacked my scatter of books and manuscripts, made up the sofa bed on which I slept and which I would give to Giselle for sleeping. I would sleep on the floor, use the throw rug and two blankets as a mattress, it'll be fine; and Giselle and I would reconsummate our marriage on the sofa bed, wide enough for one-on-one, wide enough for love. We'd often done it in more cramped accommodations.

'What the hell happened here?' Peter asked when he entered the apartment, finding his studio devoid of disorder and dustballs, his own bed in the corner of the studio made with fresh pillow-case, clean sheet turned down with precision, blanket tucked army style.

'My wife is coming home,' I said.

'Home? You call this home?'

'What else would I call it?'

'Anything but home.'

'It's not your home?'

'Colonie Street is my home. This is my studio.'

'Your studio is my home. I have no other.'

'But it's not your wife's home.'

'Home is where I hang my hat and my wife,' I said.

'That remains to be seen,' Peter said. 'You know she can't live here.'

'Why not? There's plenty of room.'

'There isn't even any room for mice.'

'Are you saying she can't come here?'

'No, I'm telling you it won't work. She wouldn't stay here with me hanging around the place all day long. Don't you know anything about women?'

'I like to think I'm an expert on the subject.'

'I once thought I knew all about the art world, but I didn't know my ass from third base, as your Uncle Francis used to tell me as often as possible.'

'My Uncle Francis?'

'You know who I mean.'

'Is he really my uncle?'

'He said I was born innocent and would grow old that way. I believed him for years, but I've outgrown his prophecy. Now I'm beginning to wonder whether I've passed my old condition on to you.'

I looked at Peter and saw myself as I might be in thirty-seven years, when I too would be sixty-six. It could be worse. I knew men of fifty-five who seemed decrepit, ready to roll obligingly down that beckoning slope. Peter was still a vigorous figure, grizzled of mien, with his voluminous gray mustache all but minimalizing the crop of gray hair that sat in wavy rumples behind his half-naked forehead; robust of torso, a man who professed no interest in clothing, but who in public wore the uniform of creaseless trousers, formless coats, always with leather elbows (where did he find them?), each coat a perfect fit; an open-collared shirt to which he added a neck scarf for dress occasions; the jaunty fedora which, no matter how many times it wore out from fingering and grease, was always replaceable by a twin from the new age; and two pairs of shoes, one for work, one for walking through the world, the latter less speckled with the artist's paint. In short, the man presented himself as a visual work of art: casual self-portrait achieved without paint or brush.

'She might not stay, but I want to bring her here.'

'Bring her, bring her,' Peter said. 'I'd like to see the look of anybody who'd marry you.'

Peter smiled. I examined the smile to evaluate its meaning. Was it a real smile? It looked like a real smile. I decided to return it with a smile of my own.

Son?

Dad?

The bright light of the day had cheered me all the way to Idlewild Airport, spring only a day old but the brilliant white clouds racing ahead of my step, even so. I felt the fire of the equinox in my chest, a sign of certainty: Orson Purcell, no longer an equivocator. I saw Giselle coming toward me from a distance, hatless in her beige suit, frilly white blouse, and high heels designed in heaven, and I quick-stepped toward her, stopped her with an embrace, kissed her with my deprived mouth that was suddenly and ecstatically open and wet. Even when I broke from her I said nothing, only studied all that I had missed for so long, reinventing for future memory her yellow hair, the throne of her eyes, the grand verve of her mouth and smile; and I felt the fire broiling my heart with love and love and love. Love is the goddamnedest thing, isn't it? The oil of all human machinery. And I owned an oil well, didn't I? Separation would be bearable if it always ended with rapture of this order.

I retrieved her one suitcase (the rest of her baggage would arrive later) while she went to the ladies' room; then we quickly reunited and resumed our exotic obeisance to unspoken love. So much to say, no need to say it. In the taxi I stopped staring at her only long enough to kiss her, and then I realized she was naked beneath her skirt, which buttoned down the front. I stared at the gap between two buttons that offered me a fragmented vision of her not-very-secret hair, reached over and undid the button that allowed expanded vision, and I put my hand on her.

'Did you travel from Europe this way?'

'Only from the ladies' room.' She kissed me and whispered into my ear: 'I've been with you for twenty minutes. When are you going to fuck me?'

I immediately undid more of her buttons and parted her skirt to each side: curtain going up at the majestic theater of lust. I loosened my own clothing, shifted and slid her lengthwise on the seat and maneuvered myself between her open and upraised legs. The cab driver screeched his brakes, pulled off into the breakdown lane of Grand Central Parkway.

'That's enough of that,' the driver said. 'You wanna behave like a couple of dogs, get out on the highway and do it, but not in my cab.'

I saw a crucified Jesus dangling from the driver's rearview mirror, and a statue of the virgin glued to the top of the dashboard. The first time in my life I try to make love in a taxi, and the driver turns out to be a secret agent for the pope.

'This is my wife,' I said. 'I haven't seen her in six months. It's her first time in this country.'

'I don't care if she's your long-lost mother. Not in my cab.'

Giselle was sitting up, buttoning up, and I tucked in my shirt. The driver pulled back onto the parkway and turned on the radio. Bing Crosby came through singing 'Bewitched, Bothered and Bewildered.'

'I'm overcome by irony and chagrin,' I told the driver. 'If I were you, I wouldn't expect a big tip.'

'Just what's on the meter, buddy. I don't take tips from creeps like you.'

Condemned by taxi drivers. A new low in moral history. I took Giselle's hand in mine and put them both between the opening in her skirt, then covered her lap with my topcoat. Clandestinely, I found the passage to the Indies, stroked it as passionately as a digit would allow, and made my wife sigh with some pleasure. Life has never been easy for immigrants.

I directed the cab to my father's apartment, and Giselle was barely inside when she told Peter Phelan, 'I must photograph you.'

'What for?' asked Peter.

'Because you cry out to be photographed. Has anybody ever done a portrait of you in this studio?'

'Never.'

'I'm surprised.'

'You're naïve. I'm not important enough to be photographed.'

'I disagree,' said Giselle. 'I love the paintings of yours I've seen. I like them better than some of Matisse. I took photos of him a month ago in Paris. He was a charmer.'

'Orson,' said Peter, 'I know why you like this girl. Her lies are as beautiful as she is. How did you convince her to marry you?'

'He didn't convince me,' Giselle said. 'He *wooed* me, and carried me away to Never-Never Land.'

'You still hang out there?' Peter asked.

Giselle looked at me. 'I don't know, do we? Don't answer that.'

'Why not answer?' Peter asked.

'I want to talk about Matisse,' Giselle said. She opened her camera bag, took out her Rolleiflex, and looped its strap around her neck.

'I'm struck that you know Matisse,' Peter said.

'When I went to see him he was in his pajamas. I fell in love with his beard.'

'He says light is the future of all art,' Peter said. 'I thought that was pretty obvious, but he must understand darkness in some new way or he wouldn't think that was an original idea.'

'The only thing I understand is photographic light. I once heard a lecturer say that without light there is no photography. How's that for obvious?'

'I avoid lectures on art,' Peter said. 'It's like trying to ice-skate in warm mud.'

'Orson,' Giselle said, 'I'm falling in love with your father.'

'Gee,' I said, 'that's swell.'

Peter leaned on the table and stared at Giselle. She focused her camera, snapped his picture.

'Orson,' she said, 'stand alongside your father.'

'Father in a manner of speaking,' I said.

'However,' said Giselle. 'Just move in closer.'

I so moved, and there then came into being the first photograph ever taken of Peter Phelan and Orson Purcell together. In the photo, it was later said by some who saw it, the two men bear a family resemblance, though Peter's mustache destroys any possibility of establishing a definitive visual link. My full head of dark brown hair has a torsion comparable to Peter's, and our eyes both shine with the dark brown pupils of the Phelan line. By our clothing we separate themselves: Peter, in his bohemian uniform, I a spruced dude in double-breasted, gold-buttoned black blazer, gray slacks (retrieved that morning from the cleaners) with razor-edge creases, black wingtips burnished bright, black-and-white-striped shirt with winedark four-in-hand perfectly knotted, and red-and-black silk handkerchief roiled to a perfect breast-pocket flourish as the finishing touch.

I had not groomed myself so well since I'd arrived in New York as a basket case. This was a gift to Giselle: a vision of myself in meticulous sartorial health: no longer the manic, self-biting spiritual minister to the rabble; now Orson Purcell, a man in command of his moves, a surefooted, impeccable presence ready to enter, at a highly civilized level, the great American future, with his beautiful wife beside him.

It had been my plan to use the one hundred dollars my mother gave me to pay for a weekend at the Biltmore with Giselle, maybe even ask for the room where Zelda and Scott Fitzgerald had spent their honeymoon. This was a harebrained idea, but I thought the ambience of that outlandish marriage might serve as a psychic prod to our own marital adventure, which seemed as blasted from the outset as the Fitzgeralds' most vulnerable union.

I broached the matter in the taxi back from the airport, but Giselle had scant memory of Scott or Zelda (though I had lectured her on both).

'Anyway,' Giselle said, 'we already have an apartment on the West Side. Twelfth floor, three bedrooms, view of the river. A *Life* editor I met in Paris offered it to us. He was doing a story on Matisse the same week I was there to photograph him. You know I knew Matisse when I was little, did I ever tell you that?'

'No,' I said. 'Lots of things you've never told me.'

'The editor's in Japan for two months,' Giselle said. 'We can have his place for the whole time, if we want it.'

Giselle's steamer trunk had arrived ahead of us, and was already inside the apartment. I wanted only to make love to her, immediately and fiercely, but she flew into instant ecstasy at seeing the place, which was a triumph of modern decor, full of paintings, photos, books, mirrors, bizarre masks, pipes, stuffed birds, shards and estrays from around the world, the collections of a cultured traveler, Picasso on one wall, a sketch by Goya on another.

'It's such a stroke of luck he and I were both in Paris at the same time,' Giselle said.

'You're good friends, then,' I said.

'Well, we're friends.'

'He's most generous to you.'

'He's like that.'

'Are you lovers?'

'Orson, please.'

She opened the steamer trunk and rummaged in it for a folder with several dozen photographs. She stood them on end, one by one, on the sofa and on chairs, laid them on the dining-room table for viewing.

'This is why they want me to work for *Life*,' she said.

I looked through the photos Giselle had not put on exhibit and found more quality work; also two portraits of one Daniel Quinn, in uniform sitting on a pile of rubble, somewhere in Germany, and in mufti at a sidewalk café, somewhere in Paris? I then looked carefully at each of the photos Giselle had put on display, a photo of my sugar whore fellating the handless man; a photo of me biting myself; a group portrait of the rabble in the Garden of Eden; a photo of a smiling Henri Matisse in pajamas on his sofa, and on the wall above the sofa a painting of a cross-legged nude woman; industrial images – great gears and machines of unfathomable size and function in a German factory; a barge on a German river with a deckhand waving his hat and pissing toward the sky; a woman sitting in a *Bierstube* perhaps exposing herself to two American soldiers; two seated women in their seventies, elegantly garbed, aged beauties both, in tears.

'I can't imagine *Life* running most of these pictures,' I said.

'What they like is that I seem to be present when strange things happen. Keep looking.' She stood beside me as I looked.

A farmer was plowing his field behind an ox that had been branded with a swastika.

'When *Stars and Stripes* printed this one,' Giselle said, 'somebody went out to the farmer's place and killed the ox.'

To my eye the photos all had quality. The woman had talent for capturing essential instants, for finding the precise moment when the light and the angle of vision allow an act or an object most fully to reveal its meaning or its essence. These pictures set themselves apart from routine photojournalism. Giselle, six months ago an amateur, was suddenly light-years ahead of so many of her peers. Obviously she had a future in photography. Her beauty would open every door of all those male bastions, and this artistic eye, perhaps developed in childhood in her mother's art gallery, would carry her forward from there.

'This looks familiar,' I said, and I picked up a photo whose locale I recognized: the stage of the Folies Bergère. A dozen near-naked chorus girls and the beautiful Folies star, Yvonne Menard, were in seeming full-throated song, all watching, at center stage, an American-army corporal kneeling in front of a statuesque beauty in pasties and G-string, the corporal wearing a handlebar mustache for the occasion, his face only inches from the dancer's crotch.

'It looks sillier than I imagined,' I said.

'It is quite humiliating,' Giselle said.

'How did you arrange it? They never allow photos during the show.'

'I told them I was on assignment for *Life*, and they let me do anything I wanted. I did get others but this is all I really was after.'

On our first trip to Paris, before we married, I took Giselle to the Folies and, because I was in uniform, an easy object of derision, I was dragooned from the audience onto the stage by the beautiful Yvonne, put in the same situation as this kneeling corporal, then pulled to my feet, drawn to the abundant bosom of the dancer who had stuck the mustache on my lip, twirled about to a few bars of music, and then abandoned as the stage went black and the dancers ran into the wings. Like a blind man, I felt with my foot for the edge of the stage (a six- or eight-foot drop if I missed my footing), found the edge, sat on it with legs dangling, and slid sideways toward the stairs that led to the audience level. I was still sliding when the lights went up and I was discovered in yet another ridiculous position. I scrambled down the stairs and back to Giselle, who was so amused by it all that she kissed me.

'You were very funny,' she had said then. 'It was just as funny when I took this picture,' she said now. 'The poor boy didn't even know he was being humiliated. Neither did you, did you, my love?'

'If you have a mustache to put on me, I'll be delighted to be *your* fool and give a repeat performance,' I said. 'I'll even do it without the mustache. I'll even do it in public.'

I embraced her and undid her blouse and knew that she and I would separate, that something fundamental had gone awry and very probably could not be fixed. With her every breath she revealed not only her restlessness but her faithlessness. I saw in her that surge of youth and beauty that was so in love with itself and its imagined possibilities (they must surely be infinite in her imagination now) that even the fetters of marriage were not only ineffectual, they were invisible to the logic of her private mystique.

Standing before me in her uniform of love, she was voluptuosity itself: books could be written about the significance of Giselle in her garments, and how, together, she and they communicated their meaning. The word 'noble' came to mind. What could that possibly mean? I backed away and studied her.

'Do you think we married too soon?' I asked.

'I didn't,' she said.

'You seem so certain.'

'I never make a wrong decision on things like that.'

'Are there any other things like that?'

'I know what I want,' she said.

'And do you have it?'

'I have some things. I have you.'

'Well, that's true enough.'

'Why do you want to talk? Why don't you make love to me?'

'I'm discovering what a noble creature you are. I understood it at the baths in Wiesbaden but I didn't put the word to it until now. Noble. How you carried that remarkable body of yours, the way you sliced the water with your arms when you swam, the way you sat beside me on the bench in the steam room with all those other ignoble nudes, enveloped in clouds of love and heat, and you a presence as brilliant as the fire that heated the rocks. The way you looked when you lay on that cot behind the white curtain to take your nap, the erotic extreme of your arched back when I knelt by your cot and offered you worship.'

'Nobody ever made me explode the way you did then. If I said skyrockets you'd scold me for using a cliché. How did you learn so much about women?'

'I've been a lifelong student.'

'I wonder what will happen to us.'

'Everything,' I said.

'It must be valuable.'

'Very true. If it isn't valuable it's a malaise.'

'I don't ever want to do anything to hurt you.'

'But you might.'

'You really think I might?'

'Giselle is an undiscovered country.'

'So is Orson.'

'No, not any more.'

And this was true. I knew what was in store for me, felt it coming. I decided to blot it out and I pulled Giselle toward me.

3

'I am desperately weary of contemplating the fact that I have nothing to contemplate except the weariness of having nothing to contemplate.'

The sentence took form in my mind as I sat in the anteroom of the publishing house that had hired me to edit the pretentious subliterary drivel of Meriwether Macbeth. On the walls of the anteroom, whose floor was covered with a solid dark red carpet suitable for red-carpet authors, I looked up at the giant faces of writers whose work had been published by this house, and who had very probably trod this carpet, or these bare floorboards in pre-carpet days, hauling in their MSS. in briefcase, suitcase, steamer trunk, wheelbarrow, or perhaps only jacket pocket if the author was a poet. A pantheon is what one might call the epiphany on these walls: Dreiser, Dos Passos, Yeats, O'Casey, Wharton, Frost, Joyce, Steinbeck, Sherwood Anderson. We or our work have all passed through these hallowed halls, they say; and we are what hallowed them. Which boards, which carpet will Orson Purcell hallow in his future? None at all should my present frame of mind continue, for I knew that line of mine – I am desperately weary et cetera – was hardly the mind-set required of hallowed hangables.

My editor was in conference but would be available soon, the receptionist said. I waited, trying to conjure a way out of the conversational cul-de-sac any statement about literary weariness would lead me into, and returned always to the magnificence of my morning romp on Giselle's sacred playing fields. But it is written:

one may not raise with one's editor such uxorious delight unless one's editor raises the subject first. Better to speak of the upcoming Hemingway, the Salinger phenomenon.

I walked to the rack of books on display for visitors, found the Cassirer, leafed in it, always wanted this. I'll ask Walker for it. I went back to my chair, opened the book randomly to an early page, and read: 'No longer can man confront reality immediately; he cannot see it, as it were, face to face. Physical reality seems to recede in proportion as man's symbolic activity advances. Instead of dealing with the things themselves man is in a sense constantly conversing with himself.'

A book about me, I thought, and I put it in my pocket. The use of the word 'symbolic' brought Malachi to mind, and also what Peter had said when I asked if Malachi really was a madman, as Mother had suggested.

'The man had madness thrust upon him,' Peter said. 'The poor son of a bitch lost his cow to a Swedish cardsharp in a poker game and never got over it, blamed his wife, the devil, all Swedes, half his relatives. I never got the full story, just hand-me-down snatches from Sarah and what Molly got from Mama. As to madness in the family, Tommy's not all there, but that's not madness. And who's to say I'm not nuts? We're an odd lot, boy, we Phelans.'

I wasn't sure whether I was included in that grouping; and I let it pass.

Walker Pettijohn, venerated editor, emerged from his inner sanctum with the durable particularities of his presence in place: the wild crown of the whitest of white hair, the face flushed not from booze but from the wrong shaving cream, the corporate stomach made round by the most exquisite restaurants in New York, the smile known round the world of international publishing, and the genuine glad hand that was as reassuring to me as the very light of day when I awoke at morning. The Pettijohn handshake drew me into the sanctum and toward the boar's nest of books and paper that was the workspace of this legendary discoverer and shaper of American literature.

'Did your wife arrive?' he asked me.

'She did. Indeed.'

'And all is well?'

'Let's not get into wellness,' I said. 'She may go to work for *Life* magazine.'

'How fine.'

'Yes, perhaps.'

'Ah, you're in your gloom still.'

'It's gloomy, this life.'

'Meriwether Macbeth had a good time all his life.'

'All right, we're around to that.'

'Are you ready to talk, or should we do this next week? I can wait.'

'Now is the time.'

'Then what I need is more of that wildness of Meriwether, that silliness, that absurd boyishness that kept him floating in that crazy, artistic, and erotic world of his. Peter Pan de Sade.'

'He wasn't really erotic. He was just a satyr.'

'Same thing in print.'

'No. He's an asshole.'

'Of course, that's his charm.'

'Assholes are now bookishly charming?'

'This one is. He did whatever came into his head.'

'Infantile behavior to be cherished.'

'You know what I'm talking about, Orson. Don't get remote. Use that brilliant brain of yours.'

'If I were brilliant I wouldn't be dealing with this fool.'

'What I want is more of the stupidity of the man's life, the empty nonsense, the ridiculous logic, the romancing of worthless women, the publishing of rotten poetry. I think of that masterpiece you tossed out: "Naked Titty Proves God Exists."'

'My life is full of error,' I said. 'I stand corrected.'

'We're not trying to be objective here about poetic values, we're revealing Macbeth for what he was, and if we do this book right the whole world will have a fine old time seeing through his façades.'

'They're not worth seeing through.'

'Orson, you're being difficult. You don't want to quit this, do you?'

'Of course not. It's my life blood.'

'If you say you'll do it we'll move on to more serious matters, like your own work. Shall we do that?'

'Let's do that.'

Pettijohn reached into a pile of manuscripts and pulled out one bound in a yellow cover (after Giselle's hair), and opened it, revealing handwritten notes clipped to the first page of the manuscript. He looked at me and I instantly understood that here would come a true judgment on my would-be work and my surrogate self. Now would come the revelation of my flawed brain, errant heart, rapscallion soul. The eradication of the future was at hand.

'This is absolutely brilliant,' Pettijohn said. 'I love it.'

I was stunned.

'There's a very original voice in these pages,' said Pettijohn, 'and nobody writes dialogue better than you. You're the best since O'Hara.'

I could not speak.

'There's a potentially great book here,' said Pettijohn, 'and I want you to know I'm behind it one thousand percent.' He paused, stared me in the eye. 'But I can't get anybody else in the house to back me up. Nobody sees what I see in it.'

The iceman finally cometh.

'I've made notes on it, and I've included what others say about it, so you'll know the negatives.'

'Then you're rejecting it.'

'Not I,' said Pettijohn, 'not I. But I'm only one opinion here, and one opinion does not a novel publish.'

'A rejection by any other name.'

'Consider it temporary. Let me see it again when you've gone further with the story.'

'What do people fault?'

Pettijohn cast his eyes toward the ceiling. I anticipated a rain of slush from anonymous editorial heights.

'People like the story up to a point, but they think the writing lacks the necessary poetry. And they say it lacks a verve for life, that it's life seen through a black veil of doom. The truth is, Orson, that people do occasionally laugh, even on the gallows. But this book is absolutely joyless all the way. This doesn't bother *me*, but others it does. To hear them talk you'd think nobody had ever written negatively about life before you. But my arguments convince nobody about this manuscript.'

'No poetry, no verve for life, eh. They should've seen me in bed this morning. I was poetry in motion.'

'A wonderful way to avenge yourself on your enemies. Fuck them all to death.'

I stood up and so did Pettijohn, who picked up the manuscript.

'You want to take this?'

'I'll get it another time.'

'What about these notes?'

'Their essence is enough for one day.'

'You'll fatten up Meriwether's book, won't you?'

'I'll make it obscenely obese.'

We nodded and shook hands across the desk and then I found my way out through the warren of corridors to the waiting room. I kept my gaze level and steady, did not glance upward toward the epiphanic walls.

Lacking in my work, and perhaps in the deepest reaches of my person, the necessary poetry, the necessary verve for life, I decided to acquire some of each, or, that being impractical, to discover, at the very least, where, how, and from whom verve and poetry were dispensed to seekers.

When I came out of the lobby of my publisher's building and stepped onto Fifth Avenue I felt the pulsation of a new vibrancy, putting me at one with possibility in the land of opportunity. I knew this was a wholly unreasonable attitude in the face of what I had just gone through, but one must not look too closely at what liberates one into excitement. I assayed the sky and found it clear, blue, and glorious. I welcomed the snap in the early spring breeze, and I crossed to the sunny side of the avenue to confront the warmth and light of the noonday sun, which was just slightly past its zenith.

I was hungry and I envisioned food of delectable piquancy, served in luxurious surroundings by punctilious and servile waiters. I would order veal, possibly venison, perhaps duck. But I did not yet want to become stationary, however tempting and elegant the atmosphere. I would walk now, but where? I had almost three hours to spend before meeting Giselle. I'd told her to meet me about three o'clock in an Irish bar on Sixth Avenue, not far from her point of rendezvous with the editors of the greatest picture magazine in the world. Should I now walk north to Central Park, embrace the natural world of trees, of soft spring earth and new greenery, or weave my way among the sumptuous lobbies and cafés of the hotels on Central Park South? No, I longed for something grander and with more verve than those, something even more poetic than nature.

I strode southward on the avenue and knew the instant pleasure that came from the high elegance of the windows of the great stores. In Saks' window I saw a suit that I instantly coveted, a double-breasted gray glen plaid, one of the grandest-looking suits I'd ever seen. In the window of The Scribner Book Store I found two books that suited my mood: *Life Is Worth Living* by Fulton Sheen and *The Power of Positive Thinking* by Norman Vincent Peale, wise men both. I would buy both books when I had the money. I turned, decided to say hello to Jesus at St Patrick's Cathedral; and I remembered the flustered Methodist cleric who protested to his Irish taxi driver that he had asked not for St Patrick's, but for Christ's Church, and the driver advised him, 'If you don't find him here he's not in town.' There's verve.

I crossed the avenue at 49th Street and walked west between the British Empire building and La Maison Française toward the sunken plaza in Rockefeller Center. I stopped and read the credo of the great John D. Rockefeller, Jr, carved into a slab of polished black marble: 'I believe in the sacredness of a promise, that a man's word should be as good as his bond; that character – not wealth or power or position – is of supreme worth.' Wonderful. And more: 'I believe that the rendering of useful service is the common duty of mankind and that only in the purifying fire of sacrifice is the dross of selfishness consumed and the greatness of the human soul set free . . . I believe that love is the greatest thing in the world . . .' And so do I, John, so do I.

I continued my walk through the Center, the greatest concentration of urban buildings in the world. I remembered coming here with Peter when I was a child to see the tallest Christmas tree in the world. I followed my shoes and found myself in the lobby of the Time-Life building, home to the greatest concentration of magazines in the world, and considered going up to the office where Giselle was being seduced away from me, but descended instead into the underground world of Rockefeller Center, the most labyrinthine subterranean city since the catacombs, passing stores and restaurants and murals and sculpture, far more exciting to a refined sensibility than any underground passageway anywhere, including Mammoth Cave, or the sewers of Paris. I took a stairway up into the RCA building, home to the greatest radio and television networks in the world (and next door the Associated Press building, home to the greatest news service in the world). Nothing in urban, suburban, or rural history could compare with this achievement, and as I moved through the magnificent corridors I noted shining brass everywhere: in the floors, the hand railings, the revolving doors; and the thought of the cost of such elegance exalted me.

The very idea of selfless munificence in the service of the architectural imagination was surely a pinnacle in the history of man's capacity to aspire. And aspire I did, assuming the poetry of all this grandeur into my eyes, my ears, my sense of smell, the poetry of man the master builder, the poetry of man who climbed to the skies with his own hands, the poetry of Babel refined into godly and humanistic opportunity and respect and mortar and stone and endeavor and joy and love and money and thickness and breadth and luxury and power and piety and wonder and French cuisine and the American novel and jazz music and (oh yes, Meriwether, oh yes) the naked titties of ten thousand women. Oh the immensity of it all!

I taxied back to the apartment where Giselle and I were staying and, from the desk where our host kept his financial records, expropriated two checkbooks, two dozen of the host's business cards, several letters that would verify my identity if the business cards and the checkbooks did not, assorted press credentials from the U.S., West Germany, the Soviet Union, Brazil, and an Arab nation whose name I did not immediately recognize, all identifying the owner as a writer for *Life* magazine. I folded these items into one of the host's several empty breast-pocket wallets, dialed the number at *Life* Giselle had given me, and left a message for her: 'Meet me at either the Palm Court or the Oak Bar of the Plaza Hotel, the greatest hotel in America, when you are free,' and I then set out in further quest of poetry and verve.

The first thing I did was register and establish my credit with the Plaza's front desk, then equip myself with ready cash. I engaged a corner suite that looked out on Fifth Avenue, Central Park, and the Grand Army Plaza, and then I descended to Fifth Avenue and on to Saks, where I bought three new shirts and ties, pocket handkerchiefs, shoes, belt, socks, and the gray glen plaid suit I'd seen in the window; but I would accept it all, I told the clerk, only if alterations were done within the hour (cost not an obstacle) and delivered to my suite at the Plaza, which they were.

I bought two pounds of Barricini chocolates for Giselle, and back at the suite ordered two dozen yellow roses from the hotel florist and four bottles of her favorite French wines from room service. I went back downstairs and explored the lobby, found the Palm Court too crowded, sought out an empty corner of the Oak Bar, and ordered my first drink in five and a half months, a Scotch on the rocks with water on the side. I sipped it with care, waiting for my system to feel the first alcoholic rush of the new year, and wondering if Dr Tannen's prophecy would be correct: that, should I ever again drink alcohol, the flood controls of my brain would let the madness cascade back into my life.

I affirmed my disbelief in this diagnosis with another sip of whiskey, and only then did I look about me at this walnut-dark, wood-paneled male saloon, with its murals out of the storied past of the Plaza – a horse and carriage in a snowstorm in front of the old hotel, water spilling out of the fountain's dish while a full moon is all but covered by clouds. By the light from the room's wall sconces and copper windows this country's Presidents, giants of capital, movie stars, and great writers had drunk for half a century. I recognized no one. I took another sip and knew the ease that drink had always provided me, a flow of juices that wakened dormant spirits and improbable values. The first sips alone did this. Consider, then, the potential of an entire bottle.

For months I had not seen anybody through the auroral brilliance that those summoned juices could generate. My life had been repetitive ritual: rise from narrow bed, dress in sordid clothing, eat meagerly and without relish, go out into the world to edit a book you loathe, confront what you now knew to be an unpublishable novel of your own making, come home in darkness to reinhabit your father's bohemian gloom, and write your daily letter to Giselle.

I knew the danger of imposing too much trivia on my letters and so, one by one, I outlined the lives of my putative relatives to her, also wrote her short essays on the values assorted poets and writers imparted to the world, even if they never published a word. The task, of itself, I wrote her, was holy, the only task atheists could pursue that was buoyed by the divine afflatus. As for myself, the afflatus was flatulent.

I realized with each new sip of Scotch that Dr Tannen was wrong. I had, since Germany, accepted the doctor's rules and entertained no temptation to suck on a whiskey bottle. But here again came that most wondrous potion into my life, already sending enriched phlogiston into my internal organs, upthrusting my spirit to an equivalency with Presidents, giants of capital, movie stars, and great writers, and providing me with all this not through fraudulence, bravado, delusion, or hallucination. None of that was on the table. This was real. I saw the future unrolling itself before me, knew phlogiston, fraudulence, badness, chocolates, yellow roses, and new neckties when I saw them, Mr Plaza.

I ordered another Scotch.

A man of about forty years sat at the next table and placed his folded *New York Times* on an adjacent chair. I could read one headline: U.S. – South Korea Units Lash Foe; Jet Bombers Cut Routes Far North. The owner of the newspaper ordered a martini and I asked him, 'Could I borrow your *Times* for a quick look?'

The man shrugged and nodded and I looked through the paper: Senate will confirm Chip Bohlen as ambassador to Moscow despite McCarthy attack. Alfred Hitchcock melodrama, *I Confess*, is panned by reviewer. Twenty-three killed, thirty wounded in Korea, says Defense Department. *Salome*, with Rita Hayworth, Stewart Granger, and Charles Laughton, opens at the Rivoli Wednesday.

It all served to incite informational depression in me, especially the opening of *Salome*. We all know what Salome does to John the Baptist, don't we, moviegoers? I folded the newspaper and returned it to my neighbor.

'The news is awful,' I said.

'You mean out of Korea?' said the man, who had a look about him that Orson seemed to recognize.

'Everywhere. Even Alfred Hitchcock isn't safe.'

'Who's Alfred Hitchcock?'

'He's a Senator. A Roman Senator. He looks like Charles Laughton.'

'Oh.'

'He's married to Rita Hayworth. You know her?'

'The name has a ring.'

'I agree,' I said. 'Reeeeee-ta. A ring if there ever was one.'

'I *beat* Korea,' the man said.

I now realized that this man looked very like Archie Bell, the warrant officer I had served with at Frankfurt. It wasn't Archie, of course, but there was something about the mouth; and the eyes were similar. But the face, the hair – nothing like Archie.

'They sent me to Korea,' Archie said, 'and they thought they were givin' me tough duty. You know what I did? I beat the shit out of my knee with an entrenchin' tool and got a medical discharge. They thought I caught shrapnel. Got the pension, all the musterin'-out stuff, and right away I invested it in Jeeps. Willys, you know the company?'

'The name has a ring,' I said. 'Wil-yyyyyys.'

'Today Kaiser-Frazer bought Willys for sixty-two mill. You know what that means?'

'Not a clue.'

'That's major-league auto-making. My broker says I could double my money.'

'Smart,' I said. 'Very smart. I had a pretty good afternoon too. I started out with a hundred, and it's ten times that now, maybe more.'

'Hey, buddy, this is a good day for the race.'

'The human race?'

'Noooooo. The race race. We're beatin' the niggers.'

'I noticed. They don't have any in here. But then again Lincoln used to drink here,' I said.

'Izzat right?'

'Every President since Thomas Jefferson drank here.'

'Izzat right? I didn't think the place was that old.'

'Who's your broker?'

'Heh, heh. You think I'm gonna tell you?'

'You know who my broker is?'

'Enhhh.'

'Thomas Jefferson.'

'A two-dollar bill.'

'My card, friend,' I said, handing him the business card of the *Life* editor. 'Call me anytime. Let's have lunch and plan some investments.'

'Watch out for falling rocks,' the man said.

'Here?'

'Everywhere,' he said, and he smiled a smile that I recognized from the poker games in Frankfurt. This was the Captain, invested with Archie Bell's smile. I left the Oak Bar without looking back, knowing my past was not far behind. I took the elevator to the suite, put on my new clothes, opened a bottle of Le Montrachet to let it breathe, then descended to the Palm Court to meet the most beautiful, most sensual, most photographic, most photogenic wife in the history of the world.

* * *

'You look *merveilleux*,' Giselle said, stroking the waves of my hair, feeling the silk of my pocket handkerchief between her thumb and forefinger. I had been sitting alone in the Palm Court, sipping whiskey, listening to the violin and piano playing Gershwin's 'Summertime,' when the livin' is easy, a perfect theme for this day. The song wafted over the potted palms, over the heads of the thinning, mid-afternoon crowd.

'I never expected this,' Giselle said.

'I decided to reward myself,' I said.

'Reward? What happened?'

'My editor loves my book. I asked him for an instant advance and got it.'

'Oh, Orse, that's beautiful.' She leaned over and kissed me, pulled away, then kissed me again.

'And what about *your* day?' I asked.

'They hired me. I go to work whenever I want. Tomorrow if I want. I told them I wanted to go to Korea and cover the war.'

'I knew it would happen. Why *wouldn't* they hire you?'

'I thought they wanted more experience.'

'They buy talent, not experience. Everybody buys talent.'

'Isn't it nice we're both so talented?'

'It's absolutely indescribable,' I said.

'I always knew you were going to be famous,' she said. 'My wonder boy. I knew it. That's one of the reasons I married you.'

'*Merveilleuse*,' I said.

'I was so surprised when you said to meet you here,' Giselle said. 'I thought we'd meet in some terrible Irish café.'

'There are no Irish cafés, my love.'

'I'm so happy,' she said. 'Order me something.'

'Port. You love port in the afternoon.'

'And Le Montrachet,' she said.

'I know.'

She looked at the wine list, found half a dozen port wines listed, their prices ranging from one dollar to eighteen dollars. She ordered the four-dollar item, and the waiter smiled.

'You know,' said the waiter, 'this is the wine Clark Gable ordered when he proposed to Carole Lombard. Right at that table over there.' He pointed to an empty table.

'It's fated,' said Giselle.

'You two seem to be very much in love,' the waiter said. I looked up at him and saw a Valentino lookalike, a perfect waiter for the occasion.

'What's more,' the waiter added, 'the first day this hotel opened, a Prussian count proposed to his American bride in this room. So you see, this is where happy marriages begin.'

'What a waiter!' I said. 'I'm putting you in my will. What's your name.'

'Rudolph Valentino,' the waiter said.

'I thought so,' I said. 'Bring us the port. Two.'

Giselle kissed me again. 'My wonder boy,' she said.

The light in the Palm Court was pale beige, my favorite color on Giselle. I looked at the display of desserts the Palm Court offered: raspberries and strawberries, supremely ripe and out of season, bananas, grapes, peaches, plums, pineapples, and fruit I could not call by name. This was the center of the fruitful universe. All things that happened within its confines were destined to change the world. Values would tumble. The rain of money and glory would fall on all significant consumers. There was no end to the sweetness of existence that was possible if you ordered a bowl of raspberries in the Palm Court.

'This is what your life is going to be like from now on,' I said. 'This is what success looks like. The absence of money will never again interfere with your happiness.'

Giselle beamed at me the most extraordinary smile ever uttered by woman. I considered it for as long as it lasted, tucked it away in the archives of my soul, and raised my glass of port to hers. We clinked.

'May our love live forever,' I said.

'Forever,' said Giselle.

'And if it doesn't, the hell with it.'

'The hell with it,' said Giselle.

'There's Ava Gardner over there,' I said, pointing to a woman in close conversation with a man whose back was to us.

'Really?' asked Giselle.

'Indubitably,' I said, but then I looked again and corrected myself. 'No, it's not her. I was mistaken. It's Alfred Hitchcock.'

Giselle's laughter shattered chandeliers throughout the Palm Court.

I stood next to the yellow roses, staring out of a window of our suite at Fifth Avenue below. The fading light of this most significant day (such frequent confrontations with significance were a delight) was troublesome to my eyes, but I could see a roofless motorcar stop at the carriage entrance to the hotel, saw Henry James step down from it, adjust his soft hat, then extend his hand to Edith Wharton, the pair bound for dinner in the hotel's Fifth Avenue Café. Teddy Roosevelt struck a pose for photographers on the hotel steps, his first visit to the city since shooting his fifth elephant, and Mrs John D. Rockefeller waded barefoot in the Plaza's fountain to raise money for widows and orphans spawned by the oil cartel. As I stared across the avenue at the Sherry Netherland, I saw Ernest Hemingway in the window of an upper floor, his arm around Marlene Dietrich. The great writer and great actress waved to me. I waved back.

At the sound of a door opening I turned to see Giselle, wrapped in the silk robe and negligee I'd bought her when she learned we were staying the night at the hotel. I poured the Montrachet and handed her the glass, then poured my own. Never had a married man been luckier than I at this moment. By virtue of the power vested in me I now pronounce you husband and traitor, traitor and wife. God must have loved betrayals, he made so many of them.

'I think you are probably at this moment,' I said, 'the most fucksome woman on this planet.'

'What an exciting word,' Giselle said.

I opened her robe and peeled it away from her shoulders. The perfection in the placement of a mole on her right breast all but moved me to tears. She stood before me in her nightgown, beige, the color of pleasure, and as I kissed her I eased her backward onto the sofa, and knelt beside her. I put my hands on the outside of her thighs and slid her nightgown upward. She raised her hips, an erotic elevation to ease my task, and revealed the bloom of a single yellow rose, rising in all its beauty from the depths of her secret garden.

'Are there thorns on this rose?' I asked.

'I eliminated them,' Giselle said.

'You are the most resourceful woman on this planet.'

'Am I?'

'You are. Did Quinn ever tell you you were resourceful?'

'Never. Say the word.'

'Resourceful?'

'The other word.'

'Ah, you mean fucksome.'

'Yes. I like that word. Don't get any thorns in your mouth.'

'I thought you said there were no thorns.'

'I don't think I missed any.'

'Did Quinn ever have to worry about thorns?'

'Never. Shhhhh.'

Silence prevailed.

'Aaaahhhh.'

'Was that the first?'

'Yes.'

Silence prevailed again.

'Aaaahhhh.'

'Was that the second?'

'Yes.'

Silence prevailed yet again.

'Aaaahhhh. Aaaahhhh.'

'Third and fourth?'

'Yes. Say the word.'

'Fourth?'

'No. Fucksome. Say fucksome.'

'I'd rather you say it.'

'Does your stripper say it for you?'

'Never.'

'Is your stripper fucksome?'

'Somewhat.'

'Do you tell her she's somewhat fucksome?'

'Never.'
'Why are you still wearing your suit?'
'It's my new glen plaid. I thought you liked it.'
'I do, but you never wear a suit when you make love.'
'This is the new Orson. Natty to a fault.'
'I want to go onto the bed.'
'A sensational idea. Then we can do something else.'
'Exactly. Are you going to keep your glen plaid on?'
'Yes, it makes me feel fuckish.'
'Another word.'
'Do you like it?'
'Somewhat. I think I prefer fucksome.'
'They have different meanings.'
'Does your stripper make you feel fuckish?'
'Somewhat.'
'Have you told her?'
'Never. What does Quinn say that you make him feel?'
'I couldn't say.'
'I think I'll take my suit off.'
'I prefer it that way. It makes me feel fucksome.'
'You mean fuckish.'
'I prefer fucksome.'
'Language isn't a matter of preference.'
'Mine is.'
Silence prevailed again.
'Is this better?'
'Much better. And a better view.'
'How would you describe the view?'
'Classic in shape.'
'Classic. Now that's something.'
'And larger than most.'
'Larger than most. That's *really* something, coming from you.'
'It also looks extremely useful.'
'You are a very fucksome woman, Giselle.'
'Fucksome is as fucksome does,' Giselle said.

4

Giselle and I walked along 57th Street and down Broadway, a change of scenery, a move into the murderous light of eschatological love and sudden death. I had convinced her after five hours of lovemaking that the walking was necessary to rejuvenate our bodies for the next encounter. Master the hiatus, I said, and you will regain the season. I did not tell her where I was taking her. I told her the story of Meriwether Macbeth, protagonist of the memoir I was putting together from a chaotic lifetime of journals, notes, stories, poetry, letters, my task being to create the quotient of one man's verbal life.

'He lived with a woman who called herself Jezebel Jones, a name she adopted after meeting Meriwether,' I said. 'She was a slut of major calibration, but quite bright and extremely willful; and together she and Meriwether cut a minor public swath through Greenwich Village for the better part of a decade. She was known for bringing home strangers and creating yet another ménage for Meriwether, who had grown bored with Jezebel's solitary charms. She turned up one night with a hunchback who called himself Lon because his hump was said to look very like the hump Lon Chaney wore in *The Hunchback of Notre Dame*, and Jezebel found the deformed Lon enormously appealing. But it turned out Lon was a virgin, a neuter, who had never craved the sexual life, was content to move through his days without expending sperm on other citizens. Jezebel tried to change this by teaching the game to Lon and his lollipop. She enlisted Meriwether's aid when Lon visited their apartment, and Meriwether, through deviousness, bound Lon's hands with twine, then tied Lon's legs to the bedposts as Jezebel, having unsuited the hunchback, aroused him to spire-like loftiness, and mounted him. Released from bondage, Lon fled into the night, returned the next day with his Doberman, and sicked the dog on Jezebel and Meriwether. As the dog bit repeatedly into various parts of Jezebel, Meriwether took refuge behind the sofa, his face buried in his arms. Lon moved the sofa and, with the hammer he had brought with him, crushed Meriwether's head with a dozen blows. Jezebel survived and provided enough detail of the attack to put Lon into the asylum for life, and Meriwether moved on to a posthumous realm that had eluded him all his life: fame.'

'This is where I spend a bit of my social life when the world is too much with me,' I said, pulling out bar stools for Giselle and myself.

We were in The Candy Box, a 52nd Street club that featured striptease dancers from 6:00 p.m. till 3:00 a.m. It was eight o'clock and the low-ceilinged room was already full of smoke that floated miasmically in the club's bluish light. Four young women in lowcut street dresses sat at the bar, two of them head-to-head with portly cigar smokers. The other two, on the alert for comparable attention, turned their eyes to us, recognized me, gave me greetings.

I called them by name and sat beside Giselle. On the dance floor, Consuela, a busty platinum blonde, awkwardly unhooked her skirt to the music of a four-piece band, while three other club girls cozied a table full of men, and another dozen solitary males watched the blonde with perfect attention.

'This is so depressing,' Giselle said. 'Do you come here to be depressed?'

'I know the bartender,' I said.

'You know more than the bartender.'

'He's a friend. He lost his leg at Iwo Jima. A colleague in war, so to speak.'

'And your stripper, she works here?'

'Five nights a week.'

'Are we in luck? Will we get to see her?'

'It turns out we will.'

'Is that her trying to make herself naked up there?'

'No, that's Consuela, one of the new ones, still a bit of an amateur. My Brenda is a talented stripper.'

'Your Brenda,' said Giselle. 'Your behavior is ridiculous, Orson. It's the way you were back in Germany. You seem to like living in the sewer.'

'Orson the underground man.'

'What'll you have, Orse old buddy?' the bartender asked. He was tall and muscular, with a space where his left canine tooth used to be, a casualty of a bar fight. But you should see the other guy's dental spaces.

'Port wine, Eddie,' I said. 'The best you have. Two.'

'Port wine. Don't get too many calls for that.'

'It's a romantic drink, Eddie. My wife and I are celebrating our reunion. I brought her in to meet Brenda.'

'Yeah? Now that's a switch, bringin' the wife in here. You don't see much of that either.'

'Wives have a right to know their husbands' friends,' Giselle said.

'Not a whole lot of husbands buy that idea,' Eddie said.

'It's trust, Eddie,' I said. 'There has to be more trust in this world. Shake hands with Giselle.'

'A pleasure,' Eddie said, taking Giselle's hand.

'When is Brenda on?' I asked.

'She's next.'

'We *are* in luck,' Giselle said.

'Eddie, would you ask her to come out and say hello before her act?'

'Right away, old buddy.'

'Eddie is certainly a friendly bartender for a place like this,' Giselle said.

'You should avoid categorical thinking, Giselle. There are no places like this.'

'They're all over Europe.'

'The Candy Box is different. Trust me.'

'Why should I trust you?'

'Because basically I'm a good person,' I said.

'That's another reason I married you, but I've decided that doesn't mean I should trust you.'

'In God we trust. All others should be bullwhipped.'

I saw Brenda walking toward us from the back of the club, wrapped in a black dressing gown that covered less than half of her upper significance. On the stage Consuela was removing, as a final gesture, her minimal loin string, revealing a shaded blur that vanished in the all-but-black light that went with that ultimate moment.

I stood to greet Brenda, her eyes heavily mascaraed, her red lipstick outlined in black, her shining black hair loose to her shoulders. I bussed her cheek, offered her my bar stool, then introduced her to Giselle as 'my good friend Brenda, who has done everything a woman of her profession is ever asked to do by men.'

'And what is your profession, Brenda?' Giselle asked.

'She's a dancer,' I said.

'I didn't ask you, I asked Brenda.'

'Is this really your wife, Orson?'

'She really is,' I said. 'Isn't she lovely?'

'I'm a dancer,' Brenda said to Giselle. 'What's your profession, honey?'

'Giselle is a photographer,' I said.

'You take my picture,' Brenda said, 'I'll take yours,' and she parted the skirt of her gown and spread her legs.

'Is that what you'd like me to photograph?' Giselle asked.

'No,' said Brenda. 'That's my camera.'

'She has a sense of humor, your Brenda,' Giselle said.

'She's had dinner with Juan Perón, she's stripped for the Prince of Wales. Is there anything you haven't experienced, Brenda?' I asked.

'True love,' said Brenda. 'Men only want my body.'

'What a pity,' said Giselle.

'It's good for business, is how I look at it,' said Brenda. She stood up from the bar stool. 'Business calls me.'

'Happy business,' Giselle said as Brenda left us.

'A lively mind, don't you think?' I said.

'I'd say her tits were her best feature,' Giselle said.

On stage Brenda worked with a film of herself dancing, and a stage spotlight. The film and her live dance were the same but in the film she was seducing a shadowy male figure. As she removed a garment on stage the camera moved in for a close-up on the area about to be revealed, then cut away as the stage garment was tossed. The spotlight dimmed progressively as nudity impended, and then the camera focused in grainy close-up on the parts of Brenda that were illegal in the flesh.

'Clever juxtaposition, isn't it?' I said. 'It was Brenda's own idea.'

'Two Brendas for the price of one,' Giselle said.

I turned my back to Brenda's performance and faced Giselle. 'I have something I must tell you,' I said.

'Don't you want to see how Brenda comes out?'

'I know how Brenda comes out. My editor didn't buy my book, he rejected it. The money I spent belonged to your friendly editor from *Life*. I took two of his checkbooks and his identification to cash them. It's really quite simple to assume a new identity.'

Giselle stared and said nothing.

'The care and feeding of love and beauty should be a primary concern of the human race, but if I can't afford it at any given moment, it doesn't follow I should abandon my concern. Making love to you this afternoon, I argued with myself about confessing the deed, but confession would have destroyed the aura of love that we'd created. I also tried to understand whether my fraudulence was enhancing or diminishing my excitement, and decided it wasn't a factor, that I existed for you apart from my fraudulence. But I knew the confession would change *your* view of what was happening, and I didn't want that. I wanted you to see what lies in store for you in America, the future of your ambition, which we both know is formidable. You will have a successful career, I'm certain of that. Given our marriage and our love, I suspect you'd be inclined to tuck me in your pocket and carry me along with you, or park me in an apartment on the Upper East Side while you circle the globe with your camera. But I would rather have no Giselle than half of Giselle. I could never survive the madness that would follow such a raveled connection.'

I knew that as I talked Giselle's vision was framed by the real and the filmic visions of Brenda's performance, naked on screen, all but naked on stage. I turned to see Brenda remove her G-string and, unlike Consuela, stand before the club crowd without a garment, letting all eyes find what they sought while she danced another sixteen bars, and then, lights out, she was gone.

'Brenda looks naked, doesn't she?' I said. 'More fraudulence. She never lets herself be naked. She's wearing an all-but-invisible G-string she puts on with adhesive. It covers her opening, and has a bit of hair that matches her own. She provides the illusion of nudity while she retains the protective integrity of the larger G-string, and so the customers never see the complete Brenda. I find a fascination in this betrayal of the public trust, don't you? Most of the time in this life when you see a naked pussy you assume it truly is a naked pussy. Since we all live in the great whorehouse, and since we all give a fuck whenever we can, no matter what the cost, the discovery that even the most openhanded lewdness is only another act of cynicism seems just right, admirable even. Dr Tannen used to chide me for my quest for innocence, or at least that's how he described it. He said my time underground, or in the sewer as you put it, was really a search for something that didn't exist in the world, not now, not ever. How far back in darkness do you want to go to find that innocence? he asked. The womb? Amniotic innocence? Do you really think the womb was such an innocent place? Maybe you'd like to go back beyond the womb to the soul's descent *into* the womb, or back even to the soul's creation. Personally, he said, I don't think you can get there from here.'

Giselle put her hand on the right side of my head and held it. 'Do you still get the headaches?' she asked.

'Once in a while,' I said.

'How often do you see the doctor?'

'We're quits. I can't afford him. But I understand. He doesn't run a free lunch counter.'

'It was beautiful, what you did for me,' Giselle said.

'I'm glad you liked it,' I said. 'I'll pay your friend back when I get the advance on the Meriwether book.'

'Don't worry about it. I'll take it out of my paycheck.'

'You are a generous woman, Giselle.'

'You're a loving husband, Orson.'

'Yes. That's true. Isn't it a pity.'

Giselle dropped her hand from my head, took my hand in hers, and was smiling her smile of rue when the shooting began in the street. One shot broke the window in the club's door, and Eddie the barman yelled, 'Get down, folks, they're shootin' out there.'

I could see someone huddled in the doorway until the lights went out, heard a pistol fired twice, three times, four, heard a volley of return shots, and then the doorway went silent. Eddie switched the lights back on and when he opened the door a man in a light-gray overcoat rolled down from the two steps where he'd been huddling. Two uniformed policemen with drawn pistols stood on the sidewalk observing the situation. Both holstered their pistols and one went elsewhere.

'Who is he?' Eddie asked the policeman.

'He just held up the joint next door.'

An Interview with the Corpse on 52d Street
by Orson Purcell

The interview took place on the threshold of The Candy Box, a Manhattan nightclub on 52nd Street, a crosstown artery that is home to two dozen jazz bars and exotic dance clubs along its neon way. The corpse was male, reasonably well dressed, without a necktie, but wearing a shirt with starched collar, double-breasted dark gray suit, gray overcoat, and a gray fedora that had fallen off when the man was shot. Two policemen had come upon him almost as soon as he emerged, gun in hand, from an adjacent nightclub, where he had stolen an unspecified amount of money.

The door of The Candy Box remained open throughout the interview at the suggestion of police, who were awaiting the homicide photographer. A woman customer in The Candy Box was actually the first to photograph the corpse, using a

Leica thirty-five-millimeter and natural light. This dramatic photo received wide currency, appearing in *Life* magazine six days after the shooting.

The corpse lay on its right side during the interview, bullet holes in its head, neck, chest, and other parts of the upper torso. The eyes were open, and the expression on the face (which was free of blood) was one of inquiry, as if the man had died asking a question. This was the first interview the owner of the corpse had ever given, either in life or in death.

O: Is there any single reason why you are dead?
C: The cops shot me eight times.
O: Why did they do that?
C: I shot at them.
O: Isn't that a crazy thing to do?
C: You could say that.
O: Do all hoodlums behave this way?
C: Not everybody. It's somethin' you decide.
O: Was your decision prompted by the fact that you're suicidal?
C: Hey, whatayou sayin'? I was raised a Catholic.
O: Then maybe you were just stupid.
C: Nobody calls me stupid, buddy.
O: This is speculative conversation. Crime is often an aggressive form of stupidity. Don't be upset.
C: You think stupid guys get away doin' what I do? You think the boss'd trust me if I was stupid?
O: Maybe you were doing it to escape.
C: Now you're talkin'.
O: But you didn't escape.
C: I had a chance.
O: You gambled with your life. You're a gambler.
C: I never win nothin'.
O: Would you consider yourself an unlucky man?
C: Yeah, could be. But, shit, luck ain't everything. I know a lot of unlucky guys who got nothin' but money.

O: Perhaps it was madness.

C: I'm as sane as you are, friend.

O: That's not saying a whole lot, but we won't go into that here. Perhaps it runs in your family. If your entire family was mad then possibly you are as well.

C: My old man wouldn't let any nuts run around in the family.

O: What about fear? People get their backs up when they're afraid, when they think something might destroy them, or what is most valuable to them.

C: Balls. I been in half a dozen shootouts. You want the rundown?

O: No need. Consider that you may have been foolhardy. More brave than smart, in other words. Is that why you did it?

C: We do what we do because we gotta do it. You don't like that reason I'll give you another one. We do it because it's gotta be done.

O: A compulsive, responsible hoodlum. That's rare indeed. But shooting it out with the police all but presumes a belief in your own unkillability.

C: Oh yeah?

O: One might describe it as hubris, which of course means challenging the gods to destroy you.

C: You're one of them smart bastards.

O: If I may sum up, you enter into this sort of contretemps with total awareness, and you do it because you decide it's the valorous thing to do, because it proves that at your center you are a courageous individual, because it is your obligation to a world you mistakenly believe you understand, and that, no matter what the odds against you or your ideas, you are the final arbiter of your own action. Captain of your soul, so to speak. Am I wrong?

C: What the fuck are you talkin' about?

O: It remains to be seen. One final question. Do you think it's possible that you're not really dead, that you have a chance at resurrection, I mean coming back to life.

C: Nah, I'm dead.
O: Thank you, Mr C.

I decided that not only was I an eschatophiliac, but also an eschatophile. It seemed to be the healthiest of all possible conditions. In this most illuminating darkness of the city's night I could distinguish the last weakened light of end times, could see, with my heightened vision, that in The Candy Box's sign the ionized neon had grown sooty in its finality, a soiled and fading flickering of the city's last artificial light. Above my head the sky had turned increasingly frigid and black in a sunless world, and I knew that death was on the prowl. Could judgment, heaven, or hell be far behind? Even scavengers cringe in light such as this, for it destroys even the *appetite* to survive. Only solitude, and the contemplation of the ease of existence in the face of futility, are viable now. Suicide is pointless, for the entertainment value of terminal events exceeds that of the vapid flight to oblivion.

I now realized how much I loved to lose. Acquisition had invariably brought with it the anxiety of loss, and the settling in of that anxiety had always proved to be a prelude to harsh reality for me. This was how I had lived. I created the highs and lows of my life. I accumulated the Giselles and Les Montrachets of my days, and then I lost them. I would never again enumerate all that had been taken from me, and I blamed no one for this recurring phenomenon. I was beyond blame and had come to understand that this was the natural curve of life, especially for the Phelans. This knowledge elevated my spirit, for I knew I would live under no more delusions. I would be prepared for the worst that life could offer. Solitude, contemplation, and waiting for the finale: these were the meaningful pursuits. And also, oh yes, the elimination of the past. I would throw out all that I had written, all my letters (including those from Giselle; especially those from Giselle). I would throw out all books that did not enhance solitude. I would throw out memory. I would throw out the memory of Miss Nelson, in whose home I roomed when I first went to Albany to live. Demure, old, white-haired Miss Nelson, retired schoolteacher, had lost her connection to significance long ago. Where had it gone? There, under her canopy bed, I saw one day the bright light of yesterday's loss shining on forty empty bourbon bottles. Goodbye, memory of Miss Nelson. I would also throw out the memories of Quinn. That would take time, there were so many. I would begin with the night at the Grand View Lake House when I was with Joanie Mac in the boat house, my hand down at Joanie's place, when we saw Wanda, the new waitress, come back to the hotel's servants' quarters with Liver Mason, back from the movies in Saratoga. Let me kiss you, Liver said, and as he threw his arms around her, Wanda peck-pecked his liverly lips and pushed him away. Tomorrow again? pleaded Liver. Tomorrow maybe, said Wanda, and she ran up the stairs to bed. Getting some air, Quinn came out the back door of the hotel bar, whistling, searching in life for the elusive meaning of his solitude, and Wanda, after less than eight bars of the whistling, bounded down the stairs, took Quinn's arm, and – just as if it were planned – they came into the boat house, his hand already up at Wanda's, and he said later he never expected it to happen, didn't know she was there, hadn't been following her and Liver, was surprised out of his socks, was just out for a walk, and other genuinely true lies he told himself. Quinner the sinner. Quinner the winner. Goodbye, Quinner at the boat house. Goodbye, Quinner in Europe with Giselle. And I felt lightened already. It would be a pleasant thing to unmemorize my life. It would prove I was no longer afraid of time. I would sit in my window and watch the garbageman take away the evidence that Orson Purcell had ever existed.

And so I moved on, ever deeper, into the lovely, lovely darkness, thrilled by it all as only a true eschatophile can be.

Book Four

1

In the early spring of 1953, and with blinding illumination on through the fall of 1954, Peter Phelan came to perceive this: that individuals, families, or societies that willfully suppress their history will face a season of reckoning, one certain to arrive obliquely, in a dark place, and at a hostile hour, with consequences for the innocent as well as for the conspirators. Peter saw this first in my collapse, and then in the rolling boil of divine vengeance visited upon his brothers and sisters in these years.

In much the way that he had left Colonie Street in 1913 to escape what he saw as the shallow morality of his mother, only to discover that a tissue of other reasons had contributed to his move (and her behavior), so in November, 1954, did he return home to cope yet again with the Phelan family shallows, again pushed to doing so by ancillary reasons: the death and departure of so many friends from his changing Greenwich Village neighborhood and his near isolation as a result of this, his diminishing bank account, deficient income, and the appealing prospect of free rent in Albany, his growing problem with arthritic hips, which prevented him from standing at his easel and had sat him prematurely in the novice invalid's chair, his unflagging love for his brothers and sisters, and, not least, his distance from me, about whom he had begun to fret in unreasonably paternal ways.

Peter's return home was brought on by a series of events that began with a modestly scandalous public moment; but also by the climax of long and bitter discord in the lives of Sarah, Tommy, and

Chick Phelan, and finally by the death of Sarah. The return would also transform Peter's work radically and set him on a quest not only to understand the chain of causation that had led the family to a crisis of sanity and survival, but also to memorialize it in art.

For Chick the year 1954 was full of crisis, a climactic time in his life. A failed priest in Sarah's eyes, Chick had been introduced to Evelyn Hurley, a handsome cosmetics saleslady at the John G. Myers Department Store, during a New Year's Eve party at the Knights of Columbus in 1937, by the *Times-Union* newspaper columnist Martin Daugherty. The introduction was followed first by Chick's privileged glimpse of Evelyn Hurley eliminating a wrinkle in her silk stocking by the most modest elevation of her skirt, that elevation the equivalent to Chick of a wild aphrodisiac; and second, by Chick's intense and private conversation with Evelyn immediately thereafter, during which he became acutely aware of the audible friction created when she crossed her legs under the table, her silk stockings sliding one upon the other and creating, in Chick's heart and soul, the phenomenon of love at first sound.

Chick then pursued her with ardent respect and found his ardor reciprocated, but found also that Evelyn, a widow, was a woman of the world in ways that Chick only hoped to be a man of the world; and so for seventeen years the Chick-and-Evelyn courtship frequently approached, but never arrived at, ardor's ultimate destination. Chick was too loyal a Catholic to use prophylactics, Evelyn too alert to possibility to allow access to herself without them.

Marriage was, of course, the answer, but impediments prevailed, principally in Chick, who, even after he bought Evelyn an engagement ring in the tenth year of their courtship, chose to believe he was seeing her circumspectly. None in the city except himself thought it much of a secret, not even his sister Sarah, the chief impediment, who for years refused to acknowledge that Evelyn existed on the planet, and announced often at dinner that the Phelan credo, in the abstract, allowed no truck with widows, or divorcees, or women of loose character. Sarah, at a neighbor's wake, overheard a man describe someone she assumed to be Evelyn as 'loose as ashes and twice as dusty' and, understanding the import of the statement without grasping its particulars, thereafter actively did all she could to discourage Chick from his pursuit, never, for instance, allowing him to bring Evelyn into the house during the seventeen-year courtship.

It was during the very early twilight of a June evening in 1954 that Chick found himself in a duel of screams with Sarah, he reacting to Evelyn's ultimatum that if he did not marry her she would leave Albany and go alone to Miami Beach to take work as the hostess of a luxurious new Collins Avenue delicatessen that was about to be opened by a friend who had moved to Florida and, with prudent investment, found himself with money to burn. And how better to burn it than cooking corned beef and blintzes?

Sarah and Chick each lacked novelty in their arguments – the much-discussed moral position on widows and designing women, the depravity of men's desires, the holy priesthood ('Once a priest, always a priest'), maternal wishes, Catholic antipathy to Florida and especially Miami Beach, and, the ultimate appeal, family loyalty: 'What will become of us if you leave?' – being Sarah's enduring salvos; and Chick's – his fury at being thought of as a priest ('I was never a priest, only a seminarian'), the right of men, even Albany Irishmen, to marry, the right not to be interfered with by sisters, the love for Evelyn (newly announced within the past week), the last chance for happiness, the only love he'd ever known in this goddamned life ('Don't you swear at me over your concubine'), and the ultimate truth: that he was goddamn sick and tired of being a slave to this family, goddamn sick and tired of not being appreciated, goddamn sick and tired of this stinking town and this stinking street and . . . and there Chick's tirade was interrupted by the front door bell; and he opened it to see a policeman standing on the stoop holding Tommy by the arm.

'Mr Phelan?'

'Yes.'

'Is this man your brother?'

'He is. What's the problem?'

'Well, he's more or less under arrest. It'd be better to talk inside.'

Chick saw another policeman sitting in the squad car parked in front of the house and recognized Eddie Huberty, who used to play left field for Arbor Hill in the Twilight League. Chick waved a small hello to Eddie and backed into the house to let Tommy and the policeman into the parlor.

Molly, who had been upstairs in her room trying to shield her ears against Sarah's and Chick's eternal arguing, came down the stairs at the sound of the doorbell, and stopped behind Sarah as the policeman entered and took off his hat. He stood beside Tommy, who could look only at the floor, while Chick, in his shirtsleeves and suspenders, commanded the moment.

'Has he done something, officer?' Chick asked.

'It seems he has. We had a complaint from a woman on Ten Broeck Street that he followed her home from Downtown.'

'He always walks on Ten Broeck Street,' Chick said. 'All his life. Did he do anything to the woman?'

'It seems he did,' the policeman said, and Chick detected a small smile on the man.

'It was Letty Buckley, wasn't it,' Sarah said.

'Matter of fact it was,' said the officer. 'How'd you know?'

'I know that one,' said Sarah. 'She's a troublemaker.'

'I don't know about that,' said the officer. 'She called us and said your brother followed her two days in a row, always walking behind her, so the third day we followed along and saw him behind her, sure enough, carrying a cane, and when she got to her front stoop he hooked the neck of the cane under her skirt and lifted it up, up to her hips, and she screamed. He tipped his hat to her and kind of twirled his cane, and then he walked away. That's when we picked him up.'

'Did you do that?' Sarah asked Tommy, poking his shoulder with one finger.

Tommy made no acknowledgment, stared at the floor.

'Did you, brazen boy? Did you?' Sarah screamed, and Tommy, crying, nodded yes.

'Don't yell,' Molly said, pushing past Sarah and taking Tommy by the arm. 'Come and sit down, Tom,' she said, and she led him to the love seat and sat beside him.

'Is he under arrest?' Chick asked.

'Not yet,' the policeman said, and added in a whisper, 'Mrs Buckley hasn't filed a complaint, and I'm not sure she really wants to. Probably get in the papers, you know, if she does. She just thinks he oughta be kept under control.'

'We can guarantee that, officer,' Chick said.

'You bet your life we can,' Sarah said.

Tommy whimpered.

The policeman offered a faint smile to Chick and Sarah. 'More of a joke, really. He didn't hurt her, and nobody saw what he done except us. And, o' course, Miss Buckley. Quite a surprise to her, musta been.' And he laughed. 'Just keep him close to home.'

Chick nodded and smiled, and as they walked out to the stoop the policeman said softly to Chick, 'Really was funny. Her skirt went about as high as it could go. He's pretty clever with that cane.'

'We'll see it doesn't happen again, officer. And you wanna bring over a coupla tickets to the Police Communion Breakfast I'll buy 'em from you.'

'I'll do that,' the policeman said, and he got back in the prowl car. Chick waved again to Eddie Huberty.

Tommy's head was still bowed, his sisters watching him in silence, when Chick reentered the parlor, feeling that the policeman's smile had broken the tension. Chick tried to convey that in his tone. 'Tom, what the hell did you *do* that for?'

Tommy shook his head.

'You know Miss Buckley? You ever been in her house?'

'No,' Tommy said.

'You just like her looks, is that it?'

Tommy nodded yes.

'Where'd you learn to do that business with the cane?'

'Charlie,' Tommy said.

'Who?' said Sarah.

'I'll handle it,' Chick said. 'Charlie who?'

'Charlie, the movies.'

'Charlie, Charlie. Charlie Ruggles? Charlie Chan?'

'No,' said Tommy.

'Charlie Grapewin? Charlie McCarthy?'

'No, Charlie with the derby,' Tommy said.

'Charlie Chaplin he means,' Molly said.

'Right. Charlie Chaplin,' Tommy said.

'You saw him do that with a cane?' Chick asked.

'People laughed when he did it. People liked what Charlie did,' Tommy said.

'When'd you see him do that?'

'Saw it with you.'

'Me?' Chick said. 'I haven't seen Charlie Chaplin since the 1920s, silent movies.'

'Down at the Capitol,' Tommy said. 'You and me, we saw Charlie, and everybody liked what he did. They laughed. We liked him, you and me did, Chick.'

'Jesus,' Chick said. 'He sees somethin' in the movies and then imitates it twenty-five, thirty years later. I *do* remember Chaplin used to do that with his cane. Did it all the time. It *was* funny.'

'It was not,' Sarah said. 'Don't you dare encourage him. It's a filthy thing he did to her, even if she isn't any good.'

'There's nothing wrong with her,' Molly said. 'She's always pleasant to us.'

'She has men in, what I hear.'

'She's single, what's wrong with that?'

'I don't want to talk about it any longer,' Sarah said. 'You come upstairs with me, young man.'

'What're you gonna do?' Chick said.

'I'm going to punish him.'

'Let him alone, won't ya? He's scared to death already.'

'You want him to do it again?'

'No, of course I don't.'

'Then he has to be taught a lesson.'

'He's scared,' Molly said. 'He wet his pants.'

'Get off the love seat,' Sarah said. 'Go upstairs and change. You're a bad boy.'

Tommy quickstepped through the back parlor and went up the back stairs. Chick and Molly exchanged smiles as Sarah went up the front stairs.

'Brazen boy,' Molly said.

'Sixty-three-year-old brazen boy,' Chick said.

There is a photograph taken of Molly by Giselle in early September, 1954, sitting on the porch of the Grand View Lake House on Saratoga Lake, cupping a bird in her hands. She is looking with an oblique glance at the camera, a small smile visible at the corners of her mouth but not in her eyes. The photo is black and white and arrests the viewer with its oddness and its mystery: first the bird, a cedar waxwing whose tan, yellow, and red colors are not discernible, but whose black facial mask is vivid; and then the puzzling expression on the face of this obviously once-beautiful woman in her sixty-fifth year.

A facile interpretation of the photo is that the woman is perhaps saddened by the fact that the bird is injured, for it must be injured or else it would fly away. But this interpretation is not accurate. The memories and secrets that the bird evoked in Molly were what put the smile on her lips and the solemnity in her eyes; and it was this contradiction that Giselle captured in the picture, again proving her talent for recognizing the moment of cryptic truth in people she chose to photograph. Molly had been declining into melancholia before the photo was taken, the onset of decline dating back to the day Tommy was arrested for imitating Charlie Chaplin.

On that day, after the policeman left the Phelan home, Tommy went up to his bedroom to remove the underpants that his terror had caused him to wet. In the front parlor, Chick, awash in anger, pity, frustration, anxiety, and other emotions too convoluted to define in a single word, straightened his necktie, snatched up his seersucker sports jacket, and announced to Molly that he was going to dinner and a movie with Evelyn, goddamn it, and maybe he'd be home later and maybe he wouldn't.

When Chick left, a sudden isolation enveloped Molly: alone again in the company of Sarah, who could raise at will the barricades between herself and the rest of the family: a perverse strength in the woman to do what no one else wanted done but was always done nevertheless. Sarah would spank Tommy, as her mother had spanked all the children for their transgressions of rule. Tommy would cry openly, would wail and sob in his imposed shame, imposed because he was incapable of generating shame in himself, was without the guile, or the moral imperatives that induced it in others, was, in fact, a whole and pure spirit who had had the Commandments, and the punishment for transgressing them, slapped into his buttocks for six decades, but who still had no more understanding of them than when he was an infant. All he knew was that he should avoid the prohibited deeds that provoked spankings. Raising a woman's skirt with a cane had never been prohibited, but now he would realize he could never do it again. Now, truly; for his crying had begun and Molly knew Sarah was at her work.

The situation was old, Molly's guilt was old, the themes that provided the skeleton of the events taking place this minute were older than Molly herself, and she was sick of them all, sick of her helplessness in the face of them. She heard the sobs and loathed them. It was like kicking a dog for chasing a bitch in heat. Tommy had instincts that no amount of punishment would turn aside; they would always find a new outlet. But what of *your* instincts, Molly? Did you ever find another outlet for *your* stunted passion? It seems you did not, alas. No future for it. Animal with instincts amputated. But no. They were still there. Orson had raised them again last year, had he not? Bright and loving young man, prodding your memory of pleasure, revisiting feelings long in their grave. Orson is Peter's. Even Chick said he probably was. 'Orson,' Chick said, 'anytime you need a place to hang your hat you're welcome here.' Chick so easygoing, the trouble she gives him. He said he was sick of this stinking street. I know he was going to say this stinking house too, and this stinking family. These stinking brothers and sisters. Chick doesn't mean it.

But he does.

We all do.

Molly laid her head back on the sofa and closed her eyes to shut out Tommy's sobbing and Sarah's screaming. She tried to replace those sounds with the face of Walter as he stood tall before her, waiting for her kiss, expecting it, inviting it. Walter loves Molly's kisses. Loved. Don't pity yourself, Molly. Remember poor Julia, dead at twenty-two, Julia who never knew passion, Julia who was kissed by boys twice in twenty-two years and neither kiss meant any more than a penny's worth of peppermints. I was truly kissed, Julia. Your sister knew kisses and love and more. Much more. Never again. Other things. Never again.

Molly plunged into the blackest part of her memory to hide, to shut out the thoughts that were coming back now. So much wrong. So many evil things the result of love. Why should it be that we are gifted with love and then the consequences are so . . .

Tommy squealed and Molly rose up from her black depths, sat upright on the sofa, heard the squeal a second time, a third, the squeal of an animal in agony, and she was racing up the stairs in seconds toward the wretched sounds. She saw Tommy face down on his bed, Sarah striking his naked buttocks – she had never hit him naked before, never; nobody was ever hit naked, ever – her hand coming down again and again with the two-foot rule (and Molly saw that Sarah was hitting him not with the rule's flatness but with its wide edge and screaming, 'filthy boy, brazen boy, filthy boy, brazen boy'), the Tommy squeals and Sarah screams beyond Molly's endurance.

But as Molly moved toward Sarah to snatch away the ruler Tommy suddenly rolled onto his back and with both feet kicked Sarah in the stomach as she was raising the ruler yet again, and Sarah flew backward across the room, her back colliding with Tommy's three-drawer dresser, knocking his clown lamp to the floor and throwing the room into darkness. And Sarah sat suddenly on the floor, breathless, her glasses gone, her expression not pained as much as incredulous that such a thing could happen to her.

So began Sarah's awareness of her mortality.

* * *

In her rage, Sarah damaged Tommy's spine so severely that he could not walk, could not stand or lie straight, could not bend over, could only rest and sleep sitting on cushions. Dr Lynch, the family physician for thirty years, prescribed pain pills, a wheelchair, and X-rays, and accepted without question the explanation that Tommy had been attacked on the street by wild kids who hit him with sticks. Tommy would not eat or drink, would accept nothing from Sarah, and so Molly assumed control of his life and convinced him to take some bread pudding and tea. She put whiskey in the tea to soothe this grown-up child who never drank whiskey, or even beer or wine, in a house where it went without saying that a drop of the creature improved every living thing, including dogs and fish.

Tommy calmed down and Molly busied herself so totally with him that she could, for hours at a time, forget how dreadfully hostile she was to this house, this family, especially to the absurd and brutal Sarah, who could not only do such a thing but who could stand for the doing for decades, Sarah who felt no remorse, only mortal pangs of ingratitude that she should be isolated by her family after giving her life over to its care and feeding, its salvation from damnation.

Chick was the first to isolate her. When he learned what she had done to Tommy he immediately picked up the telephone, called Evelyn, proposed to her and was accepted, told her he would give two weeks' notice at the *Times-Union* and take whatever severance pay he had coming, then they would go to Miami as she wanted, she could work at the deli, he'd get a job somewhere, and they'd start a new life and never look back.

He said all this in earshot of Sarah, who was sitting in front of the television watching 'Death Valley Days,' a western series to which she gave loyalty because it advertised 20 Mule Team Borax scouring powder, which Sarah used for cleaning, as had her mother before her. Sarah said nothing to Chick when he hung up, did not acknowledge that he was in the room. He walked in front of the television and said to her, 'Sarah, you and your mad ways are out of my life. And Tommy's life too.'

The latter threat was not to be carried out. Chick had concocted an instant pipe dream that he would take Tommy to Florida with him, care for him, let him grow old in the sun. But Tommy could not move, and would not; said he didn't want to leave Colonie Street in such nice weather. Tommy, in a week, seemed to have forgotten the beating Sarah gave him. He did not really remember why he couldn't walk right, yet he shunned Sarah even so, leaving the room when she entered. He did not talk to her about the beating, or about Letitia Buckley, and when Molly tested him and asked what happened to his back he thought a while and said some bad boys hit him with sticks down on Pearl Street.

After six weeks in the wheelchair and sleeping on the sofa in the back parlor to avoid going up and down stairs, Tommy began to improve. Despite this, Molly felt herself sliding back into the melancholy mood that had enveloped her after Walter's death. She barely talked to Sarah, who had withdrawn into her cocoon of injured merit, and nurtured herself with silence and television. Also, with Chick being gone, probably forever, the house never seemed emptier to Molly.

She took short walks in the neighborhood, visited with neighbors, Martha McCall across the street, who was supervising the movers who would take her and Patsy and their household of forty-four years out of the neighborhood and up to a new house on Whitehall Road, and Libby Dolan, who said she was selling her house to a Negro woman. Would Molly know anybody on the block in another year?

Molly also bumped into Letty Buckley, to whom she had apologized coming out of church the first Sunday after Tommy's cane trick, and found Letty sweet, even forgiving, knowing how simple Tommy was, a bit abashed it was a simpleton who had done that to her, and even worried for him. Will you have to put him away? No, never, said Molly. And she came home in a fog of emptiness.

Coming into the house made it worse. Talk to Tommy? Talk to Sarah? Talk to the walls? She called her niece, Peg Quinn, just to hear a family voice, and Peg was strong, as always. Molly updated her, leaving out the cause of Tommy's injury, and Peg immediately offered to come down and visit, or take Molly to supper Downtown, or a movie maybe? But no, that wouldn't solve anything. And then, after a half-hour of speculating on what would become of Chick in Florida, and analyzing Sarah's sullen isolation, Peg said, 'Why don't you go up to Saratoga and spend some time at the hotel? The weather's beautiful, and Orson's there, isn't he?'

'He is,' said Molly.

'Then call him and tell him to get a room ready for you, and one for Tommy, and for Sarah if she wants to go. Get a change of scenery. Do it, Molly, do it.'

Do it. Molly understood the advice. Do it, Molly, Walter told her, Chick told her, Peter told her. And did she do it? In her way. But she didn't weigh much. Ha-ha.

'Maybe I will,' Molly said. The hotel, the lake, Orson. 'But Tommy needs his wheelchair. I couldn't handle it alone.'

'I'll send Billy down to give you a hand getting him and the chair into the car,' Peg said. 'And Orson can help you at the other end.'

Molly called Austin McCarroll at the Texaco station and told him to come and take her car down off blocks and make it drivable. Walter had given her the car, a 1937 Dodge, and taught her to drive it. In seventeen years Molly had driven less than four thousand miles, drove it back and forth to Saratoga, took Sarah and Tommy for drives in the evening to get ice-cream cones, went riding Sundays after the war. This year she didn't even bother to take it off blocks when the good spring weather came. No place to go any more.

But now Molly could see herself again at the wheel, driving up Route 9, going up the hill into the Grand View driveway, a thrilling prospect, something she hadn't done as a vacationer in years. Even though so much time had passed, the Grand View had never been out of her mind for long, and whenever she did find herself turning into its driveway she knew that it would be like going home again, going home to love.

2

The Grand View Lake House: An Old Brochure

Situated on the eastern shore of Saratoga Lake, fifteen minute ride from railroad station, our car and porter meet your train; the hotel and cottages offer beautiful vista, eighty rods from and 110 feet above lakeshore, avoiding excessive dampness at night, free from miasma and malaria; convalescents accommodated, consumptives not entertained. Rolling lawns, shade trees, canoeing, boating, fishing, bathing, tennis court, croquet, clock golf, eighteen-hole golf course nearby, bird sanctuary in woods, small game and bird hunting in season, tents available for camping in nearby woods, thousands of flowers, garage on premises, motor parties welcome. Dining room screened, strictly home cooking, all eggs, milk, cream, poultry, and vegetables from our own farm. Wide, 200-foot long veranda, two fireplaces, casino for dancing, piano, phonograph, talking pictures every Sunday night, shower baths, inside toilets, long distance telephone connection, cars carry our guests to nearby Catholic and other churches. Proprietors Patrick and Nora Shugrue, William Shugrue full partner. Hotel open from June 1st to October, 105 rooms, three cottages, special rate by the week, write for terms.

Molly and Giselle: A Colloquy, September, 1954

'I must tell you about love,' Molly said.

'I must tell you about marriage,' Giselle said.

'You seem to know nothing about love.'

'I know everything.'

'It would not seem so.'

'Peter loves you.'

'And I him. But he loved Julia more. I wonder did he ever love Claire.'

'And Orson loves you.'

'And I him,' said Molly.

'I haven't loved much in my life, but I know I love Orson with a full heart,' Giselle said.

'It would not seem so.'

'You should know me, should be in my head. Then you would understand.'

'You left him alone last year.'

'We'd been apart for six months, but even so we were always together.'

'It would not seem so.'

'You are old. You don't understand the young.'

'You must never leave them alone for long if you love them,' Molly said.

'Then you live for them, not yourself.'

'You seem to know nothing about love.'

'You should have seen us together.'

'It looks alike sometimes. It looks alike.'

'You should have seen us together at the Plaza.'

'You were not together then.'

'But we were,' Giselle said. 'Even there in The Candy Box with his stripper I felt no jealousy. There was a woman in Germany he went with one night, and he must have had others in New York, but I was never jealous of any of them. But this night I loved him and yet I was jealous of the vision he had of me, for it wasn't me. That loving, successful, talented, noble woman, that was his invention of me. Orson hallucinating again. Orson of the brilliant imagination. Orson the fabulous lover, like none of the others. Orson the marvelous, loyal dog of a man.'

'And that is what you think love is?' Molly asked.

'I knew he might go away from me, but I also knew it wasn't me he was leaving but the idea of me. And when I looked at his face I wanted to photograph what I saw. There was an uncertainty in his eye, a calmness, with that old wildness banished. There was something in him I didn't understand.'

'As he didn't understand you.'

'When we left The Candy Box after the shooting we took a cab back to the Plaza. He saw me to the elevator, then went out for a walk, to clear his brain, he said. He didn't come back, and after an hour I feared he wouldn't, so I got dressed again and scoured the lobby and the hotel bars, because I couldn't believe he'd left me. I preferred the *Life* editor's apartment, where my things were, if I was going to spend the night alone, but I still thought there was a small chance Orson would return. And I knew he knew I'd wait for him in the hotel. And so I did. I phoned Peter and found Orson had neither been there nor called. Peter said he knew an all-night bar where Orson sometimes went and offered to go there alone, or with me if I wanted. He said he'd call Claire, but I knew that would achieve nothing, and it did.'

'We were up at Saratoga Lake for three weeks. Mama was dead six months and it was a suffocating summer. We were sitting on the veranda talking about I don't know what, and I saw that a new arrival, a good-looking fellow who had struck up a conversation with Sarah yesterday, was talking with her again. Then I saw a bird fly into a tree on the lawn, and it must've hit something, because it fell to the ground. I ran out to get it and picked it up and started to cry. The newcomer squatted down beside me and said, "May I see it?" And I showed him this beautiful creature that he said was a cedar waxwing. "It seems to have an injured wing," he said. "We can help him." I asked how that was possible and he said, "We'll keep him alive while he gets well." And that's what we did for the rest of the week. We fed him and made a nest for him in the birdcage the hotel gave us and he became the pet of the guests. I loved him so, that little creature. Everybody came to my room to see him. We took him out of the cage and he did fly a little inside the room at the end of the week, but not very well. On the tenth day he seemed ready and, when I carried him to the veranda, a dozen guests and waitresses came out to watch him go. I released him over the porch railing and he flew so well, right up into the same tree he'd fallen from. We were all so happy. He perched there in the tree for a minute and then he fell again, not injured, but dead.'

'Orson was gone two more nights before we found him. Peter had the idea to call Walker Pettijohn, Orson's editor, who suggested looking in Meriwether Macbeth's apartment. He said Orson sometimes worked there among Macbeth's papers that Macbeth's widow still kept intact, though she no longer lived there. And Orson was there all right, and as close to death as he ever will be until his time comes. He was in an alcoholic coma, five whiskey bottles, all empty, strewn around the room. Peter lifted him up and slapped his face but he didn't come to, didn't react at all. Death in life. And if he did live he wouldn't remember anything of this moment. I went out to a pay phone and called the ambulance.'

'It was sad that the bird died. I cried so hard. But I've been grateful to it ever since, because that's how I met Walter. The cedar waxwing introduced us. Walter picked the dead bird up and took it into the hotel and wrapped it in a handkerchief and put it on ice and we called around till we found a place, down home in Albany, that stuffed birds. We drove down together and gave the waxwing to the little man, who said he'd never stuffed such a small bird before, usually folks only stuff the big ones they shoot, owls and hawks, or their pet parrots. I still have the bird. I always bring it when I come up here.'

'Who is Walter?'

'Walter Mangan, my husband. He taught Latin in a boys' high school. He died in 1937.'

'And you miss him still.'

'We were so in love. Nobody loves you like an Irishman. He read me poetry about the bird.

'". . . A sparrow is dead, my lady's sparrow,
my own lady's delight, her sweetest plaything,
dear to her as her eyes – and dearer even . . .
I'll attend you, O evil gods of darkness.
All things beautiful end in you forever.
You have taken away my pretty sparrow,
Shame upon you. And, pitiful poor sparrow,
it is you that have set my lady weeping,
Dear eyes, heavy with tears and red with sorrow."'

'I went mad for Orson when we met. He wasn't like anybody else I'd ever known. He made me laugh and he was smart and he was crazy and I loved it.'

'You sent him home alone.'

'He was sick and I knew he'd get well in New York. I had a chance at a career, and I knew if I had to nurse him and abandon the career I'd hate him. And what kind of marriage would that turn into?'

'Walter was never sick. You must never leave them alone for long. You would've gotten your career.'

'Did you ever leave Walter alone?'

'Did I ever leave Walter alone.'

'Orson left me alone and then he went off to drink himself into oblivion. He stole the world for me, put himself in jeopardy, facing jail, really, and then he went off to die. I love him so for that.'

'You love that he wanted to die for you?'

'He wanted to die for the *image* of me. He was too crazy to see I was only a bright, immature woman out to save herself, which is really all I knew how to do. He wanted to make me into a goddess and I helped him, because I loved the idea of such a man, and loved what his love did to me.'

'But the love was a lie.'

'You should have seen us in bed.'

'But you didn't stay in his bed.'

'No.'

'Did he ever understand how you were leading him on?'

'I wasn't leading him on. I was trying to be equal to his dream. I'd deceive him again if it meant keeping that love alive.'

'Are you brighter than Orson?'

'Would it make any difference if I was?'

'You know something, but love isn't what you know.'

'I know everything about love.'

'Walter and I made love in a tent the first time. He set up his pup tent in the woods one night after supper, and went out to stay in it as soon as it got dark. I went down the back stairs and met him in the spot where we watched the birds, and Walter had a flashlight. We went to his tent and he loved me and made my heart bleed with joy . . . like . . . holy and blessed Jesus . . . like nothing else. There was never *anything* like that, ever before, in anybody's life I'd ever heard about. Have you? I'd bleed every night if I knew we'd both feel like that when we were done. Wouldn't you?'

'Yes. Maybe.'

'He never came right out and asked me to marry him. We were walking on Pearl Street one day and he says to me, "How'd you like to be buried with my people?" I said I'd like that just fine. But we didn't marry then, because I couldn't. We married when I was able and we took a flat up in the Pine Hills, and I was never happier, ever. A year passed and Tommy fell crossing a street and broke his wrist, and Sarah got sick and couldn't cook for Chick and him, so I went back home and ran things till Sarah could get on her feet. But she couldn't. The doctor tried everything, but she was so weak she couldn't get out of bed, and she wouldn't go to the hospital. Walter got impatient with me after two months of it, me being with her more than I was with him. And we fought. He said Sarah was faking sickness to keep me there, that she never forgave me for taking his attention away from her that day on the porch. But I couldn't believe that. Why would she ever do such a thing? Walter never meant anything to her. There was no sense to it. Walter said I should hire a woman to cook and keep house for two weeks so we could drive to Virginia to see his brother, and also break in my new car. He'd bought it for me, but I hardly drove it. It just sat in the alley on Colonie Street while I took care of Sarah. Sarah wouldn't hear of hiring anybody, wouldn't allow a woman in the house that wasn't family, so I didn't go to Virginia. Walter went with one of his friends from the school, and the friend fell asleep at the wheel and went over a ravine and they were both killed.'

'Orson didn't die.'

'He might have.'

'No. He has things to do. With or without me.'

'I fell apart when I heard the news. I couldn't do anything. Walter's family took over and had his body shipped home. They were furious with me and none of his sisters even called me. They sent the undertaker to tell me where the wake would be.'

'I wonder which of us will bury the other.'

'I went in and sat for the last hour of the second night of the wake and never spoke to any of them. They were cool to me, nodded at me when I came in, and one came over and tried to talk, Lila, the youngest, who I always liked. But I didn't say much, even to her. I just watched, and then when the undertaker came in to tell us to say good night to Walter, that he had to close up, I went and told Walter this was not good night, that we were leaving this place. Then I told his sisters, "I am the widow. He was my husband. I have my own undertaker, and he's right there in the hallway." And there was Ben Owens, standing there with three helpers, waiting for me to tell him what to do, and I told the others, "I'm taking him to our home, and he'll wake from there, and I hope none of you try to stop me, because I have a letter my lawyer got me from the courts" – I really didn't have a letter; I made that up – "and if you raise one finger against me I'll have the police on you. I don't know what you thought you were doing taking Walter, but a widow is not without her rights." They couldn't believe it. They thought he was theirs. But he'd left them and married me, that's what marriage is. And so Ben Owens put him in the coffin I bought for him and carried him out to the hearse and we went to our house and had the second wake. They didn't come. They drove behind to make sure where we were going. They thought I was totally mad, but I was never saner in my life. And I sat up with him all night long and then at five in the morning I called Sarah to tell her what I was doing, that she could come to the church if she wanted, seven o'clock mass at St Joseph's, where we were married. And we had the mass, and Sarah got out of her sickbed and never went back to it, and Chick and Tommy came with her, and Peter would have too, but it was too short notice. And then we went to the cemetery, with Father Mahar saying the prayers at the grave. Us and Billy and his mother, and all the Quinns, and a few neighbors who'd heard about it were all the ones that came, but then almost nobody knew what I'd done. His family came to the cemetery and stood off to one side and nobody talked to them. And then we buried Walter in the Phelan family plot, right next door to where I'll be buried, not with his people at all. We always had too many empty graves in our family. We always prepared for death, never for life. So I did that for him anyway.'

Giselle focuses her camera, Molly framed in her lens, the now mythical cedar waxwing cupped in her hands. Molly sits in the first rocker in a line of thirty rockers on the Lake House veranda, the rocker in the same place as when Molly first saw the waxwing fall from the tree, injured but still alive. The tree is still giving shade to the lawn, although Molly says it has lost many branches since that day nineteen years ago. Part of the tree is visible in the background of the photo (what is not visible is Tommy in his wheelchair, under the tree) about to be taken by Giselle, who is trying to record some part of the secret being of this sixty-four-year-old woman her husband loves: his aunt, if you can believe that; and Giselle is looking for a clue to what has generated this love, and what sort of love it could be, and why she is profoundly jealous of it. After all, the woman is thirty-four years older than Orson, forty years older than Giselle, a fragile and fading page of history, a woman who purports to know everything knowable about love, although she has probably known only one man and was married to him less than two years, which isn't much more than Giselle has been married to Orson; and Giselle has known more than one man, to be sure. Not *so* many more, but more. Giselle sees the family resemblance between Molly and Orson and Peter and she knows that her jealousy is irrational and that Orson is not about to break any taboos, but on the matter of taboos she also knows that there is the possibility of her own dalliance with Orson's father. The man is strong-minded, knows who he is. He's a talent and Giselle respects that above much else. He's taken with her as well, which she saw during the hours they spent looking for Orson in the Village bars and coffeehouses and movie theaters. In a Bleecker Street movie he took her hand, held it, told her, 'Don't worry, he can't hide forever, we'll find him,' and kept holding the hand as they sat in the back row looking over the audience. She had sat in back rows before, holding hands, and it was just like this, and she did not take her hand away. You carry on with a thing like that and if you're not careful you'll cross the line. Sitting beside Peter, she felt she understood his life as a painter, as a bohemian, for in spite of her bourgeois life she was free in the world (working for *Life* was not working, it was soaring), and she was pursuing her photography the way he pursued his art. They were kindred, if not kin, as Orson may be with Molly. But there is more between those two than blood. Orson says to Molly from his vantage behind Giselle, 'Look at me, Moll, this way,' and Molly turns her head and when she sees him she looks again at the bird and then at the camera, and the smile is there now and Giselle captures it, that smile: the soft currency of Molly's soul.

The things we do when we're alone, without a perch or a

perspective, and when there is no light in the corner where we've been put. The things we do.

When I left Giselle at the Plaza, I walked the streets until I came to Meriwether Macbeth's corner. Then I went upstairs and sat in Meriwether's darkness and drank myself to sleep with whiskey. I awoke to dismal day and assayed the work I had previously done on Meriwether's jottings and tittlings, then set about the task of concluding it as Walker Pettijohn had suggested: expanding the jots, fattening the tittles. I read and culled for two days and two nights, breaking stride only to forage for an editorial survival kit: two sandwiches and three more bottles of whiskey. I decided I was done with the editing when only half a bottle of whiskey remained, and I knew then I had an excellent chance of dying of malnutrition, darkness, and Macbethic bathos. I wrote Pettijohn a note, told him to give to Giselle all money due me for this editing, and also to give the manuscript of my novel to the Salvation Army for public auction, any money realized from its sale to be used to purchase ashes, those ashes to be given free of charge to unpublished authors, who will know how to use them. Then I drank myself quiet.

Giselle is jealous of Molly. The attention she shows me in Molly's presence is different from the attention she shows me when we are alone. Giselle is always smarter than I judge her to be, no matter how smart I judge her to be. It doesn't really matter that she is jealous of Molly, though it's a change for both of us. It truly does matter that I love Molly.

A full day had passed before I realized that it was Giselle and Peter who had found me in my alcoholic coma. I opened a sobering eye to see her standing over my hospital bed, a tube dripping unknown fluid into my arm, my body in original trouble: nothing like this sort of pain ever before.

'You're still alive, Orson,' was her first sentence.

'That's not my fault,' I said.

'You idiotic bastard,' she said. 'It's one thing to be crazy, but it's another thing to be dead.'

'Don't call me a bastard,' I said, and I lapsed willfully into a coma-like sleep for two more hours. Giselle was still there when I again surfaced.

'You're getting better,' she told me. 'We're taking you to Albany. You obviously can't live in this city.'

'Are you coming with me?'

'Yes,' said Giselle.

And I slept then, sweetly, ignorantly.

I put undeservedly great faith in hollow objects. What is the purpose of this?

I thought of the Grand View Lake House, which was at the edge of hollowness; all but empty of significance; 'dead' would soon be another viable adjective. But it would not *really* die as long as the Shugrues stayed alive, and the loyal handfuls kept coming in season in enough numbers to cover expenses; and it would not die as long as I moved through its hollowness as helpful artisan, wood-cutter, sweeper of leaves and dead rats, scraper of paint, mower of lawns, outwitter of raccoons, magus of empty rooms.

The Phelans had been coming to the Grand View for more than half a century. Pat Shugrue had worked with Michael Phelan on the New York Central, but quit in '91 to build three cottages on the shore of Saratoga Lake. Michael took his brood of seven (Tommy, the youngest, was one; Francis, the eldest, was twelve) to one of the cottages (three bedrooms) for a week the following summer, the first annual Phelan Saratoga vacation. When Shugrue upgraded the cottages to a Lake House, the Phelans were there for that first season.

The Phelan boys grew up with Pat Shugrue's son, Willie, who inherited the hotel and added two wings when Pat and Nora phased themselves out; grew up also with Willie's wife, Alice, who at first supervised the cooking at the Lake House in the late 1930s, but by the early '40s was the organized brain behind the business. Alice was also Molly's closest friend, ever since their days at St. Joseph's Industrial School, where Catholic girls from Arbor Hill learned cookery and needlework.

Giselle brought me to Albany in early April, 1953, stayed two nights with me in the Phelan house, and in that time revealed such a restlessness that I insisted she go back to her career. 'You weren't put here on earth to be a nurse,' I told her, 'nor could I abide watching you try to become one against your will.'

It fell to Molly to oversee my reentry into the human race. An instrument of angelical mercy, she soothed my psychic wounds with gentleness, brought me food and the newspapers, told me stories of her life, convinced me I could trust her with my troubles.

But Molly perceived, as others in the family did not, that my recovery was static; that to recover fully I needed more than this household could offer; and it was she who in the late summer of that year called Alice Shugrue and asked whether she could use me at the hotel, provided I worked for my keep. She said I'd been raised by Peter (the Phelan handyman) and could do carpentry, plumbing, electrical work, and more; that I needed no wages, only a place to stay and something to do with my hands.

And so now, October, 1954, a year and months after that salvational intercession by Molly, something new can begin. The nights are beyond autumn, and beyond even that by the woods on the lakeshore, cold into the marrow, the morrow, reading *Finnegan*, yes, *carry me along, taddy, like you done through the toy fair!* And then doesn't the kerosene for the heater vanish entirely from the world? It does. Himself alone with that book and his own book, a writer and a woodsbee, a man in a manner of wondering, what manner of wondering man is this? A man in love with his wife and his-aunt-your-sister, tadomine. Of all love there is, this has been the most strange, leaving nothing undesired, nothing sired, the lover bald to the world, no heir. Was ever a family so sonless, so cold, dark, and bereft of a future as these fallow Phelan *fils?*

I was used to being alone here in the cottage, relieved to discover that one did not wither in such solitude; that it really could be a nurturing force. What I did not expect was this onset of winterish night without heat. I put on my overcoat, muffler, hat, and one glove, the other hand free to turn the pages, and

I kept reading, ranging now through the book's final pages, the glorious monologue of Anna Livia Plurabelle: *Why I'm all these years within years in soffran, allbeleaved. To hide away the tear, the parted. It's thinking of all. The brave that gave their. The fair that wore. All them that's gunne. I'll begin again in a jiffey. The nik of a nad. How glad you'll be I waked you! My! How well you'll feel! For ever after.*

Words alone, language alone, not always penetrable (like women with their mysteries; and how they do fill this life with spectacle and wonder), now filling the reader-and-writer with infeasible particulars, always the great challenge, is it not, to fease the particules and not malfease? Giselle was gone again, yet again, but in transition to something other than what she once was; and who knew how that would come out?

'I'll be up next weekend,' she told me.

'That soon?'

'I like it up here.'

'Not much action.'

'I'm saturated with action,' she said. 'I like the calm of this place. I want to photograph it, and Saratoga too.'

So, you see, that's a change in Giselle. I make no plans on the basis of it, however. Giselle is as mercurial as the early autumn in Saratoga: sunlit day become gelid night. Apart, we move together slowly into the future. But since coming here I do perceive a future, with or without the woman. Molly did this; brought me to see Alice and Willie Shugrue, Alice a tightly wrapped Irish whirlwind who holds the hotel together by dint of will and want: wanting nothing but this place now, living in the South Cottage with the rheumatoid Willie, a waning wisp of a fellow who can no longer afford artisans to stave off the decay of the buildings, can no longer climb a ladder himself. And all the while your man lives in the North Cottage, reading, learning to write, learning how to be alone. And out our windows we all watch the Lake House begin its struggle through yet another winter, and we wonder: Is this the year it collapses of its own hollowness?

When I first came to live at the Lake House in 1953, Molly drove me with my baggage, helped settle me into the cottage, helped Alice Shugrue cook dinner for us all, and when Molly was leaving to go home she presented me with forty ten-dollar gold pieces to help finance my life while I waited for my survival advance from Walker Pettijohn. My manipulation of the Meriwether papers had pleased Pettijohn so much that when he learned I was neither dead nor dying he turned me loose to edit the fustian out of a pop-scholarly study of the love theories of Lucretius, Ovid, and Henry Miller.

The gift of gold from Molly was a stunning surprise, not least because it was gold, but also, as I would discover, because she had been hoarding it for two and a half decades, giving it away, five dollars at a time, to relatives and select friends on special occasions.

The August racing meet had ended at the Saratoga track, and most of the Lake House's last guests had gone home, except for a few couples who would stay through Labor Day; and so Molly really didn't go home that night. She decided to stay overnight when the Shugrues and I suggested it. This was when I first heard the story of the cedar waxwing, and Walter's sudden courtship of Molly on that late-summer day in 1935.

I'd been here once before, in the early 1940s, on a long weekend with Peter and Danny Quinn, and knew the place somewhat. But Molly now gave me her own private tour of the grounds and buildings, each weighted with memory.

'Right here,' she said of an area now grown over, 'was the clock golf that Walter and I had played every day. Here's where we played croquet and once I beat him. Here's the path into the bird sanctuary where we used to meet. There's the boat house where he first kissed me, and there's the barn that was our dance hall, isn't it wonderful? And because it's so away from the hotel we could play our music all night long if we wanted to, and nobody would yell at us for keeping them awake.'

The barn had been a cow barn, sturdily converted to a weatherproof building in the early 1930s. It was a cavernous place with exposed beams, its never-painted dance floor now a challenge because of warped boards. The barn was redolent of raw wood and of the pine groves that bordered it outside, and Molly said it was the purest odor she ever knew, that it always turned her memory to those summer days with Walter; that in eighteen years this perfume of love never changed. The place is really just like it always was, she said, the phonograph still there on its table, and the old records (hundreds loose on shelves and in albums), some so old even I remember playing them on the wind-up Victrola. Some were cracked from careless use, but the Shugrues never threw any away, for this music was as much a part of the history of the place as their guest register. You expected the same records to be there, year after year, even the cracked ones.

Molly took down a pile of them, all scratched, no envelopes to protect them, shuffled through them, and found one. 'Here,' she said, and gave it to me to put on the turntable: 'When I Grow Too Old to Dream,' by Ray Noble and his orchestra, a waltz. And we sat then in two of the chairs that lined the barn's walls, and we listened to it all through. Then Molly said, 'Put it on again and we'll waltz,' and so we did. Step, slide, pivot, reverse.

'It was like this,' she said. 'Even when others were here watching, it didn't matter. We were alone in each other's arms and just with the holding we made our pact of love.'

Step, slide, pivot, reverse, my hand on Molly's back, her full breasts against me, our thighs touching through her dress and my trousers as we spun around the floor, she so young, and I so beyond age of any number, just keepers of love in our arms, we creating love with our presence, my cheek against hers, her hair touching my eyes. When the music stopped I started it again, and we heard the scratchings and skips of the song and we danced to that too, and then I replayed it again, yet again, and neither of us said anything, nor did we fully let go of one another while I moved the needle back to the beginning. Her hair, its yellow all but gone into gray, was what Giselle's would be like years from now, her body in its age fuller than Giselle's.

'Do you love her very much still?' Molly asked.

'I do. As you still love Walter.'

'We are serious people about our love.'

'We love. It's what we do.'

And then I kissed her as one kisses one's love, a long kiss, and then I stopped and we held each other, neither of us there, of course, both of us looking at love, of course. And it looks alike sometimes.

I turn the page and I find: *But you're changing, acoolsha, you're changing from me, I can feel . . . Yes, you're changing, sonhusband, and you're turning, I can feel you, for a daughterwife from the hills again . . . I pity your oldself I was used to. Now a younger's there. Try not to part! . . . For she'll be sweet for you as I was sweet when I came down out of me mother. My great blue bedroom, the air so quiet, scarce a cloud. In peace and silence. I could have stayed up there for always only. It's something fails us. First we feel. Then we fall.*

'We'll go make a fire,' Molly said, 'and I'll tell you.'

'Tell me what?'

'I'll tell you about me.'

I shut off the phonograph and Molly took my arm and we walked to the main entrance of the hotel, up the stairs, and into the main parlor with yesterday's rustic furniture and scatter rugs and shelves of forgotten books and the great stone fireplace and its stack of wood and old newspapers, and no people but us two, the other guests all in bed. I moved the screen of the fireplace and built the fire. Molly knew where to find the matches and then we sat on the sofa and watched the fire grow, me keeping my distance from her, yet close, close, and we looked at one another and we smiled at what we saw. I had to touch her face, and then her hair, and then her neck, and I had to let my hand move down to her breast and I touched that, and she said, 'Yes, do that,' and I felt the softness and the fullness with just that one hand. She touched my face and ran her fingers through my hair, kissed me with the fullness of her mouth, then took my hand and put it back in my lap.

'We must find a way not to be naughty,' she said.

And I read this: *I'll close me eyes. So not to see. Or see only a youth in his florizel, a boy in innocence, peeling a twig, a child beside a weenywhite steed. The child we all love to place our hope in for ever.*

'Walter and I made love every day for a week, sometimes twice a day,' Molly said. 'The family hardly saw me and they knew, though they didn't know exactly what they knew. Sarah hated it, scolded me every day, warned me, "You'll be sorry," but I didn't care. Then we all went home and love was over for the time being, though I found ways to meet him. And I did get in the family way. It'd have been a holy miracle if I hadn't. Me forty-five and him a year older, latecomers both of us to this, but I never told him. He died without ever knowing. When I was two months in I found ways to stay home, said I was sick and I was. We talked often on the phone and he couldn't understand why I wouldn't see him, and I always told him, "I will see you, I will when I can." I stopped eating so the weight wouldn't show, had a ketchup sandwich once in a while, and tea, and I was weak. Very. Nobody knew. I never let Sarah or my brothers know anything, didn't even let them see me unless I had a big robe on. And I could never in a million years tell Sarah. She always said after Tommy was born simple that there shouldn't be any more Phelan children. That was Mama's idea, of course. Mama stopped sleeping with Papa after Tommy. No more, no more, it's a sign, I know it. We all heard them fighting about it. Did I want the baby? No. Not for Mama's reason but because I wouldn't want any man marrying me for that, could never raise a child alone, and couldn't ask for help. And so I started to take things to force the birth: medicines, potions, what I'd heard about through the years, pills I saw advertised once, and I knew I could hurt myself. I knew a girl once took a douche of gin and naphtha to get rid of it and she screamed for two hours, all by herself, until they heard her, and she kept screaming until she died. I wouldn't be that foolish. I tightened my corset as much as it went, but I kept growing. And then I called Mrs. Watson, the midwife, and asked her what a woman had to do if she was alone and the baby came, and she told me. "But don't stay alone," she said. "Come and see me." I doubted I'd be able. I always thought I'd have it alone. Not a soul in the world I could ask for help. Not a soul. *First we feel. Then we fall.* It was past four months when it came on its own, a boy, and dead. I cut the cord and mopped the blood when I could, never a scream or a moan out of me, can you believe that? In the night it was. No light till it was over with and I wrapped up the blanket and sheet and the towels and all, and put the baby in the steel box from the closet shelf, where I kept some valuables, and went down the cellar and buried it. I don't know where I got the strength to dig the hole. We don't know how strong we are, do we? I called the baby Walter Phelan and baptized him with water from the sink in a teacup and he's down there still, in a far corner of the cellar, with boxes of horseshoes and jam jars on top of him all these years, God forgive me. You're the only person in the world knows this. God was with the Phelans, don't you think? He took the baby but saved us from scandal and he let me have my love back. I was well in a week and Walter came and took me down to Keeler's for dinner and I remember he ordered a half-dozen clams and when they came he started to eat one and at the same time asked me would I marry him right away, not waste another day, and I said I would before the clam got to his mouth. I will marry you a hundred times, a thousand. And I did.' *I done me best when I was let. Thinking always if I go all goes. A hundred cares, a tithe of troubles and is there one who understands me?*

One.

I turned the page.

The things we do when we're alone.

3

In the year after Molly and I fell in love with each other's failed love, I could at last say without equivocation that I had acquired a family, although a failing one. Sarah and Tommy passed on, Molly fell into her melancholy, and my father, mad with art, and obsessed with his imagery of pernicious life – this rage of creative excess being the condition to which he had aspired all his artistic career – nearly died of a heart attack. That attack reduced him to part-time madman, immobilized and weak, but insistent on working an hour a day, at least. It was because of his condition, and Molly's, that I eventually moved down from Saratoga to become magister of the Phelan house on Colonie Street.

Sarah died first. Molly encountered the beginnings of her sister's decline upon her return from her and Tommy's Labor Day visit with Giselle and me at the Grand View. She found the interior of the Colonie Street house in total darkness at late afternoon, every window barricaded against the light by black drapes Sarah had nailed to the walls. Sarah had also unplugged all lamps, and removed all bulbs from the ceiling fixtures Peter had installed twenty years earlier. Molly found her in her room, sitting in her chair reading, by the light of a solitary candle, an old yellowed newspaper. Sarah seemed not to hear Molly enter the bedroom, but when she saw her she folded the newspaper and put it in the drawer of her bedside table. Then she blew out the candle, moved onto the bed, and pulled the covers up to her chin.

'What happened, Sarah?' Molly asked. 'Are you sick?'

'You left me alone,' Sarah said.

'I asked you to come with us. We went to Saratoga.'

'I know where you went.'

'Billy helped me bring Tommy's wheelchair into the house. He's downstairs. Don't you want to say hello? Don't you want to see Tommy?'

'No. You left me alone,' Sarah said, and that's all she said for two days.

Billy and Molly plugged in the lamps, put the bulbs back in the chandeliers, pulled the nails out of the drapes and woodwork, some of which had splintered, the first serious damage to it since the house was built seventy-five years earlier. As Molly was trying to understand what could have possessed Sarah to do such a thing, she realized that being left by herself was reason enough; for it came to Molly that never in her life had Sarah spent one night alone in this house. Molly knew that she herself could be alone forever, *would be* alone forever, with or without other people, and that it wouldn't kill her; intensify the sadness she was never without, yes; but I am not going to die from such a thing, is how she put it when we talked about Sarah.

The decline of Sarah seemed uncharacteristically abrupt. We all thought she would struggle more vigorously against the cabal of forces that had beset her, but we misread her plan. All her strength and will centered on the downward rush to death, and she clenched her jaws against even minimal nourishment, ripping out of her arms the tubes that carried the life-sustaining fluids Dr. Lynch had ordered for her. She had a deadline for her death. She calculated her weakness until it was the equivalent of a newborn: helpless, pulled into a realm not of its own choosing, the newborn and the imminently moribund bound for an encounter at the symbiotic boundary of life and death. And she died two hours into November 17, 1954, her mother's ninety-fourth birthday.

Sarah left explicit instructions for her wake. She was to be laid out in the same style dress that Kathryn Phelan wore to her grave, and in the same style coffin, which was to be placed in the same position in the front parlor. A solemn high funeral mass should be said for her, as with Kathryn Phelan, and with Father Mahar, the pastor, to be the celebrant. She left the bankbook of the family savings account in the drawer of her bedside table, and it revealed a balance of $840.22. Sarah had no bank account of her own. What little money she earned sewing she always deposited to the family account.

Molly did not find the newspaper Sarah had put in the bedside drawer, nor had it been thrown away. Molly resolved to search for it when the funeral was over. She also chose to countermand Sarah's request for the ancestral dress.

'She'll wear her good Sunday dress,' Molly said. 'I won't have us a laughingstock, people thinking we're old-fashioned.'

Tommy saw Ben Owens and another man carrying Sarah's body down the front stairs and out to the waiting hearse.

'What're they doing, Molly?' Tommy asked.

'They're taking Sarah,' Molly said.

'Where they taking her?'

'To the funeral home,' Molly said, and she sat down beside Tommy on the sofa. 'Sarah died, Tom.'

'She did?'

'She died this morning.'

'Will they bury her?'

'Yes, they will.'

'Why'd she die?'

'She was sad,' Molly said.

'What was she sad about?'

'Oh a lot of things, Tom.'

'Is she dead? Really, really dead?'

'Yes.'

'I didn't think she'd die.'

'Neither did I.'

'Will you die, Moll?'

'Some day.'

'How about me? Will I die?'

'I hope not.'

'Me too,' Tommy said. 'I don't think I wanna die.'

Molly called Peter and he said he'd be up the next day. When she called Peg to tell her the news Peg immediately came down and helped clean the house. I also came down after Molly called me, and made plans to stay over through the funeral.

Ben Owens brought Sarah home at early evening. There would only be one night of waking, the two-night wake going the way of gaslight and woodstoves. Molly had ordered two pieces of flowers and had them delivered immediately, which I found odd, for surely they'd look fresher if they were delivered the day of the wake. We imposed order and polish on the house, then ate the turkey sandwiches Peg brought for us. When Peg went home Molly put Tommy to bed, and then she and I sat alone in the back parlor, I expecting the full story behind Sarah's death. But Molly only sat with her hands folded in her lap, still wearing her kitchen apron, staring at the coffin in the front parlor.

'I should do it now,' she said. 'I may not have another chance after Peter gets here.'

'Chance for what? What should you do now?'

'Bury my baby,' she said. 'Put him in hallowed ground.'

'Jesus, Moll, are you sure? You want to go back and relive that whole thing?'

'I relive it every day of my life,' she said.

'You mean you want Ben Owens to go down cellar and dig up the bones and buy a grave and have a mass and all that? It could turn into a police matter. Can you seriously want that?'

'That's not what I want. Do you love me the way you did the night we danced?'

'I do, Moll,' I said, 'I think it's a permanent condition.'

'I thought so. That's why I want you to dig up the baby for me.'

Access to the cellar was through a trapdoor in the kitchen floor. The stairway was of narrow, warped boards, without a banister, and one achieved the bottom either in darkness or with a flashlight. The place had obviously been designed by a lunatic, the foundation a crazy collage of brick and fieldstone, the dirt floor never leveled, the place never wired for electricity, despite the former need for access to the now defunct coal furnace (oil now heated the house). The cellar gave off the cloistered odor of coal dust, dry earth, and crumbling mortar from the foundation walls, which were in a decrepitude parallel to that of the denizens of this house. Dozens of empty jelly and Ball jars lay in boxes on shelves, and beside them dusty rows of pickled cauliflower, tomatoes, onions, preserved fruit and jellies, and I wondered were these still edible, and how long had they survived in this dismal grotto?

Molly followed me down the steps, more surefooted than I, more used to the stairs' rickety incline. Some light from the kitchen shone through the open trapdoor, and so we could see each other dimly. She looked back up to the light.

'Imagine me holding the box with the baby, and finding my way with a flashlight because I didn't dare put on the kitchen light, and then coming down those stairs in my condition. I don't know how I did it.'

'You're a strong-minded woman.'

'Not strong-minded enough.'

She took the flashlight from me and shone its beam into the area behind the stairs. Three more boxes of jars, a box of tools, a crank for an old automobile, a box of horseshoes, a few lengths of pipe, rusty plumbing fixtures, and a backless chair occupied the space. Molly shone the light onto the horseshoes.

'That's the spot,' she said, and she reached into the coal bin, lifted a spade off a nail, and handed it to me. I moved the horseshoes and began to dig. It was a shallow grave. I struck the box on the spade's third thrust.

'Is it just one box, nothing else?'

'It was wrapped in a towel.'

I scraped dirt away, exposing the box and small, decayed fragments of cloth no longer recognizable as anything in particular.

'No towel here any more,' I said.

The light disappeared from the grave and I turned and saw Molly facing away, shining the light on a far wall.

'I need the light, Moll,' I said.

She focused it on the dig but again looked away.

'I don't want to see it,' she said.

'You won't have to.'

I raised the box with one end of the spade, then lifted it out with my hand. Only with its touch did the next question arise: What do we do with it? Hallowed ground where? And how? Climb the cemetery fence at night, babe in hand and the spade strapped to my back? But Molly had already thought it through.

'We'll put the baby in the coffin with Sarah,' she said.

I could only whistle my admiration at the tidiness of this.

'Put the box on her chest and fold her hands over it,' I said, brushing dirt from the box.

Molly took off her apron and handed it to me.

'Wrap the baby in this, and then put the box back in the ground,' she said. 'I can't watch. Bring it up to the kitchen when you finish.' And up the stairs she went.

I spread her apron on the lowest empty shelf and set the box beside it. In close light I saw the box was of a type that locked with a key, and it *was* locked, or sealed by rust under its eighteen-year-old layer of silt. I found a hammer and chisel in the tool box, easily broke the lock, and raised the top to see the remnants of a cloth of indeterminate type: a muslin pillowcase? a linen blouse? I tipped the box upside down to empty its contents onto the apron, but it would not release, the remains wedded to the interior rust. I did not want to touch anything, more out of sacredness than revulsion or fear of curruption. I nudged the edges of the cloth with the chisel and, as gently as the task demanded that I do this, scraped the swaddling cloth out of its coffin. It was far more intact than the towel, its underside discernible as linen, tanned by time and stained by blood and afterbirth. There was almost no shape to the remains of the child: no torso, no shoulders or rib cage, no limbs, no bones at all that I could see except the half-curve of the tiny skull that raised a doll-like protuberance under the cloth. I would make no inspection of what lay beneath the linen. I folded the apron around it and the odor that arose from the closure was neither of blood nor decayed flesh, but rather a singular emanation more powerful than the fused odors of earth and disintegrating metal: a pungent assault on the senses by the mortal remains of love.

In the kitchen Molly had prepared the burial packaging: a length of brown wrapping paper, a roll of Scotch tape and another of adhesive tape, and a white linen napkin with the scrolled letter P on one corner. I took the remains out of the apron and put them in the wrapping paper, this movement revealing that there remained nothing but human dust and the fraction of skull, and I wrapped and sealed this completely with the tape. I wrapped it then within the napkin, exposing the letter P, and wrapped that twice around with adhesive tape. The entire package was about the size of a poppy-seed roll from the Grand Lunch, and when I finished with it Molly took a small purse from the top of the refrigerator, put the remains inside it, and handed it to me.

'You decide where to put it,' she said.

The logical place was under Sarah's head. I raised the head cushion, and Sarah as well, and fitted the purse snugly into the space. The change in Sarah's angle of supinity was negligible.

'Do you think people will be able to smell anything?' Molly asked.

'Your flowers should take care of that. Isn't that why you ordered them?'

'It is.'

'You've thought about this a long time.'

'For years. I knew I'd send Walter along with whoever went next in the family. I prayed I wouldn't go first.'

'What do you think Sarah would say if she knew she was having company in her coffin?'

'She'd find fault. She found fault with everything.'

'It gives a new meaning to "virgin with child."'

'We all would've been happier if Sarah wasn't a virgin.'

'You really think that would have made a difference?'

'Virgins think about heaven,' Molly said. 'They don't care about what goes on down here.'

Our neighborhood was in a stage of vanishing tradition, dying to its old self, an influx of Negroes creating a new world order, displacing the old Irish and Germans in the same way those two groups had displaced the Dutch and English gentry who so shortsightedly thought that bucolic Arbor Hill was to be their private garden forever. And so for this reason, and also because of the all-but-cloistered life Sarah had led, fewer people came to her wake than were expected, the most notable absence being Chick, who did not even telephone after he received Molly's telegram, but merely sent a modest basket of flowers, the card with them bearing nothing other than the names *Chick and Evelyn Phelan*, the first announcement to the family that Chick had married, and simultaneously an act of distancing Molly took to be spiteful.

'Chick will regret this to his dying day,' Peter said when he read the card, 'not because of Sarah, but because he'll eventually realize what we think of his gesture. Anger makes people stupid.'

Anger did not make Peter stupid. And surely it was at least anger, perhaps even rage at the power of an abstraction as cruel, remote, and inviolate as God, but not God, that propelled Peter toward his masterworks. He saw, in the story of Malachi and Lizzie, and then in the way that Kathryn and Sarah had nursed that story and secretly kept it alive, a pattern that need not have been – a wrong to two generations that might have been preventable, if only . . .

I've generalized about cause and effect in this family, but one proximate cause of what made Kathryn, Sarah, Peter, and the rest of us behave in such diverse but consistent ways was chronicled in that newspaper story Molly saw Sarah reading by candlelight. Molly found the cache of old papers in a crawlspace that opened off the closet of Sarah's room (Kathryn's and Michael's room before Sarah took it over) into an unusable area of the attic. As children, Molly and Julia had discovered the crawlspace and hidden in it to elude Sarah, or merely to exist in a secret place no one else could enter; but Sarah caught them coming out of it one day and the secret place lost all value.

Molly found the papers in the small brown leather suitcase Michael Phelan had used when his work on the railroad required him to stay overnight in another city. There were a dozen newspapers in all, telling day by day the story of Malachi and Lizzie, the marriage destined for enshrinement in a lower circle of hell.

'So this,' Molly said to me when she showed me the papers, 'is what she was reading at the last. Gone back to the first.'

What happened with Malachi was hardly the first, but I do believe that that's how Molly and others in the family thought of it. Molly wasn't even born when it happened, nor were Julia and Tommy. Francis was seven, Sarah four, Chick one. Also Kathryn was pregnant with Peter when she went through the Malachi ordeal in 1887.

In the 1930s Peter had found his artistic vision in *The Itinerant* series, but then in subsequent years he foundered badly, dabbling in cityscapes, portraits, and in the new non-figurative, non-representational abstract mode, whose exercises in symbolic color and form, devoid of the human being, he could admire when done by others, but only loathe as pretentious failures when he created them himself.

In the weeks after Molly and I showed him the Malachi newspapers, Peter returned to figurative drawing, sketches of people closest to him, and felt instant strength, saw the abstract elements of these lives not as layers of scumbled space and violated line, but as the cruel specifics of eyes and jaw, the mournful declension of a lip line, the jaunty elevation of a leg. For years he had sketched the family, either from photographs or memory, or by cajoling his siblings (even Sarah one afternoon) into modeling for him. He never showed any of these works publicly, though he completed a dozen or more paintings from four or five score of sketches. Perhaps he was waiting for the moment when the visual reunion of his kin would make exhibitional sense.

That came to pass when the family, as he saw it, osmosed its way into his *Malachi Suite*, that manic outpouring of genius (I give him no less) that eventually drew me, and even Giselle, into its remarkable vortex. He sketched with a passion and painted with a fury that bespoke his fear of time, his full awareness that he had so little of it left in which to complete this now obsessive work. But he also painted with a sure hand, all errors deemed fortuitous and made part of the painting. His brush never wavered, these works of pain and poignancy stroked into existence with swiftness, certainty, and a realism that arrested the eyes of the beholder, held them fast.

In early childhood Peter had heard the Malachi events spoken of in cryptic bits by his mother, later heard more from Francis, who was seven when it happened, and in time heard it garbled by street-corner wags who repeated the mocking rhyme:

If you happen to be a Neighbor,
If you happen to be a witch,
Stay the hell away from Malachi,
That loony son of a bitch.

When the story took him over, Peter moved out of portrait sketching into scenes of dynamic action and surreal drama that in their early stages emerged as homage to Goya's *Caprichos, Disparates*, and *Desastres de Guerra*. But in his extended revelation of the Malachi-and-Lizzie tragedy (and mindful of Goya's credo that the painter selected from the universe whatever seemed appropriate, that he chose features from many individuals and their acts, and combined them so ingeniously that he earned the title of inventor and not servile copyist), Peter imposed his own original vision on scandalous history, creating a body of work that owed only an invisible inspiration to Goya.

He reconstituted the faces and corpora of Lizzie and Malachi and others, the principal room and hearth of the McIlhenny three-room cottage, the rushing waters of the Staatskill that flowed past it, the dark foreboding of the sycamore grove where dwelled the Good Neighbors, as Crip Devlin arcanely called those binate creatures whose diabolical myths brought on that terrible night in June of 1887.

His first completed painting, *The Dance*, was of Lizzie by the sycamores, her bare legs and feet visible to mid-thigh in a forward step, or leap, or kick, her left hand hiking the hem of her skirt to free her legs for the dance. But is it a dance? In the background of the painting is the stand of trees that played such a major role in Lizzie's life, and to the left of her looms a shadow of a man or perhaps it is a half-visible tree, in the dusky light. If it is a tree it is beckoning to Lizzie. If it is a man perhaps he is about to dance with her.

But is that a dance she is doing, or is it, as one who saw her there said of it, an invitation to her thighs?

In the painting it is a dance, and it is an invitation.

4

Why would Lizzie McIlhenny, a plain beauty of divine form and pale brown hair to the middle of her back, choose to dance with a tree, or a shadow, or a man (if man it ever was or could be) at the edge of a meadow, just as a summer night began its starry course? Aged twenty-six, married five years to Malachi McIlhenny, a man of formidable girth whose chief skill was his strength, a man of ill luck and no prospects, Lizzie (née Elizabeth Cronin) had within her the spirit of a sensuous bird.

Malachi imposed no limits of space on their marriage, and so she came and went like a woman without a husband, dutiful to their childless home, ever faithful to Malachi and, when the bad luck came to him, his canny helpmate: first trapping yellow birds in the meadow and selling them to friends for fifty cents each, but leaving that when she found that fashioning rag birds out of colored cloth, yarn, thread, feathers, and quills was far more profitable; that she could sell them for a dollar, or two, depending on their size and beauty, to the John G. Myers Dry-Goods and Fancy-Goods Store, which, in turn, would sell them for four and five dollars as fast as Lizzie could make them.

At the end of a week in early June she made and sold sixteen birds, each of a different hue, and earned twenty-seven dollars, more money than Malachi had ever earned from wages in any two weeks, sometimes three. The money so excited Lizzie that when crossing the meadow on her way home from the store she kicked off her shoes, threw herself into the air, and into the wind, danced until breath left her, and then collapsed into the tall grass at the edge of the sycamore grove, a breathless victim of jubilation.

When she regained her breath and sat up, brushing bits of grass from her eyelashes, she thought she saw a man's form in the shadowy interior of the grove, saw him reach his hand toward her, as if to help her stand. Perhaps it was only the rustling of the leaves, or the sibilance of the night wind, but Lizzie thought she heard the words 'the force of a gray horse,' or so it was later said of her. Then, when she pulled herself erect, she was gripping not the hand of a man but the low-growing branch of a sycamore.

Malachi's troubles crystallized in a new way when he lost his only cow to a Swedish cardsharp named Lindqvist, a recently arrived lumber handler who joined the regular stud-poker game at Black Jack McCall's Lumber District Saloon, and who bested Malachi in a game that saw jacks fall before kings. Lindqvist came to the cow shed behind Malachi's cottage and, with notable lack of regret, led Malachi's only cow into a territorial future beyond the reach of all McIlhennys.

The lost cow seemed to confirm to Malachi that his life would always be a tissue of misfortune. At the urgings of his older brother, Matty, who had come to Albany in 1868 and found work on a lumber barge, Malachi, age seventeen, had sold all that the family owned and left Ireland in 1870 with his ten-year-old sister, Kathryn, and their ailing father, Eamon, who anticipated good health and prosperity in the New World. In Albany the three penniless green-horns settled in with Matty at his Tivoli Hollow shanty on the edge of Arbor Hill. Within six months Matty was in jail on a seven-year sentence for beating a man to death in a saloon fight, within a year he was dead himself, cause officially unknown, the unofficial word being that a guard, brother of the man Matty killed, broke Matty's head with an iron pipe when opportunity arose; and then, within two years, Eamon McIlhenny was dead at fifty-nine of ruined lungs. These dreadful events, coming so soon after the family's arrival in the land of promise and plenty, seemed to forebode a dark baggage, a burden as fateful as the one the McIlhennys had tried to leave behind in County Monaghan.

Malachi did not yield to any fate. He labored ferociously and saved his money. And as he approached marriage he bought a small plot of country land on Staats Lane, a narrow and little-used road that formed a northern boundary of the vast Fitzgibbon (formerly Staats) estate, and built on it, with his own hands, the three-room cottage that measured seven long paces deep by nine long paces wide, the size of a devil's matchbox. In 1882 Malachi moved into the cottage with his bride, the sweet and fair Lizzie Cronin, a first-generational child of Albany.

After five years the marriage was still childless, and Lizzie slowly taught herself to be a seamstress as a way of occupying her time, making clothing for herself and Malachi. But with so few neighbors she found other sewing work scarce, and her days remained half empty, with Malachi working long and erratic hours. And so Lizzie looked to the birds, the trees, the meadows of the Fitzgibbon estate, and the Staatskill, a creek with a panoramic cascade, churning waters, and placid pools, for her pleasure. Malachi saw his wife developing into a fey creature of the open air, an elfin figure given to the sudden eruption of melodies off her tongue that Malachi did not recognize. She began to seem like an otherworldly being to Malachi.

In the spring of 1887, two days after he lost his cow, the waters of the Hudson River, as usual, spilled over their banks and rose into the lumber mills, storage sheds, and piles of logs that were the elemental architecture of Sage's lumber yard, where Malachi worked as a handler. One log slipped its berth in the rising waters, knocked Malachi down, and pinned his left shoulder against a pile of lumber, paralyzing his left arm and reducing the strength in his torso by half, perhaps more. So weakened was he that he could no longer work as a handler, that useless left arm an enduring enemy.

He found work one-handedly sickling field grass on the Fitzgibbon land, work that provided none of the fellowship that prevailed among lumber handlers. He worked alone, came home alone, brooded alone until the arrival of his wife, who grew more peculiar with every moment of Malachi's increasing solitude. He topped her at morning, again at evening after she returned from her communion with the birds of the field, and he failed to create either new life in Lizzie or invincible erectness in himself.

To test himself against nature he sought out the woman known to the canalers and lumber handlers as the Whore of Limerick, her reputation as an overused fuckboat appealing to Malachi's free-floating concupiscence. After several iniquitous successes that proved the problem existed wholly in Lizzie, Malachi abandoned the fuckboat and sought solace again in Lizzie's embrace, which cuddled his passion and put it to sleep. He entered heavily into the drink then, not only the ale that so relieved and enlivened him, but also the potsheen that Crip Devlin brewed in his shed.

Drink in such quantity, a departure for Malachi, moved him to exotic behavior. He lay on his marriage bed and contemplated the encunted life. Cunt *was* life, he decided. Lizzie came to him as he entered into a spermatic frenzy, naked before her and God, ready to ride forever into the moist black depths of venery, indeed even now riding the newly arrived body of a woman he had never seen, whose cunt changed color and shape with every nuance of the light, whose lewd postures brimmed his vessel. Ah love, ah fuckery, how you enhance the imperial power of sin! When he was done with her, the woman begged for another ride, and he rode her with new frenzy; and when he was done again she begged again and he did her again, and then a fourth ride, and a fifth; and, as he gave her all the lift and pull that was left to him, his member grew bloody in his hand. When the woman saw this she vanished, and Lizzie wept.

The following morning, when he awoke, Malachi found not only his wife already gone from the house, he found himself also bereft of his privities, all facets of them, the groin of his stomach and thighs as hairless, seamless, and flat as those groins on the heavenly angels that adorned the walls of Sacred Heart Church. Here was a curse on a man, if ever a curse was. God was down on Malachi now – God, or the devil, one.

Malachi clothed himself, drained half a jug of potsheen, all he had, then pulled the bedcovers over his head. He would hide himself while he considered what manner of force would deprive a man not only of his blood kin, his strength, his labor, and his cow, but now, also, his only privities. He would hide himself and contemplate how a man was to go about living without privities; more important, he would think about ways of launching a counterattack on God, or the devil, or whoever had taken them, and he would fight that thief of life with all his strength to put those privities back where they belonged.

In the painting he called *The Conspiracy*, Peter Phelan created the faces of Malachi and Crip Devlin as they sit in Malachi's primitive kitchen with their noses a foot apart, the condiments and implements of their plan on the table in front of them, or on the floor, or hanging over the fireplace. The bed is visible in the background, a crucifix on the wall above it.

Malachi is in a collarless shirt, waistcoat and trousers of the same gray tweed, and heavy brogans, his left arm hanging limp. Crip Devlin wears a cutaway coat in tatters, a wing collar too large for his neck, a bow tie awkwardly tied.

These men are only thirty-four and forty, Malachi the younger of the two, but they are portraits of psychic and physical trouble. Malachi's face is heavily furrowed, his head an unruly mass of black curls, his black eyes and brows with the look of the wild dog in them. Crip is bald, with a perpetual frown of intensity behind his spectacles, a half-gray mustache, and sallow flesh. He is moving toward emaciation from the illness to which he has paid scant attention, for at this time he considers all trouble and trauma to be the lot of every man born to walk among devils.

Crip was in a late stage of his pox veneris, not knowing how close he was to death, when he brought his mystical prowess to bear on the lives of Lizzie and Malachi. He had studied for the priesthood briefly as a young man, and later taught primary school, but was unsuited for it, lacking in patience toward eight-year-old children who could not perceive the truth. In recent years he had worked as a lumber handler with Malachi, and in the winter they cut ice together on the river. But his disease in late months kept him from working and he lived off the sale of his homemade liquor, which, by common standards, was undrinkable, but had the redeeming quality of being cheap.

Crip had brought the recipe for the potsheen with him from Ireland, as he had brought his wisdom about the Good Neighbors, those wee folk who, he insisted, inhabited a hilly grove of sycamore trees and hawthorn bushes not far from Malachi's cottage. Crip was a widower who lived with his nine-year-old daughter, Mab; and he taught her all the lore of the Good Neighbors that he himself had learned from his mother, who once kept one of the wee creatures (a flute player) in the house for six months, fed it bread and milk on a spoon, and let it sleep in the drawer with the knives and forks. And didn't Crip's mother have good luck the rest of her life for her generous act? Indeed she did.

When Malachi listened to Crip Devlin talk, something happened to his mind. He saw things he knew he'd never seen before, understood mysteries he had no conscious key to. When Crip stopped talking Malachi also felt eased, relieved to be back in his own world, but felt also a new effulgence of spirit, a potential for vigorous action that just might give back a bit of its own to the foul beast that was skulking so relentlessly after his body and his soul.

In Ireland, Crip boasted, he'd been called the Wizard, the Cunningman who could outwit the Good Neighbors. And when Malachi heard this he confided to Crip that he had lost his privities.

'Did you ever lose them before?' Crip asked Malachi.

'Never.'

'Was there pain when they went?'

'None. I didn't know they were gone till I looked.'

'It's a shocking thing.'

'I'm more shocked than others,' Malachi said.

'I've heard of this,' said Crip. 'Somebody has put the glamour on you.'

'Glamour, is it?'

'A spell of a kind. The Neighbors could do it. I read of a man who lost his privities and thought he knew who did it, and it was a witch and he went to her. He told her his trouble and also told her she had the most beautiful bosoms in the village, for he knew how witches love flattery. And she took him out to a tree and told him to climb up it and he'd find what he needed. When he did that he found a great nest full of hay and oats in the treetop, and two dozen privities of one size and the other lying in it. And the man says I'll take this big one, and the witch says no, that belongs to the bishop. So the man took the next-smaller size and put it in his pocket, and when he got to the bottom of the tree and touched the ground with his foot, the witch disappeared and his privity was on him. And he never lost it again.'

'You're thinkin', is it, that a witch did this to me?' Malachi asked.

'It well could be. Do you know any witches yourself?'

'None.'

'Have you had any in the family?'

'None that I know of.'

'And your wife's family?'

'I've never heard it spoken of.'

'They don't speak of it, don't you know.'

'I'll ask her,' said Malachi.

'I saw her up on the Neighbors' hill two days ago.'

'Is that so?'

'It's so, and she was dancing.'

'Dancing, you say.'

'I do. Dancing with her skirts in the air.'

'No.'

'Didn't I see it myself, and the shape of a man in the woods watching her?'

'The shape of a man?'

'Not a man atall, I'd say.'

'Then what?'

'One of the Neighbors. A creature, I'd call it.'

'Lizzie dancing with a creature? You saw that. And were you at the potsheen?'

'I was not.'

'Did you go to her?'

'I did not. You don't go near them when they're in that mood.'

'What mood?'

'The mood to capture. That's how they carry on, capturing people like us to fatten their population. They like to cozy up to them that come near them, and before you know it somebody's gone and you don't even know they're gone, for the creatures leave changelings in place of the ones they take. But there's no worth atall to *them* things. They melt, they die, they fly away, and if they don't, you have to know how to be rid of them.'

'You know how to do that, do you?'

'I've heard how it's done. I have the recipes.'

Two books lie on the table in Peter's *Conspiracy* painting.

The first is the *Malleus Maleficarum.* Its subtitle, not visible in the painting, is *The Hammer of Witches Which Destroyeth Witches and Their Heresy as with a Two-edged Sword*. The book is a fifteenth-century theological analysis of the anarchical political forces that for centuries sought the overthrow of civilization through witchcraft, plus abundant remedies for this evil; and it is a work that had motivated Crip Devlin since the days of his priestly intent, for its divinely inspired misogyny conformed to Crip's own outlook, especially after his infection with the pox by his wife. And did she give it to him, the witch? Well, she did. Didn't she die of it herself, and die before Crip? Was that proof or was it not?

Malachi, when he listened to Crip's wisdom, handed down from the sages of history, felt like a chosen man, one who would yet again do battle with the dark spirits, the lot of the true warrior in every age. Malachi accepted the role without complaint, for its rules and its goals were as familiar to him as the streets and the fields of Albany. He agreed with them, he understood them, and he knew from his wound that he had been singled out for this challenge. As the *Malleus* pointed out so clearly, devils existed only with God's permission, and Malachi perceived that God had allowed these devilish things to happen to him, allowed his life to be taken away piece by piece, in the same way He had allowed Job and Jesus and the martyred saints to be warrior sufferers for His sake.

Without ever having heard the phrase, and with small capacity for understanding it if he had, Malachi had become an ascetic idealist, as obsessed by his enemy as Peter would be by his art; and when you look at the eyes Peter gave the man, you know that both Malachi and Peter understood that the world was inimical to them and to their plans of order and harmony, that their lives existed at the edge of disaster, madness, and betrayal, and that a man of strength and honor would struggle with the dark armies until he triumphed or died on the battlefield.

Malachi truly believed he would win this struggle with the black villain. He had done as the *Malleus* counseled, had said his Aves and his Our Fathers, had made the Stations of the Cross on his knees, had talked to the priest and confessed his sins (not his loss for that was an affliction, not a sin), and had gone to mass so often that the women of the parish thought he must be either very guilty, or dying. But, in truth, he was coming to understand that some sort of action that went beyond heavenly recourse was called for, action beyond what was known on earth – except by a chosen few whose courage was boundless and whose weapons were mighty.

The second book on the table in the painting is a slim volume that is open to a sketch of a plant with leaves and berries that any herbalist would recognize as foxglove. Also in the painting Crip is holding a chicken by the neck with his left hand and from its anus is receiving droppings in his right palm, some of these already floating in a bowl of new milk on the table.

Crip, before the moment shown in the painting, has enlightened Malachi on the things witches fear most, things that cure enchantment and banish the witch back to her own devilish world: foxglove and mugwort, white mullen and spearwort, verbena and elf grass, the four-leaf clover and the scarlet berries of the rowan oak, green and yellow flowers, cow parsnip and docken, a drawn sword, the gall of a crow, the tooth of a dead man, rusty nails and pins, the music of a Jew's harp, a red string around the neck, the smoke of burned elder and ash wood, the smoke of a burned fish liver, spitting into your own shirt, pissing through a wedding ring, and fire.

Crip mixed half a dozen potions for Malachi and he drank them; the two men burned ash wood and fish liver; they found foxglove and cow parsnip and made a paste of it and Malachi went off by himself and rubbed that on his groin. He thought of pissing through his mother's wedding ring, but then he remembered he had nothing to piss with. More things were done, all of them failing to restore Malachi's privities.

Crip then moved to the next logical step: an inquiry into the behavior and the physical properties of the women around Malachi (his sister Kathryn, the Whore of Limerick, Lizzie), for it was well known that witches sometimes assumed the shape of living people, especially women. Even so, they could be found out, for they always had marks and traits that were not human. Crip knew of one witch who had an extra nipple on her stomach, and another with nipples on each buttock. A third witch always lived with two creatures sucking her, a red one at her left breast, a white one at the inward walls of her secrets.

When Malachi heard these revelations he immediately undertook a thorough but surreptitious study of his wife, and for the first time he realized that she had shrunk in height by four inches, that the mark on her left thigh could well be an extra nipple. He remembered that she brought a succubus to their bed and encouraged him to copulate with it until he was bloody. Also, Crip swore to him that, on the night he watched Lizzie dancing on the Neighbors' hill, her partner, the shadowy creature, had the webbed feet of a goose.

And so Malachi made ready to launch his counterattack against the demon (and all its hellish consorts) that inhabited his wife's body.

Book Five

1

As the time grows closer for it, I'm becoming obsessed by the fact that Giselle is coming here, and that my life is about to change yet again. She now tells me she's pregnant, and that she didn't plan it. It's July, she's two months gone, and I did it to her in May, she says, when she came up to take the final photo of Peter for the *Life* profile she did on him. She was here all weekend, we went at it in my room, what, two, three times? And bingo! She left then to travel for two months, and I didn't hear from her until last night, when she said she'd be up today, with an enhanced womb, for the family meeting Peter had invited her to attend.

She also told me that, after five years of it, she's had enough and is leaving *Life* – as soon as she finishes her current project. She'll have a baby, then free-lance, giving *Life* first look at whatever she photographs. She no longer wants to be at the beck and call of magazine editors, now says she's willing to rejoin the nuptial bed, which she'd hinted at when last we bathed in the steam of our malfunctional wedlock.

I'd often given her my spiel, that the quotidian life is the most important element of our existence, and although she didn't accept that in the early days of our marriage, she now says I was right, that a career is indispensable, but it makes for a very sterile life if that's all there is. She says she envies me the family ties, and that she's come to understand she and I might be divorced now if it weren't for Molly.

Of course I don't believe much of what Giselle says. Such

conversions are for minds more simple than hers. It will be a major change having her with me all the time, but it is true that she's grown closer to the family since the *Life* profile on Peter, and the book project that grew out of it. Walker Pettijohn suggested an art book on Peter, a book suitable for coffee tables, with Giselle doing the photos, me doing text blocks plus interviews with the artist (he thought the father-son link would enhance the book's appeal, but I pointed out to him the awkward disparity in our names), and a critic yet to be chosen analyzing Peter's work and putting it in historical perspective. Such is the man's fame, now that he's close to death (though not yet moribund), that this was one of four book offers prompted by the *Life* article. Peter has managed to jump through the flaming hoop of high art and come out the other side as a potential creature of the popular imagination.

I was still at the dining-room table, cheating at cards for Billy's amusement, when I heard Peter's hoarse voice call me.

'Orson, can you come up?'

And so I excused myself and went up. Peter was in bed, just reawakened after a mid-morning nap. He'd had his matinee with Adelaide, then attacked his easel until fatigue pulled him back to his pillow. He looked tousled and very old for his seventy-one years, his gray-haired torso going to bone, his hair and mustache almost solid white, and more scraggly than usual.

When I entered his bedroom he was sitting on the side of the bed gripping the sturdy blackthorn walking stick Michael Phelan had bought in Ireland. His room, the same one he'd slept in all his life in this house, was full of books, newspapers, and three unfinished sketches, this being his pattern: to keep incomplete work at his bedside, study it before sleep, and wake perhaps to find a solution that would let him complete it. I thought he might now be ready for a second go at the work-in-progress, but he had another plan.

'Anybody here yet?' he asked.

'Just Billy and myself.'

'So you nailed him.'

'He's here but he's itchy to leave.'

'Keep his curiosity aroused and he'll stay.'

'That's what I'm doing.'

'Get him to help you move some paintings downstairs.'

'He's got a cast on his foot.'

'How'd he get here? You carry him?'

'He can walk.'

'If he can walk he can climb stairs.'

'Which paintings do you want?'

'*The Dance*, *The Conspirary*, and *The Protector*.'

'Not the new one?'

'No, I don't want to shock them. Maybe later. Those'll do for what I have to say.'

'Done.'

I called Billy and he hobbled upstairs immediately. I took him through the rooms, which he hadn't seen since the day Sarah went crazy because Molly left her alone. Billy and Molly then had to repair all Sarah's damage and chaos, and that was the first Billy had ever been above the ground floor. He'd told me more than once he never wanted anything to do with the house, or its people, after his father's experience, the exception being Molly, who always gave him five dollars in birthday gold, as she gave others in the family. Like most people who knew her, Billy projected a ray of love toward Molly. 'Good old dame,' he called her. He liked to tease her about her hemorrhoids, a problem he also lived with.

'Christ, what a wreck this joint is,' Billy said when he came upstairs.

'It's not a wreck. It's an artist's studio, all of it except my room and Molly's. And he's even moving things into her room, now that she's not using it.'

'Molly's not livin' here no more?'

'Not for months. She's up at Saratoga with the Shugrues, living in the rooms I used to live in. She couldn't take care of Peter, couldn't go up and down the stairs twenty times a day. She's got all she can do to take care of herself these days, and so we swapped rooms. I came here, she went there. Alice Shugrue's her best friend in the world, great company for her.'

'I didn't know Molly was sick. I don't hear what goes on.'

'She's not sick, just weary. She's in good enough shape that she's cooking lunch for us. You like roast lamb?'

'Are you kiddin'?'

'Good.'

'What's this lunch business all about?'

'About all the Phelans, and their ancestors.'

'Not interested.'

'Don't be so quick, Billy. We need you, and I really mean that. We need what you know.'

'I don't know nothin' you don't know.'

'You know about your father. You know when he came home in '42, and what he did. I don't know any of that. I was in the army already. You see what I'm saying?'

'I see what you're sayin', but I don't know what you're talkin' about. What's my father got to do with anything?'

So I showed him all my photos of *The Itinerant* series, in which Francis played the central role. I told him how Francis showed up all of a sudden, then fought with Sarah, and how Peter tracked him down and asked him to come back, and that I saw this with my own eyes.

'But he didn't come back,' Billy said.

'No. He kept walking. He didn't come back to stay till the war. Do you know whether he ever came here in the war period?'

'He wouldn't put a foot on the stoop.'

'Did he ever talk to Peter, or Molly, or Chick, or anybody?'

'Maybe Pete went to see him at a Senators game when he was coachin', but if he did my father never mentioned it.'

'He saw you, and Peg, and Annie.'

'That's why he came home. He called my mother and found out I was goin' in the army and he said he'd come home and be around if somethin' needed fixin'. He took a room up near the ball park. He'd come down to the house once a week and sit with my mother, bring her a pint of vanilla ice cream, or pineapple sherbet, talk an hour, have a meal with us, then disappear for another week. But he'd come by in a minute if Ma called him. He shoveled snow, cut the grass for her, put up screens and storm windows, fixed a busted asbestos pipe on the furnace.'

'He was a strange guy.'

'He was an *all-right* guy,' Billy said with an edge to his voice.

'I didn't say he wasn't.'

'Everybody else in this joint did.'

'I just told you that wasn't true. Stick around, Billy. You'll learn something about your relatives you didn't know.'

'Yeah,' he said.

But I knew I'd hooked him. I took him into Peter's studio and found the paintings Peter wanted as props when he delivered his remarks to the assembled kin. Billy looked at the paintings the way he looked at everything else in the house: not interested. Then we carried them, one by one, down the hallway to the dining room.

That Malachi was still influencing our lives like this supported my idea that we are never without the overcoats, however lice-ridden, of our ancestors. This luncheon was going to be an expressionistic occasion, offering graphic imaginings of where we came from, what we might expect of ourselves (and our children), and what we might do to our greatest loves, given our inherited propensities. I tried to imagine whether and, if so, why Malachi was predisposed to disaster, and all I could do was project myself backward into my own disturbed history, into the isolation where I had been able to triumph privately in social, financial, marital, and artistic realms, no failure possible in that utopia where all eccentricity is justified, where ineffectuality is not only acceptable, but desirable as a badge of defiance, where there is no need to engage the actual world because the private world is always sufficient to the day. Reality conquered by the ego: Malachi's story precisely.

I now like to think that I am coming out of this benighted condition, and in my own peculiar way am again an engaged citizen of the bright day, working within the race. I see evidence of this in my ability to function in the publishing world without either the hem-kissing subservience of the acolyte, or the wound-licking reverie of the early failure.

I feel pride in my restrained reaction to Giselle's pregnancy, never once voicing those Strindbergian doubts that had dropped into my mind like henbane: never inquiring whether it truly was I who seeded her furrow; never offering the suggestion that it was perhaps an anonymous creativist at *Life*, or possibly Quinn the traveler who had left his enduring mark on her during one of his New York visits. Did I suggest, as the young Strindberg ruffian, Nojd, put it, that 'it wouldn't be much fun slaving all your life for another chap's brat'? No, I did not. If it was Quinn who'd done the deed, then at least the Phelan ontogeny was now at work in Giselle's inner sanctum, and I might become father to my first cousin twice removed. But I am no more likely to have certitude on any of this than Nojd, or Peter Phelan.

Molly pulled the doorbell and stood on top of the stoop with her arms full of groceries. She turned to the curb, where Alice Shugrue waited behind the wheel of her Chevrolet, idling until Molly had gained proper access to the homestead; and then I opened the door and took a bag from Molly ('Be careful, there's breakables,' she said). I hugged her and bussed her cheek, then waved to Alice.

'Come in and see us when you come back for her,' I said, 'and we'll catch up on all your news.' Alice smiled and waved me down, saying, 'You're not to be trusted with my news, now that you're writing a book,' and off she went.

Molly stepped into the hallway and tapped the bag of groceries I was holding. 'You're not to be trusted with breakables either,' she said. 'I've seen you with dishes in the hotel kitchen.'

'There are things I never dropped,' I said, 'so get your dirty tongue off me.'

Molly, kittenish, kissed my cheek with her arms full as we moved toward the kitchen. 'I miss this house,' she said.

'Well, come back to it, then,' I said.

'Easy to say.'

'Easy to do. There's change afoot in the world.'

'Afoot me foot,' said Molly. 'All that'll change this place is an earthquake.'

'Exactly what we've got planned for lunch,' I said.

'It's a scheme, I knew it. What's he up to?'

'I'll tell you when it's time to tell you.'

I thought Molly looked well, though a bit more frail than when I'd last seen her. Her north-country exile seemed to be sapping her energy, but she was wearing one of her dressy summer dresses, the pink one, so I sensed she was trying to rekindle her old self for the occasion. We put the groceries on the kitchen table and I then took her by the elbow and moved her toward the dining room and Billy. Her gaze went instantly to *Banishing the Demons* on the wall, then to *The Conspiracy*, which I'd leaned against the back staircase. She had seen, and fully understood, the content of both paintings, but made no comment on their presence. She turned and looked at Billy in his plaster cast.

'It's a long time since I've seen your handsome mug, Billy boy,' she said. 'I heard you might be here today.'

'That's more than I heard. Who told ya that?'

'I'm no squealer, kiddo,' Molly said. 'And whatever did you do to your leg? Are you all right?'

'I can't kick,' Billy said. 'You're lookin' good, Moll. How's the old bareedis?'

'I'm fine in all respects, and I'll answer no more impertinent questions.'

'How's Saratoga?'

'The hotel is busy. The track opens next week.'

'But no more gamblin' casinos.'

'None that I hear of. It's not like it used to be.'

'Nothin' is,' Billy said.

'How many are coming for lunch, Orson? We have to set the table.'

'Us three and Peter, and Peg is coming with Roger Dailey, the lawyer, and Giselle. Seven.'

'Giselle is coming?'

'Peter invited her. She's been up fairly often lately.'

'How is she?'

'She's pregnant. I guess that makes it eight.'

'Oh,' said Molly, 'oh.' And she looked at me with that hybrid smile of hers: knowing smile of love, and comprehension, and loss.

'First tremor of the earthquake,' I said.

'Hey,' Billy said, 'you gonna be a papa.'

'Looks that way,' I said.

'The lawyer,' said Molly. 'Why is the lawyer coming?'

'I'll tell you when it's time to tell you,' I said.

'Well, I'll tell *you* what it's time for. It's time to make lunch. Bring me the potato dish, two big platters, a vegetable dish, and the pickle and jelly dishes. And the bread plate. And set the table with whatever's left of the good china.'

Molly's reference was to the remnants of a set of china that Peter had bought for Kathryn with his mustering-out pay from the first war, a belated acknowledgment that he had been partly responsible for Francis's fall into the china closet. And I wondered how much of that episode in his father's life Billy knew, and I decided he probably knew nothing at all.

'Have you taken a good look at these paintings?' I asked Billy, indicating *The Conspiracy* and the *Demons*.

'Unhhh,' Billy said, and he craned his neck to look at both, then moved his chair for a better look, and he stared.

'That guy looks like my father,' he said, indicating Malachi in *The Conspiracy*.

'Right. And a little like my father too,' I said.

'Yeah,' said Billy. 'What the hell is it?'

'It's Peter's vision. Your father's been important to him all his life. He's painted him many times.'

'This is the first one I saw.'

'Not the last. He's in that one too,' and I pointed to the *Demons* painting.

'Who's that guy supposed to be? It ain't really my father.'

'It's your great-uncle, Malachi McIlhenny.'

'I heard of him. Wasn't he nuts?'

'Totally, but there's more to it.'

'Yeah,' Billy said, 'when people go nuts they got a reason.'

'You never uttered a truer word,' I said.

I heard footsteps on the porch and went to see who was coming. But it was only the afternoon paper, stuck between the jamb and the doorknob by the thoughtful paperboy to keep it dry. It had been cloudy for an hour and now a fine drizzle was beginning. I was closing the door when I saw a taxi turning off Pearl Street onto Colonie, and I thought, Giselle, accurately. She paid the cabbie and slid out of the back seat with her arms full, offering me her knees in the drizzle, constantly smiling, moving with small steps back into my life. I held the door for her, and she kept going down the hallway to the kitchen.

'Don't I even get a hello?'

'Yes,' she said. 'Follow me.'

And so I did, as I always have, and in the hallway she gave me a serious kiss and went into the back parlor to deposit one of her bags next to the player piano. She said hello to Billy without introducing herself and delivered her gifts for the meal (goose-liver pâté, a wheel of Camembert, English tea biscuits, two bottles of Haut-Brion, and two pounds of Whitman's chocolates for Peter) to Molly in the kitchen.

'That's Giselle,' I said to Billy, and I handed him the afternoon paper. He nodded and looked at the front page.

'They got a story on the shootin',' Billy said. 'They picked up Johnny Rizzo at the railroad station, leavin' town, and Morty's in the hospital. He might lose a leg.'

'That's a tough one.'

'Yeah, but he loses a leg means the card game's off. That son of a bitch'll do anything not to pay me what he owes.'

'If they have to reschedule the game let me know. I'll go with you anytime.'

'Nah, forget that. I'll do it on my own.'

'All right, whatever you say.'

Giselle came in from the kitchen. 'You're Billy,' she said. 'I've seen your picture.'

Billy stood up and shook her hand.

'I'm Billy,' he said, 'and you're pregnant.'

'My news precedes me,' she said, and with both hands she arced a bulbous abdomen onto herself. I then took my first look at her body, which was sheathed in a smart white linen dress that gave no indication of the two months of new life that functioned beneath it.

'A kid in the family,' said Billy. 'That's something new.'

Giselle had pulled her hair back tight in a ponytail, more severe than I'd ever seen her look. Was she already shedding glamour to befit her incipient motherhood? Throttling down her sex appeal for the sake of the family gathering? I heard the closing of a car door and then saw through the parlor window Peg getting out of a Cadillac convertible (its top up), abetted by a soulful caress of her elbow by Roger, the lawyer, that bespoke something beyond a lawyer-client relationship. I noted Peg's coy smile, the retreat of her elbow, and their mounting of the stairs together (Peg carrying a fat bag of fresh snowflake rolls and a strawberry pie from the Federal Bakery), and this instant gave me more insight into the femininity of my cousin Margaret than I had ever had heretofore. I could see the appeal she held for Roger, a man twenty-two years her junior, who was to be married in three weeks. But impending marriage was not an obstruction to fun for Roger, who en route to this luncheon meeting offered Peg an afternoon of pleasure at a hotel of her choice, a movie (*Indiscreet* was playing at the Strand), or an evening at an out-of-town summer theater (*Silk Stockings* was playing at Sacandaga, and he told Peg she had elegant legs, and she does).

Peg told me all this when I taunted her with what I had seen as they arrived, adding that she had declined the offers, even though she thought Roger was 'a doll.' And I believe her, cannot think of her as an adulterous woman, though of course what do I know? Also, I marveled at how quickly she offered up all this information to me, such frankness unheard of in this family, wherein affectionate elbow-stroking, had it been observed by Kathryn or Sarah, would have led to unexplained excommunication of both pairs of elbows from these sanctified rooms, not to mention the cancellation of lunch.

* * *

Peter came down the front stairs to the parlor and sat in his leather chair, which was still where I'd seen it in 1934, though hardly in the same condition. He had tried to transfigure his appearance, banish the scraggle by wetting and combing his hair, perhaps even trimming his mustache; and, despite the heat of the day, wore an open-collared white shirt with a tan paisley neckerchief, brown corduroy sport coat with leather elbows, tan pants, and paint-speckled dress shoes.

'Who's here?' he said as he was easing himself into the chair, favoring his bad hip.

'Everybody,' I said, and we moved toward him and took all the available seats in the room. I brought a dining-room chair for Molly, who came in wearing her apron, drying her hands on a kitchen towel. Peter surveyed the assemblage with a constant smile, then fixed on Giselle.

'And how is Mother Gigi?' he asked. I had never heard anyone call Giselle Gigi before.

'She's sick every morning,' Giselle said, 'but otherwise fine.'

'Margaret, how's the family?'

'About the same,' Peg said, 'except for Danny. He called me at the office this morning to say he's getting married.'

I looked at Giselle, who blinked at the news about Quinn. I wonder why? She did not look at me.

'A Cuban girl,' Peg said.

'New blood in the family,' Peter said.

'Is she a Catholic?' Molly asked.

'Who gives a royal goddamn?' Peter said.

'All I know,' Peg said, 'is that he's very much in love.'

'I should hope so,' said Peter. 'Roger, I'm glad you could arrange your schedule to be here. And, Billy, it's good to see you. It really is good to see you.'

'Yeah, well,' Billy said, and he worked up half a smile.

'Molly, you're losing weight, but you look grand.'

'And so do you,' said Molly, 'with your kerchief.'

'But you should take off that apron. A day of some formality requires the proper costume.' And as Molly untied her apron he looked at me. 'And you should have a tie on for your guests, Orson.'

'I'll dress for lunch,' I said.

I was wearing my usual shirtsleeves, slacks, and loafers; and who needs more in this weather? The answer is Peter, who was demanding proper tribute be paid to the patriarchal rite he was now conducting, and which I had organized. When it became clear that he would be getting a great deal of money for his *Malachi Suite*, he said to me offhandedly, 'I don't want to keep all that damn money. I won't live long enough to make use of it. And when I go they'll probably take half of it in taxes.'

'What's your alternative to being well off?'

'Give it away.'

'To needy painters?'

'The family.'

It began with that; then I called Peg to get a lawyer, for she had legal contacts I lacked. Enter Roger Dailey, perennial eligible bachelor, three-handicap golfer at Wolfert's Roost Country Club, a junior partner in one of the city's best law firms, member of an old Irish family with links to Arbor Hill when it was the neighborhood of the lumber barons and other millionaires. I talked him into coming to the house to see Peter, then left them alone. That was a month ago, and now here he was in his creamy Palm Beach suit, bringing us legal tidings.

I hadn't invited Giselle, for I'd evolved into thinking we were all but finished. But Peter took the matter out of my hands and invited her himself, which fixed the day of the event. It then fell to me to round up the others, which was a problem mainly with Roger, because today's visit cut into his golf schedule (the rain would have canceled it in any case), and with Billy, who, as we all knew, loathed this house. But I got around everything and here we were, wondering what was about to happen, imagining what was in Peter's mind, imagining Peter.

'You have the goods, Roger?' Peter asked.

'I do,' said Roger, taking a document from the legal-sized envelope he'd brought with him.

'Then let's not drag it out, just go ahead and read it.'

'This arrangement isn't unheard of, but it's a bit unorthodox,' Roger began. 'Then again we shouldn't expect conformity from a major artist like Peter Phelan, whose last will and testament I'm about to read to you. Peter has decided its provisions should be made public not posthumously but today, here and now.' And then Roger read Peter's ideas translated into legalese:

'Because money has never been a source of anxiety in me, and because the pursuit of money was never what this family was about, I, Peter Joseph Phelan, have chosen to divide my modest, newfound wealth among my siblings, and the heirs of my siblings, for I do believe that my career turn toward financial reward and artistic recognition, which, however belated, has made me feel blessed with good fortune, has been a consequence of my knowledge of this family. And because I further believe that out of the collective evil to which so many members of this family have been heir, heiress, and victim (the scope of which I have only in very late years begun to understand) there can come some collective good, and because one known form of good is the easing of the financial woe that periodically besets us all, I therefore make the following bequests:

'To my brother, Charles Edward Phelan, the sum of eleven thousand five hundred dollars;

'To my sister, Mary Kathleen Phelan, the sum of eleven thousand five hundred dollars;

'To my nephew, William Francis Phelan, the son of my late brother Francis Aloysius Phelan, the sum of five thousand seven hundred and fifty dollars;

'To my niece, Margaret Mary Phelan, the daughter of my late brother Francis Aloysius Phelan, the sum of five thousand seven hundred and fifty dollars;

'To my former concubine, Claire Theresa Purcell, in acknowledgment of two reasonably good years, and two decades of thoroughly unsatisfactory relationships, the sum of two dollars;

'Further, concerning Orson Michael Purcell, my unacknowledged son by Claire Theresa Purcell, I do now fully and publicly acknowledge him as my true and only son, and appoint him the sole benefactor and executor of the remainder of my estate, after the bequests specified in this will have been distributed, and do invest him also with artistic and financial control over the future of all forty-seven finished, unsold paintings of mine, thirty-six other unfinished works of mine, and any new works I may undertake before my death, all profits from any sale or exhibition of these works, or any other of my worldly goods, holdings, or inheritances, to accrue to Orson alone, provided that he legally change his name to Orson Michael Phelan, and that he thereafter remarry, forthwith, his present wife, Giselle Marais Purcell, to insure that her unborn child of this moment, July the twenty-sixth, nineteen hundred and fifty-eight, will legally bear the Phelan name; and that if this issue be not a male child, that Orson pursue yet again the conception of a male heir with his wife of the instant, or, if that marriage is terminated, with a subsequent legal spouse, in order to insure at least the possibility of the Phelan name continuing beyond Orson's own demise, this latter contingent action thus ending his responsibility for the Phelan line; for more than this no man should be asked to do.'

In the silence that followed the reading we glanced where we had to, me at Giselle, all the others at Peter; and Peg spoke up first to say, 'Uncle Peter, thank you, thank you. I don't think you know how much this will mean to our family.' Fifteen hundred down: easy as apple pie.

Molly walked over to Peter and kissed him on the cheek, said, 'You have a good heart,' and went back to the kitchen tying on her apron. Billy stared at Peter with what I took to be puzzlement: Why is this guy givin' money away? And why to me? But Billy made no statement except with his eyes.

I caught Peter's eye and I nodded at him. And then he nodded.

Giselle stared at me, and in her look I saw more comprehension of what the will had said about us than I myself possessed at this moment; for while I'd known Peter planned to dispense money, and suspected I would get a bit of it, no thought of a paternity clause ever crossed my mind. I believed he would die without acknowledging me, and I had decided long ago that that was all right. Who needed legitimacy? The answer again was Peter. He needed it now that he was going public. He needed to tidy up his life, organize his death.

He had not expected the professional and financial success that was now coming to him at such a late hour. But it happened that a few perspicacious gallery owners and museum people began to see that his work, despite the varied modes and genres in which he had painted and drawn, had about it a prevailing quality that now seemed to be singular. Recognition came to him as does the fixative an artist acquires at death: No more innovation for you, my friend; we read you at last. This handful of influential Peter-watchers saw him neither as sectarian of any art movement of his era, nor as yet another gadfly among trends. Now they saw an artist who had vaulted beyond his matrix, fused the surreal, the natural, the abstract, and the figurative, and produced an oeuvre that was as cumulatively coherent as his motivation had been in creating the work.

Peter Phelan, obsessive artist of Colonie Street, subsumed in the history of his family, all but smothered under his ancestors' blanket of time, had willfully engaged it all, transformed history into art, being impelled to create, and purely, what Picasso had called 'convincing lies'; for Peter believed that these lies would stand as a fierce array of at least partial Phelan truths – not moral truths, but truths of significant motion: the arresting of the natural world at an instant of kinetic and fantastic revelation; the wisdom of Lizzie's lofted leg in her dance with the shadows; the wizardly acceptance of chicken droppings by the demented Crip Devlin; the madly collective flailing of arms in *Banishing the Demons*.

This latter painting, the largest in the *Malachi Suite*, treats of the collective Peter mentioned in his will. By the light of an oil lamp, a candle, and a fire in the McIlhenny hearth (shadowed homage to La Tour), the players in the Malachi drama are enacting their contrary rituals: Kathryn Phelan (abundantly pregnant with Peter, the arriving artist) is sitting on the bed in the background, holding the hand of the beset Lizzie, who is supine in her calico chemise, blue flannel nightgown, and black stockings, her hair splayed wildly on her pillow; and the Malachi minions – the wizard Crip Devlin; Crip's daughter, Mab (the image of the child who led me to Francis at the railroad tracks); Lizzie's father, old Ned Cronin, who badly needed a shave; Malachi's ancient cousin, Minnie Dorgan, with her dropsical stomach, and her stupid son, Colm, whose hair was a nest of cowlicks; and, central to it all, Malachi himself, with his wild curls and his wilder eyes, all these clustered figures pushing upward and outward with their arms (Colm gripping a lighted candle in his right hand and thrusting upward with his left), ridding the house of any demons that may have been summoned by the archdemon that Lizzie had become. The entrance door and two windows of the house are open to the night, and those errant demons, who well know that this room is inimical to their kind, are surely flying fearfully out and away, back to their covens of hellish darkness.

Malachi had gathered his counsel, his blood kin, and his inlaws about him for a communion of indignation at what was happening to Lizzie, and also to people his house with witnesses to his joust with the evil forces. He'd begun that joust with interrogation of Lizzie.

'What is your name?'

'Lizzie McIlhenny. You know that.'

'Is that your full name?'

'Lizzie Cronin McIlhenny. In God's name, Malachi, why are you asking me this?'

'We'll see what you think of God's name. Why are you four inches shorter than you used to be?'

'I'm not. I'm the same size I always was.'

'Why are you asking her these things?' Kathryn Phelan asked.

'To find out who she is.'

'Can't you see who she is? Have you lost your sight?'

'Just hold your gob, woman, and see for yourself who she is. Don't I know my wife when I see her? And this one isn't her.'

'Well, she is.'

'Are you Lizzie McIlhenny, my wife?'

'Of course I am, Malachi. Can't you see it's me? Who else do you think I am?'

'Do you believe in God the Father, God the Son, and God the Holy Ghost?'

'I do, Malachi, I do.'

'You do what?'

'I believe in God the Father, Son, Holy Ghost.'

'She didn't repeat it exactly,' said Crip Devlin.

'Let me ask her,' said Ned Cronin. 'Are you the daughter of Ned Cronin, in the name of God?'

'I am, Dada.'

'She didn't repeat it,' said Crip.

'Repeat it,' said Malachi.

'Dada.'

'Not that, repeat what he said.'

'I don't know what he said.'

'Ah, she's crafty,' said Crip.

'You'll repeat it or I'll have at you,' said Malachi. He grabbed her and ripped her nightgown, then pushed her backward onto the bed. When she tried to get up he held her down.

'Ask her where she lives,' said Crip.

'Do you live up on the hill with the Good Neighbors?'

'I live here with you, Malachi.'

'Who are you?'

'I'm Lizzie, your wife.'

'You're four inches shorter than my wife.'

'I'm not. I'm this same size since I was a girl.'

'You really are insane, Malachi,' said Kathryn. 'You're torturing her.'

'We'll see who's insane. Do you believe in Satan?'

'I don't know,' Lizzie said.

'Crafty again,' said Crip.

'By the Jesus,' Malachi said, 'we'll get the truth out of you,' and from the table he took the cup of milky potion he and Crip had prepared for this encounter, set it on the bedside table, and lifted a spoonful to Lizzie's mouth. 'Take it,' he said.

She smelled it and turned her head. 'It's awful.'

'Drink it,' Malachi said, lifting the cup to her lips. Lizzie pushed it away and some of the potion spilled onto her nightgown.

'Oh you'll take it, you witch,' Malachi said, shoving the cup to her lips and pouring it. Some of the fluid entered her mouth and she screamed and spat it out.

'She won't take it,' said Crip. 'And if any of it falls on the floor she's gone forever.'

'She'll take it or I'll break both her arms,' said Malachi. 'Hold her legs, Colm.' And the dimwit flung himself crosswise on the bed, atop Lizzie's legs.

'Like this?' Colm asked.

'That's it,' said Malachi.

'There's rewards in heaven for them that beats the devil,' said old Minnie Dorgan, rocking her body on a straight chair in the corner, plaiting and unplaiting two strips of cloth as she watched the exorcism. She blessed herself repeatedly, and dipped her fingers into a jar of holy Easter water she had brought with her. She sprinkled the water at Lizzie and then at Malachi.

'If you get the drink into her, the witch is dead,' said Crip.

'We'll get it,' said Malachi.

'That's enough of this crazy talk,' Kathryn said, putting herself between Malachi and Lizzie.

'Get out of my way, Kathryn.'

'I'll get out and get the police if you don't leave her be.'

Malachi walked to the door, locked it, and pocketed the key.

'You'll go noplace till I say you will,' he said. 'And neither will anybody else in this house. Build up the fire, Mab.' And Crip Devlin's child, silent and sullen, threw twigs and a log on the dying fire. It crackled and flared, creating new light in the bleak room, into which not even the faintest ray of a moonbeam would penetrate tonight.

Kathryn whispered into Lizzie's ear, 'I won't let him hurt you, darlin', I won't let him hurt you.' And she stroked the distraught

Lizzie's forehead and saw that her eyes were rolling backward out of their rightful place.

'You're a vile, vile man to do this to her,' Kathryn said.

Malachi looked at the women and walked to the hearth. He picked up a long twig and held the end of it in the fire until it flamed; then he pulled it out and shook out the flame and walked toward the bed.

'You bring that near her,' said Kathryn, 'you'll have to burn me too, Malachi,' but he quickly put the stick between his teeth, grabbed his sister with his good right arm, and flung her off the bed and into the lap of Minnie Dorgan, who sprinkled holy water on her. 'Mother of God,' said Minnie. 'Mother of God.'

'You'll not be burning her, Malachi,' said Ned Cronin. 'You won't burn my daughter.'

'It's not your daughter that's here, it's not the wife I married. It's a hag and a witch that I'm sleeping with.'

'It's my daughter, I'm thinking now,' Ned said.

'Have you no faith, man?' said Malachi. 'Don't you know a demon when it's in front of your eyes?'

And he had the twig in his hand again, and he lighted it again, blew out its flame again, and put it in front of Lizzie's face.

'Now will you drink what I give you?'

When she threw her head from side to side to be rid of the idea he touched her on the forehead with the burning stick, and she screamed her woe to heaven. 'Now you'll take it,' he said, and with terrified eyes she stared at the madman her husband had become; and she knew no choice was left to her.

'Leave her be!' screamed Kathryn, and she tried to move toward Lizzie. But Minnie Dorgan and Ned Cronin held her.

'Give her the drink, Mab,' Malachi said, and the child raised the cup to Lizzie, who stiffened at the odor of it and, retching dryly, said weakly, 'Please, Malachi.'

'Drink it, you hag, or I'll kill you.'

And she took the cup and drank and screamed again as the foul concoction went down her throat, screamed and spat and drank again, then fell back on the bed as the cup's remnants splattered on the floor.

'It's done,' said Malachi.

'And it's spilled,' said Crip. 'There's no telling what it means.'

Colm, lying across Lizzie's legs, sat up. 'I'm goin' home now,' he said.

'Indeed you're not,' said Malachi. 'You'll stay till we're done with this.'

And Colm fell back on the bed with a weakness.

'When will we be done?' Ned Cronin asked. 'For the love of Jesus end this thing.'

'We'll end it when I've got my wife back,' Malachi said.

'How will you know?' asked Ned.

'We'll see the demon leave her,' Crip said. 'But time is short. Ask her again.'

'In the name of God and heaven,' Malachi said, 'are you Lizzie McIlhenny, my wife?'

All in the room watched every inch of Lizzie, watching for the exit of the demon. But Lizzie neither moved nor spoke. She stared at the wall.

'We've got to go to the fire,' said Malachi. 'We've no choice.'

'It'll soon be midnight,' said Crip, 'and then she's gone for sure, never to come back.'

'We'll carry her, Colm,' said Malachi, and the dimwit rolled off Lizzie's legs. Then he and Malachi carried the now limp figure toward the hearth as Mab stoked the fire with a poker. Lizzie's nightgown was off her shoulder and Malachi ripped it away and it fell on the floor. Mab moved the grate back and Malachi sat Lizzie on it so she faced the fire.

'Are you goin' to make a pork chop out of me, Malachi?' she asked. 'Won't you give me a chance?' And on the dark side of the room the women fell on their knees in prayer.

'Do you know what I'm doin' here, Ned Cronin?' Malachi called out.

'Jesus, Mary, and holy St Joseph,' said Ned, 'I pray you know what you're doing.' And he knelt beside the women.

Malachi leaned Lizzie toward the fire and when it touched her it set her calico chemise aflame. Kathryn Phelan wailed and screamed at her brother, 'You'll live in hell forever for this night, Malachi McIlhenny. It's you who's the demon here. It's you that's doing murder to this woman.'

Malachi let go of Lizzie and she fell away from the fire, burning. He watched, with Crip beside him, and Colm holding the now unconscious Lizzie by one arm.

'Away she go, up the chimney,' Malachi said. 'Away she go!' And he waved his good arm into the flame.

'I saw nothing go,' said Crip.

'Hail Mary, full of grace, the Lord is with thee, blessed art thou amongst women,' said Kathryn on her knees.

'Come home, Lizzie McIlhenny!' yelled Malachi, waving his arm, watching his wife's body. The room was filling with smoke from Lizzie's burning clothes and flesh.

'Beast!' screamed Kathryn.

'Do you think that's Lizzie that's lyin' there?' Malachi asked.

'I saw nothing leave her,' said Crip.

'More fire,' said Malachi, and Colm leaned Lizzie back toward the flames. Another edge of her chemise caught fire and now half her torso was exposed, the flesh charring from below her left breast to her hip.

'Let her down,' said Malachi, and from the floor beside the fireplace he took a can of paraffin oil and threw it onto Lizzie's stomach. Her chemise exploded in flame.

'Away she go!' yelled Malachi, waving his arm. 'Away she go!' And he threw more oil on her.

Kathryn Phelan ran to the wildly flaming Lizzie and threw herself on top of her, snuffing the fire, burning herself, and sobbing with the grief known in heaven when angels die.

The last painting Peter put on exhibit for his luncheon guests was *The Protector*, a portrait of Kathryn Phelan smothering the flames on Lizzie's clothing, her own maternity dress aflame at one corner, the smoke obscuring half her face, the other half lit by firelight.

Kathryn's burns were not severe but her act did precipitate, two days later, the premature birth of Peter Phelan, child of fire and brimstone, terror and madness, illusion and delusion, ingredients all of his art.

I had asked him why he chose to resurrect Malachi, such a dreadful figure in the family's life, and he said he could not answer with any accuracy, that the Malachi he was painting wasn't the Malachi of history, that, in whatever ways his paintings reflected reality, they would fall far short of the specifics of that reality, which was always the fate of anything imagined. 'We try to embrace the universe,' Peter said, 'but we end up throwing our arms around the local dunghill.' And yet he felt that whatever he imagined would somehow reflect what was clusive in the historic reality, elusive because its familiarity and its ubiquity in real space and time would make it invisible to all but the imagining eye.

In this context, what he had intuited from the Malachi story was the presence of a particular kind of thought, a superstitious atmosphere aswirl with those almost-visible demons and long-forgotten abstractions of evil – votive bats and sacrificial hags, burning flesh and the bones of tortured babies – the dregs of putrefied religion, the fetid remains of a psychotic social order, these inheritances so torturous to his imagination that he had to paint them to be rid of them.

He had always rejected as extraneous any pragmatic or moralistic element to art, could not abide a didactic artist. Nevertheless, his work already had an effect on the moral history of the family, and would continue to do so through the inevitable retellings of the story associated with the paintings; and these retellings would surely provide an enduring antidote to the poison Malachi had injected into the world. The work would stand also as a corrective to the long-held image of Kathryn in the family's communal mind.

'As much as we loved her, none of us can undo the two generations' worth of trouble and anguish she caused,' Peter said, and he quoted Francis as saying long ago, 'She didn't really know nothin' about how to live.' Peter agreed there was some truth in this, but he added that Kathryn surely knew how *not* to live under the mad inheritance that had destroyed Malachi and Lizzie; and that the thing she knew best was denial, the antithesis of Malachi's indulgent madness. After Malachi, Kathryn had even denied herself the pleasure that had probably been hers with the conception of Peter (the subsequent children were conceived under duress).

And, by convincing her husband to make the deathbed request to Sarah, she had imposed on the girl the scullery-nunnery existence that made Sarah deny and eventually destroy her own life rather than admit that lives of sensual pleasure were not only possible, but sometimes eagerly pursued outside the cloistered innocence of this house. She became a mad virgin, Sarah, the dying words of Michael Phelan her dungeon, the courage of her saintly, sinless mother the second-generational iron maiden of her fate.

No chance at all to rescue Sarah. No bequest for Sarah.

No chance to rescue Tommy either. His spinal injury turned into a plague of unpredictable immobility and, when he went back to his job as a sweeper at the filtration plant, the pain struck him so severely that he collapsed and rolled into the thirty-five-foot depths of one of the plant's great filtering pools; and, having been unable to learn to swim any more than he could learn to think, he drowned, another martyr to the family disease.

And not much of a chance to lure the maverick Chick out of his Floridian indignance and back to the family circle. He telephoned Peter from Miami Beach, acknowledged the bequest, offered lively thanks for what he said would be his hefty down payment on a sporty inboard motorboat he'd been longing to buy, invited his brother to come down and go ocean fishing, said Evelyn sent her best, and hung up, maybe forever.

By the time lunch was about to be served, the light rain had become heavy, a storm gaining strength, according to Peg's reading of the weather story in the *Knickerbocker News*.

'It's going to rain all night, and some places might get floods,' she reported. She was at the table, where Peter had told her to sit. The rest of us were standing half in, half out of the dining room, waiting for Peter to seat us. Molly was still in the kitchen, organizing the meal.

'The Senators won't play ball tonight,' Billy said.

'George's Democratic picnic must be rained out too,' Peg said.

'Democrats like the rain,' Billy said.

'The Irish like the rain,' Peter said. 'Three days of sunshine and they start praying for thunderstorms.'

The roast lamb lay in slices on the platter in the center of the table, and on the sideboard the leg itself, on another platter, awaited further surgery. Molly had asked me to carve but before I could begin Peg suggested Billy do it, for he did it so well. And so he did, and when only half finished he asked Molly, 'You got any mint jelly to go with this?'

Molly looked in the pantry and the refrigerator, reported back, 'No mint jelly, I'm sorry, Billy.'

'There's mint jelly in the cellar,' I said, and I took the flashlight, opened the trapdoor, and found dusty jars of mint jelly and strawberry jam.

'Sarah put those up,' Molly said, 'after the war. We got the strawberries from Tony Looby's store, and Sarah grew the mint out in the yard.'

'You certainly know your way around this house,' Peg said to me. 'How'd you know they were down there?'

'I was fixing something one day and I saw this stuff.'

'This house would fall apart if it wasn't for Orson,' Molly said. 'He also kept the Lake House from collapsing around its own ears. Orson is a treasure.'

'Just waiting to be dug up and spent,' I said.

'You'll never be spent, Orson,' Giselle said.

'Oooh-la-la,' said Peg, and everyone looked at Giselle, who smiled at me.

'Orson,' said Peter, 'take control of your wife.'

'I would prefer not to,' I said. 'I like her the way she is.'

'We're ready to eat,' said Molly, coming in from the kitchen with the potatoes, hot from the oven.

And then, one by one, we sat where Peter placed us, and we were seven, clockwise: Peter sitting where his father had always sat, in the northernmost chair in the room, the first formal resumption of the patriarchal seating arrangement since Michael Phelan died in 1895; Giselle next to Peter to have the impending grandchild in the closest possible proximity to the grandfather, then Roger, Peg, me, Molly in Sarah's chair (her mother's before it was hers) nearest the kitchen, and Billy at Peter's right, completing the circle.

Giselle's pâté, Camembert, and English biscuits lay in tempting array on the sideboard, forgotten, and alien, really, to the cuisine of this house. But we made ready to devour Sarah's mint jelly on Molly's leg of lamb, with the marvelous gravy made from the drippings, small new peas out of the can, the best kind, potatoes mashed by Peg (she said Billy mashed them better), bread by Peg out of the Federal, and the two bottles of the rich and robust Haut-Brion 1934 (a momentous year for both the Bordeaux and the Phelans) that the extravagant Giselle had brought. Peter contributed the saying of grace, which he pronounced as follows: 'Dig in now or forever hold your fork.'

I suggest that this luncheon was the consequence of a creative act, an exercise of the imagination made tangible, much the same as the writing of this sentence is an idea made visible by a memoirist. If Peter brought it about, I here create the record that says it happened. If, through the years, I had been slowly imagining myself acquiring this family, then this was its moment of realization, and perhaps the redirection of us all.

I think of Peter's creative act (though I am not so modest as to deny my own contribution to the events) as independent of his art, a form of atonement after contemplating what wreckage was left in the wake of the behavior of the males in the family: Malachi's lunacy, Michael's mindless martyring of Sarah, Francis's absence of so many years, the imploding Chick, Peter's own behavior as son, husband, father: in sum, a pattern of abdication, or flight, or exile, with the women left behind to pick up the pieces of fractured life: a historic woman like Kathryn, an avant-garde virgin renegade like Molly, a working girl like Peg, and, to confirm this theory with an anomaly, there is the case of Giselle.

'I have to say it,' Roger said. 'This is the most unusual lunch I've ever been to.'

'Perfectly normal little meal,' Peter said. 'Last will and testament with lamb gravy.'

'Those here, we've never sat down together like this before, never,' Molly said.

'That's hard to believe,' said Roger. 'You look like such a close family.'

'Get your eyes examined,' Billy said.

'Don't mind my brother,' Peg said. 'He's a perpetual grump.'

'What this gathering is,' I said, looking at Roger, also at Peg to discover where her eyes went, 'is the provisional healing of a very old split in this family.'

'What's that mean, provisional?' Billy asked.

'For the time being,' I said. 'More to come later. Like having the first horse in the daily double.'

'Yeah,' said Billy.

'And it's about time,' Molly said. 'We should have done this years ago.'

'The point is it's done,' said Peg. 'I love you for it, Uncle Peter,' she said, and she blew him a kiss.

'I'm not takin' the money,' Billy said.

Peter looked my way, caught my eye, chuckled. I'd predicted that Billy would say this.

'Don't be hasty, now, Billy,' said Peter.

'Don't be stupid, you mean,' said Peg.

'The hell with stupid,' Billy said. 'My father couldn't live here, I don't want no money outa here.'

'It's Francis's money as much as it's mine,' Peter said. 'I made it in good measure because of him.'

'I showed you those photos,' I said to Billy, '*The Itinerant* series, and you know Francis inspired that. Peter only painted it.' Peter gave me a sharp look. Nothing worse than an ungrateful child.

'And Malachi's face is the face of Francis in the new paintings.

You've seen that for yourself,' Peter said. 'And that's where the money for these bequests really came from.'

'So you paint his picture? What the hell is that? He wasn't welcome here and all these years neither were we.'

'I came here plenty of times,' Peg said.

'I didn't, and neither did he,' Billy said.

'You're gonna ruin it,' Peg said. 'You'll be like Sarah, spoiling it for everybody else.'

'I ain't spoilin' nothin' wasn't spoiled years ago,' Billy said.

'Have some mint jelly, Billy,' said Molly. 'Sweeten your disposition.'

'I'm sayin' my father never got nothin' outa this house and neither did we, and I don't want nothin' now.'

'You told me Molly gave you gold on your birthday,' I said.

'Yeah, that's right.'

'And she gave me gold too,' Peg said.

'You know where I got that gold, Billy?' Molly asked.

'You never said.'

'You remember Cubby Conroy?'

'I remember his kid, Johnny,' Billy said. 'They shot him over highjacked booze and dumped him in the gutter.'

'Cubby was a good friend of your father's. They grew up together on this block.' Molly paused, looked at Roger. 'Mr Dailey,' she said, 'do lawyers keep secrets?'

'If they don't, they're not very good lawyers.'

'I can't tell my story unless you keep it a secret.'

'I'll carry it silently to my grave,' Roger said.

'Good,' said Molly. 'Cubby Conroy was a bootlegger.'

'Right,' said Billy. 'He was also a con man. He and Morrie Berman got badges and flashed them at Legs Diamond and convinced him they were dry agents. They almost copped a truckload of his booze before he caught on.'

'I did hear that,' Molly said. 'And then somebody shot Cubby. Perhaps it was Mr Diamond, who was upset by what they did.'

'Maybe so. Diamond was like that. But how do you know all this tough stuff?'

Billy was smiling, and I marveled at the way Molly had turned him around so quickly. She was wonderful at human relationships and I loved her.

'Well, you know, don't you,' Molly said, 'that they killed Cubby up in Glens Falls in one of those roadhouses. Then they killed Johnny, and the only one left was Charity, Cubby's widow, who had a collapse of some sort, afraid they'd come after her, I suppose, or maybe just living alone and drinking alone. I used to cook her a dinner every day and bring it over, but it didn't help much. She got sicker and sicker and one day she told me she had this bootleg money she wanted me to have. All her relatives were dead, she didn't know where Cubby's people were, but wherever they were she hated them, and so the money was mine. I thanked her a whole lot and took it home.'

'Where'd she have it hid?' Billy asked.

'Inside an old mattress in the cellar.'

'How much?'

'Twelve thousand dollars,' Molly said, and we all wheezed our awe.

'She let you take twelve thousand home?' Billy asked.

'She did. I had to make six trips in the car with my suitcase. Maybe seven.'

'Wasn't she afraid of goin' broke?' Billy asked.

'She wasn't broke.'

'How'd you know that?'

'When she died,' Molly said, 'I found another fifteen thousand in two overstuffed chairs and a sofa. That took twelve trips.'

We all wheezed anew.

'Twenty-seven grand,' Billy said.

'Very good arithmetic, Billy,' Molly said.

'What'd you do with it?' Roger asked.

'Everything I wanted to do,' Molly said. 'I went to Philadelphia for two weeks to visit our cousin and I looked at the Liberty Bell, and I bought curtains for the house, and I went to Keeler's twice a month and had oysters and lobster, and I paid for the new oil furnace when the coal furnace cracked in half, and I gave money to special people, and I turned it all into gold and put it in safe-deposit boxes because I didn't trust paper money.'

'You have any of it left?' Peter asked.

'If I do will you take back my bequest?'

'Of course not,' said Peter.

'I have nineteen thousand.'

We all looked carefully at Molly now, a woman worth scrutiny, the true and quixotic mistress of this house, the secret financial power behind Sarah's imperious, penurious throne, the self-sufficient dowager, ready with the quick fix for family trouble, the four hundred dollars she gave me a case in point.

'You know, Billy,' said Molly, 'when your father came home during the war I called and invited him for dinner, lunch, anything, just to get him back in the family. But he hung up on me and wouldn't answer my calls.'

'I went to see him at the ball park,' Peter said. 'He told me he was too busy to talk to me. He wasn't a forgiving man, your father. Always difficult.'

'I got along with him,' Billy said. 'So did Peg.'

'I'm glad somebody did,' Peter said.

'He gave Billy his old baseball glove,' Peg said.

'Sure, why not?' said Peter. 'Can you imagine him telling Billy not to take this money?'

Billy fell silent.

'I'm going to take some pictures of the table,' Giselle said with perfect timing. 'I'll use your camera and tripod, Orson,' and she went up the back stairs, knowing exactly where my camera equipment was.

'I feel like an interloper,' Roger said, 'but I might as well get it straight. What was Francis doing at the ball park? I thought he lived on the road.'

I pointed to Billy for the answer, and he gave me the back of his hand.

'Don't bug out on us, Billy,' I said.

'Who's buggin' out?'

'Francis came home in 1942 to help the family when he thought

Billy was being drafted,' I said. 'Francis stayed close to Annie till he died, didn't he?'

'Yeah, he did,' Billy said.

Giselle came down with the camera and flash and set them up on the tripod in the back parlor. Nobody spoke while she did this. We waited for her to say she was ready, but she'd heard our conversation and she left the camera standing and came back to the table.

'Francis lived up by Hawkins Stadium, the ball park,' I said, 'isn't that so, Billy?'

'Hoffman's Hotel,' Billy said. 'Eight rooms with a saloon. Old-timey street guys and barflies, newspapermen with no teeth and dyin' ballplayers, an elephant graveyard. But Francis was in good shape for a guy who bent his elbow so much, and he went to all the Senators' home games. Johnny Evers was one of the bosses of the club and he and Francis both played big-league ball at the same time, so Evers gave Francis a season pass. Those were tough days for baseball, all the young guys gettin' drafted, and you hadda fill their shoes with kids, or old guys, or deaf guys, or guys with one arm, or one eye. Francis tells Evers he knows a guy doin' short time in a Buffalo jail hits the ball a mile and does Evers want him? Evers says hell yes and hires the guy when he gets out and hires Francis as a coach. Francis, he's sixty-two and he suits up, ain't played a game of ball for maybe twenty-eight years and he's out there telling kids and cripples never to swing at the first pitch, and how to steal bases and rattle the pitcher, when to play close in, when to go deep. Ripper Collins is managin' and he pinch-hits Francis, puts him in for the hit and run, or the sacrifice, because Francis can still bloop it to right once in a while, and he's champ with the bunt, lays it down the line, soft, easy, never lost the touch. He runs like a three-legged goat, takes him two weeks to get to first base but it don't matter. He's out from the go but the runner gets to second or third. I seen him do this half a dozen times before they drafted me, December, and I'm gone eight months I'm back out with a bad eye. Francis is coachin' third, and they're writin' stories about him, and the con he talked Johnny Evers into signin' is knifed dead on a dance floor hustlin' somebody's wife. Dangerous game, baseball. And there I am in a box behind third and there's the old man, movin' like a cricket, and while I'm watchin' him he falls over in the baseline. You can't get up? I'm up and over the fence, on the field, and they got a stretcher comin', take him down to Memorial. I'm in a cab behind the ambulance but it don't make no difference. He's dead before his chin hits the dirt.'

Giselle said, 'The chocolates,' and got up from her chair and went to the kitchen. When she came back with the box of candy I saw she'd been crying. Molly saw it too.

'Everything all right, dear?' Molly asked.

'Oh, sure,' said Giselle.

'What is it?' Peter asked.

'Nothing,' she said.

'It's Francis,' I said.

Giselle opened the candy and put it in front of Peter. 'There's strawberry pie for dessert,' she said, 'but I know you love chocolate.'

'Francis?' Peter said, looking at her.

'It was more Billy,' she said. 'The image I had of him climbing the fence to help his father.'

'Wire fence,' Billy said. 'Keeps you from swallowin' foul balls.'

'Nobody in my family would've done that, climbed a fence, or even thought about it,' Giselle said. 'We were so full of hate for one another.'

'Your mother?' said Molly. 'Your father?'

'When my mother died my oldest brother cremated her the same day with no funeral service, so no friends or family could see her.'

'Stuff like that happened here,' Billy said.

'But today everybody's at the same table,' Giselle said. 'That never happened in my family after I was six and it never could. Hate is a cancer, and even when it fades, something awful takes its place. I know, because I hate my brothers. I hate them.'

When no one chose to ask her why, she said, 'So I want to take a photo now. Turn your chairs and look toward the camera.'

'Oh, good, a picture,' Peg said. 'Danny raves about you. He says you take wonderful pictures.'

'Danny is just being friendly,' Giselle said, and I agreed. Danny was compulsively friendly.

'You should be in the picture,' Peter said to Giselle.

'I will be.'

And so another formal photograph in modern Phelan family history came into existence; my second with my father, Peter's first with Billy and Peg, and so on. The new combinations were quantifiable. Giselle, eminently photogenic, set the shutter, hurried back to her chair, and imposed a smile on the film that was as natural as sunshine and equally radiant.

We were a family soon to disappear from this form, from these chairs, from this place. The diaspora would be complete in, what, four, three, two years? Barring a miracle, Peter would die in the months ahead. Molly could go on for years, but even with a house-keeper (and she could afford one) she wouldn't stay here alone. And Giselle and I? Ah, now, there's a rub.

Whether or not we would now stay here for an extended time was a new question. But she was responsible for my being here (I see no need to run through the tissue of causation) and therefore obliquely responsible as well for this day of reunification, this time of our dawning into unity (as Keats put it), if indeed it was unity, if indeed it was dawning; and perhaps she would also be responsible for us reordering the house to accommodate a modern married couple, with nursery. The very thought of these things was so exotically afield of my present consciousness that I could only look at it all as a freakish turn of fate. The lives we had known for five years were about to be superseded. But by what?

My personal agenda was to finish the book on Peter's art, and finish also this memoir, of which Walker Pettijohn had seen two-thirds. He professed to admire it, this time with editorial associates supporting publication, but a contract awaited completion of the manuscript, and I detected no confidence in Walker that the book would sell more than forty copies. I no longer needed survival money, but I yearned for proof that I was not chattering to myself in the forest, making no sound.

Giselle said the book made her weep, a rare occurrence (her weeping at Billy climbing the fence was the only time I'd ever seen her in tears). She'd read it the weekend I threaded her needle's eye with such rare, if unverifiable, significance, and told me this book was the fulfillment of the intuition that had helped convince her to marry me: that she knew, without understanding why she knew, the value of the way I wrote and thought about this family. I'd shown her the early version of the book and talked to her about the family as if I'd owned it, when I was actually drawing out unknown, unspoken impressions of people to whom I had only tenuous connection, none of my impressions really authentic, all of them as much a creation as one of Peter's sketches. Yet this talk insinuated itself into some receptive corner of Giselle's imagination, and she concluded that one day I'd write a meaningful work about the family; and she wanted to be part of that. And all along I'd thought it was my romantic charm that got her.

'Why didn't you tell me you liked what I wrote?'

'I didn't know how to say it. Maybe I didn't like it so much either. Maybe I only liked how you talked about it. But now you write better. And I think I think better.'

'My artistic soul drew you to Colonie Street.'

'You might say that.'

It ran through my mind that I might also say it was her desire for a safe haven in which to ride out the pregnancy that drew her here; or the lure of this new money coming my way (in fair measure because of her work) as a cushion for the future; or her weariness with being a pioneer feminist in a man's world; or the realization that one-night stands only exacerbate solitude; or perhaps she'd had advance knowledge that Quinn was about to settle down with one woman. ('Does that change your mind about him, now that he's getting married?' she asked me, to which I replied, 'Why should it? It didn't change his when I got married.')

There was always the possibility that she genuinely perceived her psychic transformation into motherhood as an idea whose time had come. But even if she *was* luxuriating in it (Mother Giselle: it landed with an oxymoronic bounce in my consciousness), what was her view of remarriage? Perhaps it was as ambivalent as my own view of this particular paternity.

The proposed renaming of the putative grandson, the unnamed fetus, would be the occasion for reaffirming the matrimonial vows and the sacrament; but a year or more ago I had decided that fathering a child with Giselle could turn into a crime against the unborn, predestining trouble for the product of this all-but-doomed union. I had also anesthetized my anguish glands, had learned how not to be a Giselle addict, how not to fall into a neurasthenic droop when she left the room. I had, in reaction, found abundant, even raucous solace with other women, for, without ever having proof of Giselle's infidelity, I believed in it. How not to, knowing her as I had? 'I never did anything bad,' she once said with moderate conviction, but that changed nothing for me; and this vast unknown, this black riddle, I do believe, was the erosive element that had destroyed my acceptance of the marriage as a temporary game of long-distance singles.

But now here she came with her renovated interiors, telling me that she had learned how to think, had learned how to be a mother; in effect, that she had grown into the marriage the way a child grows into a garment two sizes too large. But she could know little of how her physical condition would transform her in the months ahead, or what it would be like not to work at what she did so well, or what remarriage and the fusion with this family in the name of a name would do to her, or what our arm's-length connubiality had done to me. She might even come to think of her own name (Gisel in Old English, Giall in the Old Irish) as her fate: for the word means 'hostage.'

The ring of the telephone broke our concentration on our communal photographic image, and Molly answered it. Alice Shugrue.

'She can't pick me up,' Molly said when she hung up. 'It's raining so hard the sewers are backed up and the streets are flooded. Her engine got wet and they had to tow her out of a huge puddle. She's at her cousin's in the North End, and she's not even going to try to go home tonight.'

It was truly a fierce storm. Great sheets of water were flowing off the roof past our windows, and you could barely see Pearl Street.

'So you'll stay here tonight,' Peter said to Molly.

'If it keeps up we'll all have to stay,' Peg said.

'If it keeps up,' said Peter, 'it won't come down.'

'Oh dear,' said Molly, 'my brother is telling Papa's jokes.'

'As paterfamilias he's entitled,' I said.

'As what?' Billy said. 'Whataya givin' us all these twenty-dollar words.'

'Just means the "father of the family,"' I said, 'Also means he's liberated from his own father – and mother too, you might say. Am I right, Father Peter?'

'I hope we're all liberated,' Peter said.

'I'm liberating Molly from the kitchen,' Peg said.

'Don't be silly,' said Molly.

'I'll help in the kitchen,' Giselle said.

'No you won't,' Peg said. 'You take it easy. I'm drafting Roger to dry dishes.' And I said silently to myself, 'Ah ha, Margaret, ah ha.'

'It rained like this,' Peter said, 'the day I left home in 1913. You remember that, Billy?'

'You mean the rowboat?' Billy said.

'Right. You and your father rowed down to rescue me.'

'I remember,' Billy said. 'We took you to the railroad station. Where were ya goin'?'

'New York, but anywhere would've been all right with me. I was just getting out from under. And yet I never really left this place.'

'It can be a trap,' Molly said, and she turned to Giselle. 'So be careful, my dear, if Orson decides you should live here. You *are* going through with the second marriage, aren't you?'

'It's not for me to say,' Giselle said. 'Are we, Orson?'

'It somehow seems as though deuterogamy is an idea whose time has come,' I said.

'There he goes again,' Billy said.

Molly smiled. 'Why am I not surprised?'

Peter was nodding his head at the completion of something, the beginning of something else. It seemed facile to think of the remarriage as a beginning when it was merely the supercharging of an old steam engine that might or might not make it over the next rise. The new name, the child, the remarriage as confirmation that the first marriage was a bust, which it was, these thoughts also saddened me: the sadness of the completion of anything, a book, a marriage, a life. Or a sad painting.

'There's one more painting,' Peter said. 'It's upstairs, and it's not a pretty picture. I warn you against it, but Orson will show it to anybody who wants to see it.'

'Have I seen it?' Molly asked.

'No,' Peter said. 'Only Orson.'

And so we all, including Giselle, who had photographed it two months ago when it was embryonic, went up to Peter's studio to see *The Burial*, his major unfinished work. If he lived on, it would very probably not be his last in the *Malachi Suite*. He'd already made several sketches of Malachi and Crip in hell, and was trying to assign a fitting punishment for them; but as of today, *The Burial* was as far as he'd gone with his great graphic leaps through those abominable events.

It is raining in the painting, and Colm Dorgan, with the point of a spade, and Malachi McIlhenny, with his muddy right brogan, are pushing the half-folded corpse of Lizzie into her muddy grave, which is too short for her. The grave's borders are a sea of mud and Malachi and Colm are drenched. Lizzie is naked except for her black stockings and a burlap bag over her head. Colm is pushing her feet into the grave. Malachi is stepping on her right breast with his foot. The left side of her chest is a broad, raw crevasse of flesh, her charred rib cage and parts of her internal organs protruding, the flesh burned off two fingers of her left hand, leaving the burned bones visible.

A small cottage, Malachi's, wherein the other witnesses to Lizzie's burning are locked and awaiting the return of Malachi, is visible in the distant background, as are a sky and a landscape full of demonic figures, including the lithe form of Lizzie dancing on a hill with a web-footed creature with the head of a goat.

Piles of dirt beside the grave will be heaped on Lizzie and on the secluded grave, which is at the side of a ditch, with a high fence on one side and trees on the other. When the grave is covered with dirt it will be hidden by leaves and twigs, and Lizzie will lie scrunched in it for five days before searchers find her corrupted body, tortured even in death.

Upon his return from the grave to the cottage, Malachi will, with a long knife in his hand, swear all present to secrecy, and will invent the story to be circulated: that Lizzie ran away from the house in a crazed condition the previous night. Malachi will be especially threatening to his sister, Kathryn, whose throat he swears he will cut if she peeps a word of what happened. When Kathryn swears this out of fear, Malachi will then scrape his trouser leg with the blade of his knife and say, 'Oh Kate, that's the juice and substance of poor Lizzie I'm scraping.'

And Kathryn will say, 'Malachi, even if you scrape off your skin, God will not let the stain be off you. You're damned, my brother, and I hope the devils in hell never let you draw a painless breath.'

Upon public revelation of this story, neighbors will sack and burn Malachi's house, and Malachi and Crip Devlin will be tried and convicted of murder and sentenced to twenty years in jail. Colm Dorgan will be sentenced to ten years, will serve all ten, and emerge toothless, hairless, mindless, and without a family. Ned Cronin will be given, and will serve, one year in prison, and live six more months before dying of public shame. Minnie Dorgan, though guilty of conspiracy to murder, will be set free because of her advanced age, and will sell all that she owns to move away from Albany.

In the first six months of his incarceration Crip Devlin will sicken from the pox, develop intolerable headaches and lightning pains to the legs. He will vomit and become incontinent, will develop ulcers of the heels, soles, toes, and buttocks, blockage of the penis, and rubbery tumors in the testicles. At the moment when his memory vanishes and he can no longer remember who he is or what he did to Lizzie, he will die of suppressed urine and an exploded brain.

In 1890, during the third year of his sentence, Malachi, with leather thongs he created in the shoe shop of the Albany penitentiary, will hang himself in his cell, swearing to the moment of his death that it was not Lizzie but a demon that he burned, and he will be buried in a potter's field. On the day after his burial his grave will be violated and his corpse stabbed through the heart with a wooden dagger in the shape of a cross, a suitable implement for destroying the soul of a heretic.

Kathryn Phelan will be the chief witness against Malachi. Already the mother of Francis, Sarah, and Charles, she will give birth to Peter within two weeks of Lizzie's death. She will also have three subsequent children, in this order: Julia, Mary (Molly), and Thomas.

Mab Devlin will become a charge of the city, but will escape confinement and become a vanished child.

The family's mood, after viewing the painting and listening to my recounting of the details, was so bleak that Giselle suggested putting on some music, and she then unwrapped the gift she'd found in a second-hand store and bought for the house: three player-piano scrolls of the songs 'They Always, Always Pick on Me,' 'After the Ball,' and 'Won't You Be My Little Girl.' I put on the first one under the hopeful gaze of Julia, whom Peter had etherealized in the sketch of her at the seashore, about age twenty-one, a year away from death, abounding in her virginal glory; although I noted Peter had emphasized the ample bust line that was common to all the Phelan girls. But even with Julia as a prod, I could not bring myself to pump the piano's pedals, could not so easily turn my mind from Lizzie to music.

George Quinn called to tell Peg he had asked Patsy McCall for work, something he had never done before; for city and county jobs paid only pittances, and George always believed that the ban on gambling was temporary, that the okay would come down from on high one sunny day and all the gamblers in town would go back to work. But he could afford this fantasy no longer, and so he finally popped the question, and Patsy told him to go down to Democratic-party headquarters in the morning and talk to Tanner Smith, and they'd probably put him to work canvassing the Ninth Ward for the next election. Peg said the prospect of a political job so excited George that when she told him about her bequest from Peter and her plan to buy the house he said only, 'That's great, I gotta go. Patsy's giving me a ride to my car.'

Peter finally relaxed, took off his neckerchief and his coat, and sat alone at the table, smiling. I leaned across and asked him, 'After all these years, what do I call you? Papa?'

He considered that, then shook his head no. 'Sounds like an alias,' he said.

Billy stood up from the table and, with cane and gimp leg, hobbled into the front parlor.

'Shall we adjourn?' I said to Peter.

'You go ahead. I'll sit here a minute with the chocolates.'

So I joined Billy, and when I did he said, 'I ain't even gonna collect my elephant bet if they take that bum's leg off.'

'You were pretty sure they weren't elephants.'

'One of the workers was up there came by Brady's saloon. All them guys knew the bones was owned by a mastodon, whatever the hell that is. It's big like an elephant, but it ain't an elephant.'

'You're pretty shrewd, Billy. You shrewd enough to use that money to get married? Money *was* the main obstacle, wasn't it?'

'Who said I was takin' the money?'

'Nobody.'

'Right,' Billy said.

'Maybe we could have a double wedding,' I said, and that made Billy laugh.

Doing people favors isn't always easy.

If I really was a magician and could command the spirits the way Malachi thought he could, I'd build a skeleton that would have Lizzie's ribs and fingers, Tommy's chipped backbone, Francis's all-but-gangrenous leg with the bone showing, Billy's broken ankle, Sarah's near-fleshless arms with bones pushing through skin and with tubes dangling, Peter's arthritic hips, Walter Phelan's partial skull, Meister Geld's toe and thumb, the handless armbone that my sugar whore loved to suck, and I'd have the creature dance to the 1911 tune Giselle brought us to lighten things up with music from the past. Remember the lyric?

They always, always pick on me,
They never, never let me be.
I'm so very lonesome, I'm so sad,
It's a long time since I've been glad.
I know what I'll do, bye and bye.
I'll eat some worms and then I'll die.
And when I'm gone, just wait and see.
They'll all be sorry that they picked on me.

It's about four o'clock in the afternoon now, and outside the rain is as torrential as it was at three. Colonie Street is a river. Here, in the midst of this performance by nature, we have no reversal, no ironic sunshine about to dawn. The day is crepuscularly gray, as it seems to have been forever in the life of this family; and there is something so profound in that grayness, in that cloud of unexpungeable horror and loss, that, even when the sun finally does come our way, we grieve at the change, and we pray for thunderstorms.

Poor hubristic Malachi, think of it. When you cross the border out of the real world, as he did, the way back, if you can find it, is perilous, at best; and not only for yourself. I think of the itinerant Francis, walking abroad in a malevolent world, never knowing what lay beneath the exile his mother and sister had forced upon him; and of the subterranean Molly, burying and resurrecting her sins, and living on to regret everything forever; and of myself, Orson Phelan-to-be, fugitive from the isolato's disease, about to reinvent marriage with an ambiguous wife of a second dubious dimension; and of all the others in this family: collective of the thwarted spirit, of the communal psyche that so desperately wants not to be plural.

I am one with the universe, we Phelans say; but I am one.

The universe answers us with black riddles of the past that refuse to yield their secrets: lost faiths and barren dogmas that weave the web and the winter that the poet of order had seen: the web is woven and you have to wear it, the winter is made and you have to bear it . . . It is all that you are, the final dwarf of you.

I remember Molly telling me that her mother was always afraid her daughters would meet someone, and in a single night would ruin their lives. But it takes longer than that.

I left the contemplative Billy and walked to the dining room. I watched my father choosing between a chocolate-covered nougat and a vanilla cream. In the kitchen I saw Giselle drying the dishes alongside Molly and Peg and Roger, the four of them discussing a prolonged kiss that Cary Grant had given Ingrid Bergman in a movie, and I took my cue from that. I gripped Giselle's face in my right hand and kissed her, did the same to Molly, kissed the radiant Peg, shook Roger's hand, and I then said to them, 'It's all that we are.'

They looked at me as if I had gone back into isolation, but when I smiled at them they knew I was as sane as any of them.